LINDSAY McKENNA

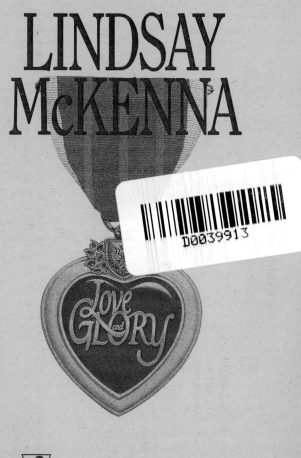

Silhouette® Books

Published by Silhouette Books
America's Publisher of Contemporary Romance

SILHOUETTE BOOKS

ISBN 0-373-20173-7

by Request

LOVE AND GLORY

This edition published by arrangement with Harlequin Books S.A.

Visit Silhouette at www.eHarlequin.com

Printed in U.S.A.

MEET THE TRAYHERN FAMILY!

From powerful storyteller Lindsay McKenna,
Silhouette Books is proud to present

Love and Glory

The series that started the gripping and passionate saga of Morgan Trayhern and his mercenaries!

A QUESTION OF HONOR: When Coast Guard officer Noah Trayhern offers battle-weary undercover agent Kit Anderson a safe house, he unwittingly endangers his own guarded emotions.

NO SURRENDER: Navy pilot Alyssa Trayhern's assignment with arrogant jet jockey Clay Cantrell threatens her career—and her heart—with a crash landing!

RETURN OF A HERO: Strike up the band to welcome home Morgan Trayhern, whose top-secret reappearance will make headline news...with a delicate, daring woman by his side.

LOVE AND GLORY

The Trayherns

Chase "Wolf" Trayhern
U.S. Air Force
General, retired

m.

Rachel McKenzie
U.S. Army Nurse Corps
First lieutenant, retired

Morgan Trayhern
aka Morgan Ramsey
Foreign Legion
officer
U.S. Marine Corps
Captain

m.

Laura Bennett
writer and
researcher,
U.S. military

Noah Trayhern
U.S. Coast
Guard
Lieutenant

m.

Kit Anderson
Miami Police
Department
Former narcotics
agent

Alyssa Trayhern
U.S. Navy
Second
lieutenant
and pilot

m.

Clay Cantrell
U.S. Navy
First lieutenant
and pilot

CONTENTS

Dear Reader,

No one knows more than I do how many of you have been pleading for the original LOVE AND GLORY series to be reissued! To say the least, I'm overjoyed that Silhouette Books is putting all three stories in the series together in one special volume. For those readers who are not aware of how MORGAN'S MERCENARIES began, you'll find the foundation in LOVE AND GLORY.

With the publication of this 3-in-1 volume, readers who love Morgan Trayhern can now go back to the beginning and see him in his younger days, meet his sister, Aly, and his brother, Noah. The Trayherns have a proud military history that goes back to almost the time our country was born, two hundred years earlier.

In *LOVE AND GLORY,* tragedy strikes the Trayhern family and threatens the honorable family name. Over the course of the three books, we learn what has happened to Morgan Trayhern, the oldest son, and how the rest of the family's lives change as a result of Morgan's trials.

In the last book, *Return of a Hero,* you get to meet Morgan himself. Those of you who have followed Morgan Trayhern and the men and women of Perseus, the company Morgan created, will have your heart's desire fulfilled by this opportunity to read Morgan's story and learn about the wonderful Trayhern family. I'm bubbling over with enthusiasm about the publication of this special volume featuring three powerful novels. I hope you enjoy reading these stories as much as I did writing them. And after you are through with *LOVE AND GLORY,* you and I can look forward to more of Morgan's adventures with his mercenaries in an upcoming, brand-new book in the MORGAN'S MERCENARIES series available from Silhouette Special Edition in July 2000, as well as a longer-length single title release, *Morgan's Mercenaries: Heart of the Warrior,* available in August 2000. Then, just wait until you see what I have in store for Morgan and company in 2001—another new Special Edition novel and an exciting new single title. Enjoy!

Warmly,

Lindsay McKenna

A QUESTION OF HONOR

Chapter One

May, 1975

"There's no way you can talk me into taking this job, Chuck," Kit said tightly.

"We'll see, Detective Anderson," her superior shot back. He pushed a sheaf of recently signed papers forward to emphasize his intention. Chuck Cordeman's blue eyes caught and held Kit's gaze as she stood tensely on the other side of the desk. "You wanted to get away from the scum of Dade County, sweetheart, and you got your wish. This new assignment is yours." His gravelly voice softened slightly. "Narc division is a lousy place for anybody. And for a woman..." He shrugged his meaty shoulders, rounded by the weight of responsibility after fifteen years on the police force. ''I sympathize with you, Kit, but this is the best I could come up with.'' He nudged the documents closer to the edge of the desk.

Kit reached hesitantly for them. ''What's the assignment?'' she asked tiredly.

Chuck's face brightened, and he sat farther back in his well-worn chair. ''Congratulations, Kit. You have just officially joined the Coast Guard as an adviser. You're gonna act as liaison between their department and ours.'' A small grin tugged at his mouth. ''You're gonna learn how they drug-bust at sea. I hope you don't get seasick easily.''

Her eyes narrowed in disbelief. ''The military?'' she croaked as she slowly began to read the orders before her.

''You're now officially part of the South Florida Task Force,'' Chuck continued. ''You'll interface as a member of both the Drug Enforcement Agency and the Coast Guard.'' He smiled slightly. ''And you thought you were getting out of the excitement.''

Despair caused Kit's already aching stomach to feel as if it were on fire. She ran her hand across it, trying to ease the pain. ''I don't want a lateral transfer, Chuck!'' Her nostrils flared. ''I want out of narc completely. I thought I'd made that clear.''

Chuck held up his hands in self-defense. ''Listen, Kit, I tried. Honest I did. But—''

Kit's lips felt stiff with anger.

''The captain said you were too damned good to lose. Let's face it, you've been one of our best undercover agents. You've survived when others haven't. You're bright and young—not to mention that you're part of a police family. The captain sees you going places with the department.''

"Over my dead body!"

"Easy, Kit. I know how you feel. Everybody in narc gets a gutful at some point." His voice became soothing. "Look, the captain likes your work. You've busted your tail and made some damned fine collars. Now you're getting this cushy assignment to take the pressure off you. Believe me, Kit, *everybody* has been bidding for this job. Hell, I'd rather chase smuggling dope boats into our country than get shot at every few days by some junkie in Dade." His eyes glittered. "Wouldn't you?"

Kit clamped down on her rising anger. *Turn it inside,* she told herself. *Don't show any emotion.* Wasn't that what she'd learned from five years of living in the trenches as a narcotics agent? Show any emotion and you were on a morgue slab faster than you could snap your fingers. Her stomach burned as her ulcer acted up again. But Kit had more immediate concerns. She eyed her boss.

"Chuck, I told you—I want out. Out of narc. Out as an undercover agent. I can't take it anymore."

Chuck shook his head. "Everybody here develops either stomach ulcers or permanent migraines—or both. It comes with the territory. I'm tellin' you, Kit, one more year in narc and Cap will promote you to that desk job you've been wanting. Just hang in there."

Kit sighed. Maybe he was right. Her father would be disappointed if she quit an assignment. Hadn't she and her three brothers all followed his footsteps into police work? Family tradition came first, her Irish father had gravely told her the day she'd been accepted to the Florida Police Academy.

Focusing her attention back on Chuck, Kit couldn't

muster any anger toward him. He was a rumpled, solidly built man with a weathered face. That face had seen a lot of action, she reflected. Beneath that lined flesh were hidden scars born of ten years in the narc trenches. Somehow he still belonged there, even though he'd been allowed to move up the ladder to the safety of a desk job.

She cared for this man. He would never say, "Kit, I know you're hurting. I know you're tired. And I'm worried about all the weight you're losing." Chuck only knew how to be supportive by being gruff. But she knew he cared for her. Kit sighed.

"It's a one-year assignment, Chuck? Are you sure?"

"Yeah, just one. You were chosen because you're the only one who can identify Garcia, the Colombian kingpin, on sight. Word's out that he's going to be making a big drop either here, the Bahamas or Puerto Rico. We want him, Kit. Real bad. And so do you. All you have to do is cruise around on this cutter and check out every druggie they bust." He managed a sliver of a smile. "You'll get one hell of a nice tan. Most of their work is done during daylight. Hell, you'll be able to live like a normal human being, sleeping nights and working days instead of the other way around."

A corner of her mouth quirked. "So Garcia is finally going to make his move."

"Yep, and you can collar the bastard for us."

"Yeah...maybe." Tiredly Kit ran her fingers through her short black hair. Her voice trailed off into a quavering whisper. "Maybe..."

Chuck produced a severe frown. "All right, get your rear over to CG Headquarters at the Port of Miami. There's a Lieutenant Noah Trayhern who's expecting you."

The name sounded familiar, Kit mused. "Right now?" she asked, turning her attention back to Chuck.

Chuck consulted the watch on his thick wrist. "It's 10:00 a.m. Go clean out your locker. Lieutenant Trayhern requested you meet him at noon."

Kit shook her head morosely. She was twenty-eight going on eighty and feeling every minute of it. Releasing a long breath, she waved the papers that still needed to be signed at Chuck.

"Okay. Or should I practice saying aye, aye, sir?"

"That's my girl. You'll be okay, honey. Stay in touch?"

A genuine smile crossed her lips. "You're in my heart forever, Chuck. You know that."

"Ha! The man who gets your heart is going to be a lucky guy."

Kit grimaced, slowly pulling the leather strap of her purse across her slumped shoulder. "The only men interested in me are pimps who'd like to see me out on the street working for them when I'm undercover as a hooker. No thanks."

As she made her way down the noisy, crowded hall toward the locker rooms in the basement, Kit felt as if one heavy stone had been lifted off her and another put in its place. The narc division was filled with police officers who had learned to be actors and actresses. They could play the part of dope peddler, junkie or pimp to infiltrate organized crime in Dade County. Kit herself had become an actress for much larger stakes: she had posed as a rich Colombian landowner's daughter interested in connecting with the top of the drug hierarchy in southern Florida. She had been perfect for the part with her black hair, flawless Spanish and deep tan. She had lied and said her mother was American to explain her gray eyes. And because of her bravado, skill and courage, she had been able to infiltrate Jose Garcia's drug empire in Colombia. The information she'd gathered had dealt Garcia an almost lethal blow to his million dollar business. And the damage she'd caused them had cost the Mob stateside even more in drug sales. Yes, she had fooled them all and managed, thus far, to stay alive.

Kit found little in her locker worth retrieving. As she emptied the last of its contents, she dug out the address of the CG station. *Lieutenant Noah Trayhern,* she repeated to herself. Where had she heard that name before?

"I hope you don't have any bones to pick with me, Lieutenant Trayhern," she whispered softly, "because I'm down and out."

Something prompted Noah Trayhern to raise his head. The cubicle that served as his office sat opposite the entrance, and he looked up and saw a tall young woman standing just inside the main doors of the Coast Guard station. There was a decided air of loneliness around her that seemed to wear like a coat of armor, he thought, his green eyes narrowing in inspection. And her ill-fitting beige blazer over a plain white blouse and blue jeans indicated some carelessness about appearance.

Noah's gaze moved to her face, seeking a redeeming quality to counteract her initial image. Her eyes were large and expressive but held no life. They were slate gray and weary looking, with dark telltale shadows beneath them. Her finely sculpted chin held tension, warning him that although she might appear vulnerable, she had a stubborn streak. She was also underweight for her height, Noah observed, her cheeks hollow beneath her high cheekbones. Now his gaze was drawn to her mouth. She had beautifully formed lips that, despite her tension, pulled upward. That was good. It was her saving grace, Noah decided.

She was on guard, her feet planted slightly apart—a fighter's stance that Noah recognized. He, too, knew the value of keeping balance in devastating situations.

Kit noted the Coast Guard officer's appraisal and bridled inwardly as his impassive green eyes roved the length of her. But she coolly did a similar stocktaking of this tall, obviously athletic man. There was something about him that suggested calm, she decided. In fact, as she looked around, Kit began to register that the difference between the military headquarters and the police station was shocking. The noise level here was almost nonexistent. People working at nearby desks were actually smiling and joking with one another. And the smell was antiseptic clean, with a touch of ocean breeze to make it worth inhaling deeply.

"You're looking for someone," the officer said from the desk where he sat. "May I help you?"

Kit regarded him with growing interest. This man's well-modulated voice would soothe even the most violent junkie. Her stomach slowly began to unknot. And his sea-green eyes revealed a keen vitality with undeniable sparks of intelligence. Humor lurked at the corners of his well-shaped mouth—a mouth that looked accustomed to giving orders and having them carried out. Kit swallowed dryly, unable to break eye contact.

She moved closer to the desk. "I'm Detective Kit Anderson. I was told to be here by noon to meet a Lieutenant Trayhern."

Noah swallowed his shock as he stared up at her. A *woman* was being assigned to him? He sat for several seconds, digesting his surprise and anger. His commanding officer had told him that a police officer who could identify Garcia would be assigned to his cutter. Noah had leaped at the opportunity. Anything to retrieve his family's honor over his brother Morgan's tragedy. He rose hesitantly, bitterness coating his throat. The writing was too clearly on the wall: once again his superiors were going to try to railroad his career. This time they were handing him a woman agent to work with. She didn't appear capable of much. She looked more like a bedraggled stray in need of some care. She couldn't possibly be an undercover narc—one savvy enough to know Garcia. It must be a trick. An ugly calling card to remind him that the military hadn't forgotten about his brother.

Forcing his hand across the desk, he muttered, "I'm Noah Trayhern."

Automatically Kit placed her hand within his. The contrast was startling as her cold, damp hand disappeared in his warm clasp. For a moment she felt the latent power in his grip, then she disengaged her hand, puzzled at the sudden sense of loss she felt. She'd watched surprise, anger and then a sullen look enter his assessing eyes. Confused, she took an aggressive stance in an attempt to protect her weary emotions.

"Why noon, Lieutenant? I barely had time to clean out my locker and—"

Scowling, Noah threw the report back on the desk. Right now he wanted to wrap his hands around his commander's throat. "I thought we might get acquainted over lunch," he muttered. *A woman, of all things.* He'd just been given one of the finest boats the Coast Guard had to command. And now his hopes of distinguishing his career for the honor of his family name were going to be sabotaged once again.

"Lunch?" Kit stalled, disconcerted by his apparent anger.

He tossed her a sharpened look. "It's the meal between breakfast and dinner. What's the matter? Don't the people over in narcotics ever see the light of day?"

Although she managed to remain impassive on the outside, Kit flinched internally when he opened and shut a desk drawer with force. His anger was directed at her. With a sinking feeling she realized that he didn't want a woman on the job with him. There was so little strength left in her, but Kit dredged up shreds of it, standing her ground. The kindness she'd seen in his face earlier had disappeared, and her heart cried out at the unfairness of the situation. "Look... Lieutenant, I don't like this any more than you do." Kit tried to make her voice sound firm and strong. "And I can see you're upset."

Noah glanced up after putting away the report and the pen. There was a pleading tone to her husky voice and in her eyes. Frowning, he nodded. "'Upset' isn't the word for it," he ground out. He felt the barely leashed tension within her; she was a mine ready to detonate. Noah tucked the observation away and held up his hands in a peacemaking gesture. ''Okay—truce, Detective Anderson. You look pretty beat, and I've been up all night on a drug bust. I'm tired, but I'll try to be more responsible for my actions and less the little boy. Deal?''

''It's better than the alternative,'' she muttered. When he smiled, Kit felt as if the sun had come out again. Even if it was a grudging smile. Even if he was forcing it for her benefit. Still, her heart sank at the knowledge that he didn't want her around. Well, she didn't want him, either, she thought grimly. A year with this officer was likely to put her right over the edge.

Struggling to maintain an air of neutrality, Noah nodded. So many emotions were rising within him. Anger at the continued harassment by the Coast Guard was primary. But this woman officer was behaving like a prickly cactus, too. Shoving his reactions back down inside, Noah forced himself to be civil. He knew if he went to his superior and asked for the woman to be replaced, it wouldn't work. Whether he liked it or not he was stuck with her. Somehow, as he had on the other messy assignments he'd been given in the past, he'd have to make the best of it. Judging by the wariness still in her huge gray eyes, she hadn't sensed his decision.

''Let's start over,'' Noah suggested.

Was he really trying to make amends? Or was this a sham? Kit stared at him hard, allowing her instincts to take over. How long had it been since she'd spoken with a man who had such ease of bearing? There was no doubt he was a leader. And right now she felt the overwhelming urge to lean on someone stronger. Her senses told her Noah was such a man. Kit nodded. "Yes, let's start over. But why lunch?"

"Narc agents are shadow people. You sleep during the day and work all night. I figured you probably hadn't been out to lunch in a long time."

"I'm not really hungry, Lieutenant Trayhern, but if you are, let's go."

"Okay." Noah wanted to dislike her, but there was something ethereal about Kit Anderson that tugged hard at his heart. His emotions were automatically reaching out to her, but his mind was in turmoil about what to do with the situation in general. He wasn't going to have his career scuttled by this police detective. He intended to find Garcia. It would help his career and, perhaps, begin to remove the stain from his family name.

He moved around the desk, walking toward the doors. He stopped at the entrance and picked up his cap, hanging from a peg. She walked hesitantly at his side, and he could feel her withdrawal. Settling the cap on his head, he briskly opened the door for her, and they stepped out into the brilliant sunshine. "Do you mind if I call you Kit? It's less formal than Detective Anderson."

Startled, Kit retreated. His demeanor was suddenly warm, almost as if he'd never had his earlier negative reaction. Her mind went blank.

"Do you mind?" he repeated quietly.

"N-no...of course not."

Ignoring her stammer, he placed his hand on her elbow, guiding her down the walk and toward the parking lot at the rear of the building. "Call me Noah."

"I can't do that, Lieutenant," Kit replied tensely.

His fingers were firm on her elbow. The desire to lean against him for just a moment was almost overpowering.

He gave her an amused glance as they left the walk and headed toward the rows of parked vehicles. "Sure you can."

Her lips thinned. She jerked her elbow from his hand, pulling to a halt. "This isn't a date we're going on, Lieutenant. I was assigned to DEA to interface between narc and the Coast Guard. You're my boss."

Noah threw his hands on his hips. Damn, but she was a contrary person! "That's right, I am. And a little civility is in order. You've been in those trenches too long."

Stung, Kit glared up at him. Her stomach began to knot again. "Now look, Trayhern, you can cut out the flirting act right now. I've got five tough years behind me in that drug jungle they call Dade County. I handled it, and I can handle you and this new assignment they threw at me. Keep your distance, be professional, and we'll get along."

Cocking his head, Noah studied her, gauging the fervent tone of her voice. The fire in her gray eyes interested him. "You think I'm flirting with you?" Her quicksilver temper intrigued him, and he liked her boldness and honesty. Of course professional conduct must rule. For just a moment he sensed the potential danger in letting himself think of Kit Anderson as a woman.

Kit gave him a flat look. "If the shoe fits, wear it."

"You are attractive," Noah admitted, "but I didn't ask to call you by your first name because I was flirting."

She watched him wearily. "We might as well get the rest of this settled right now."

"What else is eating at you?"

"Not me. You. I'm a woman being dropped into a 'man's job,' and I don't want to put up with chauvinism from you or your crew. I'm a police officer, Lieutenant Trayhern. A damn good one. You give me orders and I'll carry them out—or die trying. It makes no difference whether I'm male or female—I'll do the job for you."

Anger lurked beneath the surface in Noah and it came out in his voice. "You always spit bullets, Anderson?"

"Only when I'm fired upon."

"Are you always this tough?"

"When I have to be."

"I'm trying to patch things up between us, and you keep insisting on destroying my attempts."

Kit resisted the warmth in his eyes. She set her jaw, flashing him a dark look. "Then be honest. You didn't expect a woman on this assignment."

"Hell, no, I didn't!" Noah compressed his lips into a single line. "I got a file with 'K. Anderson' on the label. I assumed you were a man." He searched her upturned face. He was a good judge of people, and he sensed she was emotionally exhausted, though she kept it well hidden. "When your superior, Cordeman, called earlier, all he said was that you had one hell of an impressive record. He neglected to tell me you were a woman."

Touching her brow, Kit struggled with the rawness she felt. "Look, there's no way out of this assignment for us," she muttered. "If I could, I'd go back to Chuck Cordeman and ask for a transfer. But I'm the only one who can identify Jose Garcia.'' She raised her eyes, holding his hard stare. ''Whether you like it or not, I'm here to stay. Maybe you can request a change of orders. Maybe there's another cutter captain who'd have less hostility about working with a woman.''

Noah took off his hat, running his fingers through his military-short black hair. He settled the cap back on his head. ''I wish the hell I could,'' he growled, glancing down at her. ''But I'm just as stuck in this assignment as you are.'' If he requested a change because he didn't want to work with a woman, his career would be down the drain, and he knew it. ''We're both going to have to bite the bullet on this one, Detective.''

''Okay.'' Kit closed her eyes, feeling dizziness overwhelm her momentarily. She placed her feet slightly apart to steady herself. Chuck had thought this would be a plush, easy assignment. He'd been wrong. She didn't have the strength to be hard and tough with Noah Trayhern. That was an act she put on when undercover. In real life she wasn't anything like that. In real life the trauma of her undercover life had brought her close to an emotional breakdown. Kit knew she needed time to heal, but Lieutenant Trayhern wasn't going to give it to her. He was looking at her as if she were a noose around his neck.

''Come on,'' Noah muttered, ''let's go to lunch.''

''You're hungry?''

''No. But I need a drink.''

Chapter Two

Kit felt more at ease in the darkened surroundings of the restaurant with Noah at her left elbow. She gave him a curious look after he ordered his drink.

"Did you purposely choose a corner where we could sit with our backs against the wall?"

"No. Why?"

"It's a good defensive position."

Noah gave her a keen look. "I see your back's to the wall. Do you find that preferable?"

"Of course," she confirmed. "Walls can't sneak up behind you and slide a knife between your ribs or fire at you when you aren't looking." Kit noticed Noah's hands. His fingers were long and capable looking. She could imagine him at the helm of a tall, four-masted sailing ship instead of a modern-day Coast Guard cutter.

"Why don't you just sit back and relax instead of

eyeballing everyone who walks through that door? This is a restaurant, not a dive where drugs are being exchanged under the table.''

''I've survived five years because I'm alert, Lieutenant. I'm not about to drop my guard just because you're with me.''

Noah clamped down on a rejoinder. The waitress delivered his drink and Kit's large glass of milk.

Kit took a gulp of it, hoping it would quell her screaming stomach.

''Milk?'' Noah goaded, eyeing the glass she clutched between her hands.

''Why not?'' Kit asked defensively. ''Do you have a problem with me drinking milk instead of liquor?''

Noah's mouth tightened momentarily as he held her stare. ''No. But it could mean you have stomach ulcers. Do you?''

Her composure ruffled as Noah's open expression suddenly slid beneath an unreadable mask. It shook Kit, and her street instincts took over. Here was a man who could be generous, she suspected. Yet he wasn't to be trifled with, her gut warned. ''It doesn't matter why I drink milk, Lieutenant. As long as I do my job, you shouldn't care what I eat, drink or do within reasonable limits.''

Noah gave her a cutting smile. ''Look, Detective Anderson, I don't know how Chuck Cordeman treated you, but I consider the people aboard the cutter my extended family. I try to treat each person the way I would want to be treated.''

''So far that quaint rule of conduct doesn't apply to me, does it?''

He throttled his mounting anger toward her. Noah

knew she was right. "I'm applying it right now. I'm concerned about the state of your health."

Kit shook her head. "My drinking milk isn't the real issue. Since when does an officer get friendly with the people beneath him? You and I both know there's a forbidden zone there. The military has a hierarchy just like the one over at the police department."

"You do have a perverse attitude, don't you?" Noah ground out.

Kit glared at him. "And you really get under my skin, Lieutenant." She took another swallow of the soothing milk. Licking her lips, she continued. "I've never met anyone like you in my entire life, and I've met some real winners."

In that instant Noah saw her tough street mask slip. "Do you ever smile?" he asked suddenly.

Kit jerked her head up. "What?"

Noah gave her a calculating look. "What the hell have they done to you, Kit, to make you so damned paranoid?"

The words, holding a hint of genuine tenderness, drove deeply into Kit's walled, aching heart. She blinked once, feeling the rush of hot tears. Noah's concerned face blurred before her. This time he wasn't acting. This was the real man beneath the hardened facade of the officer. *Care* was a foreign word to her. No one cared for her but herself. Her lips parted in response and she sat frozen beneath his searching gaze, suddenly overwhelmed by the human side of Noah Trayhern. Bowing her head, she fought against the tears, willing them away.

"No you don't," he growled, gently capturing her

nearest hand and placing a handkerchief in it. ‘‘It’s not a crime to cry, you know.’’

Kit shoved the handkerchief back across the table. ‘‘I’m not going to break down like some soap opera character. Women don’t always cry at the drop of a hat.’’

‘‘I’m not going to answer your sarcasm, Kit. How long has it been since you last cried?’’

Her eyes clouded with pain as she looked up at him. ‘‘Stop it!’’ she whispered, wanting to escape. At the tenderness burning in his eyes she rasped, ‘‘Cut the pity. There’s nothing wrong with me!’’

‘‘Care is not pity,’’ Noah grated out. He sat back grimly, watching her struggle with the deluge of emotions he’d unwittingly triggered in her. Stunned that he was drawn to her, he could say nothing. Kit Anderson touched him on so many levels that words escaped him, and silence hovered heavily between them.

Kit found it sheer agony to sit through lunch with Noah Trayhern. She ate little, her fingers visibly trembling as she lifted the glass to finish her milk. Occasionally she would catch him staring at her, sadness evident in his green eyes. Finally she could stand it no longer. After the waitress had cleared away the dishes, Kit placed both hands on the table and faced him squarely.

‘‘Look, Lieutenant Trayhern, I know you must think I’m some kind of—’’

‘‘First,’’ he interrupted sharply, ‘‘you’re a woman, something the narc division conveniently overlooked. They’ve used you up and abused your qualities. You’ve been sucked dry emotionally.’’ Noah’s mouth became grim as he held her embarrassed gray eyes.

"I'm not the new boy on the block when it comes to the drug world," he reminded her tersely. "I've been up to my neck in it since 1970. I'm one of two skippers who command the Bell Halter Surface Effect Ship. I interface with Drug Enforcement Agency headquarters, DEA agents in South America, the FBI, the CIA and local authorities to help halt drug trafficking. I've seen a hell of a lot of agents come and go in the past five years, and I know the narc type. I also know what working this dirty business has done to them." His voice deepened. "You've got ulcers, your hands tremble and you expect danger when there's nothing to fear."

Kit sucked in a sharp breath, feeling as if he'd glimpsed secret places in her that no one else suspected. Shakily she started to rise, but Trayhern gripped her arm, and she sank back down again.

"No," he ordered quietly. "First things first." His green eyes bore into hers. "You're taking a week off, Kit. Go home and get some sleep. And I mean deep, uninterrupted sleep. Lie in the sun. Learn how to relax. Consider this a minivacation in order to pull yourself back together again."

She sat stiffly, unable to speak. Who was this man? He'd just probed her from top to bottom and discovered a truth she'd been avoiding for a long time. Drawing in a ragged breath, Kit became achingly aware of him as he released the grip on her arm. "And then?" she rasped, looking up into his face. Noah's eyes glittered with anger and a frown creased his forehead. He was angry with her, she thought in confusion, and disappointed.

"I'll call you sometime next week and we'll go over the details of your new job. We'll begin your integration into my unit slowly, provided we're given the time."

"I've never failed any assignment I've undertaken."

His mouth tightened, as if he were experiencing her pain. "That's not what's at stake here, Kit," he countered less harshly.

"Then what is?"

Noah's eyes softened momentarily. "You." He got to his feet. "Come on," he coaxed, "I'm taking you home. You need the rest." And then he added to himself, *I need time to think this thing through.* Maybe when he got back to the office, he could objectively evaluate Kit Anderson, her role and their assignment with each other. Like it or not, Noah had to acknowledge how powerfully he was drawn to her.

Noah had no sooner gotten back to his desk at headquarters than the phone rang. Muttering an oath under his breath, he picked it up.

"Coast Guard Headquarters, Lieutenant Trayhern speaking."

"Noah?"

He sat down. "Aly?" It was his younger sister, Alyssa, and she sounded depressed.

"I'm sorry to call you at work, Noah, but I just needed to hear a friendly voice."

"I know what you mean."

"Thank God for our family," Aly said fervently.

"Yeah," Noah agreed. The Trayherns were as tight as a family could get. They had to be. Since the events of 1970, Noah had watched his own blossoming military career go sour. Alyssa, who'd just entered the naval academy in 1970, had been given the silent treatment. Now she was in flight school at Pensacola, in northwestern Florida. ''So how's it going, ace? Are you flying the wings off those planes up there?''

Aly's voice was low. ''I'm trying to, Noah.''

He gripped the phone a little tighter. ''Pretty bad?''

''Yeah, really bad. God, Noah, I'm getting the silent treatment from the students all over again. I've got one instructor who does nothing but scream at me for an hour in the cockpit. He's trying to wash me out, make me quit. I—I don't know if I can hold it together....''

His throat tightened. ''Hang in there, Aly. The Trayherns are made of tough stuff. We've got a two-hundred-year family military tradition to uphold. There's too much riding on both our shoulders to let go of that honor.''

''I'm getting tired, Noah. And I didn't want to tell Mom or Dad what's happening here at Pensacola. They worry too much about us, anyway.''

Noah tried to smile. ''I'm glad you called. Any chance you might cut free for a weekend soon and visit me? Getting away from the name-calling and stares might help.''

''That would be wonderful, Noah. I really need a break. And I know Mom and Dad would die if they saw me right now. You know how they expect a monthly visit from each of us. I have dark circles under my eyes and I've lost a lot of weight since starting the flight program. These instructors really want me out, Noah. They want to disgrace me in retaliation for Morgan.''

''I know,'' he said softly, hurting for her. ''Look, you get down here at the first opportunity, okay? My house has two guest bedrooms, and one of them has your name on it.''

Alyssa's tone was strained. ''Thanks, big brother. I owe you one. I'll drop in to see you just as soon as I can.''

''Do that, Aly.''

''How are things with you? Are they still putting pressure on you?''

Noah managed a choked laugh. ''Yeah, same old stuff.'' And then he told her about Detective Anderson and his latest assignment.

''Maybe this week off will get her in shape to be an asset instead of a problem for you,'' Aly offered.

Rubbing his face, Noah said, ''God, I hope so. If she screws up, my career will be torpedoed. I fought so damned hard to get this SES billet. And now I've got a woman with a chip on her shoulder toward men.''

''Just turn on some of that famous Noah Trayhern charm and she'll come around. I know she will.''

He closed his eyes, buoyed by Aly's teasing warmth. ''I hope you're right. I'm going over to her house on Friday and lay out the basic assignment to her.''

''She'll be fine by then.''

''Oh? You a psychic now?'' he asked, chuckling.

''I've got a good feeling about her, Noah. Don't know why, but I just do. You'll know Friday for sure....''

There was no answer at Kit Anderson's bungalow door. Noah stood and listened, then rang the bell again. He'd tried to call earlier, but there'd been no response. Walking around the stucco one-story home, he spotted a high-walled wooden fence. Maybe she was in back, getting that suntan. Taking a chance, he opened the gate and moved quietly inside the closure.

Over the past few days Noah had tried to reconcile himself to the fact that Kit Anderson was going to be a part of his hardworking crew. Although still unconvinced that assigning a woman to this project was a good idea, Noah realized he'd treated her poorly upon first meeting her, and owed her an apology. Getting off on the wrong foot was no help to either of them. Gazing across the lawn, he spotted Kit in a lavender bathing suit, lying on a chaise lounge. His hand tightened automatically around the briefcase he carried.

The late-morning sun had lulled Kit into a twilight of peace. Fragrant oleanders ringed the yard, scenting the late-morning air. Idly she ran her fingers across her lower arm, amazed at how deeply tanned she had become. Closing her eyes again, Kit enjoyed the call of the birds that made their homes in those ten-foot-high flowery bushes. In the years she had spent living at night, she'd missed their melodic songs.

Her languor ended at the sound of approaching footsteps. Instantly alert, Kit jerked into a sitting position, on guard. Noah Trayhern looked devastatingly handsome in his light blue shirt and dark blue slacks and garrison cap. He carried a briefcase in his left hand. Kit searched his face for signs of anger but saw none.

"I called earlier, but there wasn't any answer," Noah offered. "I thought I'd take a chance you might be back here." She looked slim and elegant in the revealing bathing suit. Puzzled as to why he hadn't realized how pretty Kit really was, Noah realized she was no longer in the baggy clothes that hid her innate femininity. His heart thudded hard in his chest, and he felt that familiar stirring that was beginning to seem inevitable whenever her name or face came to mind. And that had been often. Too damned often.

Kit lowered her lashes, hotly aware of a strange intensity to his inspection of her. She reached for her light blue beach jacket, quickly shrugging it across her shoulders. "It's better to get a tan in the morning," she said. Tying the sash, Kit stood. "I thought you'd conveniently forgotten about me."

Noah managed a crooked smile. "I had that coming, didn't I?"

Nervous beneath his continued stare, she crossed her arms. "Yes, you did."

"I'll try to change that."

Relief swept through Kit. There was something in his voice that said he was telling her the truth. "All I want to do is catch Garcia and survive this year with you, Lieutenant. I don't want any battles. I'm tired of fighting."

"I don't like to fight, either. Well," he amended, "only druggies. I didn't call you because I didn't want to disturb you."

Kit remained on guard. Noah was a man of incredible insight, and it unnerved her to suspect that he probably knew as much about her as she did herself. "If we've got business to discuss, come on in the house. I've got some sun tea made. Would you like a glass?"

"Sounds good. And yes, we've got business to discuss."

She nodded, seeing the undisguised hunger in his face. It rattled her badly. "I'm ready to work. I've had my fill of soap operas and crossword puzzles."

He walked easily beside her, and Kit admired his aura of confidence. It gave her a sense of stability when she had none left within herself. Somehow Noah Trayhern made her feel safe. Right now she didn't want to probe the reasons why too deeply.

"You needed this time, though," Noah reminded her.

"Maybe," Kit hedged, walking into the cool interior of the small, neatly kept house. "The kitchen's that way," she instructed. "I'll change into something more appropriate and be out in a minute. Why don't you pour us some tea?"

Noah busied himself in the kitchen. When Kit emerged from the bedroom ten minutes later, she was dressed in a pair of pale pink shorts and a sleeveless blouse. Its pink-and-fuchsia print with burgundy accents highlighted her golden skin. He found it difficult not to stare. Picking up her glass of tea, he met her halfway.

"I like what you've done to your hair," he noted, handing her the cool glass. Their fingers met and touched.

Kit fingered the wispy bangs over her brow. She had coaxed her black hair into soft waves around her face. "Thank you," she muttered nervously, and took the glass, barely able to endure Noah's examination. Heat rushed into her face. My God, was she blushing? Touching her flaming cheek, Kit was at a loss for words.

Noah fought himself, but he lost out to the driving need to touch her. He placed his hand beneath her chin and gave her an approving look. "No circles under your eyes, either." Her flesh was soft and far too inviting. It was the shock in her eyes that forced him to drop his hand back to his side. He wasn't behaving professionally, and that irritated him. What was it about her that invited this kind of familiarity?

Kit's skin tingled where Noah's hand had fleetingly rested. Despite an initial hesitancy, she found herself responding to him like a flower parched for water, drawn helplessly to him. He seemed to put her in touch with her own vulnerability and restore the sense of femininity that had long been buried by her undercover career.

"Come into the living room," she said, shaken. She took a chair opposite Noah. The coffee table acted as a barrier between them, allowing her to relax slightly. Clearing her throat, she said, "I still don't know what to make of you, Lieutenant."

Giving her a wry glance, he selected several groups of papers from his briefcase and spread them across the coffee table. "Call me Noah."

"Even in front of the DEA, FBI and CIA people?" Kit taunted. Every second spent with him was dissolving her barriers. Noah was too much like Pete, she admitted to herself. The Coast Guard officer appeared driven, probably a superachiever, just as her partner, Pete, had been. Noah reminded her too much of the recent past, but she had no way to stop his encroachment on her life, either professionally or, even more frightening, personally.

"Even with them," he agreed affably, hearing the disbelief in her voice. Glancing up, he said, "My crew and I work well together, Kit. They all know who's boss and we know our responsibilities. I came out of a very tight-knit family myself, and I know the benefits of one. I apply that same philosophy to my crew."

She gave him a strange look. "Family?" His last name struck a memory chord within her once again.

Noah looked up. "Why not?"

"Wait a minute..." Kit snapped her fingers, finally remembering where she'd heard his name. Her eyes rounded. "My God, you aren't from *the* Trayhern family with the traitor, are you?" Kit saw Noah's eyes go dark with hurt, then anger, and she instantly regretted how she'd framed her question.

Noah's hands stilled over the reports spread before him. He struggled with the grief and loss of Morgan, and then the anger that she or anyone would dare call his older brother a traitor. Kit was just one more person to parrot what she'd been fed by the press. She hadn't grown up with Morgan, didn't know how loyal he was or how much integrity he possessed. Wrestling with an avalanche of stripped feelings, Noah whispered tautly, "Yes, Morgan is my brother." Funny, he never could say was. He didn't accept that Morgan was dead. He couldn't. And neither did anyone else in his family.

Kit placed a hand across her mouth, the huskiness in his voice tearing at her. "Oh, no..."

Noah misinterpreted her reaction as negative and sighed roughly. "We might as well hash this out right now." He tried to prepare himself for her outrage at having to work with the brother of a supposed traitor. He'd gone through this scenario for five years now. Would it never end?

"No...I mean, I'm sorry. It's just that the memory hit me so hard and out of nowhere," Kit blurted. She desperately wanted peace between them, not more dissension. Some of the hardness left his eyes, replaced with grief. Kit ached for him, realizing the pain he'd carried because of his infamous brother. "It must be awful to have endured the names and blame for something you didn't do."

Noah searched her flushed features, her eyes soft and dove gray. He'd expected anger and accusations from Kit. Instead she was desperately trying to mend the fence between them. His voice came out low and tortured. "First of all, my family and I don't consider Morgan a traitor. He was a captain in the Marine Corps in charge of a company of men in Vietnam. Something happened over there, and his entire company was wiped out, except for him and one other man."

Kit bit her lower lip, feeling the magnitude of his anguish. "Everything I read in the papers and saw on television said he deserted his men, leaving them to die. They said he deserted to North Vietnam—the other survivor swore he ran away."

Noah shook his head, as if trying to shake off an invisible millstone he carried. "Morgan would never desert anyone. Our family prides itself on taking care of those under us. He was raised to be loyal to a fault, and we feel he's been made a scapegoat for something that went wrong. My father, who was a general in the air force at the time, tried to investigate, but he was stopped at every turn. That's why we believe Morgan was somehow framed." Raising his chin, Noah caught and held her gaze. "There's no way to prove it. Besides, it's the past, and we've got to work in the present."

"I remember something about your family having a two-hundred-year military tradition. Every child of each generation went into one of the services."

"That's right. In my generation, Morgan went into

the Marine Corps. I went into the Coast Guard and our younger sister, Alyssa, went into the navy as a pilot. She's in flight training in Pensacola right now."

Kit saw the pride in his eyes, heard the pride in his voice for his family and its name. "If Morgan didn't desert, then your whole family must be bearing a terrible burden."

"We've all paid for it in some way," he muttered, unwilling to discuss it any further. "But I guess everyone has his or her personal set of problems to carry around."

"Some have more than others," Kit said softly, overwhelmed at the immensity of Noah's load.

His eyes bore into hers. "Is my family history going to be a problem between us?"

Shakily Kit rubbed her hands together, unable to meet his gaze. "No," she whispered tightly, "it won't. It just helps me understand you, that's all."

Noah wanted to say, *Understand me how?* But he didn't. Kit looked genuinely apologetic for her outburst. Rallying because he believed her, he said, "Come over here. Let's get this briefing over with."

Slowly Kit rose. There was a dangerous edge to Noah Trayhern that triggered the flight mechanism within her. She sat down on the couch, far enough away to avoid any direct bodily contact. But she was less nervous now that she realized that she and Noah shared similar unhappy, gut-wrenching pasts. Pete had abandoned her. Morgan had abandoned his family. She had paid for Pete's supercop heroics, and Noah had paid for his brother's horrifying mistake.

Noah pulled out an eight-by-ten black-and-white photograph and handed it to her. "This is our ship, the *Osprey*. It's an SES."

Kit studied the photo, admiring the clean, sleek lines of the Coast Guard cutter. "She's beautiful." In an effort to lighten the atmosphere, Kit added teasingly, "I assume you still refer to ships as 'she'?"

He rallied beneath her obvious attempt to smooth things out between them. There was an endearing quality to Kit, Noah decided sourly. And it wasn't helping him maintain his professional demeanor with her. "The day any ship quits behaving like a fickle, beautiful woman is the day I'll start calling it 'he,'" Noah admitted. "The *Osprey* will be your home for one to seven days at a time. We have cramped crew quarters, a galley and all the social amenities packed into a small space. Quite a bit of room is reserved for the boarding crews, rifles, ammunition. There's also a hold for the storage of confiscated drugs."

Kit's eyes grew large. "Seven days?" She'd never set foot on a boat in her life.

"Most of the time it's one-day missions, five days a week. But we're going to be hunting for Garcia, so our trips will be longer in order to be in his backyard when he decides to do business with the smugglers. We'll be off the coast of South America or in the Gulf of Mexico from time to time because of our assignment."

Kit grimaced. "Chuck was right—I'll turn into a sailor."

"It's better than being a narc patrolling back alleys."

Sobering, Kit muttered, "You're right, I suppose." She tried to shake off the gloom of five years in the trenches and Pete's desertion. "I've never been out to sea, Noah," she warned him, unease plain on her face.

It was the first time she'd called him by his first name. Noah relaxed slightly. Maybe, with time, Kit would call a truce between them and they could both quit carrying a chip on their shoulders. "We've got Dramamine aboard," he reassured her. "I'll let you in on a little secret, though."

"What?"

"Even the crew gets seasick sometimes. It gets pretty rough out in the Gulf and Caribbean at certain times of year. So you'll be in good company."

"This is like an unfolding nightmare. I'm a land-lubber. And I'm not a great swimmer, either."

"I'll give you a tour of the *Osprey* and maybe that will help." He handed her a report. "You're going to have to learn what we do and where you fit into the scheme of things. Let's get down to the business at hand."

Chapter Three

How can I concentrate? Kit wondered distractedly. She tried to remain objective as the briefing continued, but Noah's presence sabotaged her attempts. Pete had been dead a little less than a year now, and Kit was painfully aware of how much she missed having a man in her life. Not that she and Pete had been lovers. No, it had been strictly professional—but undeniably personal. They'd been an unbeatable team on the streets until…

Kit tried to squelch the horrible images that rose in front of her. She shut her eyes tightly, trying to control the sudden surge of grief and loss.

"Here's the map of the territory we have to patrol," Noah pointed out, interrupting her thoughts. He placed the chart before them on the coffee table, using his index finger to trace the areas of activity. "There are four major choke points where Garcia might appear. These are also where we tend to intercept most of the drugs en route to the United States. We've got the Yucatán Channel, the Windward Passage, the Mona Passage and the Anegada Passage.''

Kit managed to surface from the mire of grief. ''What happens at those points?''

''Our chances of intercepting Garcia in a sixty-to two-hundred-foot class of mother ship are much greater.'' Noah rested his strong chin on his clasped hands as he gazed over at her. ''Mother ships carry the bales of marijuana, dropping them off by crane to small ships and boats that try to smuggle them into our waters. The Coast Guard plies 1.8 million square miles of open seas, but the DEA feels Garcia will show up at one of these choke points.''

''And we'll be there?''

''Sometimes. It depends on weather conditions. It's May now, and beginning in August we're building toward hurricane season. No one knows when Garcia might make his move. We know it will be within a year, but not when.''

''And you need me on board to identify the bastard, right?''

Noah watched her face grow tense. ''Yes. We could end up catching him, then turning him loose without even being aware of who he is. You were the only agent to successfully infiltrate his organization in Colombia and can identify him on sight. That's pretty impressive when you consider Garcia can smell an agent ten miles away.''

Kit's breathing grew harsher, and she tried to control the hatred welling up inside her. Running her fingers agitatedly through her hair, she whispered,

"Don't get me started on him. He's the key man in all my nightmares."

"It must have been rough on you." Instinctively Noah reached out and placed his hand on her arm in a gesture of comfort. Her skin was warm and smooth, sending an ache through him. There was something mysterious and primal about Kit that had nothing to do with her being a police detective. Noah had spent all week mulling over his unexpected attraction to her. She seemed unaware of her own sensuality. Yet he sensed it—still, powerful and profound. Reluctantly he released her arm and focused his attention back on business.

Shaken by the sudden intimacy Noah had established with her, Kit retreated inside herself—the only place of real safety she knew. "Garcia's rough on everyone."

"No argument from me. We've been wanting him a long time. The DEA is calling this 'Operation Storm,' because Garcia will, in all likelihood, take his mother ship out during hurricane season. But we can't be sure. That's why we need you with us on every bust. Only you've survived to make a positive ID. The only other person who knows his real identity is his accomplice, Emilio Dante."

Kit's mouth thinned. "Him," she stated flatly, a cold shiver moving up her back.

Noah nodded grimly. Garcia was known for his cold-blooded murders of agents who had tried over the years to infiltrate his vast drug empire in Colombia. Kit had been the only agent to successfully accomplish it and live to tell about it.

Lady, you're very special. And how I admire your courage, Noah thought, glancing over at her bent head. But her bravery had taken a terrible toll on her, and Noah sensed her fragile hold on her emotions. "You can read the report on Operation Storm between today and tomorrow. If you're not doing anything tomorrow afternoon, I'll take you over to the *Osprey* and you can get acquainted with the ship."

"I'll warn you right now, Noah, I don't care for boats." Kit tried to appear calm despite the adrenaline pumping through her. When Noah had touched her, she had wanted to melt into his arms. But her attraction to him wasn't clear or simple. In fact, she wasn't at all comfortable with these newly emerging feelings. Who was he, anyway? In her undercover work she met only the worst of men. Noah seemed like a knight in shining armor by contrast, incorporating Pete's driven quality with a special underlying gentleness. How could she fight this attraction and still do her job as a cop?

Resting his arms against his long, muscular thighs, Noah managed a slight smile. "I think you'll find the *Osprey* a solid vessel. Sometimes when we board the druggie boats, the action can get tight. More than one member of our boarding party has been pushed overboard and had to be rescued."

"I guess it can't be more dangerous than Dade County," Kit ventured wryly.

"On a small, cramped boat there's no place to hide from bullets," Noah warned, his brows dipping. "You'll be the DEA representative aboard our ship. We have radio com-nets with the Miami police, the air force, navy, customs and other CG units. Since you speak fluent Spanish, you can be our interpreter when we need one. You'll also relay info to IOIC—

Interdiction Operations Information Center—and help us identify suspects as we pick them up off boats.''

''Then I'll be part of the boarding party?''

Noah firmly shoot his head. ''No, you'll stay aboard the *Osprey* until we've secured the boarding. No rough stuff for you, lady.''

In a way Kit was relieved. For five years she'd worked undercover without any kind of protection. If she'd carried a pistol, she would have blown her cover and been recognized as a cop. She'd lived by her wits and her ability to survive. ''Then all I'll need is my shoulder revolver.''

''You won't need to carry one.''

Kit gawked at him. Was he crazy? She almost said it but caught herself in time. ''Look, you're painting a pretty dangerous picture. I want to carry a revolver on your ship, just in case.''

Noah gave her an unruffled look. ''The only people who carry weapons on the *Osprey* are the boarding party. No one else has one. That's the rule. Besides, I don't intend to have you close enough to the action to get shot at,'' he explained patiently.

''I hear male chauvinism talking, and I don't like it. I'm not some helpless female who—''

''You're under my command, Kit,'' he interrupted firmly. ''I intend to make sure you'll be safe. My crew is specially trained for boarding procedures. You're along as liaison.'' Her gray eyes were glittering angrily and he tried to defuse the tension between them. ''What's the matter, don't you think I'll keep my promise?''

''Experience has taught me to be leery of trusting men's promises, Noah. They're capable of breaking their word when it suits them.''

Noah held on to his disintegrating patience. ''As long as you're under my authority, you'll have to live with my orders. I'll make sure you're properly protected.''

''I can take care of myself,'' Kit gritted out.

Moving his shoulders to release the accumulated tension, Noah said, ''Can't any man or woman, up to a point?''

''Don't play word games with me!''

Noah slowly sized her up, realizing he was striking at the core of her stubbornness. ''You're so damned independent that you don't know when to lean on someone for support.''

Kit reared back as if struck. ''That's your opinion, Lieutenant Trayhern. Just because I'm a woman doesn't make me less capable of surviving. I learned the hard way that a man can't even protect himself, much less me!''

She got up and turned angrily, then marched down the hall. Taking deep breaths, she walked out into the backyard to cool down. Not more than ten seconds passed before Kit heard the back door open and close. She turned, still trembling with anger, her arms belligerently crossed over her chest.

Noah Trayhern's features were thundercloud dark as he approached her. Kit tensed, uncrossing her arms, allowing her hands to drop to her sides as he halted inches from where she stood. His eyes were the color of a stormy sea as he appraised her in the icy seconds afterward.

''I swore I wouldn't let myself be affected by your negative attitudes,'' he began, his voice low with fury. ''But I am. For some reason, you don't trust men. And whoever caused that kind of damage to you ought to be hung out to dry.'' His voice became more coaxing. ''The only thing that will make our relationship bearable is total honesty. Don't project on me the images of previous men in your life.''

''I'm sorry, Noah,'' she offered, confusion in her gray eyes. ''You hit a sensitive chord in me. I shouldn't have overreacted like that.''

He hung his head and released a long sigh. ''I've tried to figure you out, Kit. You're a woman in a man's world as an undercover agent. That's a harsh kind of life for anyone, much less a sensitive person like you. Second, I think a man has damn near destroyed you emotionally in the past.'' He narrowed his eyes with concern. ''Am I right?''

Kit nodded painfully. ''Right on all counts.'' She turned away and went to the chaise lounge, sitting down. Noah followed and crouched beside her, sympathetically placing his hand on her knee. She accepted his gesture for what it was, and openly studied his face. It was generous and trusting, and Kit felt a desperate need to trust him right now. ''What are you, an amateur psychologist?'' she asked, attempting lightheartedness.

Noah took her hands and held them in his own. ''I think in our business it becomes second nature,'' he offered quietly. ''Level with me, will you?''

''Why?'' Just the warming touch of his strong, protective hands sent a burst of stability through her.

''Because I care.'' Far more than he should, Noah added inwardly. Far more than she would ever know. ''Is that reason enough?''

Kit looked up guardedly. Her heart ached, and need finally won out over her fear. ''Okay, what do you want to know?''

The grip of his fingers tightened momentarily. "Who made you so distrustful of men?"

Fighting a deluge of emotions, she stammered, "Is—is this necessary, Noah?"

"Kit, we're going to be working closely together," he explained, his eyes never leaving her taut features, "and I need to know your strengths and weaknesses, just as you'll know mine."

She searched his face. Her heart thrashed about like a bird caught in a trap. Pain began to ebb from that tightly walled chamber. Kit withdrew her hands and buried her face in them. She felt Noah's reassuring hand sliding across her shoulders in a gesture of support.

A ragged breath escaped her lips, and she lifted her chin, staring blindly past Noah. "I'm sure my personnel file shows that Pete Collins was my partner for four years out of the last five."

Noah searched his mind; he'd read her file thoroughly, committing it to memory. "It does."

She gulped unsteadily. "The last three generations of my family have been police officers. I have three older brothers and they were already police graduates. I followed that family tradition. Except I had all those pie-in-the-sky dreams about helping people."

"You were a supercop with a high degree of patriotism, and you wanted to strike at the roots of one of our worst problems."

Kit winced and nodded miserably. "Supercop. You hit the nail on the head..." Gathering her courage to go on, Kit continued in a strained tone. "When I graduated and demanded narc duty, Chuck Cordeman gave me Pete Collins for a partner. He was a supercop, too. Only he had ten years experience and all kinds of commendations. He was a hotshot, just like you are. As an impressionable twenty-three-year-old, I emulated him in almost every way.''

''Your file shows four years of impressive collars, Kit. And you've got a lot of commendations.''

Sadness overwhelmed her. ''My father's proud of me. That's all that counts.''

Noah understood what she meant. All his life he'd striven to live up to the glorious thirty-year military career that had won his father, Chase Trayhern, nearly every conceivable medal. ''You said you emulated Pete.''

''Not quite.'' Kit's voice turned harsh with agony. ''Pete had a family—a lovely wife and two kids. He had me as his backup and partner. He had everything, Noah, but he threw it all away.''

''What do you mean?''

''His wife divorced him the second year I was with him because he took too many chances. We were always mixing it up with the Mob collars, and there were a lot of shots fired. Finally Valerie couldn't stand his John Wayne tactics, and she took the children back to California. She couldn't live in the constant fear of him dying.'' Kit rubbed her aching brow. ''I tried to tell Pete he should have cared more for them, for his wife and kids. But he just kept taking chances....''

Grimly Noah looked at her. ''He was taking constant chances with your life, too,'' he suggested softly.

''Yeah...I guess he was....'' She closed her eyes. ''But I was too naive to know that at the time. I was so caught up in the image he presented that I was like his shadow. And I was too inexperienced to see that he was a heavy drug user himself.''

Noah frowned, his grip tightening on her shoulder. ''Hard drugs?''

''Yeah.'' Kit laughed hollowly. ''I was so intent upon cleaning up the streets of Miami that I failed to see Pete and his problem! God, how could I have been so blind?''

''We're all blind at some point in our lives. So when did you discover his habit?''

''It was just a few months before he died. Pete's bravado and risk taking were sort of a death wish. The thing he hated most in the world had control over his life. When I put two and two together, I tried to talk to him about it.''

''And?''

Kit shook her head, giving Noah a grief-stricken look. ''When I confronted him with it, he denied it.''

''Typical of a junkie.''

Kit valiantly tried to stem the rising tide of anguish that threatened to shut off her breathing. ''Typical,'' she croaked.

''You're doing fine. What happened next?''

Her shoulders dropped, and her eyes remained fixed on him. ''Those months were hell,'' she rasped. ''Once Pete knew I was aware of his drug problem, he didn't care what he did. He just kept taking stupid chances.''

''Were you emotionally involved with him?''

''If you're asking if we were lovers, the answer is no. I was emotionally involved from the standpoint that he was my partner. He'd been like a hero to me, and we'd spent too many years together not to have feelings of intense loyalty.''

Noah studied her tortured features. At a gut level he sensed that Kit *had* been in love with Pete Collins. Had she been naive about love before meeting the larger-than-life supercop? If so, then Pete Collins could have had an almost mesmerizing effect on Kit and her young, untutored emotions.

"Was he like a father to you?" Noah asked, trying to put their relationship into some kind of focus.

"More like a big brother." She managed a sad smile. "He was wonderful, Noah. So proud, brave and strong. And then he became just like the filth we were busting."

Noah's stomach knotted. "Did he become violent with you?"

"Not physically. But brutality comes in many forms, Noah. You know that and so do I. Pete beat me down emotionally and mentally until I began losing it."

"So narc duty and your home life became one and the same?"

"I never had a home life. Narc was my life. I—I never could talk to Dad about this. I'm sure he'd have expected me to turn Pete in. I felt guilty about not being able to talk Pete into getting help. I was walking a tightrope with Pete in the middle of the Garcia undercover operation. I posed as a Colombian, and Pete was my older brother who handled things stateside."

"I remember reading in the paper how Emilio Dante was collared. You were responsible for that, weren't you?"

A shudder worked up her spine, and Kit hid her face in her hands to hide the emotions etched on it. "Dante was Garcia's main man. I lured Dante to Miami for capture. At the last moment, just before the bust went down, Pete took an unbelievably stupid chance and Dante gunned him down.''

Noah felt as if a fist had slammed into his heart. ''Right in front of you?''

''Y-yes. Damn Pete Collins!'' she sobbed. ''He should have cared more about his family, himself or even his partner, me! And he didn't! All he could do was grandstand, adding another commendation to his record and having the other cops look up to him. I really believe he was more afraid of them finding out he was a junkie than he was of getting killed.''

Her anguish scored his chest. She was trembling, and he guessed that she hadn't cried for a year. He wrapped his arm around her. ''I'm sorry,'' Noah soothed, ''I didn't mean to make you hurt this way. It's over, Kit. Just let go of the pain. I'll hold you…''

Noah's gentleness shattered her immobility. Fear vomited through Kit, and she tore out of his embrace with a cry. She saw the surprise on his features as he looked at her.

''Just leave me alone!'' she begged hoarsely. ''Just go away!'' Hanging on to the grief and tears, Kit whirled around, running for the safety of her house. Blindly she ran down the hall to her bedroom, closing the door behind her. With shaking hands, she locked it. Knees wobbly, she made it to the bed and curled in a tight ball, unable to release the past because Noah Trayhern reminded her too much of Pete Collins.

As she lay there, eyes tightly shut, Kit saw too many similarities between the two men. Only this time, Noah's gentleness and understanding had made her vulnerable in a way she'd never encountered. Pete had never been tender, much less sensitive to anyone but himself. But Noah had some of Pete's other attributes—a drive to be the best, to overcome a personal failing, although in Noah's case it was to compensate for his brother, Morgan. He was a supercop in a Coast Guard uniform.

Muffling a cry, Kit rolled onto her stomach, clutching a pillow, buried in a mire of past and present anguish. There was no way out, no answer. Somehow she'd have to stop the unraveling emotions that Noah had jerked free within her, and try to work with him. But where was she going to get the strength? And what would Noah do about her past? She'd trusted him enough to tell the truth. What would he do with that volatile information?

"Are you Chuck Cordeman?"

Cordeman raised his head from the mound of paperwork that seemed to attack him from every direction. "Yeah, I'm Cordeman. Who are you?" he shot back in an irritated tone. The noise surrounding them couldn't be blocked out, although the narc supervisor's office was enclosed by a sturdy glass panel. Phones were ringing constantly, and men and women in plainclothes with police IDs hanging on their shirts milled around in the larger outer office.

"I'm Lieutenant Noah Trayhern of the Coast Guard." Noah didn't offer his hand.

Leaning back in his lumpy chair, Cordeman studied him a moment. "Have a seat."

"We've got some business to discuss."

"Look, I'm pretty busy, Lieutenant. If you can make it quick I—"

"Stow it, Cordeman. What I've got to tell you isn't going to wait." Noah took a deep breath, trying to control his emotions. "I left Kit Anderson's house an hour ago."

Cordeman's bushy eyebrows drew into a heavy scowl. "So?"

Noah's expression hardened as he placed both hands flatly on Cordeman's desk, glaring down at the pudgy supervisor. "When I met Kit, I knew she was in bad shape. That's why I fought IOIC to give her a week's rest before we initiated Operation Storm." His nostrils flared. "She hasn't improved. Now you're going to throw your considerable departmental weight into this lopsided battle to help get her two or three more weeks of rest. She's not anywhere close to being ready to step into this damn snake pit of an operation!"

Cordeman glared up at him. "I think you'd better calm down!"

"You really don't care if Kit Anderson can survive this bust, do you?" Noah asked angrily.

Cordeman shot out of his chair and leaned across the dilapidated desk. "Now just one damn minute, Trayhern! Who the hell do you think you are, coming in here with accusations like that?"

"I'm responsible for Kit Anderson," Noah countered. "She's officially part of my team, Cordeman. And *I* do care what happens to my people. Particularly when so much is at stake." His eyes narrowed to slits of fury. "You knew Kit was broken emotionally before you sent her to us, didn't you? You knew it, and sent her, anyway. Why did you do it, Cordeman?"

Cordeman's jaw jutted outward, and his face turned red. "Kit is a damn good agent!" he breathed. "The best! The captain wanted her on this operation because she's the only one who can identify Garcia. She's the only one to come back alive from his fortress. That's *why* she's been assigned to you, Trayhern. Is that clear enough?''

Noah dug his fingers into the desk, his knuckles whitening. ''A lot of good her knowledge is going to serve if she's mentally and physically on the edge. You know that and so do I!''

Cordeman reared back, glowering at Noah. His raspy breathing heated up the silence lengthening between them. ''Okay,'' he muttered. ''So she's almost washed up. Kit will hold together for you. She's tough. She's got what it takes.''

''She bought it less than a year ago, Cordeman! Kit's been running on raw nerves and ulcer medicine since then. Who the hell are you trying to fool?''

The narc supervisor's shoulders dropped. ''Okay, okay,'' he groused, ''so Kit's been going downhill for a while.''

Noah straightened, his eyes blazing. ''Kit lost her partner, Pete Collins. And you didn't even have the humanity to give her time to recover. You just pushed her back into the trenches, hoping she'd forget about it.''

Cordeman's gaze moved to the floor. ''Look, I feel badly about this.... Kit's like a daughter to me.''

''No father in his right mind would have done what you did,'' Trayhern snarled. ''She looked to you for support, Cordeman, and you ignored all the warning signs. I don't buy the father figure routine.''

The older man sat heavily on his chair, not meeting Noah's eyes. ''Kit was hysterical after Pete's death.''

''Did you know he was hooked on drugs?''

Cordeman studied him harshly. ''At the time, no.

And if I had, I'd have hauled him off duty, taken his badge and sent him into rehabilitation. Kit kept that knowledge to herself and tried to help him, but she failed. What she did was wrong. She should have come to me. But she was too young and too loyal to Pete.''

''So you found out after he died?''

''Yeah. I went over to the hospital and that's where she spilled the whole ugly story.'' He shook his head. ''They had a special relationship, Trayhern. It wasn't love, but it was a commitment to each other to be the best at what they did. They were one hell of a team. Ever since Kit lost him, she's been sliding.''

''So after Collins's death you sent her right back out there?''

Cordeman glared at him. ''What else could I do?''

''You could have gotten her some therapy, for God's sake!'' Noah spit out. ''Emotionally, she was *never* cut out for narc duty, but she was trying to please her father, Collins and you.'' Noah grimaced, fury racing through him. ''Kit Anderson shouldn't have been a cop. She hasn't got what it takes to deal with the brutality of it all. You've used up her strength, her spirit and her will to live. Right now, she's close to an emotional breakdown.''

''So what the hell do you want me to do about it?''

''You side with me against IOIC and get Kit three more weeks of recuperation time before we initiate Storm.''

''Three weeks?'' he cried. ''You're out of your mind!''

''Three weeks,'' Noah ground out, ''or she'll be dead on this bust and we both know that.'' He rested his hands against the desk, hovering over the narc supervisor. "And I'm not going to allow that to happen, Cordeman. You hear me? Either you side with me, or I'll throw so many wrenches into this operation that you'll scream like a stuck hog. I know your captain is going up for promotion soon. And I suspect he's counting on Storm to make him look like a regular tin god in front of the good city fathers. I carry weight over at the CG. I'll screw your department so damn hard that your captain will bury you so deep you'll never see the light of day."

Cordeman's eyes grew round. "Do you know how hard it is to get something like that approved? The paperwork alone will weigh ten pounds!"

"I refuse to knowingly put one of my people's lives on the line. Kit is part of my team, Cordeman. Side with me or else. Her life is more important than any drug bust or captain's promotion."

Cordeman continued to glower at Noah, but his tone admitted defeat. "You've got balls, Trayhern."

"See that Kit gets those three weeks," Noah repeated grimly.

"If it will make you feel any better, I tried to get Kit off this assignment."

Noah was sure his eyes indicated his distrust. He had worked with Cordeman from a distance on several occasions in the past. He knew the man's reputation for integrity and an unwavering attitude toward drug smugglers. Cordeman also ran one of the toughest narc divisions in the country. He was good at his job and had a decided talent for getting the best out of the people who worked under him. Maybe a little too good, Noah decided. Kit had returned to work instead of taking time off to adjust to the death of her partner. "Just how hard did you try?"

Cordeman motioned him toward the chair. "Sit down," he growled, his blue eyes narrow. "You're gonna find out, Trayhern, that I do take a great deal of interest in my people." He paused as Noah sat. "I had plans to force Kit to take a leave of absence from the department before Operation Storm was created by DEA. I knew she was hurting, and I tried a number of times to persuade her to talk about it. But she wouldn't. She kept insisting she was all right. About six months ago, she began to make mistakes. It was little things, but she realized as well as any of us that in this business details can get you killed. Finally she came and asked me for a transfer out of the department."

Noah frowned. "Out of narc completely?"

"Yeah. Kit admitted to me that she'd had it. She wanted a desk job—anything to get her off the streets. I promised her I'd do my damnedest."

"With her record of commendations, it should have been easy," Noah pointed out tightly.

Cordeman met his glare. "I went straight to the captain with it. I told him she was at the end of the line emotionally and needed the rest. That was when he told me about Storm." He shook his head sadly. "You know how important Kit is to the success of this operation. If we can get Garcia out of the picture, the Colombian government will cooperate with us in prosecuting him. Garcia's smart—he stays out of the limelight. Anybody trying to take a photo of him can kiss his life goodbye."

Noah rubbed his jaw. "So what kind of deal did you wrangle for her?"

"A lateral transfer to your ship as a liaison observer."

"And after that?"

"After Storm's completed, Kit gets her wish. She gets a cushy desk job as a detective in homicide upstairs."

"Maybe I've misjudged you, Cordeman. And maybe I haven't."

The supervisor sank wearily back into his frayed leather chair. He mopped his brow with a limp white handkerchief. "I'll get Kit those three weeks. Somehow."

Rising, Noah muttered, "Call me as soon as it's official."

Chapter Four

Noah had barely gotten back to headquarters to finish up some paperwork, when Cordeman called. Sitting down at his desk, he took the call.

"Coast Guard. Lieutenant Trayhern speaking."

"This is Cordeman. I've got some bad news for Kit."

Automatically Noah placed a clamp on his emotions. "What's wrong?"

"Plenty. Emilio Dante was just released from prison. Kit was the one who put him away, Trayhern. And he swore that when he got out he'd settle the score with her. Well, he's out, and our snitch just told one of my undercover officers that he's planning to go after her."

Cold fear washed through Noah. "How in hell did that happen? Dante was supposed to be put away for fifteen years."

"His lawyers got him out on bail due to a technicality. There will be another trial. Until then, he's walking around free and vowing revenge. With him out, Operation Storm takes on new importance."

"That's the least of our problems," Noah shot back, irritated. His mind whirled with options on how to protect Kit. She'd have to go into hiding. She was a sitting duck at her home. His heartbeat quickened at the thought of Kit in danger.

"Listen closely, Trayhern. There's not much time. The captain, DEA and IOIC have decided Kit has to go underground. We don't have the manpower to provide her twenty-four-hour protection. She's going to have to disappear completely."

"Of course."

Cordeman's voice grew aggravated. "You still don't get it, do you? Kit's your responsibility now. I just talked with your commander, and we're all in agreement on the action to be taken."

"Fine, I'll go along with it. Just spell out the plan, Cordeman. Dante isn't going to waste any time getting to her."

"Tell me about it. Okay, here are your new orders. Kit is to go underground at your residence for the duration of Operation Storm. Since I haven't initiated the paperwork transferring Kit to the CG yet, that will be the ideal place for her to hide. It's been decided to issue fake orders transferring Kit up to Atlanta on special assignment. That will throw Dante off her trail. I'll be the only police contact with you and her. No one, other than me, the captain and your commander will know Kit's true whereabouts. Your residence will become a safe house for Kit. From there, she can ride with you to the ship and home again. It dovetails perfectly with the operation.''

His fingers tightening around the phone, Noah whispered an epithet. How the hell could he keep a professional distance from Kit when she would be in his personal life? ''There's no way you're putting her on my doorstep, Cordeman.''

The supervisor laughed sharply. ''Tell that to your commanding officer, Trayhern. Listen, this is coming down fast. You can't buck these orders. They've been approved all the way up the line. If I were you, I'd get over to Kit's home pronto, pack a few of her clothes and get her out of there before Dante shows up.''

Kit heard the doorbell ring. She wiped her hands on a towel and placed it on the kitchen counter. It had to be Noah. Why had he sounded so grim on the phone earlier? Opening the door, she looked up at his hard features. He appeared harried—and aggravated.

''Come in,'' she invited. Her heart began a slow pound of dread as she read some undefinable emotion in his stormy eyes.

Taking off his officer's cap, Noah moved into the living room. Kit looked achingly beautiful in the raspberry-colored floor-length cotton gown she wore. Her hair was tousled, framing her oval face, her gray eyes large with concern. As she approached, he said, ''I couldn't talk on the phone when I called you.''

Kit tensed. ''Something's wrong.''

Obviously agitated, Noah ran his fingers across his chin. ''Very wrong. Cordeman called me half an hour ago. Emilio Dante has been sprung from prison.''

Gasping, Kit stared up at him in disbelief and confusion. Dante was free...and he had sworn to kill her the first chance he got! She shut her eyes tightly, trying to fight through the flood of fear. "My God..."

Noah saw her weave unsteadily. He reached out, gripping her arm. "Come on, sit down," he entreated huskily, leading her over to the couch. He sat down next to her.

"Dante's free. But how?" she cried.

Her fear became his. Until that moment, Noah hadn't realized just how much Kit had started to become someone important to him in an emotional sense. The feeling made him reel. Struggling to keep his voice calm and neutral, he told her what Cordeman had said.

"That means I have to disappear. I can't stay here...." Kit looked around the room. She'd spent little time in this house over the past five years, yet within one week she had grown to love its quiet beauty.

"I know. Cordeman and the DEA have already decided what's to be done," Noah began heavily.

"They want me to go to a motel under a fictitious name?"

"No. To my home. It will be your safe house for the duration of Storm."

"What?" Kit stared at him, her mouth dropping open. "You can't be serious!"

"I wish I wasn't," Noah confided, getting to his feet. "The DEA feels you'll be safe at my place. The paperwork transferring you to the CG was never processed. For once the slowness of bureaucracy is a blessing. Cordeman will issue fake orders sending you TAD to Atlanta. Besides, with you going out daily on the *Osprey* this will avoid a lot of transportation difficulties. You can ride to and from work with me." He saw the shock deepen in Kit's features.

Kit looked down at her hands. Her fingers were trembling. She might be physically safe at Noah's home, but her emotions were in danger. "But," she began in a strained voice, "can't you do something? Anything? I don't think us living together under one roof is such a good idea. We can't seem to spend an hour together without arguing."

"There's nothing either of us can do about it," he muttered. "Look, let's get you packed and out of here. There's no time to waste."

Rising, Kit turned to him. "This isn't going to work, dammit!"

All Noah's aggravation and frustration dissolved beneath the desperation in her gray eyes. Why the hell was he acting like this? He could see she was badly shaken by the news. Kit needed his maturity and protection right now, not his anger. "We'll make it work."

Her gaze followed every curve of his face. Despite the harsh set of his mouth, she found compassion in his eyes and heard it in his voice. Her heart said yes to the plan, but her wary mind screamed no. "Noah…this is going to be disastrous."

"I don't like it any more than you do."

Kit wanted to continue to protest, but she knew it was useless. Uncertain, she walked toward the bedroom. Too emotionally exhausted to argue further, she said, "Okay, but I'm not going to be your housekeeper and cook, Noah Trayhern."

He managed a curt nod. "You're a guest at my home. I'll treat you like one."

Kit swallowed against her constricted throat. "Give

me a few minutes and I'll be ready to leave," she uttered tiredly.

"I feel ridiculous," Kit said to Noah as they drove toward his home.

He glanced over at her, struggling to sound optimistic. "As soon as you get over the initial shock, you'll be fine."

She had her doubts. The scenery along the freeway didn't impinge upon her inner turmoil, and Noah's closeness did nothing but emphasize her fragile emotions. She wasn't prepared for any kind of relationship with a man—professional or otherwise. Kit stole a quick glance at Noah's profile, lingering on his mouth. It turned up, and there were laugh lines at the corners of his eyes. The men she worked with didn't smile often.

"You know everything about me," she began awkwardly, "and I know nothing about you."

His sea-green eyes lightened. "I'll give you a hint—my friends refer to my home as 'Noah's ark.'"

Her brows drew down. "I'm in no shape for guessing games today. Mind explaining?"

"I'll let that be a surprise. What else do you want to know?"

Kit refused to yield to the implication in his husky voice. Further, she chose to ignore the word "home." She had always lived in a house, never a home. "Tell me about yourself," she insisted.

"Twenty-nine, single, black hair, green eyes—"

"Cut the stats. You sound like a sales pitch for some dating service."

"With my job responsibilities, I don't date much."

"Are you complaining?"

"Just a roundabout way of letting you know you won't be a third wheel at home."

Kit sank against the car seat, and as she closed her eyes, she suddenly felt very tired. "The more I get to know you, Noah, the less I understand about men," she admitted softly.

"You've worked with men all your life," Noah returned. *The dark side of them,* he thought. "Maybe I can show you a more positive side." He saw a slight upward curve of her lips. That was enough for him. Even in the bright afternoon sunlight that cascaded through the car window, Kit appeared drawn. "Go to sleep," he coaxed. "I'll wake you when we get home."

Kit released a sigh, the warmth of the sunlight making her drowsy. There was an incredible sense of protection surrounding her and she knew it was due to Noah's presence. Even with Dante free, she knew she was safe with Noah. His words were like balm to her exhausted state and Kit quickly succumbed to sleep.

Noah glanced at Kit from time to time, keeping most of his attention on the traffic. In sleep she looked younger. It was hard to imagine that she was close to his own age; she looked twenty-four. Maybe that was why she had an ulcer: instead of allowing the tension of her job to show, she turned it inward on herself, like a dagger.

Groggily Kit forced her eyes open after a third gentle shake of her shoulder. Noah's male scent drifted into her sensitive nostrils and she inhaled it like a lost memory.

"Kit?" he called. "We're home."

Home...the word struck a responsive chord. If only she were really home...

"Come on, or I'll have to carry you in."

Viewing that as a threat, Kit forced herself to move, unbuckling the seat belt. She blinked, her lids heavy with sleep. "I feel as if I slept forever."

Noah opened the door to the Trans Am. "It was only about half an hour's worth."

She suppressed a yawn. "That long?"

"You needed it," he growled softly, climbing out of the sports car.

Kit was going to open her car door, but Noah got there first. "You don't have to do that," she protested, getting out.

He gave her a patient smile, cupping her elbow as he guided her up the walk.

Kit ignored the trace of irony she saw in Noah's face, looking instead at the house he called a home. It was a single-story brick bungalow with well-manicured hedges and several palms gracing the yard. Towering hibiscus bushes surrounded the house itself, their profusion of multicolored flowers creating a look of Eden.

Kit cast a glance up at him. "You do all the yard work alone?"

"Will wonders never cease?" Noah drawled, opening the latch on the gate and allowing her to enter the front yard.

"That tells me something about you."

Noah frowned. "What?"

"You may spend a lot of time at sea, but you also like putting your hands in the earth, as well."

"I like putting my hands on any living thing," he

remarked cryptically as he fished the house key out of his pocket.

"That sounds threatening," Kit muttered.

"Relax. Okay, brace yourself," he warned, pushing the door open.

Kit frowned and began to ask why, when a barrage of brown, black and gray furry bodies assaulted her. The joyous bark of a dog and the meowing of two cats blended into a cacophony of greetings. Kit's eyes widened enormously as she was swamped by the cats running madly in circles between her legs. She heard Noah laugh and he gripped her arm, guiding her skillfully through the animals.

The dog barked, leaping midair before them in the red tile foyer, and Kit realized with amazement that he had only three legs. A flood of compassion surged through her. Noah reached out, speaking in an authoritative, but nonetheless gentle tone. Immediately the black Doberman ceased his antics and calmly positioned himself in front of them, panting happily.

Kit looked up at Noah. "What is this? A zoo?"

He grinned, taking off his officer's cap and tossing it on the small mahogany desk nearby. "Noah's ark, remember?" He gestured toward the dog and two cats. "Meet my extended family. The dog's name is Tripoli. He's the general boss of my home when I'm not here and he's an outstanding watchdog."

Kit barely heard Noah's explanation, a pained expression on her face. "But look at him, Noah. He's got only three legs! My God, that's horrible...the poor thing."

Noah reached over to caress Kit's cheek, then chastised himself at the instinctive gesture. Kit invited intimacy. Disgruntled, he growled, "Let's look at the positives, shall we? No negatives. So his right front leg is missing. Tripoli gets around fine without it.''

''But he's crippled!'' Kit protested, a catch in her voice.

''He doesn't know that,'' Noah returned, catching her startled expression. ''If you make him a cripple, he'll become one for you, Kit.'' He patted Tripoli affectionately, scratching a favorite place behind the dog's ear. Then Noah gave her a serious look. ''But if you treat him as a whole dog, he'll be whole for you and won't know the difference.''

Noah's philosophy rattled Kit. There was truth to his quietly spoken observation. She turned her attention to the cats, who milled about her feet, meowing out their own kind of welcome, begging for her attention. ''It's a good thing I love animals,'' she groused, crouching in the hall to pet all of them.

Noah knelt beside her, acutely aware of the tenderness in her expression. ''I knew you would.''

''Did you, indeed?'' Kit replied, hiding behind sarcasm.

This just wasn't going to work. She was snapping and defensive over his every comment. He picked up the first cat. ''You hear that, Calico? This beautiful lady thinks I'm pulling her leg. What do you think?''

Calico promptly released a mournful meow as if on cue. Kit couldn't help but laugh as she reached over and petted the animal. She heard the cat wheezing heavily with each breath.

''Something's wrong with her....''

Noah nodded, placing Calico in her arms. ''She came crawling up on my back porch last year during a hurricane. The vet diagnosed distemper. I thought she was going to die from it.''

"And you pulled her through."

"Actually," Noah admitted, "Calico pulled herself through. She's got a good heart, and if you don't watch this little lady, she'll snuggle up beside you on the pillow at night. Callie prefers the softer things life has to offer."

Kit laughed helplessly, placing Calico on the highly polished red tile floor. Her heart softened as she stood watching Noah with his animals. Anyone who had this kind of devoted following couldn't be all bad. Animals were said to be living mirrors of their owner's temperament. "I wouldn't mind a furry body sharing my bed."

Noah's brow arched inquiringly.

Flushing, Kit stood nervously beneath his gaze. She could almost hear his rejoinder about him joining her in bed. The thought was startlingly heated. With every new discovery about Noah, her defenses melted just a little more, leaving her vulnerable to his appealing nature.

Picking up the second cat, Noah grinned. "This dainty little morsel is Tuna Boat." He placed her in Kit's waiting arms.

"She weighs a ton!" Kit exclaimed, hefting the twenty-pound long-haired gray cat.

"Yes, well, Tunie has never missed a meal in her life, as you can tell."

Kit tried not to be swayed by Noah and petted the worshipful cat. She studied the cat's face. "Oh, Noah..." she whispered, distraught. "Don't tell me she's—"

"Blind," Noah finished. "Some teenage boys were chasing her with sticks and struck her in the head down by the dock one morning before I went aboard the *Osprey*. I happened to see it, but by the time I got over there, the damage had been done. I took her to the vet and he said she was lucky to have survived the blow at all.'' He stroked the cat's head fondly as she nestled contentedly in Kit's arms. ''She'll be blind the rest of her life.''

Kit's gray eyes glittered with unexpected tears. ''How can people pick on poor, defenseless animals that have no way to protect themselves?''

She was emotionally unpredictable. One more minus to their unworkable situation, Noah told himself. But Kit's unexpected compassion touched him deeply. ''Tunie has the run of the front yard and back. She's in seventh heaven—she owns me, chows down twice a day and has a home.''

''But she's blind!''

''Tunie doesn't know that. Put her down, Kit, and watch her navigate for a moment. This cat has memorized the entire layout of the house and yard.'' Noah shook his head, mystified. ''I swear Tunie has all-terrain avionics inside that head of hers. She never runs into a tree or bush.'' He ruffled the cat's fur affectionately. ''She's quite a little lady.''

Kit rested her fingers against her throat, swallowing hard.

He gave her an intense look. ''Animals touch you, don't they?''

She glared at him, then fixed her gaze on the cat. ''Of course! Why should you be so surprised?''

''Now calm down. That wasn't meant as an accusation.''

''It sounded like one.''

''It was an obtuse compliment. Truce?''

Kit gave him a disgruntled look as she tore her eyes

from Tunie. ''All right,'' she relented. ''Truce.'' Her voice lowered with feeling. ''I don't believe all this. They're all disabled.'' And her eyes darkened upon him. ''Am I one more cripple coming to your house, Noah?''

The tenor of her voice caught him off guard. His green gaze softened as he held her wavering stare. ''In my eyes, no one here is crippled. Does that answer your question?''

Kit gulped down a lump, holding Tunie tightly. For some unknown reason, she identified strongly with the loving cat. ''I feel like Tunie here,'' she admitted rawly. ''Only my blindness to the narc business has left me spinning.''

Noah nodded, understanding far more about her condition than he could let on. ''You're surrounded by courage. Each one of these animals has pulled itself back to life with its own inner strength.'' He gave her an unsure look. Kit was too mercurial for his tastes. ''Listen, let's get you settled. I've got some business to attend to back at the office. When I get home around seven, I'll make dinner. Deal?''

How could she say no? Kit wondered numbly, looking down at Tunie happily snuggled within her arms. Noah brought in her luggage and placed it in the brightly colored guest room that would be hers. Sunlight filtered through the pale green curtains. The bedspread was patterned with white daisies, yellow marigolds and rust-colored asters. The furniture was crafted from cherry wood, which added to the overall sense of richness of the decor. Kit stared at Noah's broad back as he placed the suitcases on the bed for her. Those shoulders could conceivably carry the weight of the world, she thought. Her heart blossomed with hope—a feeling she thought had been taken from her forever. Looking down, she realized the animals had crowded around her feet once more. She managed a laugh.

"Looks like I'm going to have all the help I need to unpack."

Her laughter was lilting, stealing through the barriers Noah had tried to erect. He straightened, forcing a smile. "Just watch Tunie. She has a terrible habit of plopping down in opened suitcases, open bureau drawers or on clothing that isn't hung up." Noah grimaced. "And I can't tell you how many times I've picked gray cat hairs off my uniform."

"Typical man—you throw your clothes anywhere it suits you."

Smarting under her observation, Noah halted at the entrance. "Get used to your new home while I'm gone," he muttered. "With all these characters here, I keep it clean or else. The bathroom is over there," he said, pointing toward a closed door.

"And your room?" Kit asked. The words were out before she could take them back.

Noah acted as if there were nothing wrong with her question. "On the other side of your bathroom." He gazed down at the animals, then up at her. "Take your time unpacking, get the layout of the house. Then I suggest a hot bath and some rest. You're still pale."

Kit wrinkled her nose. "I don't like being mothered, Noah."

His green eyes glinted with devilry. "Oh, yes, you do. You just don't know it. I'll see you later."

He was so sure of himself, and in her present state that unsettled her. "I'll see you at seven."

The lack of enthusiasm, even friendliness in her tone, left him uncomfortable. ''Yeah. Seven.'' And he turned, leaving her bedroom.

After Noah left, Kit chastised herself. Her voice had sounded clipped and hard. Noah Trayhern was making her emotions fluctuate like a roller coaster. As she put away her jeans and tank tops and hung up what few dresses and skirts she owned, Kit attempted to sort out the past week.

Noah was a catalyst, she decided, for everything he came in contact with, judging from the animals sitting expectantly around the bed, watching her with aplomb. And whether Kit wanted to admit it or not, she felt protected with Noah's animal family. Taking a deep breath, she walked over to the bed, giving each cat a quick pat before wandering through the house. *Home,* she corrected herself. *Noah calls it a home.* It was going to be a battleground with them forced to live in such close quarters.

Kit mulled over that thought as she ambled down the hall. The feeling in his house made her admit it really was a home. She looked over her shoulder: Tuna Boat waddled in the lead, with Calico and Tripoli bringing up the rear. A tender smile pulled at her lips as she watched them follow her like a gaggle of loyal geese. Noah was right: they didn't recognize they were crippled, blind or shortchanged. Was love the ingredient that made them feel whole again?

Deep in thought, Kit wandered into Noah's bedroom by accident. Tuna Boat came and rested her plump fanny on Kit's foot. Calico wheezed on by, leaping up on the multicolored afghan spread across the large bed. Noah was like a prism, Kit decided as her gaze ranged around the room. Sunlight, when refracted through a crystal, revealed all the colors seen by the human eye. This room, this house, did not mirror the dark side of masculinity. Instead, like a prism, it showed light, color and sensitivity.

Several luxuriant Boston ferns hung from the ceiling, and potted plants graced the finely crafted cherrywood dresser. The warmth of the highly waxed mahogany floors only enhanced the feeling of life that made Kit want to stay in his room. A flood of guilt surged through her: she felt as if she were trespassing. Yet it was as if he had invited her to explore this personal side to himself. He trusted her!

By the time she had completed her exploration of the house, Kit was tired. Glancing at her watch, she saw it was almost three o'clock. Noah's suggestion of a hot bath sounded heavenly. At the door to the bathroom, Kit turned to the two cats tagging along with her.

"No," she told them firmly. "You are not following me in here."

As Kit shut the bathroom door and slid out of her clothes, her mind drifted back to Noah. She realized as she stepped into the hot, fragrant water that she had been on the receiving end of his hard, efficient side. This new and unexpected aspect involving his love of animals that had suffered beckoned to her. Noah was healing, whether she wanted to admit it or not. But could she keep her personal feelings for him at bay and maintain the decorum demanded of both of them in this unusual circumstance?

Getting out of the bath, Kit slipped into a silky lavender nightgown. Drowsy and feeling relaxed, she padded to the bed and lay down. As she tucked her hands beneath the pillow and closed her eyes, her last thoughts were of Noah and the miraculous effect he had upon her.

The sun was hot, making the humidity seem even higher than usual. Noah brushed a light film of sweat off his brow as he eased himself out of the Trans Am. He saw Tripoli at the picture window of his house as he sauntered up the walk. Glancing at his watch, he realized he was half an hour late. Kit was probably furious. Starving women made poor companions. Unlocking the front door, he was greeted by the Doberman. Noah leaned over to pet him, then took off his officer's cap and dropped it on the small desk.

"Where's Kit?" he asked. The dog leaped away, his claws clacking noisily on the wooden floor as he raced to the end of the hall toward the bedrooms. Noah followed him, steeling himself against Kit's anger at his lateness.

To his surprise, Kit didn't come out to meet him. He halted at the entrance to her bedroom, allowing his eyes to adjust to the gloom. The venetian blinds behind the green curtains had been pulled shut, and Noah felt his features relax. Kit lay asleep, a light quilt drawn up to her waist. Both cats were napping beside her.

Quietly entering the room, Noah stood over Kit and watched her sleep. He shouldn't be standing here; he ought to pretend she wasn't even in the house. But that was impossible, he admitted harshly to himself. While at dockside with the *Osprey* crew, he'd thought constantly of Kit being here in his home. Oddly, just getting to see her helped evaporate the confusion of his feelings. He narrowed his eyes with concern. Even in the semidarkness her skin was pale, drawn tightly across her cheekbones. The shadows beneath her eyes were still in evidence, and Noah tried to curb his worry. Her lips were parted, stress no longer drawing in the corners. *So,* he thought, *you really do want to laugh.* She looked like a lost, helpless waif on the huge expanse of the bed. Noah leaned over and pulled the quilt up around her shoulders, tucking it in so that she would remain warm despite the coolness of the central air-conditioning.

Straightening, Noah ordered himself to leave. He had to before he reached out to caress her cheek. Every time he got around Kit, he seemed to go into a tailspin. She must have taken a bath—her hair was slightly curled, easing the angular planes of her face and creating a softer look to her features. The powerful need to will away the pain she still carried caught him off balance.

He didn't want to leave Kit's room, but he made himself move. How Kit, as a woman, had survived five years in the narc trench warfare was beyond him. He kept the door to her bedroom open so that the animals could come and go as they pleased. As he walked down the hall to his own room, Noah admitted that Kit affected him deeply. No woman had ever reached out and unraveled him like this. Somehow, he was going to have to hide all those feelings from her. But how?

Kit felt the warm roughness of a man's hand moving across her shoulder. Drowsily she forced open her eyes. Even in the darkness she was aware of the intensity of Noah's gaze as he leaned over her.

"I thought I'd better get you up for a bite to eat,"

he explained in a low voice. "Then you can go back to bed."

She fought the drugged feeling of tiredness, slowly becoming aware of his presence. A fresh ribbon of emotion squeezed from her heart as she silently stared up at him. Noah gave her stability, and something more. "Wh-what time is it?"

"Almost 9:00 p.m."

"Nine?" Her eyes widened and she struggled into a sitting position. It dawned on her that she was wearing a revealing gown with a low-cut neck, and heat rushed into her cheeks. What was he doing in *her* bedroom? And then, with a pang, Kit realized she hadn't shut the door, so how could he knock and announce his presence? She pulled her knees upward. Sudden shyness gripped her when she saw the undisguised hunger in his eyes.

Noah placed himself in check. Gone were all of Kit's defenses. She sat shyly before him like a child-woman just awakening from a wonderful dream. Grimly he forced himself to step away from the bed.

"I wanted you to get something to eat before we tucked you in for a good night's sleep," he told her, his voice gruff.

"'We'?" Kit asked, her voice husky.

Noah gestured to the foot of the bed. "The cats slept with you."

Kit laughed. It was a clear, uninhibited laugh, straight from her heart. And the rich sound coming from her filled her with an inexplicable joy. Her eyes crinkled as she met Noah's green gaze. "I don't believe this, Noah. I feel as if I'm in some kind of dream. Your animals are like little guardians." Her smile died on her lips as she searched his shadowed face.

"You're coming out of a five-year tunnel of darkness."

"I'm just beginning to realize how badly I buried myself in my work. You're right. It was a horrible tunnel."

"Life doesn't have to be a dark, moody scene, Kit. There can be light and laughter in this crazy-quilt world of ours." He managed a smile. "There can be light even in the worst sort of darkness."

Kit shut her eyes and turned her head away. "At first I thought you were just like Pete."

Noah shoved his hands into the pockets of his jeans. "Oh?" What she thought of him meant more than he cared to admit.

Kit rested her cheek against her drawn-up knees and stared blankly at the wall. "You're driven just as he was. And you have something to prove because of your family tragedy. Pete was always striving to prove he was better than anyone else. His work was his entire life." Releasing a broken sigh, Kit raised her head and gazed up at Noah. "Maybe I'm wrong about you to a degree. This house is lived in and cared for. All the plants are healthy and trimmed. I noticed you had a bunch of seedlings on the windowsill in the kitchen.... Your officer image doesn't fit the Noah Trayhern who lives in this house."

Relieve to hear she didn't think he was another Pete Collins, Noah grinned. "Don't take my officer image too lightly. Remember, I come from a family with a two-hundred-year tradition of military service."

Although hungry for information about him, Kit

quelled her curiosity. Even in the shadows, Noah had a kind face when he allowed that officer's mask to slip. The man who stood relaxed in front of her was her boss. Kit couldn't still the suffused happiness that surfaced unexpectedly within her. ''Let me put my robe on, and I'll join you in a few minutes,'' she promised.

Chapter Five

Kit shuffled into the kitchen. Hands thrust deeply into the blue velour pockets of her robe, she stood uncertainly at the entrance. Noah had just placed a seafood salad at the table, and he motioned for her to come and sit down.

He saw a smile light her eyes, erasing the tension around her mouth. "Come on in," he invited.

"Somehow," Kit commented, sitting down and picking up the royal blue linen napkin, "I think I've got the better end of our deal. This is more than a safe house. This salad looks pretty good."

Pouring her some coffee, Noah sat down opposite her. Funny, how Kit made the house feel warm and comfortable with her quiet presence. "My mother made all three of us kids learn how to cook," he noted wryly.

Smiling, Kit picked up the fork. Suddenly she was

famished. The combination of crab, lobster and shrimp on a bed of fresh lettuce was incredibly appealing. "Good for her."

"Did yours?"

She grinned and scooped a forkful of crab into her mouth. There was amusement in Noah's thoughtful green eyes. The rapport he established with her was molten, heating the inner fires of her heart. "Yes, me and my older brothers."

"Good for her," he repeated.

"I'll help around here with house duties, Noah. I don't intend to be a bad house guest."

"This house is just like a ship. Every crew member has responsibilities. We'll set up a system and share the chores. You're not the type to escape duty, anyway," he mused, sipping his coffee.

"You're right. Noah, this is really disconcerting."

"What is?"

Kit jabbed her fork into a piece of lobster. "You have an entire personnel file on me. I have absolutely nothing on you."

"I'm an open book."

Kit gave him a dark look. "Sure you are."

He sat back, the silence pleasant despite her growling. "I figure with the time we're going to have to spend with each other, you'll probably find out more about me than you'd like to know."

Kit wasn't so sure. "To tell you the truth, I'm feeling bad about cluttering up your personal life by using your place as a safe house."

Noah toyed with his cup, turning it slowly around. "I don't have much of a personal life, except that I visit my parents in Clearwater once a month, or open up one of the guest rooms to my sister, Alyssa."

Kit finished the salad and pushed the plate aside, then picked up her coffee cup. ''It sounds like you're close to your family, the way I am to mine.''

He snorted softly. ''Believe me, if we hadn't been close in these five years since Morgan disappeared, I don't know how any of us would have survived.''

She nodded sympathetically, recalling the press about Morgan Trayhern's defection to North Vietnam. Every time the topic came up, Noah's eyes reflected grief and sadness. Kit hurt for him.

''My father just retired from the Minneapolis Police Department,'' she offered, not wanting to dig into something so sensitive. ''I have three brothers who are in the highway patrol.''

''Family tradition runs strong in you, too.''

''Don't sound so unhappy about it. They like what they're doing.''

He shrugged, wanting, unsuccessfully, to keep their talk impersonal. ''I wasn't thinking about them. Take a look at you— I think family pressure pushed you into a career you really weren't cut out for.''

Kit studied him for a long time before answering. Noah had made the comment with feeling, not hurled it as an accusation. ''Lately I've been thinking about that possibility,'' she admitted quietly. ''What about you? Are you happy in your chosen career?''

''Yes. I put in long hours to keep my record spotless. You get ahead in the Coast Guard by making yourself outstanding in some way. I've had to work extra hard because of what happened to Morgan.''

''You work at your job twenty-four hours a day, leaving no time for a personal life.''

''You've done the same thing,'' he parried.

Kit got up and went to the drain board, leaning

against it, coffee cup in hand. "Maybe we're both like Pete Collins and don't want to admit it."

"Maybe you project Collins on every man you meet."

"Touché. Maybe I do."

Disgruntled, Noah rose and arranged the dirty dishes in the dishwasher. Why did he get nettled when she compared him to Collins? He was nothing like him!

"What's on the agenda for tomorrow?" Kit asked, realizing he was upset.

"It's the weekend," he snapped.

"I didn't know it made any difference to you." Kit saw the anger flash momentarily in his eyes and knew she'd blundered into sensitive territory. Wearily she said, "I guess it does."

"I try to work five days a week, Kit, not seven. But I've had to prove myself. Other times we're at sea for an extended period." Noah felt some of the anger drain away as he noticed Kit struggling to smooth over the tension between them.

"So what do you usually do on weekends?" Kit knew that since she was in hiding, she would have to remain solely at the house or on the *Osprey*.

"If I haven't taken on any extra projects at headquarters, I work with wood and make furniture, or take my boat out to a cove and snorkel for dinner. What do you do?"

She shrugged and set the cup on the drain board. "Lately I've watched too much television. This is the first time I've had a series of weekends off in years. I guess I'll find out, won't I?"

The sudden unhappiness in her eyes bothered him. He rested his hands on his hips, studying her. "I was going to plant those seedlings tomorrow along the front of the house.''

''I like the idea of you planting flowers. Need some help?''

There was life in her eyes, and Noah found himself drowning in their soft dove-gray color. Jerking himself back from his spiraling attraction to Kit, he muttered, ''If you want to help, you can.''

''I'd love to. It's been a long time since I've dug my fingers into the earth, or even sat in the sunshine doing something like that.''

He heard the enthusiasm in her tone and was unable to stop a smile from curving the corners of his mouth. ''Get some sleep, Kit. I'll see you in the morning.''

Cordeman's call at eight in the morning rousted Noah out of sleep. He turned over, groping for the phone.

''Trayhern,'' he muttered.

''This is Cordeman. I'm calling from a pay phone because I don't want our conversation tapped by the wrong parties.''

Noah sat up, instantly alert. The sheet fell away, exposing his naked chest. ''What is it?'' He wiped the sleep from his eyes, his heart taking on an urgent beat.

''Nothing's wrong, Lieutenant. I'm just calling to make sure your house guest arrived safely.''

Eyeing the clock on the dresser, Noah bit back a curse. ''She's fine,'' he ground out.

''Good, because word is Dante's out lookin' for Kit. Another one of our snitches brought us the news late last night. I don't want her to show her face in

Miami. You understand, Trayhern? She's not to make phone calls, or answer your phone, either.''

Pushing strands of hair off his brow, Noah dangled his legs over the edge of the bed. Sunlight streamed through the windows. ''Look, Cordeman, I know standard operating procedure on this, so don't lecture me like I was some rookie cop.''

''I just want to make damn sure she's safe. The only place she goes is to and from the dock.''

''I've got a boat at a marina outside Miami. Some weekend I plan to take her out on it for the day. Any problem with that?''

''Just keep her low profile, Trayhern. I have a DEA agent who is in position to retrieve info on Garcia—if he's able to get it back to us. Operation Storm is officially initiated as of now. That three weeks you wanted for her is out of the question with Dante loose.''

''Dammit.'' Noah rubbed the growth of beard on his face savagely. Cordeman was right. Dante would renew activity with Garcia now that he was out on bail. ''I'm planning to get her on board the *Osprey* Monday.''

''Fine. She's got this weekend to rest up then.''

Noah wanted to say that Kit needed a hell of a lot more than that, but it was useless. ''Anything else?''

''Yeah, one more thing.''

''What?''

''Keep all this stuff about Dante from Kit. She saw the bastard blow Pete away.''

''Don't worry, I intend to try to allow her a place to heal, Cordeman.''

The supervisor chuckled. ''Yeah, the word's out on

you, Trayhern—you're a real in-fighter for your people. I oughta know.''

Grimly Noah said, ''I still want you to do everything in your power to make the next three weeks as easy as possible on Kit. She's fragile....''

''I'll do my best. You two have a good weekend. I've got a feeling Kit needs a Sir Lancelot right now.''

Sir Lancelot. Noah dropped the phone back into the cradle, his mood black. Grumbling, he got up, took a hot shower, shaved and then dressed in a pair of old, faded jeans and a red polo shirt.

Opening the door, he waited for the rush of animals that always came. No one was in sight. The entire house was still. Frowning, he wondered where everyone was. Usually the cats were meowing at his bedroom door, with Tripoli nearby. Padding down the hall in his bare feet, Noah saw that Kit's bedroom door was ajar. The scent of coffee wafted on the air, and he inhaled the delicious aroma.

Moving to the kitchen, he saw that coffee had just been put on to brew. Kit must be up. Glancing out the back door, he frowned and drew to a halt. There in the yard was Kit, playing Frisbee with Tripoli. The two cats sat on the sidelines like little spectators. Dressed in a pink tank top and jeans, she was laughing as the Doberman raced after her, chasing her merrily around the huge yard, trying to grab the Frisbee out of her hand.

Noah's eyes narrowed as he watched Kit play tag with the frolicking dog. Her cheeks were flushed, her eyes alive with joy, and her laughter was like music to his ears. He poured two cups of coffee and edged open the door, standing at the screen. Tripoli lunged at the Frisbee in Kit's right hand, trying to tug it free.

Startled by the dog's unexpected move, Kit tripped over her own feet and fell.

She hit the dew-soaked lawn with a thud, rolling to take any shock from the fall. Laughing as Tripoli raced around her, Frisbee in his mouth, Kit tried to snatch it back from the dog. Tears ran down her cheeks at Tripoli's endearing antics. Finally he came and lay at her side, dropping the toy nearby. Panting happily, Tripoli licked her hand.

"Oh, boy," Kit gasped, sitting up and running her fingers through her unruly hair, "you are one tough dog, Tripoli." She reached out, throwing her arms around his neck, pressing her cheek against the dog's head. "What a love you are... I never realized how much I missed animals until just now...."

Kit pulled deep drafts of air into her lungs. She wasn't used to fifteen minutes of running and jumping like this. But Tripoli had brought the Frisbee to her while she was making the coffee, and she hadn't been able to resist his silent plea. She closed her eyes, running her hands down his sleek black back, thanking him silently for his companionship.

Noah moved out into the yard, stopping just short of where Kit and Tripoli sat on the grass together. He was suddenly envious of the Doberman as he watched her stroke the dog with such obvious affection. "If I'd known you liked exercise, I'd have made plans to take you jogging with me."

Kit's head jerked up and her widened eyes settled on Noah. She shivered, wildly aware of that green flame of hunger in his gaze once again. Tripoli left her arms, going to his master's side. "Noah..." she began lamely. Again she felt as if she were invading his private life.

He crouched in front of her, handing her a cup of steaming coffee. Did Kit know how pretty she was? She looked like a young girl right now, her hair tousled and eyes shining with happiness. ''Do you always get up this early on a Saturday morning?'' he demanded, sipping his coffee.

''Thanks,'' she whispered, taking the cup. Lowering her lashes, she was unable to meet his disapproving gaze. ''Uh...well, I usually sleep all day.'' A nightmare about Emilio Dante had awakened her at six, but she didn't want to tell Noah that. She forced herself to look up. Noah made her feel good about herself as a woman. No, he made her vibrantly aware that she *was* a woman. ''It was just such a beautiful morning that I couldn't resist Tripoli's invitation to play Frisbee.'' She grinned. ''As you can see, he won.''

''He's a keen player.''

''Like his owner, no doubt.''

Noah nodded, enjoying the intimacy that had sprung up between them. ''I play for keeps,'' he said amicably. His gaze dropped to Kit's parted lips, and he wondered for the hundredth time what it would be like to kiss her. She was so damned provocative and appealing, sitting there in the yard with bits of grass entangled in the ebony strands of her hair. Against his better judgment, he leaned forward and began to pick the green bits from her curls.

Stunned by Noah's gesture, Kit inhaled sharply. He was utterly male, his jeans hugging his lower body, effectively outlining his well-developed thighs. The polo shirt revealed just how powerful his chest really was. His arms were tightly muscled and covered with dark hair. Noah was built like a boxer: lean, tight and well proportioned, standing at least six-two. There was nothing to dislike about him physically, she decided lamely.

"It's nice to see an adult who can play like a child," he teased, plucking the last of the grass from her hair.

Shaken by his nearness, Kit said, "When you've got three brothers, you learn to tumble with them, not play with dolls and stay clean."

"A beautiful woman in tomboy's clothes."

Kit had never thought of herself as beautiful—until now. "I guess growing up with brothers brought out the tomboy in me," she murmured, getting to her feet. Noah was too close, too male for her ever since he had touched her hair. She had to keep her distance.

Disappointed that Kit had scrambled to her feet, Noah rose and straightened. He saw her sudden nervousness and decided that she was right: this was a business arrangement, not a friendship or love relationship. "You make a good cup of coffee," he said, trying to get on neutral ground with her once again.

Kit brushed off the seat of her pants. "Coffee's something I can't live without."

"Makes two of us." Noah smiled down at her. "Hungry? I make a pretty mean breakfast of whole grain pancakes with maple syrup."

Groaning, Kit fell into step with Noah. "Don't tell me you're one of those health nuts!"

"Afraid so."

"I'm a junk food addict."

He caught her rueful smile, thinking how sweet her lips looked when they curved upward. "Opposites attract, they say."

Kit wasn't sure what he meant by that enigmatic statement. "Opposites or not, I'm starved."

Her enthusiasm was infectious. Noah couldn't recall feeling this elated. Even his step felt lighter. "Well, you'd better eat plenty, because I'm going to put you to work in the flower garden after breakfast," he threatened good-naturedly.

Noah chastised himself; he was getting friendly with her again. But how could he help it? There was a refreshing quality to Kit. She simply invited a man to lower his walls and be himself with her.

"I can help you with breakfast," Kit offered once they were in the kitchen.

"No, that's all right. Just sit down and relax."

Her mouth quirked. "Noah, I don't expect to be waited on hand and foot."

Busying himself gathering the ingredients, he nodded. "Fair enough. You can clean up the dishes afterward and put them in the dishwasher."

The warmth they had shared dissolved as they fell back into their assigned roles. Dejectedly Kit sat down at the table. One minute Noah was like the warmth of sunshine around her, the next he was grumpy and defensive. Why was he shifting from one extreme to the other? Frowning, she asked, "Are you *sure* I'm not a royal pain in the rear for invading your personal space?"

Pouring milk into the pancake mixture, Noah stirred the contents in a bowl. "Positive."

His guard was up and well in place again. Kit sighed. "Don't you have a girlfriend who comes over here every once in a while?"

"No girlfriend. The kind of life I lead doesn't encourage many long-term relationships. Most women don't like their men at sea three to seven days at a time."

Kit found that hard to believe, but didn't say so. Besides, she felt an unexpected monumental relief at his admittance. Rubbing her eyes, she sank into silence. She didn't have the strength to overcome Noah's sudden retreat from her.

After breakfast, which took place in stilted silence, Kit said, "I need to talk to Chuck Cordeman. I know the routine about not using the phone, but I've got to talk to him."

Scowling, Noah got up and poured himself another cup of coffee. "Why do you need to speak to him?"

Girding herself, Kit met his troubled gaze when he came back to the table and sat down. "Look, Noah…this isn't going to work."

"What isn't?"

"This," she said, gesturing around the kitchen. "You and me under one roof together. Ever since I got here, I've felt this tension around you. I feel trapped. I feel odd about doing anything for fear you'll disapprove. Like this morning, when I was playing with Tripoli. I felt as if I were somehow trespassing." She shrugged, gripping the mug in her hands. "You're one of those men with his life in a certain order, and you don't like someone coming in and messing up the continuity. I understand that. I even agree." Kit gave him a pleading look, noticing the turmoil in his eyes. "Let me go to some motel nearby and stay there. I can handle it. This isn't the first time I've had to do a safe house routine."

Getting a grip on his emotions, Noah held her gaze. "Look," he began in a low voice, "I don't mean to make you feel you have to be a shadow here." Noah couldn't tell her the real reason for his abruptness: if he didn't put that wall between them, he would pull her into his arms. A white lie was better than the truth in this case, he decided. Kit didn't need any more pressure on her, and yet, he realized, he was unintentionally applying it to her. "I'll admit that having someone here is different, but I'll adjust, Kit. Just ride this out with me, okay? I'll get used to you being underfoot." He snorted. "Besides, there's no way you're staying in a dingy motel room like a trapped animal in a cage."

Searching his face hard, Kit sensed his ambivalence. Her voice came out soft. "I don't want to intrude on your life, Noah. Neither of us expected to be thrown together like this. I—I just don't know how to act around you."

Picking up her hand, Noah squeezed it. "Listen to me, Kit. You do what feels right for you. I promised Cordeman a place for you to heal, and I mean it."

Just his touch sent unexpected tears to her eyes. She hastily lowered her gaze so he couldn't see them and pulled her hand out of his, poignantly aware of the warmth and strength of it. "Are you sure?"

"Yeah, I'm sure," Noah said, getting to his feet. "Don't take my change of moods personally, Kit. Right now, my sister, Alyssa, is under a lot of pressure at Pensacola. She's got a flight instructor who's trying to wash her out of the program. I'm worried for her."

It was on the tip of her tongue to whisper that Noah cared a great deal about the people in his life. Looking up, Kit managed a wan smile. "If Alyssa's anything like you, I know she'll hang in there."

Relief washed through Noah. He and Kit had just

surmounted a small crisis. Somehow he had to wall off his moodiness from her so she could relax and heal. "Aly's going to be coming down here one of these weekends soon. I'm sure you'll get to meet her." He managed a genuine smile. "In fact, she's a lot like you."

"How do you see me?" Kit asked, getting up to attend to her portion of the kitchen chores.

"Loyal, hardworking and overresponsible."

"And Alyssa's like that?" She picked up the plates from the table.

Chuckling, Noah nodded. "Very much so. I think you two will have a lot in common." Wanting to add that Kit had that same kind of vulnerability Aly possessed, Noah decided to remain silent. However, Kit didn't have Aly's bulldog attitude, he reminded himself. Their tenacity was a Trayhern hallmark. Kit had run out of emotional stamina and strength after four years with Pete Collins. There was nowhere else for her to pull that extra strength from in order to survive, as Aly had done in the past. As all Trayherns had done at some point in their lives, he admitted.

After she finished loading the dishwasher, he said, "Let's go plant those seedlings, shall we?"

Kit nodded, wiping her hands on a towel. Whatever had been bothering Noah was now gone. His face was open and expressive once again. "You don't know how much I've looked forward to this, Noah."

Noah's heart wrenched in his chest at her quietly spoken admittance. Once again the desire to reach out and take her in his arms was excruciating. But Kit needed a little attention, a little care right now. Instead he squeezed her shoulder momentarily and then said, "Come on, let's find out if you've got a green thumb or not."

Chapter Six

It was Monday morning and time to go to work. Noah smiled to himself as Kit walked at his right shoulder down the long, concrete dock. At the end of it was the *Osprey*.

"Excited?" Noah asked. The morning sky was bathed in colors of pale peach and flaming orange.

Kit breathed in the salty air. "No, I'm worried about seasickness." The sun was up, creating a glare across the quiet channel waters where the Coast Guard station sat near the Atlantic Ocean.

"You've got that seasickness patch behind your ear?" Noah glanced down at her. Kit had worn her one-piece dark blue police uniform replete with revolver. He had relented and allowed her to wear the weapon. Sometimes orders could be bent. And because she was in uniform, the revolver seemed a natural addition. Nevertheless she looked feminine as hell, her unruly black hair emphasizing her dancing gray eyes. His mind wandered back over the weekend. There had been a truce of sorts. He had taken all the strain upon himself, making Kit feel she was an indispensable partner around his home. She had responded beautifully, and her laughter was all he'd needed as a reward.

"Yes, it's in place." Kit pressed the small bandage hidden behind her left ear, hoping it would stop any seasickness. She looked at the SES that sat like an elegant steed at the end of the dock. Painted a medium gray color, the *Osprey* was huge. Crewmen were already on board, moving around on the decks, performing the jobs that would ready the *Osprey* for a day at sea.

On the enclosed bridge of the vessel, Noah introduced Ensign Joe Edwards, his second-in-command, to Kit. The younger officer, who had just graduated from the academy, blushed deeply when he shook her hand. Joe was just as taken with Kit's quiet demeanor and natural beauty as he was, Noah decided. If Kit noticed Joe's blush, she didn't react to it as she took a seat not far from the helm.

"What's on the hot sheet today?" Noah asked, taking his place at the large steel helm. He always guided the *Osprey* out of dock and into the channel that led to the ocean.

Joe picked up the hot-sheet list. "The DEA has added two more vessels is all, Skipper." He smiled over at Kit, handing her the clipboard. "You might as well take a look at this, ma'am. They list names of boats or ships that have been known to carry marijuana bales. Sometimes we run into the vessels out at sea, and we order them to drop anchor so we can make a search.''

Noah ordered his crew to cast off. The morning was clear and cloudless, and he found himself happy that Kit was with them. Under his hand the *Osprey* moved away from her berth. The hull of the ship sliced cleanly through the waters of the channel. Up ahead was the greenish-blue expanse of the Atlantic Ocean. Once clear of the channel, Noah would let Edwards take over and they'd head south, moving around the tip of the Florida peninsula to begin their hunt for boats carrying drugs.

Kit felt her stomach begin to roll the moment the *Osprey* moved out into the ocean. She swallowed hard, praying that her reaction was only temporary.

After Noah turned over the *Osprey* to Edwards, he walked over to her. ''You're looking a little green,'' he noted, taking in Kit's once flushed features, which were now drawn with tension. He rested his hand on the back of the steel chair where she sat, aware how much easier he found it to deal with her professionally in the atmosphere of his boat and crew.

''It's nothing,'' Kit murmured, swallowing hard. She forced a smile. ''How about giving me the grand tour of this lady?''

''Sure?'' He looked intently into her trusting, soft gray eyes, and took a deep breath, controlling the surge of feelings she aroused in him.

Slipping off the seat, Kit nodded. ''Very sure.''

Both bulkhead doors to the bridge were open, allowing the warm, humid ocean air to circulate. Noah stepped out onto the deck. The *Osprey* was barely moving up and down; the ocean was glassy smooth. If Kit was seasick now, would she handle the moderate sea that usually came up every afternoon when the winds picked up?

Kit fought valiantly to ignore her roiling stomach as Noah led her around the deck. On the bow sat a fifty-caliber machine gun on a tripod, reminding her that the Coast Guard's mission could turn ugly. And then she looked down at the revolver she carried at her waist. She hadn't been in uniform since her graduation from the academy five years ago. It felt strange to be wearing the bulky black leather belt and holster around her waist. But it was necessary, she reminded herself. Still, the idea of a gun battle sickened her.

"Below deck we have crew quarters, a small galley and the weapons area," Noah said, gesturing for Kit to climb down the stairs. With each passing minute Kit looked worse, her face paler.

"This is quite a ship," Kit admitted once on the lower deck. The SES was immaculate. Noah Trayhern ran a tight vessel from what Kit could tell, and the men obviously respected him. He was a natural leader.

Taking her by the elbow, Noah led her down one passage. "The *Osprey* is the new generation cutter designed for drug work. Her hull is built to take the waves without a lot of yawing or rolling."

"I feel like everything's rolling."

"You're looking worse. Do you want to lie down for a while?"

Kit shook her head. "I'm sure it will pass, Noah." They arrived amidships, where several rows of bunks were built into the hull.

"These are the crew's quarters. They're cramped to say the least."

"Looks like a can of sardines if you ask me," Kit

joked. The *Osprey* rolled beneath them and instinctively she placed her hand on her stomach.

The gesture wasn't lost on Noah. "Let's go to my cabin," he suggested, leading her past the crew's quarters. He pushed open a bulkhead door halfway down the narrow passageway, revealing a small room with a bed, a table and chair and a desk, all bolted to the floor. "Go on in."

Nausea stalked her and she didn't try to argue. He led her to the bunk and sat her down. "Rest awhile. When people get seasick they either want to stay up in the fresh air or lie down."

The bunk was inviting. Kit gave him a sheepish glance. "I think I'll lie down. I'm sorry, Noah."

He reached out, barely caressing her hair in a gesture meant to give her solace. Kit looked positively miserable. "Don't be. Just take it easy. I doubt if there will be any action today, but if we need you, I'll send one of the crew down to get you. Otherwise, rest."

Feeling as if she had disappointed him, Kit nodded. "Thanks." After he left, Kit unbuckled the cumbersome belt and holster, placing them on the desk. Lying down did help to a degree, but the fact that even the most modern drug wasn't going to help her was a big disappointment. She'd warned Noah she was strictly a landlubber.

"Where's Detective Anderson?" Joe asked when Noah reappeared on the bridge.

"Lying down in my cabin."

Nodding his sandy-haired head, Joe said, "She doesn't look very seaworthy, does she?"

Sitting down, Noah picked up the hot-sheet list. "No, she doesn't."

"Pretty, though."

"Very."

"For being from the police department, she's got a nice way about her," Edwards added, checking the compass and lightly turning the helm to keep the *Osprey* on course.

Kit was nice in many unexpected ways, Noah grudgingly admitted. "Especially for having been an undercover cop for five years."

Edwards whistled, his blue eyes crinkling with surprise. "Her? An undercover agent? You gotta be kidding, Skipper."

"I wish I was. She's not cut out for it."

"No kidding. Man, we've seen some hard agents, and Kit—I mean, Detective Anderson—just doesn't fit that bill of goods."

Smiling to himself, Noah returned to the paperwork at hand. He noticed Joe had slipped and called her Kit. She had the same mesmerizing effect on everyone, it seemed, himself included. The rows of radios surrounding them on the bridge were fairly quiet. They would get noisy if a drug boat were spotted.

"Don't let her fool you, though," Noah warned him. "She's survived five years in the trenches and is alive to tell about it."

"Yeah, but what's it done to her, Skipper? We both know the undercover world is hell on an agent."

And Kit had gone over the edge, Noah wanted to add, but he didn't. He had gotten permission to tell Edwards that his home was a safe house for Kit. But the rest of the crew would never know; as far as they were concerned, she was just another police officer interfacing with the Coast Guard. A well-kept secret would keep Kit safe. ''Her health isn't what it should be,'' he said in answer to Joe's question. That wasn't a total lie, but it wasn't really the full truth, either. Noah felt himself becoming even more protective of Kit, wanting to shield her in every way possible.

''Well, she's quite a lady in my book. I'm kind of glad she's going to be with us during Operation Storm.''

Placing the clipboard on the console, Noah watched his crewmen on deck for several moments before responding to Joe. ''I don't know if she's going to be glad to be with us,'' he finally said ruefully.

Edwards chuckled. ''Yeah, if she's seasick even taking that drug, she might get to hate this assignment real fast.''

The brilliant blue-green depths of the ocean were darkening, telling Noah they were moving away from the coast. The waves were barely two feet in height; it was a perfect day. ''I'll check on her around noon. Maybe she'll be feeling better by then,'' Noah said. He could send one of the crewmen to look in on Kit, but he wanted to do it himself. Glancing at his watch, he saw that it was 8:30 a.m.

In some respects, the day was going to drag because Kit wasn't there at his side. Musing on how much Kit had already made herself a part of his life, Noah shook his head. What kind of magic did she wield? He felt as if his life were spinning completely out of his control. Yet he had to maintain a professionalism or jeopardize his career. He had enemies who wanted to embarrass him because of Morgan. No, somehow he had to walk that razor-fine line, help Kit back on her feet and carry out his duties in the meantime. He glanced at his watch one more time, restless and wanting to make sure Kit was all right.

The bulkhead door opened, then closed. Kit stirred from sleep and drowsily opened her eyes. Noah stood nearby, his face etched with shadows.

"Uh..." Kit struggled into a sitting position. "I didn't mean to fall asleep."

Noah sat down on the lone chair in the room, studying her intently. Kit's eyes were still heavy with sleep, her mouth soft and inviting. The urge to reach out and brush the hair off her brow almost got the better of him. He kept his hands resting on his thighs. "When you get seasickness, sleep is the best thing. How are you feeling?"

Groggily Kit took stock of herself. "My stomach's more settled, thank God."

Smiling slightly, Noah nodded. "Good. It's noon and we're going to be dishing up chow pretty soon. Do you feel like joining us?"

She didn't, but Kit refused to allow her present condition to control her. "Sure. Just give me a minute to freshen up." She ran her fingers through her hair, trying to tame it back into place.

Rising, Noah opened the door. Kit still didn't look too good. The walls she usually kept erected were gone. Maybe she was finally trusting him enough to be herself. "I'll see you in the galley, then," he said, his voice strained.

The tension between them was broken. Kit watched him disappear out the door, shutting it quietly behind him. She hadn't slept at all the night before, with dreams of Emilio Dante plaguing her. As she stood up and pressed her hand against her stomach, she wondered if some of her reaction to the ocean was really fatigue in disguise. Ever since she had found out Dante was loose and hunting for her, she barely slept at night. Kit ran her fingers through her hair one more time.

The mirror image staring back at her wasn't that of the Kit she used to know. Even in the dark blue uniform replete with silver badge and name plate, Kit didn't feel very much like a police officer anymore. What was happening to her? Being around Noah was exposing all her soft and feminine emotions. She no longer felt strong and confident. Instead she had an urgent need for some gentleness and peace in her life. Noah gave her that. Touching her arched brow, Kit looked deeply into her shadowed eyes. The old Kit Anderson was dying. In her place was this new person, this new woman, who had a serenity the old Kit hadn't felt in five years.

Confused by the myriad changes within her, Kit turned around. She stared at the revolver in the holster. Her mind told her to put it on and wear it. The rest of her recoiled from the ugly-looking weapon that could take a life. Fingers trembling, Kit reached down and reluctantly strapped on the hardware. The belt and holster hung heavily around her waist like an anchor. Disturbed and not understanding why, Kit left the cabin, heading toward the galley.

Four *Osprey* crewmen sat at one of three tables, eagerly consuming their noontime meal. Noah sat alone, his full tray in front of him. Kit nodded to the crew and made her way across the steel deck.

Noah stood as she approached, noticing her shyness

in front of his men. ''Sit down, Kit. Freddy is our cook on board. He's made—''

''Please,'' Kit protested quietly, ''I don't want any food, Noah.'' She gave him an apologetic look as she sat down opposite him. ''I can't handle it right now.''

''How about some fruit juice?'' he suggested.

Her stomach was beginning to roll once more. Was sleep the only way to spare herself this misery? When she saw Noah's frown, she knew she'd have to eat or drink something in order to erase the worry she saw in his eyes. ''I think I can get down some tomato juice.''

Freddy, a red-haired, freckle-faced crewman, brought over a small glass with a slice of lemon for Kit. She thanked him and busied herself squeezing in the citrus juice. Noah began eating with relish. Swallowing hard, Kit cast about for some topic that would get her mind off her damnable stomach.

''Spotted any drug boats yet?''

''No, it's quiet so far.''

The tomato juice was cold and tasted good. Kit sipped it slowly. ''How do you intercept these smugglers?''

Noah smiled lightly. ''Sheer luck, usually. No, that isn't always so. Sometimes a Navy P3 subhunter airplane will be flying at high altitude and spot possible boats. They'll call in the coordinates to us and we'll head in that direction.''

''And the rest of the time?''

''We're pretty familiar with the smugglers' favorite sea lanes. So we ply those waters and wait around to intercept them.''

''And you do this during the day?''

Nodding, Noah buttered another roll. He offered it

to Kit, but she shook her head. "Until about five in the afternoon. Then we head back to port. Why?"

"I'll be glad when five rolls around," Kit confided huskily.

"Don't be hard on yourself," Noah soothed. "Getting your sea legs could take several weeks."

With a pained look, Kit muttered, "What if I don't get those sea legs? I don't want to feel like this every day of the week for a year!"

"It took Joe Edwards five months before he stopped getting seasick. People adjust to sea life at different rates, Kit."

The thought of five months of this kind of feeling left Kit devastated. "You're kidding me."

"I'm not," Noah promised.

"Two weeks," Kit muttered to herself, rubbing her eyes as she sat on the edge of Noah's bunk aboard the *Osprey* after waking from her normal afternoon nap. Well, two weeks had passed and she was still miserable with seasickness every day. It was wearing badly on her. She got up shakily and put some cold water in the small basin, feeling a bit better after she'd washed her face.

Patting her face dry with the towel, she reached into the purse she kept in the drawer of Noah's desk and took out her makeup. Without it she looked positively ill. Well, wasn't she? Applying it, she noted that the blusher gave her skin a rosiness, some liquid foundation beneath her eyes erased those ever-present shadows and the lipstick made her look halfway alive.

Out of habit, Kit donned her holster and revolver. The first two weeks had been fairly routine, except for interdicting three drug-smuggling boats. Duty aboard the *Osprey* was deadly boring with intermittent moments of high tension whenever a druggie's boat was apprehended.

There was an urgent knock at the door and Kit opened it. Freddy stood there, struggling into the protective flak jacket they all wore when a boarding took place.

"Detective Anderson, we're preparing to board a ship. The skipper asked that you come to the bridge right away."

"I'll be right there, Freddy." Her heart began a slow pound, as it always did at these moments.

"Yes, ma'am!" and he ran down the narrow passageway toward the stairs.

Moments later Noah turned his attention toward the doorway. He saw the grim set of Kit's mouth as she entered the bridge. "Get your flak jacket on," he ordered. "We've got a hot-sheet yacht we're pulling over to search."

Shrugging into the heavy jacket, Kit walked over to him. Joe Edwards and the helmsman, Carter, were also on the bridge. "That's a big yacht," she commented.

"One of the biggest around. It's the *Sea Devil*," Noah said. "Do me a favor and take a look through the binoculars. See if you recognize any of the men aboard. We'll be boarding the *Sea Devil* in about ten minutes."

Her mouth grew dry as she scrutinized the four crewmen up on deck of the yacht. None of them were very savory-looking characters. As she scanned the cockpit at the rear, a gasp escaped her.

Noah frowned, focusing all his attention on Kit. She had paled considerably. "Kit?"

"My God, that's Brett Davis on board."

He watched as she placed the binoculars on the console, her eyes suddenly dark with real fear. "Davis? Who's that?"

Kit tried to control the iciness flowing through her. "Davis is a contract killer," she croaked. "He works directly for Garcia. When I was at Garcia's fortress posing as a buyer, I met him a couple of times."

Gripping her elbow, Noah guided her to the chair. He'd never seen Kit react so strongly. Wanting to put a hand on her shoulder but not daring to because of the situation, he soothed her with his voice, instead. "Take it easy. If Davis is one of Garcia's hired guns this could mean Garcia's closer to making a move to sell off his latest crop of marijuana."

Turning his attention back to the bridge, Noah ordered Edwards to prepare the boarding party. The *Sea Devil* had lowered its sail and was now heaving to as the ensign had ordered. Within minutes, the *Osprey* would dwarf the yacht as it settled alongside it. Lines would be thrown across the *Sea Devil*, mooring it to the port side of the Coast Guard vessel. Once secured, the boarding party would leap to the other deck.

Trying to think clearly, Kit watched the unfolding drama. "You're not going on board, are you?" she asked, her voice strained.

"No, it's Joe's turn."

"Thank God..." Kit whispered, and averted her eyes from Noah's sharp glance in her direction. Twice Noah had boarded boats with his team, and twice Kit had died an agonizing death, afraid that one of the smugglers might shoot instead of surrendering. No matter how many times he tried to persuade her that ninety percent of the boardings were safe, she was still left shaky in the wake of one.

"Relax," Noah urged her, taking up the portable radio. He instructed the helmsman to stop all engines, watching as the *Osprey* was brought alongside the *Sea Devil.* "Stay in here out of sight until after we've secured the situation."

Kit nodded, trying to get a grip on her rioting fears.

"Joe," Noah called on the portable radio, "keep an eye on the bearded man in the cockpit. His name is Davis, and he's one of Garcia's contract killers."

"Roger, Skipper. We'll be real careful."

Hands knotted, Kit watched from her vantage point on the bridge. Noah had moved out to the deck rail for a closer view, staying in touch with Edwards by radio. She saw Davis's square features screw up in fury as Joe cautiously approached the man, the M-16 in his hands ready to be fired.

Without realizing it, Kit got to her feet and moved quickly outside. Noah had his back to her, unaware that she was near the railing, all his attention on Davis. "Be careful, Joe..." she whispered under her breath. Davis was an angry man, yelling curses at Edwards, backing up and out of the cockpit. He refused to raise his hands above his head.

The hair on the back of Kit's neck stood on end. She turned to warn Noah that Davis wasn't going to give up without a fight. The words never left her mouth. Davis screamed a curse and pulled out a .350 Magnum from his belt, firing off a series of wild shots. The bullets whined past the bridge, burying themselves deep within the skin of the *Osprey*.

Noah lunged forward, jerking Kit to the deck to keep her from getting hit. He saw Edwards drop to the deck and fire off several more shots. In seconds the showdown was over. Davis lay on the deck, unmoving.

''Joe, get the corpsman!'' he shouted over the radio. Dammit! Worriedly Noah turned his attention to Kit. She was slowly getting to her knees.

''Stay down!'' he commanded harshly. Turning, he ordered several more crewmen to force all five *Sea Devil* sailors to lie on the deck, hands behind their necks. This was an armed lot, and Noah didn't want to take any more chances that they'd draw against his men.

Kit remained on the deck, breathing in gulps of warm, humid air. Her stomach turned violently, and she felt like vomiting. Had Davis killed anyone? She heard Noah's voice, crisp with authority over the radio, and she closed her eyes. Noah could have been killed—any of them could have. Shivering with apprehension, Kit lay there until Noah told her it was safe to get up.

''You okay?'' Noah asked, dividing his attention between the action on the *Sea Devil* and Kit.

''Y-yes. Fine, just fine.''

''I told you to stay on the bridge, dammit. Go below deck, Kit. I don't want you anywhere near the action.'' He glanced down at her. Her eyes were huge with horror. ''Go on,'' he said less harshly. ''We'll get this situation secured and then head back to port.''

Numbly Kit nodded. ''Home sounds awfully good right now,'' she admitted, her voice unsteady.

Kit clasped and unclasped her sweaty hands on the drive home. She was painfully aware of Noah's gaze occasionally settling on her as they drove from the pier to his house in silence. Her uniform was drenched with sweat, and she longed for a long, hot bath to unknot the kinks in her neck and shoulders.

Noah pulled into the driveway and shut off the car engine. Then he put his arm around her shoulders, noting how damp the material of her uniform was. ‘‘How you doing?’’

‘‘Okay.’’

He knew she was lying. Where did professional conduct begin and end? he wondered. Right now Kit needed to be held. The terror in her eyes told him everything. He sensed how close she was to exploding, five years of horror dogging her heels. Managing a slight smile for her benefit, he awkwardly patted her shoulder, then removed his arm. ‘‘Come on, let's get inside.’’

Kit escaped to the bathroom after greeting the animals, who met them at the door. With trembling hands, she stripped out of her uniform. Blips of past scenes involving Dante and Davis flashed through her mind. Why did this have to happen? Unable to cope with her turbulent feelings, Kit turned on the bathtub faucets and settled into the filling tub of hot water. But it was Noah's arms that she wanted around her. Kit knew that within them she would find solace. Closing her eyes, she pressed the washcloth to her face, taking in a ragged breath.

Noah had changed into a pair of jeans and a chambray shirt and was preparing to get dinner on the table. Just the nightly routine around the house had calmed his nerves. Getting shot at wasn't the norm, and as much as he himself had been shaken by the confrontation with the *Sea Devil*, he knew it had torn open a scar in Kit.

An hour passed, and he got worried when she didn't appear as she usually did after her bath. Normally Kit would come into the kitchen and help him by setting the table and making them a pot of fresh coffee. Noah had just finished preparing their individual salads, when Kit walked through the entrance. Despite her tension-lined face she looked beautiful in a pale pink cotton gown that brushed her bare feet. He'd come to look forward to her companionship in the evening, when she shed her masculine work clothes for the simple cotton gowns she wore so well.

Kit avoided Noah's searching look, going to the cabinet and pulling out the dishes to be set on the table. Her hand slipped, and one of the plates crashed to the tile floor, shattering.

With a cry Kit pressed her hand against her mouth, staring down at the broken earthenware.

Noah tensed, hearing the crash, and turned toward her. Kit stood with her back against the drain board. He walked over to her and pulled her into his arms. She was trembling, and he held her tightly against him. "It's all right," he murmured soothingly against her ear. "It's over, Kit, and you're safe." He rocked her gently, whispering words meant to heal, wanting to draw from her the fear she had carried so long by herself.

Kit collapsed against him, burying her face in the textured cotton of his shirt, longing to hide forever in his strong arms. She felt Noah's hand begin to stroke her damp hair, and she wrapped her arms around his waist, losing herself in his gentleness.

Noah's heart was beating raggedly in unison with

his breathing as he pressed a kiss to her fragrant hair. Right now, Noah knew he was strong and Kit was weak. ''That gun battle brought back a lot of bad memories for you, didn't it?'' he asked.

Kit nodded once, realizing that their breathing was synchronizing. His arms were supportive, holding her tightly, the cranberry fabric scratchy beneath her cheek. ''Y-yes.''

''Want to talk about it?'' Noah reluctantly loosened his embrace so he could look down at Kit. He shouldn't be holding her, because he wanted her too damn much. His body was tightening with hunger.

Fighting her own desires, Kit moved out of his arms, backing nervously away. This shouldn't have happened. None of it. Touching her brow, she stammered, ''Noah, I don't feel well. I think I'll go to bed.'' And she fled the kitchen, hurrying down the hall toward her room before he could protest.

Dammit! Noah stood in the kitchen, staring at the entrance. He was torn between going after Kit and giving her the room she needed to work through her reaction to the shooting. Frustrated, he knelt and began retrieving the broken bits of plate. The phone rang. Rising, he picked up the kitchen extension.

''Trayhern,'' he growled.

''This is Cordeman.''

''What do you want?''

''Considering you nabbed one of Garcia's men this afternoon, you're in a foul mood, Trayhern.''

Noah gripped the receiver. ''What the hell do you want, Cordeman?''

''DEA wanted me to call you and tell you that Davis is gonna make it. I imagine Kit's pretty happy about getting one of Garcia's contract gunmen.''

Anger boiled up through Noah. ''Kit's not happy at all,'' he ground out. ''Seeing Davis and then getting shot at has really shattered her.''

''What are you talking about?'' Cordeman demanded testily. ''Doesn't she realize what this means? Garcia putting one of his lieutenants like Davis in action means he's gonna make his move. That hired gun never leaves the Colombian fortress unless something big is in the offing. We figure Davis was going to meet up with Dante for future planning.''

Hanging on to his temper, Noah snarled back, ''I'm sure you're all pleased as hell. Kit's the one I'm worried about.''

''She'll pull through for you, Trayhern. She always has in the past.''

''Cordeman, this phone call is boring the hell out of me. You got anything further about Davis, you contact my commanding officer. Right now, I've had a gutful of drug-busting activity.''

He slammed the receiver down, realizing how perfectly childish he probably seemed to Cordeman. But no one was worried about Kit's emotional state or frame of mind. Running his fingers through his hair, Noah returned to picking up the pieces of pottery. What should he do? Go to Kit's room and force her to talk? Or should he remain in the shadows, allowing her to come to him?

It was impossible to get their brief embrace out of his mind. Noah threw the pieces of plate into the trash. He wasn't hungry, either. Shutting off the oven, which held a casserole, he went into the living room to pour himself a drink. Perhaps later, Kit would emerge from her room and they could talk. Somehow he had to get her to trust him enough to lean on him and release all those bottled-up fears that haunted her. Somehow....

Chapter Seven

Kit was on the bridge of the *Osprey* when Joe Edwards spotted a small boat with a tattered sail on the horizon.

"Looks like a Haitian refugee boat," he said, handing Noah the binoculars.

Studying the boat for several minutes, Noah muttered, "Yeah, and not in very good shape. It's sitting low. I can see people bailing water. Let's pick them up."

"Yes, sir," and Edwards pointed the *Osprey* in that direction.

Noah set the binoculars down on the console, glancing over at Kit. Ever since the Davis shooting incident three weeks earlier, she had withdrawn deeply within herself. There were shadows beneath her haunted eyes. And nearly every night, he'd hear her get up before dawn, leave the bedroom and pad down the hall to the living room, unable to sleep. The ache in his heart intensified and so did the need to help her. Kit filled his waking, and now his sleeping, state.

Tearing from his own inner turmoil, Noah explained what was going on with the boat they would intercept shortly. "The poor of Haiti will gather on an old, leaky tub and try to make it to the U.S., hoping for a new and better life for themselves."

Kit nodded. Through her binoculars she could see the small sixteen-foot boat loaded down with human cargo, including many nearly naked children. "What will you do?"

He heard the worry in Kit's husky voice. "Let them board. Chances are, they're probably out of food, maybe even water. Depending on ocean currents and weather conditions, they may have been out to sea a good seven to ten days. Their supplies have to be running low."

Relief flowed through Kit. Nothing touched her heart like the destitute and elderly. "While I was undercover, I got a chance to work with a group of orphaned Colombian children for almost six months." Kit lowered the binoculars, searching Noah's face. He gave her strength, whether he knew it or not. "I love children. All of them."

The yearning in her voice didn't go unnoticed. "You came from a large family, so you probably want a big one yourself," he teased.

A trace of a smile crossed Kit's lips as she watched the Haitian boat drawing closer and closer. "At least three kids, maybe four."

"No basketball team?" he said, still teasing.

Drowning in Noah's warming gaze, Kit sobered.

The need to walk into his arms once again to kiss him, was driving her to distraction. Tearing herself from her torrid thoughts, Kit murmured, "I love all kids. No matter what their color or nationality. They're the ones who get caught in situations beyond their control."

Noah agreed. "Well, when we get them on board, I'm sure we're going to need your help as an interpreter. They usually speak French and little else. Maybe some pidgin English, if we're lucky."

"For once I'm looking forward to our boarding a boat," Kit said fervently. Every boat they'd searched after the Davis gun incident had made her break into a sweat, her fear a palpable, living thing within her.

Noah's voice lowered with feeling. "I can tell you are."

Kit's heart went out to the fifteen Haitians in that leaky tub they called a boat. It was a miracle they hadn't sunk. She watched as Noah and his men transferred the five families to the *Osprey*. And he'd been right: the Haitians spoke little English, so she became the organizer, more or less, of getting the people comfortable.

She saw the desperation and fear in the eyes of the women as they kept asking her if they could remain in the U.S. Kit didn't know the answer. She stayed busy in the hold of the cutter while Noah was up on the bridge, placing the *Osprey* on a course for Miami. One young woman, no more than seventeen, was decidedly pregnant. Another child, Marie, hung shyly at Kit's elbow, her brown eyes huge with fear.

Getting them fed and providing space in the hold where they could rest or lie down on blankets was the main course of action. Kit crouched at the pregnant mother's side when she saw Noah enter the hold.

Noah nodded to the families, huddled in small groups. The children were far less frightened now, thanks to Kit's obvious affection and care. He halted, watching Kit as she tended to the frightened teen. Miraculously all the tension was gone from Kit's features, and her eyes were sparkling with life. He saw one little girl steal beneath Kit's left arm, snuggling close to her.

Kit looked at Noah when he knelt opposite her. His eyes were warm with pleasure. "Looks like you've already got a family," he noted, motioning to the little girl in Kit's arms.

Embracing Marie, Kit nodded. "She sort of took to me, I guess."

Moved because she had shared her feelings with him, Noah realized the child was drawing Kit out of her shell. "Anyone in their right mind would," Noah admitted, a catch in his voice. And when he saw the surprise in Kit's eyes, he quickly changed the subject. "You can tell these people that we'll be taking them to Miami, not back to Haiti. Immigration will see that they're given food and shelter. There's a good chance they'll be staying in the U.S."

Tears surged into Kit's eyes unexpectedly. Embarrassed that Noah had seen them, she wiped them away with the back of her hand. "That's wonderful," she whispered in a strained voice. "They were all so fearful you were going to return them to Haiti. Let me tell them."

Noah got to his feet, watching hope spring up to the faces of the refugees as Kit told them the happy news. It made him feel good. In his daily life he often saw only negativity. This time there was something positive, and he relished the Haitians' reactions to Kit's announcement. He frowned, noticing that tears continued to stream down Kit's face. She placed Marie beside her mother and turned to him.

"I—I have to pull myself together, Noah. May I use your cabin for just a—"

"Come with me," he told her huskily, putting his hand on her elbow and leading her down the passageway. She was trembling.

"I'll be okay," Kit stammered, trying to stem the flow of tears. Why was she crying like this? Why couldn't she stop? Noah's firm touch on her arm only made her want to cry more. Blinded by the onslaught of tears, Kit didn't try to pull out of his grasp.

"Hang on," Noah said, opening the door to his cabin. He drew her inside, guiding her to the bunk, where she sat down. Picking up the phone, he called the bridge and told Edwards to take command for now. When he turned back to her, she was hunched over, hands clasped in her lap, head bowed. Removing his officer's cap he placed it on the desk, then crouched in front of her. The instant his hands came to rest on her slumped shoulders, a sob tore from her.

"Oh, Noah..."

He maintained a firm grip on her arms. "It's about time," he said thickly.

More sobs punished her, and Kit raised her head. Noah's face was nothing but a blur. "Wh-what are you talking about?"

"You're burned out, Kit. And you've been holding a lot of ugly stuff inside you." He pushed a wayward strand of hair behind her ear. "I've been waiting and wondering when you were going to let it all go." His voice grew dark. "Don't fight it. I'm here, and I'll help you."

She hadn't cried in almost a year. Kit clung to his tender gaze, feeling as if she were coming apart from the inside out. Just the husky tenor of Noah's voice dissolved the last of the barriers that held her grief and fear captive. Noah rose and sat down on the bunk beside Kit, opening his arms, drawing her to him.

As she sank against him, Noah groaned, wrapping his arms tightly about her, rocking her gently, as if she were a hurt child. "It's okay, Kit, let it out, let it all go...." And he shut his eyes, pressing his cheek against her hair, allowing her to weep freely. Her fingers dug deeply into his chest, and Noah rubbed her shoulders and back, willing out the horror she'd held so long in abeyance.

Every stroke of his fingers on her back took a little more of the pain away from her. Kit surrendered her trust to him, something she'd never done with a man before. She felt Noah move slightly, his strong, sensual mouth pressed against her temple in a soothing kiss. Kit instinctively nuzzled upward, finding refuge in the feathery touch of his mouth. A soft moan of surrender slid from her as he barely grazed her mouth.

Giving free rein to his feelings for Kit, Noah cradled her chin, imprisoning her. He leaned down to kiss those full, glistening lips, and tasted the bitterness of salt on her flesh. A fire lit explosively within him. She was soft and inviting.... He grazed her lips with his tongue, and his body tightened with desire as he molded his mouth hungrily to hers. At first there was no response from Kit, but he continued his gentle seduction. And then her lips moved shyly against his, sending a soaring sheet of flame through him. He felt the hunger of wanting to love her physically gnaw at him. But his heart instructed him differently.

Body hard and throbbing, Noah tore his mouth from hers. Kit was breathing raggedly. He saw wonder and some unknown feeling in her wide, gray eyes. She was just as shocked by his kiss as he was.

The silence eddied around them. Kit drowned in Noah's turbulent green gaze. She read so much in his eyes, a richness of feelings that flowed through her like a gentle wind in the wake of a destructive storm. Kit swallowed hard, unwilling to leave Noah's embrace. The unsure smile that tipped the corners of his mouth endeared him to her even more.

"All right now?" he asked, his voice little more than a rasp. His senses were vibrantly alive because of her, because of everything she was and was not. She had been so sweet and feminine in his arms. Noah knew his kiss had not been out of pity for her condition. Just the lustrous quality in her eyes sent him reeling. He had to get up and leave. He had to staunch the flow of this molten ribbon that so powerfully connected them.

"Y-yes, fine..." Kit whispered. She tried to wipe her cheeks dry but didn't succeed very well. "I feel so stupid, breaking down like that for no reason."

"Don't you think it was good to cry and get rid of all that poison inside you?"

Sniffing, Kit couldn't meet his gaze. But his deep voice was a balm to her ravaged state. "I guess so, Noah."

"Maybe you'll be able to sleep better at night from now on."

Stunned that he knew of her nightly wakenings, Kit

stared up at him. His eyes were gentle with understanding.

"I haven't met too many agents who didn't have some sleepless nights," Noah said soothingly. "From now on, if you need a shoulder to cry on, look me up."

Taking a deep breath, Kit nodded. "I will."

"Promise?"

"Promise."

Noah rose—the last thing he wanted to do. Keeping a hand on her shoulder, he said, "Stay here awhile and work through the rest of it, Kit. Okay?"

She lowered her lashes, her heart squeezing with fresh pain. Noah was retreating rapidly. His voice had taken on that familiar authoritative quality. "I'll be fine," she promised in a rasp. "Go ahead, I know you have things to attend to."

The disappointment in her tone was very real. Noah wondered why, but didn't ask. Reluctantly he allowed his hand to slide from her shoulder. "I'll see you later."

The door shut quietly, and Kit looked up. All her senses focused on the wonderful kiss they had shared. It had been so unexpected, but so right. Getting up, Kit ran some water in the small basin and washed her flushed face, hoping to get rid of the signs of crying. What she couldn't wash away was Noah's tenderness or her physical need to love him.

As she dried her face with a towel, she tried to understand what had happened. Ever since she'd met Noah, some undefinable tension had simmered hotly between them. And every day it seemed to heighten, making her excruciatingly aware of being a woman. All these feelings were new and disturbing.

Placing the towel on the bracket, Kit took in a deep breath, trying to steady her roiling emotions. Nothing worked. She sat back down, burying her face in her hands. A young Haitian child had broken through the barriers behind which she had hidden so many old hurts and griefs from past wounds. Somehow Noah had known what was happening and taken her aside so that he could hold her while she worked through that terrible storm of feelings. But he didn't have to kiss her. And she didn't have to respond, either. Kit's eyes grew troubled with the implications. They had to work together, and this shouldn't be happening.

If she was any judge of the situation, Noah was just as surprised by the kiss as she was. But both of them had wanted it, needed it. Kit tried to tell herself that Noah had kissed her out of compassion, nothing else. There could be nothing else between them right now. Her entire life was focused on trying to collar Garcia.

Rising, Kit studied herself in the mirror. Her eyes were a soft gray color, her mouth still tingling in the aftermath of Noah's kiss. She saw none of the old Kit Anderson left as she searched the face in front of her. In the past month Noah had brought out her vulnerability. And as the tides of the ocean ebbed and flowed because of the moon's pull, she was responding in kind to him.

"You've got to get a hold on yourself," she whispered. It was Friday. Thank God Alyssa Trayhern would be visiting this weekend. Kit felt incredibly susceptible after Noah's kiss. She had no idea how she would behave if they had to spend this weekend alone together. Yes, Aly's presence was essential.

* * *

"Aly!" Noah grinned and threw his arms around his tall, slender sister. He hugged her fiercely, laughing as she wrapped her arms around him.

"Oh, Noah." Aly sighed, standing back and looking up at him. "It's so *good* to see a friendly face. I'm sorry I'm early, but I had to escape from Pensacola for a while or lose what little's left of my mind."

"Friendly and glad that you're here. Come on in." Noah ushered his younger sister inside. It was eight in the morning, and Aly was right on time. She was dressed in a short-sleeved bright green blouse that emphasized her auburn hair, and a pair of khaki-colored slacks. And she looked very tired. Almost as tired as Kit.

Aly leaned down to pet Tripoli, then gave each of the cats a ruffle on the head before following Noah from the foyer.

"You're just in time for breakfast, sis. I was fixing some of my world-famous Trayhern omelets."

Chuckling, Aly followed her brother into the kitchen. "Noah, my stomach isn't up to a wild omelet today."

"I'll make you a tame one, then. Fair enough? Sit down. Coffee?"

Placing her purse on another chair, Aly nodded. "A stiff drink would be more like it."

"That bad at Pensacola, huh?" Noah handed her the cup and returned to his cooking.

"That bad." Aly looked around. "Hey, you said you had a roommate. Where is she?"

With a grimace Noah turned and faced his sister. "I couldn't say much on the phone when you called last week, Aly. She isn't exactly a roommate."

Aly raised an eyebrow, her eyes sparkling. "Been

a long time since you had a serious relationship, if my memory serves me correctly.''

Stirring the egg mixture, Noah muttered, ''It's not what you think.''

Aly tittered delightfully, and sat back in the chair, enjoying Noah's sudden discomfort. ''Oh...okay. Tell me all about her.''

''There's not much to tell. Detective Kit Anderson is here on police business I can't talk too much about. This is a safe house for her.''

Aly frowned. ''A safe house?''

Noah set the bowl on the drain board and added a number of vegetables, then some shredded cheese to the mixture. ''Yeah. There's a Mob contract out on her, and everyone concerned felt she'd be better off here.''

''My God, Noah, that's dangerous! This is something new. I mean, I've heard of taking work home with you, but isn't this going too far?''

Chuckling, Noah said, ''Don't overreact. Being a safe house isn't really all that dangerous.''

''What's she like?''

''Kit is...'' Noah struggled with adjectives. If he allowed his heart to talk, he'd say that she was incredibly beautiful, with eyes that shone like the ocean touched with moonlight. That ever since the kiss yesterday, there had been a new unsureness between them.

''Yes?'' Aly goaded, watching her brother's face closely.

''She's been an undercover agent for the narc division for five years.'' There, that was a safe, impersonal comment. ''Kit should be joining us shortly for breakfast.''

"Great. Frankly, I need a family situation to unwind from that murderous flight school."

He gave her a dark look as he poured the first omelet into the skillet. "It's not a family situation between me and Kit, Aly."

She grinned at his defensiveness. "Okay, big brother, anything you say. But I see that look in your eye, and I hear it in your voice."

Heat flowed into Noah's cheeks, and he was acutely aware of Aly's appraisal. She sat there with a silly know-it-all grin on her face. He had never been able to hide much from his sister. "You're barking up the wrong tree," he growled unhappily.

Kit entered the kitchen, dressed in a pale pink blouse and a pair of threadbare jeans. She halted, seeing a red-headed woman at the table. It had to be Alyssa. Grateful for her presence even though she really didn't know her, Kit gave her a warm smile. "You must be Alyssa," she said, moving to the table and extending her hand.

Aly rose, shaking her hand. "And you're Kit Anderson. Call me Aly. It's good to meet you." She shot a glance over at Noah, who had his back to them. "My brother has been telling me all about you," she said in a conspiratorial tone.

Uncomfortable, Noah turned and gave his sister a warning look. "You'd better explain yourself, Aly. And in a hurry."

Aly sat there, a pleased look on her face, deliberately ignoring Noah's remarks.

Kit poured herself a cup of coffee, vibrantly aware of Noah only a few feet away from where she stood. He looked magnificent in a forest green polo shirt and faded jeans. And when he glanced in her direction to mutter "Good morning," her heart squeezed, then began to pound.

"Good morning," she murmured in return, retreating hastily to the table, where Aly sat.

"I understand you're in navy flight school," Kit began, trying to move to a safe topic of conversation, aware that Aly had a special look of alertness in her startling blue eyes. She was very pretty, Kit thought, taking in the cute pixie-style cut of Aly's auburn hair that emphasized the fine qualities of her facial features. Kit liked her immediately. There was a tension to Aly, as if she were a clock that had been wound too tightly. Her movements were quick, concise and sure, shouting her obvious confidence.

"Yes, I'm battling my way through Pensacola," she griped good-naturedly.

Noah placed a plate in front of Kit. "This one's for you," he said.

Kit looked down at the omelet, hash browns and toast, distraught at the quantity of food. "Noah—"

"Looks like he's trying to fatten you up," Aly noted wryly, then added, "Noah has this thing about always helping out the underdogs of the world. If you're too skinny, he wants to fatten you up. If you've got a problem, he'll loan you his shoulder to cry on. If you need a place to hide, he'll throw open the doors to his home." She smiled warmly over at Kit. "He takes in stray animals, too, as you can see." She gestured at the two cats and dog sitting patiently around the table, waiting for scraps.

Kit lowered her lashes, unable to stop a smile. "Yes, Noah helps people and animals in many ways."

"Here, eat this and quit talking," Noah muttered to his sister, putting a plate in front of her.

"You must think I'm skinny, too," Aly teased, picking up the fork.

"You both are."

"Uh-oh, watch it, Kit. My brother is stalking us. If we keep eating like this, we'll balloon to a hundred and thirty in no time."

Laughter spilled from Kit. She was delighted with Aly's quick retorts. Noah was terribly uncomfortable, and if she wasn't mistaken, that dull red color on his cheeks meant he was blushing. Suddenly, with Alyssa's effervescent presence, the weekend was taking on a wonderful new quality.

"So, what's on the agenda for the rest of the day?" Aly wanted to know after breakfast.

Noah didn't like the way Aly was watching him—especially whenever he talked with Kit. It was only polite table conversation, but she was far too interested to suit him. She obviously thought there was something between them, when there wasn't. He was about ready to throttle her. "*I* was going to work in the garage on that bureau I started building three months ago. I've got some sanding to do on it before I start rubbing it down to bring out the highlights in the wood."

"And I was going to weed the flower beds," Kit said, rising to clear the plates from the table.

"What a homey twosome you are."

Noah glared at Aly, but said nothing.

"Tell you what, Kit," Aly began with enthusiasm, "I want to catch up on what my handsome brother has been doing, and later I'll help you weed. It's about time I did penance in the form of ground duty."

Kit grinned. "Sounds good. There are enough weeds for both of us."

Chuckling, Aly followed Noah out of the house to the garage. She placed her hand on his shoulder. "She's really beautiful, Noah."

He opened the garage door, and sunlight spilled into the gloomy depths. "Just what the hell were you trying to do in there, Aly?" he demanded, walking over to the chest of drawers he'd fashioned out of cherry wood.

"What?"

He sized up his spunky sister. "You know damn well what."

Aly picked up some sandpaper and handed it to Noah. "Come on, Noah! I'd have to be blind not to see you like her."

He snorted and sat down to begin sanding the wood. "You're way off base."

Kneeling and starting to sand the other side of the bureau, Aly muttered, "Noah, you never could hide a thing from me. So don't sit there and tell me you don't like Kit Anderson! I can see it in your eyes and the way you talk to her."

"You're nuts."

Tittering, Aly caught his glance. "Your voice gets soft when you speak to her, Noah."

"Why don't you just sand, and we'll talk about something else."

"How long have you known Kit?"

"A month."

"She married?"

"No."

"A boyfriend?"

"Dammit, no! Can we get on another topic?"

"No. Hey, I like Kit! She may be a cop, but there's a special quality about her."

He sanded with more intensity, refusing to look over at his sister. "Yeah, she is special," he grumbled.

"See?"

"Shut up and keep working."

Laughing delightedly, Aly did as she was told for about five minutes. Breaking the pleasant silence, she asked, "How can Kit take that kind of dangerous pressure?"

The scowl on Noah's forehead deepened. "That's what I've been wanting to know myself. Frankly, I thing she took up police work because her family's like ours—bound by tradition."

"Oh, I see. Several generations of cops, huh?"

"Yeah." Noah wiped off the sweat gathering above his upper lip and concentrated with renewed vigor on the bureau. He wished with all his might that his eternally nosy sister would drop the subject. "Kit isn't cut out for police work. Never has been. Yesterday she broke—" Noah caught himself. Dammit, he never meant to talk to anyone about that! He saw Aly's eyes grow gentle.

"What do mean, 'broke'?"

"Forget I said it."

"No." Aly reached out and gripped his arm. "Noah, it's obvious to me you care an awful lot for Kit. Come on, I'm your sister. If you can't talk to me, who can you talk to?"

Noah sat back, staring down at the sandpaper in his dusty hands. "Kit has been carrying a lot of past grief and terror in her from her years as an undercover agent,'' he said finally. ''Yesterday we picked up a bunch of Haitian refugees, and it got to her.'' He sighed, staring out the opened door of the garage. ''There was one little girl who absolutely adored Kit. When I went below to check on everyone, she had the girl in her arms. Kit was acting as interpreter, and I told her to tell the group they would be going to Miami.''

''And then?'' Aly stopped sanding and watched her brother's face intently.

''Once they understood they would be going to the U.S., the people started to cry and thank Kit. She started crying with them. And then she couldn't stop, so I took her to my cabin for some privacy.''

''She was finally letting go? Getting it out of her system?'' Aly guessed.

Noah nodded, exhaling. ''Yeah…''

''Something else happened?'' Aly pressed gently.

He folded the sandpaper methodically in his hand. ''Something happened,'' Noah admitted heavily. ''She felt so good in my arms. It was like a shock to me, Aly.''

''What was a shock?''

Noah compressed his mouth into a thin line, looking over at his sister. ''I kissed her.''

Brows arching, Aly grinned. ''What's so shocking about that? Kissing's pretty natural and normal between a man and a woman.''

''Smart ass.''

Swallowing her smile, Aly asked, ''Did you do it out of pity, because she needed help?''

''No. I don't know…'' He snorted. ''I don't know much of anything right now with Kit around. I've got a job to do, and I'm supposed to be professional about all this. Kit's on the *Osprey* with me five days a week. And then she lives here.''

''Kinda close quarters with each other all the time, huh?''

With a curt nod Noah returned to the job of sanding the bureau. ''Very close.''

''I see.''

''I wish to hell I did. That kiss came out of nowhere, Aly. I haven't been thinking about Kit in those terms.''

She began to sand again, watching Noah closely. ''Maybe you were, but weren't aware of it.''

''We came together like an explosion. I've never been so shaken, Aly. And I've had my fair share of relationships. Kissing a woman isn't something new to me.''

''Kit is different.''

''She sure as hell is.''

With a smile, Aly reached over and patted her brother on the shoulder. ''Hang in there. I have a hunch all this will become crystal clear to you after a while.''

Noah wasn't so sure. He hadn't been able to forget, much less erase, the kiss he'd shared so hotly with Kit. All night he'd tossed and turned in bed, replaying that molten moment. her mouth had been so soft and inviting, and he'd drowned in her arms for that one stunning moment torn out of time. In a monumental effort to put Kit out of his mind, Noah changed the subject to Aly's progress at flight school. She complied, telling him about the instructor who was trying to wash her out because she was the sister of a traitor.

It was almost noon when Aly finished talking about

the incidents at Pensacola. The bureau had been sanded, and now needed a second sanding with a finer grit. "Why don't you go help Kit for a while?" Noah suggested, standing and brushing the dust from his jeans.

"Better yet, I'm thirsty. How about if I make us all some lemonade and bring it out to you and her?"

"Sounds great. Thanks."

Kit was on her hands and knees when Aly came out the front door, bearing two glasses of lemonade. Kit smiled gratefully, sitting back on her heels.

"I was dying of thirst. How did you know?" Kit said, taking the glass. "Thanks."

"I was getting thirsty out there in the garage, so I figured you were probably even thirstier working out here in the sun." Aly sat down on the grass, admiring the flowers.

"I'm taking a break." Kit motioned to the border surrounding the front of the house. "Got half of it weeded so far."

"I'll help you with the second half."

Sipping the sweet, ice-cold lemonade, Kit groaned with satisfaction. "This tastes wonderful." She wiped the sweat off her forehead with the back of her arm. "You're a mind reader like Noah."

"Oh?"

Kit smiled over at Aly, who sat cross-legged in front of her. "He's forever surprising me with his ability to know what someone needs."

Aly sipped the lemonade and nodded. "Noah's always had a special sensitivity to everyone around him." She pursed her lips, holding Kit's friendly gaze. "I imagine working and living together is a bit of a strain on you."

Absently Kit picked at a few weeds between the marigolds. "In some ways," she admitted. "I feel I've become a real burden to him."

Snorting, Aly stretched out on her stomach. "You're the best thing that's happened to him, Kit."

"I find that hard to believe."

Choosing a blade of grass, Aly put it in her mouth and chewed on it thoughtfully. "I'm sure he told you about Morgan and what happened."

"Yes. Knowing you and Noah, I find it hard to believe that your brother would be capable of such an act."

"Exactly. Morgan didn't defect, and he didn't leave his men to die alone on that hill." She grimaced. "That aside, the past five years have been hell on all our family. Noah got it broadside because he was already an officer in the Coast Guard. A lot of people went out of their way to try to derail his career because they thought Morgan was a traitor and they wanted to punish a Trayhern for it. Noah became their target."

"I understand you've had your share of hell with that particular item, too," Kit said, noting the pain in Aly's eyes.

"Yeah, nobody escaped the full-scale attack by the press and Pentagon," she muttered bitterly. "Because of it, Noah's had to double his efforts to keep his record clean. He's had to become like Superman and overachieve just to be grudgingly accepted by his superiors. I'd hate to add up all the overtime and special assignments he's taken to keep our name clean and his nose out of trouble."

Kit frowned, weaving invisible patterns in the short grass where she sat. ''You mean he isn't really a workaholic?''

''No. Have you seen his carpentry out in the garage?''

''Yes, he showed it to me one time. There are some beautiful but unfinished pieces of furniture out there.''

''Precisely. Noah's been good with woodworking since he was in his teens. At one time he wanted to be a wood craftsman.''

''But family priorities got in the way?'' Kit guessed.

''Bingo. Before Morgan disappeared and this whole mess erupted, Noah had his life laid out. He likes the Coast Guard, but loved his woodworking even more. I remember he and I used to talk about his dreams.''

''What dreams?'' Kit asked softly, seeing Noah in a new, more positive light.

''Oh, you know.'' Aly rolled over on her back, closing her eyes and absorbing the warmth of the July sunlight. ''He wanted to make his living doing woodworking. And he wanted a wife who wanted lots of kids, because he loves kids.''

A lump formed in Kit's throat, and she stared down at the grass. ''But then family obligations got in the way.''

''Noah figured he'd put in the mandatory twenty years, retire, then pursue his real dream.'' Aly opened one eye and looked over at Kit. ''Of course, he wanted to marry and have that passel of kids before that.''

''I see...'' Kit said faintly.

''Funny how family tradition can change things,''

Aly went on quietly. "I mean, I love the navy, and even more, I love to fly. Noah wasn't really in love with the military the way Morgan and I were. That's why he joined the Coast Guard."

"Because it's the least militaristic?"

"Right. He's always been good at helping others, and felt the Coast Guard was a perfect answer for him. They do a lot of rescue work, and he's happy in that capacity."

With a sigh, Kit got to her knees and began to pick at the weeds once again. "It looks like we've both been trapped by tradition."

"Noah said he didn't feel you belonged in police work."

"He's right. I wish I'd known that five years earlier."

Aly slowly got up and came over to join Kit at weeding. "I think being here with Noah is going to be good for you," she confided. "Let him take care of you. It's what he's best at." A smile filtered through Aly's serious demeanor. "Right now, you need a little attention and care. And Noah needs someone to care for."

Chapter Eight

"Thank God it's Friday and we've got the weekend ahead of us," Kit said, meaning it as she climbed into Noah's Trans Am. Behind them, the *Osprey* sat docked in the shadowy dusk.

Noah gave her a quick glance while buckling up. "Ever since Aly visited, all hell has broken loose for us," he griped. Driving slowly down the parking lot, Noah took off his officer's cap, tossing it in the back seat.

"Three weeks of incredible work," Kit added tiredly. "I really think Garcia's deluging U.S. shores with boats to get our attention so he can make his big drop elsewhere without law enforcement interference."

"I think you're right." Noah turned the car onto the street, heading for the on-ramp to the freeway that would take them home. The *Osprey* had intercepted at least two boats a day. It was as if someone were sending them in droves toward the Florida coast. His and Kit's days started before dawn and rarely ended before nine or ten at night.

Kit leaned back and chuckled. "I don't know if we want Aly to visit this Saturday, Noah. She was the harbinger of all this boat activity," she teased.

Grinning, Noah nodded. "I'll tell her it's all her fault." His eyes darkened. "Are you sure you don't mind if she visits us again?"

"Of course not. I like your sister." Aly had been the perfect buffer between Kit and Noah, easing the tension between them. Kit didn't want to admit that living with him was like a wonderful dream come true. It was as if they were married—without the physical intimacy.

"She thinks an awful lot of you, too." Noah studied Kit's face in the light and darkness for a moment. Ever since she had cried in his arms, she had changed markedly for the better. No longer did she get up at night to pace the house. The shadows were almost gone from beneath her sparkling eyes, and she smiled more often. With a monumental effort Noah returned to the task of driving. Kit's mouth was far too delicious, and there was too much danger in thinking about the one kiss they'd shared.

Yawning, Kit muttered, "I don't know about you, but I'm dead on my feet. As soon as we get home, I'm going to have a bath and go to bed."

"Good idea, because I'm sure Aly will show up bright and early on our doorstep tomorrow morning," Noah said with a chuckle.

"She's good for us. We need a laugh or two," Kit returned with a smile. A feathery feeling tremored through her as Noah said "our" doorstep. The past few weeks had bound them inexorably to each other in simple but telling ways. And she knew without a doubt that Noah wasn't really like Pete at all. Leaning back, she closed her eyes, looking forward to Aly's effervescent visit. Yes, they all needed to laugh, kick up their heels and have a good time.

"Psst, Kit!" Aly leaned forward from where she sat on the couch with Noah, a bowl of popcorn in hand.

Kit roused herself from the floor, where she lay on her stomach. They were watching a movie on television together on a Saturday night. "What?" She saw the look of devilry in Aly's eyes.

Aly set her bowl of popcorn aside. "Did you know that my brother is ticklish?"

Before Kit could respond, Aly stretched across the couch and began tickling Noah unmercifully beneath the arm. Thoroughly engrossed in the movie and oblivious to their banter, he let out a yelp of surprise.

Kit sat up, watching the popcorn Noah had held in his bowl go flying all over the couch and carpet. Aly pressed her attack, tickling Noah until he fell off the couch and onto the floor.

"There!" Aly crowed triumphantly, getting to her feet with a grin. She beamed at her brother, who was still laughing from his prone position on the carpet.

"What was that for?" Noah demanded, sitting up and grinning, too.

"Things were getting too quiet around here," Aly announced. "I'm going to get some soda pop. Anyone want some?"

Noah looked around with dismay at the scattered popcorn. ''We drank it all.''

''Then I'll drive down to the corner store and get us some more,'' Aly said. ''Be back in a bit, gang. Kit, why don't you help Noah pick up all the popcorn he spilled?''

Giggling, Kit crawled over on her hands and knees to where Noah sat. She began to pick up the popcorn, one piece at a time, putting it back in the emptied bowl. Both Calico and Tuna Boat were getting their share before she could rescue all the kernels.

Noah scowled at her. ''What's so funny, Ms. Anderson?''

''Nothing,'' she said, giving him a merry look. ''Big, bad old Coast Guard officer is reduced to Jell-O by his teeny little sister...'' and she started laughing so hard she had to hold her hand to her stomach.

A mischievous grin spread across Noah's face. He heard Aly close the door on her way out. ''It's a good thing we're alone,'' he growled, and then lunged at Kit.

Startled, Kit let out a yelp and tried to escape, but Noah pinned her to the carpet, anchoring her hands above her head. ''Noah!'' she gasped. His body was so close to hers.

''Let's see what a big, bad police detective does under the same circumstances,'' he threatened as he began to tickle her ribs.

A cry broke from Kit, and she curled up, laughing hysterically. It was impossible to get away from Noah, and all she could do was try to protect her sensitive rib cage from his attack. Finally tears were streaming down her cheeks.

''Uncle! Uncle!'' she gasped, giggling. Kit placed

a hand against his chest, wildly aware of his masculinity. Noah's face loomed close, and she could feel the warmth of his breath fanning across her cheek. ''I give… I give…'' she pleaded breathlessly.

Capturing Kit's hands once again above her head, Noah straddled her with his body. ''Uncle, huh?'' he gasped, smiling down at her. God, but she was beautiful, her eyes lustrous with happiness. Taking his hand, he smoothed several strands of hair from her eyes.

Kit's breasts rose and fell rapidly. Noah was so close that she could feel the heat from his body. Although he had captured her, he wasn't hurting her. Far from it. Kit drowned in his sea-colored eyes. The memory of his kiss flowed to the surface of her heart and mind.

Noah saw her lips part provocatively as she held his gaze. This need for her was excruciating, her slender form taut beneath his. ''Next weekend,'' he rasped, ''I want you to come with me.''

Puzzled, Kit asked, ''What's so special about next weekend?'' His fingers traced her brow and a tiny shiver arched through her.

''We both need a rest from work,'' he decided. ''I want to take you to a special place for a day.'' Tightening his hold on her wrists, Noah allowed his other hand to drop threateningly to her rib cage. ''And if you don't agree, Ms. Anderson, I'm going to tickle the daylights out of you.''

A breathy laugh escaped her. ''If you start tickling me again, Noah Trayhern, I'm going to wet my pants and you know it!''

He gloated, his gaze never leaving her soft, sparkling eyes. He wanted to drown himself in their depths. "Then agree to be pirated away for a day."

It was impossible to relax beneath him. The urge to lean upward and touch his mobile mouth was too much for Kit to ignore. Everything about Noah excited her, and she inhaled his special scent, closing her eyes. "I'll go. Anything not to be tickled."

"Good." Noah released her wrists and forced himself to move off her. Kit was too enticing, too close, and he could feel heat building in himself. He knelt at her side and helped her sit up.

Giving him a wary look, Kit ran her fingers through her short hair. A tremor of longing sang through her as she sat next to him. "Where are you taking me?"

"It's a surprise," he replied enigmatically. "One that you deserve."

"I don't believe this is happening," Kit muttered, trading a glance with Noah as he drove.

His smile was one of pure devastation. "Just one of life's little bonuses. How could I possibly leave Tripoli behind while we enjoy this special Saturday?"

Tripoli hung his head between the seats, panting to emphasize the point. Kit stifled her laughter, shaking her head. "We're going on your boat with a dog!"

He shrugged his broad shoulders, the white polo shirt he had on emphasizing their breadth. "Sit back and relax. This is our day to enjoy."

Kit ran her fingers through her black hair, smiling. When Noah had confided that he was going to take her out on his boat to a beautiful cove for a picnic, she had been excited. He'd promised her it would be a short trip by water, knowing that she would get seasick as always.

She curled up on the seat, rested her chin on her arm and watched Noah. "If I didn't know better, I'd say Tripoli is looking forward to our outing."

Noah grinned, guiding the car slowly down the quay toward a small bay that sheltered over a hundred privately owned boats and yachts. "He should. Every time I get a chance, I take him with me."

"And he likes boating?"

"Why not? In the days of sailing ships, they used to carry cats on board to catch rats. Why not a dog?"

"I certainly hope you're not hinting there are rats aboard your boat!"

Noah laughed, his green eyes flecked with gold as he looked over at her. "Trust me. Tripoli has sea legs and he isn't with us to chase rats."

"I wish I had sea legs," Kit complained, "so I would quit getting sick every day on the *Osprey*."

Noah lost some of his merriment. "I guess you're just one of those people with an inner ear imbalance, who will never adjust to sea life." He brightened. "But we'll take a swim, catch some fish and have a fine time on the beach."

"Remember, I'm not such a hot swimmer, either, Noah."

"Trust me. I won't let anything happen to you."

"That's what they all say—'trust me.'"

Noah grinned. "If you fall overboard, I'll just toss Tripoli in the water with a rope in his mouth. He'll keep you afloat until I can reach you."

"Very funny," Kit growled.

The boat basin looked like the others she had seen dotting the coastline of Florida. The sun was hot, the August day humid, with rapidly building cumulus clouds budding into towering turrets to the west of them. Kit wore her pale lavender bathing suit with a pair of comfortable pink shorts.

Carrying a small picnic basket, Kit watched as Tripoli bounced happily around them as they walked down the wooden wharf. Despite her misgivings about being on the boat, Kit felt her fear begin to fade as she allowed the pleasant events of the day to take their course. The past week had been just as busy as the three before. And Noah was right: they needed to take a breath and relax.

Noah halted and nodded to the boat on the right. "Meet the *Rainbow*."

Kit's gaze roved appreciatively over the eighteen-foot cabin cruiser. How like Noah to name his boat the *Rainbow*. His entire life-style attested to the fact that he allowed few stormy days to inhibit his mood. Noah crossed the plankway, then held out his hand for her.

"Okay, you're next, landlubber."

Kit returned his infectious smile, gripped his hand and stepped aboard. "It's a beautiful vessel, Noah."

"Coming from you, that's quite a compliment. Climb up this small ladder and get comfortable by the helm. I'm going to cast off."

She ascended the ladder to the bridge. Two black leather chairs were bolted to the deck on either side of the wheel. Kit sat down, glancing around until Noah gingerly came up the ladder. He looked breathtakingly masculine in a pair of well-worn cutoffs. Pulling off his shirt, he set it to one side and then took the wheel. Pressing the button on the console, he brought the motors to life with a throaty growl. A slight vibration raced through the sleek craft. Noah guided them safely out of the harbor, the turquoise water beckoning, adding to Kit's building excitement. She tried to ignore the rich brown tone of his upper body as he steered them out into the beautiful waters, heading south.

"I'm jealous of your tan," Kit teased. It was true. Noah's body was a golden color, making the black mat of hair on his chest even more appealing.

He glanced over at her. "You'll get your share today. Come here."

Kit's eyes widened. "Why?"

He held out his hand. "You might as well learn how to guide the *Rainbow*. Come on, don't look so scared. It's easy."

She grimaced. "Next you'll be telling me Tripoli does it."

Noah laughed fully, leaning over and gripping her bare arm, pulling her to her feet. "Come on, my hesitant sailor."

Grudgingly Kit placed her hands on the wheel, her feet slightly apart to compensate for the gentle rolling motion of the vessel. Noah stood behind her, both arms around her as he helped Kit get the feel of the helm. She was agonizingly aware of the warmth of his male body against her, of having nowhere to break contact with him. Her heartbeat rose and she tensed.

"Relax," he said close to her ear. "I don't bite, contrary to popular feminist opinion."

Kit twisted her head, trying to give him a dirty look. "As I've said before, no man is unarmed."

Noah's green eyes danced with laughter, his smile teasing. "As if women don't have their own arsenal," he taunted.

"Such as?" Kit challenged, enjoying their repartee.

He rested his head on her shoulder for a moment,

amusement lacing his rich, husky voice. "Such as, 'I've got a headache tonight, Fred' or—"

Kit gave him a jab in the ribs. "You—"

Noah stepped away, laughing. "Don't say it! I know I'm a chauvinist. Let's face it," he said, coming back and standing dangerously close to her again as she gripped the wheel, "if you didn't have me around to tease you a little, you'd get serious about feminism."

Kit gave him a black look, an unwilling grin tugging at the corners of her mouth despite everything she could do to stop it. "You can go, but Tripoli can stay."

He feigned being wounded, coming up and sliding his hands suggestively across her shoulders. "You mean you'd make me walk the plank?"

"Where's the plank?" Kit called in a loud voice.

Noah looked over at the dog. "Tripoli, I think she means it! You're going to have to save me from getting torn apart by the sharks. Quick! Be my life raft!"

Kit laughed in gales, unable to stop. It felt so good to laugh, to let go of that professional barrier that always existed between them while on board the *Osprey*. The last month had altered their relationship subtly, and she relished the new intimacy with him. Finally Noah took the helm, guiding her to the chair so she could sit and giggle. The wind was brisk, and the tangy scent of the ocean was a delicious intoxicant. Occasionally Noah would cast a spurious glance in her direction, one brow crooked at a questioning angle. He guided the boat along the coast, rarely more than a mile offshore. Tripoli lazed at Kit's feet, sleeping.

"Truce?" Noah hedged finally.

"You think you deserve one after those earlier remarks?" Kit demanded.

He shrugged his broad shoulders. "Let's take a democratic vote by the crew." He glanced down at Tripoli. "I'm sure I'll get reinstated that way."

"Let's not and say we did. I don't think there's much democracy aboard this boat of yours."

"I think you're right. Feel like going down to the galley and getting us something cool to drink?"

Kit shrugged indifferently, feigning a yawn. "Sorry, I have a headache."

It was his turn to grin. "Touché. I wish I had a mirror right now."

"Why?"

"To show you just how lovely and relaxed you've become."

Kit groaned, getting to her feet. "I'll be back in a minute."

Opening the doors to the cabin of the boat, Kit stepped carefully down the polished mahogany steps. Bunk beds were built into one wall, the deep golden wood burnished and smooth beneath her fingertips as she made her way toward the tiny galley. Passing the bathroom, Kit spotted a mirror. Out of curiosity, she ventured in and looked at her reflection. The difference was startling! Noah was right—her gray eyes sparkled with happiness, her cheeks were flushed with life and her lips curved upward, free of tension.

Climbing back up to the deck with their refreshments, Kit handed Noah a soft drink and sat down in her chair.

"Thanks," he said, meaning it.

"You're welcome. You really do have a beautiful boat, Noah."

"It's my sanity when things start closing in on me over at the Coast Guard."

Kit understood what he meant—the brutal number of hours and days he'd put in since Morgan had been branded a traitor. "You don't get to do this very often, though, do you?"

"No, maybe three or four times a year." He shared a warm look with her. "But until Garcia is caught, this is now officially your second home."

Kit eyed him speculatively. "Maybe," she hedged. "That's all I need—a boat as a second home."

"You're teaching me to take time out from the job and relax."

There was a difference in Noah, Kit conceded. When she had first met him, he'd been a driven officer who was married to his carèer for good reasons. But since she'd been living with him, he'd been taking more and more time away from his job. Weekends were spent relaxing whenever possible. They had a positive effect on each other, she decided.

Noah turned, catching her thoughtful gaze. "Besides, I like to fish for our dinner. Saves on grocery bills," he teased.

Kit tried to ignore the fact that he'd said, "our" dinner. She tilted her head. "Tell me, Noah, why aren't you married?"

Noah turned the boat in a westerly direction as they rounded an outcrop of rock, heading toward a small cove ringed with palm trees and a white beach in the distance. "I was planning on a family about five years ago, and then this fiasco with Morgan blew up in our faces. Since then I've had to devote all my spare time to keeping my own career intact from officers who wanted to see me leave the Coast Guard. No one wanted the brother of a traitor in the ranks. So, for a long time I slaved twelve hours a day, seven days a week to salvage my career and ensure that no one could drum me out before I put in the twenty years required for my pension.''

''It's not fair that you or Aly should be punished like that,'' Kit growled unhappily.

''Life is never fair. We just have to learn how to roll with the punches.'' His eyes crinkled with sudden amusement. ''Besides it's only been recently that I've felt like settling down. I had plenty of wild oats to sow.''

''I'll bet you did.''

''Now there you go again, accusing me.''

Kit grimaced. ''With your good looks, I'm sure you have an army of women waiting in line to snag you.''

''Jealous?''

She clamped her mouth shut, embarrassed by his gentle taunting.

''Let's put it this way. I've had a few serious relationships in the past and I enjoy women. Are you going to hang me for that?''

Kit approved of his honesty. ''No. I'm the one who should get hung out to dry for the way I've fouled up my life.''

Noah shook his head. ''Mistakes are allowed, Kit. It's when you keep making the same mistake that it becomes stupidity.'' He shared a smile with her. ''Ignorance is forgivable. Stupidity isn't.''

''For once we agree.''

Noah guided the boat into the cove. The blue-green water sparkled a crystal invitation as he slowly approached the sandy white beach. About ten feet offshore, he cut the engine and heaved the anchor overboard. He looked up at her.

"Well, are you ready to go snorkeling with me to catch our picnic lunch?"

She smiled and nodded, following him to the lower deck, where the equipment was stored in a large wooden locker. Kit slid out of her shorts. She felt immediate heat in her cheeks when she noticed Noah watching her with a hungry glimmer in his eyes. Almost immediately he veiled his gaze, and she took a deep, shaky breath in relief.

Noah pulled out several articles from the box. "Okay, here you go. One set of flippers, a face mask and a snorkel." He handed them to her, then retrieved his own set of gear.

The rest of the day was a little slice of heaven for Kit. It started when she eased herself into the warm, welcoming waters of the cove with Noah's steadying hand on her waist. She learned quickly with his instructions, and in no time they were swimming around the cove, watching hundreds of brilliantly colored tropical fish. The entire floor was carpeted with a fortress of coral. Tripoli had leaped off the boat earlier, immediately swimming to shore, happily exploring his new domain. Kit laughed as she saw the Doberman collecting fallen palm fronds on the beach as if they were prize bones.

For more than an hour, she experienced an intense joy with Noah at her side. He speared two sea bass. Afterward they swam to shore to roast them over the open flames of a small fire. Kit sat on a blanket sharing a lunch of fish, cantaloupe and potato salad with Noah. His body gleamed from the recent swim, and she enjoyed the play of muscles each time he moved.

''Sure you aren't a fish?'' Kit asked between flaky bites of sea bass.

''Probably am. I was born in Clearwater and learned to swim when I was five years old.''

''It's nice to see someone really enjoy himself,'' Kit said.

Noah sat cross-legged, balancing a cup of wine in one hand and his plate in the other. ''I learned early on in this game to keep some distance between drug busting and my personal life, Kit.'' He looked gratefully around the cove. ''This place has been a real haven and heaven to me when the pressure gets rough.''

''I believe it,'' she whispered. Her appetite over the past month had improved markedly, and Kit ate with relish. ''I never separated narc work from my home life.'' And then she added with a grimace, ''I really didn't have a home life.'' Finishing off the meal, Kit put the plate aside and wrapped her hands around her legs to rest her chin on her knees. The cove was alive with color.

''You do now,'' Noah said. ''In all fairness to you, though, doing undercover work is totally different from sea-busting activity. I don't live in the trenches the way you did. If we find one low-profile boat a day, that's usually good hunting for us. You lived with the element, rubbing elbows with the pimps, the junkies and the dealers.'' He gave her a keen look. ''And you paid the price for it, too.''

Pleasantly tired, Kit closed her eyes, turning her head in his direction. ''Too much for one, looking back on it,'' she admitted.

Noah repacked the picnic basket, his lips thinning.

"Kit, if you had a choice right now, would you quit narc?"

The question startled her. That, plus the carefully concealed strength in his voice. She lifted her lashes to study him. "Want the truth?"

Noah gave her a gentle smile. "Has there ever been anything but that between us?"

Managing a short laugh, Kit stretched out on the blanket before him, luxuriating in the rays of the hot sun. "That's one of our unfailing attributes as a team, I'm afraid."

"I find it an important one," he countered.

Kit eyed him suspiciously, deciding not to ask him why. "That aside, yes, I'd quit narc today if I could."

"Why don't you?"

She frowned. "You read my personnel file. I'm up to my hocks with Garcia and the Colombian connection." She rested her arm against her eyes, muttering, "Chuck needs me on this bust, Noah. I told him it would be the last one. I can't take it anymore."

Noah forced himself to sit quietly at her side, his heart contradicting at the pained admission slipping from her lips. He stared down at her. Kit looked almost ethereal, but he could also see strength and courage in the set of her full, promising lips. Not to mention that telltale flash of silver in her large gray eyes from time to time. He reached over, running his fingers lightly down her arm, and captured her hand briefly, giving it a squeeze.

"What would you do if you quit?"

Kit thrilled to his unexpected touch. As always, Noah had caught her off guard. She removed her arm from across her eyes and looked up into his strong, clean face. The intimacy between them was one of silent, mutual agreement, and it rattled her completely.

"I have a minor in teaching. I'd like to go back to college and get my certificate. Then I'd like to work with kids in the elementary grades."

His green eyes darkened. "You'd be one hell of a teacher." Noah felt himself growing hard with desire and fought to restrain himself. Frustration curdled in his throat. Reluctantly he forced a smile. "Let's rest for an hour and then we'll go for a swim," he suggested, rolling over on his belly and lying next to her.

Kit's lips parted, and she was aware of her rapidly beating heart. The need for Noah filled her. Without another word, she lay on her back and closed her eyes, excruciatingly aware of Noah's body only inches away from her.

Chapter Nine

"Come on," Noah coaxed, "let's take one more swim around the cove." He rose and offered his hand to Kit. After an hour's nap, both were refreshed. Kit's gray eyes shone, and as Noah saw desire lingering in their depths, it hit him physically. His strong, bronzed fingers wrapped around her hand and he pulled her gently upward. It would be so easy…so easy to pull her those last few inches that separated them into his arms, lean down and…

"No—" Kit whispered, alarmed as she looked into his hooded eyes and read his intent. Some small part of her fought her desire because it was wrong to entangle their professional relationship with a personal one. But the protest dissolved as she became helplessly ensnared within his sea-green gaze.

Noah maintained a hold on Kit's hand, poignantly aware of her warmth. He saw her eyes grow dark, and felt himself being drawn into a vortex of heat. His grip tightened and he pulled Kit forward until their bodies met and touched like hot, molten steel. He knew he shouldn't, but another part of him, the part that wanted to give her the happiness she had long deserved, won out. He reached out and gently caressed her cheek. Placing his finger beneath her chin, he gently forced her to meet his mouth. The dangerous world they lived in no longer existed. Only Kit and her beautiful gray eyes telling him so much did.

Something old and painful broke loose in Kit's heart as Noah's mouth gently brushed hers. She felt his hands cradle her shoulders, bringing her fully against him. Her breathing grew chaotic as she slid her hands up his arms and across his shoulders.

"Kit..." Noah whispered against her lips, his breath moist, fanning across her cheek. He ran his tongue across her lips, tasting the ocean salt, feeling her quiver. "Yes," he coaxed thickly. "Yes..."

Kit uttered a small cry, melting against his sun-warmed body, her breath stolen from her as Noah deepened his kiss. His mouth was strong, plundering her ripened senses, evoking one major explosion after another throughout her yearning body. She was wildly aware of the hard muscles tensing across his chest, the wiry hair beneath her palm, the clean male scent of him mixed with the sun and the salt tang of the ocean. His tongue caressed the corners of her lips, inviting her to join him in the exchange that sent a wave of exultation racing through her.

Her breath came in short, shallow gasps as she hungrily returned the questing pressure of his mouth. The world anchored to a halt, the lapping of the waves on the beach heightening the dreamlike cocoon he was weaving around both of them. Noah tasted good. And clean. Her lashes fell softly on the planes of her cheeks, and she slid her arms around him, relinquishing all her disintegrating control to this man who had fanned the fires of her body to life. The experience created a storm of exhilaration, making her crave even more of him.

Noah's hands moved upward from Kit's shoulders to frame her face, and his mouth gloried in her returning passion. Time melted into infinity and Kit leaned heavily against him, caressing the inner softness of her mouth, sending a tumult of wavelike sensations that shuddered deliciously throughout her. Slowly Noah lowered her back to the blanket.

His green eyes were dark, searching hers. Fingers trembling as he caressed her cheek, he whispered, "I need you, Kit."

Wordlessly she nodded. Every nerve in her begged for his continued touch, his fiery onslaught. As his hands moved along the straps of her lavender bathing suit, she sighed deeply, surrendering to him.

Peeling the thin straps from her shoulders, Noah eased the suit off Kit. She was exquisitely perfect—for him. Wanting to worship her, he stood and divested himself of his suit, dropping it to one side.

Kit's heart mushroomed with a suffused glow. She welcomed Noah into her arms as he slid down beside her, and captured her face in his large hand, cradling her chin, forcing her to look up at him. She read so much in those green eyes flecked with depths of gold fire. Kit shivered at the coiled power she felt building explosively around him. She wanted him as much as he wanted her.

Noah outlined her lips with small, hungry kisses.

He nibbled at the corner of her mouth and then sent his hot, claiming lips down her slender nape. "You're beautiful," he rasped. "More than beautiful. Perfect..."

A shiver fled through her as his tongue wove wet patterns in the valley between her taut, aching breasts. A moan rose in her throat as he goaded the already hardened nipples into fiery life. Somewhere in the delicious hazy state of her mind, Kit wanted to return the love he was giving her in equal measure. Her hands moved knowingly, down the expanse of his tightly muscled chest, from the flat of his stomach to the rich, carpeted area below. She heard him groan, then felt him tense beside her.

"God, how I want you," Noah gasped, smothering her awaiting lips. He cupped one breast, delighting in its proud, crescent curve, and leaned over to tease it. He felt Kit's nails dig deeply into his shoulders, her body becoming a taut bow against him as he gently tugged on the yielding nipple. Kit tasted good, her perfume and the ocean scent intoxicating to his senses. She felt like firm velvet beneath his exploring hands. His body shrieked for release, but he quelled his own desires in order to bring her pleasure, instead.

Noah rained kisses down the expanse of her stomach, across her slightly rounded abdomen, and gently parted her thighs with his hand. He heard her cry out in fierce need as he tantalized the very core of her being. As he drove her beyond the edge of ecstasy, he realized that she was the most inviting, passionate and willful woman he'd ever met. Her breath was shallow and gasping as he placed his knee between her damp thighs. Her body had a sheen to it and he gently ran his hands upward from her hips and ribs to her beautifully formed breasts and, finally, to her flushed face. Kit's eyes were wide and dazed with fulfillment. He covered her with his male body, moving in accordance with the woven web of desire throbbing heatedly between them. Leaning over, he caressed her full, eager lips and responded to her hungry urgency, glorying in her uninhibited response.

"Now...please now," Kit keened softly. "Please... I need you, Noah..."

He was aware of the boiling heat within him, his own primal animal desire clashing savagely with his control. He eased into her warm depths, dragging in a deep, ragged breath of air. Kit tensed, her fingers clutching his shoulders. She felt like life itself—yielding and fertile to his starving body. Urgency thrummed through him, and all his powerful control exploded in a raging thirst. He thrust deeply, and a growl tore from him.

They were one as they must be, for there was no other way with them. With each matching movement of her responsive body, Noah gloried in their shared joy. He felt Kit tense beneath him and heard a small cry bubble upward from her throat. A look of utter rapture crossed her face, and her lashes lay like sooty fans against her cheeks. He reveled in her climax just as he yielded to his own need to send his seed of life deep within her moments later.

Kit lay gasping against him, spent in the aftermath. "I never knew..." she whispered, moving her hand across Noah's damp chest, giving him a weak embrace.

Noah kissed her temple. "That it could be this good? It can be when it's right," he said thickly, gathering Kit up against him. Their hearts thundered in unison against each other. He kissed her eyelids, her nose and, finally, her wet, full lips.

"You're beautiful, Kitten," he admitted softly.

Kit raised her lashes. A tender light burned deep in his jade-colored eyes and her heart somersaulted with joy. Words were useless. She could feel the depth of his feelings radiating toward her, and she felt humbled by it, swept upward on a rainbow of ecstasy because of it. Loving Noah was without comparison. He made her feel as if the human body were a vessel rendered sacred through their loving act. Kit caressed his cheek, her eyes wide with the wonder of this new discovery.

"You make me feel beautiful."

Noah nodded, understanding. The bond he felt with Kit was almost tangible. He was aware of it with every touch of his hand on her. Tenderly he placed his mouth on her lips, drinking deeply of her. "You've given me so much," he told her, stroking her hair.

Kit shook her head, her voice trembling with emotion. "No, Noah. You've given me a new and better life."

He smiled and rested his cheek against hers, inhaling her sweet scent. "Maybe, maybe not. We've got a lot of tough days ahead of us."

Fear niggled through her as she slid her arms across Noah's shoulders. As she buried her face against his neck, Kit couldn't ignore that seed of terror.

After taking a shower once they arrived home that evening, Kit sat on her bed, worried. Noah's lovemaking had left her feeling vulnerable and exquisitely feminine. It was as if he had taken away the last of the old Kit Anderson's toughness and bravado forever. Wandering over to the dresser mirror, Kit hesitantly lifted her lashes to stare at herself. She wore a sleeveless light blue blouse and a pair of jeans, but that didn't detract from her as a woman. No, one look into her own eyes and Kit realized how much more had happened. And the future was uncertain. And dangerous. With a sigh Kit opened the door. Regardless of how she felt, dinner had to be made.

In the kitchen she took a checkered apron from one of the drawers and tied it around her waist and began preparing a meal of fried chicken with wild rice. Kit heard a bedroom door open, and then close, and realized Noah was coming.

Turning her head, she saw Noah saunter into the room. He was heartrendingly handsome in the dark blue polo shirt with a pair of khaki shorts, and he gave her a devastating smile of silent welcome. Kit trembled beneath the mesmerizing warmth of his eyes as he walked over to her.

''Can I tell you how happy you look?'' Noah whispered as he leaned down and placed a kiss on her lips. It was a long, welcoming kiss meant to convey more than the lightness of his words. Not a second had gone by without Kit in his thoughts. He would never forget the power of their lovemaking. His fingers. tightened on her shoulder briefly. ''And I'll also make a decidedly male chauvinist comment and tell you how utterly ravishing you look wearing an apron.'' He dropped another more coaxing kiss. This time he lingered, his mouth barely grazing her warm lips. ''Mmm, I think we ought to have dessert before dinner,'' he teased. He brushed his mouth more strongly against her, delighted by her returning pressure.

Kit gave a low laugh, trying to extricate herself gently from his continued charm. ''Noah Trayhern, you're the most enticing man I've ever met, but the answer is no,'' she murmured, smiling. ''Besides, we need to sit down and have a serious talk.''

His brows dipped. ''Oh?'' He caressed the slope of her cheek. Did Kit know how delicious she appeared to him? Her eyes held a special spark of life for the first time, her cheeks were pink from the heat of the kitchen stove, and that smile... He expelled a heavy sigh and tried to be dramatic. Looking down at the assembled animals sitting expectantly at their feet, he addressed them with a twinkle in his eye.

''Okay, gang, what do you think? Is this ravishing woman going to tell me I have to cook dinner, instead?''

Calico meowed sonorously as she got up to rub against Noah's leg.

Kit giggled. ''You are the most manipulative person I've ever met! And yes, we're going to talk. And no, I don't mind doing my fair share in the kitchen.''

Noah's green eyes darkened with a mischievous glint. He grabbed Kit and imprisoned her seductively against his body. ''Okay, would you agree to live here forever and ever if I continue to help you with all the kitchen chores?''

Kit eyed him speculatively. The strength and hardness of his male body sent new waves of surging, hungry awareness through her, and she craved his closeness and his wonderful ability to love her. ''Let me go, Noah, before I lose my train of thought!''

She was magical, Noah decided, still bound up in

the desire of their explosive lovemaking on the beach. But that was another world, a world of dreams, not reality. And looking into Kit's worried eyes, he felt some of his euphoria begin to evaporate. Releasing her, he went to the refrigerator and pulled out a bottle of chilled white wine. "I think this is going to call for a drink," he murmured, taking down two glasses and setting them on the table.

The mood altered, and Kit lost her smile. "This isn't going to be easy, Noah."

He matched her seriousness, pouring wine into one of the glasses, then handing it to Kit. "Okay, honey, what is it?"

Just the tenor of his voice sent a shiver of renewed longing through her. Kit expelled a long breath before beginning.

"This afternoon—"

Noah reached across the table, his hand covering hers. "It was special, Kit. For both of us."

She moistened her lips, raising her eyes to meet his honest gaze. "Yes. Yes, it was, Noah. And more than anything, I want to be honest with you." She swallowed hard, removing her hand. "In my job as an undercover agent I lied all the time, Noah. I lied to stay alive. I've got five years of lying under my belt. Worst of all, I find it easy to lie to myself more than anyone. When I'm scared on a narc job, I lie to myself and pretend I don't feel the fear. And when I was at an emotional breaking point I used to stick my head in the sand by working harder, hoping to forget it." Kit took a fortifying sip of the wine to shore up her raw emotional state. One look at Noah's open face gave her the courage to go on. "So that brings it around to us."

“Go on,” Noah said softly.

Kit closed her eyes. “This afternoon was the most beautiful experience in my life, Noah. It was one positive against so much negativity I’ve lived with for five years. But—” She chewed on her lower lip for a second. “This is so hard,” Kit confessed, seeking his silent assurance.

Noah grimaced. “Just say it, Kit. Let your feelings speak. We can handle it.”

Kit shook her head. “You’re always so positive.”

“Do you like the alternative?” Noah probed.

“No. Okay, the bottom line is...until this thing is settled with Garcia, I can’t sleep with you, Noah.”

He sat back, digesting her comment. At that moment Kit was searching and unsure. He offered her a slight smile meant to reinforce her honesty. “You’re right. For both of us. It won’t be a problem.”

Her eyes widened slightly. “No?”

Kit’s tensed shoulders fell and she took a deep breath. “I thought you would be angry, Noah. Hurt, maybe—I don’t know.” She gave him a soulful look of utter relief.

Leaning his elbows on the table, Noah said, “Let’s talk about your decision to stay in your bed and out of my arms.”

Kit was caught off guard by his concern and calm reaction to her ultimatum. She found it easy to respond. “We’re in a terrible predicament with Garcia, complicated by this contract out on my head. We both need to remain clearheaded about our priorities until Operation Storm is over.” She stared down at his hands around the wineglass. They were so strong, so loving. “I haven’t been with a man for two years.

And when I met you, I had no intention of—of—well, going to bed with you."

"It just kind of happened," Noah admitted quietly. "When I first saw you, I wondered why you dressed in oversize baggy clothes to hide that beautiful, skinny body of yours. Then I realized it was to conceal your obvious femininity. Working in the trenches had made you wary of men in general."

Kit blushed. "You're right. After years of protecting myself from the male criminals I had to live with, you walked into my life and made me feel like a woman again."

Noah's eyes grew warm as he studied her. "You've always been a woman. We just seem to bring out the best in each other."

"I've never before felt the things you've brought out in me. And I mean more than just in bed," Kit hastily added.

"That's a wonderful compliment. Thank you."

She shot him a knowing look. "I have the distinct feeling that everything you touch is in some way better for the experience."

Noah laughed, pouring them both more wine. "You're no slouch, either, Anderson. My life hasn't been the same since you arrived." And then he added, "It's been better. And you're right. We both need to keep our focus on our job and place our personal needs aside for now."

"Yes," Kit agreed. She wanted to tell him that being in his arms was heaven. It was healing and wonderful and… She gave him a tender smile. "You've given me so much in such a short time, Noah. And all of it has been so—" Kit groped for the words to convey her feelings. "I don't know how to say it. Only that you've made me feel again. And feel good about myself for the first time in years." She reached out, shyly touching his hand, aware of the wiry texture of hair that covered its broad expanse. "You've given me so much in precious little time, and I want and need time to assimilate it all. To adjust to this new me." Kit's eyes grew cautious. "Our future is like a box of explosives that could detonate in our face at a moment's notice until we collar Garcia. I don't know where we're going with each other, Noah. I only know that we're both worth too much to throw this away on a whim. I need time to iron myself out emotionally. In all fairness to you, I don't feel I've contributed much to our unique arrangement beyond being a moody house guest."

A smile curved the corners of his mouth. "If you're talking about getting up and pacing the halls at night, don't give it a second thought."

She withdrew her hand from his. "The nightmares have finally stopped. Ever since you held me when I cried, I've been able to sleep nights."

"Listen to me, Kitten," Noah coaxed huskily, "you're made of silk. You're tough, resilient, beautiful and exotic. Right now you don't know it, but you're one of a kind. I saw that right away in you, and you're in the process of realizing it yourself."

Tears marred her vision, and Noah's face blurred as Kit looked at him. "In the time I've been here with you, I have changed for the better. With your help, I've gotten rid of a lot of my past."

"You're on the road to recovery," Noah agreed. And if he was willing to admit it, he thought, he wanted to be a continued part of Kit's healing process. She brought out the best in him.

Kit got to her feet and went to the drain board, staring out the window for a long moment. Finally she turned and leaned against the counter, meeting Noah's patient gaze.

"I'm glad we could talk this out. I feel better."

Noah wanted to go to her and hold her, but it was impossible. He had given his word to back off and wait. Trying to ignore the sensual tension strung tautly between them was going to be tough. The phone rang, breaking that tenuous cord that bound them.

Noah rose and answered the call on the kitchen phone. "Lieutenant Trayhern speaking."

"Trayhern, this is Cordeman."

Flicking a glance over at Kit, Noah found himself automatically wanting to protect her from any more narc activity. His voice hardened. "It's Saturday evening, Cordeman."

"Can't help it. How's our house guest getting along?"

Angry because the police supervisor had interrupted the tenderness he and Kit had shared, Noah growled, "Just fine. What's going on that I deserve the honor of this phone call on the weekend?"

"Just wanted to let you know that the U.S. Navy is picking up an awful lot of activity at all the major choke points. Also, our DEA undercover agent had brought back word that Garcia is getting ready to move the *Marie-Elise*, his personal two-hundred-foot yacht, out for a meeting with smaller drug dealers' boats."

His hand tightened on the phone, his eyes never leaving Kit's face. "When?"

"No sure answer to that, Lieutenant. All we know

is that Garcia is behind the increased drug trafficking you've been meeting head-on the past few weeks. We think he's going to continue this onslaught to try to keep the attention of the CG cutters—clearing the way for him to drop his bales of marijuana in some safe harbor without the possibility of a bust.''

''So the pond's heating up.'' That meant sixteen-hour days and probably weekend duty.

''You got it. The U.S. Navy P3 will be doing a flyover of the Colombian coast to keep an eye on Garcia's ship. When it moves, we know he's going to meet with the dealers. You'll be notified as soon as possible so you and the *Osprey* can get into position.''

''Fine,'' Noah answered.

''Tell your house guest hello for me, will you?''

''Yes.'' The word came out clipped, and Noah hung up the phone, glaring down at the tiled floor.

Kit moved over to where he stood. ''That was Chuck. What did he want?''

Grudgingly Noah filled her in and he saw some of the old terror coming back to Kit's eyes. Unthinkingly he reached out, placing his hand on her shoulder. Damn! Reluctantly he removed his hand. ''It's going to be hard not being intimate with you,'' he muttered, a sour smile on his mouth.

''I know,'' Kit whispered, moving to a safer distance from Noah. Struggling to maintain a professional demeanor with him, Kit changed subjects. ''So Garcia's going to step up the pace of boats smuggling drugs to our coast.''

''Yes. He's trying to pull a decoy maneuver so his drop of bales to the dealers will go unimpeded.''

Kit turned to face the counter. Their dinner needed

to be finished, although in all honesty, she was no longer hungry. She went through the motions of preparing a salad. Noah moved around the room, tightly wound with energy. It felt as if he were going to explode any second.

"Did Chuck say how he's doing?" she asked, wanting to defuse Noah's tension.

Shrugging, Noah sat down, staring moodily at the glass of wine. "Fine, I guess."

"You don't like him, do you?"

"I don't exactly see your old boss as a nice person, no."

She peeled a carrot, slicing it into the bowl. "Why?"

"Cordeman's more concerned with results than he is with his people."

"Isn't that a bit cruel?" Kit demanded, taking issue with his abrupt assessment.

"He used you, Kit. I don't respect someone who burns out his best people."

Kit rested her hands on the sink, feeling she had to defend Chuck. "Look, no one's perfect, Noah. Chuck has his shortcomings, but I'll never forget that he was the only one there for me when the chips were down. He's gruff, yes, but he's not really callous." She chewed on her lower lip, watching Noah's face darken.

His mouth thinned. "Let's not fight, Kit. Particularly over Cordeman. It isn't necessary."

She began to slice a ripe, red tomato. "Okay," she whispered. "Life's too short to spend it on disagreements. God knows, we do enough fighting with the druggies."

"Our home is a haven against that."

She raised her eyes. ‘‘That’s an understatement. It’s the only place where we can escape.’’

The noose was closing around them. Noah sensed it. ‘‘Well, as long as Dante doesn’t discover where you are, that’s a big point in our favor,’’ he groused, more to himself than her.

She put the tomatoes in the salad, choosing a scallion to add to it. ‘‘Every month I lived at Garcia’s fortress with Dante at his side, I sweated. I knew the longer I stayed, the higher my chances were of being discovered.’’

‘‘No wonder you ended up with stomach ulcers.’’

Kit pursed her lips. ‘‘Well, Chuck told me ulcers and migraines are the occupational hazards of an undercover agent.’’

‘‘So much for Cordeman’s philosophy. If he’d taken better care of you, the ulcers wouldn’t have been the outcome.’’

Kit ignored the jab, realizing that no matter what she said about her other boss, Noah wasn’t going to agree. A shiver coursed down her spine.

‘‘What’s wrong?’’

‘‘Nothing,’’ Kit muttered, wiping her hands on a towel.

Noah got to his feet, placing his hands on her shoulders and turning her to face him. God, she looked incredibly unguarded at that moment. He couldn’t stop himself from reaching out and caressing her flushed cheek. ‘‘Tell me,’’ he commanded.

Kit shivered beneath Noah’s low, disturbing voice. She took an unsteady breath, aware of the desire within her to kiss that male mouth that tore her senses apart. He lifted her above every fear and depression into the yearning euphoria she hungered to explore with him again. She saw so much in his eyes, wanting to lose herself within them and know that she was safe. A broken smile came to her lips.

"It's Dante," she admitted.

He searched Kit's very still face, and his hands tightened on her shoulders. "And?"

"Dante's a snake, Noah." Her eyes glazed with the remembrance that had haunted her nightly dreams with regularity. "I worked with that sick bastard for a year down there at the Colombian fortress. I sweated around Dante more than all of them put together. I never knew if he was going to pull a knife on me or what."

"Did he try to—"

She grimaced. "No, thank God. He had other preferences besides women. I suppose I should be thankful, but..." Her voice trailed off as she relived one frightening episode with Dante. She felt Noah's hand sliding down her hair in a reassuring gesture. Forcing a smile, Kit said, "I'm too old for this business, Noah. I've seen too much."

"Maybe you ought to resign," he murmured, "and go after that teaching certificate."

Reluctantly Kit withdrew from him, turning to put the salad on the table. "Maybe I should."

Frustrated by the vise Kit was caught in, Noah busied himself setting the table. He wanted to say; *Dammit, Cordeman has pulled out every human emotion you had and then put it through a blender, Kit. You need a nice safe job like teaching. You don't need street action to tear holes in your stomach and shatter your senses.* But he remained silent, realizing Kit would no more quit Operation Storm than Cordeman would. Was her life worth getting Garcia? He didn't think so, wishing mightily for an escape for her. But there was none. They had to take things one week at a time, netting the drug dealers trying to reach the Florida coast, waiting and watching for Garcia to make his move.

Chapter Ten

Something was wrong. Kit could sense it. After another grueling month of seven-day weeks, she had come down with stomach flu on Friday and stayed home. Noah had left that morning without her for the first time. She glanced at the clock on the kitchen wall: it was now 8:00 p.m. He'd promised that if he was going to be late, someone from Coast Guard headquarters would notify her. But no call had come. Where was he?

The police portion of her brain began to work overtime. Dante and his contract killers were making every effort to find her, according to the snitches. Had they discovered that Noah was protecting her? Had they kidnapped him as he stepped off the *Osprey*? Killed him? She escaped to the living room, a deep sense of anguish searing through her.

Biting her lower lip, Kit stared at the front door.

Come through the door, she begged silently. *Please, Noah, just come home....* Burying her face in her hands, Kit forced herself to take a deep breath. What was happening to her? Living with Noah since they had made love had been like a never-ending dream. The warmth between them was undeniable, just as the longing in his stormy green eyes when she caught him staring at her during quiet moments at home was nearly unbearable. They wanted each other so badly. But if they allowed their emotions to rule their heads, it would take their alertness away from the danger that surrounded them, and possibly get them killed.

Kit paced back and forth from the living room to the foyer. She had planned a special dinner for Noah tonight to let him know how much she missed being at his side. Her lips thinned, and she walked over to the phone sitting on the lamp table in the living room. She had to call someone...but whom? She picked up the address book on the table and flipped to the last page where Noah had scribbled the number he could be reached at in an emergency.

Her hand hovered over the phone. She wasn't supposed to make a call for any reason! The line might be tapped, and her cover would be blown. Snitches who worked for Dante could be anywhere. Kit's eyes narrowed as she stared down at the phone. Swallowing convulsively, she made the decision. Just as she touched the receiver, the phone rang. Startled, Kit jerked her hand back, her heart slamming against her rib cage.

The phone rang four times before she reached out to pick up the receiver. She wasn't supposed to answer the phone either, but Kit couldn't combat the terror she was experiencing....

* * *

"We've got a live one, Skipper," Joe said excitedly.

Handing the hot list to the ensign, Noah smiled grimly. "The *Sanchez* is registered in the U.S. This is our lucky day."

Noah motioned for the ensign to take over the helm, and watched the hundred-foot ship bobbing a mile away from them. "This is the second one today," he muttered, thinking that this meant he wasn't going to make it home before midnight. The sun had already set. Worried about Kit all day, he hadn't been as alert as he might have been. She had been deathly sick all night. This morning when he'd gone to her bedroom, she'd still been weak from the flu.

"She's definitely low profile," Joe said, pointing at the ship.

"Yes." Twisting around, Noah ordered the boarding party to prepare for another search.

The *Osprey* came alive, but Noah remained seemingly immune to the sudden activity surrounding him. The thrumming of the *Osprey*'s mighty engines accelerating to close the distance between it and the *Sanchez* filled the air. He pulled his baseball cap an inch lower, his gaze intent on the other boat.

"You taking this boarding, Skipper?" Edwards wanted to know.

"Yes. I'll run it from the deck of the *Sanchez*. You stay on the bridge and coordinate the radio and other necessary communications."

Edwards's blue eyes danced with excitement. "I wish it was my turn."

A thread of a noncommittal smile pulled at Noah's mouth. He was aware of everything at the moment. Adrenaline was surging through his bloodstream, heightening his five senses and giving him that extrasensory perception that might be needed—might save him or one of his men from death by a smuggler's bullet. "Next time, Joe," he murmured.

Noah took the binoculars and watched the activity aboard the *Sanchez*. The ship listed and wallowed like a pregnant whale, far below the safety waterline. Noah counted three open hatches on her deck. Scowling, he put down the binoculars.

"I've got a bad feeling about this one, Joe."

The ensign nodded, skillfully easing the *Osprey* alongside the *Sanchez*. "Three hatches. Not good. The hold must be huge. They could have gunmen hiding down there anywhere." Edwards passed a quick look to his skipper. "Just be careful..."

Noah was handed an M-16 rifle by a member of the boarding party. A slight grin touched his mouth. "I've got everything in the world to live for, Joe. I'm not about to waste my life on a drug runner." He placed the portable radio on his belt and stepped from the bridge. "I'll stay in touch once we get aboard," he promised.

Vaguely Noah heard Edwards's commanding voice coming over the PA system, ordering the *Sanchez* to heave to and allow them to board. Noah's mind was on his work, but his heart lingered on Kit. It was true. He did have everything to live for. He'd found Kit. Noah walked down the immaculate deck of the *Osprey* to join his waiting five-man party. Like the crew, Noah was dressed in the one-piece dark blue Coast Guard uniform. They all wore flak jackets.

Petty Officer Jack Formen approached him. "We're ready, Skipper."

"Good. Lock and load," Noah ordered his men

quietly. The metallic sound of ammunition magazines being loaded into the lethal weapons was heard. The *Osprey* loomed over the *Sanchez*. Noah saw only two half-naked crewmen in sight. They were dark skinned. Probably Colombian. His jaw clenched as his gaze swept across the vessel. His instincts told him the rest of the motley crew was down in the hold, waiting.

"What do you think?" Noah asked Formen.

The petty officer of forty-five shook his graying head. "Not good, Skipper. This tub's too big to be run by those two dudes."

Noah's mouth quirked as he nodded, bracing himself to compensate for the movement of the *Osprey*. "Yeah...okay, men, let's watch ourselves very carefully," he warned the party.

Noah gave Formen a nod, and the six men leaped from one ship deck to the other. The three hatches looked like yawning, cavernous mouths to Noah. He ordered McMorrison, the youngest crewman, to detain and search the two *Sanchez* men standing on the bridge. Noah's sensitive nostrils detected the sweet odor of marijuana. He motioned Formen to his side.

"You take the first hatch."

"Yes, sir."

Noah looked at the other two men. "Dawson and Crinita, you take the second hatch. I'll take the third."

"Yes, sir," Dawson said.

Noah turned to the last man, Sullivan. "You wait up here in case we get into trouble," he commanded.

"Yes, sir."

The silence became deafening as Noah walked lightly across the cluttered deck laden with coils of rope. The *Sanchez* was a garbage scow, with rust in evidence everywhere. In the gray light of dusk, everything became indistinguishable. They would have to descend those wooden ladders into either total darkness or dimly lit areas where precious seconds would be lost until their eyes adjusted.

Noah's heart began a slow pound as he released the M-16's safety, readying the weapon. His hand tightened around the rifle and he slowed his step, trying to discern if anyone was waiting with gun in hand at the bottom of the hold. His eyes couldn't pierce the gloom. Noah walked cautiously around the hold, lifting his head momentarily to see if Formen or the other team had descended yet. They were getting ready to go down. Sweat trickled down his temples. Gripping the splintered ladder and swinging over the hold entrance, he winced at the powerful odor of marijuana. Grimly Noah glanced around. The feeble light from several electric light bulbs left huge areas of gray shadow throughout the cavernous hold.

Noah descended to the lower deck, turning, his back against the ladder. Silence. He pulled the radio from his belt. Putting his mouth close to it, he pressed the button. "Nothing so far, Joe. Stay alert," he ordered.

Replacing the radio, Noah allowed his hearing to do the work for him. His eyes were adjusting and he saw his other three men coming down into the hold. Bales of tightly wrapped and freshly dried marijuana were packed everywhere with the exception of a few key aisles.

There was the sound of a metallic click. Cold horror washed over Noah. "Formen!" he yelled, "look out!" and assumed a crouched position.

Before Formen could react, the roar of gunfire shattered the silence. The petty officer was knocked off his feet. He slumped to the deck, wounded. The smell of spent ammunition stung Noah's flared nostrils as he raced down the central aisle toward his wounded crewman. Screams, curses and more gunfire mingled in earsplitting explosions all around him. Noah saw four *Sanchez* crewmen hiding behind bales, firing away at his men. Everything blanked out in his mind except the imperative to pin down the enemy.

"Crinita, Dawson!" he roared, "four men at eleven o'clock!" He threw himself flat on the hard surface of the deck, rolling over twice as his men fired in that direction. Finding protection against a bale, Noah glanced toward Formen, who lay unconscious only twenty feet away. Blood was pooling rapidly to surround the area where he lay. The bluish haze of gunfire drifted through the poorly lit hold, the vicious red-and-yellow flames from the muzzles of the rifles ripping through the air.

Sweat covered Noah's face as he gestured for Dawson and Crinita to outflank the *Sanchez* crewmen. Grabbing his radio, Noah shouted orders back to Edwards.

"We need help! Get a medic over here. Formen's down!" Dammit, Formen was bleeding to death! Noah shouldered the M-16, aiming carefully, firing. Dawson and Crinita were working their way into position to pin down the enemy. If only... Noah flipped the rifle on full automatic, spraying at the *Sanchez* crewmen. He lurched to his feet, laying down a blistering wall of fire that gave him cover as he sprinted to where Formen lay.

Noah looked up as he stood over his petty officer. Sullivan was waiting anxiously at the top of the hold.

"Get ready to take him up!" Noah yelled. "I'll push him up the ladder!"

Dropping his weapon, Noah pulled Formen into his arms. He had to get him topside or he would die! Grunting from the weight, Noah maneuvered Formen to the ladder and pushed him upward. Helping hands reached downward, hooking beneath Formen's armpits. With one mighty shove, Noah boosted the unconscious petty officer up and out of the hold to safety. Another spate of gunfire erupted. Wood splintered and exploded all around him. Noah clenched his teeth, dropping to the deck below. In those horrifying seconds, he knew he was the target they were gunning for. Suddenly life became precious as Noah leaned down to grab his rifle. But a bullet found him and he was slammed to the deck. He felt a searing flame of white heat in his left arm as an electric jolt ripped up into his shoulder and neck.

He shook his head to clear the shock of being hit and hung on to his weapon with his right hand. A *Sanchez* crewman suddenly leaped from behind a bale and ran toward him, his revolver lifted. As Noah tried to raise his left arm to steady the wavering barrel of his rifle, he found he couldn't move his fingers.

The crewman sprinted closer, screaming curses. He waved the revolver wildly in his right hand and bore down on Noah, who stood between him and freedom via the hold ladder. Noah gasped as he forced his left arm to move. He had to lift the rifle or he'd be dead in seconds. Blood flowed heavily from his arm, staining his uniform, as he forced his numbed left fingers to steady the weapon.

The crewman was lowering the revolver. Aiming it directly at Noah's chest as he leaped the last few feet toward the ladder. Noah heard Dawson scream at the crewman to drop the gun. He didn't. Noah lifted the M-16. Pain raged through the left side of his body as he squeezed the trigger. The jerk of the rifle tore through him and he cried out, dropping the weapon after firing it, rolling onto his side and grabbing his left shoulder. The *Sanchez* crewman was hurled backward by the impact of the bullet, dead.

"Son of a bitch," Noah sobbed between clenched teeth. Blood. He was bleeding heavily. His mind was clearing, but he knew he was in shock. One look at his forearm and he knew the bullet had severed a major artery. He would bleed to death right here. *No!* his heart screamed. *Kit. What about Kit? Dammit, you can't bleed to death!* He was aware of Dawson running down the aisle, kneeling at his side.

"Get me a tourniquet," Noah gasped. "Anything…for God's sake, hurry!"

Dawson's eyes widened as he stared down at his skipper. "Yes, sir!" he breathed, scrambling up the ladder and yelling for the corpsman.

Noah fell back, pressing as hard as he could on the injured area. Closing his eyes, he fought off the first tidal wave of blackness. *I don't want to die in this lousy hold. I want to live. Kit… Dammit, I want to live! Got to have time for Kit… Isn't the bleeding going to stop?* Noah groaned as he felt his strength begin to ebb. He'd lost too much blood and his eyesight was dimming. If he lost consciousness, his hand would slip from the wound. Where was help? Where the hell was Dawson with a tourniquet? And Jack…Jack Formen. God, was he still alive? *Kit…I need you…* Anger mingled with despair and Noah felt coldness seeping into his lower extremities. He knew what that meant. He lay sprawled on the splintered wooden deck between huge bales of marijuana, wondering if he was going to die without being able to tell Kit just how much she meant to him....

Kit wrapped her hand around the receiver shakily, then finally jerked it off the cradle. "Hello," she croaked, trying to steady her voice.

"Kit, this is Cordeman."

Her knuckles whitened as she tightened her grip on the receiver. "What's wrong, Chuck?" she gasped.

"There was a firefight involving the *Osprey*. Trayhern and another Coast Guard crewman were wounded in the action. They're being brought to the trauma unit of the naval hospital in Miami."

No! her heart screamed. The trauma unit was reserved for critical cases only. Noah had been involved in a gun incident. "Oh, my God," she cried.

"They'll be arriving shortly by Coast Guard helicopter. There's an emergency team standing by and—"

Kit dropped the phone and raced to her bedroom to grab her purse. She didn't care if she blew her cover by showing up in a public place. Noah was injured and she wasn't going to wait patiently at home for further word on him. She took the keys to the silver Toyota, which Noah used as a second car. Using the automatic garage door opener, Kit waited impatiently for the door to lift. *Hurry! Hurry!* Her world was suddenly blown apart. Noah, loving, trusting Noah, who always smiled and looked on the positive side of life, had been shot. How bad was it? What kind of gun? Depending on the type, the bullet could do minimal or maximum damage. She swallowed against the lump in her throat as she backed the Toyota out of the driveway, intent on only one thing: being with Noah.

Kit tore through the trauma unit, almost colliding with Chuck Cordeman as he stood outside the double doors to the restricted area where the critically injured were treated.

Cordeman's eyes narrowed. "Kit? What the hell are you—"

Anxiously she looked around. "Noah. Where is he, Chuck?" she demanded breathlessly.

Cordeman jerked a thumb toward the doors. "In there."

Kit started to push by him, but he grabbed her arm and pulled her back.

"Have you lost your mind?" he demanded. "What the hell's gotten into you? You're supposed to stay out of sight!"

Kit was sobbing breathlessly. She had run all the way from the parking lot after hearing more details on the radio about the gun battle at sea. "Let me go, Chuck." She turned, fully intending to go through those doors with or without Cordeman's consent.

"You're outa your mind!" Cordeman snarled. "Trayhern's the least wounded. Just a bullet through his left arm. They're prepping him for surgery right now. There's nothing you can do—"

Kit glared at him. "Like hell there isn't!" Wresting her arm from his hand, she pushed through the doors. Adrenaline poured through her bloodstream, heightening her senses to an incredible degree. In one sweep of the room she spotted a doctor and two nurses working feverishly over a man in a dark blue Coast Guard uniform. Kit immediately walked across the room before an orderly could accost her. She saw Noah's pale face, the pain pulling at his mouth. Tears jammed into her eyes once more. As she stepped up to the gurney, Noah's eyes widened slightly.

"Kit..." he rasped thickly.

"I'm sorry," the blond nurse said, turning to Kit, "you're going to have to leave."

"Let her stay," Noah begged weakly to the doctor on his left.

The physician hesitated, took one look at Kit and decided to let her remain. "You can only stay for a minute or so. We've just given him a shot and we're taking him to surgery. He'll be unconscious shortly."

Nodding, Kit swallowed hard. She slipped by the nurse and into the cramped cubicle. Tears slid down her cheeks as she surveyed Noah. Blood was splattered all over the front of his uniform; his left forearm was wrapped in a blood-soaked bandage, indicating the area of the wound. A pint of plasma hung from the IV unit above his head, and the needle was inserted in his right arm.

"Oh, Noah..." she whispered, leaning over, placing her trembling hand on his forehead. His brow was damp with perspiration and she saw the ravages of pain lingering in his dark green eyes. He stared confusedly up at her.

"You came..."

"You knew I would." Anxiously Kit searched his drawn features. "God, I was so worried, Noah—"

"So was I," he whispered, closing his eyes momentarily. He reopened them, gazing darkly up at her. "It was bad. Jack Formen's really hurt, Kit. I don't want to lose him." His mouth thinned with pain.

''I've got to talk to Wanda, Formen's wife. I've got to tell her how he is...''

''Hush, darling,'' she murmured, running her hand gently across his hair. ''You've been wounded. They're taking you to surgery soon.''

Noah shook his head, becoming groggy from the effects of the drug. ''No, Kit, I've got to tell his wife... God, they love each other so much—'' His voice cracked and he closed his eyes.

Kit reached out, gripping his good hand. ''I'll talk to her, Noah. I'll tell her. Go to sleep, darling. When you wake up, you'll feel better.'' She felt the fingers clutch weakly at her hand, and watched helplessly as grief and pain furrowed his brow.

''Kit?'' he mumbled, his voice slurring now.

''Right here.''

''Kit, I need you. Out there today, when the gunfire started, all I could think of was you....''

She fought back a sob, leaning over the gurney, placing her mouth against his lips. His flesh was cool beneath hers as she pressed a kiss on them. ''I'll be here, Noah. Stop fighting the drug. Everything will be taken care of, I promise you.''

Kit stared dully at Chuck across the Surgery floor's visitor's lounge. He gave her a disgruntled look in return. Already two hours had passed since they had wheeled Noah into the operating theater. Wanda Formen sat opposite in another plastic lounge chair, waiting in silent anguish, her face drawn. Kit had consoled her earlier as well as she could. With a sigh she rested her elbows on her thighs. She felt like a quagmire of emotions. Noah's last statement had shaken her almost as badly as finding out that he'd been wounded in a gun battle. As they'd wheeled him away and the nurse had guided her toward the elevator, Kit had fought back the tears. And on the way up, Chuck Cordeman had glared at her obvious lack of control of the situation.

He rose ponderously now and walked over to where she sat.

"Mind if I join you?"

Kit shrugged. "If you're going to discuss my being here, you can save your breath."

Cordeman sank heavily into the chair beside her. He stared at her for a long moment before speaking. "You've changed, Kit."

She roused herself with effort. "Maybe I have."

He frowned. "Yeah. It's not like you to blow your cover over something stupid like this."

Kit sucked in a sharp breath, rounding on him. "*Something like this* just happens to be Noah!" she whispered angrily. "He's not some damn statistic, Chuck!"

"You're touchier than a—"

"Go to hell."

"What's gotten into you, Kit? Does this guy mean something to you? I know you've been living under his roof for quite a while. The way you're behaving, I'd think you'd fallen in love with him."

She had to get a grip on herself. "I know this is hard for you to grasp, Chuck, but Noah has helped me more in the past few months than any human being I've encountered in the past five years. Does that make sense? He helped pull me out of a year-long depression, and he fought to get me time off to rest." She glared at him. "Which is something you never did."

Cordeman's mouth turned sour. "Okay, okay. I had that one coming," he growled. "So he's a nice guy in our rotten little business."

Kit wrung her hands, allowing her head to fall forward. She stared blankly down at the polished black-and-white tiles beneath her feet. "He's a better man than either of us has ever had the privilege of knowing," she gritted out. "Or are ever likely to meet in our business."

Chuck snorted. "Enough of the hearts and flowers, Anderson. If you've got an ounce of sense left, you'll get your rear out of here before you're recognized."

"I'm staying," she hissed between clenched teeth, "until hell freezes over, Chuck. And I don't care if you don't like it. You're not my boss anymore."

Kit rose and began to pace the length of the corridor. Her heart was lost in a cauldron of emotions. The gun battle had ripped away all pretense of how she really felt toward Noah. Halting, Kit closed her eyes, her hand pressed to her chest because it hurt so much. She loved Noah.

A trembling sigh broke from her as she allowed the realization to sink it. When had it happened? How? Just living with Noah had dissolved those wary walls around her heart.

The look in his dark, agony-filled eyes had told her she meant much more than she'd dared admit to him, too. They'd both been fighting to ignore what they really felt. Raising her head, Kit knew what must be done: Noah couldn't know that she loved him. Not until Operation Storm was completed. It would be too hard on both of them.

And did Noah love her? She knew that what she felt was love. A love that had gently captured her and would never let her go. Noah had shown her that real, caring people existed. Did he love her, or was his attention and care merely that, and born of his proximity to her the past months? Uncertain, Kit shuffled slowly back down the hall. Nearly losing Noah had torn away any self-deception she'd cloaked their relationship in. And the future held nothing but more danger. Her love was going to be brutally tested.

A surgical nurse was the first to leave the operating room, and she headed in Kit's direction.

"Ms. Anderson?"

Kit anchored herself to the spot, her heart thrashing in her breast. "Yes?"

She smiled tiredly, taking off the face mask. "Lieutenant Trayhern is going to be fine. We're putting him in recovery and it should be about an hour before he's conscious."

Relief flooded Kit and she closed her eyes. "When may I see him?" Her voice sounded faint to her ears.

"Just as soon as he's conscious and in his private room."

"Thank you," Kit whispered, reaching out and touching the nurse's shoulder. She turned away so that Cordeman couldn't see her face or the tears that dribbled down her cheeks.

Noah groaned, the sound reverberating like a kettle drum through his head. Dizziness was interwoven with nausea as he fought to surface from the powerful anesthetic. His mind was shorting out, with blips of the gun battle, Kit's anxious face and the hammering recoil of an M-16 combining to rip through his semiconscious state. His whole being centered on Kit. He loved her, dammit! And he was bleeding to death in a dark hold. Was he going to slip over the edge to oblivion without ever having told her how damn much he loved her?

Kit, I need you! I don't want to die! You have to know—

"Noah," Kit soothed, leaning over the bed, caressing his sweaty brow, "it's all right. You're safe and you're going to live."

Noah concentrated on Kit's unsteady voice. His eyes felt weighted, and it took every last vestige of strength to force them open. Kit's face danced out of focus before him. He felt the warmth of her breath against his face as she pressed her lips to his. Did she know how good she felt to him?

"You're here," he rasped thickly. "I'm alive..."

Kit cradled his bristly cheek with her hand. "You almost bled to death, Noah. But the doctors fixed the artery." Tears welled up in her eyes.

He saw her tears, a broken smile pulling at his mouth. "Just a close call. God, I'm glad you're here. I kept thinking I'd never get to see you again."

She traced his wrinkled brow with her fingertips. "Welcome back," she whispered.

Exhaustion lapped at Noah. Even now, he knew that with his wound, it would probably be at least six to eight weeks before they'd allow him to skipper the *Osprey* once again. And during that time, Kit would be going out to sea every day without him. Sliding into unconsciousness, he felt his joy over living snuffed out by nightmares. Kit would be out on the pond, a possible target herself. The world was closing in on them like a noose around their necks.

Chapter Eleven

Kit boarded the *Osprey* as she had for the past three months. The only difference was, this time Noah was at her side again, completely recovered from his gunshot wound. She traded greetings with the crew as they walked across the plank and went to the bridge.

Kit stood aside as Joe Edwards thrust out his hand to Noah. "Good to see you back, Skipper. The *Osprey* is all yours."

Noah smiled and shook Joe's proffered hand. "Thank you. You took good care of her in my absence."

A grin spread across Joe's affable face. "I took good care of both your ladies while you were shorebound, Skipper."

Laughing, Noah agreed.

"How you feeling today, Kit?" Joe inquired.

She mustered a proper grimace. It was always the

first question asked, because there wasn't a day that went by that she didn't become seasick. "The usual, Joe."

"You'd think that in time you'd adjust to this," Edwards jibed good-naturedly, trading a look with his skipper.

Noah gave a soft snort, stowing the navigation charts beneath the console. "She's the first person I've ever met who's never adjusted to sea life."

"Just proves I'm not a mermaid, Noah Trayhern," Kit reminded him tartly, making herself comfortable on one of the bridge chairs.

Noah gave her a wicked look in return, one filled with longing. How had three months since he'd been wounded pass so quickly? Noah drank in her fragile form. Kit had never regained the weight she should have, due to her constant seasickness.

Sipping the coffee that the second mate had given her, Kit watched Noah pilot the *Osprey* out of the berth and into the channel. His eyes were narrowed in concentration, his sensitive hands gripping the helm, monitoring every slight change in the ship's course. Hands she now longed to have love her again.... Kit closed her eyes, savoring the ache in her heart. Their home life had changed, their affection toward each other deepening. Noah had worked at headquarters while his arm was healing, while Kit had gone to sea every day aboard the *Osprey*. And every night Noah was there, waiting on the dock for her to disembark. Their weekends were special, spent in the quiet of their home or out at the cove. Their home... Kit smiled to herself. Funny how she thought of everything in the plural now. Their home, their cats and dog.

Her stomach began to roll in warning. Kit put the coffee down and stood. "Excuse me, I'm going down to the cabin."

Noah glanced worriedly over at her. Kit's face had grown pale. "Seasickness?"

"Yes. And right on time. I'll be better around noon, Noah." She smiled lamely into his concerned green eyes. "Don't worry."

An hour later, Noah made his way from the bridge down to his cabin. He knocked once on the bulkhead door and entered. Kit had just emerged from the bathroom, looking waxen.

Grimly he gripped her arm, leading her over to the bunk. "You look like hell," he muttered, going and getting a warm washcloth.

Gratefully Kit took the cloth, wiping her face. "I hate throwing up."

He gave her a fierce look. "Look, something needs to be done about this, Kit. It can't continue. It's bad for your health."

The amount of care in his expression sent her heart soaring with joy. Kit placed her fingers on his arm. "Okay, I'll go to the base dispensary."

"It's about time. Stay home tomorrow and go to a doctor." He tunneled his fingers through her black hair, which now hung shoulder length. He saw Kit's eyes go soft with longing. The need to take her into his arms and make love with her was excruciating. Stilling his desire for her, Noah tucked away those clamoring feelings. When Operation Storm was over, he was going to admit his love for her.

"Okay, okay. I'll take the day off and get to a

doctor. But really, Noah, I don't think he'll be able to do much.''

He caressed her cheek. ''Maybe you're anemic. You never have any color in your face anymore,'' he muttered.

It was rare that Kit would allow herself the gift of putting her arms around Noah's shoulders and hugging him, but she did now. Closing her eyes, she felt his arms slide around her, and she moaned softly. Their careful avoidance of each other had been torturous. ''I'll be okay,'' she whispered, leaning tiredly against him.

''You'd better be, lady,'' he growled, pressing a chaste kiss to her hair.

Kit walked into the Coast Guard dispensary at nine the following morning. Feeling wretched with the usual nausea, she carefully made her way between a number of waiting patients. Most of them were pregnant women or worried young mothers coping with their sick charges. Kit found a seat next to a red-haired girl who was obviously pregnant.

The girl, probably no more than nineteen, was dressed in a pink cotton maternity dress and smiled encouragingly over at Kit. ''How far along are you?''

''Along?''

The girl ran her fingers across her swollen belly in a loving gesture. ''How many months before you have your baby?''

Kit gave her a startled look. ''I'm not pregnant. I'm here to see if something can't be done about my seasickness.''

The girl gave her a shy smile. ''Funny, I thought you were pregnant. You have that look.''

"What look?"

"You know what they say about a woman who's with child—her skin becomes real glowing."

Kit smiled gently, taken by the girl's interest in her. "I'm sure it's a case of seasickness."

"You're nauseated now?"

Pressing her hand to her stomach, Kit nodded. "Terribly."

"And you're not on a boat. How could that be seasickness?" she pointed out, still smiling.

Closing her eyes tightly, Kit felt a sinking sensation in the pit of her stomach. My God, she couldn't be pregnant! Not now! Oh, God, not now! Dante still had that contract out on her. She was living on borrowed time until Garcia was captured. But Noah had made beautiful, wonderful love to her a little more than three months ago. And her menstrual cycle was erratic at best because of the stress of her job.

Slowly opening her eyes, Kit stared blankly ahead, her mind whirling with the possible options she'd face if she was pregnant. Hard, terrible choices would have to be made to help her and Noah's child survive the coming confrontation.

Kit heard her name called. Rising, she took a deep breath and grimly threaded her way through the groups of children and their mothers.

"Congratulations, Kit," Dr. Ann Whitten said, coming back into the small room.

"I'm pregnant?"

"Indeed you are," the gray-haired woman said, smiling.

Kit's fingers trembled as she buttoned up her blouse. "How far along am I?" she asked hollowly.

"I'd say three and a half to four months. Further, you're anemic. I'm writing you a prescription for some iron tablets to get your red blood count back up."

Letting out a shaky breath, Kit rubbed her brow. "I can't believe it."

"You need rest, Kit," Dr. Whitten said, coming up and standing in front to her. "You're working too hard."

Kit avoided the doctor's probing gaze. "What happens if I keep working, Doctor?"

"Your uterus is slightly tipped, Kit. If you want to keep that baby, you're going to have to rest. Some women can push hard for nine months and deliver a strapping young tyke, but you can't. With your underweight condition, anemia and a body that isn't fully cooperating in carrying this child, you need rest. And plenty of it."

Kit drew in a painful breath. She wanted this baby more than life itself. Her gray eyes mirrored the turmoil she was experiencing. "But if I had to work, Doctor, wouldn't it be better *now* rather than later? I mean, wouldn't my chances of a miscarriage rise if I were farther along in my pregnancy?"

Ann Whitten nodded, placing the clipboard on her desk. "The farther along you are, Kit, the greater the chance that you may have to opt for total bed rest until your baby's born."

Silence engulfed them while Kit mulled over her limited options. "Doctor, there are certain things I have to do in the next couple of months. I don't have a choice."

Dr. Whitten handed her the prescription. "There are always choices, Kit. If you want to carry your baby to full term, you'll have to do something to alter the work you feel has to be done.''

Kit touched her brow, anguish filling her heart. If they didn't capture Garcia and Dante, her life would be worthless. Dante had fled the U.S., jumping bail and escaping to Colombia but leaving a contract out on Kit, according to the undercover agent trailing him. She stole a look over at the kind doctor's face. ''You're right,'' she whispered. ''I'll do the best I can.'' Kit slid off the table and stood. Picking up her purse, she decided to visit Chuck Cordeman. Only he could help her now.

''What the hell are you doing here?'' Cordeman demanded as Kit walked into his office.

''We have to talk, Chuck,'' she announced without preamble. ''Let's go into one of the interrogation rooms.''

Cordeman reluctantly pushed his football-shaped body out of the dilapidated chair. ''You look like hell,'' he observed.

Kit gave him a bitter smile. ''Thanks for the compliment.''

Cordeman walked like no one else Kit had ever seen. He seemed to list from side to side. As they moved down a long, poorly lit hallway, she wondered if he would ever get seasick. Probably not, because of the way he mimicked a ship bobbing on the ocean. Chuck was used to that kind of motion.

''Okay, what's so important that you've broken your cover by coming here?'' Chuck demanded, pointing to one of two chairs in the small, barren room as he shut the door.

Kit sat down, facing her old boss. ''I need some information, Chuck.''

''About what?''

''When is Garcia going to move his mother ship?''

He shrugged. ''We've got an undercover agent in place and we're hoping to find out soon.''

Her heart pounded heavily in her breast. ''I've got to know.''

Cordeman regarded her darkly. ''What's going down, Kit? You look like death warmed over. In fact, you look worse than when you left us. What's Trayhern doing? Working you too hard?''

She bit her lower lip. ''No, Chuck. It isn't Noah. I—'' She swallowed hard. ''Make me a promise?''

His face softened slightly. ''What's wrong, Kit? You're shaking.''

''I need a promise from you first, Chuck,'' she said, desperation in her voice.

''Okay, okay, I promise. What is it?''

Kit fought back her tears. ''Chuck, I'm four months pregnant with Noah's child, and there's a contract out on my head. I know the odds are in Dante's favor of finding me sooner rather than later.'' She reached out, gripping his meaty hand. ''Promise me you'll tell no one about my condition,'' she rushed on. ''I've got to help find Dante and Garcia before they get to me first.''

Chuck's face betrayed his emotion. His eyes grew round and he stared at her in disbelief. ''Oh, God,'' he muttered. And then he got heavily to his feet, giving her a sorrowful look. ''Ah, Kit, why now? Pregnant? Of all the bad timing—''

She blinked back the tears. ''Okay, so it was lousy

timing, dammit! I didn't plan this, Chuck. It was an accident. But I can't help that now.''

His eyes grew squinty. ''Does Trayhern know?''

''No, and he's not going to find out, either. If he knew, he'd never let me continue to participate in Operation Storm.''

Cordeman snorted vehemently. ''He'd pack your rear out of Dade County so fast it'd make your head spin. He's protective as hell.''

''And getting me out of Dade isn't going to improve my chances of surviving, Chuck. You and I both know that. And you need me to identify Garcia.'' Kit rubbed her face tiredly. ''That's why I ask you, when is Garcia going to make his move? The sooner the better.''

''Yeah, no kidding. Damn, Kit, this is bad.''

''No one's more aware of that than I am.''

''You're not the narc detective I used to know,'' he muttered, shaking his head sadly. ''You're not the tough broad who could be counted on to carry anything through with success. Kit, you've changed.'' And then he added, ''For the better. You're more feminine. More—'' Words failed him, and he shifted to his official tone. ''Okay,'' he muttered gruffly, ''what do you want me to do? Where are we going with all these confessions?''

Kit gave him a wobbly smile. ''The original plan was for me to board the mother ship in search of Garcia and Dante.''

''After the scum has been rounded up,'' he put in.

''But there could be firefights on the mother ship, Chuck. I don't want my baby exposed to gunfire.''

''We're bringing several decoy craft piloted by DEA agents into the bay during the trading. They'll be taking the names and registry of drug-buying ships so we can hunt them down later. Knowing Garcia the way I do, I'm betting he won't be on board the *Marie-Elise* during the buying. He'll play it smart and be on a smaller boat hanging somewhere around the bay. How about if you stay on one of our DEA decoys? I'll be boarding the *Marie-Elise* as soon as the bust goes down. I can get in touch with you by radio once we've got everything secured and then you can come on board."

"That sounds better," Kit answered, relief in her voice. Then she frowned and rubbed her temples, hating herself momentarily. "The last thing I want to do is hold off telling Noah about the baby—" she glanced over at Chuck "—but until Dante and Garcia are identified and behind bars, I'm still on their hit list."

"I understand. You been to a doctor yet?"

She got up, pushing her fingers through her hair in an aggravated motion. "Yes. She said something about me having a tipped uterus and that I stand a good chance of losing my baby if I don't get off my feet soon."

Cordeman grimaced. "Damn, Kit—"

Her eyes were dazed with fatigue. "I don't have a choice, Chuck. I just hope Garcia makes his move soon."

He grunted, getting to his feet. "Makes two of us. Well, come on, let's get you home. You really look wiped out."

Kit walked over and put her arm around Chuck's sloped shoulders. "Thanks," she whispered, meaning it.

He gave her a thin smile. "For what? If Trayhern

finds out I knew you were pregnant and didn't pull you out of this operation, *he'll* put a contract out on *me*.''

Kit's heart wrenched at the sound of Tripoli's joyous bark. Noah was home. She glanced at the wall clock: 9:00 p.m. Scrubbing the potato with renewed nervous energy, she thought, *God, give me the strength to lie to him. Please, please don't let him see I'm not telling him the whole truth. I have to carry this off! For all of us....*

Noah ambled into the kitchen, a smile on his handsome face. ''Are you feeling better?'' he asked, coming over to the sink and placing his arms around her.

Kit trembled, shutting her eyes, biting back the words that wanted to flow from her heart. ''Better,'' she said in a strained voice. It was unlike Noah to embrace her like this, but she understood, needing his strength right now.

''Mmm, you smell like jasmine,'' Noah whispered seductively rocking her gently in his arms. ''And you look a hundred percent improved from this morning.''

''I just took a bath.'' That wasn't a lie. She raised her head. Was any man as strong or compassionate as Noah? Her lips parted in unspoken joy as she saw the corners of his mobile, sensual mouth turn up as he gazed down at her. And his eyes...oh, God, she could be forever lost in their changing sea color. Kit saw tenderness in the golden flecks mingled with the green and felt her heart melting with unparalleled joy. The words *I love you* wanted to tear from her. Kit closed her eyes, fighting them back, fighting everything back.

''What did the doctor say?'' he asked, splaying his

long fingers down her back, gently following the curve of her spine.

Kit took a deep, ragged breath, feeling her heart rip in two, screaming to be released from the bondage of a secret that must be kept buried deeply within her. "She said I was anemic."

Noah eased his embrace, studying her. "How anemic?"

She shrugged, making light of it. "Enough to put me on some iron pills for a while."

"What about the nausea? Anemia doesn't cause that, does it?"

Kit's heart pounded violently to underscore her loathing to betray Noah. "No," she murmured, closing her eyes so that he couldn't see the lie. "She said it was an inner ear imbalance and that nothing could be done about it."

Noah stroked her silky hair, disgruntled. He studied her troubled features. "Could you use some good news then?"

Hurting inwardly at deceiving him, Kit whispered, "Something…anything…"

Noah traced the clean line of her jaw. It was so easy to become lost within the facets of Kit's face. She had a wonderful bone structure, wide-set eyes that were now shadowed with pain and seriousness. Her mouth was one of her most beautiful features, Noah thought. And he hungered to kiss her. He roused himself from his torrid reverie and realized that Kit was waiting for him to answer her.

"We had just pulled into the dock when we got word from the undercover agent in Colombia that the *Marie-Elise* had heaved anchor. She's in the Gulf of Darien. From the looks of it, she's heading in the direction of the Windward Passage choke point. It's a little early to confirm that yet, but right now it appears to be her bearing.''

Kit's knees jellied. ''The *Marie-Elise* is—''

Noah watched her cheeks stain with color. ''Yeah, Operation Storm is in full gear.''

Her prayer had been answered! Kit gasped. ''When do we go to the *Osprey*?''

''I've got my crew outfitting her right now. It means a number of days at sea.'' Noah's features grew worried. ''Are you sure you'll be able to take this? It's going to be rough.''

Sinking against him, Kit buried her face in his chest. ''I'll do whatever it takes, Noah,'' she whispered. ''I just want this part of my life wrapped up.''

Noah felt the urgency in her voice, understanding. ''I know,'' he soothed. Holding her away from him, his voice grew husky. ''And just as soon as this damned operation is ended, Kit, you and I have some serious talking to do.''

She drowned in the darkness of his eyes. There was unspoken warmth in them. ''Yes,'' she said faintly, ''we're going to have a long talk....'' Now, if only Noah would agree to go along with Chuck's change in plans, she and her baby would be safe. Safe for a future she would die to protect.

''There's been a change in plans, Lieutenant.'' Cordeman's face was shadowed as he stood at dockside, close to the *Osprey*.

Kit stole a glance at Noah's scowling features. The lighting carved his face into harsh planes.

''What change, Cordeman?'' he growled, standing close to Kit.

For a second Cordeman's gaze locked with Kit's. There was a silent exchange and then he broke contact, directing his attention to the officer. "I want Kit safe on the *Guayama*. It's one of our DEA decoy boats that will be tooling around in the bay, getting names and the registry of the dealer doing business. You'll transfer Kit over before pulling into Cap Haitien, which is where Garcia is headed. I'm sending Barnes, one of our narc agents, with her. There's no way in hell I want her life jeopardized on this mission."

Noah's mouth relaxed slightly. "For once we agree on something, Cordeman. You feel Garcia's going to be in a boat hovering near the *Marie-Elise*?"

"That's right. So Kit can use the binoculars to check out the smaller craft, and stay safe."

Nodding, Noah looked toward the *Osprey*. It was nearly one in the morning and time to go. "I like the idea."

Kit started to sway, but caught herself. Relief surged through her as the three of them walked toward the ship. Dawn would bring the confrontation with Garcia. Soon the showdown would come. Shoring up her broken emotions, Kit walked up the plank and stepped onto the *Osprey*. *Hurry,* she prayed. *Hurry and get this over with....*

A bloodred dawn greeted Kit's eyes as she moved up the steel steps toward the bridge of the *Osprey*. Kit found Noah, Cordeman, Edwards and Barnes hunkered over a map spread across the console.

Noah glanced up, his heart wrenching with anxiety. Kit looked ethereal in the dawn's light. "Things are firmed up," he told her. "Come and join us."

Chuck nodded in her direction, a question in his eyes. Kit forced a slight smile for his benefit, wedging herself between Noah and him.

"What's going on?" she asked, her voice still husky with sleep.

Noah pointed to the map, circling the area. "The *Marie-Elise* has dropped anchor in a cove near Cap Haitien." His voice betrayed his aggravation. "Garcia wasn't stupid. The bay is shallow, with little room to maneuver a larger ship. It means that the *Sea Eagle* and the *Osprey* are going to have to choke off the only escape route in or out of the bay. They'll barricade the entrance by positioning the cutters horizontally across it. We aren't going to be able to sail into the bay at all."

A sheen of perspiration showed on Noah's hardened features as he studied the map with fierce intensity. Kit realized timing was critical to capturing the *Marie-Elise* and the drug dealers like fish in a net. A shiver shot down her spine and she tried to throw off the cape of dread that settled around her drawn shoulders.

"It's going to be vital that Kit be able to find Garcia," Cordeman said. "With the shallow waters, I'm positive that the bastard will be aboard a smaller boat."

Straightening, Noah studied Kit. "The *Guayama* is already alongside. We'll transfer you and Barnes now, and then Henri Galera, the DEA agent, will take you into the bay. After you're in there, we'll wait until he calls us to take our position to trap all of them."

"Fine," Kit said. She told the crew on the bridge goodbye, and then Noah took her arm, leading her to the lower deck.

Like everyone else, Kit wore a flak jacket and a shoulder holster. The sun had just peeked over the horizon, sending shafts of glaring light across the choppy waters. The tension she felt in Noah put her on edge.

"It will be over soon," she told him.

"No one's happier about it than me," he confided. Stopping at the ladder, he pointed toward a small tug that bobbed beside them. "The *Guayama*."

The small boat was nothing more than a rusty scow sitting high in the water. Kit saw a black man at the wheel, who waved up at them. "Not much to it, is there?"

"No." Noah turned Kit around, his hands on her shoulders. He didn't give a damn who saw them at that instant. Fear hovered around him, and he couldn't shake the feeling. He wasn't sure if it was for him or Kit. "Listen, you be damn careful, Kitten," he rasped, holding her gaze.

"I'll be very careful, darling."

His face relaxed slightly. He couldn't kiss her. He couldn't tell her he loved her—yet. There was a slight tremble to his voice. "Stay safe. We've got everything to live for."

Barnes came walking up. Kit couldn't hide her disappointment. She had wanted to kiss Noah one last time. But that was impossible now. "I'll see you when this is all over, Noah. Please, *you* be careful."

Releasing her arms, Noah stepped back. He gave her a warm smile meant only for her. "Very careful, Kitten."

Turning away, Kit stepped distractedly down the steel ladder and took Galera's waiting hand.

"Welcome aboard, Detective Anderson."

Kit stepped aside, allowing Barnes to board. "Thank you, Henri." Her eyes lifted upward, and she saw Noah standing far above them, silhouetted by the growing light, his face grim. Anguish overwhelmed Kit. Out of habit, she touched her stomach. Was it because she was pregnant that she was more fearful than usual? Dread stalked her. Every time she felt that ugly sensation crawling through her, it meant danger.

"Cast off!" Galera ordered Barnes, who released the lines to the *Osprey*.

A lump formed in Kit's throat. She raised her hand. Noah raised his in return. Tears blurred his stalwart figure and Kit turned away, no longer able to stand the pain of their separation. Heading to the bridge, where Galera was, Kit wanted to focus all her attention on the forthcoming bust. Her life, the life of her baby and Noah's, depended on it.

"There they are," Henri said grimly as they moved into the shallow cove.

The *Marie-Elise* was anchored as close to the shoreline as possible, lying heavy in the water. Clusters of boats bobbed next to one another at the ship's starboard side as huge bales of marijuana were crane-hoisted onto the smaller ones.

Kit counted at least fifty smaller boats in the cove. Taking the binoculars, she began to scan the *Marie-Elise*. She heard Henri make a call to alert both Coast Guard cutters to come in and close off escape from the bay. In half an hour they would arrive on station, and then all hell would break loose.

"Man, they're doing a booming business," Henri said with a chuckle. His skin glistened with perspiration.

People in ragtag outfits of gaily colored shirts and jeans were running up and down metal stairs at the bottom of the loading platform of the *Marie-Elise*. "I don't see Garcia or Dante," Kit muttered. As soon as one boat was loaded, another zipped up to take its place. Her heart pounded with anxiety as she continued to make a slow, thorough appraisal of each boat near the mother ship. Where were they? She saw flags of all nationalities being flown.

Henri glanced at his watch. "In ten minutes the Coast Guard will be on station," he warned, maneuvering the chugging tug toward the beach to get a closer look at another group of boats anchored there. "Take a look at this next bunch, Kit."

She swung her binoculars toward the shore. There were more than thirty sleek inboard cruisers, beat-up rusty tubs and yachts huddled together, all waiting their turn to get the bales. Could she spot Garcia and Dante before the Coast Guard closed off the cove? Tension thrummed through her as she frantically searched each boat in turn.

"Five more minutes," Henri warned, "before these boats split like a flock of startled birds. The moment they see the Coast Guard, they're gonna panic." He gave the wooden wheel a hefty turn, urging the *Guayama* around so that the bow was aimed at the mother ship.

Kit glanced up; the shore was no more than fifty feet away from them.

Barnes crowded in on the bridge, unholstering his revolver and releasing the safety. "Man, this is going to be a mess in a few minutes. Where are all these boats going to go when they find out they're all trapped?"

Chortling, Galera asked, "You ever seen druggies walk on water?"

Kit grinned sickly, continuing to rapidly scan the boats. Suddenly her heart thudded. "Oh, my God!" she breathed. "It's them. Garcia! And Dante!"

"Where?" Henri demanded.

"Over there," Kit said, pointing. "That red-and-white charter boat about two hundred yards east of us." Her throat ached with renewed fear as Barnes took the binoculars.

Henri grabbed the microphone, calling the *Osprey* and *Sea Eagle*, giving them a clear description of the boat. Kit listened in stunned silence, watching the boat. Her pulse was strong, her heart beating wildly in her breast.

"They're sitting on two-hundred-fifty horsepower of boat," Barnes growled, lowering the binoculars.

"They ain't gonna go anywhere," Henri said with a booming laugh. He glanced at his watch and then over his shoulder. "They're here."

Kit jerked her attention to the only entrance to the cove. Both the Coast Guard vessels had just hoved into view, stationing themselves like a barrier across it. She turned back to the smugglers. Suddenly, without warning, the entire cove rippled with fear. Kit saw smugglers sprint into action as soon as they saw the *Osprey* and *Sea Eagle*. Shouting and cursing filled the air. It was as if a huge tidal wave had smashed through the cove. Boats fled in all directions.

All her attention was riveted on the red-and-white boat. Suddenly the huge, thunderous engines roared to life, water foaming and swirling madly around the rear of the boat. From the corner of her eye, Kit saw four other DEA boats of varying sizes, shapes and power closing in on Garcia to cut him off and surround him. Henri thrust the two throttles forward, causing the little *Guayama* to leap ahead with surprising adroitness. They were closing the net around Garcia.

Barnes cursed and gripped Kit's shoulder. "Look out!" he screamed. "He's trying to escape!"

Kit's lips parted, a cry lurching from her throat. In the blinding split seconds that followed, the red-and-white monster of a boat careened wildly, its bow pointed directly at the *Guayama*, which blocked its only remaining route of escape.

The snarl of engines and the sudden crunching sound of bows meeting, folding and cracking shattered the air. Kit was thrown heavily against Barnes, who was slammed into the rear bulkhead. The explosion that followed punctured the cove like an artillery barrage.

Kit remembered wave after wave of broiling heat from the explosion, screams, then the smell of diesel fuel in the air. She crawled to her hands and knees, blood dribbling from her nose and mouth. Water rushed into the destroyed bridge of the listing *Guayama*. Blindly she reached out, gripping Barnes's limp arm. She yelled at him, realizing in her dazed condition that he was unconscious.

Staggering to her feet, Kit turned. Nausea overwhelmed her and she jerked her head away, unable to cope with the grisly scene that met her eyes. Henri was dead. But Barnes was still alive. Kit heard gunshots all around them, ignored the angry firing and dragged the agent off the bridge and onto the deck of the sinking *Guayama*.

Barnes revived just in time. Kit stared disbelievingly as diesel fuel and fire raced across the surface around the two wrecked boats. She gasped for breath, realizing that several people were flailing nearby in the water, all of them heading for shore to escape.

"Come on!" she begged Barnes. She jerked his arm, and they both jumped overboard.

The water was surprisingly warm, and Kit coughed wildly, floundering toward shore. The heavy flak jacket weighed her down, and she swallowed water as she struggled to stay afloat. Barnes was having equal trouble. They touched bottom minutes later.

Kit's hair hung limply around her face as she staggered toward the beach, Barnes weaving unsteadily on his feet in front of her.

"Kit!" Barnes screamed in warning.

Automatically Kit flattened, throwing herself into the shallow water as the crack of a gun sounded very close to her. Barnes was thrown backward into the water, a red stain moving across his head. Kit rolled on her side, fumbling to unsnap the revolver that rested beneath her left armpit.

"Hold it!" a voice snarled.

Her hand froze on the gun and Kit looked up. Into the viperous eyes of Emilio Dante.

Chapter Twelve

Cordeman was the first to discover what had occurred. It had been one of the many messages coming across the bridge of the *Osprey*. He had seen the two boats collide close to shore and heard the resulting earsplitting explosion. Moving with unaccustomed quickness, Cordeman got a ride on another DEA decoy boat and made it over to the *Marie-Elise* to locate Noah and his boarding crew.

Cordeman found Trayhern, his face blackened by grime and sweat, down in the hold. He grabbed Noah's arm and jerked him around to get his full attention. The roar of several fire hoses and shouts of the men directing water on the blaze mingled with Cordeman's raised voice.

"Kit's in trouble!"

Noah wiped a trail of sweat from his eyes, blinking once. "What?"

Cordeman's grip tightened. "The boat Kit was on was rammed by Garcia and Dante!"

Noah's mouth opened and closed. He stared disbelievingly at Cordeman. Everything had happened so fast. The boarding party from the *Osprey* had been the first to engage in gunfire, and he had led the initial attack aboard the bristling mother ship. He pointed toward the hold ladder.

"Get topside so I can hear you," Noah ordered. He turned, giving orders to Chief Stanton to continue battling the blaze, then quickly climbed the ladder. He took a deep breath of clean air, and his eyes pinned the narc supervisor.

"What the hell are you talking about, Cordeman?"

"We got a call from the *Guayama* seconds before it was rammed. Kit spotted Garcia and Dante on a red-and-white charter boat near them." He gritted his teeth, watching the officer's face pale beneath the tan. "I don't know if they rammed the *Guayama* on purpose or not. Anyway, an agent on one of the other DEA decoy boats watched the whole thing through binoculars. With Galera's description, he was able to identify Garcia and Dante."

Noah felt his heart tearing apart inside his chest, and he looked toward shore, where two vessels were still mated and burning from their collision. "No—" he croaked. "No!"

"Get hold of yourself, Trayhern! They saw Kit, Barnes and Dante make it to shore. Dante shot Barnes and he took Kit prisoner."

Noah tensed and glared toward the scenic beach lined with palm trees. Beyond the grove of palms, the rocky land rose sharply, dotted with gnarled trees and cactus. He swung around.

‘‘He’ll kill her.’’

‘‘Not yet. She’s his ticket to safety until he can get to the other side of the hill above us,’’ Chuck growled. ‘‘Come on, let’s get a rescue party together. If Dante reaches some means of safety before we can get to him, he will kill Kit.’’

Grimly Noah tightened his lips to a thin line of pain. ‘‘What about Garcia?’’

‘‘Dead. We just recovered his and Galera’s body from the area of the collision.’’

Noah uttered an expletive and moved quickly toward the debarkation area. Cordeman reached out, pulling him to a halt. ‘‘Look, there’s one more thing you gotta know before we try to rescue Kit.’’

‘‘What?’’ Noah snarled, tired of Cordeman feeding him bits and pieces of information. All he wanted to do was find Kit. He glared at Cordeman, confused by the look on the man’s sweaty face.

‘‘I promised her I wouldn’t tell you.’’ He breathed harshly, mopping his brow with his handkerchief. ‘‘But things didn’t go right. Trayhern, she’s four months pregnant with your baby.’’

Stunned, Noah froze. *Four months pregnant?* Tears welled in his eyes. ‘‘When?’’

Cordeman swore. ‘‘I don’t know what your love life’s like! You answer those questions, dammit. She went to the doctor recently and it was confirmed.’’ His voice lost its angry tone as he saw the officer’s face turn ashen. ‘‘Look,’’ he went on, ‘‘the doc told her she’d have a tough time carrying the baby to full term.’’ He mopped his brow nervously. ‘‘Dammit, what I’m trying to tell you is that even if we’re able to rescue Kit, she still might be in serious danger of a miscarriage!’’

Shakily Noah touched his brow, trying to force his crowded, cartwheeling thoughts into some semblance of order. Kit was pregnant with his child! A deluge of joy was shattered by terror for her and the baby's life. He had to think straight! He could not allow his emotions to get the better of him. "Yeah...okay," he muttered, forcing himself to think, not feel. "Come on, we'll get a boarding party together."

Noah's green eyes were dark with despair as he looked around at the group of six volunteers. Each man's face was tense, anticipating. They all knew the score—Dante would use Kit as a shield, kill her at the first opportunity and escape. Further, she was pregnant, and even if they could find Dante, it might be too late. Noah made sure a corpsman came along, just in case, and a helicopter from a hospital in Port-au-Prince was on its way.

Two Haitian drug agents would guide the party ashore and help them track Dante. They knew their island better than anyone and were aware of all the nooks and crannies in the rocky foothills that loomed above the beach. Noah tried to shove aside his personal suffering, but it was impossible. He rubbed his grimy, sweat-streaked face, fighting to keep his escaping emotions under control. Picking up his M-16 and jamming the baseball cap back on his head, he growled, "All right, let's get Dante."

Dante wheezed brokenly, giving Kit a push that sent her sprawling on the hillside. He rested the gun on his knee as he sat for a minute and tried to catch his breath. Glaring at her, he snarled, "Don't move, or I'll blow your damned head off your shoulders."

Kit sobbed for breath and dragged herself into a

sitting position. She dared not speak back to Dante, dared not aggravate him into shooting her as he had Barnes. How far had they come in the past half hour? Turning her head, she saw the chaos down below them in the small, cluttered cove. Smoke was still pouring in thick black clouds from the *Marie-Elise.* Fear made Kit tremble as she sought to fight down the panic eating at the edges of her mind. Dante had jerked her up by her hair, forcing her to run out of the water toward the line of palm trees on the beach. Once there, he kept shoving the snub nose of the gun into her back and forcing her to keep running up into the hills. Her hands and knees were bleeding where she had fallen several times, trying to scramble up the steep slopes. And Dante was close to losing what little patience he had.

Kit weakly leaned her head against her drawn-up knees, gasping for breath. Her clothes clung to her sweaty body. She was a hostage, she realized bleakly. *Dante will keep me alive for as long as I'm useful to him.* Tears stung her eyes and she fought against a burgeoning sob caught in her throat. Dante despised weakness in any form.

"Damn!" Dante swore, leaping to his feet. His narrow face hardened, his brown eyes growing black.

Kit jerked her head up, following his gaze. Down below on the beach was a contingent of men armed with rifles. Her heart soared as she recognized Noah among them. Tears drifted down her dirty cheeks as she also saw Chuck Cordeman with the group. They knew! Someone had spotted Dante taking her prisoner! Hope escalated with fear. Wildly Kit glanced over at Dante's ferretlike face. A snarl had lifted his thin lips away from his small, sharply pointed teeth.

He looked like a snake ready to strike. He turned slowly, his opaque eyes burning into her.

"Get up," he demanded coldly.

Kit rose, unsure of what he was capable of doing next. Her mind spun with options, choices. How fast could Noah and his squad move? Would it take them the same amount of time to traverse the trail she and Dante had taken? Kit doubted it. She watched as Dante raised the ugly black barrel of the gun toward her.

"You'd better pray you can run even harder, Anderson, because that's what we're going to do. I ain't lettin' the Coast Guard catch me."

Kit stifled a scream, watching as his finger stroked the trigger. Her throat was parched, dehydration stalking her thirsty body. Her only ounce of satisfaction was that Dante was going to be equally deprived of water. Hopefully this would slow him down enough so that Noah could reach them in time. "I'll do the best I can," she rasped.

Dante cursed, motioning for her to turn around. "Shut up and get moving!" He jabbed the barrel savagely into her neck. "I'm gonna enjoy puttin' you down, Anderson. All I need to do is find a boat on the other side of that cliff, and then you're dead meat."

Noah wasn't aware of anything except catching up with Kit. Those few moments watching her struggle up the hill with Dante on her heels made his stomach turn. Leaping over a series of vines, he pushed his body to its maximum, disregarding the pain in his lungs and the stinging sensation of cacti as it tore at his lower legs. *I love you, Kit! Just keep going, don't try anything with Dante. Just survive! Survive!*

* * *

Kit sobbed for breath, feeling the punch of the gun barrel in her bruised back again. Dante cursed her, giving her a shove forward.

"Keep moving!" he panted.

Sweat blinded her, and she stumbled over another vine. The summit to the hill seemed so far away. And the heat...she heard Dante gasping behind her. The man must be made out of steel, she thought. He never slowed down. They reached an outcropping of granite eight feet high with gaping fissures, which crowned their escape point in front of them. They would have to either go around it, losing precious time, or try to climb it. Kit turned, eyeing Dante. He cursed, having come to the same conclusion as her.

He glanced over his shoulder. The six men in uniform were climbing steadily toward them. Dante probably had five shots left in his revolver, Kit thought. It wouldn't pay him to fire wildly at this distance. The rescue party would take cover in the rocks, completely safe from his useless attack.

"We're gonna climb this face and save time. If I find a boat down in that harbor once we're on the other side of this hill, I won't need you any longer."

Kit gasped, leaning over and trying to recover her breath.

She raised her chin, a sheen of sweat on her flushed face. A dull ache was beginning in her lower abdomen, sending a thread of fear through her. She placed her hand across her belly, anguish clearly written on her face. *No...no,* her heart screamed. She tried to concentrate on Dante and on giving Noah a clear shot at him. If the drug dealer foolishly decided to climb the rock wall, he would become an obvious target for an M-16 rifle. It was a long shot, Kit realized. If her blurred memory served her correctly, even a SWAT team sharpshooter couldn't place a bull's-eye at over six hundred yards. And right now, if she estimated accurately, Noah was at least eight hundred yards behind them. Would he try anyway? It would be her last chance before they started up the cliff that led down to the other cove.

More pain shot raggedly up through the center of her body and Kit doubled over, dropping to her knees. Tears squeezed from beneath her lids as she wrapped her arms around her middle, her head resting against the dirt and stones.

Dante growled. ''Get up! Dammit, get up! We're climbing. You first!''

Kit gasped, lifting her head, tears streaking down her cheeks, making silvery paths through the dirt. Dante's eyes were wild as he waved the gun at her head. ''I—I can't!''

He gripped her shoulder, his long fingers digging into her flesh. Placing the revolver at her temple, he snarled, ''I said, get up.''

The pain increased as Kit swayed to her feet. She tottered toward the wall, blindly lifting her foot into the first crevice, finding a handhold above her. Tears blurred her vision as she hoisted herself upward. Her baby—oh, God, her baby...the pain...no, it couldn't happen! *Don't let me lose our baby....*

''Hurry up!'' Dante shrilled, climbing right up behind her.

Kit forced herself to take another step and then another up the face of the cliff, sweat rolling down her brow. Her hands were bloodied and scraped as she hunted frantically for another handhold above her. Dante jabbed the revolver repeatedly into her lower back. *Noah!* she screamed in her mind. *Please take a shot at Dante. Hurry! Please, hurry!*

Noah made a slashing motion with his hand, a silent order for his men to halt behind him. He dropped to one knee. He had his target. He saw Dante start to climb the wall. His heart was pounding achingly in his chest as he wrapped the sling of the M-16 around his upper arm, steadying the rifle, willing his body to stop trembling so he could draw a bead. What direction was the wind coming from? And how many knots? He knew from much experience with weapons that wind direction played a key role in the trajectory of a bullet. If he estimated windage incorrectly, the bullet could easily strike Kit, instead. Or, he could miss Dante completely, and he and Kit would be over the wall before he could fire off another careful shot. Sweat stung his eyes. His face hardened, his mouth pursed as he raised the rifle into position. *Stop breathing. Don't move. Kit—Kit, I love you.* His finger squeezed back against the trigger, and he increased the pressure, willing the rifle barrel to remain steady despite the agony tearing through his heart.

Kit heard Dante swear directly below her. She gripped the granite, hugging the rock surface as pain arched through the core of her body, blanking everything else from her mind. Somewhere in the haze of agony, she heard the crack of a rifle in the humid afternoon air. Dante let out a groan and dropped to the ground.

Gasping with relief, Kit sobbed, unable to hold on any longer, the pain tearing at her, robbing her of all senses. It felt as if she were falling in slow motion, and when she hit the earth below it was like hitting a lumpy mattress. Rolling onto her side, Kit curled into a tight ball, feeling the warmth of blood flowing down her legs. A scream tore from her as she frantically tried to keep the baby whose life hung in precarious balance within her trembling, exhausted body. Blackness engulfed her.

Noah scrambled the last three hundred feet ahead of everyone else, leaping over the unmoving Dante to where Kit lay. When he'd seen her fall, it had torn him apart. They had called immediately for helicopter assistance, and even now, as he knelt at her side, he could hear the whapping rotor blades puncturing the air as the helicopter sped toward them.

Noah's hands trembled as he leaned over, barely touching Kit's shoulder. His eyes blurred with tears as he saw blood staining the legs of her jeans, and knew…knew what was happening. Her face was pale, tense even in unconsciousness, her arms wrapped protectively around her belly.

A sob tore from him as he dropped his rifle and gathered Kit into his arms. More sobs wrenched from deep within him as he held her while the chopper sat down on the small landing area below the cliff. Gently picking her up, Noah carried her to the helicopter and the waiting medics on board. The two men quickly laid her on a gurney. Noah climbed into the helicopter, positioning himself near Kit's head. No one said anything as tears drifted down his face. The engine whined and the helicopter lifted off, heading for Port-au-Prince.

Noah watched in silent horror as the two medics worked in unison. Kit lay unconscious in the severely limited space. The roar of the engine, the heaving, bucking motion of the aircraft in the thermals increased his anxiety as Noah watched them put a blood pressure cuff on her left arm. He placed a hand on Kit's head.

"Not good!" the first medic shouted to the second. "Seventy over fifty."

"Dammit!" the second medic yelled, ripping open a pouch containing an IV.

No, Noah thought. *Don't die on me, Kit. Don't.* His hand tightened against her shoulder as he stared down at her colorless features. Tears coursed down his face and he sobbed at his helplessness as she lay bleeding. His own brush with death rushed back to him. He remembered lying on that dark deck, the life draining out of him. Noah jerked his chin up, glaring at the medics, who labored to stabilize her condition.

"She's pregnant," Noah shouted over the din of the closest medic. "Can you save the baby?"

Sweat beaded the medic's forehead as he shot a glance up at the officer. "Don't ask for miracles. I'll be lucky to save her!"

"No!"

"We're doing all we can!"

Noah swallowed back a cry of sheer terror. "Then do more!" he screamed above the earsplitting sounds of the helicopter.

The medic shoved a second IV into Kit's other arm and took another blood pressure reading. Noah watched as the chief medic twisted around to the pilots.

"Blood!" he yelled at them. "Tell the hospital to stand by with whole blood! We can't stabilize her!"

Noah groaned and leaned over, resting his sweaty brow against Kit's limp hair. "No," he begged hoarsely. "Don't leave me, Kit. I love you! Fight back, dammit! You hear me? Fight back!" His hands dug into her shoulders as he willed his own vital force to flow into her limp body.

Wave after wave of agony flowed through Kit, from the bottom of her feet up to her head. It felt like one engulfing, hot, searing pain after another. The pain centered in her lower abdomen, and in that hazy in-between state that straddles consciousness, a moan slipped from her throat. Weakly she tried to raise her hand to place it against her body. Strong, cool fingers caught her hand in midair, captured it and gently brought it back down to her side. Strength. The word, the sensation, imprinted itself on her confused state as she fought to surface, to regain consciousness. The pain reminded her of her baby. A baby who had been created out of love. A frown formed on her brow and she moved her head slowly from side to side as if to deny what her aching body was telling her.

"No," Kit mewed weakly, "no..."

A cool hand touched her brow and she felt some semblance of steadiness. Kit stopped mumbling and concentrated on that hand that stroked her hair, bringing a balm to her tortured state. "My baby...my baby."

As he leaned closer, Noah's features reflected the anguish he heard in Kit's voice. He glanced up at the doctor standing on the other side of her bed.

The physician gave a brief nod. "Just stay with her, Lieutenant Trayhern. She's regaining consciousness. I'll send a nurse to check on her in half an hour. If you need anything, just press that buzzer."

Tiredly Noah sank into a chair next to Kit's bed.

"She'll be okay now?" he asked. His voice was a monotone; it sounded as if it belonged to someone else.

"She lost over two pints of blood, Lieutenant. For someone in her condition, that's plenty. We've replaced the blood. The rest is up to her body. She'll be coming around shortly. Just stay with her."

Noah anxiously searched Kit's pale features. Had it been only two hours ago that he had held her on that rocky outcrop far above the ocean? He wiped his watering, bloodshot eyes and searched her taut face. *Kitten, sweet, harmless kitten. I love you. No matter what happens now, just know I love you.* His long fingers trembled as he stroked her cheek in a caressing gesture meant to give comfort. Kit had almost died.

He shut his eyes tightly, more tears squeezing from beneath his dark lashes. She could have been cold-bloodedly murdered by Dante, who was now dead. Or if he'd missed the long-range shot, Kit could easily have been killed by Noah himself.

A ragged sigh tore from Noah as he raised his head and studied her in the dim light. He cupped her cheek and leaned over, placing a small, tremulous kiss on her cool, unmoving lips. So much else could have happened. But she was alive, and he was alive, and the threat of Garcia and Dante had finally been removed.

"Come back," he called softly, "Kit, come back. Come on, be here with me. It's all right, honey. I love you."

Noah's voice penetrated the fog that enveloped Kit. She opened and then closed her mouth. The name Noah formed on her lips. Her eyelids were simply too heavy to raise, but she felt his mouth upon hers:

warmth against cold, life against death, love against loneliness. Another tidal wave of pain forced her into a greater state of wakefulness. A moan came from deep within her throat.

"Noah?"

"Right here, Kit."

His voice was unsteady and thick with tears. Her own tears slid down the sides of her face and soaked into the black hair at her temples. Slowly Kit opened her left hand, clasping Noah's strong, warm one. She forced her eyes open, and saw that Noah's skin was tautly drawn over his cheekbones, the corners of his mouth tucked in with pain, and his eyes…oh, God, his eyes mirrored anguish.

More tears slid down her cheeks and Noah made an effort to dry them with his fingers. Kit forced herself to turn her head. The pain was so great that it hurt to move.

"The pain's worse?" he asked in a hushed voice.

Kit bit down on her lip, barely managing a nod. "Noah—our baby…" she cried softly, gripping his hands. "Our baby…did I lose her?"

Noah leaned close, kissing her tear-soaked lashes, his breath moist against her face. "You're still carrying our baby, honey. It was close. The doctors say you have to be very still and rest." He carefully gathered her limp form into his arms, holding her gently. "I love you so much, Kit," he rasped. "I have for the longest time, but I couldn't say anything." He kissed her damp temple. "Neither of us could admit it."

Relief jagged through Kit. Their baby was safe! She was too weak to lift her arms to put them around

Noah's shoulders, but she rested her hands against his arms. "I love you," she whispered.

As carefully as he could, Noah laid Kit back down. He rested one arm near her shoulder, his other hand stroking her hair. Her eyes were like soft gray diamonds. "You're going to be the mother of our child, Kitten." His voice caught. "There's nothing else I want in this world but the two of you. Understand?"

Kit closed her eyes. "I—I lied to you, Noah—"

"I know why you lied, honey. And I understand."

Her eyes widened as his hushed words were soaked up into her heart. He was telling her the truth. Kit could see hope flickering in the depths of his green gaze. Her heart contracted with relief, with love for his understanding. "I had to make sure Garcia and Dante were apprehended, or we'd never have a life of our own. I—I thought I was going to die out on that cliff, Noah. How did you know what happened in the cove?"

He took a deep, unsteady breath. "Chuck told me everything. Including the fact that you were pregnant. I know you tried to do the best you could under the circumstances." Admiration shone in his eyes. "You possess a kind of courage I've rarely seen, Kit."

She closed her eyes, moving her hand across her belly. "Not courage," she said softly, slurring the words. "I fell in love with you, Noah, and I wanted a decent life for us. My courage was nothing more than surviving to make that dream come true."

Noah stood there, watching her fall into a deep, uninterrupted sleep. Gently he placed his larger hand over her smaller one covering her abdomen. "Always dream for us," he told her softly.

Epilogue

A mournful meow split the quiet of the house. Kit gasped, rushing from the kitchen and hurrying into the living room, wiping her damp hands on her apron.

"Melody Sue Trayhern!" she scolded softly. Stifling a laugh, Kit lifted her fifteen-month-old daughter into her arms, rescuing Tuna Boat from further attack.

Tuna lifted her head, offering Kit a pitiful look that asked, *Why won't she leave me alone?* Kit returned her attention to her dark-haired daughter, ready to deliver a gentle reprimand. But one look into those wide, heart-stealing green eyes and Kit relented as usual. Nuzzling Melody, she gave her a kiss on the cheek and held her tightly to her chest.

"What am I going to do with you, squirt?" she whispered, smiling down at her. Kit was forever stunned by how much Melody resembled Noah. It was true that Melody had Kit's black hair, but those wide, guileless green eyes and her laughter-filled smile were Noah's. Kit scowled, trying to make her daughter realize that she couldn't keep stalking Tuna Boat.

"Now listen, young lady, you're not supposed to pick on poor blind cats. Do you hear me?"

"Kitty?"

Kit suppressed a smile that was begging to be released. "Yes, kitty. You pet her, Melody. Tuna Boat isn't one of your stuffed animals, honey. She's alive and sometimes she doesn't want to be held, even if you want to hold her."

Melody's attention zeroed in on the front door as it opened. Kit rolled her eyes. Everything she had just said to Melody had gone in one ear and out the other! But her smile broadened as she saw Noah step into the foyer. Her heart somersaulted, as it always did, when he greeted her with that devastating smile of welcome.

Kit rocked Melody in her arms, watching as Noah eased through the tangle of welcoming animals. He dropped his hat on the desk and made his way down the hall, careful where he placed his feet. She marveled at how much more handsome he had become with each day, each month of their marriage.

"What's this, a conspiracy in the living room?" he teased, leaning over and placing a kiss on Kit's lips. He lingered a moment longer. "Mmm, you taste good, Mrs. Trayhern. You been nibbling on an apple, maybe?" His green eyes glimmered with a tender smile.

"It's about all I can keep down."

Noah placed his arm around Kit, leaning over her shoulder and ruffling his daughter's curly hair. "What have you been up to, Melody?'' he asked, lifting one tiny hand. ''Gray cat fur?'' And then he raised an eyebrow, giving a very unhappy Tuna Boat an understanding look.

''She was after Tunie—again,'' Kit muttered, handing Noah his daughter. ''Here, you talk to her while I finish getting our supper ready.''

Noah hugged Melody with a fierce growl. His daughter squealed with delight, stretching her arms upward. Noah held Melody at arm's length as he followed Kit into the kitchen.

''Tuna is not a stuffed toy,'' he told her, planting a kiss on her brow.

Melody giggled, happy to be nestled against her father's broad shoulder, her small, pudgy arm encircling his neck. Noah gave his daughter a good-natured smile. He slipped his free arm around Kit's waist as she stood at the drain board, making his nightly salad to accompany his meal.

''How are you feeling?'' he asked, some of the teasing leaving his voice.

Kit felt her heart contract with love as he pulled her against his strong, steady body. Closing her eyes, she allowed him to take her full weight for a moment.

''Exhausted,'' she admitted, and then lifted her chin, meeting his worried gaze. ''But deliriously happy.''

A smile edged his sensual mouth. ''It's getting close to the fourth month. That nausea ought to be stopping soon. You can't keep eating apples and crackers forever.''

She grinned. ''Have I turned into one yet?''

Leaning down, Noah placed a kiss on her parting lips. ''Never,'' he whispered against her. ''But you do taste sweet.'' He inhaled her feminine fragrance and sighed deeply. ''God, how I love you,'' he told her thickly.

Melody squirmed, giggling in Noah's arm and forcing him to give her all his attention. Noah spotted Tuna Boat at the kitchen entrance and a gleam came to his eye. Putting Melody down, he pointed toward Tuna.

''Go pet kitty for a moment, squirt,'' he urged, winking up at Kit, who was standing there shaking her head.

''Kitty?''

''That's right, honey. Go pet Tunie. She'll love it.''

Happily Melody toddled through the kitchen calling, ''Kitty, kitty, kitty....''

With an unhappy yowl, Tuna Boat promptly did an about-face and left for parts unknown.

Kit dried her hands on the apron and then threw her arms around Noah's shoulders. ''You're terrible! Using poor Tunie like that.'' She laughed, pressing her body against his hard length.

Noah grinned, leaning down, claiming her lips in a hot, provocative kiss that made her entire body yearn with desire for him. He drew away, laughter lurking in the depths of his sea-green eyes. ''I guess I should feel guilty.''

''But you don't.''

Grinning, he said, ''No, I don't.''

Kit gave him a warning look. ''That smart little daughter of ours is going to catch on to your trickery, Noah Trayhern.''

Noah produced an innocent expression. ''All I'm doing is practicing military tactics—a diversionary measure for a moment so I can take my beautiful, pregnant wife into my arms for a well-deserved welcome home kiss.''

She laughed with him as he rocked her gently in his arms. ''One of these days your deceit is going to be rewarded,'' she threatened softly, nuzzling his ear.

A low growl vibrated from within him as he ran his splayed fingers down across her swelling belly. His mouth caressed her awaiting lips, tasting deeply of her. Finally he drew away, his green eyes stormy with desire. ''We're going to be rewarded again for the love we hold for each other, Kitten,'' he said huskily.

Her black lashes fell against her flushed cheeks and a sigh of happiness escaped her wet, throbbing lips. One month after nearly losing her life and Melody, they had been married. And four months after that, their daughter had been born. Kit sighed in memory of those beautiful months waiting for her child. Noah had been with her in the delivery room, and the tears they'd shed together had been ones of pure happiness. Noah was life. He gave life. He shared it with her, Melody and now another baby, who rested within her body. When Kit reopened her eyes, they shimmered with unshed tears and met his deep, loving gaze. ''Living with you is all the reward I'll ever need, darling,'' she told him in a trembling voice filled with love.

Noah's embrace tightened, and he held her, never wanting to let her go. ''Never stop dreaming for us, Kitten,'' he said, kissing her gently.

* * * * *

NO SURRENDER

To Midge Wagner—
a special and dear friend.

Chapter One

January 1976

"What now?" Clay Cantrell growled under his breath. He swung through the huge open bay doors of an old blimp hangar. Exhaustion from an arduous twelve hours as pilot on the United States Navy P3 Lockheed Orion was making his mind fuzzy. Clay didn't want to look too closely at his emotions. This past mission had been a bitch. They'd busted an oil line in one of the four turboprop engines.

Staying to the left of the yellow safety line, he glanced toward the center of the busy complex. Several P3s were in for maintenance checks, mechanics crawling all over them. Clay took off his garrison cap and ran his long fingers through his military-short black hair. Those who knew him well could recognize that particular gesture as a sign of frustration. Just what the hell did Commander Joe Horner want? Clay knew he'd been walking a dangerous line for the past year, ever since—

He brutally rejected the memory. Rejected the rush of violent emotions that came with it. He swallowed against a forming lump, his gray eyes growing cold and distant. *Screw the past. You've got to forget it. What counts is now, Cantrell.*

With a muttered oath, Clay opened the door that would take him into the outer office of VP 46's commanding officer. Chief Yeoman Jo Ann Prater looked up. She was a woman in her late forties with red hair tucked neatly into a bun at the base of her neck. Women with red hair always intrigued Clay. It was as if the gold and copper highlights woven into the auburn strands promised complexity of character. And he liked complex women. Women—not situations. But right now, judging from the suddenly concerned look in Prater's hazel eyes, he was about to step into one.

"Good afternoon, Lieutenant Cantrell," she greeted him briskly, rising. "Have a seat." She pointed toward the leather couch to the left of her desk. "I'll let Commander Horner know that you've arrived."

"Thank you," Clay said, taking off his garrison cap and tucking it into a pocket of his dark green flight suit. He sat as gingerly as if he were sitting on a carton of eggs. He noticed that his hands were sweaty as he clasped them. Often, they shook—but so did any carrier pilot's hands. Clay reminded himself that he was no longer an F-14 fighter pilot. He'd been relegated to the slow, matronly P3s. It was a safe transfer—safe and out of the way. His old squadron commander aboard the *Enterprise* had said it was best under the circumstances.

Running a hand wearily over his face, Clay tried to ignore a burgeoning headache. What was up? His mind raced with possibilities—all of them making him uneasy. For the past year, he'd been unable to think in positives, only negatives. Funny how one plane crash could change his entire outlook on life. Well, that was the past. What did Horner want? Clay had made a lousy landing three days ago after a rough twelve-hour mission out over the Pacific Ocean, and the bird would have to have extensive maintenance on the port landing gear assembly, as a result. Could that be it? Or was it something worse?

Their antisubmarine warfare squadron base, at the tip of San Francisco Bay, was shorthanded. All pilots were working more missions than was advisable. The squadron commanding officer was trying to remedy the situation by bringing new pilots on board, but it had been a slow process. Navy pilots, the cream of the crop of aviators, didn't just grow on trees. They had to wait for the next group of pilots to graduate from Pensacola, the U.S. Navy flight school. Too many missions and not enough time off was everyone's problem right now.

Since coming to U.S. Naval Air Station Moffett Field, Clay had felt abandoned. Not even San Francisco's magic spell could lift his depression. Maybe that was it. Clay admitted he wasn't the pleasantest person to be around right now. Could it be that his crew was complaining about his constant snarling and the sharp, angry orders?

Running his hand through his hair, Clay realized that he'd lost the prankster side of himself at the time of the crash. He never smiled or joked anymore. He didn't see much to laugh about. Yeah, the CO was probably going to chew him out about his attitude problem. *Damn.*

"Lieutenant Cantrell? The CO will see you now."

Clay rose, forcing a smile in Prater's direction. "Thanks." *Here it comes.* Clay knew no way to brace himself emotionally, because he had nothing left with which to defend his vulnerable feelings. Prater's eyes gave her away. She looked almost sad for him as he walked by her desk.

Joe Horner was standing when Clay entered the inner office. Snapping to attention, Clay announced himself. Horner, a man in his early forties with graying hair, nodded.

"At ease, Lieutenant." He pointed brusquely to a leather chair in front of his huge maple desk. "Have a seat."

"Yes, sir."

Horner sat down, his blue eyes never leaving Clay's tense features. "I've got some good news and bad news, Clay."

Great. Clay nodded. "Sir?"

"As you know, we've been flying shorthanded around here for the past quarter. Transfers and a computer screwup in D.C. have left us holding the bag."

Relaxing slightly, Clay tried to ferret out Horner's strategy. What was this preamble leading up to? "Yes, sir, it's been tough on everyone," he said cautiously.

Horner's narrow face thawed slightly. "Well, D.C.

is finally starting to remedy the situation. They've given us two of the top graduates from Pensacola."

"That's good news, sir." Even a rookie pilot out of Pensacola was better than nothing. They could be taught cockpit procedure here. Clay brightened. Maybe he was getting a new copilot!

"Very good news." Horner sat down and tendered two files sitting in front of him on the desk, holding his gaze on Clay's suddenly hopeful expression. "I'm assigning one of the pilots to you."

"Great!"

"Perhaps," Horner hedged. His thin mouth tightened. "Second Lieutenant Alyssa Trayhern is being assigned to you, Clay. And yes, she's the sister of Morgan Trayhern, the traitor who cost an entire Marine company their lives." Horner sat up, folding his hands and leaning forward. "I know your brother Stephen was the assistant company commander for the company that was wiped out, and that he was killed along with everyone else." Joe pushed the orders toward Clay, continuing to watch him closely.

Clay sat, stunned. First rage, then numbness hit him. He stared at Horner, his mouth falling open. Snapping it shut, he rose. "No," he rasped hoarsely. *"No!"*

"I'm afraid so, Clay." Horner gestured toward the orders. "Read them yourself: direct from D.C. You're to train her."

Reeling with shock, Clay stood, breathing in sharp gasps. His chest hurt, his heart ached. Tears wedged unexpectedly into his eyes, but the instant it happened, he jerked himself back to the present. Fighting for control, he uttered harshly, "I won't take her! *Sir.* There's no way in hell I'm working with the sister of the traitor who murdered my brother. Not now. Not ever!'' He spun, dazed, to leave the office.

''Lieutenant!'' Horner's voice rolled through the office like a shot being fired.

Clay froze, his hand inches from the brass doorknob. *Grab it!* his subconscious shouted. *Grab it, twist it and jerk it open. Get out! Escape!* This was a nightmare. He had to be dreaming. Clay's hand shook perceptibly, his fingers still reaching out.

''Get a hold on yourself,'' Horner ordered coldly, ''and get back here.''

Hatred poured through Clay as he slowly pulled his hand back. He gulped for air without success, and he could no longer jam his shredded emotions deep inside where he'd always kept them prisoner. Bitterness coated his mouth as he stood stiffly, his back still to his CO.

''Look, I had nothing to do with this pairing, Clay. These are orders from Washington.'' Horner's voice grew soothing. ''Come on, have a seat. There's nothing either of us can do about the situation. It's just one of those things. I'm sorry.''

Sorry? Clay turned slowly, his eyes narrowing with anguish and burning rage. What little pride he had left intact after the crash, he used to salvage himself in front of his commander. With a monumental effort, he straightened, throwing his shoulders back as if ridding himself of some invisible load.

''Have a seat,'' Horner invited one more time. ''I know this comes as a shock, Clay. I know how you feel about your brother dying in such a useless tragedy.''

''No, sir, you don't.'' The words were ground out—a dog crushing a bone between his massive jaws. That was how Clay felt about this new assignment. He wanted to savage Trayhern. He wanted to hurt this brat of a woman who thought she could be a Navy pilot.

Horner's face grew closed. Insistent. "Sit, Lieutenant. Histrionics isn't going to change one damn thing about this assignment for you or me."

The CO's cold analysis was like ice hitting Clay. He sat, his knees suddenly shaky. He gripped the arm of the chair, his knuckles whitening. "This can't be real, sir. Someone's got it in for me back at the Pentagon." Were they trying to drum him out of the service? Get him to retire after his first six years? Clay had wanted to make the Navy his career. He had only a year to go before fulfilling the mandatory six-year enlistment, but he intended to reenlist—providing he was recommended for it. Ever since the crash, though, Clay had wondered if they might politely railroad him out of the service. There were many ways to accomplish it, and this was one of them: make the environment so miserable that he wouldn't think of reenlisting.

"Let's not overreact," Horner was saying. He paced the length of his small office. Outside, they could hear the whistling whine of a P3's turboprop engines revving up to trundle down the ramp toward takeoff.

"Then give me one reason why Trayhern was assigned to me," Clay demanded. His voice cracked, and he felt a warm flush crawling up his neck into his face.

With a shrug of his thin shoulders, Horner said, "I can't give you one."

"Sir, with all due respect, I can't handle this assignment. She's the sister to the man who killed my brother. My God—''

''Look, I know this is tough.'' Horner pointed to a board hanging on the wall, showing the names of pilots to fly the missions. There were many more flights than pilots. ''You can see I'm strapped. I don't have many pilots with more than a year's experience in P3s, and I can't put a green pilot and a copilot together. We'd be asking for disaster.''

''But—'' Clay grasped at straws, any straw ''—why can't I have the other graduate? Couldn't we make a trade?''

Tapping the file with Trayhern's name on it, Horner said heavily, ''Orders are orders.''

Helpless rage entwined with real panic deep within Clay. ''Then make a phone call. Surely this is a mistake. Whoever paired us didn't realize Stephen was my brother.''

Compassion showed in Horner's taut face. ''I've already made a call, Clay. And I *did* explain the situation.''

''And?''

''No go. The pairing stays as is.''

Somebody's got it in for me. Clay almost said it out loud, but bit down hard on his lower lip to stop himself from blurting out the words. The handwriting was on the wall. They wanted him out. He was a washed-up F-14 driver. In some head honcho's eyes back in D.C., he was no longer a valuable commodity to the Navy. They didn't want him to reenlist.

Horner's voice cut through Clay's spinning revelations. ''...Trayhern got top grades. She finished at the head of her class both at the Naval Academy in Annapolis and later at Pensacola. I think she's a credit to the U.S. Navy, regardless of what her brother did five years ago. You should let the past remain there, Clay. Don't confront her on the issue. Let it stay buried.''

Buried. The word haunted Clay. Trying to maintain a poker face, which he was usually good at doing, he straightened in his seat. His stomach was knotted so tight, it hurt. Horner was asking for a miracle from him. Stephen had been murdered by Morgan Trayhern's cowardly act, and their mother had died two days after receiving the news, as surely as if Trayhern had left her, too, on that hill. Clay had never known his father, so in two days he had lost his entire family. Morgan Trayhern had ripped the heart out of him by snuffing out the lives of the two people he loved most in the world.

''Do you hear me, Lieutenant? Leave the past alone. You deal with lieutenant Trayhern as you would any green copilot trainee coming out of Pensacola.''

Clay fought his anger, his utter anguish over this unexpected trial. He didn't know how he was going to overcome the palpable hatred he felt. ''Yes, sir,'' he choked out. He wondered obliquely if Alyssa Trayhern knew she was being assigned to him. How would she react to the news? As he looked out the window, he saw a storm gathering in the west. Any moment now, it would begin to rain at the station. Was there *ever* a storm coming....

''I hate rain,'' Aly said to no one in particular as she drove her red Toyota MR2 sports car down the freeway. It was eight in the morning, and traffic speeding into the city of San Francisco was at its peak. She slanted a quick glance at the passenger seat where Rogue sat. The black and white Border collie whined, as if in answer.

"The landlord of our new apartment said they call this the Bloody Bayshore. He mentioned it has more bloody accidents than any other highway system leading into the city. What do you think about that, Rogue?"

The collie tilted his head and wagged his tail in a friendly fashion.

Aly chuckled. "God, Rogue, I'm really beginning to feel free. Sometimes, I think this is all a dream after the past five years." She narrowed her eyes in memory as she stayed alert on the rain-slick freeway. Were her trials really over? she wondered. Were the taunting, the insults hissed in her direction calling her a traitor, really over? Her hands tightened momentarily on the wheel. Aly knew she didn't dare allow all her hurt and anger to surface. Like a true Trayhern, she had kept her head high and her shoulders squared, pretending to be impervious to the slings and arrows hurled at her because of Morgan.

The Marine Corps had never officially listed her brother as missing in action or dead. His body had never been found after the 1970 slaughter on Hill 206 at the close of the Vietnam war. The only survivor, a private, had said that he saw Morgan escape into the arms of the North Vietnamese, a traitor. But Aly violently rejected that scenario. No way was Morgan a traitor! He'd *never* leave 180 men—his men—on a hill to be decimated by their enemy. He'd have died with them.

So what had happened? Aly's head spun with questions, and with obvious answers that she instantly denied. She knew her brother. He was a good man, a strong person with a streak of undying loyalty toward those he was responsible for, bred into him just as it was bred into the very bones of Aly and her other brother, Noah. Morgan would never have left that embattled hill just before the dawn attack, taking with him the only working radio in the company. That radio could have put them in contact with air protection and kept the company from being overrun. The press had repeatedly accused Morgan of turning coward and surrendering himself to the enemy in order to live, instead of dying with his men, but there were so many unanswered riddles and dead ends to Morgan's disappearance.

Agony sliced through Aly, tears surfacing unexpectedly in her eyes. More than two hundred years of Trayhern military service were permanently stained. And so were the lives of Noah, of herself and of her parents.

Wiping away the errant tears with the back of her hand, she muttered, "We're supposed to be happy, Rogue. We just leased an apartment. Today we shop for groceries, and tomorrow I sign on board at Moffett Field. This is the start of my career. Mom and Dad are so happy and proud of me." She looked over at her Border collie, feeling not triumphant but only tired and drained. "We've made it, Rogue. This generation of Trayherns is on its way—hopefully—to brilliant military service. Maybe Noah and I can erase some of the black mark put on our name by the Defense Department and the press. We've made it—"

The rest of her words were torn from her as a large white car slewed sideways in front of her as it tried to change lanes too quickly.

Everything slowed down to single frames in front of Aly's widening eyes. The white car's brakes screamed, water spraying in high sheets. The water slammed against the windshield of her Toyota, temporarily blinding her. Cars were braking and swerving ahead and around her, as if the six lanes in front of her had become nothing more than a bumper car track.

Aly's reflexes were fast and skilled. Acting only on instinct, Aly wrenched the wheel to the right, moving quickly into the lane closest to the shoulder of the freeway. A blue car suddenly loomed ahead, skidding sideways, coming directly toward her. Sucking in a breath, Aly slammed on the brakes, putting her car into a spin. The red sports car spun once, twice. The screech of tires, the odor of burning rubber entered Aly's brain. In seconds she found herself and the sports car off the road on a wet grassy slope, safe.

Sudden silence overtook her. She blinked once in amazement. All the cars involved in the crisis had straightened out. No one had been hit! It was a miracle. Her heart pounding in her chest, Aly leaned back and closed her eyes.

She took long slow breaths, trying to calm her racing pulse. At the sound of a sudden decisive knock on the window of her car, Aly opened her eyes and looked up in surprise.

The concerned face of a man in his late twenties stared back at her. It was still raining lightly, and she could see the darkened splotches appearing on his well-worn leather jacket. It was his eyes that mesmerized Aly. They were large and gray, with huge black pupils, and fringed with thick lashes. Somehow they seemed to penetrate her deepest, most secret self.

Strangely she wasn't put on the defensive by the intensity of his stare. Instead, Aly felt a powerful wave of concern for her emanating from the stranger.

Shakily, she rolled down the window. He crouched, hand on the door.

"Are you okay?" he asked.

His voice was husky, a balm to her jittery nerves. Aly nodded dumbly. "I—yes, I am."

Clay pulled a handkerchief from his back pocket. "I'm not so sure. You've cut yourself," he said as he reached in and pressed the cloth to the woman's bloodied hairline. "That was a fine piece of driving you pulled off. I thought for sure you'd bought the farm." He smiled slightly as she raised her hand, pressing her cool fingertips to where he held the handkerchief in position on her temple. God, but she was pretty. Red hair, too. And then Clay laughed to himself, feeling lighter and happier than he could recall in a long time.

"I got lucky," the woman admitted hoarsely.

"Red sports car, red hair. It all fits," he told her, withdrawing his hand from hers. She was pale and shaken. But who wouldn't be? Hell, her tiny little car had stood every chance of getting smashed between a couple of those careening behemoths. Clay liked her wide, vulnerable blue eyes, and her nose was aristocratic with small, finely flared nostrils. But it was her mouth that he couldn't drag his gaze away from. Her lips weren't full, but they weren't thin, either. It was the delicate shape, maybe, that entranced him. There was utter sensuality about them, and it sent a sheet of heat flowing through him.

She lifted the handkerchief away, staring at the red

blood on it. "I don't even remember hitting my head," she said softly.

"Probably hit it against the window when you deliberately threw that car of yours into a spin to miss that blue Buick sliding at you. You'd make Parnelli Jones look like a rookie with the moves you put on this girl." He patted the door fondly, as if to reward the car for its part in the effort.

With a sigh, Aly leaned back, closing her eyes. She kept the cloth pressed firmly against the wound. Head injuries were notorious for bleeding heavily even if this one was a mere scratch. And that was all it was—a little cut on her left temple. The adrenaline was making her weak and shaky in its wake. She needed at least another fifteen minutes to recover. Rogue whined, nosing her gently. Patting him reassuringly, Aly returned her attention to her rescuer.

An unfamiliar warmth surrounded Aly's pounding heart as she lifted her lashes, drowning in the care exuding from his dove-gray eyes. He had a square face, a stubborn chin, a flexible, intriguing mouth and a nose that had obviously taken some punishment earlier in life. Aly liked his hard, intelligent eyes. He wasn't a huge man—moderate build and about six-two in height. There was a nice balance to him, she decided. More than anything, she liked his long, expressive, large-knuckled fingers. Hands capable of molding and shaping.

"I—I owe you so much for stopping to see how I was."

He grinned. "My pleasure. If I'd known it was a beautiful redheaded lady in front of me, I'd have put my Corvette between you and those bruisers that wanted to play bumper cars on the Bayshore."

A hesitant smile pulled at Aly's mouth. There was so much warmth radiating from him. She noticed no ring on his left hand. For the first time in five years, Aly felt herself responding to a man on a strictly feminine level. It felt good—right. "I just moved here," she explained. "My landlord warned me that they call this the Bloody Bayshore." She shivered, sitting up slightly. "I almost became a part of its legend, didn't I?"

Out of instinct, maybe need, Clay placed his hand on the woman's small shoulder. She was getting paler, if that was possible. "Close, but no cigar. Hell of a welcome to this area, wouldn't you say?" He gently kneaded her left shoulder and neck, feeling her visibly relax beneath his ministration.

"Y-yes, a hell of a welcome," she agreed faintly. She took the handkerchief away from her head. The bleeding had stopped. "I think I'm going to live, now. Thanks." She handed the cloth back to him. "You'd better get that home and into some cold water or the stain will never come out."

Clay folded the handkerchief and placed it in the pocket of his jacket. "I'll do that. You said you just moved here?" Clay wanted to drown in her dark blue eyes. Her face was porcelain, with freckles sprinkled across her nose and cheeks. Her red hair was shaped into a flattering pixie style that barely brushed the bottom of her delicate earlobes and emphasized the oval contour of her face. Small pearl earrings and a single pearl resting against her throat simply multiplied her femininity.

"Yes, just a week ago," Aly said, "from Florida." She turned, realizing suddenly that Rogue must have been tossed around, since he couldn't wear a seat belt as she did. The Border collie sat, panting, enjoying the sudden attention as Aly ran her hands carefully over him just to make sure he hadn't broken any bones.

"Your dog okay?"

Aly liked his concern. She liked people who liked animals. It said something good about them as far as she was concerned. Giving Rogue an affectionate pat, Aly returned her attention to the man. "He seems fine. Probably got a few bruises we'll never know about."

Clay glanced at the traffic zooming by them. The rain had stopped, leaving only a pall of gray clouds hovering about a thousand feet above them. Typical January weather for the Bay Area. He noted the color creeping back into her face. Her pupils weren't as dilated. "Looks like you're feeling a bit better."

"I am, thank you." Aly met and held the gray gaze that seemed to silently caress her. Her heart wouldn't settle down, and she realized that it was *him* affecting her so strongly, not the reaction to the near accident. "I don't even know your name. My friends call me Aly." She offered her hand through the open window.

"Clay. Clay Cantrell." Clay took her hand, surprised at the firmness of her grip. Grinning, he said, "You've never been to California before, eh?"

"I'm brand-new. No, I've never been to the state, much less to the fabled city of San Francisco. Rogue and I were going to go shopping for our groceries this morning and stock the shelves of the apartment I just rented."

Reluctantly, Clay released her fingers. Her flesh was soft and inviting, like the rest of her. She lured powerful emotional responses from him, and it puzzled Clay. No woman had ever affected him like this. Was it the shimmering red hair entwined with gold strands that enticed him? Or those huge blue eyes filled with every feeling she was experiencing? And then he groaned internally, his gaze falling to her parted lips. Lips that were begging to be pleasured and seduced. To his chagrin, he felt himself growing hot and turgid. If he kept up this line of thought, she'd soon know just how she affected him, too. Heat crept into his cheeks.

"Look, I know this is a lousy introduction to the Bay Area, and you're new. If you haven't got too many irons in the fire, how about if I give you the grand tour of our city this coming Saturday? I'll even treat you to the best pizza in the world, afterward. We could have dessert at Ghirardelli Square."

Aly laughed, delighted by Clay's candor. His eyes crinkled, a smile burning in their depths that stole her heart. His mouth curved deliciously upward, and molten fire stirred deep within her. "As long as we're both free, I'll accept your invitation."

Laughing, Clay dug out notepaper and a pen from the breast pocket of his light blue shirt. "Free, eligible, good-looking and one hell of a good deal."

Aly couldn't stop the laughter from bubbling up within her. My God, how *great* it felt to laugh again! Her world had consisted of nothing but darkness and pressure for so long that she had forgotten that light moments could exist. Clay was like sunlight.

"Here's my phone number, Aly. Give me a call Friday, after five. Get settled into your new home, and we'll set up that tour tomorrow evening." Never had Clay so much wanted any woman to say yes.

Aly liked his style and his easygoing confidence.

Clay reminded her strongly of the instructor pilots back at Pensacola. They were cocky veterans, brazenly confident of themselves on every conceivable level. Clay had that same virile bearing—that mark of the lone eagle flying the blue sky in triumph. She liked his lack of pressure about a possible date. "Aren't you even going to ask me for my address and phone number?"

Giving her a wink, Clay slipped the paper into her waiting fingers. "No, ma'am. I learned a long time ago through the school of hard knocks not to pressure a lady."

"Sure this isn't some new line?" Aly teased, meeting his confident smile. He *knew* she'd call him!

Clay patted the door of the sports car. "I don't think so. But I'll let you be the judge of that." He sobered slightly. "You sure you feel up to getting back into traffic?"

"Yes, thank you." She held up her hands. "See, they're not shaking anymore."

Clay wondered what it would be like to have those long, delicate fingers moving across his body. The thought was startling, intense. Normally, he didn't think of a woman on such a sensual level, but Aly was incredibly heady stuff. He was happy, he suddenly discovered. Her smile was a rainbow to his dark existence.

Finding his voice, Clay said, "I'll look forward to your call."

Aly tucked his phone number into her small black leather purse. "You'll be hearing from me, Clay." And then her voice lowered with feeling. "Thank you for stopping. It means a lot to me...."

Clay rose to his feet and threw her a salute. "I'll

see you later, pretty lady. You go ahead and climb back up on the Bayshore and I'll follow you a ways to make sure you're doing okay.''

He had to be a military pilot! That stance, that carelessly thrown salute and confident grin smacked of his unknown career. Aly almost called Clay back to ask him if he was a Navy pilot. Of course, he could be Air Force, too. Travis Air Force Base was just north of San Francisco. Shaking her head at the sudden turn of events, she rolled up the car window.

As she maneuvered her Toyota back into the morning rush-hour traffic, Aly told Rogue, ''Well, this is quite an interesting start to our life here at Moffett Field. And tomorrow morning I sign on board at the station. I wonder what kind of adventures that will bring?''

Chapter Two

"Welcome on board, Lieutenant Trayhern." Lieutenant Jack Donnelly stretched his hand across the desk toward her.

Aly took his hand, shaking it. "Thank you, Mr. Donnelly." All morning she'd filled out forms, signed them, and then filled out some more at the base personnel office. Her hands were sweaty, and she realized that Donnelly had noticed. The sandy-haired officer obviously didn't like her much. As usual, her Trayhern name had preceded her.

"Take a seat." Donnelly reached for a file on his desk. "In a minute I'll have our driver take you over to your new home, VP 46. The CO, Commander Horner, is aware that you're here, and he wants a few minutes of your time. Induction and all—you'll get your squadron assignment through him."

"Sounds good," Aly said.

There was a savage twist to Donnelly's smile as he ended the monologue. She glanced around the small office, photos of the graceful P3 Lockheed in a picture frame behind his desk. Moffett was primarily a sub-hunting base, little else. On another wall was a photo of the powerful F-14 Tomcat, the fighter utilized aboard all naval carriers.

"I understand we have an F-14 squadron here," Aly said.

"Huh?" Donnelly looked up. "Oh, yes. The past five years Moffett's had a training squadron based here. Normally, F-14s are on a carrier, but because we're close to the Pacific Ocean and near a deep-water port, the base is utilized as a training site for graduates out of Pensacola before they begin flying those babies onto carriers for the first time."

"They practice their landings here," Aly guessed.

"That's correct. We've got some instructor pilots on board who work with the greenhorns. One of them, Lieutenant Jeff Starbuck, is a pretty amusing character."

Aly managed a small smile. What fighter jock wasn't colorful?

F-14s made her blood race. If she had been a man, with her top grade-point average at Pensacola, she would have been given the plum assignment of becoming a fighter pilot upon graduation. Instead, because women weren't allowed to fly combat aircraft, she was appointed to fly the land-based P3. She curbed her disappointment. The chance to fly *anything* was enough for her. It was her life's ambition.

"Just sign this last set of papers, Lieutenant Trayhern, and you're free of us."

Aly leaned forward and dutifully placed her signature one last time. Finally! Now, she'd get to tour the station, her new home.

The men's and women's barracks, the chow hall and Operations, which consisted of meteorology and the control tower, were located on one side of the base. On the other side were three huge blimp hangars that had been modified to serve as the home of Anti-Submarine Warfare Squadron, VP 46. Only the three long, massive airstrips separated the outdated hangars from the more modern side of Moffett. Aly got her first look at the NASA installation on board the station, sitting right across the street from the WAVE barracks. The driver told her that NASA had one of the world's largest wind tunnels at the state-of-the-art facility. A silly smile curved Aly's lips. How could the enlisted women sleep when that wind tunnel was revved up right across the street from them? The entire station must shudder when it was activated.

Aly's eyes widened as they drove around the end of the main runways and toward the gaping mouths of the blimp hangars. The graceful P3s, gray on top and white beneath, had long booms that looked like dangerous needles, extending ten feet from the tail assembly, much like the stinger on a hornet. In the tail boom, she knew, was highly responsive radar equipment. It was sensitive enough to locate and track Soviet submarines far beneath the surface of the ocean. The P3s looked like such graceful steeds. She itched to sit at the controls and feel what it was like to fly one.

"We're here," the driver announced, braking the vehicle to a halt. He'd pulled up at the side entrance to Hangar One, the largest of the three. "Just follow that yellow safety line, Lieutenant. About halfway down on the left is Commander Horner's office. You can't miss it.''

''Thanks.'' Aly climbed out. She was in her black wool uniform, with a white blouse and black tie. Placing the garrison cap on her head, she pulled the black leather purse over her left shoulder. The right hand had to be free to salute with. Shutting the door, Aly took a deep breath, trying to stabilize her wildly fluctuating emotions.

As she walked down the concrete expanse toward her destination, her black heels clicking sharply, Aly absorbed the spectacle to her right. At least four P3s were in for maintenance. In the 1930s, the driver had told her, Moffett had been the largest blimp station on the West Coast. With the advent of propeller-driven planes, the blimps had met a slow and eventual death. The hangars were now used for the more advanced aircraft that succeeded them.

Horner's office was easy to find. His chief yeoman looked up when Aly entered. She felt instant camaraderie with the woman because she had red hair, too. Trying not to appear nervous, Aly offered her a small smile.

''Hi. I'm—''

The yeoman broke into a genuine smile. ''Don't say it, I know.'' She pointed toward the gold aviator wings that rested over the top of Aly's left breast pocket. ''You're Lieutenant Trayhern. I'm Chief Yoeman Jo Ann Prater. Welcome aboard.''

Relief flowed through Aly. This woman was the first person at the base to smile and sound as if she was honestly glad to see her. Was Prater unaware of the blackened Trayhern history? Probably. Anyone who carried the memory never treated her with such unabashed cordiality. In the military mind and heart, the worst thing one could be was a traitor to his country.

"Thanks, Chief." Aly took her hand, shaking it.

"Commander Horner is expecting you. Go on in."

Swallowing hard, Aly nodded and walked past the desk and through another opened door. This was her new boss. *Dear God, don't let him hate me. Let him judge me on my own merits, not the past. Not—*

"Lieutenant Trayhern, come on in." Horner rose, extending his hand.

A weight formed in Aly's stomach as she appraised Horner's narrow face. A cry started deep within her as she saw barely veiled animosity in the CO's narrowed eyes. He hated her. For the past? For the fact that she was a woman in his male world? Probably both, she decided with disappointment, shaking his hand. "Commander Horner," she said, her voice firm and unruffled-sounding. A far cry from all the violent emotions clamoring deep within her.

"Have a seat, Miss Trayhern." And then Horner cocked his head in her direction, pulling out a pipe and beginning to fill it after he sat down. "Or, do you prefer Ms.?"

It was game time again. As always. How many times had her male instructors at Pensacola jabbed her with the same question? Aly looked Horner straight in the eye. In the military, they respected an adversary's strength, not his weakness. "Either is acceptable to me, Commander."

Horner lit a match, holding it close to the pipe, puffing on it. Bluish-white smoke rose in a cloud around his head. "I see." He sat down, flipping the match into a glass ashtray nearby. ''Well, welcome to VP 46.''

''Thank you, sir.''

Picking up her file, Horner said, ''Your record at Annapolis and Pensacola is outstanding. I'm glad to have someone of your caliber on board.''

Liar. Her heart was beginning a slow beat of dread. There was coldness in Horner's eyes. He was saying the right things, but there was no enthusiasm or sincerity in his voice. ''I'm planning on at least thirty years in the Navy, sir,'' Aly responded. ''This is my home, my way of life. I tried to get off on the right foot with good grades.''

''You certainly did that.'' Horner puffed a few more times before continuing. ''Now, as to your assignment. Because we're shorthanded, I'm going to be putting you into intensive Link cockpit training immediately.'' He saw the surprise on her face. ''You've been assigned to one of our best pilots, who is also the Link instructor for our squadron. I have every belief that between his education of you in the cockpit and the ground training, you'll qualify for copilot status in record time so that we can put your flying skills to work in the P3. I need every able-bodied pilot behind the yoke as soon as possible.''

Aly blinked once. Usually a new pilot spent at least three months in a ground trainer, flying under the hood with various difficult situations that might be encountered with that particular aircraft in the air.

After her brother Noah had graduated from the Coast Guard Academy, he'd had two terrible years under a commander who wanted to railroad him out of the service because his name was Trayhern. She slowly closed her right hand into a fist, realizing that

Horner was possibly gunning for her, too. There was no way he should be putting a green copilot in a plane in such a short period of time, no matter what the personnel problem with the squadron.

"Sir, while I respect the fact that VP 46 is short on pilots, don't you think this is rather—"

"Lieutenant," Horner droned, "the manpower situation with VP 46 is critical. Ordinarily, I wouldn't throw a green pilot into a P3 this soon. But—" he got up, scowling "—in the past quarter we've had more Soviet sub activity down in the Baja region of Mexico, and we've been pressed to fly twice the missions anticipated. Something's up." He turned and buttonholed her with a dark look. "The other new pilot coming on board tomorrow will get the same treatment. I'm not singling you out."

Aly had the good grace to blush. Horner wasn't one to beat around the bush. "I see, sir."

"Believe me, you've been paired with our best man. He's a capable pilot, a damn good instructor, and he's been in on most of the hunts this past year."

Her hopes rising, thinking that perhaps she was wrong about Horner's intention to sandbag her career, Aly said, "I appreciate you putting me with someone like that, sir."

"Don't worry, Clay will help you make up for any deficiencies of learning about this bird of ours in Pensacola. I've also assigned him as your liaison officer. He'll be in charge of helping you get situated on and off station. He'll show you around, get you set up for Link training and, in general, make your transition here to Moffett as easy as possible."

"Clay?" The name rang a definite bell with Aly.

He couldn't possibly mean the Clay she'd met yesterday on the Bayshore, could he?

Horner came around the desk and faced her. He methodically tapped the pipe against the ashtray. "Lieutenant, there's one more thing you need to know," he began heavily. His scowl deepened as he met and held her gaze. "You aren't going to like this. I don't, either, but it's out of my hands."

Immediately, Aly went on guard. Her fist tightened until her short nails dug into the palm of her hand. "Sir?"

"Before I tell you more about your assigned liaison, and your instructor pilot in the cockpit, I'm going to need your understanding."

Just what the hell was he going after? Aly wondered bleakly. By the set of Horner's jaw and the funeral sound of his voice, he was acting as if someone had just died. "Go on, sir."

Horner folded his arms against his chest. "I've got a situation on my hands, Lieutenant Trayhern. And you can either make it easier or tougher on me, on yourself and on the crew you'll be flying with—depending on how you handle it."

"What's going on, Commander?" she demanded huskily.

"Washington, D.C., sent specific orders to pair you with this pilot."

Frustration ate at her. "So?"

"So I want you to realize from the outset that this was out of our hands. I've already tried to change the orders or in some ways rectify the situation, but it's a no-go situation."

Aly's eyes narrowed. What could possibly be such

bad news? "Sir, why don't you just tell me the gist of these orders?"

Horner smiled briefly. "You've got that shoot-from-the-hip Trayhern trait, don't you?"

"It's a family tradition, sir. We've served two hundred years with honors in the various military services. My father passed on his endurance and candor to me."

"Obviously." Horner sighed. "Well, you're going to need both, Lieutenant. Your mentor is a pilot by the name of First Lieutenant Clay Cantrell." He drilled a look into her widening eyes. "His brother was Stephen Cantrell. One of the men who died on Hill 206 five years ago."

Aly started to rise. And then she fell back into the chair, a gasp escaping her. Clay Cantrell! His brother was Stephen! *Oh, my God!* She sat for frozen seconds, assimilating the news. The man she'd met on the Bayshore *was* the same man. She'd been so drawn to him. For those precious minutes, he'd eased the coldness that had inhabited her for so many years.

The sting of reality replaced that wistful memory. Judging by Horner's reaction, Clay Cantrell was going to make it very tough on her. How could he not dislike her? Morgan had supposedly gotten his brother killed on that infamous hill. She bit down so hard on her lower lip that she tasted blood. And Clay was her IP in the Link trainer. And once she qualified as copilot, she'd be flying with him on every mission. She'd be spending hours at a time every day with him....

"Oh, God," Aly whispered, pressing her fingers against her brow.

"Get hold of yourself, Lieutenant."

Her head snapped up, her eyes narrowing. "My reaction is warranted, *sir*. And don't worry, I'm not going to faint or get hysterical."

Horner nodded and slowly made his way around the desk to sit down. "Glad to hear it, Miss Trayhern."

Swallow it, Aly. Swallow everything. Just like you did before. Real anguish flowed through her as she realized that there was never going to be a time or place in her career where she could afford to be her real self or show her true feelings. Horner was watching her closely. She had to shore up and wear that impervious military facade. Internally, Aly girded herself, playing the game, denying so much of herself.

"Does Lieutenant Cantrell know about this assignment, sir?" Her voice was husky again, but in charge. Emotionless.

"He does."

"His reaction?"

"Negative."

Aly wanted to cry. She wanted to scream out at the unfairness of the situation. She came from a military family that knew the military way of life. It hadn't escaped her that someone in D.C., probably some admiral, wanted to wash her out of the Navy because she was Morgan's sister. There was no room for a traitor's family in the service. God, how many times had she heard that?

"Can he separate his personal emotions from his duty toward me?" she demanded tightly.

Horner shrugged. "I told him he'd better."

Great. "And if he can't, sir?"

"Come and see me. But," Horner growled, "I'm expecting both of you to behave maturely about this.

After getting cockpit qualified, you've got a P3 and a crew of ten other men on board. *That's* your focus, your responsibility. I won't tolerate any bickering, sniping or back-stabbing coming from either one of you. Is that clear, Lieutenant Trayhern?''

Aly rose unsteadily. She locked her knees, coming to attention. ''Yes, sir, it is. Permission to leave, sir? The sooner I meet with Mr. Cantrell and clear the air, the better.''

Again, Horner gave her an amused smile that didn't quite reach his eyes. ''Bulldog tough. That's what they said about your father, Chase Trayhern—he was one tough son of a bitch in a fight. I wish you luck, Lieutenant.''

''Thank you, sir. Where can I find Mr. Cantrell?''

''He's in the Link Trainer office across the way. When he's not flying, his duties include scheduling continued Link trainer education for all pilots of VP 46.'' Glancing at his watch, he said, ''It's 1130. Usually, Clay heads to the chow hall about noon. You'll probably catch him before he leaves.'' Horner got up, extending his hand. ''Good luck and welcome aboard, Lieutenant.''

Aly gripped his hand, her fingers icy cold. She said nothing, coming to attention and making an about-face. Blindly heading out the door, focusing on the worst confrontation she'd ever come up against, she didn't even say goodbye to the friendly red-headed Chief Prater.

The day was cloudy, but patches of blue sky could be seen between the fleecy gray and white stratus overhead. Bits of sunlight slanted through, striking the revetment area where the squadron of P3s stood like gallant, silent chargers waiting to be called into battle. But Aly couldn't enjoy any of it. Her heart hurt, her head ached. Somehow, she had to gird herself for the collision with Clay.

As she walked around the perimeter of the hangar, Aly wrestled with a gamut of feelings. Clay had been friendly and likable yesterday. Thank God, she'd seen his good side, because it might be the last time. No matter what happened, she would keep reminding herself that he had stopped to help her when no one else had. There was integrity and humanity in his soul and heart. She liked the warm gray smile in his eyes, and that mobile mouth that drew into such a careless, little-boy grin. But yesterday he hadn't realized that she was Morgan's sister.

Taking a deep breath, Aly entered a door that had a sign posted: Link Trainer Officer. The door led to a narrow passageway lined by at least ten offices up and down the east side of the hangar. Straight ahead, through the glass-paned window, she saw Clay sitting at his desk, buried in paperwork. Glancing around, Aly saw no one in the passageway. She took the few seconds of reprieve to put a tight clamp on her feelings. Her father had always counseled her never to allow her emotions to enter the field of any battle. Keeping a clear head was the only way to win, he'd told her time and again. For five years Aly had used his wisdom with success. But could she now?

Taking a look at Clay, her heart unraveled, heedless of her father's stern warning. He appeared tired, one hand resting against his head as he scribbled something on a yellow legal pad in front of him. His short black hair shone with blue highlights in the lamplight from overhead. The desk was cluttered, and Aly wondered if the responsibility as Link Trainer Officer combined with his many flights was wearing him down. His mouth was pursed, almost as if he were in pain. And today his skin appeared washed-out, darkness shadowing beneath his eyes.

Aly released a shaky breath, knowing she couldn't hate this man—not even remotely. But instinctively she knew he'd hate her. It was just a question of on what level and how much. There was something else, something gossamer and fleeting that had touched Aly's aching heart. The vulnerability in Clay Cantrell held her captive. She had no explanation, no proof of that; it was simply something she *knew*. And because of that, she was going to be exposed to him emotionally. That meant he could get to her, hurt her.

Give me the courage, give me whatever it takes to handle this. Please... And Aly placed her hand with determination on the doorknob.

Clay heard the door open and close. He looked up. A rush of breath was expelled from his lips as he stared up...up into that angelic face once again. It was her! The woman he'd stopped to help on the Bayshore! The pen dropped from his hand. His eyes narrowed as he took in the uniform she wore. Shock rocketed through Clay. His gaze flew to the gold name tag over her right breast pocket: A. Trayhern. *No!* The words were almost ripped from him. My God, what kind of fate was stalking him? She couldn't be Alyssa Trayhern! She just couldn't be! He sat for almost a minute, wrestling with his violent emotions.

"You!" The word exploded from him. He rose ominously to his feet, his hands resting in fists against the surface of his desk. *No!* his heart shouted. Fury tunneled through him like molten lava flowing up

from a fissure deep in the earth. She was so damned pretty, her blue eyes wide and pleading. That irresistible mouth was parted, looking incredibly sensual. But it was her name that screamed at him. How could someone so damned fragile-looking be the sister of the man who'd killed Stephen? There had to be a mistake. Some kind of sick, twisted mistake!

Clay drew himself up, watching her stand before him. Part of him admired her. The other part hated her. "Just what the hell is this?" he snarled.

Aly wanted to die. She saw the shock, the anguish and then the fury in his burning pewter-gray eyes. That wonderful vulnerability that had drawn her effortlessly to Clay was buried in the mire of old memories and old hate dredged up by the guttural tone of his voice. Her stomach turned with nausea. "I'm sorry," she began, her voice unsteady. "I didn't know who you were. I mean, yesterday..."

Words jammed in Clay's throat. He glared at her. "You're sorry?" he whispered hoarsely. "No, I'm the one who's sorry. Sorry that you got assigned to me. Sorry that your traitor of a brother got Stephen killed. Sorry that—"

"Now you wait just one damn minute!" Aly walked up to the desk, breathing hard, her voice trembling. "Morgan *was not* a traitor! I know my brother! He'd *never* leave a company of men exposed!"

Real hatred raged through Clay. He wanted to wrap his hands around her slender neck and choke the life out of her—just as Stephen's life had been choked from him. "Your brother—" he breathed harshly, leaning forward, not more than six inches from her face "—was a goddamned traitor! He allowed nearly two hundred men to die that morning on that miserable hill in Vietnam. Your bastard of a brother left with the only radio that could have gotten his men safely out of that situation and disappeared into the jungle. He left Stephen and his Marine company wide open to NVA attack. The only survivor, in case you don't happen to remember, *saw* your brother hightail it to the other side.'' He punched a finger toward her. ''So don't you come waltzing in here telling me Morgan Trayhern wasn't a traitor. I know different! The whole damn country does!''

Agony warred with Aly's anger. She felt herself unraveling before him. Each word, spit forth with such virulent loathing, plunged through her undefended heart. ''My brother is *not* a traitor, Lieutenant,'' she rattled. ''And I won't stand here and be insulted by you.''

''Oh, yes, you will. Because your brother killed my brother.'' Clay smiled savagely. ''Do you know how many years I've lived with the nightmares? I have dreams about going to your family's home in Florida and knocking on the door. Your father answers and I'm screaming at him, wanting to kill him the way Morgan killed Stephen.'' He leaned forward, his voice flat with disgust. ''Five years, Trayhern.''

Get hold of yourself, Aly. He's losing it. You've got to keep your cool. Aly slowly straightened, deliberately placing her hands at her sides. ''All right, Lieutenant Cantrell, now's your chance.''

Startled by her sudden composure and the throaty coolness of her voice, he scowled. ''What the hell are you talking about?'' he grated out.

As much as it hurt, Aly held his blazing gray gaze. ''If you've still got that much hatred from that many years, it needs to be released. I'm my father's daughter. You can't punch him out, but you can me. Go on, take a swing at me if it will help.''

Her voice was utterly devoid of emotion. Clay was shocked at the change in her. Yesterday... He closed his eyes, remembering her wide, trusting blue eyes and the smile that could steal the heart of the most hardened men. He trained his gaze back on her. Now she was pale, calm and almost detached. Almost. He saw the pain in her eyes.

''I was taught never to strike a woman,'' he whispered.

Her voice hardened. ''Make an exception, Cantrell, because I'm not going to put up with your anger from here on out.''

He saw her set her jaw, as if braced for a possible blow. The whole thing would have been ridiculous under any other circumstances. Her spine was ramrod straight, her blue eyes challenging, her voice no longer soft. This was the Annapolis graduate. Clay had come up the hard way: through college and then flight school at Pensacola. But Aly was a ring knocker, an Annapolis graduate—one of those elite few who had the ''right stuff'' to make it through four of the toughest years ever thrown at an individual.

Her courage tempered his hatred of her just enough. A lazy smile pulled at the hard line of Clay's mouth. ''Lucky for you that you're in a woman's body. Otherwise, I would invite you out back.''

The tension in the room was frantic. Aly was thrown off guard by his amused smile. And when he straightened, throwing back his shoulders, she grew afraid. Really afraid. Her ploy to meet him head-on had defused some of his anger. But not all of it. She saw a flicker in his eyes of some emotion she couldn't name. But it sent a chill of apprehension through her, knotting her stomach.

"I think for the good of everyone concerned you'll forget I'm a woman."

Clay threw his hands on his hips, studying her, sizing her up. Impossible, he decided. She filled out the black officer's uniform to sweet perfection. Alyssa Trayhern was a looker, there was no doubt about it. And he liked the tousled pixie haircut that gave her a girlish quality. She was small breasted and waisted, her hips boyishly slim, but most of all, Clay liked her long, slender thoroughbred legs. His gaze moved deliberately back up to her face, back to those blue eyes that blazed with—what? Hurt? No, that couldn't be. This woman was as tough as they came. She was from the Trayhern military dynasty, there was no doubt. Her famous relatives had fought in America's struggle for independence, blazing a two-hundred-year record of prestigious and Congressional Medal-winning service. Until 1970. Sweet angel face and the heart of a pit bull, he thought, seeing the strength in her compressed lips, in her tense stance. Even her hands were wrapped into fists.

Some of the tension flowed out of his shoulders and the back of his neck. Clay rubbed his neck, studying her ruefully in the thickening silence.

"If you could try and judge me on my own merits, not my family name, it would help both of us," Aly whispered in a strained tone.

"As far as I'm concerned, you're Morgan Trayhern's sister. That's all. Your gender or first name has nothing to do with anything." He stabbed a finger at her again. "You're the sister of a murderer and traitor."

Blood sang through Aly, heated and furious. She stared at him. God, but he could be one cold bastard when he chose to be! She tried desperately to remember their first meeting, remember his warmth and openness. "I won't respond any longer to your name-calling, Cantrell." Aly leaned forward, only the desk separating them. "Whatever ax you have to grind with me will be done in private. I won't tolerate this kind of behavior in front of our crew or the enlisted people. I don't like this situation any more than you do, but let's try to make the best of it."

Clay smiled lethally. "You can bet your sweet face that I'm not having my fitness report screwed up because of you. Don't worry, Trayhern, our private war will stay private. I have one of the best crews in VP 46, and they aren't going to know how I really feel about you."

Aly nodded. "Fine, I can cope with that." But could she cope with his continued nearness? Dear God, Clay affected her powerfully. She was hurting. Aly wanted to see that carefree smile, to watch his gray eyes glimmer with sunlight. She was so tired of fighting…of defending Morgan and her family name. "Look," she uttered, "all I want to do is get along, Lieutenant. I don't expect any favors. I've worked hard all my life for everything I've ever gotten. I'll do my best to weave into the situation here at the squadron. You give me orders and I'll die trying to follow them."

The sudden exhaustion in Aly's voice caught Clay off balance. He saw the bleakness in her blue eyes and heard the raw pleading in her husky voice. For a split second, Clay felt guilt. But just as quickly as it came, he smashed it. ''As I said—I'm not screwing up my career because of *you*.''

''Likewise.''

Clay almost smiled. What a little hellcat she was. For her size and weight, which couldn't be more than 120 pounds, she was a fighter. He allowed himself to admire her for that. ''Okay,'' he muttered, looking around his desk, ''let's get this miserable show on the road.''

The puncturing of the tension nearly unstrung her. Aly sat down, her knees shaking. She hoped Clay hadn't seen it, because he'd probably wonder if she was up to the task of flying as his copilot on the multimillion-dollar aircraft.

Tossing a file folder across the desk, Clay said, ''I've been ordered to set up your Link training for the next quarter. You'll start tomorrow. Aviation Engineer Chief Random is assigned to start running the computer programs for you. I'll be 'flying' as your IP and take you through an introductory phase on the P3.'' His eyes grew dark. ''And I hope for your sake you're a fast learner, Trayhern.''

Aly opened the folder, quickly scanning the first page. Link training would take place every day, five days a week, for at least two to three hours at a time. She began to sweat as she had before every flight at Pensacola. It was a fear sweat. ''Isn't this schedule a little demanding?''

''Yes, it is. But so is the position the squadron's in. VP 46 flies from the Bering Strait of Alaska down to the tip of Baja, Mexico. We protect the entire West Coast from Soviet subs that ply off our twelve-mile limit. I'm sure Commander Horner told you that there's been a lot of unusual activity in the Baja California area lately. More Soviet subs are in that region. Civilian shipping is frantic because the Reds are ghosting their movements. There have been some close calls.''

''In what way?'' Aly was relieved to get on a neutral topic. But it in no way lessened the hatred she saw burning in his eyes every time he glanced over at her.

Clay moved to a wall map of the West Coast and Pacific Ocean. He circled an area with his index finger. ''We've got Soviet freighters plying their trade to the Central American countries here. The Soviet subs dogged the heels of friendly U.S. freighters in that area. One Red sub took a torpedo shot at an American-registered ship last week.''

Aly's eyes widened. ''And they got away with it?''

With a slight, triumphant grin Cantrell said, ''No. We dropped a depth charge from the P3 I was flying, right in front of the bastard's nose, to let him know we weren't going to allow him the privilege of a second shot. The ship wasn't in any real danger. It was only harassment by the Soviets. But we're there to make sure they know we'll interdict any game they want to play with U.S. shipping.''

Excitement thrummed through her. ''Then what happened?''

''The sub dived and hightailed it back out to sea.''

''Does this kind of thing happen often?''

Clay tried to ignore the sudden enthusiasm in Aly's voice, the shine in her azure eyes. What would it be like to see that same warm glow in them after he'd made love with her?

Where the *hell* did *that* thought come from? He gave himself an internal shake. Alyssa Trayhern was doing things to him he had no control over, and that shook him. No woman had held that kind of power over him. Ever! Angry at the train of his thought, he snapped at her.

"It happens a lot. And for your sake, Lieutenant, you'd better be up to the demands of it. Flying a P3 at fifty feet over a raging ocean and knowing that any second a down-draft could suck you and your entire crew into a watery grave isn't for weaklings. Or women," he added viciously.

Chapter Three

Clay's words haunted Aly. It was a barely veiled threat that if she screwed up, he'd be the first to point out her error and log the mistake into her fitness report. And blots on her fitness report, issued twice a year on every officer, could hurt, even destroy, her budding career. No, Clay held the sword of Damocles above her head and they both knew it. Aly hefted the three large manuals he'd given her just before she left the training office. They were manuals that covered cockpit procedures, emergency procedures and defense measures for the beautiful, graceful P3.

It was noon, but Aly had lost her appetite. If she studied nonstop over the weekend, she *might* gain an edge on cockpit procedure for Monday morning so that she'd impress Clay. The plan was a lot better than the opposite possibility—disappointing him.

As Aly hurried down the safety walk toward the

side entrance, she heard a long, loud wolf whistle. She ignored it. Probably some enlisted man, she thought, irritated. But again came another long whistle.

Slowly, Aly turned and saw a pilot in a green flight suit, his garrison cap at a cocky angle on his head, following close behind her. He was smiling, his brown eyes sparkling. His walk was jaunty, self-assured. Aly saw a patch on his olive-green flight suit that identified him as an F-14 Tomcat pilot. And then she saw the inspector pilot's patch on the other side of his chest. She frowned as he ambled up to her and threw his hands on his hips.

"Hi, there. The name's Starbuck. Jeff Starbuck. Scuttlebutt was flying around the hangar this morning that a good-looking lady was on the premises." His grin deepened as he met and held her defiant gaze. "I said, 'Nah...' And they said, 'Yeah!' So the chief of maintenance said he saw her go into that lucky bastard, Cantrell's office. I decided to scope it out for myself."

Starbuck drew himself up and snapped off an impressive salute. "You've got to be Alyssa Trayhern," he said and offered his hand. "Damned glad to have you on board."

Aly refused to take his hand. "Lieutenant Starbuck, your manners are not impressive."

Starbuck looked crestfallen, his oval face losing some of its joviality. "What?"

"I'm sure you've been in the Navy long enough to realize that whistling at an enlisted woman or a woman officer is considered sexual harassment."

His mouth tightened. "Well, gosh, I meant it as a compliment, Miss Trayhern." He cocked his head to one side, deliberately checking out her legs. "I mean, what a set of legs!"

He was irrepressible, Aly decided, and she relented. Starbuck's demeanor was typical of fighter jocks. Typically male chauvinistic, egotistical and self-serving. Despite that, Starbuck was a bright spot in her gray day. His brown hair was neatly cut, and he had large, hawklike eyes. The devil-may-care smile on his full mouth enhanced the youthful appearance of his face, although he had to be in his late twenties. There were crow's-feet crinkling at the corners of his eyes and deep grooves around his mouth, indicating that he smiled and laughed a great deal.

"Okay, Mr. Starbuck, thank you for the compliment."

"But?" His smile deepened.

"Look, I just spent four years at Annapolis and a year with you guys at Pensacola."

He rubbed his chin. "Hmm, sounds like something serious. Betcha you're going to tell me I'm just like all the rest, eh?"

"Roger that."

"But," he said dramatically, "I'm the best-*looking* F-14 driver at Moffett." He jerked a thumb over his shoulder. "The trash haulers who fly the P3 are a pittance compared to me. I got the looks, the time and—" he held up his left hand for her to observe "—I'm free."

"And I'm not. Sorry, Starbuck, I've got things to do. If you'll excuse me?" Not waiting for his response, Aly turned and walked toward the mouth of the hangar.

"Hey! Wait up!" Starbuck trotted up alongside and

grabbed the manuals she was carrying. "At least let me help the lady with her books."

Aly groaned, wavering between stopping to wrest the books from him and giving in. Starbuck wasn't going to be easy to get rid of. "If I didn't know you had ulterior motives, Lieutenant, I might be impressed with your thoughtfulness, but I'm not."

"Can I at least carry these to your car—ulterior motives or not?"

He was an engaging character, Aly decided. "Oh, all right." And she took off at a fast walk. Her red Toyota was parked halfway down the other side of the hangar, a long walk to endure with the fighter jock.

"Beautiful day, isn't it?" Starbuck asked, gesturing to the sky. "Man, I just got done flying up there. Air's smooth as a woman's—" He flushed. "Sorry, I'm used to talking to male pilots, not female ones."

Aly gave him a flat look of disapproval. "I can tell, Lieutenant."

He grinned self-consciously, color heating his neck and cheeks. "Sorry, Alyssa. Do you mind if I call you by your first name?"

"No, I don't care," she answered. Her mind, and if she was honest with herself, her heart were dwelling on the confrontation with Clay Cantrell. They were at a terrible impasse with each other. How could she overcome the barriers he'd thrown up and get him to wave a white flag of truce so that they could survive their time together?

"Well," Starbuck said, noticing she was ignoring him, "as I was saying, it was great flying up there this morning. We've been hearing about a woman pilot being assigned to Moffett for the past two weeks. I was really excited about the opportunity.''

''I'll bet you were,'' Aly answered dryly. Probably thought he was going to be the first to bed her down, and then go around strutting and bragging about his latest conquest to every man on the station who would listen.

''Ahh, there you go again, Alyssa. You don't trust my intentions, do you?''

''Not in the least, Lieutenant.''

''You can call me Jeff if you want. My buddies call me Iron Eagle.''

''In or out of bed?'' Aly flinched inwardly. Now she was trading tit for tat. Offense was the only defense against someone like this arrogant jock.

Laughing heartily, he said, ''Good sense of humor, too. I like that in a woman.''

''I'm not keeping score, and neither should you.''

''You must have met that sour bastard, Cantrell,'' Starbuck said, glancing at the stack of manuals under his arm. ''And it looks like he's thrown the homework at you.''

He was right on that account, Aly acknowledged silently. ''Lieutenant Cantrell is my mentor for my training-in period.''

''Yeah, I heard you got stuck with him.''

An ocean-scented wind blew in off the bay, and Aly inhaled the fragrance. She could see the salt marshes that grew right at the end of the airstrip. A lot of sea gulls were wafting on the unseen currents over the station. Right now, all she wanted to do was fly. Fly and forget. Let the sky take her into its arms and hold her for a while.

"I don't know what you're talking about," she retorted sharply.

Chuckling indulgently, Starbuck watched a sea gull sail overhead. "Well, sooner or later you're going to hear about the infamous Cantrell."

"From you, no doubt, whether I want to or not. Isn't that correct, Lieutenant?"

He curbed his smile, seemingly struggling to remain serious. "What I'm going to say isn't gossip, Alyssa. These are things you should know. I mean, after all, you've been assigned to fly with him, right?"

"Yes." She shot Starbuck a warning look. "I don't like gossip, mister. Especially the malicious variety. If that's what you've got on Lieutenant Cantrell, you can stow it."

He nodded, growing somber. "Fair enough. I imagine you've had plenty of gossip about yourself, so you're a little sensitive in that area."

Aly was stunned by his sudden insight. "Well—yes," she stammered.

"See, we aren't all the insensitive jocks stuck on our egos that you thought," he teased, smiling again.

Aly smiled unwillingly. "You're a big tease and I know it."

"But a harmless one," he pleaded. "Really."

"Sure."

"You know how we fighter jocks talk. I mean, we're bred to have confidence. You gotta have a healthy ego in order to lift a fifteen-million-dollar aircraft off a pitching carrier deck in the middle of an ocean."

"That's the truth," Aly agreed. She pointed toward the Toyota. "That's my car."

Starbuck drew to a halt while she fished around in her purse for the keys. "Look, I meant what I said about Cantrell. There are some things you need to know. It might save that nice-looking rear of yours, someday."

Aly ignored the remark and jammed the key into the lock. "I don't want to discuss it."

Starbuck handed her the manuals, which she stowed in the rear of the sports car. "Give me just five minutes, okay?" He held up his hands in a sign of truce. "I promise you, everything I'm going to tell you is true."

Sighing, Aly muttered, "Five minutes, Starbuck, and that's it."

"A year and a half ago, Cantrell was an F-14 driver like me. We flew off the *Enterprise* together. He was one of the hottest pilots in our squadron, and we were both vying for the top-gun slot at Miramar. Then he screwed up on a deck landing. Cantrell ended up crashing the bird he was flying into the deck. He ejected, but his radar officer bought it." Starbuck's voice dropped with feeling. "Cantrell ended up in the hospital for a while, and the flight surgeon grounded him. He'd lost his nerve. Every time he tried to requalify as a carrier pilot, he failed. The Navy finally rerouted him to a land-based aircraft. He's been here at Moffett for a year." Starbuck pointed to the P3 parked closest to them. "That's his bird. It's been downed. Three days ago he made a rookie pilot's landing and did some major damage to the port landing gear. The whole strut is going to be replaced later today."

Instead of being worried about Clay's past, Aly felt her heart ache for him. She'd heard of fighter pilots losing their nerve out on the carrier. They flew under the toughest, most demanding of flight conditions possible. "Look, Starbuck," she said coolly, "his past is no concern of mine."

"It is if you're sitting in that cockpit with him," he challenged, his eyes flashing with irritation. "Look, you've worked hard to get this far. I'd hate to see your career screwed up because that guy's in the process of losing his touch."

"You don't know that—you don't fly with him!" What the hell was she *defending* Clay for? Aly didn't have time to analyze her response.

Starbuck lifted the garrison cap off his head and settled it back on with feeling. "His *crew* knows it. His copilot, Randy Hart, just transferred out of here to his next assignment. Hart is a damn fine pilot. Every once in a while we'd have a beer or two over at the Officers Club after a mission, and he'd tell me what it was like to fly with Cantrell."

Aly threw her purse into the passenger seat. "That's enough, Lieutenant. I told you: I won't listen to gossip."

"This isn't gossip! Cantrell's hands shake so bad after a mission that his entire crew thinks he's close to the edge. All he does is bitch at them. He doesn't have a kind word for anyone."

"I suppose next you're going to tell me that he's a heavy drinker, slopping them down at the O Club after every mission?"

With a groan, Starbuck held up his long, expressive hands. "Whoa, sweet thing. I'm just trying to prepare you for what you're up against." He grinned slightly, his eyes taking on a familiar twinkle. "I just found you. I don't want you run off by a sourpuss like Cantrell.''

Aly couldn't decide what Starbuck's motives were. He'd flown with Cantrell in the same squadron, and Aly knew that competitiveness was the chief gestalt between fighter pilots vying for top-gun selection. Starbuck might hate Clay because Clay was a better pilot than Starbuck before the crash. She didn't know, and at this point, didn't care.

''Lieutenant, do you know who I am?'' she challenged.

''Yeah, you're Alyssa Trayhern.''

''I'm the sister of Morgan Trayhern. Does that name ring a bell with you?''

With a shrug, Starbuck answered, ''Of course it does. Look, I don't bear grudges. It was your brother that gave your family a black mark, not you.''

Aly eyed him in silence, evaluating. His face was free of tension, his eyes lacking guile. ''And you know that Lieutenant Cantrell's brother was in the same company with my brother?''

''I heard about that. Scuttlebutt has been thick and heavy ever since we found out you were assigned.'' He rubbed his chin, studying her frankly. ''That's another reason I wanted to warn you about Cantrell. He's not the type to forgive and forget. He bears a grudge for a long time. I know from experience, because I beat him out for top gun and went on to win the honor for our squadron.''

No kidding about Clay holding grudges, Aly almost blurted out. But Starbuck was a dangerous person to confide in, she decided. As badly as she wanted to break down and tell someone about her trials with Clay, she knew it wouldn't be Starbuck. No, she sensed a vicious streak in him, despite that disarming smile and teasing manner.

"Look, I appreciate your two cents worth on Cantrell. But if you don't mind, I don't want to hear any more war stories. Now, if you'll excuse me—"

"Hey! What about a pizza tonight? There's a terrific little parlor over in Mountain View. Mama Cara's has the best Italian food in the Bay Area. How about if I pick you up, say, around 1900, and we'll get better acquainted over some great pizza and good wine?"

A little pain stabbed through Aly's heart. She winced outwardly. Was it the same pizza place that Clay had referred to yesterday? She had been looking forward to that date with him. "Thanks, but no," she said and climbed into her sports car.

Crestfallen, but not giving up, Starbuck shut the door for her.

"Probably shouldn't, with all those training manuals to study this weekend." He smiled. "Get your beauty sleep tonight. I'll be seeing you around, Alyssa," and he threw her a salute.

Don't count on it. Aly nodded and backed the car out of the parking spot, anxious to escape the cloying attention of Jeff Starbuck. Right now, all she wanted to do was go home, have a good cry, get herself back together again and call her parents. They had been her stanchion of strength, of wisdom. And right now, she needed both. Desperately.

"Hello, Dad."

"Punkin! Well, how was your first day at your very first station?"

Aly shut her eyes, gripping the phone hard. It was

nearly six o'clock. She had come home earlier, cried, taken Rogue out for a five-mile jog around their new neighborhood, gotten a hot shower and unpacked more boxes. Needing to talk to someone, Aly had finally picked up the phone and dialed.

"Its been terrible, Dad." She explained the entire sequence of events. Just talking about it to an understanding ear helped. Afterward, Aly rubbed her face tiredly.

"What do you think, Dad? Does someone back in D.C. have it in for me?"

"Let me make a few phone calls and feel this out," Chase muttered. His voice was deep with concern. "It does sound as if some admiral has it in for you. That's why those orders were cut that way."

Aly knew her father had powerful and influential ties to all the services. He had retired a brigadier general in the Air Force just before Morgan's tragedy. Generals were power brokers, and her father knew how to infight politically with the best of them. But since Morgan's terrible tragedy, her father's awesome political clout had been brutally undermined. Despite his forty years of service, few of his friends remained such after Morgan was declared a traitor. Aly knew her father's access to the Pentagon to investigate her problem would be severely hampered, if not hamstrung from the beginning.

"Can you do it without stirring up problems, Dad?" Aly didn't want whoever was trying to kill her career to get wind of his delicate inquiry.

"I'll be careful, Punkin, you can count on it. For now, how are you going to handle this? Is Cantrell someone you can reason with?"

"No," she said miserably, propping an elbow on

the table and resting her head in her hand. "He's filled with hatred, Dad. I hurt for him. I think Clay's backlogged with emotions from five years ago, that he never released his grief over his brother's death."

Chase's deep voice softened. "You hurt for him, honey?"

Aly laughed weakly. "Oh, Dad, you don't know the other half of it," she explained, and she told him about their meeting on the Bayshore.

"I see," he murmured. "So you're attracted to him despite the situation, Aly?"

"Yes. This is the first time I've ever been knocked off my feet, Dad. He just took my breath away. No man has ever done that before."

"Sounds serious."

Aly's depression lifted. "I love you, Dad. You always know when to tease me and get me out of the hole I've dug for myself."

Chase's voice grew tender. "Listen, Punkin, you're our only daughter. Your mother and I are terribly proud of you. The past five years have been utter hell on you, too."

Closing her eyes, Aly nodded. The rest, what her father didn't say, was: because of what happened to Morgan. No one in the family believed Morgan was a traitor. They all knew something had happened that Morgan had been caught in the middle of. Chase felt his older son had been made a scapegoat. But for what? They didn't even know if Morgan was alive or dead. And her father had been thwarted from all angles in trying to investigate his son's disappearance off the face of the earth. She sighed tiredly. "I thought my hell was over, Dad. I had so many hopes and dreams about Moffett. I finally felt as if all the shadows from the past were dead and buried...."

"Take this one day at a time, Punkin. Perhaps your liking Cantrell might make it easier in one way."

"Oh?"

"You're not defensive with him. You understand where his pain is coming from, and you won't go for his jugular each time he attacks you. It might give you the patience to outdistance his hate. Sooner or later, he'll run out of hate. That's what you've got to count on."

"But by liking him I'm leaving myself wide open, Dad. Everything he said to me, I've heard thousands of times before, and it never cut me like it did coming from him."

"I know, honey," Chase soothed. "I wish I could protect your heart where he's concerned. But I can't. No one can. You have a choice: put up walls to protect your heart, or go ahead and feel your way through the situations and take the hurt that goes with the territory and the decision."

"Which would you do, Dad?" Tears stung her eyes, her voice wobbling dangerously.

Chase sighed. "A better question is: what do you want to do about it?"

Aly sniffed, wiping her nose. "Mom always counseled us to feel our emotions, don't run away from them."

"That's true. And she also taught you to listen to your gut instincts. What are they telling you?"

Aly's heart hurt, and she rubbed the area unconsciously. "Th-that Clay's like a hurt animal, biting anyone who comes remotely near him, whether they created his pain or not."

"Okay, and what do you do with an injured animal?"

"Care for it as carefully as you can, remain objective and don't try to pet it."

"That's right. A hurt animal doesn't equate a stroke on his head with comfort. He just sees it as a hand attacking him and will strike out at it."

Managing a choked laugh, Aly said, "Dad, do you ever think I'll get wise about people and their emotions the way you and Mom did?"

Chase chuckled. "I think, Punkin, that at twenty-five, you're way ahead of most women your age. You have savvy, intelligence and a world of traveling and experience behind you. My money's on you to win out in this situation with Cantrell. Just be patient. And don't get your hand close enough for him to bite."

It was drizzling rain again on Sunday. Aly felt as depressed as the low-hanging gray clouds that embraced the Bay Area. She hefted the cockpit manual under her left arm and climbed out of her car. Moffett Field was almost deserted on Sunday, except for those who had to stand the duty. Dressed in jeans, a pink turtleneck sweater and a warm beige jacket, Aly ran to the closest entrance of Hangar One.

Inside, she went to the duty chief's office. An aviation engineer first class was standing the duty office, busy with paperwork when she entered.

"Hi, I'm Lieutenant Alyssa Trayhern."

The tall string bean of a man, dressed in a light blue chambray shirt and dark blue serge trousers, straightened in the chair. His red hair was close cropped, his skin sprinkled with copper freckles. "Oh..." And then he grinned sheepishly and rose, sticking out his hand. ''Miss Trayhern, I'm your engineer on board our aircraft. The name's Dan Ballard. I'm happy to finally get to meet you.''

Aly flushed at his softened words. The man meant what he said, his hazel eyes alight with unabashed enthusiasm as he pumped her hand long and eagerly.

Reclaiming her hand, she rewarded him with a shy smile of her own. ''What a wonderful welcome. I hope the rest of the crew's as happy about me as you are.''

Ballard nodded. ''To tell the truth,'' he said in a conspiratorial tone, ''since we found out about this two weeks ago, I've been telling the crew that it's the best thing that could happen to us.''

Placing the manual on the desk, Aly dried her hands by wiping them across her jeans. ''Oh, why's that?''

Scratching his head, Ballard blushed a dull red. He avoided her gaze. ''Well...you know... My wife, Sandy, is a real feminist.'' He held up his hand, assuming Aly would take his comment the wrong way. ''We've been married some twelve years now, with four kids between us, and I've seen a woman's strength compared to a man's. She was saying the same thing I was: that you're going to add some dimensions to the crew that we didn't have before. Good things, I think, that will help....'' He stumbled, groping for the right words.

Starbuck's conversation came back to her. Maybe he hadn't exaggerated the situation with Cantrell's crew. Ballard reminded her of an eager puppy just dying for a warm pat on the head. She liked him. He was open and honest. ''Help what, Dan?'' she probed gently, hoping to get an answer.

"Ahh, don't mind me, Miss Trayhern. I just get carried away and all. Just know that the crew is going to welcome you with open arms. We need a lady's sensitivity and her gentle way of handling us. You know what I mean...."

Aly nodded and pretended to know. "Well, look, Dan, if you don't mind, since you're duty chief, I'd like to have your permission to climb on board number 7 and sit in the cockpit to familiarize myself a little. Is that possible?" The P3 was still in the hangar, and Aly could see that the old landing gear had been replaced with new on the port side of the aircraft.

"Sure. Of course. I'm sure Mr. Cantrell won't mind." He came around the desk and opened the door for her. "Would you like some help? I'm the guy who sits right behind your seats working the four throttles while you're flying. I'm also certified to taxi the gal, and qualified on engine start-up and shutdown procedures."

She warmed to his generosity. "Maybe later? Right now, I just want to sit and acquaint myself with her."

Dan opened the door, nodding. "Sure, Miss Trayhern. Want me to drop by in about an hour? The only thing I gotta do is be here in the hangar. We've only got one P3 out on track, and that bird isn't scheduled back from the mission for six hours."

"Kinda bored?" Aly guessed, smiling.

"Yes, ma'am."

"Give me an hour, Dan, and then you can quiz me on procedures, okay?"

"You got it, Miss Trayhern." He beamed.

Aly's step was lighter as she walked across the concrete floor in her sensible brown shoes. Every sound was amplified, echoing off the walls. It was ghostlike, the pall of rain and gray clouds hanging silently outside the opened bay doors of the hangar, increasing her sense of loneliness. Still, Aly felt her first real ray of hope with Dan Ballard, who was obviously delighted in her arrival.

The fuselage door was open on the port side of number 7, a ladder placed up against the hatch. As Aly approached the ladder, she reached up, running her hand across the smooth, cool skin of the P3.

"Hi there, Gray Lady," she whispered. Her eyes darkened. "Let's you and me be friends. We're both women in a man's world." The gray aluminum skin warmed beneath her palm. Aly could swear the aircraft was alive, possessing a unique personality. She'd always named her planes, her animals, her car and anything else that would stand still long enough to be given a name.

"Gray Lady, be my ally. Help me," she pleaded to the strong, silent aircraft. It was time to go on board. She'd never stepped inside a sub-hunting aircraft. Slowly Aly entered the plane. Inside, the port and starboard fuselage were a complex array of radar screens. A desk ran down both sides. So much electronic equipment was squeezed into the small working space that there seemed barely enough room for the eight crewmen at the consoles. Looking aft, past a small entrance without a door, she saw two more seats and a collapsible bunk that fitted tightly up against the fuselage wall. One seat was for the radioman, the other for a meteorological observer.

The aircraft was flawless, Aly decided with admiration. Everything was stowed neatly and efficiently. She located the sonobuoys that could detect a Soviet sub beneath the oceans if they were dropped out the rear hatch of the P3. The depth charges weren't on board, so she assumed they must be loaded on the aircraft for the mission and then taken off when the plane returned to the station.

Aly's heart beat a little harder as she moved forward into the cockpit. She saw the four throttles that Dan Ballard would kneel before and monitor. Her hands grew damp as she halted, glanced around the small instrument panel in front and overhead. Her fear dissolved as she began to look at the individual gauges. This was Gray Lady's circulatory system. The P3's heart consisted of four powerful turboprop engines. Some of the many dials would tell Aly how the fuel was getting pumped and distributed to her heart. Triumph soared through her as she sat down for the first time in the copilot seat, her position for at least the next two years of her life.

A sense of belonging swept through Aly. She laid the manual open across the throttle case. Running her hand gently across the copilot's yoke, new excitement thrummed through her. One of these days, she'd be allowed to fly Gray Lady. What she'd give to feel the plane come alive under her careful, supervised skill! Would the P3 give over her power to her? Or would she fight every step of the way like some prop and jet trainers Aly had flown at Pensacola?

''Enough daydreaming,'' she muttered, giving the aircraft a quick, friendly pat. ''Down to work!''

Clay shielded his eyes from the downpour. Having parked near the entrance to Hangar One, he dived inside. He shook the excess water from his well-worn leather jacket and headed straight for his P3. Looking around, he realized the hangar was all but deserted. The other men had families to go home to, they had wives…children.…

His family was the Navy, his woman that gleaming P3 that stood like an elegant queen before him. Eyes narrowing, he bent and moved beneath the plane's graceful undercarriage. The damage sustained in that landing had been repaired. Clay carefully checked the mechanics' work. He trusted them, but he had to be sure. Any pilot concerned with his plane's performance would do the same. Besides, as usual, there was little to do on the weekend when he didn't have the duty. Clay felt better just being on the station. This was his life.

Satisfied, he ran his hand down the steel strut. On the last mission there had been a malfunction with the low-altitude altimeter or LAA. He wanted to go on board and see if it had been repaired and checked off the maintenance sheet by the ground crew. He and his crew would be flying this girl Tuesday, and he wanted her in tip-top condition.

As Clay climbed the ladder, he could have sworn he heard a woman's voice. A husky voice. Impossible. Frowning, he halted at the lip of the P3. Confusion turned to disbelief as he looked toward the cockpit area. Although the light was dim, he could see a mop of unruly red hair glinting dully in the cockpit.

Aly! And then Clay sternly chastised himself. *No, her name isn't Aly!* He'd sworn he'd never call her by her first name again. But he couldn't help himself, and he stood mesmerized as she leaned over the manual, muttering out the names of the dials and gauges.

Closing his eyes, Clay hoped that she would disappear. She didn't. He was intensely aware of her red hair, clean profile and those parted lips. As he inhaled, he could faintly smell the fragrance she wore—something spicy, like herself. And when she placed her finger against her lower lip, studying the manual with undivided intent, he felt himself begin to tighten with desire.

Disgusted with his reaction to her, Clay moved silently up the passageway toward her, letting his anger at himself mask his real feelings. There was savage pleasure in realizing she was so focused on the manual that she didn't hear him coming until it was too late. Clay told himself he was going to enjoy this.

"Just what the hell do you think you're doing here, Lieutenant Trayhern?"

Aly jumped, her head snapping up, her eyes wide. Clay Cantrell's dark, shadowed features loomed above her. The anger in his eyes consumed and struck her viciously. She could only stare, stripped of any defense, because he was the last person she'd expected to run into today. Despite the fact that he was wearing a civilian light blue shirt, that same old leather jacket and a pair of brown trousers, he still held an invisible power over her.

Swallowing, Aly choked out, "I—I study better if I've got the real thing in front of me."

Placing his hands on his hips, Clay glared down into her frightened eyes. Blue eyes he could fall into and seek warmth from in his freezing, empty world. His voice came out in a low snarl. "I don't give a damn what your excuse is, Lieutenant. I'm your training officer. What I say, goes. I told you to take those manuals home and study them over the weekend. I didn't tell you to come here of your own volition and sit in the right seat of a P3." He saw his words land with the desired effect upon her. Why should he care if they hurt her? Fighting any sympathetic reaction to her flinch, Clay added savagely, ‘‘Lady, you may think you’re copilot material, but until I sign that piece of paper attesting to it, you don’t deserve to sit in that seat. Now get the hell out of here and go home.’’

Aly sat stunned, incredible pain welling up in her chest. Clay was like an avenging angel, hovering darkly above her in that gray cockpit. She opened her mouth to speak, but nothing would come out. Her throat was suddenly clogged with tears.

She blinked and bowed her head, afraid that Clay would see her tears. She didn’t dare let him know how badly he’d wounded her. Fumbling with the manual, she accidentally let it slip from her fingers, banging to the steel deck with a thump.

‘‘Dammit, can’t you do anything right?’’ he snarled, jerking the manual off the deck and tossing it her direction.

‘‘Hour’s up, Miss Trayhern,’’ Ballard sang out from the ladder. ‘‘I’m ready to help you with start-up and shutdown proced—’’

Clay turned, ominously facing his chief engineer, who stood frozen in the middle of the P3. ‘‘Just what the hell is going on here, Ballard?’’

‘‘Well…uh, Mr. Cantrell, I thought I’d help Miss Trayhern learn the instruments….’’ The rest of his explanation died in the icy silence of the aircraft. Ballard shrugged, seeing how upset his skipper was. ‘‘I was just trying to help her, sir.’’

Clay’s nostrils flared with fury, and he advanced upon the AE. He opened his mouth to deliver a verbal tongue-lashing to his chief, who had no business helping train any copilot unless he gave the order.

"Don't you dare chew him out!"

Clay heard Aly's strident cry. He halted, halfway between both of them. Jerking his head toward her, he saw that she had risen to her feet and climbed out of the cockpit. Her eyes were hauntingly large, pleading.

"This isn't his fault, Mr. Cantrell. I asked Dan to come and help me in about an hour."

"But," Ballard admitted, obviously noting the mounting rage on the officer's face and not wanting Aly hurt further, "it was my idea, skipper."

Clay didn't know whom to bite first. It was obvious Ballard was covering up for her. That made him twice as angry. "You're dismissed, Ballard," he ground out. "I'll deal with you later."

Hesitating, Dan looked toward Aly uncertainly before grudgingly saying, "Yes, sir."

Waiting until Ballard had disappeared, Clay slowly turned back toward Aly. She was still frozen at the entrance to the cockpit, her face shadowed and tense in the dim light. His smile was withering. "You've already wrapped Ballard around your finger," he began silkily. "But it won't do you any good. This is my plane and my crew. You try pitting any of them against me, and you'll pay, Trayhern. And in ways you never thought possible. Do you understand what I mean?" His eyes bored into hers.

A quiver ran through Aly. The sick, injured animal was biting again. It would do no good to fight back, he'd only rip her into more pieces than he had already. She tried to remember her father's words of wisdom, tried to rise above her own pain. Deliberately breaking the sizzling tension strung between them, Aly bent down and retrieved the second manual on the throttle case. She clutched both of them to her breast and slowly walked toward him. When she was within a foot of him, she halted.

"Your engineer had nothing to do with me being in this cockpit. It was my decision and my fault," she said, keeping her voice calm.

Clay stared down at her. Her jaw was set, her lips compressed with very real anxiety. He hated himself in that anguished second. And he could barely meet her shadowed blue eyes, riddled with hurt and confusion. "Ballard gave you permission to come on board because he's the duty chief this weekend. I'm not going to chew him out. Now get the hell out of here. Be at the Link trainer at 0800 sharp, tomorrow morning, Lieutenant."

"Yes, sir," she ground out.

Clay moved aside, not wanting contact with her. But the aisle of the plane was too narrow, and his breath lodged in his chest as she brushed past him. He saw her eyes narrow and heard a small gasp of air escape her. She hated him so much that she was disgusted by minimal contact with him, he thought wearily.

Clay stood, feeling little shocks move through him, long after she'd disappeared. Her arm had barely grazed his chest. But the contact had been electric. He was sure they'd both felt it, whatever it was.

Such a stupid, trivial thing, Clay upbraided himself as he turned toward the cockpit. How could a woman's arm merely brushing his chest make him go hard with longing? Running his fingers through his hair, Clay muttered an oath and settled into the pilot's seat. As he sat examining the LAA, he couldn't escape pangs of guilt.

He shut his eyes, rubbing them tiredly. Sleep hadn't come at all the past two nights—only dreams of the past involving his mother and Stephen. Alyssa Trayhern's entrance into his life had stirred up all the buried grief and loss. And yet, as he sat, leaning heavily against the seat, he knew Aly didn't deserve his hatred and anger. One look into those distraught blue eyes and he knew....

Chapter Four

Damn! He was late for work! Clay rolled out of bed, glaring at the alarm clock. It read 0745. It was Monday, and he wasn't going to be on time to meet Aly at the Link trainer.

As he staggered toward the bathroom, rubbing his eyes, he stubbed his toe on the edge of a rocker he kept in the corner.

"Ouch!" He hobbled the rest of the way, his left toe smarting. Fumbling for the electric razor in the drawer, he finally found it and shoved the plug into the outlet. He had to hurry. He tried to shave without looking in the mirror.

The rest of his Sunday had been spent at his apartment, studying some new training procedure manuals for the P3. Dismayed by his cruelty to Aly, he'd wanted to hide from those feelings of guilt, shifting his mind to technical demands. Last night he'd tossed and turned, unable to erase Aly's hurt features from his mind. Getting up at 0200, he'd downed a shot of Scotch, thinking it would numb the dirty feelings inside himself. It hadn't. Somewhere around 0400 he'd finally dropped off. Vaguely, Clay remembered the radio alarm clock beeping at 0530, his usual time to get up, but he'd hit it, shutting off the alarm.

His hand shook now as he placed the shaver on the tile expanse. Risking a look into the mirror in order to quickly comb his short hair into place, Clay winced. He looked like hell. He felt like hell. What was he going to do about Aly?

"Dammit!" he breathed, throwing the comb down on the counter. It skipped along the tile, falling into the washbasin. He didn't want to think of her as Aly. She was Trayhern—just another pilot. Pilots always called one another by their last names or by the nicknames they'd received at Pensacola, denoting some special feature. When Clay graduated at the top of his class, his squad mates had dubbed him Wolverine, because he was relentless and tenacious in the air.

Placing his palms against the surface, Clay ruthlessly studied himself in the mirror. His eyes were bloodshot and there were puffy bags beneath them. With his mouth pulled into a slash, he looked like a grim reaper, in his estimation. Why couldn't he just refer to her as Trayhern? Why did some miserable part of him automatically call her Aly? Clay turned away, automatically going through the steps of donning the loose-fitting olive-green flight suit.

The sun was already up, and the Bay Area was going to enjoy one of those cool but sunny January days. Clay drove hell-for-leather, pushing his Corvette along the Bloody Bayshore, weaving expertly in and out of traffic. So, okay, he'd grudgingly call her Aly to himself, but never out loud. If some part of his mind refused to coldly classify her by her last name, he wasn't going to fight it anymore. But she was still the sister of the man who had murdered the two people he loved most in the world. And for that, he could never forgive her.

Rubbing his eyes because they ached, Clay wondered what Aly would think of his being late for their first training session. Would she automatically think he was arriving late on purpose? Another ploy to make her nervous and unsure of herself? His conscience needled him. His hands tightening on the wheel, Clay felt backed into a corner as never before. Ordinarily, he was never cruel. It wasn't his nature. But every time he got around Aly, he was aware of an incredible tension that sizzled like fire between them. He rejected the idea of being drawn to her. She was the sister of a murderer. And so, there was no alternative but to treat her coldly and jam the rest of these new and unexpected feelings down into some deep, dark corner of himself—as he had with his grief for the past five years.

At exactly 0800 Aly arrived at the Link training facility, which was located at the rear of Hangar One. The room was large and spacious. The control booth, which held hundreds of computerized disks, was enclosed with glass. Chief Bill Random, who sat at the large computer terminal, came out and introduced himself. He was about fifty-five, small and brisk. But a smile wreathed his face when he pointed toward the two-seat Link trainer that would serve as her home for the coming months on a daily basis.

"I think somebody's already sweet on you, Lieutenant Trayhern."

"Oh?" Aly saw Random gesture toward the opened canopy on the Link. The trainer sat on a single movable steel pylon. When they climbed in and closed the hood, that pylon would move in any direction, simulating flight.

"Yes, ma'am. Go take a look at what's on the copilot's seat."

Mystified, Aly walked over to the trainer. Her eyes widened considerably when she saw a single red rose lying across the seat. There was a small white envelope tied to the stem with a pink ribbon.

"Clay..." she whispered, and reached down, gently cradling the rose in her hands. Having slept poorly last night, Aly had wrestled with a gamut of feelings. She had seen Clay's eyes go from anger to regret once during their explosive confrontation Sunday in the P3. Some part of him didn't want to be the bastard he was to her. Was this his way of apologizing?

Eagerly, Aly opened the envelope. Inside, neatly printed were the words: *I'm sorry.* Her heartbeat quickened, underscoring her unleashed emotions. Turning away so that Chief Random couldn't see her face, she caressed the rose, inhaling its delicate scent. Her fingers trembled as she followed the smooth curve of the large red bud. Maybe there was hope after all. Maybe...

Turning, Aly walked to the control room where Random was setting up the computer tapes that would be played for them during the training session.

"Chief, where's Mr. Cantrell?" she asked, deciding that she wanted to thank him in private.

Random punched in a program and glanced in her direction. "Oh, I'm sure he's around here somewhere. Mr. Cantrell practically lives in this place. He comes in around 0630 every morning. Probably got caught up in some last-minute scheduling problems over at his office." He waved her toward the trainer. "Why don't you climb aboard the trainer, strap in and get comfortable? I'm sure he'll be here any second."

Pressing the rose to her breast, Aly nodded. "Okay, Chief." Much of her nervousness had abated with the knowledge that Clay had chosen such a wonderful and romantic way to apologize for his behavior yesterday.

In the cockpit, Aly began to refamiliarize herself with the instrument panel. Just having an hour in Gray Lady had helped her confidence immensely. From time to time, she glanced down at the rose in her lap. More of her anxiety dissipated as she began to focus on the dials and gauges in front of her. By 0830, Aly had relaxed a great deal in the mock-up of the P3 cockpit.

She heard the door to the training room open and close. Glancing out of the Link, she saw a harried Clay Cantrell come through the door dressed in his flight suit. There was a scowl on his face and his eyes were dark and angry. Automatically, Aly tensed. What was he upset about now?

Not wanting to risk being seen, she ducked back under the hood and waited patiently for Clay to come over to the trainer. She heard him and Chief Random talking in lowered voices. Clay sounded positively irate. What had happened? Her fingers tightened around the stem of the rose, her heartbeat racing.

Clay stalked over to the trainer. He ran his fingers

through his hair as he approached the pilot side of the Link. Unable to ignore his unraveling feelings as he arrived at the trainer, he tried to steel himself to work with Aly.

"Good morning," she said cautiously.

Her voice was husky. Warm. Clay looked at her. How had Aly grown more lovely? Her cheeks were flushed pink, her blue eyes seemed soft, and her red hair was copper and gold beneath the bright lights. He tossed a manual into the trainer.

"It's morning," he growled, climbing into the left seat and strapping in. God, it was impossible to ignore her! The scent of her perfume encircled him, and unwillingly Clay inhaled it. She smelled so good, so clean in comparison to how he felt inside.

Nervously, Aly lifted the rose so that Clay could see it. "I—uh, I wanted to thank you for this...."

Clay stared at the rose and then up at her. Shaken by her vulnerability, he growled, "What's this?"

Aly tried to ferret out the confusion in his voice and the sudden shock registering in his dark gray eyes. "The rose," she offered huskily. "It's beautiful...and a beautiful way to apologize for yesterday."

"But—"

A shy smile pulled at the corners of her mouth. "I'm sorry, too, Clay. All I want to do is fit in around here, not fight with you."

Her admission tore a scar off the festering wound in his heart. The rose trembled in her hand as she held it out to him. Her shyness shattered his anger. And when she called him by his first name, a tendril of longing sang through him. Aly had a voice that would tame the fiercest of wild animals.

Clay had no idea who had given her the rose—a

fact that irritated him more than he cared to think about. But he wasn't going to let her think he'd given it to her. He opened his mouth to speak.

"Hey!"

Aly tensed at the sound of Starbuck's booming voice. She closed her eyes momentarily. Why did he have to show up just when there was a tentative truce between her and Clay?

Starbuck strode around to the front of the trainer, a triumphant grin on his face. He was dressed in tight-fitting G-suit chaps that hugged his lower body to masculine perfection. His helmet bulged beneath his left arm. A pair of red eagle wings had been painted on either side of it, and the name *Iron Eagle* was visible.

"Just thought I'd drop by, Cantrell, and visit your good-looking student." Jeff winked at Alyssa. "How's my favorite girl doing this morning?"

Clay glared at the fighter pilot. "Lieutenant, this trainer is off-limits to anyone not on the training roster."

The F-14 pilot's smile disappeared, his brown eyes hardening. "Ease off the throttles, Cantrell." He put back his winning smile for Alyssa's benefit, and patted the trainer. "I just wanted to steal a minute and get her reaction to the rose I left her."

"Oh, God," Aly blurted. She glanced over at Clay; his face was thundercloud-black with anger. Heat flamed from her neck into her face, and she wanted to die of mortification.

"A beautiful rose for a beautiful lady," Starbuck said. He turned to Clay. "For once, buddy, you lucked out. After that crash that took your RIO's life, I thought a black cloud was hanging over you. T'ain't so, anymore, is it? You've got this luscious-looking woman who's going to be flying with you. I'm jealous as hell, Cantrell."

Clay gripped the manual. It hurt to breathe. It hurt to feel. Starbuck's malicious attack reared memories of the crash and John's death. "Starbuck, get the hell out of here," he snarled softly.

Aly tensed, hearing the raw anger in Clay's voice. Instinctively, she reached out, her hand resting on his arm, as if to stop him from rising to climb out and hit the fighter pilot. She handed the rose back to Starbuck.

"Lieutenant, I don't approve of your tactics, either. Why don't you go play in the sky with your F-14? Mr. Cantrell and I have some serious work to do. I don't appreciate your barging in."

Starbuck took the rose, his expression suddenly stiff. He smiled, but his eyes were cold upon her. "Sure thing, Alyssa." He lifted the rose and gave them both a mock salute with it. "I'll see you later, boys and girls."

Aly suddenly remembered her grip on Clay's arm. She jerked her fingers away as if burned. The training room was quiet after Starbuck's departure.

"I'm sorry, Mr. Cantrell," Aly whispered, too embarrassed to meet his eyes. "I thought the rose was from you. It was a stupid assumption."

Clay's mouth softened as he watched Aly. He was just as embarrassed. If he was any kind of sensitive human being, he'd apologize to her. But apologies came hard when so much hurt and pain filled the past between them.

"Don't worry about it," he growled, trying to take the harshness out of his tone. He saw her head snap up, her eyes trained on him. Did he see tears in them? Swallowing against a sudden lump, Clay motioned toward the manual that he placed between them. "Starbuck's a pain in the ass sometimes."

"He's insensitive." Breathing with relief that Clay wasn't going to snarl at her, Aly was anxious to move ahead and forget her faux pas. What must Clay think of her now? His face was pale, his gray eyes narrowed and dark. He must be furious with her and it could mean only one thing: more tension and hatred vibrating between them for the duration of this training session. Suddenly, all her hope was destroyed and her exposed nerves jangled.

Clay handed her the copilot's preflight checklist. "Yeah, he's insensitive all right," he ground out.

Aly didn't dare mention Clay's crash. She saw the rawness in his eyes, and the terror from the past. There was no way she was going to wound Clay with that memory. Fumbling with the elastic strap around her leg, she managed to fit the small board on top of her thigh where she could flip through the plastic-coated pages in rapid succession. The silence was stilted and she muttered, "I don't like roses anyway."

"Oh?"

"I love irises. They're my favorite flower...." Aly's voice trailed off into a whisper. What was she saying? Clay didn't care what she liked or didn't like. He had to put up with her. "Never mind, I talk too much," she muttered.

Irises. Clay stole a glance over at Aly. Her cheeks were flushed bright red, almost matching her hair. Somehow, he had to help her settle down. Right now she was so damn tautly strung, she was ready to explode. *Get a hold on yourself, Cantrell. For once, don't jump down her throat.*

"Iris would look good with your hair color," he pointed out awkwardly, trying to establish some neutral ground with her.

Blinking once, Aly risked a look in Clay's direction. Had she heard right, or was she making up this conversation? Struck by the fact that all the darkness had disappeared from his gray eyes, Aly was thrown completely off guard. Clay's mouth had softened. There was so much happening so quickly. Aly avoided his penetrating gaze and tried to focus on the checklist. One moment he could be a bastard, the next, his voice was unhinging her, touching her aching heart with soothing reassurance. That same look of warmth lingered in his eyes—just as it had at their first meeting on the Bayshore.

Taking a shaky breath, Aly said, "I'm ready to start preflight procedures if you are, Mr. Cantrell."

Brusque and efficient. Good. Clay released a held breath, thankful to be on familiar territory once again. "Roger. Okay, let's walk through each page of the checklist. I'll do it slowly, and if you have any questions, stop me and we'll discuss them. Okay?" He drilled her with a look that demanded an answer.

Aly nodded. "Yes, sir." And then she cringed. Now she was behaving like a frightened student pilot with an inspector pilot back at Pensacola. She saw a slight grin ease Clay's set mouth.

"You can drop the 'yes, sir.' Call me by my last name."

Aly wanted to die of embarrassment. What must he think of her? That she was a silly, addled-brained woman so flustered that her emotions were getting in the way of the business at hand? Aly had no defense against him. Clay affected her so profoundly on so many new, awakening levels that she completely lost her usual composure every time she got around him. Forcing a slight smile, she nodded. "I'm ready to start, Mr. Cantrell."

Clay brought down the hood, locking it in place. "Okay, let's get this show on the road."

Two hours later, the hood latch was sprung and opened. Aly took a deep breath of fresh air, relieved to be released from the stuffy, smelly Link. She had sweated like a student pilot at Pensacola, the underarms of her flight suit wringing wet. Wrinkling her nose, she was sure Clay couldn't have helped but notice. There was no end to the humiliation she felt around him. First the rose debacle, and now her less than glorious performance under the hood.

Clay sat scribbling a number of notes on the clipboard resting against his thigh. The tension in the Link for the past two hours had been distressing. To both of them. Each time a green pilot trained in the Link, the IP had to assess and grade his or her performance. Aly had been strained, making the same mistakes over and over again. His conscience railed at him. *Let's face it, Cantrell, you weren't a good IP, either. All you did was snap at her for two hours straight.*

Whipped, her legs feeling weak, Aly climbed out of the cockpit. The feathery bangs across her brow were damp, sticking to her flesh. She had performed terribly. And judging from Clay's closed face, he was going to grade her without remorse. This was worse than the awful pressure applied to the fledgling student pilots at Pensacola. She'd had IPs who had screamed in her ear while she was flying the right-hand seat in the trainers. She'd had them badger her, taunt her, and she had stood up to them and graduated, despite their tactics to try to wash her out of the program.

Wiping her sweaty brow, Aly glanced toward the computer room. Chief Random gave her a game smile and a thumbs-up. That rallied her plummeting spirits, if only minimally. The chief would grade her performance, too. Maybe Random would be more understanding and lenient in his grade analysis than Clay would be.

God, if I keep screwing up like this, I'll never get approved to copilot. The thought tore deeply through Aly. She had fought for five years to get here. And today she'd been the worst she could ever remember behind the controls.

"Trayhern?"

Aly turned toward Clay, trying to shore up her shredded defenses to face his evaluation. Forcing herself to meet shore up her shredded defenses to face his evaluation. Forcing herself to meet his eyes, she stood, waiting for the guillotine to drop. "Yes?"

Clay leaned across the cockpit, handing her the clipboard so that she could read his comments and grading. He tried to take the harshness out his voice, noting how pale she'd become as she took the board. "If you've got any disagreement with my analysis, let's talk it over now, before I sign it off."

Taking the board in both hands, Aly tried to focus on his almost illegible scribble. What she cared about most were the four areas that she was graded upon. Her heart pounded once to underscore her disbelief.

Clay had given her seventy-five percent in all categories! Aly gasped, looking up at him.

"Well?" he goaded. "You got a problem with that, Trayhern?"

Elation leaked through her terror. Aly knew from being graded for a year at Pensacola that Clay was being generous with her. *Very* generous. She should have dragged a sixty percent, which was a failing grade. Instead he'd given her barely passing marks. Trying to read his scrawl and assessment, there was no indication of personal feelings being involved with his analysis of her abilities today.

"I—no, I don't," she whispered unsteadily.

Clay saw the life come back to her sky-blue eyes as she handed him the clipboard. Color had rushed back to her cheeks. She was excruciatingly vulnerable in that moment, and he had to stop himself from reaching out to caress her cheek. There was gratefulness in her luminous eyes. And that made his heart soar with an incredible sense of elation. And then he saw his dead mother's face waver before him, and he smashed all those fragile new emotions.

Clay glanced down at his watch. "You've been assigned to Commander Winger's office for collateral duty. He's expecting you any moment. You'd better get going."

Aly nodded, holding her manual tightly against her breasts. "I—right." She wanted to thank him for not failing her. But one look into those sharp gray eyes, and Aly swallowed her thanks.

Watching her go over to a chair to pick up her purse and garrison cap, Clay called, "Be here at 0800 tomorrow morning, Trayhern."

"Yes, sir—" Aly halted and gave him an apologetic shrug for slipping back into student-pilot vernacular. ''I mean, I'll be here, Mr. Cantrell.''

Grimly, Clay watched her leave. He packed up his manual and clipboard and climbed out of the Link. In the control room, Random handed him his grading sheet. The chief had given her seventy-five percent, too.

''Miss Trayhern was a little nervous,'' Random told him, as if to defend the percentile grade. ''Typical of a young pilot just coming out of Pensacola, wouldn't you say?''

''Typical,'' Clay agreed, signing off both sheets and handing them back to the chief.

''She's sharp, though,'' Random continued. ''I think once she settles down and realizes no one's out to sink her, she'll catch on fast.''

Clay grunted, putting his manual into the briefcase he always carried.

''You want the trainer set up for her tomorrow morning, Mr. Cantrell?''

Placing the garrison cap on his head, Clay nodded. ''Yes, I do.'' He walked to the door and opened it. ''Oh, one more thing, chief.''

''Yes, sir?''

''I want you to schedule Lieutenant Trayhern into an hour of cockpit training in a P3. Choose any one that's on the line that won't be flown that day. Assign AE Ballard to work with her. He's qualified on preflight, start-up and shutdown procedures. This week, starting Tuesday, have Ballard drill preflight procedures with her.''

Random nodded. ''She one of those people who do better in the real thing?'' he guessed. Some pilots never got used to a Link trainer. And yet in the cockpit of the actual aircraft, those same people performed flawlessly.

"I think so. I'll see you at 1400, chief."

Random nodded. The next student, a green lieutenant just out of Pensacola, was scheduled for that afternoon. "Yes, sir."

Where had the week flown? Clay wondered as he moved up the ladder of P3 number 7, where he knew Aly and Ballard were practicing in the cockpit. It was already Friday afternoon. He slowed his step as he entered the sub hunter parked out in the revetment area. Ballard was in the pilot's seat. Aly was in the copilot's seat. He stood listening to their bantering exchanges, watching her hands fly with knowing ease across the instrument panel. She'd flip a switch here, turn a dial there as Ballard called out each step. After a lousy start earlier in the week, Aly was now moving with typical Navy pilot confidence, her voice firm and sure.

Cantrell almost smiled, settling his hands on his hips, watching and listening. With the morning Link sessions and Ballard working with her every afternoon, Aly was becoming well acquainted with the P3. His heart blossomed with powerful feelings of pride toward her. And just as quickly, Clay tried to push them back down inside himself. Aly invited familiarity. He found himself longing to see her smile. Once, midweek, he'd heard in his office her beautiful laughter pealing down the hallway. It had sent a shaft of hot need through him. Would she ever laugh or smile like that for him?

He doubted it. Clay shoved his hands into his pockets, continuing to watch Ballard and Aly. There was excellent camaraderie between them. They kidded each other between maneuvers. Her laughter was breathy and light, lifting the darkness that haunted Clay. She was sunlight, he decided morosely. Sister of a murderer or not, she reminded him of anything but death.

"Not bad, Miss Trayhern," Dan congratulated Aly. "You know preflight blindfolded."

Aly flushed over his compliment and sat back, relaxing. The P3's windows were large and she could see the blue sky outside. The sun was bright, making the cockpit hot. "Thanks, Dan. You've been a wonderful teacher." She tipped her head in his direction, her eyes twinkling. "I couldn't have done it without you. I still haven't thanked you for asking Mr. Cantrell to let you help me every afternoon."

Dan's red eyebrows arched. "I didn't do anything, Miss Trayhern. That was Mr. Cantrell's idea in the first place."

Stunned, Aly sat up. "It was?"

Dan grinned, closing the large manual that sat on the throttle casing. "Yes, ma'am. I think he realized you relax in the real thing. A lot of pilots do poorly in those trainers. There's just something about them...."

Aly sat there, digesting Dan's answer. So Clay had been responsible for this. Mixed emotions threaded through her. He was so damn cold and distant with her in the Link. She would never have thought he had the sensitivity, much less the insight, to know that she trained better here. Again, he hid so much of his real self that Aly could never hope to understand him. Cantrell didn't want anyone to know anything about him.

"You know," Dan said, breaking into her thoughts, "I'll bet next week Mr. Cantrell might let you fly with us. We've got a training mission coming up next Wednesday. Maybe, if we can get you familiar on start-up and shutdown procedures, he'll give you that opportunity."

Aly rallied. "You think so?" Hope rang strong in her voice, and she didn't try to disguise her enthusiasm.

Dan collected the other manuals, leaning back to relax for a minute. "Don't see why not. Ol' number 7 here is ready to fly again."

"Number 7," Aly murmured softly. She reached over, affectionately patting the top of the instrument panel. "How can you call her that? She's so sleek and beautiful."

Scratching his head, Dan said, "Dunno. I guess you're right. Number 7 sounds pretty detached, doesn't it?"

"I've already given her a name," Aly admitted, watching Dan. He was almost like a big brother to her, and she enjoyed spending time with him.

"Yeah? What?"

"Promise you won't breath a word of it to anyone else, Dan?"

With a grin, he nodded. "Won't say a word, ma'am. Now what kind of name have you christened this gal with?"

Reaching over, Aly ran her fingers across the smooth yoke in front of her. "I call her Gray Lady, because she reminds me of an elegant swan ready to take off in flight."

Dan pursed his lips, giving the name some thought. "I like it, Miss Trayhern." And then he grinned, catching and holding her gaze. "See? I told you that having a woman on board would change things for the better."

Embarrassed because she'd divulged a piece of herself to Dan, Aly muttered, "Oh, I don't know about that. I still haven't met the rest of Mr. Cantrell's crew."

"You will shortly, Miss Trayhern."

Aly gasped, whirling around in the seat. Her eyes moved up…up into the shadowed face of Clay, who stood, his hands on his hips. Instead of finding the dark anger that usually hung in his eyes or in the set of his mouth, Aly saw momentary warmth there instead.

"H-how long have you been here?" she blurted.

Clay moved his gaze to Ballard, who nodded a greeting, unaffected by Clay's unexpected appearance. He returned his attention to Aly. She looked so damned enticing every time she blushed.

"Long enough," he answered.

She didn't dare ask what "long enough" meant. Had he heard her name for the P3? He'd probably use it against her in the future, or ruthlessly spread it around the squadron. Gathering her strewn thoughts, Aly got up. "We're done here, Mr. Cantrell. If you'll excuse me, I'll—"

Clay remained in her path so she couldn't move by him. "Have a seat, Miss Trayhern, we're not quite finished yet."

She didn't like the silky tone in his voice. This was something new. Aly gave Dan a quick look, and he appeared just as mystified.

"Dan, how about giving me my seat?"

"Yes, sir!"

Oh, no! Aly shut her eyes. Clay was going to quiz her!

When she reopened her eyes, she noticed a ground crew pulling up in a vehicle outside the aircraft. What was going on?

Clay strapped himself in and barely glanced at her. ''Miss Trayhern, I suggest you strap yourself back in.''

Dan grinned broadly and knelt behind the throttles. ''We going for a ride, sir?'' There was enthusiasm in his voice.

''I think Miss Trayhern's ready for her first flight, don't you, Dan?''

Happily, he nodded. ''She's an ace at preflight check, sir.''

Clay glanced over, positioning the board on his knee. ''Let's find out. Okay, Miss Trayhern, you ready to preflight this bird?''

They were going to taxi! Joy leaped through Aly. Learning how to fly a plane consisted of start-up, taxi and, finally, a first flight. Just getting the chance to taxi the P3 was more than Aly dared expect so soon in her training. She stared at Clay, disbelief, she was sure, written all over her face.

''Well?'' he drawled.

''I—yes…oh, yes, I'm ready, Mr. Cantrell.''

Ignoring the tremble of happiness in her voice, Clay nodded and briskly returned to the business at hand. Why should he feel light and pleased at her reaction? Her blue eyes literally danced. Getting to see her smile for the first time since their fated meeting made Clay realize just how unhappy Aly had been the past week. And just how much he longed to see that smile again.

Minutes flew by for Aly. Before she knew it, preflight was complete. She'd performed it perfectly. Her heart was pounding as Clay slowly took her through start-up procedure. Given the thumbs-up by the ground crew, he leaned over to start the first turboprop engine on the P3.

Aly held her breath as his Nomex-gloved fingers depressed the start button on engine number three. The whirling whine of the prop began. She felt a shiver run through Gray Lady as the engine caught and moved smoothly to life. Clay repeated the procedure, starting engine number two, on her side of the aircraft.

"Okay, you start the last two," he ordered.

Eagerly, Aly repeated his steps. A thrill moved through her as all four of the P3's engines moved in rpm unison. A smile curved her lips, and she looked over at Clay.

"She feels good. Solid."

Clay understood what Aly meant. The P3 was a reliable plane with heart. "Ready to taxi?"

Aly nodded. Her heart was in her throat as Cantrell waved the ground crew off to one side.

"Use throttle two and three in the center there, to taxi her. Bring up power slow, and watch your rpm gauges."

Placing her gloved hand over the two center throttles, Aly looked to her right and then left. "Clear to taxi?"

"Roger, clear," Clay confirmed. He felt Aly's unbridled excitement and it lifted his gloom. Her face was flushed with delight, her eyes shining with life. God, but she was excruciatingly beautiful. He tore his gaze from her profile, keeping his booted feet near the rudders.

Aly gently applied right rudder, inching the throttles forward, increasing rpm just a bit. *Come on, Gray Lady, work with me. Give yourself to me...please....*

The P3 rolled smoothly out of its revetment berth, moving slowly down the concrete ramp, the turboprop engines whining.

"You're doing fine," Clay assured her.

Another thrill went through Aly and she nodded, keeping her attention focused between the ramp and the engine instruments.

As they neared the end of the taxi area, Aly began to ease back on the throttles and apply rudder brakes to slow down the aircraft.

"What are you doing?" Clay asked.

She gave him a confused look. "Well, you just wanted me to taxi it, didn't you?"

"I said we're going to fly."

Her heart leaped. "Fly?"

It was impossible not to smile. Clay placed his hand over hers, easing the throttles a bit more forward. "Let's take Gray Lady to the end of the runway, and I'll walk you through a takeoff. We'll take a few circuits of the flight pattern and some touch and gos. That will be plenty for you today."

Aly wanted to cry with exultation. That one smile, and the thawing of his gray eyes, made her heart somersault with euphoria. His hand was firm, guiding hers, as he taught her how to delicately monitor the engine throttles. And he had heard her call the plane Gray Lady! But he hadn't been disgusted by it. There was, for the first time, a hint of admiration and respect toward her in his voice.

It was a dream, Aly told herself, as they sat at the end of the runway, ready to take the bird aloft. Her hand just barely spanned the four throttles as they sat there, Clay's hand firmly across her own. For once, she was glad he was in physical contact with her. She needed his assurance and support.

"Okay, everything checks out," Clay told her, catching her attention out of the corner of his eye. "I'm going to let you push the rudders and keep her nose down the centerline. You make the actual takeoff. I'll keep my hand over yours to teach you the art of talking to these throttles."

Aly nodded, licking her lower lip. "Roger." Her voice was trembling. But it wasn't out of fear, it was out of anticipation.

"We've got clearance. Let's roll, Miss Trayhern. Rotation speed is 120 miles per hour."

"Roger. Starting to roll..."

Aly's world narrowed to awareness of her boots delicately pressed against the rudders to keep the plane's nose on the centerline of the airstrip. Clay's hand guided hers, and he pushed all four throttles slowly forward until they were against the fire wall. The P3's four engines were fairly screaming around them. Gray Lady vibrated, as if she were a thoroughbred trembling to break the gate and race her heart out.

"Releasing rudders," Aly called out.

"Roger, we're rolling." Clay kept his left hand near the yoke, but didn't touch it. He would not interfere in her takeoff unless it became critical. It was important that Aly be able to have a clear victory in her battle to attain copilot status. Clay grinned to himself at the way she played the aircraft. She had it. She had the right stuff.

Gray Lady moved faster and faster down the strip, the huge blades cutting through the invisible air. She lightened as takeoff speed approached. Wind moved powerfully beneath her long, graceful wings. Aly felt the aircraft strain to break contact with the earth. She kept her hand on the yoke, and the nose remained on the ground. The moment the speed gauge hit 120, she gently eased back on the column.

They were airborne! Aly gasped as the P3 launched skyward in one graceful leap, the engine whine deepening as they climbed.

''Good takeoff,'' Clay told her in his normal IP tone. ''Now level off at fifteen hundred feet and make a ninety-degree left turn.''

She listened to his steady, calm voice. Gray Lady was incredibly responsive to her every command! So much more sensitive than any other plane she'd ever flown. Wanting to please Clay because he was going beyond the call of duty and giving her extra training, Aly worked hard.

Clay had her lightly hold the yoke, keep her feet on the rudders and her hand on the throttles as he showed her how to land the P3. It was a light, three-point landing, kissing the deck like a lover.

''Lift her off,'' he ordered Aly the instant the wheels touched the airstrip.

The second time around, Aly got her chance to land the aircraft for the first time. With the long, extended tail boom, the pilot couldn't come in nose high, or the boom would scrape against the airstrip, causing major damage to the aircraft. A three-wheel landing was demanding in comparison to the normal two-wheel landing of other types of planes. Aly worked the rudders, jockeying the P3 into the correct landing angle. Clay's hand covered hers on the throttles, helping her to monitor the incoming speed.

They were down! The P3 bumped, but not hard. Aly didn't have time to do any celebrating, because Clay immediately ordered her to take off again.

After the third landing, Aly had a good sense of positioning with the P3, and the fourth was her best. She grinned.

Clay nodded. "Nice landing, Miss Trayhern. All right, let's taxi Gray Lady back to her berth. She's worked well for us today."

"Nice landing!" Dan Ballard said, giving Aly a slap on the back as they taxied back to the revetment area.

Flushed with victory, she looked at both men after they had parked and the chocks had been placed beneath each wheel by the ground crew. "Thanks," she whispered, meaning it. "Between the two of you, I don't have any choice but to become a good copilot."

Ballard got up from his position behind the throttles. He chuckled and placed his set of earphones to one side. "Miss Trayhern, you aren't going to be just a good copilot, you're going to be a great one."

Stunned by Dan's assessment, Aly blinked. She unstrapped, nervously wondering what Clay thought of her performance.

"Isn't that right, Mr. Cantrell?" Dan asked, standing in the aisle, waiting for them.

Clay tried to ignore the bliss in Aly's eyes. He'd never seen her so joyful. More than anything, he wanted to drown in those azure eyes shining with gold highlights. Each of her breathy laughs he'd absorbed like a starving man. "Yeah, she's going to be a good addition to the crew, Dan," he said, climbing out of the seat and straightening up in the interior of the aircraft.

Nothing could dampen Aly's spirits as she got up and followed the two men out. Once on the concrete, she turned and reached up, patting the P3 with great affection. *Thanks,* she silently told the stalwart aircraft.

Ballard had gone on to the hangar. But as Aly turned, she saw Clay standing there, an odd look on his face. Avoiding his piercing look, she walked over to him. "I just wanted to thank her for giving us such a good flight."

"I see." Clay checked his normally long stride so that she wouldn't have to run to keep up with him.

The wind was blowing off the marshes, lifting strands of her red hair. Aly brushed several from her eyes, still breathless over the flight. "I know you probably think it's strange to name an aircraft or think of it as a living thing, but I do."

"I never said I disagreed with you."

Aly laughed softly, her step light. "Then you don't mind if I call her Gray Lady?"

Clay shook his head. Part of him wanted this heady moment to last forever. The other part of him said it wasn't right: Aly's brother had cold-bloodedly murdered Stephen. He studied Aly's upturned face. Was she a traitor, too? Would she cut and run when the chips were down? How would she handle the nerve-racking tension of hunting a Soviet sub, flying fifty feet above the grasping fingers of a fickle ocean?

"I just wonder, Trayhern, if you can stand the heat

in the kitchen. Your brother couldn't.'' He saw her eyes narrow with sudden and unexpected pain. ''Today, you did okay flying. But what will you do when things get tight? Will you run? Flip out? Break under the strain? What?''

Aly hung her head, wrestling with incredible anguish. Her earlier joy shattered like glass beneath a sledgehammer. She looked back up at Clay, wondering if he honestly felt that way. Or was she just too much a reminder of the past, every new experience bringing out some facet of his old memories? She drew to a halt, holding his bleak gray gaze.

''You think I'm a coward, don't you?'' she demanded softly.

''I don't know what to think of you,'' Clay admitted. ''One member of your family ran when the chips were down. How do I know you won't, too?''

Defiantly, Aly placed her hands on her hips, her voice riddled with anger. ''I guess we're both going to find out, aren't we, Mr. Cantrell?''

Clay's shoulders slumped in sudden exhaustion. He didn't want to fight with her, but there was no other way with them. ''Sooner or later, we will.''

Aly's mouth tightened. ''Thanks for the ride today, Cantrell. At least you know I won't lose my nerve on a simple takeoff and landing. That ought to make you sleep better at night!'' And she stormed off toward the hangar, fighting the hot tears that threatened to fall.

Chapter Five

"Stuck with the duty on a Friday night, Miss Trayhern?"

Aly looked up from behind the duty officer's desk. It was five o'clock, and Dan Ballard, like nearly everyone else, was ready to go home. She smiled.

"Afraid so, Dan."

"It's a lousy Friday night, anyway. April rains, and all." He scowled. "I suppose you're gonna study that manual in front of you?"

"Right again. You know me too well."

The red-haired engineer grinned. "Four months in Gray Lady with you has helped, ma'am." He opened the door. "Hope it's a quiet watch for you. I'll see you Monday morning."

"Roger that, Dan," Aly agreed. She watched the lanky engineer quietly shut the door. Through the office window, she could see the cavernous inside of

Hangar One. A number of P3s, in for general maintenance, stood silently.

Had four months really flown by? Aly had lost track of time, buried in learning the art of flying the P3 and nonstop studying of so many manuals concerned with sub hunting. Just a week ago, she'd been approved for copilot status. Now she'd be flying every mission with Clay and his crew. Happiness simmered in Aly as she leafed through the first pages of the manual on sonobuoys. *I've made it.* Aly savored the thought. Through four months of hell with Clay, she'd made it, despite their impasse over the issue of Morgan.

Clay... Closing her eyes, she pictured his face before her. Her dad had been right; Clay had lost most of his virulent anger toward her. By the end of the first month, the worst of the snipes and barbs had ended. The more she'd proved she could fly, and fly well, the less vitriolic he'd become. Still, he would take shots at her from time to time. He didn't trust her to come through in a crisis; it was that simple.

Sighing, Aly stared down at the manual, not seeing the words. For three months Clay had been a fortress of silence. He never traded a smile or a joke with her as he did with the rest of his crew. They worshiped the ground Clay walked on because of his unique abilities to relate easily with each man. In the cockpit, he was cool and emotionless with her, and that hurt.

"Let's face it, Trayhern, you like him and he hates you." Still, she stood in awe of Clay, because in the cockpit, he never allowed his personal feelings to interfere with their demanding teamwork while flying.

Sometimes she could have sworn she saw burning longing in his eyes when she looked up unexpectedly at him. Sometimes it was the softening of his mouth. Little things…but each time, it made her heart ache. Dammit, she *liked* Cantrell! There wasn't much not to like about the man, Aly decided glumly. He was a good officer, a fair man, and unlike what Starbuck's malicious gossip had suggested, Clay wasn't losing it behind the yoke. He was one of the finest pilots she'd had the honor of flying with, and he was teaching her to strive for that same level of skill.

Anger simmered through Aly as she thought of Starbuck. From Dan, she'd found out why Gray Lady had sustained landing gear damage. Clay had landed her with one engine on fire in the middle of a rare thunderstorm over the Bay Area. Dan had told her the truth—that without Cantrell's years of experience as a pilot, his extraordinary skill and sheer bravado, they would have crashed. At the last possible second, with an in-flight emergency in progress, there had been a wind shear across the airstrip they were to land on. The P3 dived earthward, and according to Dan's account, Clay had grabbed the yoke, slammed hard left rudder and settled the aircraft in just like a jet landing on a carrier. If it hadn't been for his carrier landing experience, they would have crashed. They'd walked away from that one, all twelve of them, with only a damaged landing strut.

"Hey!"

Aly's head snapped up. Starbuck, in his khaki uniform, had poked his head through the opened door. "What do you want?" she asked unencouragingly.

With a genial smile, Starbuck entered the office and closed the door. He settled the garrison cap at a cocky angle on his head. "Just dropping by to say hello to the prettiest lady at Moffett."

"Stow it, Jeff. I'm wise to you." The words came out with disgust, but Aly didn't care. If she had believed anything the fighter jock had said about Clay, it would have been dangerous to her own flight career. She would have mistrusted Clay at the controls, creating even more strain between them.

"Aw, come on, Alyssa. If I didn't know better, I'd think you're turning into a sourpuss just like your lover boy."

Rage snapped through her, and she raised her lashes, glaring at him. "That's uncalled for, Starbuck. Or is that the latest nasty gossip you're passing around the base?"

Starbuck shrugged. "So you're not denying it?"

"What?"

"You two are lovers?"

"Stop being ridiculous! I fly with Cantrell, I don't sleep with him!"

Jeff rubbed his chin, inspecting her closely. "I don't know, Alyssa...you've been on board here for four months and you don't have a boyfriend that any of us can tell. The only dude you spend time with is Cantrell...."

"Starbuck, why don't you toddle on over to the O Club like you do every Friday night, and get drunk? It's what you do best."

His brown eyes danced with amusement. "You're so much fun to bait, Alyssa. Hey! Guess who I saw pulling up over at the O Club earlier?"

She sat back in the chair, her arms crossed over her chest. How someone so handsome could have such a mean streak in him was beyond Aly. Starbuck's winning smile and geniality were a cover for his ruthless, competitive nature. "I have a feeling you're going to tell me, whether I want to know or not.''

Opening the door, Jeff said, ''Your lover, Cantrell. Didn't you know he hits the bottle every Friday night? Sits in a dark corner and nurses a couple rounds of Scotch, looking moody. He must be pining away for you....''

''Get out of here!'' Alyssa said, rising to her feet. ''And take your filthy mouth with you. I'm tired of listening to it, Starbuck.''

He threw her a salute. ''Later, Alyssa.'' And he disappeared into the passageway, whistling gaily.

''Damn him,'' Aly ground out, slamming the manual shut. Starbuck was dangerous. He was a gossiper, and it could hurt her career if anyone believed half the garbage he spread around the station. Ever since she'd made it clear she wouldn't go out with him, Starbuck had waged a campaign to get even.

Going into the back room, which had a cot for sleeping purposes, and a coffee maker, Aly poured herself a cup. After she calmed down, her heart and mind zeroed in on the fact that Clay spent Friday nights drinking over at the O Club. He was so damned alone. He wore those walls around himself like a good friend, she thought angrily. What was he running from? And why did that haunted look always hover in his dark gray eyes?

Clay blinked twice before he could read the hands on his watch. The corner where he sat was dark, and the luminous dial wavered in front of him. He had to stare at it a long time before realizing it was 0100. Good, he wasn't feeling any more pain. No, that wasn't it. He wasn't feeling any more longing for Aly.

A silly smile stretched across his face as he leaned the chair onto its back legs. He watched with disinterest as pilots hustled the women who frequented the club, wanting to snag a fighter jock. The bar was crowded—wall-to-wall bodies—and a haze of smoke hung over the place. Tonight, Clay realized in some dim portion of his slowly functioning mind, he'd really drunk far too much. He watched the single women in miniskirts hunting the eligible pilots. It was a game he never wanted to play. And that was all it was: a game.

Aly's face hovered in front of him. Savagely he rubbed his eyes, trying to erase her image. Dammit! As drunk as he was, she *still* haunted him. Frustrated, he tipped his head back and rested it against the walnut paneling behind him.

How the hell could he reconcile that he liked her, wanted her in every way, with the fact that she was the sister of a murderer? Trying to ignore her breathy laughter and the gold highlights in her blue eyes when she was happy was impossible. The past four months had turned into a twisted sort of hell for him. He'd thought it would be easy to hate Aly. Instead, he was drawn so damn powerfully to her. Her easygoing nature had a quiet, calming effect on everyone during tense cockpit situations, and she had an innate ability to get along with the crew. Clay found himself unable to remain immune to her any longer.

Aly was a thoughtful, caring person by nature, Clay sourly admitted. How many times had he been sitting in the left-hand seat and she'd come back on board after the visual inspection of the aircraft? The men at the consoles all had greetings for her when she boarded. Clay watched enviously as Aly bestowed a sunny smile here, a pat on the shoulder there, and shared a joke with someone else. And then he'd watch the joy dissolve from her face as she approached the cockpit. Aly, the *real* Aly, would die before him.

She would take the right-hand seat, her face closed, her voice devoid of feeling, and begin working in tandem with him. And he'd discovered that hate wasn't the comfortable companion he'd thought it would be. It had been his fault: he'd come out firing the first salvos at Aly. God knew, she'd tried a number of times in the first two months to make amends and establish a truce between them.

But Clay hadn't allowed it. And he didn't know why. Every excruciating minute spent with Aly made him feel the sharpened hunger just to have her smile at him. He ached to kiss those beautifully formed lips. Were they as soft as he imagined they were? As soft as her heart? There was so much tenderness in Aly. Clay saw it in little ways, important ways.

Dan Ballard had turned thirty-five a month ago, and Aly had gone to great lengths to hold a surprise birthday party for him. And then when Sam Henderson's wife had a baby, it had been Aly who'd come around gathering money for a gift for the mother and new daughter. Little things counted a lot with her, he was discovering, and Clay liked her for it. She was family-oriented and loyal to family. And the crew was her extended family. All except for him…

The pain throbbing in his chest was growing as his thoughts centered on Aly. Surprised that the liquor hadn't dulled his pain as it usually did, Clay pushed himself unceremoniously to his feet. He staggered, falling against the wall to steady himself. Dizziness nearly felled him. He saw the bar manager, Bob Hudson, give him a concerned look, watching from beneath his bushy gray eyebrows. Pressing both hands flat against the unyielding surface, Clay waited until the worst of the vertigo had passed. Then he stumbled out of the corner and raised his hand in farewell to Hudson. The manager nodded a good-night.

The rain had stopped, leaving the air fragrant with newly sprouted grass and leaves. Clay inhaled, weaving drunkenly toward his Corvette in the parking lot. Aly had the duty tonight.... He groaned. Where had that thought come from? How many times had he almost driven to Hangar One to talk with her when she had the duty? And how many times had he stopped himself?

Leaning heavily against his black Corvette, Clay fumbled to find the keys in his pocket. The asphalt gleamed beneath the lights. The ground blurred and that same tidal wave of dizziness hit him again. He threw his hands outward, trying to steady himself, but his feet got tangled and he slipped, hitting the pavement hard. Gasping, he lay there several minutes, completely disoriented.

Stupid, he thought with disgust as he found himself sprawled across the wet asphalt, flat on his face. God, if anyone saw him like this, he'd never live it down. *Drank too damn much. Got to get out of here....* As he rolled over and propped himself into a sitting position against the sports car, he shut his eyes. Aly! *God, I need to talk with you so much it hurts. I need—*

''Hey, this is a pretty picture!''

Clay dragged his eyes open. There, in the shadowy light, stood Starbuck. ''Get the hell out of here,'' he mumbled.

But Starbuck came and squatted in front of him, grinning lopsidedly. "Well, well, what do you know. You finally drank too much, eh, Cantrell? Trying to drink away your frustration, buddy? Won't Alyssa give you any?"

Anger flared to life in Clay's foggy mind. "I hope like hell you say that when I'm sober, Starbuck."

Grinning and rising to his feet, Starbuck laughed. "You won't even remember our little chat come tomorrow morning, Cantrell." And he ambled back toward the O Club.

The phone rang, waking Aly. She threw off the lightweight wool blanket and blindly reached for the phone next to the cot.

"Duty Office, Lieutenant Trayhern speaking."

"This is Bob Hudson, bar manager of the O Club, Lieutenant."

She groaned, looking at her watch. It was 0130. "Yes?" What could he possibly want with her?

"I just got a report from one of my people that Lieutenant Cantrell is drunk out in the O Club parking lot. He's so intoxicated that he can't walk, much less drive. I know he flies with VP 46, that's why I called. If shore patrol comes by and finds him lying out there, he'll be in a lot of hot water. You'd better get over here and rescue his rear before they do."

"Thanks, Mr. Hudson. I'll get over there right away." Damn! Struggling into her sensible black shoes, Aly stood. She was wearing her black jacket and slacks. Throwing her black tie around the collar of her white blouse, she headed for the front office. She didn't want Clay picked up by the shore patrol, the station's military police. The damned fool! Grabbing the keys to the duty officer vehicle, she left a message with the the officer of the day at the main gate, informing him that she'd be away from the office for about fifteen minutes.

The gray vehicle started right up. The rain had stopped, and Aly spotted a few stars between the clouds as she drove around the end of the runway, heading toward the central portion of Moffett Field.

To her dismay, she found Clay sleeping in a slouched position against his sports car. He looked like a rumpled Raggedy Andy, and her heart went out to him. His khaki uniform had huge water stains across it, indicating where he'd fallen to the asphalt. As Aly got out, her alarm increased. He had skinned his elbow pretty badly, with blood drying on his lower arm and fingers. But he didn't appear to be feeling any pain.

Stooping, Aly placed her hand on his shoulder, giving him a gentle shake. "Clay? Clay, wake up!"

Clay realized he was dreaming. A smile tugged at the corners of his mouth. This was nice: Aly's husky voice so close to his ear. He actually felt the warmth of her hand on his shoulder. God, but she felt good. Inhaling deeply, he smelled that fragrance she always wore.

"Clay! Dammit, wake up! You can't sit out in the middle of the parking lot like this."

Drowsily, he dragged his lashes upward. Aly's shadowed and concerned face danced before him. "Aly?"

She winced. He'd never called her that before. "You're drunker than hell, Cantrell."

"I-is that really you?" And then he grinned, lifting his bloodied hand toward her to find out.

Aly caught his hand, placing it firmly on his thigh. "Yes, it's me, you damn fool. Can you get up? Walk?"

His brain wasn't functioning at all. He scowled, looking up into her face. Her eyes were so large. She was so pretty. "Wh-what's going on?"

"Bob Hudson called me over at the duty office," and she explained the rest of it to him. Grimly, Aly slipped her arm around his back, placing her hand beneath his arm. "If shore patrol finds us, you'll get written up so fast it'll make that head of yours spin faster than it's already going. Come on, push up with your legs, I've got to get you the hell out of here."

Her words ran together in Clay's drugged mind. He barely comprehended one-quarter of what she was saying, but Aly's arm felt good around him, and he tried to follow her angry orders, pushing upward. He rose unsteadily, his weight resting heavily on her. Dizziness assailed him.

"God, Cantrell," Aly groaned, staggering beneath his weight, "you're too damned heavy! Straighten up! I can't carry you!"

Trying, Clay stood on his own two feet, wavering badly. He grinned at her. "See? I made it."

"Don't be so proud of yourself, jet jock. The next task is to get you into the duty vehicle."

Happiness flittered through Clay. This was all a dream. It had to be! Smiling gallantly, he gestured toward the vehicle. "Lead the way, ma'am!"

It was a tussle getting Clay into the passenger seat. He was like limp spaghetti, and Aly had to keep snapping orders at him to get him to react. After placing the seat belt around him, she climbed in. The front of her uniform was smeared with oil, water and dark blood. Angry over Clay's stupid decision to get drunk, she drove back to Hangar One.

"Where we going?" Clay slurred.

"I'm putting you on the duty office cot where you can sleep off your drunk, Cantrell." She glared over at him. "You pulled a stupid stunt. What if Starbuck caught you out in the parking lot. Aren't you concerned that he'll spread it around Moffett?"

Chuckling, Clay shook his head. "He did—I think.... Besides, that bastard wouldn't dare. He knows I'd clean his clock for 'im...."

"Boys," Aly muttered between clenched teeth. "You're all little boys. Clay, I could just strangle you! This is a bad image for you, for all of us. Just what the hell did you think you were doing?"

Her voice was low with fury, but Clay absorbed the huskiness of it. He closed his eyes, fumbling for her hand. Once he found it, he gave it a squeeze. "I was just trying to forget, Aly."

Her heart lurching in her breast, Aly pulled her hand free of his, concentrating on driving. Clay's action startled her. "Forget what?"

With a dramatic sigh, Clay made a wobbly gesture toward her. "You, of course."

Shock replaced her anger. "Me?" Of course, he hated her twenty-four hours a day. It was probably eating him up inside to have to work with her.

"Yeah," he answered thickly, staring over at her profile. "You..."

Real pain wove through Aly. "Look, we're just going to have to put our past behind us, Clay. I know you hate me. You hate my family, but you can't keep resurrecting it like this. If you're drinking every Friday night to escape the fact that you hate me, then—"

"I drink to forget you...."

She traded a quick glance with him. Strands of hair dipped across his brow, and she could see that haunted look back in his eyes once again. "I know," she answered softly. "Hate does terrible things to people, Cantrell. I wish I knew how to get you to turn it off toward me."

"N-no..." He lapsed into unconsciousness, limp against the seat.

"Great!" Aly muttered. She, too, had gone on the occasional bender over the years just to relieve the terrible tension she'd lived under. But she'd quickly learned that drinking was no escape. Judging from Cantrell's condition, he'd really be in the hurt locker for the rest of this night and well into tomorrow. Well, she had the duty until noon tomorrow. Maybe by then she could get him sober enough to drive back to his own apartment and lie around for the rest of the weekend recovering from his monumental stupidity.

The next time Clay regained consciousness, he found himself sprawled across a cot. The overhead light hurt his eyes and he squinted. "Hey," he called weakly, "what's going on?"

Aly leaned over him, still breathing hard from practically carrying him from the car into the office and to the cot. "Shut up, Cantrell." She jerked his tie open at his neck and undid the top button of his long-sleeved khaki shirt. When she saw his eyes dilate and settle on her, she softened her voice. "You're dead drunk, Clay. Just lie still, okay? You're safe here."

Safe... Aly's words flowed across him. She was leaning over him, her face inches from his as she worked the knot of the tie loose, and then began to unbutton his shirt. "Aly?"

Aly's fingers froze over the second button. Risking a look at him, she felt her heart give way. Clay's face was vulnerable-looking, without any of the previous walls to hide his real feelings, his real emotions. She tried to brace herself for his hatred, his anger. "What is it this time, Clay?"

"D-did I ever tell you how pretty you are?" His voice was thick, the words mumbled badly. He smiled into her shadowed blue eyes. "I know you hate my guts, but I think you're the prettiest lady I've ever run into...."

Aly's fingers trembled, and she couldn't get the second button undone. Her voice faltering, she whispered, "I've never hated you, Clay. Ever."

Clay scowled. As drunk as he was, he felt Aly's fingers trembling against his chest. "You—don't hate me?"

"No. Never did." She nailed him with a dark look. "You hate *me*, remember?"

He lapsed back into semi-consciousness, relief surging through him. "You don't hate me...."

"Cantrell, you're one sick puppy. Just lie there and shut up! I want to get this shirt off you so I can look at the cut on your elbow."

Once his shirt was unbuttoned, Aly moved around the cot and slipped her arm beneath his shoulders. "Sit up, Clay."

He was weak, and grateful for her help. "You're one hell of a person," he told her as she helped him sit up and take off the shirt.

"God, I don't know if I can take all these compliments from you, Cantrell. The past four months you've had nothing but bad things to say about me.'' She dropped the shirt over a chair and pulled the first-aid kit from a nearby drawer. Her heart wrenched when she sat down, facing Clay. He looked so lost and confused. Without thinking, she brushed errant strands of hair off his perspiring brow.

''I have plenty of compliments for you,'' he confided softly.

Examining his right elbow, Aly grimaced. ''Well, if you do, you've been keeping them all to yourself, Cantrell. Hold still, this is going to hurt,'' she said, and she gently applied a warm, soapy cloth to the bloody laceration.

A dull pain drifted up his arm, but Clay was barely aware of it. She was so close, so fragrant and warm. ''You make my pain go away....''

Aly tried to steel herself against his admission. ''That's all we have between us, isn't it, Clay? Pain? Bad memories? I don't see how I make your pain go away. These past four months, you've made me out to be the biggest pain in existence.''

He swallowed hard, focusing on her gentle touch, the warmth of her fingers as she held his arm to doctor it up. ''That's—my fault. I was looking for a fight.''

''I know you were. And you know something, Clay?''

''What?'' He longed to reach over and stroke her hair—to find out if it was really as silky as he thought it might be.

Aly brushed some hair from her eyes. Being this close to Clay, knowing how much he affected her, was sheer agony. And now his voice was like balm to her shredded emotions. They were talking, they were close, even if he was drunk. Come morning, Aly was sure he wouldn't remember any of this. He'd wake up just as cold and distant as before. She hungered for what she instinctively knew they could share with each other. But Clay's natural warmth and dark voice were what she craved, and right now he was giving them to her. "I'm tired of fighting you," she admitted quietly.

Reaching out with his other hand, Clay settled it on the crown of her hair, running his fingers through the clean, coppery strands. "I know," he whispered. Her head snapped up, her eyes wide and startled. Giving her a slight smile, Clay admitted, "So am I."

Taking in a shaky breath, Aly closed her eyes. She'd never dared dream of this! Of Clay touching her as if she were some priceless, fragile object to be cared for. Each trembling touch of his fingers across her hair sent a widening ache through her. Her mind screamed at her to stop him. He was drunk, and therefore not in charge of his emotions. But each caress was healing to Aly. She held his injured arm between her hands and bowed her head, unable to speak, only to feel.

"Look," Clay muttered, sliding his fingers across Aly's high cheekbone, feeling the softness of her flesh, "I don't hate you, okay?" He lifted her chin, stunned by the tears that made her eyes luminous. He saw such pain in them that he winced. "It was my fault, Aly...all of it...." He cupped her cheek, holding her wavering stare. "I couldn't help but hate you, hate what your name stood for."

"I—I know. And I never blamed you for it, Clay." His touch was incredibly light, but she felt the warmth of his palm and saw the tenderness burning deep in his eyes.

He shook his head. "I still can't separate you from the past. As much as I want to, I can't. At least...not yet. But I'm trying."

She nodded mutely, her heart tearing open a little more. "I—I understand—" A sob caught in her throat, strangling off the rest of her reply.

Clay watched two tears streak down her pale, freckled cheeks. He groaned, understanding the volume of the pain he'd caused her. "I'm sorry...so sorry...." He leaned forward, drawing her to him.

Aly's breath snagged at Clay's unexpected move. When his mouth, warm and inviting, moved across her parted lips, all of her anguish dissolved. His mouth was tentative, testing her, relishing her softness. Her mind screamed at her to push away from him. Her heart, which had bled so long without any real sustenance, pleaded with her to consummate the kiss.

A groan started deep within Clay as Aly's lips grew pliant and willing beneath his hungry exploration. God, she tasted so sweet! So warm and feminine. Lost in the texture and liquid treasure of her mouth, Clay slid his arm around her shoulders, drawing her against him. This was what he'd dreamed of for so long! That luscious mouth of hers moving in hungry accord with his own, matching, meeting his escalating desire.

Hunger swept through Aly. Real hunger. She drowned in the heated strength of his mouth cajoling hers. All her pain, their pain, disappeared in that one molten moment torn out of time. As his tongue caressed her lower lip, she trembled with the real fire raging within her. His breath was hot and moist against her cheek, and with her fingers, she caressed the thick, black hair at his nape. Oh, God, Clay was so strong and yet tender with her. His kiss seared her soul, brought her into wild, yearning life and shattered every barrier that had ever been erected between them.

"Sweet," he whispered against her wet lips. "You're so sweet and kind, Aly." He kissed each corner of her mouth. "I'd die to see you smile. I die every time I hear your laughter." Clay held her close, kissing her damp lashes, inhaling her own special womanly scent. "I'm starving for you...I need you, my sweet woman of fire...."

The duty office was quiet once again, all lights extinguished. Only the shadows and dim light from the hangar stabbed weakly through the window. Aly sat at the desk, staring into the darkness, her heart an open, bleeding wound. For the past three hours, she'd sat there alone, thinking...feeling.

Her arms wrapped around herself because she was feeling nakedly vulnerable after Clay's kiss, Aly tried to sort through the emotions he'd unleashed within her. It was impossible, she decided bleakly. Reaching up, she touched her lips gently, remembering Clay's powerful kiss, which had brought her to brightly burning life. His woman of fire... The words haunted her, taunted her, teased her. If only she could be! If only...

But reality told her differently. It was nearly 0500. Soon sunrise would come, and with daylight would come the harsh truth. Clay would wake from his drunken stupor, remembering neither what he'd said to her nor their kiss. He'd go on treating her just as before. Rubbing her aching brow, Aly let the tears fall unhindered. She sniffed, taking another tissue from the box she'd set on the corner of the desk. How much stock could she put in Clay's drunken admission? Did he really not hate her any longer? Was he just as tired of their battle as she was?

Exhausted, Aly raised her tearstained face, staring sightlessly out the window. Worst of all, she had discovered in that sweet moment out of time that she was in love with Clay Cantrell. And that discovery hurt worse than any other. How it had happened, when it had happened, Aly couldn't say. Maybe it had happened on their first meeting. Who knew? Pressing her hand against her eyes, Aly cried softly for herself and for Clay. He would never know of her love. He would never accept her love. Love couldn't turn hatred around. But this one tender, searching kiss had ripped away the truth that lay in her heart: she loved him. Unequivocally. And that was something she'd have to bear the rest of her life alone.

At 0600 Clay regained consciousness and got sick. Aly awakened from her restless slumber, head resting in her arms on the desk. Turning on the light to the bunk room, she found him in the bathroom. All her fears, her apprehension melted when she found him leaning weakly against the basin, pale and shaky.

"Hold on," she whispered, grabbing a cloth and wetting it. Her heart twinged with fear when he lifted his head, his dark eyes upon her.

He said nothing as she gently wiped his nose and mouth as a mother would her child's. She got him a cup of water, and he took it in his shaking hand.

"Slosh it around in your mouth and spit it out," she told him, keeping her arm around him. He was incredibly weak, and she strengthened her grip to steady him as he followed her directions.

"Good," she soothed, taking the cup from his hand. "Come on, you need to get back to bed."

Clay placed his arm around Aly's small shoulders, leaning heavily upon her. His mind spun, and he was totally disoriented. "Where?" he managed to rasp, resting his head against her soft hair.

Aly told him, guiding him back to the cot. His uniform was soaked with sweat, and he was shivering. "You've really tied one on," she muttered.

Collapsing back on the cot, Clay shut his eyes, and the room spun wildly. He threw an arm across them. "I—don't remember coming here...."

Aly tucked him in. "With as much as you drank, I'm surprised you even remember your name."

He was feeling too sick to respond. After she shut off the light, he muttered, "Thanks..." and fell back into a deep sleep.

The next time Clay awoke, clarity was there. The room was quiet, and his gaze moved slowly toward the entrance. The door leading into the duty office was open. His mouth tasted like mothballs, and the pain at his temples was like massive hammers striking blows inside his head. It was agony to move.

Slowly events of the night before trickled through his clogged mind. He lay very still, vividly remembering his conversation with Aly. And their kiss. He groaned softly. Sweet God in heaven, he'd kissed her! The entire sequence of events came back—every feeling, every nuance of emotion shared between them. His chest felt constricted, as if he were going to have a cardiac arrest. But he was stripped of his own armor and defense, and all he could do was feel...feel those powerful emotions sweeping through him as savagely as a dam bursting.

There was no hate toward Aly left in him. Just the opposite, Clay admitted haltingly to himself. The luminous look in her blue eyes last night had told him everything. There was only love between them, not hate. And if he was any judge of their fiery, breathtaking kiss, she wanted him, needed him, as much as he did her.

A ragged sigh escaped him. *What a mess. A miserable mess!* Clay couldn't find it within himself to overcome the last hurdle that stood between them: he could never forget that Aly's brother had murdered Stephen. The fact loomed like a ghost in his mind and heart every time he was with her. She didn't deserve any of this, his heart whispered.

Dragging his arm away from his eyes, Clay stared up at the ceiling. Aly was a casualty of the war, just as he was. She carried ghosts just as he did. But they were on opposite sides. Sides that could never meet and bury the sword. But he loved her, dammit! And Clay knew she cared for him. No one, not even Aly, deserved that kind of sentence.

Clay knew what had to be done. He would protect Aly the only way he knew how, and that was to continue the charade. Let her think that he remembered nothing of the night before, their conversation or the kiss. With time, Aly's affection for him would wither on the vine of their relationship. He loved her enough to free her from the past that would always haunt him. Never again would she suspect his true feelings for her. That way, she would be free to find someone who could truly make her happy. And God knew, she deserved a little happiness after the hell he'd put her through.

Chapter Six

"I hate September weather," Dan griped, settling down behind the throttles.

Aly went through the automatic motions of preflight with Clay. Six months ago, she'd sweated out the procedure. Now it was second nature. "Why, Dan?"

"Typhoon season down south along the Baja where we've been flying one too many missions."

"I see." Aly began engine start-up at Clay's nod. In the nine months she'd been part of his crew, they'd melded into a smoothly functioning team.

"You don't have to sweat it today, Dan," Clay said, snapping off a salute to the chief ground crewman standing outside the port window. "We're just taking Gray Lady out for a spin to test this new engine."

Dan nodded happily. "Okay by me. There's a typhoon raging in Baja right now. I want no part of it."

Aly grinned at the chief engineer. "You're hoping we don't get called out for a mission in the next five days, is that it?" P3s flew in all kinds of weather, and Aly knew from grim experience that flying below fifty feet, skimming the surface of the ocean, was dangerous at all times—good weather or bad.

"Yes, ma'am," he chortled.

"Let's get this show on the road," Clay ordered. "Miss Trayhern, you take the controls. I'm playing copilot today."

Pleased that Clay was allowing her the privilege, she smiled. "Yes, sir."

Flying the P3 was easy in Aly's estimation. She took Gray Lady off the runway, the turboprops singing deeply as the plane moved through the cloudy afternoon sky above San Francisco Bay. Dan took over the throttles, his long, sensitive fingers playing with them until all engines were perfectly synchronized. Aly's gaze swept the instruments. Keeping her hand firmly on the yoke, she guided the responsive aircraft up and out of the heavy traffic patterns that plagued the West Coast. They would be heading far out to sea to begin testing the new engine thoroughly. Aly knew that with a full load of fuel aboard, Clay intended to be out at least four or five hours. A new engine could have quirks, and through a series of prepared tests, they'd find out just how well it was functioning, and whether it needed any adjustment by the mechanics.

That was all right with her. It was Friday, and she had a long, lonely weekend ahead of her. Flying released her from the constant heaviness that resided in her chest. Aly stole a look at Clay. His profile was clean, his mouth set, as usual, into a single line. Only his eyes gave him away—sometimes.

Aly had never forgotten that morning he'd kissed her and made the admission that he didn't hate her. Their relationship had changed subtly since that time. Clay had taken fewer angry shots at her. No, he'd grown only more distant. Never a smile, never a teasing remark like those the rest of the crew traded with her. Just that haunted look she sometimes saw in his gray eyes when he didn't think she was aware of him staring at her.

Sighing, Aly had no answer for how she still felt toward Clay. His praise for her flying ability had grown over the months, and he'd given her more and more flight responsibility on each mission. For that, she was grateful. It meant that he trusted her not only with his life, but with the lives of his ten-man crew. With time, she had thought her feelings toward him would die, but they had not. If anything, those emotions clamored even more strongly to be expressed. But Clay hadn't given her one sign that he really did care for her. Not with the past in their way. With a shake of her head, Aly concentrated on the series of tasks to come. Flying was a balm to her aching heart, but not the cure.

"Salty Dog One, Moffett Control. Over."

That was their call sign. Clay signaled that he'd answer the radio transmission from the station. "Salty Dog One, over."

Aly listened intently. They were flying three hundred feet above the ocean, fifty miles off the coast, near San Diego. They had been in the air only two hours, putting the engine under a number of test stresses and logging the results on a specially prepared engine chart that Clay held. Her heart began to pound when the transmission ended. She saw Clay's features cloud.

"They want us to go down to Baja, on Jester Track, to relieve Salty Dog Three?" she asked in disbelief.

Clay nodded. "Yeah, number 3 has a broken oil line. They can't stay on track with that condition. They're going to have to shut down that engine and start back to the station immediately."

"But," Dan said, "we don't have a full crew, Mr. Cantrell. What do they expect us to do?"

"There's an Israeli frigate by the name of *Titania*, being shadowed by a Soviet sub off the coast of Baja. Operations is afraid that if number 3 leaves the area without another replacement on scene, the sub might try to make an attack on the frigate."

"They wouldn't dare," Aly muttered, scowling.

"Don't count on it," Clay answered heavily. He pulled out a map, looking at the coordinates given to him by Ops. "Put Gray Lady on this heading."

Dan scratched his head. "Sir, we don't have any weapons or radar operators on board. How are we going to discourage this Red sub from dogging the heels of that frigate?"

"Hopefully, just by showing up. The sub will know we're in the area. We'll fly low and make some radio exchanges with the *Titania*, which they can monitor. Moffett's getting the standby crew ready to take number eight. They'll be in the air within the hour. We're to hold Jester Track surveillance until number eight arrives to relieve us." Clay glanced down at his watch. "We'll be on track within forty minutes. It will take the standby crew another hour to get down here. Then we can head home.''

''Doesn't sound too bad,'' Aly agreed. She chewed on her lower lip, coaxing the P3 up into smoother air. ''We'll be a decoy. That sub will never know we're not armed and prepared to take action.''

Clay nodded to her. ''Right.''

''What about the weather?'' Dan asked, worry in his voice.

''That's the bitch,'' Clay muttered, busily planning their flight. ''That typhoon is full strength, with winds at a hundred miles an hour around the *Titania* and the sub.''

''Damn,'' Aly whispered. ''Wave height?'' That was critical knowledge, because if the P3 flew fifty feet off the surface, a twenty-or thirty-foot wave could catch a wing and smash the aircraft into the ocean, killing all on board.

''Salty Dog Three will give us an update on oceanographic conditions over the track in a minute.''

A cold shiver wound through Aly. It was the first time she'd ever experienced such a sensation. Her stomach knotted with fear. Fear! Where had this reaction come from? She had flown the P3 at fifty feet above the ocean in all kinds of stormy weather. But never in a typhoon. The only safety she felt was the fact that Clay and Dan were there. There wasn't any finer pilot or engineer.

''Looks bad,'' Clay muttered, signing off the radio with Salty Dog Three half an hour later. ''Twenty-foot waves with rogue waves up to forty feet down there, and not a prayer. Damn.''

Only the familiar vibration of the P3 soothed Aly's mounting terror. She hated rogue waves. They could crop up out of nowhere, coming from an entirely different direction than the rest. Frequently, they were ten to twenty feet higher than the other waves. They could be the death of a P3 if the copilot wasn't alert enough to see one coming and yell at the pilot in time for him to ascend to a higher altitude and miss it. They were on track, descending through the murky midafternoon soup, rain slashing relentlessly across the cockpit windows. She and Clay were tightly strapped in, with Clay at the controls. Dan had no support, kneeling at the throttle base, jostled with each bump and shudder as the plane fought its way downward through the heavy, buffeting winds.

"Aly, contact that Israeli frigate." Clay silently chastised himself at the slip. Every once in a while, when things got tense, he'd accidentally call her by her first name. But if she'd noticed his mistake, it didn't show in her voice.

"Right." Switching the radio dial to the ship frequency, Aly made contact with the *Titania*. She knew Clay was counting on the Soviet sub to eavesdrop on the plane-to-ship conversation. That would warn the sub that the frigate was still being protected, despite the deteriorating weather situation.

As Cantrell brought the P3 into a standard pattern of flight approximately four miles from the frigate, leveling off at fifteen hundred feet, the buffeting weather got worse.

Aly's job was to keep an eye on the altimeter, and on the plane's elevation in relation to the ocean that frothed like mountains and canyons not far below them. The peninsula of Baja was no more than ten miles away, but nothing could be sighted because of the heavy pall of rain that surrounded them. Flashes of lightning licked from one cloud to another, blinding her for an instant. Her palms became damp.

"Mayday! Mayday!" *Titania*'s captain screamed. "I'm under attack! Repeat, I'm under attack!"

Instantly, Aly was on the radio. "Salty Dog One to *Titania*. What is your status, over?"

"Salty Dog One, a torpedo has just been launched at us! We're trying to turn out of its way, but it's going to be close! Help us! Help us!"

Aly swiveled a glance at Cantrell. His face glistened with perspiration. She could feel sweat trickling beneath her armpits. "Clay?" She hadn't meant to call him by his first name, but it had come out in a plea.

"Radio Ops. Tell them what's going down. Dan, prepare to drop this girl to fifty feet."

"Fifty feet?" Aly gasped after making the call. That was suicide in weather like this. "That water could rip off a wing!"

Clay's mouth tightened. "You heard me. Prepare to descend immediately."

"You're gonna make that Red sub think we're going to drop a depth charge on him, sir?" Dan guessed.

"That's right, Dan. You'd better play those throttles like your life depends on it."

Dan grinned weakly. "Don't worry, sir, I will."

Shaken by the turn of events, Aly shut off her emotions. She had to become a thinking machine. She radioed the *Titania* to let them know that the P3 was going to make an attack run. Below, on the turbulent ocean, they could see the *Titania* turning to starboard, hitting high, powerful waves in order to avoid the torpedo.

"Let's go down."

Cantrell's voice was taut as he gave the order. Aly nodded. Her entire responsibility centered on the low-altitude altimeter, or LAA, that sensitively monitored the plane's height between ten to fifty feet above the ocean's surface. It was a delicate instrument, sometimes given to being inaccurate. As copilot she had to divide her attention between using her eyes to estimate the plane's altitude from the ocean and checking the LAA for possible inaccurate readings. On a number of occasions, Aly's quick observation had saved them from plowing into the ocean when the LAA had messed up.

Sweat formed on her upper lip, and she quickly wiped it away with her gloved hand. "Descending...now," Aly began hoarsely, "five hundred feet...four hundred feet..." The ocean grew closer. Each wave that reared skyward looked a little bigger, a little more ominous. The P3 bucked and quivered. And each time it did, Clay ironed out the craft's reaction with his skillful flying abilities.

"Make the turn to two-five-zero, ten...nine... eight..." Aly used her watch, counting down the seconds. The P3 always made an attack on a sub into the wind.

"Three...two...one!" The *Titania* flashed under them.

Clay brought the P3 into the wind, steadying her out.

"Three hundred feet..."

"Wing lamps!" Clay ordered tightly. Every P3 was equipped with huge, powerful lights at the end of each wingtip, plus one beneath the nose of the aircraft.

Aly reached down, gripping the switch. "Wing

lamps on.'' The bright beams of light surged through the graying light of early evening, stabbing bright patches through the blinding spray and spume thrown up by the murky ocean below them.

''Nose lamp!''

''Nose lamp on.'' Now three blinding lights emphasized the angry sea's territory, helping Aly to ascertain distance between them and a possible watery grave.

They were going to need all the help they could get, Aly thought disjointedly, her gaze swinging from the instrument panel to the LAA, and back out the window to check their elevation.

In case the sub had picked up their radio frequency, Clay went through the attack sequence as if there was a full crew on board. Aly worked with him, tension mounting in the small cabin.

''Two hundred feet—'' Aly's voice broke. The ocean looked so close!

''One hundred feet.''

''On attack run, keep her steady,'' Clay told Dan tensely.

The P3 slipped through the turbulent wind and vicious rain, her wings skimming the surface. Each tiny air pocket, each up or down draft, was a potential crash situation. Clay kept both hands locked on the yoke, sensing and correcting each of the aircraft's reactions almost before it happened.

''Easy,'' he crooned to the plane.

Aly forced a breath, some of her tension dissolving beneath Clay's deep, steadying voice.

''Fifty feet,'' she croaked.

''Roger, fifty feet. Keep me apprised of our altitude.''

"Roger." Sweat ran freely down her temples. Aly kept glancing out the window. Spume from the tops of the twenty-foot waves were flung into the sky, smashing into the P3. She could barely see! The windshield wipers labored heavily on the front windows, unable to keep them clear enough to fly by sight alone. She saw Clay switch to flying by instruments.

"One minute until depth charge drop!" she reported.

"Roger, one minute. Keep her steady, Dan!"

Sweat stood out on the chief engineer's face as he tried to maintain his balance and watch the engine gauges, continually adjusting the throttles for each draft or air pocket. "Yes, sir!"

"Fifty feet maintaining," Aly said, holding on to the handrail position on the starboard fuselage as a gust of wind hit them hard. The P3 shuddered sickeningly. They were skidding! A scream lurched up her throat.

Clay applied left rudder to halt the downward skid. He checked the yoke, bringing it an inch to the left. The P3 steadied.

"Altitude!" he croaked.

"F-forty feet!"

Too low! A hiss of breath came between his clenched teeth as he pulled back fractionally on the column. It was at that moment that the new engine faltered. With the unexpected loss of power, the P3 descended.

"Look out!" Aly screamed. She braced herself as the waves loomed higher.

"Damn!" It was the last expletive heard over the radio. Cantrell reared back on the yoke, asking the P3 to recover from the shallow dive that the engine had placed them in. Ballard feathered the engine, jerking the throttle, stopcocking it. He shoved the other three to the fire wall, asking for all the reserve power they had to give them.

The P3 gallantly tried to respond, the three engines straining. But another powerful gust of wind threw the nose up, creating a stall condition. The aircraft hovered at the angle for what seemed an eternity before sinking, tail first, toward the grasping, greedy fingers of the ocean twenty feet below them. A forty-foot rogue wave caught the P3, slamming into it on the port side, sending the aircraft skimming on its belly across the waves.

Nightmare seconds collided. Aly saw the waves coming up, felt the P3 shudder into a stall. She gripped the handrail, a scream caught in her throat. In those split seconds before they crashed, she felt sorrow, not fear. Sorrow that she and Clay would end their lives enemies, not friends.

The P3 sank downward, the tail boom entering the water first. Ordinarily, because of the Lockheed's construction, the plane would have disintegrated upon impact. But because the tail took the initial contact, it was torn from the fuselage instead. The P3 skipped sideways across the water like a stone skipping across a pond. Froth and spray shot skyward. Tons of water exploded into the air as the plane sliced through wave after wave. A rending tear could be heard for agonizing moments as the left wing separated from the main body of the aircraft. The starboard wingtip dug into the water at a much slower speed, cartwheeling the craft high into the air before it settled drunkenly on the ocean's surface, and that was what saved them.

Aly was thinking clearly. The P3 was still afloat, drifting in a trough between huge, stalking waves. Because of their training in emergency survival, she and Clay quickly unstrapped and were relatively unhurt. It was a different matter for their chief engineer.

Clay stepped over the unconscious man, who lay blocking the aisle. He leaned down. The gurgle of water could be heard entering the plane through the broken tail section. In less than a minute, the P3 would go down, slipping into the ocean's depths.

"Aly!" Clay yelled above the roar of the typhoon, "get to the raft. Get it released!"

Her knees knocking so badly that she fell onto the slippery aisle filling with water, Aly crawled aft in the listing P3. The twelve-man life raft on board was stowed in the rear. In the dimness and poor light, Aly finally reached it. Her breath came in ragged sobs as she fought her way through knee-deep water. Thousands of gallons of water were pouring in from the broken tail section. Leaning upward, she triggered the latch that would enable her to drag the raft forward toward the first hatch.

Cantrell hefted the bleeding and unconscious Ballard across his shoulders. As he turned, he saw to his relief that Aly had reached the life raft. She had thrown open the rear hatch door and put the raft into position for immediate inflation. Staggering under Ballard's weight, and from the fact the P3 was slowly turning on her side, Clay fought his way through the ankle-deep seawater.

Aly flipped the toggle switch, and the life raft began inflation just outside the hatch. Made of a tough, resilient material with a cover over the top, the raft rose in place as the entire rescue assembly took shape.

She gripped the nylon line with both her gloved hands, the ocean tugging hard at it, wanting to pull it out of her grasp. As Clay approached, her eyes widened. Dan Ballard was bleeding heavily from the face and head. She met Clay's narrowed gaze.

"Hold that raft steady," he bellowed, positioning Ballard to be dropped forward into it.

"Hurry! We're sinking!" she screamed over the roar.

The P3 groaned, listing more to port as the water burped and belched into the fuselage. Another wave hit the aircraft. Aly was thrown violently forward on her knees. The line sang through her hands, burning them. With a cry, she looped the rope around her elbow to halt the raft's movement. She was jerked forward again, and she twisted around, using her feet to throw her sideways, lodging herself behind the hatch. Her entire shoulder exploded in pain. A cry tore from her. She saw Clay make it into the raft after getting Ballard aboard.

This was Clay's chance to get rid of her, Aly realized, pain making her light-headed. She held the raft steady, using her own body as a wedge against the aircraft to do so. Clay could leave her behind and she'd die.

"Aly! Jump!"

His scream impinged upon her numbed senses. The pain drifting up her shoulder into her neck and head was nearly paralyzing her.

"Aly!" Dammit! Clay moved awkwardly to the rear of the covered raft. Something was wrong! He saw how pale her face was. Her hands were slipping! She was allowing the line to slide through her fingers. What was she doing? Looking up, Cantrell saw the fuselage moving over on top of them. One more wave would bring it smashing down on the raft and they'd all die.

Cursing roundly, Clay made a flailing leap from the raft back to the lip of the wallowing P3. He jerked Aly away from the hatch where she had lodged herself against the interior. In one motion, he literally threw her into the raft and dived headlong into it himself.

Grabbing a paddle, fumbling with it, Clay dug it into the brackish green water. They had to get out from beneath the P3! He looked over at Aly. She lay sprawled on her back, unconscious next to Ballard. This was one time he wasn't going to have their help. He wasn't a man to pray, but he did it then. Digging the plastic paddle in quick, deep strokes, he moved the raft sluggishly forward.

The P3 groaned, the scream of metal against metal shearing above the shriek of wind and the roar of the angry ocean. Clay ducked, digging harder, paddling faster, still praying. The raft floated upward, caught on another huge wave. He chanced a look across his shoulder. Gray Lady was going down! A part of him cried because she'd been such a valiant aircraft under the worst of circumstances. The last scream of metal against metal rang through the early evening like the cry of a woman dying.

Ripping pain brought Aly quickly back to consciousness. She was aware of the howling wind whistling through the open flaps, and that she was soaked to the skin, and freezing. She tried to sit up, but pain sheared through her left shoulder. With a cry, she fell back to the floor of the raft, sobbing for breath.

Clay had stopped paddling as soon as they were clear of the sinking P3. With shaking hands, he had located the first-aid kit in one of the raft's many side compartments, and he placed a battle dressing around Dan's bleeding head. Finding no other evidence of injury, Clay moved him amidships to the center of the raft. Just as he finished tending Dan, he heard Aly moan. He crawled over to her on his hands and knees. The raft moved like a roller coaster, tipping and sliding at the whim of the ocean's quixotic current and the direction of the wind.

"Lie still," Clay gasped, his breath coming in jerky sobs. Aly's face was waxen, and she was gripping her left shoulder, her mouth stretched in a silent scream. He ran his hand across her life vest, trying to find out if she'd broken her arm or something. "Where's it hurt?" he demanded, leaning over her.

"Sh-shoulder. Oh, God, I think I broke it, Clay." Aly sobbed, biting back a cry.

As quickly as he could, Clay got her turned on her side, facing him, so that she leaned against his knees for support. Sliding his hand under her life vest, he gingerly felt across her wet back. After several moments of examination, he said, "I think it's dislocated." He could feel the blade separated from her shoulder. As gently as he could under the circumstances, he laid Aly down on her back. Grimly, he said, "Hold on, this is going to hurt like hell."

Aly didn't have time to prepare. She felt his strong hands upon her shoulder, front and back. In the next second, Clay jerked her entire body in one, single movement. A cry clawed up her throat, and the pain was so intense that blackness enveloped her.

It was dark when Aly regained consciousness. She

was aware of the rolling motion of the raft, the constant pelt of rain against the roof and the roar of wind all around them. When she realized she was held in someone's arms, she stirred.

"Lie still," Clay ordered her, his voice low, "I've got you."

A dull ache throbbed through her left shoulder. Aly found herself huddled against Cantrell, his arm around her. Her right arm was wrapped tightly around his waist. Even in unconsciousness, her terror of being washed overboard had made her cling to him. Relief spread through her.

"We're alive," Clay reassured her in an unsteady voice. "How are you feeling?"

Slowly, Aly raised her head. It was so dark she could see nothing at first. Then she realized that there was a blinking red light on the bow of the raft. It would make them visible to rescue searchers. She looked up into Clay's harshly drawn face, barely visible. The rain had plastered his hair to his skull, and his eyes were dark with concern as he studied her. She noticed that he had positioned himself between the main two seats of the raft. He'd maneuvered Dan and herself on either side of him, one arm around each to keep them from getting tossed around and possibly increasing the severity of their injuries.

"Okay," she mumbled. Thirst. She was dying of thirst. "Dan?"

Clay's face softened slightly, some of the lines of tension easing around his mouth. "Concussion, I think. A bad one. We won't know anything more until daylight comes."

Aly nodded, her brain seeming spongy and disconnected. She felt so safe and secure under his arm.

Trying to think coherently, she croaked, "The radio?"

Clay offered Aly a slight smile to buoy her spirits. She looked like a bedraggled kitten, her face reflecting the faint red glow from the bow. "Up and working. I'm sure the coast guard has received our Mayday signal. It's just a matter of time until they locate us with one of their Falcon jets. I don't think they'll attempt a rescue until this storm dies down, though. Maybe we'll see them at daybreak."

Trying to protect her face from the biting, never-ending wind whipping through the flaps, Aly strained to sit up more. She placed her head against Clay's broad shoulder, her lips near his ear so that he could hear her. "What about the *Titania*?"

With a snort, Clay said, "If she saw us go down, she didn't wait around to help rescue us. I think that Red sub scared her off. She's probably halfway up the Baja peninsula by now."

Real anger wound through Aly. Tiredly, she rested her head against Clay's neck and jaw. How good it felt being in his arms. "And you? Any injury?"

"None. Just some bruises from the crash. You had a separated shoulder. How's it feeling now?"

"Like hell. Where'd you learn to put one back into position like that?"

Chuckling, Clay said. "From my days in football at college. I suffered one myself. When the coach put it back in, I thought I was going to die."

"I thought I had," Aly answered. His voice was like balm. She was more afraid than she'd ever been in her life. They were alone on an ocean in the middle of a typhoon.

"Look, there's nothing else we can do right now. Try and go back to sleep."

"But what about you? What time is it?" She struggled to look at her watch on her left wrist. When she raised her arm, pain hit her hard, making her gasp.

"Easy with that arm, honey," he crooned, gently running his hand down her left arm. "You won't have mobility for a couple of weeks. As soon as I can, I'm going to fashion a sling so you don't keep aggravating it every time you move."

Honey. Aly stared up at Clay, her lips parting. His voice was incredibly gentle, his fingers even gentler as he skimmed her injured arm in a protective gesture. She saw him frown and suddenly look away from her. Despite their circumstances, that same old pain shook her heart. It had been a slip on his part—and now he was sorry he'd said it.

"I-it's almost midnight," she whispered lamely.

"Yeah. Go back to sleep, Aly. There's nothing else to be done. The raft's riding the waves fine. According to the compass, we're heading in a northeasterly direction, toward Baja."

Baja. She closed her eyes, snuggling deep beneath Clay's supportive arm. Savoring his closeness, the warming heat of his hard, masculine body, Aly closed her eyes. Tonight, Clay would hold her. It was more than she'd ever dreamed of. He embraced both her and Dan. There was a heroic side to Clay. He didn't have to hold either of them, but he must have realized that body heat was depleted in a cold rain like this. It didn't matter what his reasons were, Aly told herself. Shivering, she placed her hand against the vest he wore. The trauma of the crash, followed by her injury, had left her utterly exhausted. Despite the banshee cry of the wind surrounding them, the pitching of the raft and the unrelenting rain, Aly slept. She was safe.

Clay jerked awake at dawn, bathed in a cold sweat of fear. He'd been dreaming of the crash all over again, experiencing a gamut of violent emotions. He lay with his shoulders against the rubber raft amidships. Dan's head rested on his right shoulder, Aly's on his left. Sometime during the night, she had crowded close, her body contoured against his. It felt good and right. No longer was she shivering, and neither was he.

Clay needed to rub his burning eyes. He moved slowly, trying not to disturb either of his sleeping crew members. Every bone in his body ached. His muscles were stiff and sore. He heard Dan groan. Instantly, his attention focused on the engineer. Was he finally becoming conscious? God, he hoped so.

Aly heard Dan's groan and groggily awoke. As she stirred, she immediately felt Clay's arm tighten about her shoulder.

''Take it easy,'' he said, his voice rough from disuse. ''It's Ballard. I think he's coming around. Can you help me, Aly?''

The rain had stopped. Aly rubbed her eyes, slowly sitting up. Her shoulder ached, but the pain was at a manageable level. Focusing her attention on Dan, she got to her hands and knees, moving awkwardly around Clay and to his side.

Trading a look with him, she wondered how badly hurt Dan was. ''Dan?'' she called, placing her hand against his shoulder. ''Dan? Can you hear me? It's Aly.''

The engineer groaned again, his lashes fluttering against his pale, drawn face. But he didn't become conscious.

Aly looked up at Clay. "I think he's got a serious concussion."

"Yeah," Clay agreed grimly. He twisted around, looking for the compartment that held three survival blankets. Glancing out the flaps, his eyes widened. "Look!"

The sudden surprise in Clay's voice made Aly look up. There, between the flaps, and no more than a mile away, was the Baja desert. Golden yellow hills of sand flowed in a north-south direction for as far as they could see. "Land!" Aly croaked, hope in her voice. That would be even better for rescue!

Moving stiffly, Clay got to his knees. "Aly, can you paddle? I don't know if this current or wind will hold this direction long enough for us to make land. Can you use your right arm to paddle with?"

Aly nodded, slipping her numbed fingers around the oar. The paddle was placed between the overhead roof and the raft. "I'll do it."

Clay grinned tiredly. "You're one hell of a woman."

His unexpected smile sent a shaft of warmth through her. She pushed the damp hair out of her eyes. "Come on, Cantrell, quit the sweet talk and put your money where your mouth is. Let's go for it."

Clay wanted to reach over and pull Aly into his arms. He loved her unflagging spirit, her courage under brutal circumstances. And the smile she gave him made him feel hot with longing. "Let's go for it," he challenged her huskily.

"Last one to the beach is a rotten egg, Cantrell!" And they began to paddle.

"Prepare to land!" Clay warned Aly nearly an hour later. His arm was numb, and his shoulder hurt from paddling for so long and hard. He knew that Aly must be close to exhaustion. If she was, she wasn't complaining. Maybe it was that famous Trayhern stamina coming through for them now. Whatever the reason, Clay knew they wouldn't have reached shore without her superhuman effort. Just as he'd suspected, the current had started moving northward half a mile away from shore. It would have swept them back out to sea. The last half mile had been hellish, but they'd forced the raft through the choppy waves, aiming it for a desert landfall.

The waves were huge from the typhoon. Clay stowed both paddles and then pulled Aly into the center of the raft with him. The darkness beneath her eyes gave away her true state. She was exhausted. "Stay down and hold on to Ballard," he shouted above the crashing of the waves. "We're liable to tip over if we don't stay low and in the center of this thing. Hang on!"

Aly slid her right arm under Dan's shoulders, holding him next to her body, trying to protect him in case they were approaching a rocky shore, or if the raft should flip over. Her eyes widened when Clay came around to sit behind her, his arms around both of them. He pressed her down until she was almost lying across Dan. When she realized that Clay was protecting both of them with his body, tears leaked into her eyes. Despite his hard facade, Clay was an incredible man. And Aly loved him fiercely for it.

Chapter Seven

Miraculously, they landed upright, sliding along the smooth, grainy surface of the beach. Clay was the first out of the raft, pulling it high up on the shore with the aid of the nylon rope.

He watched as Aly shakily climbed out of the raft. She held her left arm against her torso, and he knew she was in plenty of pain from the dislocation. Tugging the raft completely out of the grasp of the heavy waves, Clay wrapped the nylon rope around a large black rock sticking up out of the sand, using it as an anchor point.

Clay looked up as she approached. ''Aly?'' He hadn't realized the full impact on her of their bid to paddle ashore until just then. Her eyes were dark with exhaustion, shadows beneath them. And that beautiful mouth was compressed into a single line of suffering.

''Yes?''

He rose to his feet. Sliding his hand around her good arm to steady her, Clay guided her toward a large, sandy bluff that stood to the left of the landing area. ''First things first. I want you to sit down before you fall down. As soon as I can get Dan comfortable, I'll take care of you.''

The sand was packed hard from the continuous rain, but Aly stumbled, nevertheless. Clay's hand tightened on her arm to prevent her from falling. Tiredness was lapping at her, and she wasn't thinking clearly. ''I—I think I'm in shock, Clay.''

He gave her a tight smile, motioning for her to sit down. ''I know you are.''

Giving him a confused look, Aly rasped, ''Why aren't you?''

Her hair was in utter disarray around her face, curled and stiffened by the saltwater. But to Clay, she looked beautiful. Leaning down, he cupped her cheek. ''I had a crash before, remember? Maybe that experience prepared me this time. I don't know. Stay here.''

As badly as she wanted to contribute to the team effort, Aly was simply too fatigued. She sat watching as Clay briskly went about the business of setting up camp. The tarp over the large, oval raft would provide them with protection against all kinds of weather. And each raft was equipped with an array of items, from ten gallons of fresh water stored in quart plastic bottles to enough dehydrated food for two weeks, a radio, a first-aid kit and other essentials.

Aly studied the turbulent gray clouds, dark with threatening rain. The wind was warm, and her stiff, salty-smelling flight suit was nearly dry. This was

Baja, and it was September. Aly wondered how hot it would get when the storm finally passed them.

Clay was satisfied with his hour's worth of effort. Dan was resting peacefully, although still unconscious, beneath the protective tarp on the raft. He'd placed two blankets over him, to keep him warm. Setting up the radio to send out the Mayday signal was his last major chore before he could attend to Aly.

Every once in a while, Clay would look up to check on her. She had lain down, curling on her side, using her right arm as a pillow for her head. Adjusting the radio control to the on position, he set it to broadcast their plea for help. He was certain that within twenty-four hours, they'd be discovered by the coast guard. His spirts were solid, and he felt good. They had survived the crash.

As he picked up the first-aid kit and climbed out of the raft, Clay didn't try to hide from his feelings. Seconds before the crash he'd realized that he loved Aly. Regardless of her background or her family name, he loved her. Confused about what to do with that knowledge, he now trudged slowly up the slope toward her. He was scared. More scared than he'd ever been in his life. How could they ever have a relationship when he was the one who had so effectively destroyed it in the first place? There was no hope, and he sadly dismissed the dream.

Aly roused when she saw Clay coming up the hill and gave him a game smile as he knelt in front of her. His eyes were dark gray, filled with concern for her. It made her feel good, and she rallied.

"I must have dozed off."

Clay returned her brief smile of welcome and went

about the business of unzipping her vest. ''You'll need a couple more catnaps in order to shake off the shock. Let's get this vest, and part of the flight suit you're wearing, off you. I want to examine that shoulder.''

Aly tried not to flinch as Clay stripped her of the vest and then pulled the Velcro of her flight suit open. She wore only a white cotton bra and panties beneath the suit. Heat stole into her face as she allowed him to gently work the sleeve from her stiff left arm. Every movement hurt.

''Take it easy,'' Clay soothed, gathering the last of the material off her hand. He realized Aly was embarrassed at having to partially strip in order for him to check the injury. Focusing on the task at hand, he tried to ignore the soft pliancy of her flesh. Allowing her to keep the flight suit on her right arm and shoulder, he maneuvered around her so that he could look at the injured area.

''You have a nice back,'' he told her huskily. It was a deeply indented back with a strong spine. Clay lightly ran his hand across the dislocation area.

''Is that good or bad?'' Aly joked weakly, wildly aware as his hand grazed her shoulder. His touch was knowing without being hurtful as he gently pressed here and there to find the extent of damage.

Clay smiled distantly and placed his hand directly over the injury. The flesh was badly swollen and hot to his brief touch. ''A compliment,'' he assured her, only inches separating them. ''You're lucky you didn't get your arm ripped out of the shoulder socket.''

''That bad, Clay?'' It was so natural to call him by his first name, Aly thought, giving up on trying to keep the normal distance between them. She was too tired to erect those walls they both hid behind so well.

Frowning, he muttered, "Bad enough." He looked down at her. "I think the only thing we can do is put your left arm in a sling and keep the entire shoulder as immobilized as possible." His hand settled on her bare arm. "Are you in a lot of pain?"

His gentle attention was unraveling her. It was impossible to ignore Clay when he was like this. It wasn't an act—this was the real Clay Cantrell that she'd fallen helplessly in love with. The serious agony was in her heart, and there was no cure for that. Ever.

"Just a little."

He got up and came around to her left side, facing her. "You sure?" Easing her fingers and hand back through the sleeve opening, Clay helped her get the flight suit back in place. "Or are you hiding behind that tough Trayhern name?" He'd deliberately goaded her to get an honest response. From the set of her mouth, the way the corners pulled in, he knew she was in misery.

Aly flashed him an angry look. "There's nothing wrong in minimizing pain, Cantrell," she said, stung. With quick, sure movements, Aly pressed the Velcro closed, the flight suit once again in place.

Clay patiently held her blazing blue eyes. "There is when we've got medication to ease it." And then he looked down at her gloved hands, noticing a rusty color staining them. "What's this?" He picked up her left hand and turned it over.

"You little fool," he breathed, examining the glove that was shredded, exposing her badly burned palm that had bled freely. She must have gotten the wounds when the nylon line had nearly been ripped out of her hands. "Why the hell didn't you tell me—"

Aly could barely tolerate Clay's hand cradling hers. But she couldn't jerk out of his grasp—her shoulder hurt too badly. "It was just some rope burns," she muttered defensively.

Clay lifted his head, meeting and holding her defiant gaze. "Lady, you may think you're Superwoman, but this kind of damage invites infection."

"Stop haranguing me!"

There was a wobble in her voice. Clay saw the tears gather in her wavering stare. His mouth tightened, and he laid her hand across his knees. Reaching for the first-aid kit, he opened it, and took out a pair of scissors. The tension was palpable between them as he carefully cut away the rest of her glove. Part of the fibers had stuck to the oozing wound across her palm.

"This is going to hurt like hell," he warned her.

Aly couldn't stop the tears. But they weren't caused by the pain as Clay gently pulled fragments of the glove from the burns. No, they were welling into her eyes because she had no defense against his closeness or the little barbs he was throwing at her.

When Clay saw the tears drifting down the taut planes of her cheeks, he winced visibly. "These are nasty," he muttered, spreading salve across her palm. "You must have gotten them holding that raft against the hatch."

"Y-yes." She sniffed, taking her right gloved hand and wiping her eyes dry.

Cantrell risked a look at her as he gently wrapped gauze around her hand and palm. "You look pretty even when you cry. Makes those blue eyes of yours even larger, if that's possible.''

Aly withdrew deep inside herself. One minute he was insulting her, the next, praising her. Frantically, she searched for some neutral topic. ''At least we survived the crash,'' she whispered in a raspy voice.

Grimly, Clay nodded. He took some adhesive tape and finished bandaging the dressing. ''Yeah.''

''I was so scared.''

''That made three of us. Okay, let me look at your other hand.''

Reluctantly, Aly gave it to him, trying to prepare for his reaction. She knew her right hand was far worse than the left. She watched his eyebrows draw together as he examined her palm.

''Lady, you have one hell of a tolerance for pain, that's all I can say.'' He met and held her gaze. ''Do you want medication?''

She shook her head. ''No. Drugs make me groggy. At least pain keeps my head clear so I can think.''

With a derisive laugh, Clay agreed. ''Yeah, that's the truth.'' He began the same procedure of cutting the glove away from her hand. ''After I crashed that F-14 into the deck of the carrier and ejected at the last second, I didn't feel anything at first, either. It was only after I woke up in sick bay that I felt the pain.''

Starbuck had told her about Clay's crash. And knowing that he'd lied to her, Aly wanted to know the truth. There was a warmth between them right now, and she hesitantly asked, ''What happened, Clay? Dan mentioned that at one time you were a fighter pilot. What changed that?''

The glove fell away and Clay carefully examined

the palm of her hand. Aly had such exquisitely long fingers. He'd bet anything that she'd get permanent scars out of this.

Aly took his silence as a negative. "That's all right, you don't have to tell me about it. I'm sure it's a horrible memory."

"What? No, I don't mind telling you, Aly." Cantrell pointed to her palm. "I was just thinking it was a shame to have such beautiful skin scarred like this."

She flushed, unable to hold his sincere gaze. "Wh-what about the crash?"

He smiled briefly, and realized she was blushing. Any color coming back into her cheeks was better than nothing, in his opinion. Taking the salve, he daubed it across the burn. "It happened a year and a half ago while I was aboard the *Enterprise*. Starbuck was in my squadron." He looked up. "I suppose he's already told you that?"

Aly raised her head, anger in her voice. "Starbuck lied to me about a lot of things, but yes, he did mention the fact that you flew together."

Chuckling, Clay murmured, "Said I was on the verge of losing my nerve after the crash, too, no doubt."

"How did you know?"

"Because Starbuck is a jealous bastard at best, and a back stabber at his worst. He and I were in competition for the top-gun slot in our squadron. I was ahead of him in points, and he didn't like it." Clay sobered, his voice lowering. "My RIO, Lieutenant John Holding, was slated to rotate stateside. We had to fly one last mission on a rotten night. It was stormy, and winds were high and variable. The F-14 started developing an engine problem, so we came back to the carrier.'' Clay set the salve aside and began to wrap her palm with the gauze. One corner of his mouth twisted into a grimace. ''I've never seen a night like that. I was calling the ball, holding the aircraft steady. Everything was lined up. The deck on that carrier was lifting and falling more than I'd ever seen it before.

''At the last second, the wind threw the plane off course, and I had a bolter, going around for a second try. I called the ball and lined up. Everything looked good. Then, just as I dropped the hook, pulled full flaps for the landing, the starboard engine that was giving me problems flamed out.'' Clay held her hand, staring off into space, the images still vivid. ''The plane nosed down. I brought it up, but in doing so, we literally starting falling toward the deck. There was nothing I could do but yell a warning, hoping John would punch out.''

Aly wanted to reach out and touch Clay's shoulder, to somehow assuage his agony. ''Were you both able to eject?'' she asked softly.

Clay shook his head, anguish in his tone. ''John couldn't...didn't. I don't know why he didn't punch out. Maybe he wasn't fast enough. Maybe the ejection phase jammed. We'll never know.''

''So, you survived and John didn't?'' Aly guessed.

''That's right.'' Clay shook off the sorrow from the past, continuing to bandage her hand. Just the gentleness in Aly's husky voice made him want to confide in her. He'd never talked to anyone except the investigators about the accident. ''I ejected and landed in the ocean. The rescue helicopter fished me out ten minutes later.''

"How badly were you hurt?" Aly knew that ejecting could cause back and ankle injuries.

"I suffered a pretty serious concussion, some minor back trouble and the normal assortment of colorful bruises."

She studied his bent head. The urge to tunnel her fingers through his short, black hair was almost tangible. Risking everything, Aly slowly raised her left arm, resting it on his shoulder. The look of surprise in his eyes when she did it made her heart lift with joy. It had been the right thing to do.

"If I know you just a little, you probably suffered more because of John's death."

Clay met and drowned in her tender expression. In that instant, he simply wanted to take Aly into his arms and make slow, exploratory love with her. Her hand resting on his shoulder sent warmth throughout his cold, knotted gut. "Yeah, you're right. John was married to a great woman, Maggie. They have three of the brightest kids." He avoided her gaze. "They're like family to me, Aly. John and Maggie sort of took me under their wing." He managed a strained laugh, completing the bandaging. "I'm the kids' 'uncle.'" And then hesitantly he added, "I always will be. I never forget Christopher, Mark or Jenny's birthdays. I've got them circled on a calendar I carry in my wallet. It doesn't matter where I'm stationed, I always send them a card and a gift."

Aly closed her eyes. His pain and suffering was far greater than her current physical discomfort. "I'm sorry, Clay " His words about the loss of his brother serrated her: 'I lost all of mine.' Stephen Cantrell had died on that hill. "Surely, you're an uncle to your own family members?"

Clay allowed her to retrieve her hand. He remained kneeling there, hands resting on his thighs. Unexpectedly, tears stung his eyes. Tears! He hadn't cried in years. "What you don't know is that when the Marine Corps officer visited my mother with the telegram informing her of Stephen's death, she suffered a stroke two hours later that killed her."

"No!"

Clay heard the raw anguish in Aly's cry. He slowly turned his head, meeting and holding her shadowed blue eyes. "They were all I had. My brother and my mother. I never knew my father, because he died in a jet crash when I was barely a year old. My dad was an orphan who worked his way through college and then joined the Navy, attaining flight status. My mother was an orphan, too. All they had was each other." He gave Aly a twisted smile filled with sadness. "Maybe now you can understand why John's children are so important to me. They're my other family." Clay got stiffly to his feet, unable to stand the tortured look in Aly's eyes. At that moment, he didn't know who hurt worse.

The day passed slowly for Aly. Forced to huddle with Clay and the unconscious Dan Ballard in the tent when the rains came, she remained silent, replaying their prior conversation. Off and on, she slept—partly to escape the ordeal of feelings surrounding Clay's softly admitted story, partly to escape the widening pain in her heart for him.

Clay sat, Dan on his left and Aly curled up at the other end of the raft under a blanket. His arms were wrapped around his drawn-up knees. Moodily, he listened to the wind outside. The storm was slowly abating, the rain coming less often, the wind less powerful. That was good. He wanted the rescue to hurry up and happen.

Clay's gaze drifted back to Aly, as it always did. This was the first time he'd gotten a chance to observe her for any period of time without continual interruption. There was something healing about watching her, he decided. Maybe it was the way her lips parted, free of tension. Or just the way she curled up like a lost kitten, looking alone and vulnerable. He wanted to curl up beside her and pull her into his arms.

Funny, he told himself, *how a plane crash brings everything into sharp clarity.* Clay hadn't meant to tell Aly about his other crash, or the fact that Stephen's death had also taken his mother's life. Rubbing his face savagely, he felt dirty and small. The anguish in Aly's tone and eyes tore him apart. It was as if she personally took responsibility for the tragedy at that moment. Nine months ago, he'd have gleefully told her the awful consequences of Morgan's decision, just to strike out and hurt her as Morgan Trayhern had hurt him. But now he had the opposite feeling. Somehow, Cantrell wanted to take away the guilt he saw in her eyes. Aly shouldn't have to be burdened with Morgan's dirty laundry.

Clay quietly got up and went over to check on Dan, taking his pulse again, and feeling his skin to make sure he was being kept warm enough. Was the engineer in a coma? God, he hoped not. Dan had a blond hellion for a wife, whom he adored. Not to mention those four kids who were often a bright spot in the dark tapestry of Clay's life.

"Dan?" he called softly. "Listen, buddy, you've *got* to pull out of this. You hear me? You've got a great wife and kids waiting for you. Don't let it all go. Hang in there. We're going to be rescued any time now.'' Dan's lashes didn't move. Grimly, Clay kept his hand on the engineer's shoulder, as if to will him out of the netherland he drifted in.

Aly stirred, and Clay looked over at her. She was groggy, her eyes a bit puffy, but endearing. He gave her a slight smile of welcome, then tucked the blanket around Dan. If he stayed, he'd want to move those few feet and take Aly into his arms. She looked so damned lonely and hurting. He forced himself to get up and exit the raft.

Taking a deep breath, Clay studied the ocean's churning whitecaps. Where was the rescue plane? Why hadn't he even heard an airplane engine? He shoved his hands deep into his pockets, walking slowly down the beach, his head bowed in thought.

Aly took care of her personal necessities, then walked back toward the raft. The evening sky was fraught with swiftly moving clouds. The wind tugged at her loosely fitting flight suit, and she lifted her face toward the ocean. She remembered awakening, hearing Clay's lowered voice as he pleaded with Dan. And then her gaze moved to the right. She saw Clay a quarter of a mile away, a lonely, dark figure against the mighty expanse of sky and earth.

Alone…he was terribly alone in a way she'd never imagined. Her family was tightly knit and close. They'd stood together, deriving strength from one another, through every storm life had hurled at them. But Clay had no one. Rubbing her head, Aly fought back the tears. Clay wouldn't take her tears of compassion as anything less than pity. And she was sure he wouldn't tolerate that. Dejectedly, Aly walked back to the raft.

When Clay returned, he found her busy preparing two MREs—the dehydrated meals packaged in plastic bags. He nodded a greeting in her direction when he entered the raft. Tying the flaps shut, he carefully made his way down to where she sat.

"What's cooking?"

She managed a small smile, handing him the dried food packet. "Not much, believe me."

Clay sat cross-legged next to her, their knees almost touching. There wasn't much room in one of these things. "Bet your cooking's great in comparison to this stuff." He took the small bottle of water, putting a bit of liquid into the bag.

"Don't be so sure." Aly laughed softly. Her spirits rose unaccountably just being with Clay. His face was clear, and she saw less tension around his eyes and mouth.

"I'll bet you're one hell of a good cook."

"I don't poison myself, if that's what you mean," she answered dryly.

He grinned. "Spirited, aren't you?"

Aly flushed. "Not really. I just can't stand all this depression. When things get bad, I tend to get a black sense of humor in order to lift myself out of it."

"Yeah, I know what you mean." Clay picked up a plastic fork. The dried food had plumped up considerably with the addition of the water. He watched Aly pick at her meal.

"You need to eat."

"I know." And then Aly rallied. "What's your favorite meal, Clay?"

He leaned back, stretching his long legs across the

width of the raft. ''Ahh, food is one of my favorite topics.'' He grinned at her. ''I guess it is for every bachelor who struggles with boiling water or burning soup in a pan. I'm a meat and potatoes man. Nothing fancy about me.''

''Roast beef, mashed potatoes and gravy, right?'' Aly ventured.

He gave her a look of praise. ''Bingo. You're a pretty insightful lady, you know that?''

''Thanks,'' she murmured, responding to the warmth of his tone.

''How about you? What's your favorite meal?''

The MRE food was dreadful, Aly decided. She wrinkled her nose and held Clay's gray gaze, filled with amusement. His smile sent her tumbling on a rainbow of emotions. ''Me? I like Greek food. Good, tart feta cheese, those nasty-tasting little black olives and some lemon soup with rice.''

''God, that sounds good. What do you say we take a walk over the hill here, and visit the first Greek restaurant we see? I'll even spring for some retsina wine.''

Aly laughed and held out her right hand toward him. ''You've got a deal!''

Her laughter broke the pall Clay had felt around him. Gently taking her bandaged hand, Clay shook it and matched her smile. ''First thing I'll do when we get back is take you to a real Greek restaurant over in Palo Alto.''

The joy died in Aly. He was teasing her. Nothing was meant by his statement. If only they could forget their past! There was such a richness that lay between them to be explored and discovered together.

Clay saw the laughter die in Aly's eyes and on her

lips. Why? Unable to ferret out an answer, he changed topics and released her hand. "I don't know about you, but I think waiting for this rescue to come is the pits."

The food tasted like cardboard, but Aly forced herself to eat it. "Are you sure the radio is working, Clay?"

"Yeah. I checked it a while ago."

"Is it possible that because of all the storm's activity the signal might be getting shorted out in the stratosphere?"

He nodded glumly. "That's a possibility."

Aly toyed with the rest of her meal, unable to finish it. "Clay?"

He looked over at her. "Yes?"

"What if rescue doesn't come?"

Silence hung in the raft, the sound of the wind buffeting them. He poked at the food with his fork, his brow wrinkling. "The map in the rescue packet says that there's a Huichol Indian village inland over the coastal mountain range. We may have to do some walking."

Aly digested the possibility. "Baja is hot this time of year from what I understand."

"Roger that. Hot and arid. No water anywhere."

"Would we have enough water and food for that kind of trek?"

Clay nodded. "If we're careful, we'd have five days' worth. That should be enough to reach that village and find help."

Baja was such a desolate place, though. Aly kept the thought to herself, mulling over the possibilities. "We've got to be rescued." She muttered it with such feeling that Clay looked up in surprise at her. ''Dan's badly injured,'' she explained.

''Yeah, and if push comes to shove, we're going to have to leave him here with half the supplies and go inland to get help.''

''What?'' Aly's eyes rounded. ''You can't be serious. He's hurt! You can't just leave him!''

Clay measured the sudden emotion in her voice. ''We may have to, Aly.''

Anger swept through her. ''You don't just go waltzing off and desert someone in Dan's condition!''

He set aside the MRE, facing her. The word *desert* smarted. Morgan Trayhern had deserted Stephen and his men. Was that why Aly was suddenly so protective of Dan? ''Look,'' he began quietly, trying to get her to calm down, ''we've both been taught survival methods. If necessary, Dan will stay here, and we'll go for help. That way we increase our chances of being found. Dan can stay with the radio and monitor it. If he gets rescued first, he'll have our coordinates, and we'll be picked up anyway. If we get to a village, we can get help for him. Either way, it increases our chances of survival, Aly.''

Her hands knotted, and she glared at him. ''I won't leave a man to die out here alone when he could come with us.''

''Aly, be reasonable—''

''No! You're the one who wants to leave Dan behind! I won't do it, Cantrell. I swear, I won't!''

Clay set his jaw, assessing her emotional response. Obviously he had struck a raw nerve in Aly. He'd suggested many times the threat of her deserting him and the crew in the face of danger. Now he was reaping the results of his misfired anger over Morgan

Trayhern's activities. Dammit! Rubbing his jaw that was bristly with a day's growth of beard, Clay held her fiery blue gaze.

"Look, calm down, Aly. We aren't at that point yet. I'm sure that as this storm continues to weaken, our chances of being discovered increase."

Aly's nostrils flared with a caldron of tapped feelings. She scrambled to her feet, glaring at Clay as she moved by him. Right now, she needed some fresh air. Her voice was strained. "You'd better hope like hell we get a rescue, Cantrell, because I *won't* leave Dan behind." She jerked open the ties and slipped between the flaps, disappearing into the gray twilight.

"Son of a bitch!" Clay glared at the flaps. He was getting a taste of that famous Trayhern bulldog stubbornness he'd heard about. For everyone's sake, Clay hoped rescue would come by daylight tomorrow. It had to. It just had to....

By dusk of the second day, Clay knew rescue wasn't coming. He stood alone on the beach, his hands in the pockets of his flight suit. The ocean was calm now, almost glassy in appearance as the sun slid toward the horizon. What few clouds were in the sky were high cirrus, a harbinger of good weather.

The day had been filled with ups and downs. The good news was that Dan Ballard had regained consciousness. The man was seriously felled by a concussion. There was no way, if they had to trek across the mountains in the distance, that Dan could make the trip. Releasing a sigh, Clay headed back toward the raft, girding himself for a coming battle with Aly.

When he lifted the flap, she jerked a look up in his

direction. She was changing the dressing on Dan's massive head wound.

"Feeling better, Dan?" Clay asked, moving inside and sitting opposite where Aly knelt.

Dan managed a wan smile. "Yes, sir. Just a little bitty headache, is all."

Clay grinned down at him. "What is it about redheads?" he teased. "Do you all fib about the amount of pain you're in?" Glancing at Aly, he saw her scowl. All day she'd avoided him, barely saying two words. And one look into those blue eyes fraught with anger and emotion told Clay they were still at loggerheads.

"Maybe some aspirin?" Dan asked.

Clay reached for the first-aid kit. "Yeah, we can do that for you." He took two white tablets out of a bottle, and waited until Aly had completed the dressing. Slipping his arm beneath the engineer's shoulders, Clay lifted him enough that he could wash the aspirin down with some water.

"Thanks..." Dan uttered, relaxing back on the pallet that Aly had made for him earlier that day.

It was going to be dark soon. The light was fading rapidly inside the raft. Clay put the bottle back in the first-aid kit. "Listen, Dan, there are some things we need to talk over."

"We aren't going to be rescued," Dan guessed.

"Chances are looking pretty slim," Clay agreed quietly. He risked another look at Aly. She was kneeling, hands tense on her thighs, her eyes very large and very round.

"Do you think the combination of weather and ocean current has thrown them off our track?"

"Yeah, I do, Dan." Clay picked absently at his

bootlace. "I'm sure the coast guard tried to figure out where our crash occurred and flew a search pattern. But we all know that in a typhoon, ocean currents change like the wind. They may be hundreds of miles west of us, still searching over the ocean."

"That's what I thought, sir."

"What about the radio?" Aly demanded, her voice tight, accusing.

Clay glanced at it. "It only has a certain radius. If those search planes are flying too far away, they won't pick up our signal."

Dan moved his head slightly, his eyes on Clay. "So what's in the cards, Skipper? What should we do?"

Here it comes. Clay braced himself and addressed both of his crew. "I think our only chance is for Lieutenant Trayhern and I to climb that mountain range and try to locate the Indian village we know exists on the other side."

"No!" Aly exploded. "You aren't going to desert Dan! He's a valuable member of our party, too. You can't just walk off and leave him!"

"We aren't deserting him, Aly," Cantrell said in a low voice. "Now, get a hold on yourself. Hysterics aren't going to help any of us."

Aly fought her anger. "Dammit, you're not leaving Dan here to—to possibly die by himself! What if he goes back into a coma? Who will feed or care for him? What if—"

"Don't worry, Miss Trayhern," Dan protested weakly, I'll be okay here. Really, I will."

She was shaking with rage and frustration. "You aren't well enough to decide anything, Dan! You've got a six-inch gash across your head! It could get infected, you could get a horrible fever and go wandering off in delirium!''

''He'll be fine,'' Clay growled, holding her tear-filled eyes. ''Dan's as tough as they come. He's been taught survival techniques just as we have. He'll be able to tough it out here alone until help arrives.''

The heat in the raft was stifling. Both men were looking at her. Didn't they understand? No Trayhern left anyone behind! Her father had crashed in Korea behind enemy lines while trying to rescue her mother who had been taken prisoner, and he hadn't given up. Nor had he surrendered. Instead he'd fought his way back to safety. Her family sense of honor would not allow her to leave a fallen comrade behind. Ever!

''Excuse me, I've got to get out of here,'' she rattled, climbing awkwardly to her feet. With her left arm in a sling, Aly didn't have the balance she wanted. Struggling to control her anger, she wedged past Clay, escaping into the cool evening air.

Tears blinded Aly as she ran down the packed sand toward the ocean. They didn't understand! Dan could die without continued care! A sob tore from her, and she slowed, stumbling to a halt. Aly buried her face in her right hand, her weeping drowned out by the crash of waves along the beach.

Clay was on Aly's heels and closed the distance between them. He reached out, gripping her arm gently and turning her around. ''Aly, listen to me—''

She reacted as if stung, jerking her arm out of his grasp. Stumbling back a step, she screamed, ''Don't touch me!''

He froze. ''Aly, for God's sake! I'm not *deserting* Dan. And neither are you!''

''Yes, you are!'' she cried out between sobs. Her

face contorted, glistening with tears. "I was taught never to leave someone who was injured. Our family doesn't leave people behind! Not now, not ever! You go take a hike over the mountains. I'll stay here and tend Dan."

Grimly, Clay advanced upon her. He took her firmly, but gently, by the shoulders "Now look," he grated, his face inches from hers, "You'll do as I order. I can't help it if you and your family have an exaggerated sense of honor toward others. This is one situation that demands that both of us leave Ballard." His fingers dug more firmly into her arms. Aly's eyes were wide with anguish. "Dammit, listen to me! You're not deserting Dan. Not in my eyes."

"That's all you've ever accused me of!" she shrieked. "How many times did you throw it in my face that I might desert you or the crew at a crucial time?" Aly tried to break free of his grip, but it was impossible. She saw his face contort with a series of emotions. "That's right! I've heard it long enough and loud enough, Cantrell. Well, I'm not leaving Dan, and that's final! I'm not going to go back to Moffett with you telling everyone that *another* member of the Trayhern family deserted someone at a critical point, possibly causing loss of life! No way!"

He wanted to shake some sense into that red head of hers, but Clay knew he had no one but himself to blame for her reaction. "Okay," he whispered harshly, "this is my fault, Aly! I pushed you into a corner. I was wrong as hell to keep goading you about deserting us. I'm wrong, do you hear me? The past nine months you've proved yourself in my eyes. I don't consider you a quitter or a deserter. Do you understand?"

With a cry, Aly jerked away. It cost her dearly in terms of pain, her shoulder beginning to ache again. Placing her right hand against the shoulder in the sling, she sobbed, "I don't believe you, Cantrell! Not a word of what you say will make me change my mind! I was this way before I ever met you and had the miserable pleasure of being harassed daily by you calling *me* a traitor!"

Running his fingers through his hair, Clay snarled, "Your brother's a traitor—you're not!"

"It's one and the same with you, though, Cantrell. Isn't it? When you look at me, you see Morgan. You see your brother, Stephen, and your mother!" She jabbed a thumb into her chest, advancing upon him, breathing hard. "You've never seen *me*! The only thing you live with daily is the damned past. You drag it around like a good friend." Her nostrils flared. "Well, now we're all going to pay for what you've insisted upon doing. I'm not leaving Ballard. You can court-martial me after we're rescued, and I won't give a damn. My honor, my personal integrity toward others is a hell of a lot more important to me than what you deem important!"

Clay stood frozen as she shouldered on by him, stalking up the slight hill and disappearing into the darkness. Dammit! He threw his hands on his hips, clenching his teeth. Glaring out into the dark ocean, he wanted to cry. Not for himself, but for what he'd done to Aly in his blind hatred toward her brother. His chest hurt, and his throat constricted. Tears jammed into Clay's eyes. He turned on his heel, walking blindly away from the raft. His hatred had turned Aly into the shrieking, wounded woman who had stood crying unashamedly in front of him. Taking a ragged breath, Clay staggered to a stop, hot tears rolling down his cheeks.

His hatred had turned Aly's vulnerability and honesty into something twisted and ugly. God, what had he done? Sinking to his knees, he realized that the coolness of the sand couldn't stop the heat of utter guilt from consuming him. He'd hurt Aly so badly that she was going to make a last-ditch stand to salvage what pride and integrity she had left. If he forced her to go with him, he'd end up destroying that. And the last thing he wanted was to hurt Aly any more.

Chapter Eight

Half an hour before the sun rose above the rugged mountains of Baja California, Clay ended his lonely all-night vigil at the edge of the ceaseless ocean. He stripped out of his flight suit and dived into the warm water, scrubbing his skin clean with the abrasive sand. Afterward, he used a disposable razor against his dark beard, scraping his skin free of the whiskers. By the time he'd shrugged back into the uniform, he felt slightly better. But only slightly.

He spotted Aly just coming out of the raft, and waited. Waited and prayed. When he saw her returning from the bluff area, he slowly rose off his haunches and walked toward her, his eyes never leaving her drawn features.

Aly's heart started a slow pound as she watched Clay walk with purpose toward her. Her fingers slowly knotted into a fist at her side. He hadn't returned from the beach last night after their fight. She knew that, because once an hour she'd awakened to find him still missing from the spot in the raft where he normally slept.

Searching his face, Aly saw that his eyes were red-rimmed and bloodshot. There was a silver glimmer to the black gaze that he trained on her. A shiver ran up her spine, and she stood, torn between running and staying. She tensed when he reached out, capturing her right hand.

"We have to talk, Aly. Come with me?"

His voice was low and off-key, and it shook her badly. His mouth was compressed, but not in the hard line as before. Aly searched the rest of his face, and saw exhaustion present, not anger. Mutely, she nodded, trying to reclaim her icy fingers from his.

Clay refused to give up her hand, leading her away from the raft and toward the rock where he'd sat all night. A lump formed in his throat, and he tried to swallow it away, to no avail. Aly was coming hesitantly, dragging each step. Clay couldn't blame her.

Fighting a gamut of emotions on tap just below her surface calm, Aly halted at the large, flat rock in front of them. It was scarred smooth by countless aeons of time, worn down by the ocean and the wind. That was how she felt—worn down and unable to fight any longer. Clay slowly turned and faced her. She felt his fingers tighten gently around her hand. His face was tortured-looking.

"There's no way my apology is going to undo the things I've said and done to you, Aly," he began unsteadily, holding her shadowed blue eyes. "Last night—" Clay swallowed hard, forcing out the words. "I've damn near stripped you of yourself, Aly, by allowing my hatred of your brother to get in our way.''

With a small cry, Aly tried to pull away.

''No,'' Clay pleaded, placing his other hand on her injured shoulder. ''Stay, Aly. Stay and hear me out. Please?''

Tears blinded her. ''I—I can't take any more, Clay,'' she whispered hoarsely. ''I hurt too much....''

He groaned, his fingers tightening around her shoulder. Closing his eyes, he hung his head. ''It's my fault. This is all my fault. Listen to me, please.'' He opened his eyes, holding her anguished gaze. ''Ever since you came to Moffett, I've been gunning for you. Last night, I realized what I'd done. I was punishing you for your brother's act. I wanted to lash out and hurt someone...anyone, for my family's death.'' His tone grew raw as he held her wavering eyes. ''You don't know how sorry I am, Aly. A-and I know there's no way to make it up to you. I'm not going to ask for your forgiveness, even if you could find it somewhere in your heart to give it to me. I don't deserve it. I promise, things are going to be different from here on out between you and me. God,'' he whispered, reaching out, smoothing strands of hair away from her damp cheek, ''I'm sorry.''

Dizziness washed over Aly. She stood frozen, the brief touch of Clay's fingers brushing across her cheek making her heart explode with grief, with loss.

''I want you to stay here with Dan. You don't have to go with me. Understand?'' Clay's voice grew urgent, his gray eyes burning with a fierce light. ''I'm not going to question your honor or integrity in this matter, Aly. I won't destroy what's left of you.'' Reluctantly, Clay released her and forced a bleak smile. She looked as if she were in shock.

"I'm going to pack enough provisions to last five days. As soon as I get them together, I'll take off. According to the map, the village is three days northeast of here." Clay raised his hand to reach out and caress her hair, but thought better of it. He allowed his hand to fall back to his side. "No more fighting, Aly. I'm calling a permanent truce between us. It should have been done a long time ago. A war doesn't determine who's right or wrong, only who's survived. I'm going to try and salvage what's left of our relationship. Instead of creating more wounds for you, maybe I can help heal up some of the ones I'm responsible for...I don't know...I'll try, if you'll let me..." He held her luminous gaze, which was filled with tears.

Aly backed away from him, her hand pressed against her lips. "I—I never expected this. Let me...let me get over the shock."

He dug the toe of his boot into the sand, bowing his head. "I wouldn't blame you if you never spoke to me again, Aly. But there's something between us—I can feel it. Maybe it's one last thread of trust." He lifted his chin, staring over at her. "Follow your heart in this matter. I know you have good instincts; I've seen you use them on the missions. Use that same gut feeling with me to see that I'm honest about my apology to you."

Dizziness washed through Aly and she closed her eyes; Clay's sudden change in attitude overwhelmed her. "All right," she whispered unsteadily. "I'll feel my way through this."

Clay nodded, hope burning in his charcoal-gray

eyes. "It's more than I should ask of you, Aly, but I can't help myself anymore, where you're concerned." He walked on by her, heading back toward the raft, his shoulders slumped.

Dan looked up from where he was sitting in the raft when Aly returned an hour later. He looked worried.

"Miss Trayhern?"

Wearily, Aly sat down, facing him. Dan looked better. He even had some color in his cheeks. "Yes?"

"Look, I don't mean to butt in where I don't belong, but I really think you ought to reconsider your decision to stay here."

She sat down. Clay had left fifteen minutes ago, hiking toward the lower desert hills. A part of her had wanted to go with him, but another, more stubborn part, wanted to remain here. "About what, Dan?" Aly felt gutted, her feelings numbed by Clay's halting apology.

"You really ought to go with Mr. Cantrell."

"He said that?"

"No, ma'am. He said you were staying, and he felt it was best that way."

"I see."

"I don't think you do, ma'am." Dan forced a weak smile. "Look, I know you two have had your problems with each other. And I know it wasn't your fault. Mr. Cantrell got carried away, there's no doubt. But he's trying to make amends, Miss Trayhern."

Bleakly, Aly studied the engineer. "Then you heard our fight last night?"

"Yes, ma'am." Dan held up his hand. "But I can

promise you, I'm not Lieutenant Starbuck. What I hear stays with me.''

''Thank you, Dan,'' she murmured, meaning it.

''That's why it's important you go with Mr. Cantrell.''

Aly tried to busy herself by picking up the items in the raft and stowing them neatly here and there. ''Oh?''

Dan leaned forward, gripping her arm to get her attention. ''Listen to me, Miss Trayhern, no one ought to be trekking that desert for days on end alone. It's dangerous out there. What if Mr. Cantrell falls and twists an ankle? Worse, what if he slides off one of those rocky hills and breaks a leg? Where does that leave him? He'll die out there alone. He's only got enough water for five days. He has no way to signal for help. The radio's here, not with him.''

Aly blinked, assimilating the feeling behind Dan's words. ''My God,'' she whispered, ''I never thought about those things.''

''Of course you wouldn't,'' Dan agreed, ''because you were upset. You had a right to be. But you have to look at the bigger picture. I'll be fine here by myself. I've got shelter, a radio, enough food for seven days and plenty of water.'' His hand tightened on her arm. ''Please, go with Mr. Cantrell. Swallow your pride. You don't travel that kind of mountains without a teammate. You're his copilot, you're supposed to be with him. I know you're raw and hurting right now, but be strong enough to put personal feelings aside.''

He was right. Aly felt shame flow through her, and she hung her head. ''Okay, Dan, I'll go.''

''Whew! Boy, am I glad! There's another pack.

Take those extra five quarts of water and pack 'em in there. The MREs are in the corner. Hurry, and you can catch up with him."

The first hill was a killer, Clay decided, winded by the time he reached the top of the rocky summit. His boots and lower legs were coated with the yellow dust. Shifting the backpack across his shoulders, he sat down to rest. The sun was rising higher, and already he could feel the intense heat building around him. There were three series of hills, scalloped upward toward the jagged mountain range in the distance. Those peaks were close to eight thousand feet high. Somewhere on the other side was an Indian village.

Checking the compass once again, Clay got to his feet to start across the nose of the ridge and head for the downward slope.

"Clay!"

He halted, frowning. That was Aly's voice! Turning around in disbelief, he looked down. Aly was halfway up the hill, a small pack slung across her right shoulder, climbing toward him just as fast as she could. Scowling, Clay wondered what the hell she was up to. Twice, she slipped on the loose rocks and gravel because her arm was in the sling, throwing her off balance. She was going to injure herself more if she didn't slow down! Cursing roundly, he met her three-quarters of the way up the hill.

"What the hell are you doing?" he rasped, gripping her by her good arm to steady her. The flight suit she wore was coated with dust. Damp strands of red hair stuck to her brow and temples. And the sheer dark blue of her eyes, when she lifted her lashes to meet his, struck hard at his heart.

"I—" Aly gasped for breath "—I had to come. Dan was right—" She took in another couple of breaths before continuing. Despite her daily five-mile runs, this kind of climbing left her unprepared. She defiantly held Clay's dark scowl. "What if something happens to you? Who will take care of you? Dan's right—I was wrong, okay?"

Convinced she wasn't going to fall, Clay released her. "Nothing's going to happen to me, Aly. Now why don't you turn around and get your rear back down there?"

"You—you stubborn, mule headed idiot!" she shouted. "There's no pleasing you, is there?"

A grin leaked through his scowl. "Stubborn? Mule-headed? Me?"

"Cantrell, you are the most contrary man I've ever had the misfortune to meet! And I'm not going to turn around and go back. You need a partner. We're a team, remember? I'm your copilot. So just wipe that silly smile off your face and start walking. I'm not leaving!"

Scratching his head, Clay muttered, "Damned if I can figure you out."

Aly glared at him. "Don't bother trying."

"I always said women with red hair were complicated. I was right. Come on, get on up in front of me so I can catch you in case you decide to take a nose-dive into these rocks."

Blinking, Aly looked up at him. "Then, I can stay?"

"Do I have a choice?"

A tight grin crossed her mouth. "No, you don't." And she walked past him, taking the lead.

The climbing, sweating and deep breathing sloughed off Aly's pain, frustration and anxiety. By the end of the first hour, she'd relaxed. The rocky hills were dangerous to tread because of the loose stone and pebbles. She'd lost count of how many times she'd tripped or fallen. And every time Clay was there to help her back up. Once, he muttered, "You're the liability on this trip, not me. It's a damn good thing *I* came along." There'd been amusement in his eyes and tone, so she hadn't reacted except to give him a smile of thanks. His returning smile tore at her raw heart, sending joy through her.

"Aly, let's take a break," Clay called.

Gratefully, Aly sank to her knees. They were half-way up the second hill; the sun was scorchingly hot. Clay walked up and sat opposite her. Sweat was running freely down his face, dark splotches beneath each armpit of his flight suit.

"This is hard work," she confided, breathing raggedly.

"Yeah. I don't think we're in shape for it." He handed her a plastic bottle filled with water. "Drink just a little, and slosh it around in your mouth before swallowing."

"Right." The water was warm, but heavenly. "Thanks," she whispered and handed it back to him.

Clay took a swallow. Afterward, he pointed toward the Pacific Ocean. "Beautiful view, isn't it?"

Aly nodded, savoring Clay's closeness. She needed his gentleness after the storm that had broken between them last night. "Yes, very beautiful."

Quiet stole across the hill as they absorbed the

spectacle of the dark blue ocean against bright yellow terrain. Clay had drawn up one knee, resting his chin on it. Peace flowed through Aly as she studied his profile beneath her half-closed eyes. There was almost a hint of a smile to the corner of his mouth, if she wasn't mistaken.

"What are you smiling about?"

Clay closed his eyes. "I was thinking about beauty, what it means to each of us. How many of the pilots back at Moffett could find beauty in this desolate place?"

"Probably not many," Aly returned softly. She hungered for his thoughts, his feelings. Every small thing Clay shared with her, healed her a little more.

"Right." And then Clay opened one eye, looking over at her. "Like right now: you're beautiful."

Aly gave him a startled look, and then she frowned. "Oh, get out of here, Clay!"

"No, really." He pointed lazily to her hair. "The sunlight makes your hair look like fire is dancing through the strands. That's beauty. You're beautiful...."

The words, spoken so softly, caressed Aly. She looked away, unable to deal with his honesty. "Right now, I don't feel very beautiful, Clay. Inside or out."

He nodded. "I did that to you."

She rubbed the perspiration from her face, feeling the grit beneath her fingertips. "I let you do it to me," she corrected.

"I don't understand."

Aly drew her legs up, resting her cheek on them. She hesitantly admitted, "My father had a long talk with me right after I got to Moffett. I told him how much you hated me because my name was Trayhern, and the fact we were going to have to work together.'' She closed her eyes, unable to stand the look of compassion in Clay's features. ''He counseled me to treat you like a wounded wild animal, to keep you from biting me.''

''And so you chose not to confront me every time I attacked you?''

''Sometimes retreat is the better part of valor.'' And then Aly whispered, ''I never wanted to fight with you, Clay. I understood some of your pain. There was nothing I could do to take away or change the past. All I could hope for, pray for, was that someday, you'd get past your hate and see me, judge me for who I was—not for my name or my family's history.''

Clay fought the urge to reach over and caress Aly. There was so much pain in her voice. ''It took me a long time to realize that.''

''It could have taken forever,'' she reminded him. ''I mean, I have another year in the cockpit with you. Maybe the second year will be better than the first.''

Clay held her gaze. His voice was resonant and husky. ''You can count on it, honey.'' Rising to his feet, he held out his hands to her. ''Come on, we've got another hill to climb—together.''

Shaken by the intensity in his voice and eyes, Aly dumbly reached out, placing her hand in Clay's. As he pulled her to her feet, she was mesmerized by his mouth. No longer was it pulled in at the corners or compressed. There was an ease to it, and she breathed deeply in relief. ''This is all a dream,'' Aly confessed unsteadily, standing inches from him.

''What is?'' Clay asked, holding on to her hand.

"All of this. Do you know how many times I dreamed of us calling a truce?"

"Believe it. It's real, Aly. Ready?" If Clay didn't move, he was going to lean those spare inches and kiss those luscious lips that were begging to be worshiped.

"Y-yes. Let's go."

"You first."

At noon they found an overhanging ledge to hide beneath, out of the sun. The land had heated up like an oven with no thermostat to control it. Aly's suit clung damply to her, and her hair was plastered to her skull. She wished for a hat of some kind to protect her head from the brutal rays.

She sat down on one of the two rocks in the niche. Clay sat next to her, their bodies touching. He handed her the water, and she drank sparingly. Every swallow counted. Giving it back to him, she muttered, "What I'd do for a bath right now!"

"Same goes for me." Clay took a sip, capping the bottle. He looked over at Aly. "How are you doing?" Heat could be a killer if they weren't careful. Not only could they become dehydrated, but a heatstroke or sunstroke was possible.

"Okay." She wiped her face with the back of her hand, grimacing. "I've never sweated like this before."

"We've never been in Baja before, either," he pointed out dryly, opening two MREs for lunch. Mixing them with just a bit of water, he handed one plastic pouch to Aly along with a fork.

Aly thanked him for the MRE. In spite of their discomforts, the past few hours with Clay had been heaven. She looked forward to each rest stop because it gave her a few minutes to simply talk and share with him. This was the real Clay Cantrell she'd met on the Bayshore on that day so long ago.

They ate in silence, watching a buzzard flying around in lazy circles far above them.

"If that buzzard had a boom on his tail, he could be mistaken for a P3," Clay pointed out.

Aly's laughter echoed down through the series of hills. She saw Clay's eyes burn with some unknown emotion as he stared over at her.

"When you laugh," he said, "I feel light inside. The way you laugh is free and uninhibited."

She blossomed beneath his praise. "Thank you."

"Your laughter reminds me of the alto mission bells at San Juan Capistrano. Ever been down there? It's a little Spanish mission near San Diego."

"No, never been there." Aly liked his comparing her to a lovely mission bell. "Is it pretty?"

Clay leaned back against the rock, getting comfortable after finishing his lunch. "Yeah. It's right in the middle of a town, but when you walk into that courtyard, it's like walking back in time. It's peaceful...sort of like you."

Aly followed suit, relaxing against the wall, the overhang protecting them fully from the sun. She was pleasantly full and suddenly very tired. Closing her eyes she muttered, "I remind you of peace?"

Clay nodded. "I wasn't the only one to notice that quality about you. Dan and Sam did, too. We all agree you're like an island of peace when there's a storm raging around us. I think part of it is your husky voice. Another part of it is just you, the way you handle yourself during an emergency. I know it makes me feel more relaxed having you in that right seat.''

She luxuriated in his softly spoken compliment. ''I haven't felt like an island or haven of peace since we met, Clay.''

''That's going to change,'' he promised her.

''I'm glad,'' Aly whispered, barely opening her eyes. ''And I've got to tell you, it feels good to know that.''

His smile was gentle as he opened his eyes and met hers. ''It feels good for both of us.''

Aly couldn't agree more, the hot noontime air making her sleepy. ''Clay...I'm beat. Can we catch a few minutes of sleep?''

''Yeah,'' he muttered, ''go ahead. We shouldn't be walking in this kind of heat, anyway. Take a long nap, Aly. We're going to wait until 1600 before we tackle that hill again.''

Tipping her head back, Aly strove to get as comfortable as possible, glad that Clay was sensible about the trek. ''Great,'' she murmured, ''I'll see you in a few hours....'' Within minutes, she was sleeping deeply.

It wasn't hard for Clay to fall asleep, either. He'd been up all night, thinking and feeling his way through the mess he'd created for himself and Aly. Her smile wavered before his closed eyes. Her laughter had sent such a sharpened shaft of longing through him. She had laughed! With him! Ever since that first harrowing night at sea when she'd clung to him in her sleep, Clay had hungered to have her near him once again. He dreamed that Aly was in his arms once again.

* * *

Aly awoke slowly, drenched in sweat. The air was hot and dry, and as she inhaled, Clay's unmistakable scent entered her flaring nostrils. Her head lay on something softer than a rock. She rubbed her cheek, feeling the texture of cloth beneath it. Confused, she dragged her eyes open.

Sometime during the afternoon hours while she'd slept, Aly had turned to the right, using Clay's body as a pillow. Her head lay on his broad shoulder, her cheek tucked next to his jaw. Shocked, Aly lay very still. When had she turned and snuggled up against Clay? And then she realized that he was snoring softly, asleep, and unaware of what she'd done.

Relief fled through Aly, and she relaxed. Clay would never know that she craved his closeness, hungered to have his arms around her as she had the night in the raft. She gently pressed those feelings into her heart. Absorbing his scent, his quiet masculine strength, Aly lay still, more content than she had ever been.

Clay invited a sense of peace, too, she thought languidly. Little did he realize just how much he was an island, a haven in her tension-filled world of flying. Still, it was kind of him to confide that he and the crew liked her calming ability on the flights.

Unconsciously nuzzling beneath his jaw, Aly smiled softly. How could she tell Clay that she had never expected him to be able to see what he was doing to both of them, much less apologize to her? Aly knew that it took someone of incredible depth and honesty to search himself ruthlessly like that. And it said something vitally important about Clay Cantrell: although he had a strong ego, he didn't allow his pride to get in the way of making apologies. So few men had the ability to release their pride and allow themselves to be wrong, much less admit it!

Aly's interlude was interrupted when she felt something crawling across her hand that was in the sling. She frowned and raised her head, looking down. A scream escaped her. It was a scorpion crawling across her fingers!

She leaped to her feet, slapping at the poisonous creature, flinging it off her. As she did so, her booted feet slipped on the shalelike rock, and she fell backward.

Clay jerked up at Aly's first scream. Disoriented, he felt her leap away from him. He opened his eyes just in time to see her start to fall. Automatically, he threw out both his arms to catch her.

"Oh, Clay!" she cried, sagging against him.

"What? What's wrong?"

Aly trembled, finding safety within his arms as he turned her toward him. "It was a scorpion! Ugh! It was awful!" she wailed, pointing at the area where it had landed.

Worriedly, he looked down at her, sleep torn away from him. "Did it sting you?"

"N-no. I was just coming awake on your shoulder when—when that horrible little creature started crawling across my left hand. Ugh!" And Aly buried her face against his chest, closing her eyes.

"Damn," Cantrell muttered, holding her tightly to him, "that was close. Those little bastards are really poisonous down here in Baja." Automatically, Clay stroked her hair, finding it thick and warm beneath his fingers. "It's okay, Aly. It's gone, and I don't see any more of them around."

The terror began to recede and Aly was wildly

aware of Clay's arms around her, her breasts pressed to his chest. She gulped in a breath, her right hand sliding across his flight suit, feeling his muscles leap and respond beneath her palm. She pushed the hair away from her eyes. "I—I'm okay now," she whispered. "You can let go of me." She wanted anything but that!

"Sure?" Clay held her at arm's length, keeping both hands on her shoulders. Aly was pale, her eyes dark with fear.

Nodding jerkily, she muttered, "Sure." When his hands fell away, she felt bereft. "I don't want to have to use that snake-venom kit we're carrying," she stammered.

"That makes both of us, sweetheart." He watched her for a long moment, to make sure she wasn't going to faint or something. Clay tried to forget their close contact, and how good her small breasts felt against him. She was so much woman that it made him ache.

"What else does that manual say about this area? What other kinds of poisonous creatures lurk around here?" Aly demanded.

Clay grinned, leading her back to their niche and helping her to sit. "We've got tarantulas."

"Ugh! I hate spiders even more." Aly shivered.

"They aren't poisonous, really," Clay tried to assure her.

"I'll bet there are snakes, too. Probably rattlers."

"Yeah, plenty of them."

"What else?"

He grinned at her. "What is this? Punish Aly with as many ugly little creatures as we can find? Are you a masochist?"

She gave him a nervous smile. "I may be Superwoman in the cockpit, but insects are my undoing."

"Where do snakes fit in on your priority list of horrors?" Cantrell teased.

"Insects are number one. Snakes are second."

"You'd better add coral snakes, too, then."

Aly groaned. "Clay, those are the most poisonous snakes on the North American continent! Are you telling me they make Baja their home?"

He suppressed his smile. "Yes." Aly was truly shaken. But he had to admit that he kind of enjoyed her little-girl reaction. It was nice to know that she wasn't perfect, and that this was an area where he could be strong for her. Crawling creatures didn't faze him in the least.

"What else is in your Little Shop of Horrors, Cantrell? You're gloating over my reaction. I can tell you are...."

His grin widened by inches. Reaching out, he gripped her right hand, giving it a tender squeeze. "I can't help it, Aly. Snakes and such don't bother me at all."

"Good for you, Cantrell. They do me."

She was beginning to smile. That was good. If he could tease her out of her terror, that made him feel of some use in this new and tentative partnership. "There's one more—"

"Ohh, I knew it! You're saving the worst for last, aren't you?"

Chuckling, he said, "Gila monsters."

"Oh, they're lizards."

"Not all that terrible, eh?"

Aly hedged. "Well, they have four legs and they

look a little less threatening than a spider or a horrible scorpion.''

''They're the most poisonous, next to a coral snake. You'd better set them first on your list,'' he warned.

''I used to have a pet horned toad,'' Aly assured him, her fear dissipating under his attention and care. She gave him a strained smile. ''Lizards are okay in my book.''

''Well,'' he growled, ''the Gila monster isn't your friendly neighborhood lizard. He's got a set of choppers that dispense some of the worst poison known to man. That snakebite kit we carry will hardly counteract that bastard's venom.''

''You sound like an expert on the little fella,'' she taunted good-naturedly, delighted that the shoe was on the other foot.

''While you were sleeping last night, I was reading our survival manual by moonlight. Seriously, Aly, if you see a black and red lizard, stay the hell away from it, you hear me? The manual said if the lizard bites, his fangs remain sunken in you until he can close them.''

Aly had the good grace to lose her smile. ''You mean his jaws lock?''

''Yeah, and it's not pretty.''

''Okay,'' Aly breathed. ''I swear, I'll stay away from Gila monsters.''

Satisfied he'd convinced her of the danger, Clay nodded. ''Smart lady.'' He looked at his watch. It was nearly 1600. The worst of the heat was over by now. ''You ready for another stroll?''

More than ready to leave the area where the scorpion lived, Aly got to her feet. ''Let's go. I don't like the critters in this neighborhood.''

Chapter Nine

The second set of hills were crossed by early evening. Occasionally, Clay would look over at Aly, who walked at his shoulder. Right now, they traversed a small, sandy valley, the hills surrounding them like rounded loaves of golden brown bread. He was happy, he realized, almost having forgotten what the feeling was like.

After the scorpion incident, Aly had withdrawn again, remaining silent for the most part during the past two hours. Was it because he'd held her? Sadness moved through Clay. He couldn't blame her for that kind of reaction. If someone had rebuffed him for nine months solid, he wouldn't trust them much, either.

Trust… The word moved gently through him as he thought about it in relation to Aly and himself. He needed to build a bridge of trust between them again.

Why? With a snort, Clay knew the answer. He'd fallen in love with her. But he had to be out of his mind to think, even hope, that she might eventually love him. How could she, after what he'd done to her?

Still, Clay wanted to establish a beachhead of trust. He wanted to be friends with Aly, if nothing else. With his spirits buoyed, his step lightened.

"See that set of boulders?" he asked her, pointing straight ahead. Three oblong boulders rose thirty feet into the air, positioned next to one another in a semicircle.

Wiping the sweat from her brow, Aly nodded. "Yeah. We get to rest?"

"Dinner stop," Clay promised, flashing her an easy smile.

Frowning as they approached the boulders, Aly muttered, "I wonder if there are any spiders or scorpions around?" And she began to look in each nook and cranny.

"Let me look. You sit down and rest. You're beat."

"Thanks," Aly said, finding a spot relatively free of rocks, and sliding into a sitting position. The sun had sunk behind the first set of hills, the strong rays divided upward like spokes in a wheel. The sky was turning salmon pink.

"No, I don't think there are any creepy-crawlies," Clay told her, settling next to her. Bare inches separated them. "Hungry?"

"Starved."

Clay grinned at the fervor in her voice, settling the large backpack in front of him and digging out two MREs.

Aly leaned back, resting her hand against her left arm. Her shoulder ached from all the jostling and jerking it had received. Admittedly, if Clay hadn't caught her a couple of times, she'd have fallen, and possibly done more damage to it. She barely opened her eyes, watching Clay through her lashes. His face was incredibly relaxed, and there was a glint of silver in his eyes; something she'd seen only once before—and that was when he kissed her when he was drunk.

"I actually think you like this hike we're taking," she muttered.

"Yeah, I'm enjoying it."

"You must have grown up in the country," she accused.

Clay fixed up the MRE with a bit of water and handed it to Aly. "And you must have grown up in a city."

She took the plastic bag, scowling at him. "Is it that obvious?"

"It is when you shriek every time you see a little critter."

Aly had the good grace to laugh, realizing he was baiting her. Clay's answering smile tore at her senses, and she found herself wanting to move into his arms, just to be held. "You're a sadist, Cantrell. You're enjoying the discovery of my Achilles' heel a little too much." Aly wasn't able to stop the grin from crossing her mouth.

Settling back, Clay spooned into the MRE. "So tell me, what city raised you?"

She arched an eyebrow at him. "It was a number of cities, smart aleck. My father was a general in the Air Force, and we literally got transferred all over the world."

"That should have gotten you used to a lot of different situations."

"Most of the houses we lived in didn't have spiders and scorpions in them, Cantrell."

"Just where did you develop this fear, Miss Trayhern?"

She loved the boyish look on Clay's face, and she welcomed his attention and teasing. "Well," she muttered, "If I tell you, do you promise not to be like Starbuck and blab it all over the station?"

"No one's like Starbuck," Clay growled. He brightened and held up his right hand. "Scout's honor."

"Were you ever a Boy Scout?" Aly probed mercilessly. "I know how you jet jocks are. You've got lines for any and all occasions. You guys lie for a living when it comes to women."

Chuckling, Clay nodded. "Man, you've got our type pinned down, don't you?"

"It comes from experience, Cantrell. Those student jet jocks hit on me too many times at Pensacola. I got pretty good at seeing a line coming from a mile away." Aly held his amused gaze. "I even had a couple raise their hand just like you did, and swear on Scout's honor, only to find out later that they'd never been Boy Scouts. Now you understand why I question *your* gesture."

This was the real Aly, he realized humbly. A wisecracking lady who could land on her feet. His smile widened, and he fought a very real urge to slip his arm around her shoulders, draw her close and kiss those upturned corners of her provocative mouth. "First of all, I *was* a Boy Scout. Matter of fact, I made Eagle Scout."

"Impressive. You must have gotten your hand-em-a-line badge after you joined the Navy."

"Watch it, Trayhern."

Delighted, Aly hooted. "To fast for you, fly-boy?"

"No one's faster than me," he gloated, a threat in his tone.

Aly chuckled between bites, trading warm glances with Clay. What a wonderful sense of humor he'd been hiding from her all these months. Momentary sadness struck her, but Aly rallied. He was trying to change, she realized. Clay was trying to make up for all the pain and hurt he'd caused her. Her smile dissolved as she made that connection.

"Aly? Where'd you take off to?" Clay had seen the dancing gold highlights disappear from her wide, telling eyes. And her smile had disappeared, too.

"Huh? Oh, I'm sorry, Clay. I just got to thinking, was all. It's nothing."

He cocked his head, catching her gaze. "Nothing?" he mimicked, trying to cajole her into telling him what she was really thinking about.

Forcing a slight smile, Aly muttered, "Don't mind me. I nose-dive every once in a while."

Not convinced, but not knowing how to pull whatever was bothering her out into the open, Clay straightened. He took another tack.

"After my father died, my mother moved us back to Dubuque, Iowa. She loved the fields of corn and wanted to raise us in the country, away from the cities." He ate more slowly, allowing those memories to well up within him. "I guess they found my mom on somebody's doorstep around Christmas one year, and she was raised in a succession of foster families in New York City. She hated big cities, telling us that concrete, glass and steel weren't going to teach us a thing. We had to go to the country to find out what life was all about.'' He laughed softly and shared a warm look with Aly, who had stopped eating and was listening intently.

''So, after my father died in that jet crash—which I don't remember, because I was barely a year old—we moved to Iowa. My first memories are of sitting on top of this huge black and white Holstein cow. I must have been three years old at the time. My mother was holding me up there, and Stephen was taking a picture of the two of us. I was bawling my eyes out because the cow scared the hell out of me.''

''Did your mother like animals?'' Aly asked, touched that Clay would share such a personal moment of his life with her.

He finished off the rest of the MRE, stowing the bag and plastic spoon in the pack. ''She *loved* animals. Horses, especially.'' Leaning back, his hands behind his head, Clay watched the changing colors of the sky as sunset neared. ''I guess as close as she ever got to having a horse was that big old cow. We rented an old four-room house from this farmer who owned a dairy herd. And this one old cow, Bossy, was real tame. Actually, it was Stephen's idea to put me up on Bossy and pretend that she was a horse for me to ride. Mom went along with the idea. They had great fun, but I was scared to death.''

A soft smile touched Aly's lips. ''It sounds as if you had a wonderful time growing up in Iowa.'' Pain over Stephen's death made her ache for Clay. But he didn't appear unhappy right now. Instead, there was excitement in his voice, as if he were sharing these vignettes for the first time.

"Yeah, well, if you knew Stephen… He was five years older than me, and he was always plotting and planning something. Usually something that included me as the naive twit who got suckered into it."

"I know what you mean." Aly laughed. "My two older brothers, Morgan and Noah, used to blame me for whatever they got caught doing behind my parents' backs."

The mention of Morgan's name hit Clay hard. He wrestled with it, praying his face remained neutral. And when he saw the happiness in Aly's eyes over those memories, he wanted to push beyond his own painful barriers to find out more about her. "Sounds like those two were in cahoots, and you were the odd person out," he teased.

"Oh, believe me, I was! I remember one time when Morgan wanted to play Indian fort. He was always cooking up ideas, and of course, Noah and I just innocently toddled along." Aly sat up, animation in her voice. "He had the greatest ideas sometimes, Clay. That particular time, he dragged a whole bunch of cardboard boxes up from the basement, and we made this wonderful fort out of them. I mean, we had boxes strung all through the living room, one and two stories high."

"Where were your parents?"

"Dad was off flying a B-52 mission, gone for two weeks. Mom was over at the base exchange, getting groceries. Morgan was twelve, so he was baby-sitting the two of us while she was gone."

"Perfect recipe for trouble." Clay chuckled.

"You got it!" Aly set down the MRE and launched excitedly into the rest of her story. "Noah got this great idea to use sheets as a roof for our fort. So they told me to go up to the linen closet and get them. I must have come back with fifteen of them!''

Clay groaned. ''Oh, God, what did your mother do when she saw this concoction?''

Laughing, Aly reached over, her hand resting on his shoulder. The action shocked both of them. She quickly removed her hand. ''By the time Mom got home, the entire living room comprised our fort. With the sheets, we had a wonderful roof, and even had enough of them left over for curtains to hang over some of the boxes inside the fort. It was *really* a neat fort, Clay.''

He grinned. ''I'll bet it was. And I'll bet your mother had a canary, too.''

Giggling, Aly said, ''She about dropped the groceries at the entrance to the living room when she saw it. Noah and Morgan had heard her car pull up in the driveway, and they scooted into the fort to hide. They told me to go out and tell Mom all about it.''

''Uh-oh...they were setting you up for the fall.''

''You got it! I ran out to the kitchen to meet her, bubbling over about this fort we'd built.'' She slanted him a wry glance. ''Now, keep in mind, I was only six years old at the time. Anyway, Mom came to the entrance of the living room, and her mouth fell open. I was rattling on in my little voice, my arms waving here and there about how we'd built it. When she finally spoke, there was this tone in her voice that meant we were in big trouble. Mom ordered Morgan and Noah front and center.''

''Did they come crawling out of the fort and face the music?'' Clay asked, grinning.

''Not at first,'' Aly hedged, fondly recalling the

incident. ''Mom demanded that Morgan and Noah show themselves or else.''

''Did they give up?''

''Morgan had talked Noah into carrying a white flag of truce out with him, thinking Mom would find it funny and relent. She didn't. Both my brothers pointed the finger at me, telling Mom that I'd taken the sheets from the closet. They hoped to transfer the blame to me, because they knew a paddling was the next order of business.''

Clay shook his head. ''Your brothers were mean.''

Chuckling, Aly said, ''That's okay. Little sister grew up in a hurry under those conditions. I learned real fast never to be around when Morgan and Noah started cooking up another one of their grandiose plans.''

''So, what happened to the fort?''

''You haven't heard the best of it.'' Aly laughed. ''Mom grabbed Morgan by the ear and demanded to know where he'd gotten all those cardboard boxes. There must have been twenty-five or thirty of them in there. He confessed to Mom that he'd gotten them from the basement. She nearly laid an egg on that one.''

''Why?''

Aly laughed for nearly a minute, holding her sides. Wiping the tears from her eyes, she finally managed to get out, ''Morgan *unpacked* those boxes from our recent move to this new base. Twenty-eight boxes of stuff were now helter-skelter all over the basement floor. Mom almost died when she went down and looked.'' Her eyes sparkled, watching Clay grin. ''The upshot of it was that Morgan and Noah spent the next week, every night after schoolwork was done, repacking each of those boxes. They hated it! Noah was really mad at Morgan, because Noah hadn't gotten the boxes out of the basement in the first place.''

Shaking his head, Clay asked, ''What about those fifteen sheets?''

''Morgan had to not only wash and dry every last one of them, but he had to iron them as well!''

''So, your Mom read between the lines and saw that you were the innocent in their diabolical plot?''

Twittering contentedly, Aly leaned back. ''Yup. For once naive little sister got a reprieve. God, that whole thing was so funny, Clay.'' She traded a happy look with him. ''I'm really glad you started talking about your family. I haven't remembered the fort incident in years.'' Reaching out, she briefly touched his arm. ''Thanks. It feels so good to laugh again.''

They had managed to scale the third set of hills before darkness fell across Baja. Clay pulled Aly to a halt. She leaned slightly, her body brushing his.

''Let's call it a day,'' he said.

''Good, I'm beat to hell, Clay.''

He squeezed her hand. ''You're a trooper, though.'' Aly had never complained, but kept doggedly climbing hour after hour. ''I'm amazed at your stamina,'' Clay admitted, allowing the heavy pack to slide off his shoulders.

Aly stood wearily, more tired than she'd ever thought possible. Clay was the one who carried the pack, but he didn't appear to be nearly as exhausted as she felt. ''Must be the family genes,'' she offered. ''What do you want me to do?''

''Nothing, just sit down and rest.''

"Thanks...I owe you one."

Clay noted a slice of moon was coming up, providing just enough light to barely see her facial features. "And I intend to collect," he warned her huskily.

A tremble of anticipation moved through her. Aly sat facing him. He couldn't be serious. No. "Uh-oh," she baited, "my body or my life, is that it?"

Taking out the plastic ground cover, Clay laid it down after clearing a spot of rocks and pebbles. "Say, now that's not a bad trade."

She snorted. "Cantrell, you're such a male chauvinist."

He took the blanket, placing it over the plastic cover, smoothing it out. "I'd take your body in trade."

"You would."

He sat up, hands resting on his knees. Seeing that Aly wasn't sure whether he was teasing or not, Clay decided to test her, to find out just how far her disgust with him went. "Now, I'm very picky about the body I make love with."

Aly avoided his dark, probing eyes. She lowered her lashes. How many times had she dreamed of Clay loving her? Of their sharing laughter and joy together? "So am I," she parried.

"But if there was a choice between losing your life or giving yourself to me, which would it be?"

Aly licked her chapped lower lip. "Well..." she hedged.

"Is it my looks that turn you off?"

"No! Of course not." Aly risked a glance at him, realizing he was watching her intently. "What I mean is, you're not ugly or anything."

''Whew, that was close!'' Clay dramatically placed his hand against his heart.

She gave him a dirty look.

''Since I'm such a handsome devil, you wouldn't find it personally distasteful to fall into my arms?''

Aly dug the toe of her boot into the dirt, trapped. ''Okay, so you're not bad-looking,'' she admitted, refusing to answer the rest of his question.

''I love the way compliments roll off your tongue. I practically have to drag them out of you.''

''Oh, shut up, Cantrell!''

Chuckling, he got up and walked over to where she sat. He crouched down in front of her. Aly refused to look up. ''What's this? Are you blushing, Aly Trayhern?'' And he placed his finger beneath her chin, forcing her to meet his gaze. ''Why, I believe you are.''

Unable to speak, Aly held his smiling dark eyes. There was tenderness burning in them, and when she realized he wasn't laughing at her, she panicked. Clay was so close, so pulverizingly male that she ached to lean those scant inches and feel his mouth on hers again.

''My shy little violet,'' Clay said huskily, lightly caressing her cheek. He saw something in her huge blue eyes, and it wasn't fear. If he read her correctly, it was longing. Need. That shook him badly. Instead of disgust or anger aimed at him, he saw desire. In those shattering seconds strung between them, Clay realized that Aly didn't hate him at all. And then he remembered the passion of her returning kiss so many months ago. He gave her a little smile, hoping to reassure her that he wasn't going to take advantage of her.

"Come on, let's get ready for bed," he murmured, slowly rising to his feet. "I'd like to sleep until about 0500 when it starts getting light, and walk while it's still cool. What do you think?"

"That sounds fine," she whispered. It took Aly a good minute to gather her strewn feelings. Clay could have kissed her, and she would have welcomed it. Somehow, he'd sensed that she wanted him! His eyes had grown dark, and she'd seen that silver flame in their depths. Her heart was pounding erratically.

Clay shed the vest he was wearing and plumped it up for a pillow to lay his head on. He twisted around, looking over at Aly. She was shaken. Using humor, he growled, "Come on, Miss Trayhern, get your rear over here. If you don't lie down, you're going to fall off that rock and hurt yourself when you fall asleep on it."

Nervously, Aly rose. She looked at the small square of bedding, realizing that both of them would be sleeping on it. "Clay," she began in a strangled tone, "two people can't sleep on that!"

He started untying his bootlaces. "Sure, they can."

Lamely, Aly approached the foot of it. "But—it's only big enough for one person."

"You didn't bring your gear with you. We'll have to make do with mine."

Despair flooded her. Clay was right. She'd rushed off in such a hurry to catch up with him on the trek that she'd packed only the essentials of food and water, not sleeping gear. "I—uh, I think I'll just sleep on the ground. You go ahead and use that pallet."

"And let the creepy-crawlies get you?"

"Clay Cantrell!"

He struggled to give her his best innocent look.

More than anything, Clay wanted Aly near him. Tonight, he wanted to salve more of her wounds by being close, letting her know that he didn't hate or dislike her. "Well, I mean scorpions are night creatures. And they're always looking for a warm body to snuggle up to...."

With a cry, Aly moved to the blanket. She gave him an angry look. "You're such a rat, Cantrell! You know I can't stand those things!"

He swallowed his smile and returned to unlacing his second boot. Pulling it off, he set it aside. Absently patting the blanket next to him, he said, "Come on, Aly sit down. I'll help you get those boots off."

She glared at Clay, more frightened of her reaction to him than anything else. "You take off anything more than my boots, and you're in big trouble, fella!"

"Threats, threats!" Clay laughed, reaching up and pulling her gently down beside him. "Really, Miss Trayhern, I'd hope I'm the lesser of two evils." He gloated as he untied her bootlaces. "I'd hope I'm more desirable to you than a scorpion. If you chose that fellow over me, that'd really hurt my feelings."

"You're impossible, Cantrell! Utterly, certifiably impossible!"

He chuckled as he removed her boots. Aly had such small, delicate feet. There was concern and wariness in her features. Clay lay down, his back to her. "Come on, stop spitting and clawing like a cornered cat, and lie down."

Grumbling under her breath, Aly lay on her right side, facing his broad, powerful back. She had no choice but to wedge next to him, the narrowness of the blanket forcing them together. She saw him rise on one elbow, pull the blanket over them and then lie back down. She clamped her eyes shut.

Clay grinned into the darkness, hotly aware that Aly was only inches away from him. "Good night, little hellcat. Sleep tight."

Aly refused to respond to his husky voice. She tried to inch away from him, balanced precariously on the line where the blanket ended and the desert began. He was just too close, too overwhelming for her rattled senses.

Clay felt Aly move away. "Scorpions like to find the edges of blankets to crawl under," he told her.

With a little cry of fear, Aly scooted back to him. "Damn you, Cantrell!"

Clay stifled a laugh. "Better get a little closer, Aly. That way, no scorpions can wiggle their way between us." His grin widened as she hesitantly fitted her body against his back and legs. "Better," he groaned. "Much better."

Aly knew her eyes must be blazing, even in the dark. "You're going to pay for this, Cantrell. You're enjoying this at my expense."

Clay shook with laughter. God, but Aly felt good contoured against him. He checked his desire to lift his arm and place it across her hip. "Yeah, I am. But you know something?"

"I don't want to hear another word out of you!"

Smiling, he murmured, "Well, I'm going to tell you anyway. I like the way you feel against me. You're warm, soft, and all woman. What a way to go...."

Aly refused to answer him. A minute later she muttered, "You're arrogant, Cantrell. You ought to be ashamed of yourself for using a situation like this on me. I can't help it if I'm scared of those horrible insects!''

Clay couldn't help himself. He slid his hand carefully beneath the blanket until it came in contact with her slender hip. Giving it a gentle pat, he murmured, ''Good night, Aly. Sleep the sleep of the angels, because you are one.''

The gray cape of dawn was just barely edging the horizon when Clay awoke. But that wasn't what awakened him. Sometime during the night, he'd turned over on his back. Aly had somehow found her way into his arms. Her head lay in the hollow of his left shoulder, her red hair smooth and springy against his jaw. Gently, he squeezed her, delighting in her feminine length against him.

The stars hung close in the night sky above him. A coyote yipped and then cried, his howl lonely across the quiet of the desert. There was no wind on top of the hill. Everything was silent, as if holding its breath. Contentment flowed through Clay. He savored each precious second with Aly, feeling the rise and fall of her breasts against him, her breath moist across his neck. What pleased him most was the fact that her left hand, despite the sling, lay against his torso.

She was sleeping deeply, and so Clay risked everything and pressed a kiss to her hair. He inhaled her fragrance like a starved man. Wasn't he? Yes. He was starved for her. And if he was able to read between the lines of Aly's reluctance to lie here with him, she too was aware of the possible chemistry that might flare to life between them. His contentment increased, and he closed his eyes, absorbing her into his eyes, absorbing her into himself. If only…if only it could be like this every day for the rest of his life.

"We belong together, little hellcat," he told her softly. "You and me. We're a good team, and I think you're just realizing that."

Aly stirred, her leg resting across Clay's. Unconsciously, she nuzzled upward, meeting the hard length of his jaw. In her dreams, she heard him speaking to her in a low voice. His arm held her safe and protected. She reveled in the feel of his masculine body against hers. There was such strength in him, such gentleness.

Clay groaned as Aly pressed languidly against him. Sweet heaven… Just that one, innocent movement brought him to hot, burning life. He wanted so badly to kiss Aly, to feel her warm, willing mouth beneath his once again. Carefully, so as not to awaken her, Clay gently maneuvered Aly onto her back, his arm beneath her head, cradling her shoulders.

He lay propped on his elbow, looking down at her in the predawn light. Her hair was tousled, and he longed to sift through those errant waves. As his gaze moved downward, Clay realized how long and thick her lashes were against the freckled planes of her cheeks. A beginning of a smile pulled at his mouth. Lifting his free hand, he lightly traced the length of her thin, aristocratic nose. She was a lady, through and through. His fingers trailed downward, and against all his better judgment, Clay barely touched her parted lips.

Aly's torrid dream state had her lying in Clay's arms. She felt his fingertips outlining the shape of her mouth, and a smile unconsciously curved them upward. With a sigh, she turned her cheek, feeling his palm cradle her face. The longing for Clay, for his touch, continued, and she nuzzled deeply into his hand, seeking, needing his warmth.

"Sweet Aly," Clay whispered, leaning over, his mouth resting against her cheek. Her skin was delicate, inviting, and he kissed her gently.

Aly felt his mouth against her cheek, and she turned her head, seeking him. Where did a dream end and reality begin? It was so real, her heart picking up in pounding beat as she felt his hand slide across her hip, bringing her against him. She wanted him so badly. A whimper broke from her as his mouth slid across the expanse of her cheek.

With a low groan, Clay covered Aly's waiting lips. She was incredibly soft, her mouth molding hotly to his. Fire shattered all his resolve, and he drank of her, tasting her, teasing her into wakefulness within his arms.

The instant Clay's mouth touched her own, Aly drew out of the folds of the twilight she lingered in. It wasn't a dream, it was wonderful reality. Dragging her lashes upward, she met and drowned in the hungry flame in his gray eyes. His mouth was cajoling, teasing, erasing her momentary panic and fear. He tasted so male, and with abandonment, Aly responded to his offering. His hand sliding across her rear, moving her against him, increased her sense of urgency. He was hard and ready and she melted within his embrace, swept away by the heat he shared with her.

Clay's mouth was hungry, searching against hers. He tasted strong and male, his scent mixed with sweat entering her nostrils. The rough texture of his beard scraped against her flesh, sending tingles riffling through her. A little cry escaped her, his name coming out in a pleading tone. She slid her fingers upward, her arm lifting, caressing Clay's hair. The strands were soft and thick. Her heart pounded urgently in her chest, and Aly pressed herself to him, feeling him groan. The reverberation thrummed through her, exciting her, putting a keen edge on her need of him.

"I need you," he muttered hoarsely against her wet, willing lips. Blindly, Clay closed his eyes, his hand sliding downward until he cupped her breast. She was so small and firm, so completely woman, her hip melting against his, creating a fire storm of hunger within him. Without thinking, Clay pulled open the Velcro of her flight suit, sliding his hand inside it, wanting to give her pleasure instead of pain for once.

Her breast was firm, the nipple taut, expectant. Gently laying her on her back, he pulled the fabric of the uniform away. Aly's breath was coming in short sobs, her fingers digging frantically into his shoulders as he leaned over, pushing the bra aside, and capturing the erect nipple.

A cry drove from deep within her as his lips covered the aching peak, and Aly arched against him, an intense heat spreading throughout her lower body. Sobs of pleasure whispered from her as Clay worshiped her as if she were some priceless, beautiful object that might break.

Clay struggled to get hold of himself. Too much was happening too fast. Aly wasn't ready for this. He fought himself, fought to try to ignore the sweet, moist texture of her lips, the passion that was making him tremble. It was enough, he screamed at himself as he reluctantly broke contact with her, that she had so willingly responded to him. One look into those sultry eyes staring up at him, and Clay knew that her feelings toward him were genuine. Joy raced beside his guilt. He didn't deserve this kind of reward for hurting her the way he had over the past nine months. Removing his hand from her flushed, rosy breast, he brought the bra back into place. Dutifully, he closed the Velcro on her flight suit, holding her confused stare.

Gently, Clay eased Aly to the pallet, his arm still beneath her head. An unsure smile tugged at his mouth as he smoothed several strands of red hair from her brow. "When I awoke, the stars were hanging over us like huge, white lanterns in the sky," he confided huskily, continuing to caress her cheek. "And I lay here a long time, thinking how lucky I was. Most importantly, you were in my arms." His voice grew gritty. "I couldn't help myself, honey. When you moved against me in your sleep, I lost all my good intentions and kissed you." Caressing her lips with his thumb, Clay whispered, "You're as hot as the color of that beautiful hair of yours. I was so cold inside and you warmed me with your fire...."

His words seemed to fall softly through Aly, into her heart. She absorbed his shaky admission and closed her eyes. She was equally at fault in this. The crash and being stranded had made her take risks that she'd never have entertained otherwise with Clay. But one look into the smoky depths of his eyes, and Aly had felt the simmering heat within her build to an explosive point again. Clay didn't even have to touch her; all he had to do was give her that smoldering look of need, and she responded. "Oh, Clay," she whispered. "I'm so afraid...."

"I know," he said, allowing his hand to rest on her shoulder, "so am I."

Chapter Ten

Clay watched Aly withdraw deep into herself after he kissed her. She was silent, and he longed to know what was going on inside that head of hers. They were both scared. Maybe for the same reasons, maybe for different ones. He simply didn't know.

The climb across the mountains effectively drew their focus and attention. Cliffs of rock rose like sharp spires flung skyward. Taking the lead, Clay tried to find a route between them. The rocks were solid under their booted feet, and for that he was thankful. Both he and Aly were drenched with sweat, their flight suits clinging to them when they stopped to eat and rest at noon.

Aly tried to find a spot that wouldn't force them close together. Clay's kiss had unstrung her. It was everything and more than she had ever dreamed about. Her response to him had frightened her even more. Struggling to resolve the taut situation between them, Aly started a conversation after they had eaten their MREs.

"About last night...I mean, this morning, Clay."

Aly was two feet away from where Clay sat on the ground, leaning against a boulder. He saw her lick her lower lip nervously. "What about it?" he asked gently, afraid of what his kiss might have cost him in terms of Aly's trust. He wanted her on all levels and all ways, in and out of bed. The fear was very real in her blue eyes.

Aly picked up a small rock, turning it between her bandaged hands. "I'm not the type for a one-night stand, Clay. Never was. Never will be." She risked a glance at him. He was excruciatingly handsome, strands of his black hair dipping across his forehead, those gray eyes dark and fathomless. A quiver tremored through her as her gaze settled on the mobile mouth that could make her heart beat faster every time he smiled at her. He wasn't smiling now.

"A long time ago, I liked one-night stands," Clay admitted slowly, holding her unsure gaze. "Part of the fighter jock image, I suppose. But..."

Aly saw Clay smile slightly. "But?" Her heart was pounding again, and it wasn't from the brutal climb they'd made earlier.

"Well, the crash changed a lot of things for me," Clay admitted. "I almost died, and that's when I found living was a little more important than flouting death every day. The main reason I switched from fighters to land-based aircraft was because I wanted to take time to smell the flowers."

"I wondered why you got out of fighters. Most guys would die to fly a Tomcat."

He pursed his lips and nodded. ''Yeah, you're right. But I'd had two and a half years racing around the skies like Parnelli Jones. And I can't say I miss those night landings on a heaving postage stamp of a deck out in the middle of an angry ocean.''

Clay's voice was balm to her aching heart and, almost unwillingly, Aly began to relax. And with his quiet soothing, some of her fear of their future dissolved, too. ''But you still chose an aircraft that does dangerous work.''

''Sure.'' And then Clay awarded her one of those heart-stopping smiles. ''I like danger. I was bred for it, I suppose. My father had been a Navy fighter pilot. It's in my genes—the way stubbornness runs in your family.''

There was no accusation or anger in his voice when he referred to her family. Aly was still in shock over his decision to release the past and treat her as an individual. ''I prefer to call it tenacity,'' she managed to parry.

''Yeah, pit bull style,'' he chortled. ''So, what's this ultimatum about one-night stands all about?''

His softly spoken words caught Aly off guard. She eyed him for a long minute, the wind lifting strands of her hair as it wove in and around the crags surrounding them. ''I like your sensitivity,'' she murmured, staring down at the rock in her hands.

''You invite it, Aly.''

His voice was deep with promise. A promise she dared never hope for. ''I—damn, this is so hard to say....''

''You want me to back off?''

Giving him a lame look, she nodded. ''Yes.''

Instead of wanting to make her feel guilty or bad,

Clay wanted her to realize he would support her decision. "It's as good as done, little hellcat." And then he grinned, striving to lift her spirits. "I promise I won't keep using the creepy-crawlies as an excuse to get you into my arms, okay?"

"You're crazy, Cantrell."

He grinned with her, watching the shadows dissolve from her wonderful blue eyes. "Yeah, but you like me anyway."

Relief spread throughout Aly, and she was suddenly tired. Leaning back, her head tipped against the unyielding rock, she closed her eyes. "I'm taking the Fifth on that one."

"I would, too."

"Thanks for understanding, Clay."

"You deserve it. Take your siesta," he coaxed, "we aren't going to start hiking until 1600, anyway."

"And then we'll walk until it gets dark?"

"You got it, honey. Go to sleep."

Without the moon's thin wisp of light, Clay wouldn't have been able to make their bed. Aly sat on a rock, watching him in silence. The wind was howling through the mountains, the temperature dropping rapidly.

"Sweat during the day and freeze at night," he told her, placing the blanket over the plastic cover.

"Isn't that the truth," Aly said, and shivered. Clay had found a depression where they would be protected from most of the wind. "I wish we could make a fire."

"No wood. This is the most desolate place I've ever seen."

Miserably, Aly agreed. The climb today had

brought them near the top of the mountains. "Do you think we'll reach that village by tomorrow evening?"

Clay took off his vest and made a pillow out of it. "Depends on how easy it is to climb down off this mountain." Getting to his feet, he walked over to her. "I want to change the dressings on your hands before we go to bed. I'm afraid you'll get dirt in those healing rope burns."

Aly looked at the dusty gauze that encased her palms and wrists. "They feel pretty good, Clay."

Crouching and opening the first-aid kit, he placed her right hand across the surface of his thigh. "Just let me play nursemaid, okay?"

She smiled tiredly. He was so close, and all she wanted to do was rest her head against his capable shoulder. Amazed as always at Clay's gentleness as he cut away the old bandage, she muttered, "You're a good doctor."

"Maybe it's the patient," he answered, catching her gaze. Examining her palm carefully, Clay could see that the wound was doing nicely. "Maybe I did miss my calling. Your palm is looking good."

"Maybe it's the guy doing the doctoring."

Clay grinned up at her. "What is this? A mutual admiration society we're starting?" Aly was so close, and those ripe lips of hers parted, needing to be kissed again. Stifling the urge, Clay expertly rewrapped her palm.

"There's plenty to admire about you," Aly parried, "and you know it."

"Naw. I'm just a brash ex-fighter jock. Cocky, self-assured—"

"Don't forget handsome."

"That, too. Brilliant mind, great sense of humor—"

"And nice," Aly added softly, meaning it. She saw him shrug as he gently eased her left hand out of the sling.

"Trying to be. With you, it's long overdue." Clay met and held her gaze, drowning in the gold fire. The need to slide his arms around her, draw Aly to him, was almost tangible. Fighting his raging desire, Clay croaked, "How's your shoulder feeling? I haven't heard one peep about it all day."

As she allowed her arm to ease from the bent position in the sling, Aly tested it carefully. "Pretty good."

"Does it hurt to rotate your arm in any direction? Try it, but be real slow about it."

Testing her arm, Aly found she had about fifty-percent mobility. To raise it above her breasts produced excruciating pain. "Maybe if I just let the arm hang and don't put it back in the sling, I'll get more mobility," she suggested.

"Yeah, try it. Keep the sling off tonight while you sleep. If you need it tomorrow, we can always put it back on."

He looped the sling around her neck. "There, it's nearby if you want it."

"Thanks, doc."

Clay got up reluctantly. "Anytime. Come on, let's hit the sack."

Aly chewed on her lower lip, watching as he walked back to the depression where their bedding and gear were waiting for them. To lie next to him was going to be sheer agony. Would he keep his word? Would he not touch her? Could she fight her own desire to reach out to him?

Already settled on the bed, his back to her, Clay felt Aly finally slip down beside him. He sensed her tension as she got closer. Wanting to defuse her anxiety, he murmured over his shoulder, "Just how did you get this phobia about creepie-crawlies? You never finished telling me."

Grateful for his teasing demeanor, Aly snuggled close, seeking his body heat. "My two brothers bought a bunch of small black rubber spiders at a dime store one day. They laid them all over my bed one morning while I was still sleeping. And then they stood there, waiting to see me wake up. When I did, I saw my blanket covered with the horrible things."

Clay began to laugh, trying to stifle it.

"See? You think it's funny, too."

His laughter rolled out into the darkness. "I'm sorry, honey, I can't help it. It sounds like something Stephen and I would have cooked up."

"All little boys are up to no good, if you ask me."

"Well," he asked between chuckles, "what happened?"

"I screamed and leaped out of bed. Noah had put a couple in my hair, which was long at that time, and I was trying to bat them away."

Clay started laughing again.

Aly hit him in the arm. "You're just like them, Cantrell. Good night."

He reached over, patting her hip again. "Good night. Sweet dreams for a sweet lady...."

All her worries dissipated, and Aly closed her eyes, sighing softly. "I hope you get nightmares, Cantrell, for laughing at me...."

The last of his laughter dissolved beneath her husky voice. What he'd give to hear her tone drop to a purr as he made love to her. "No way, lady. Tonight, I'm going to dream you're in my arms again."

"I'm going to dream of finding that village by tomorrow evening," she muttered in defense.

"I'll bet my dreams will be far more enjoyable than yours."

"Good night, Cantrell."

"Good night, little hellcat."

They stood near the bottom of the mountain slope, the sun low on the horizon. Aly glanced at her watch: it was 1800. They were right on schedule.

"Look—" Clay pointed "—I think that's the village. See it?"

Aly moved to his side, following the direction of his finger. She squinted her eyes. Heat rolled in waves across the arid wasteland, but she could make out a dark object in the distance. "Are you sure, Clay?"

He took out the map, double-checking it. "Yeah. The map says it's a major Huichol village."

"'Major'? Does that mean they'll have a pay phone so we can call for rescue?"

He wiped the sweat off his brow with the back of his hand. The heat was stifling. "Major in terms of population. There are all of fifty people living there."

Aly's left arm felt good after being out of the sling most of the day. She rested her hands on her hips, studying the miragelike village. "Where could fifty people possibly find enough food or water to survive out here?"

"Got me." Clay looked over at Aly. Her face was pink from sunburn, but she looked damned good to him. Last night, he'd barely slept because she'd been next to him. But Aly looked as if she'd slept like a proverbial rock, he observed wryly, her eyes clear, and no shadows beneath her lovely eyes. "Well, it's five miles away. Ready?"

She gave him a game smile. In another mile they'd be off the mountain and onto a plateau scattered with a few tenacious small plants that hugged the desert. "You bet. Let's go for it, jet jock."

The miles fell away. Aly felt a new sense of exhilaration, matching every step Clay took at her shoulder. Once he awarded her one of his devastating smiles. She wanted to stop, throw her arms around his shoulders and kiss him. And he must have read the desire in her eyes because he leaned down, placed a quick kiss on her hair, then resumed his striding walk without missing a beat. Aly didn't know whether to be pleased or disgruntled about it. Clay merely smiled that cocky smile of his, completely pleased with himself.

The village took form and shape as they drew closer. There was a huge pile of yellowed rock about a mile from the Indian hamlet. They'd been walking hard and fast, and Clay called a halt, wanting a drink of water.

Aly plopped down on a flat rock next to where he sat. "Whew!"

"Yeah," Clay muttered, tipping up the plastic bottle and taking a small swallow of water.

Shading her eyes, Aly said, "I don't believe it. There's a man on a burro coming toward us."

Clay handed her the water bottle and squinted in that direction. "Damned if it isn't. They must have spotted us coming off the mountain." He smiled.

"Great, the Welcome Wagon is on the way. I hope you know some Spanish."

The water was heavenly, sliding down her sandpapery throat. Aly stoppered the bottle and gave it back to Clay. "I know enough Spanish to get by, but I don't know their Indian language."

"Doesn't matter. The survival info says most of them speak pidgin Spanish." He patted her thigh. "Well, what do you say we get this show on the road?"

Aly got to her feet, standing near him while he leaned down to stow the bottle back into the pack. Her smile disappeared. A scream lurched up her throat.

"Clay!" Her cry careened off the rocks that surrounded them.

To her horror, as Clay leaned down to pick up the pack that had been placed in a crevice between two huge boulders, Aly saw a red and black lizard leap out of the shadows toward his extended hand.

It happened so quickly, that she was unable to move to prevent it. The Gila monster attacked, its huge jaws open, hurtling toward Clay's fingers.

Clay had frozen at Aly's cry. Too late he saw the blur of the red and black Gila darting out of the crevice toward him. The next thing he felt was pain sizzling up the side of his left hand. With a croak of surprise, Clay jerked back. The Gila monster clung to his hand, its two-foot-long body swinging back and forth, its jaws locked firmly into Clay's flesh, releasing its virulent poison into his bloodstream.

With a grunt, Clay staggered forward. His eyes bulged as he tried to fling the lizard off his hand. Its jaws were locked! His mind worked like a steel trap, now. Aly's screams drifted into his narrowed focus as he whirled around on his heel. Clenching his teeth, Clay took the hand the lizard clung to, and with all his might, smashed it into the side of the rock face.

Aly shrieked as the Gila monster's jaws popped open, as it was killed on impact. Clay staggered and fell to his knees, holding his mangled left hand. She raced to his side. His flesh was already beginning to lose color. His eyes were large and dark. Sobbing his name, she knelt over him.

"The sling!" Cantrell rasped. "Get that sling on my upper arm. Make it into a tourniquet!"

Her hands shaking, Aly did as he ordered. The poison injected into Clay's hand would be moving rapidly up his arm. She took off the sling, wrapped it quickly around his arm, tightening it into position with a stick.

"Oh, God, Clay!" she cried. "What—"

"The venom kit," he whispered harshly, trying to force his hand to bleed. If he could make the four puncture holes bleed, some of the poison would drip out instead of being absorbed into his bloodstream. "Get it! Hurry!" The first wave of dizziness struck him. He could die! Clay tried to steady his ragged breathing. He had to stave off his panic. Aly's sobs heightened his fear. She fumbled through the pack, her hands shaking so badly that she dropped the kit once she'd located it.

"The shot," he told her, feeling his arm going numb because of the tourniquet on his limb. "Give me the shot as fast as you can, or I'm dead—"

Aly tore open the venom kit. Inside was an antivenin shot. She jammed the needle portion into the tube containing the solution. "Where?" she cried.

Clay's breathing was becoming labored. He had to force each breath he took. God, but the poison was working fast! Sweat ran down into his eyes. He was so cold, and yet his entire body was wringing wet with sweat. "Anywhere!" he croaked. "My leg..."

She shoved the needle through the fabric of his flight suit and it sank deep into his left thigh. Pushing the plunger, Aly looked up at him. Clay was becoming semiconscious. Jerking the needle out, Aly tried to cushion his fall as he pitched forward. "Oh, God, Clay. Fight to stay awake! Fight!"

Aly's voice was like an echo in his head. Clay felt his hand slipping from his injured one. His mouth fell open and saliva drooled out the corner of it. He'd barely been aware of the needle entering his leg, or of Aly's hands settling on his shoulders to turn him onto his back.

"No!" Aly begged hoarsely, "Clay, don't die on me! Don't you dare! Fight back! You hear me? Fight!" She shook him hard.

Terror ate at Aly as she watched Clay struggle to stay conscious. His flesh was pasty, almost gray. His breath was coming in halting gasps, and he labored for every one he took. Aly released his shoulders, turning her attention to his injured hand. She retrieved the razor blade from the kit, slicing into two of the puncture wounds. There was a suction device, but her hands were shaking too badly to use it. Placing her lips over the now bleeding punctures, she sucked hard, spitting out the contents gathered, again and again. The poison would have pooled at the bottom of each hole the Gila monster had made. In moments, Aly had pulled as much out as possible from all four wounds.

She shakily got to her feet, looking around. The rider on the burro was much closer. Anguished, she knelt at Clay's side. His lashes fluttered, his breathing becoming shallow and fast.

"Clay? Clay, listen to me!" She gripped his shoulder, placing her mouth next to his ear. "I'm going for help, you hear me? I've got to get help! I'll be back. I promise I will!" She looked down at him. His flesh was beaded with sweat. "I'll be back—I won't desert you. I promise. Oh, God, Clay, hang on! I love you! You can't die on me!"

Sobbing, Aly staggered to her feet. She turned on her heel, and began running across the hard pebbled desert toward the man on the burro in the distance. Her throat burned with tears, her vision blurred. *I love you, Clay! Oh, God, please don't take him from me! We've just found each other!*

It was dark when Clay regained consciousness. His vision was blurred, and he was seeing double. The flicker of candles provided the only light in the darkened place. The first face he saw was that of a rotund Indian woman dressed in a blue cotton dress, with feathers and beads around her neck. She looked ageless, her black eyes glinting liked polished obsidian as she studied him in the thick silence.

"Clay?"

Aly! Her voice was terribly off-key, and he realized she was crying. Unable to move his head because he was simply too weak, he shifted his eyes to the right. Taking each breath was like inhaling fire into his lungs. It hurt to try to pull the air in or to force it out of his body. Aly's face was contoured with anxiety, her eyes large and filled with fear. Her cheeks were wet and glistening beneath the light of the candle.

"No, don't talk," she whispered, leaning forward, touching his damp brow with a cool cloth. "We're here at the Huichol village. Señora Madalena is their doctor, and she's going to help you."

He was so thirsty. Clay felt Aly's hand cradling his, holding on to it as if he would slip away. His throat was constricted, and he could no longer swallow. Blackness began to stalk him again, and he closed his eyes, focusing on Aly's cool hand, on her tremulous voice.

"I love you, Clay. You've got to fight back, you hear me? Please, don't leave me. I love you...."

Madalena nodded. "He returns to the Between. The Land of the Shadows beckons him," she grunted out in poor Spanish.

Aly looked over at her. Madalena's husband, José, was the one who had brought Clay to their village on the back of the burro. That was an hour ago. It had seemed like an eternity to Aly as she'd struggled to hold Clay on the animal's back. José had led the beast to the hamlet, bringing them to his wife. "Wh-what can be done to save his life? Surely, you must know. You live out in this godforsaken desert with those Gila monsters."

"That is true, *señorita*. My ally told me of your coming. He warned me that a man would be bitten." Her eyes narrowed in her dark brown face, leathery from years in the brutal sun. "That is why I sent my husband." She sighed heavily. "The bite of a Gila monster is fatal."

Fighting her anguish, Aly continued to grip Clay's listless hand. She didn't understand how Madalena could possibly have known of their arrival. Right now, it didn't matter. Madalena had met them at the door of her adobe home, a pallet already prepared for Clay. "No! Please, can't you do something else for him?" Already, Madalena had cleaned out Clay's gruesome-looking wound with a special medicine from one of the many jars on the shelves behind them, and bandaged it. The old woman had told Aly that she was the shaman for her people. Right now, help from anyone was better than nothing in Aly's mind and heart. Already, José was riding as quickly as possible toward a Mexican army outpost two and a half days from the village. Aly had given him written instructions to carry with him. The army would call the coast guard, and a way would be cleared for the rescue not only of Clay and Aly, but also of Dan Ballard. But any outside help would be too late to save Clay's life, and Aly knew it.

"You must fight to return his shadow to us." Madalena spoke slowly, wagging her finger at Aly.

"What do you mean?"

"I will perform a ceremony to call back his shadow from the Land of Death. You must be part of this, for your love of him is strong and unblemished." Madalena frowned, her gravelly voice dropping to a bare rumble. "Already he prepares to depart. His skin grows gray. Next, it will turn blue, and then he will be gone."

Aly hung her head, gripping Clay's hand. "He *can't* leave!" Tears welled in her eyes. "We've gone through so much with each other, Madalena! Through so much hell. A-and when we finally discovered we did care for each other, I—I got frightened."

"Humph," Madalena snorted, slowly rising to her

thickly callused bare feet. Although the home was sparsely furnished and had a dirt floor, it was scrupulously clean and neat. She waddled ponderously to the rear wall of the small one-room adobe house, searching through the many fetishes that lay on shelves and hung from hooks. "Your love for him must outweigh your fear, *señorita.*" She chose a gourd rattle covered with the feathers of a great horned owl, goddess of the night. The handle was beaded in a red and black design. Turning, she came back, her eyes slits. "Be prepared to see and hear and feel many unnerving things, *señorita.* The Shadow Song I will sing will call the spirit of the Gila monster, and I will ask his forgiveness, so that he will remove the poison from your man's body. And then you must close your eyes and see Señor Cantrell's shadow. When he comes to you, embrace him. No matter how much he struggles or resists you, hold on to him." She leaned down, staring deeply into Aly's large, frightened eyes. "You will want to run and scream. You must stay here, at his side, while I sing. Your courage and love must outweigh the Darkness I call."

Aly gave a jerky nod. "I don't understand what you're going to do, but if it'll help, I'll do anything you say, *señora.* Please, hurry, will you?" Under other circumstances, Aly would have pooh-poohed the ancient Indian ritual. But now, she welcomed any help that might improve Clay's chances of surviving. There was a wisdom and knowing in Madalena's eyes that outstripped present-day medical knowledge, and Aly's hope strengthened.

Madalena grunted, a satisfied glint coming to her eyes. Settling down slowly on her knees, she faced

Aly and Clay. She raised the rattle, muttering in her own language, moving it clockwise over Clay four times. With a flick of her wrist, she snapped the gourd once, the stones rattling violently.

Aly jerked. It felt as if a sonic boom had smashed against her, and yet the shaman hadn't touched her with the gourd. Her eyes widened enormously as the shaman began a low, vibrating chant that rolled through the house like a reverberating drum. Aly's hands tightened around Clay's. The room felt as if it were tipping, losing its square shape. She blinked as the sonorous voice of Madalena rose and fell like waves crashing and beating against an unseen shore. Darkness and shadows began to dance around them. Aly blinked rapidly, thinking she was seeing things. She had heard of medicine men and women, of their powerful abilities, but she'd never been confronted with them before.

She tasted her fear as the song grew in volume and power. Each time Madalena made a circle around Clay's body and shook the gourd, Aly winced. It felt as if an invisible hand were slapping her hard each time, making her mind spin and tilt a little more out of control. Clinging to Clay's hand, wanting him to live more than anything else in her world, Aly accepted the distorted reality swirling around her that deepened and expanded every second, as the song thundered through the room.

Clay felt as if someone were pulling him back from the abyss he floated in. He felt light, a feather wafting on air. It no longer hurt to breathe or to struggle to get air into his lungs. The darkness gradually turned to light, and he saw Aly walking toward him, a serious expression on her face. He smiled, waving to her. He loved her so damn much that it made his heart ache with joy.

Why was Aly looking so solemn? He laughed and bounced like a deer toward her. Her walk was cadenced, sure. "Look!" he shouted, "I'm floating! Isn't this great?" And he circled around her as she came to a halt.

"Clay, you've got to come back with me."

He floated lightly to the ground, facing her. When he realized she wasn't smiling or feeling his happiness, he sobered. "But it's great here, Aly. I mean, I'm like a bird, flying free."

"You can't stay, Clay. I love you. I want you to come back with me."

The anguish was in her eyes and in her husky voice. Aly reached out, opening her arms to him. "Come to me, Clay. Come home with me. I need you, even if you don't need me. Please?"

"I need you, too, honey," he said, and he walked into her arms, sliding them around her small, strong shoulders. He kissed her hair. "God, I love you so much, Aly."

With a sob, she tightened her arms around him. "I know you do. Now, come on, let's go back...."

Aly sat at Clay's side, her head dropping to her chest. The movement awoke her. Madalena had left hours earlier after singing the Shadow Song. Aly roused herself, fatigue slowing each of her movements. Taking a cloth, she squeezed it out in the red pottery bowl at her side, and then wiped Clay's perspiring body as he lay naked and unmoving beneath a blanket.

Had a miracle occurred? Aly wasn't sure. At the

height of Madalena's song, she felt totally disoriented, pulled out of her body. Aly remembered meeting Clay and their conversation. He'd come back willingly with her. When she'd awakened later, having no idea how much time had passed, she was lying on the floor next to him. Madalena had placed a pillow beneath her head and left them alone.

Tiredly, Aly sponged Clay's clean limbs, memories flooding her. Awakening after the song, Aly had scrambled to her knees, going immediately to Clay's side, wondering if he was alive or dead. To her surprise and joy, he had more color to his skin, and he was breathing a great deal more easily. Aly had removed his smelly flight suit and made him comfortable on the pallet. For the past hour or so, she had awakened off and on to bathe his sweaty body.

''You've got to live,'' she whispered, placing her hand on his shoulder. His flesh was warm again to her touch, not clammy as before. ''I don't care if it was the antivenin shot taking hold or Madalena's song, Clay, you've got to pull through this. I love you....''

It was the middle of the next day when Clay became conscious. Incredibly weak, he felt as if it hurt even to barely lift his lashes. Light was filtering in from an unknown source behind him. Where was he?

''Clay?'' Aly leaned over him, her voice hushed as she met and held his dark, hooded eyes. Anxiously, she touched his bearded cheek. ''It's all right. We're here at the Indian village. Help's on the way. I—I think you're going to be okay.''

He blinked, assimilating her trembling voice. She was no longer in her flight uniform. Instead, she was wearing a white knee-length shift belted at the waist with a multicolored sash. Her hair was clean and recently washed, too, framing her lovely but strained features. Nothing made sense. His mind refused to work.

"...where..." he croaked.

Slowly, Aly covered the events of the past day and a half. Clay was having difficulty absorbing her explanations. Slipping her arm beneath his shoulders, she gently maneuvered him upward, his head resting against her shoulder and breast. Madalena had prepared a special juice for him to drink, to help wash the poison from his body. Aly placed the cup against his cracked, dry lips.

"Drink," she urged him softly.

He was dying for water, slurping the drink noisily, some of the contents spilling from the corners of his mouth.

She smiled and pressed a kiss to his hair. "Madalena said you'd be thirsty when you woke up. More?" Aly removed the cup and blotted his mouth and chin with a cloth. Her heart swelled with so much love that she thought it might burst.

"Y-yeah...."

Dipping the cup back into the bowl, she allowed Clay to drink as much as he wanted. Four cups later, he was sated. Aly laid him back down. He looked more alert, taking in his surroundings. His gaze moved back to her.

"The dress..." Clay began with an effort. "You look pretty...."

Sliding her hand down his arm, she laced her fingers into his. "And you're a sight for sore eyes. Madalena is washing out my flight suit. Her daughter,

Nina, loaned me something to wear in the meantime."

Exhaustion stalked him. Clay clung to Aly's husky voice and the coolness of her hand in his hot, sweaty one. Closing his eyes, he whispered hoarsely, "I love you...."

Aly knelt there, hearing the words and watching Clay sink back into a deep, healing slumber. The words she'd thought would never be spoken by him hung gently suspended in the house. Clay was barely conscious when he'd said them, perhaps still a bit delirious. But it no longer mattered to Aly. Nearly losing him had torn away any last barriers erected during their nine-month war. Their future was uncertain, but fear of losing Clay outweighed her fear of never having had a chance to tell him that she loved him. What he would do with that information, she didn't know.

Sighing, Aly released his hand and lay down next to him, her arm across his chest to comfort him, even in sleep. She knew how much Clay loved to have her next to him. Tiredness overtook Aly, and in minutes, she was sound asleep, her head nestled next to his shoulder.

Chapter Eleven

Aly's clean scent entered Clay's nostrils. He stirred, inhaling her fragrance deep into his lungs. This time he was able to breathe easily. Lifting his lashes without much effort, he saw a sputtering candle sitting on a shelf opposite where he lay. Shadowy light danced and wavered throughout the quiet room. The wind could be heard, but the house was warm and protected from the desert elements.

His senses were sluggish and disconnected as he worked hard to remember where he was. Clay's attention focused on the warmth against his right side. Barely turning his head, he felt a slight smile pull at the corners of his mouth.

"Aly?" His voice was rough from disuse. She was lying beside him, her arm across his chest.

At first just stirring, Aly snapped awake when she heard Clay call her a second time. Getting to her knees, she tried to shake off her sleepiness. Automatically her hand went to his shoulder. His flesh was warm, not fevered as before.

Clay watched her from beneath half-closed eyes. She was wearing a thin cotton gown that fell to her knees. He could see her body outlined by the candlelight through the shift. "I didn't mean to wake you," he croaked, clearing his throat.

"It's all right," Aly reassured him in a hushed tone, reaching for the cup. "Are you thirsty?"

"Very."

With a slight smile, Aly brushed several strands of hair from her eyes and dipped the cup into the bowl.

Clay savored each of her ministrations, his head sinking against her shoulder and breast as she cradled him upward enough so that he could drink without spilling the water from the mug. After three cups, he nodded.

"Thanks, honey."

Quiet settled around them. Aly looked at her watch. It was nearly 0500. Soon dawn would break, and another day would begin in the village. "You're welcome," she whispered, laying him back down on the pallet. Maneuvering herself around so that she sat facing him, Aly felt Clay's forehead.

"Your fever's gone."

"I had one?" Clay hungrily absorbed her beauty into his heart. She looked incredibly frail and exhausted.

"Yes, for about twelve hours. Madalena, the shaman, assured me that it wouldn't last long." Aly reached over, sliding her fingers down the length of his forearm, holding his hand. "As usual, she was right."

Clay weakly squeezed her fingers. "But as usual, you worried?"

Aly rested her cheek against one knee that she'd drawn up against her body. Looking at him through her lashes, she admitted, "You know me too well."

His fingers tightened around hers. "I want to know you a lot better."

Aly's eyes widened, her heart racing momentarily.

He smiled gently. "When that Gila monster bit me and I started slipping into unconsciousness, I thought I was going to die, honey. And then I heard your voice, far away, telling me that you loved me." His smile dissolved, and Clay held her vulnerable blue gaze. "Was I making it up, or did you say it?"

She shut her eyes, afraid as never before. "No...I said it."

"Did you mean it?"

"Yes."

"Come here," Clay whispered huskily, pulling on her hand. "Lie next to me. I want you close."

She opened her eyes, staring down at him. The tenderness burning in his gaze told her so much. Aly slipped to his side, propping herself on one elbow, her face very near his.

Clay slid his bandaged left hand down her arm, coming to rest on her hip. He gazed at her, memorizing her shadowy features. "I've never met anyone with the courage you've had," he began quietly. "I nearly destroyed you in nine months, and yet you took every beating, every insult and dig I could throw at you, and kept your head up. Looking back on it, I think I figured out why you were able to do that."

"How can you hate someone you've loved from

the moment you met him?'' she asked, her voice strained with tears.

''I fell for you the day we met, too, Aly.''

She nodded, her throat constricted.

''It was your love for me that allowed you to take my hatred, wasn't it?''

''Yes.''

Clay sighed deeply, feeling the pain that she'd carried so long in her heart. ''I don't deserve you, but I'm not going to throw this chance away.'' He raised his hand, outlining the contour of her cheeks, watching her tears drift silently down them. ''It took my almost dying for me to realize that my biggest fear was of losing you after I admitted how much you meant to me.''

Aly sniffed, and held his burning gray gaze. ''It was my biggest fear, too.''

He snorted derisively. ''Figure it out—we both didn't want to admit we loved each other because we were afraid the other would say 'no.'''

''Will you?'' Aly quavered, fear at its height in her. She'd admitted her love to Clay, but he'd whispered his love to her as he'd fallen unconscious a day ago. Did he remember saying it?

Murmuring her name as if it were a reverent prayer, Clay slipped his hand across her shoulders, asking her to lean down so that he could kiss her. Aly came, a willow bending to his desire, her breath moist as she shyly touched his mouth. Although he was incredibly weak, Clay framed her face with his hands, molding his mouth to hers, showing her just how much she meant to him. Aly was willing and vulnerable to his campaign to convince her, his mouth claiming hers in a fiery kiss that consumed both of them in those explosive seconds.

"There," he growled thickly, holding her captive inches from his face, "does that answer your question?"

Aly managed a bare nod, dazed in the aftermath of his hungry desire.

His eyes glinted with an unknown emotion. "After we get rescued, and after I get back on my feet, you and I are going to do some serious talking, Aly." A weak semblance of a boyish grin split his serious features. "I'm so damn weak, I can't even undress you with my eyes. But that's going to change once we get home. You can count on it."

"Doc, if you don't release me today, I'm going to climb these damned walls." Clay stared at the Navy doctor who stood at the end of the bed, studying his chart. After being rescued by the coast guard a day after he'd confessed his love to Aly, Clay's world had changed drastically. Another rescue team had flown across the mountains and picked up Dan Ballard. They had all been flown to Oaknoll Naval Hospital, situated in San Francisco, for treatment.

Dan was recovering quickly from his serious concussion in another wing of the huge hospital. And Clay was being monitored closely for the first week after his arrival. The doctors were unable to understand how he'd survived the Gila monster bite. Clay tried to explain Madalena's care of him, but they didn't want to believe that an Indian shaman might have been responsible for saving his skin.

Clay had a deep belief in the power of the unknown, and readily accepted that Madalena's ancient skills had helped to some degree. Aly didn't care who had saved him, just as long as he survived the experience. After one day in the hospital, Aly had been released for two weeks' recovery time. She had flown back to Florida to be with her family.

"According to all reports from the nurses, Lieutenant Cantrell, you've been peeling paint off these walls for at least a week already in your efforts to get out of here," Dr. Kenneth Black answered dryly, looking over his spectacles at Clay.

"Aw, come on, doc. Give me a break, will you? I've been in this place for two lousy weeks. My lady's due back from Florida three hours from now."

Black smiled slightly, penning his initials on several sheets of paper he'd brought with him and had attached to the clipboard. He hung the board back on the hook at the end of the bed. "I hear Lieutenant Trayhern has been spending her recuperation time with her parents down in Florida."

Clay got up, pacing the small white naval hospital room. He was dressed in a pair of light blue pajamas and a blue robe. "That's right." He shot Black a dark look. "And if you guys had released me a week ago, I could have spent a week with her in some Florida sunshine recovering there instead of being locked up in this box they call a room."

"You badger the nurses like this every day, Lieutenant?"

Cantrell stopped pacing and grinned. "A hundred times worse. I'll stop badgering them if you'll release me, doc."

"That's blackmail."

"But your people would breathe a big sigh of relief if I was gone."

Black rolled his eyes. "Normally, someone who's been poisoned as you were doesn't bounce back this rapidly."

Clay looked out the window that overlooked the colorful autumn gardens surrounding the huge hospital. "I had a big reason to get well in a hurry! Look, if you release me right now, I can just make it to the San Francisco Airport in time to meet her plane." He shot a look over his shoulder. "Get rid of me, Black. I'm a pain in the ass to everyone here. You know it, and so do I. I'm fine. I'm in the pink of health. That medicine woman gave me a hell of a start back on the road to recovery."

Chuckling, Black headed toward the door. "Get out of here, Lieutenant. You've tongue-lashed my people to death for the past week. Go meet that woman of yours."

Rubbing his hands together, Clay grinned. "Thanks, doc. You're a prince."

"I'm doing this to protect my nurses and orderlies from you, Cantrell."

Clay didn't take the doctor's dry teasing to heart. He headed for the closet where a set of civilian clothes hung. Late last week, Lieutenant Miles Cartwright had brought over clothes, and parked Clay's Corvette in the visitors' lot. Clay grinned over at the physician. "You're doing the right thing, believe me."

Black opened the door and smiled. "I've also approved your thirty days' leave."

Clay pulled the door open, grabbing his slacks. "How about Lieutenant Trayhern's leave? Were you able to swing it with that sourpuss officer over at Moffett Personnel? Did you convince him that Aly needed another month of recovery time before she sits back in the cockpit of a P3?''

Black shook his head. ''Both sets of orders are approved, signed and on the clipboard, Cantrell.'' Black stood a second, watching Clay throw off the robe, draping it across the bed. ''Tell me something, Cantrell.''

''What?'' Off came the pajama top. Clay slipped a fresh white T-shirt over his head, and then shrugged into a plaid shirt, rolling up the sleeves on his forearms. Only a small bandage remained around his left hand to remind him of his brush with death.

''Do you always get what you want? This past week, I've seen you pull strings and manipulate people like nothing I've ever witnessed before.''

Smiling wolfishly, Clay climbed into his dark brown slacks, zipping them up. ''Doc, when you want something bad enough, you'll do anything to get it. I'm in love with a beautiful lady, and I've got big things in store for us. I spent two weeks lying in this bed with nothing do but think, scheme and dream.'' Clay glanced up after slipping his belt through the loops on his trousers. ''I owe you one. Thanks for all your help.''

With a wave of his hand, Black disappeared out the door, laughing. ''Any time, Clay, any time.''

Hurry! Clay glanced at his watch, his mind racing ahead. It would take thirty minutes via the Bayshore to get to the airport. Great! That meant he had just enough time to get the rest of his plans set into motion. Whistling happily, Clay sat down, pulling on his dark brown socks, then pushing his feet into his favorite loafers. In quick movements, he reached into the closet, pulled out the corduroy sport coat, threw it over his shoulder and grabbed the clipboard. Wait until Aly saw him at the bottom of the ramp, waiting for her as she disembarked from that commercial flight! She thought he was still a prisoner in a hospital bed.

Aly's exhaustion over the six-hour flight was torn away when she saw Clay standing at the bottom of the ramp with two dozen purple, yellow and white irises in one hand, and the biggest welcoming smile on his face that she'd ever seen.

A day after their rescue, Dr. Black had told her that her family was worried sick about her. Clay had cajoled her into leaving him to fly back and visit with her parents while he was in the hospital. After all, he'd argued reasonably with her, he couldn't fool around with her under those circumstances, being so weak and all....

"Clay!" she cried now, throwing her arms around his broad shoulders.

"Mmm," he whispered, picking Aly up and holding her so tightly that the air was forced out of her lungs, "I missed the hell out of you, lady!"

Laughing, Aly kissed him repeatedly, not caring who was watching them.

He lowered her back to the floor, molding her close to him, his mouth hotly claiming hers. For that moment, nothing else existed in Clay's world but her ripe, sweet mouth moving in hungry abandon against his. Finally he broke free, breathing hard, laughing with her.

"Here," he said, bringing the bouquet between them, "these are for you."

Aly blushed and gently held the flowers. "They're

beautiful, Clay. This is September. Iris doesn't bloom now. How did you—''

''Never mind,'' he gloated, pleased that she was enthralled with his gift. Actually, it had taken several long-distance phone calls to Mexico City to have the flowers flown up. Clay threw an arm around her, and they walked leisurely through the dissipating crowd. ''I like it when you blush.''

Aly inhaled the flowers' fragrance, leaning against Clay. ''And you make me blush constantly. Clay, thank you for the irises. They're so beautiful!''

''You're welcome. And you,'' he said, kissing her hair, ''love every second of my teasing.''

''I can't deny it.'' Aly looked up, studying him in confusion. ''Clay, you weren't supposed to get out of the hospital until tomorrow! What happened? Did you browbeat those poor people on your floor until they released you?''

He shrugged bashfully, walking on air because Aly was in his arms, where she belonged. ''Something like that,'' he answered vaguely. God, she was beautiful in that long-sleeved gold silk dress. It brought out the gold highlights in her hair and in her sparkling eyes. The black leather belt only emphasized her gorgeous legs. She was all elegance.

''Are you feeling okay?'' Aly asked, concerned.

Clay tried to cover his leer, not succeeding.

''You're fine,'' she muttered, trying to hide a smile.

Clay squeezed her, bringing her close and kissing the top of her head. ''You're gorgeous—'' he looked down ''—and what a pair of legs! Lady, you'd put a thoroughbred to shame.''

''Now you're calling me a horse, Clay!''

''You're right!'' He swept Aly off her feet, irises

and all, and swung her around and around. Her laughter was sweet music to his ears as he finally set her back on her feet. They were both so dizzy that they had to lean against each other to stay upright. Clay barely gave any attention to the people who made a wide circle around them. But those he saw were all smiling.

Breathless, Aly leaned against him. "What am I going to do with you?"

"Well, for starters—"

She laughed. "I knew I shouldn't have given you an opening."

Clay ignored her, digging out two sets of orders, waving them under her nose. "As I was saying, the good doctor who handled my case managed to wangle thirty days' leave for both of us." He placed the orders in her hand, watching the shock set in.

Aly read the orders in disbelief. "This—this is incredible, Clay!" She looked up at him. "How did you manage this? I called Moffett Personnel to talk to Donnelly, but he turned me down flat."

"Guess it's just my silver tongue," Clay congratulated himself, watching the joy come to her eyes. "Thirty days of vacation, honey." He took the orders, neatly folded them and put them in the breast pocket of his sport coat.

Dazed by all the good news, Aly shook her head. "It's all like a dream, Clay...."

Placing his arms around her shoulders, he rested his brow against Aly's hair. "And that's not all. I've got my 'vette out front in a No Parking zone. Provided they aren't towing it away yet, we'll grab your luggage and head south, along the coast. There's a nice little bed-and-breakfast inn overlooking Monterey Bay. It's quiet, beautiful and private. How's that sound for starters?''

Tears filled Aly's eyes. Since their rescue, they'd never had the time they'd wanted together, always driven apart by orders or needs of others. She reached out, caressing his recently-shaved cheek. ''I think it sounds wonderful,'' she quavered.

Clay lost his smile, pressing his lips to her temple, cheek, and finally finding her mouth. He tasted the salty tears on her lips, kissing them away. ''And I love the hell out of you. Come on, we're going to Monterey Bay. Just you and I, little hellcat.''

Hampton Inn stood beneath the twisted Monterey pines, a hundred feet away from a sheer cliff that dropped off to a beach below. The inn overlooked one of the most scenic bays on the West Coast. Aly stood beneath Clay's arm, watching the red sunset, the ocean glassy and calm. The wind was gentle and warm, filled with the fragrance of the sea.

''It's lovely,'' Aly breathed.

''No,'' Clay corrected, looking down at her, ''you're lovely. That bay hasn't got a thing on you, lady.''

Standing on tiptoe, Aly pressed a shy kiss to his wonderfully mobile mouth. ''Mmm,'' she murmured moments later, ''you taste so good.''

He rocked her gently back and forth in his arms. ''Must be all the champagne we drank earlier, huh?''

She giggled. ''Yeah, on an empty stomach, Cantrell. That wasn't such a wise idea. I'm feeling giddy and silly.''

''So am I.'' And he kissed the tip of her nose,

content as never before. ''You make me happy, Alyssa Trayhern, you know that?''

Closing her eyes, Aly leaned against his strong body, her mouth resting against his cheek. ''No one can be happier than me.''

''Wanna bet?''

She giggled and held Clay at arm's length. ''You're such a rogue.''

''No, Rogue would say that about himself,'' he teased, referring to her Border Collie. He saw the sudden concern in her eyes. ''And don't worry, Dan Ballard and his wife *promised* to take loving care of Rogue for you while we're on vacation. You know his kids will love the collie.''

That was true. Aly gave him a mischievous look. ''You thought of everything, didn't you?''

Clay sobered slightly, running his fingers slowly through her short, silky hair. ''I hope I have....''

''What's next?''

''Dinner with my best lady down at a very fashionable restaurant, and then dancing at a very trendy place a bit farther down that same road. Game?''

''Am I ever!''

''Well, let's go. We're going to do some heavy celebrating tonight!''

Aly made a face, dancing close to Clay. ''Do I look like a turkey?'' she asked.

He chuckled and studied her. She wore an incredibly beautiful pink silk dress that had a scoop neck, showing off her perfect collarbone and slender neck. The dolman sleeves moved like ripples in the breeze each time he swung her around to the slow beat of the music. Arching an eyebrow he said, "Definitely not a turkey. Why?"

"I feel like one. I ate too much, Clay."

"That was a good dinner," he agreed. The lobster in drawn butter had been superb, but her company was his dessert.

Aly settled against him, head resting on his shoulder, and closed her eyes. "I'm so happy, Clay."

He caressed the length of her spine, so supple yet so strong. "No regrets?"

She shook her head. "How can you have regrets when your dreams are coming true?" she whispered, looking up into his warm gray eyes. Aly ached to make love with him, each movement of his body inciting her, teasing her.

Getting serious, Clay said in a low voice, "You talked to your parents about this roller-coaster relationship of ours?"

"Yes. I told them everything, Clay."

"Our stormy beginning and middle?"

"They understood," she told him softly. "Both my parents are sorry that Stephen lost his life. And I am, too."

He sighed and nodded.

"My parents are very understanding people, Clay. They're sensitive, and they have an ability to see *why* people act or react the way they do. They don't blame you."

"They sound special," he admitted almost wistfully.

"My mother is a nurse," Aly explained. "She saved my father's life behind enemy lines in the Korean War. My father says he learned a lot from her about sensitivity."

"What's her name?" Clay asked.

"Rachel."

"Pretty name, but not half as pretty as you."

Aly tried to ferret out why Clay was retreating. "Clay? What's wrong? Are you upset because of the past?"

He leaned over, kissing her cheek. "No, I'm worried about the future. Come on, let's get out of here. I need a place where I can do some serious talking with you."

Aly felt Clay's tension on the drive up the coast toward Hampton Inn. The moon was full, casting its radiance across the desolate beauty of the Monterey Bay. Aly sensed Clay's worry and reached out, sliding her hand into his to reassure him. He squeezed her fingers, offering her a forced smile.

Nervously, Aly smoothed the light flannel floor-length granny gown she wore. It was all she had—the only sleepwear she'd taken with her to Florida. Deep inside, she fretted over Clay's unexpected somber mood. Taking a deep breath, she opened the door from the bathroom and stepped into their spacious bedroom suite. She saw Clay standing at the sliding glass doors that overlooked the ocean. He had taken off his sport coat and tie. As she rounded the bed and walked to his side, she saw that his shoes had been tossed to one side, too.

Clay heard Aly approach, pulled his hands out of his pockets and turned around. Some of his terror abated as she halted and stood shyly before him.

"I know this isn't very sexy—"

"It's perfect," he whispered, moving to her, placing his hands on her shoulders. "With your tousled red hair and freckles, it suits you.'' She looked vulnerable in the simple gown, and so very, very beautiful.

Clay's tender smile drove some of the nervousness out of her. She slid her hands around his waist, pulling him to her. His groan of pleasure was music. ''This is all I want,'' Aly whispered.

He embraced her tightly for a long moment, resting his jaw against her hair. ''Sure?''

''Very sure.''

''For how long?''

Aly nuzzled beneath his jaw, savoring Clay's closeness, his ability to share his complex emotions with her. ''As long as you want.'' She sighed softly, feeling his mouth moving temptingly along the length of her jaw.

''I warned you once before, I only like long-term commitments,'' he growled, inhaling her spicy fragrance.

A small moan came from her throat as he sought and found her mouth, cherishing it with small nips and kisses. ''Fine,'' Aly agreed breathlessly.

Clay said a prayer, his mouth hovering against her smiling lips. ''Forever?''

Aly opened her eyes, looking dazedly up at him. ''Forever?'' she whispered, perplexed.

Clay's hands tightened around her, molding her form against him. ''I want to marry you, Aly.'' There, the words, the need, were finally out in the open. Clay watched her blue eyes widen enormously, and she struggled briefly in his arms, but he wouldn't let her go.

''Marry me?'' Aly repeated dumbly.

''I told you I liked long-term commitments,

honey.'' Clay didn't know how to read the confusion he saw registered in her eyes. Aly's cheeks had gone bright red in reaction.

Faintness swept through Aly, and she leaned against Clay for support. ''Oh, Clay... I never expected this....''

''What? Ever getting married, or me asking you?''

If she hadn't been so shocked by his proposal, Aly would have found that funny. But she was breathless as she sought his turbulent gray eyes, which were fraught with anxiety. ''I had hoped someday to marry,'' she began lamely.

She wasn't going to say yes! Clay froze, fighting the terrible cold filling him. ''Then it's my name? My past, that you object to?'' The words came out in icy monosyllables of pain.

The awful clarity of their conversation struck Aly directly. ''No, Clay. God, no!'' She framed his face between her hands, drowning in the pain she saw in his features. ''Is that what you were afraid of? I loved you, but not enough to marry you because of your name? My name? Our complicated past?''

He nodded, words unable to come out because they were stuck in his throat.

Aly placed a warm, inviting kiss on his mouth, feeling him tremble in the wake of her sweet assault upon him. ''I love you, you crazy jet jockey,'' she breathed, nipping at his lower lip, cajoling him to join her. ''And I wouldn't care if your name was Humpty-Dumpty. None of that matters! You do, darling. Do you hear me? There's nothing more I want than you as my husband.'' She crushed her mouth against his, breathing life, breathing fire into the coldness that had inhabited him.

Gently, Clay lifted Aly into his arms, his mouth ravishing her moist, giving lips. She was going to marry him! As he carried her to the bed, he murmured, "You're going to be my wife, Aly. I can't live without you. I need you—your sweet fire."

As he laid her on the bed, Aly sat up and pulled Clay down beside her. Her fingers trembled as she unbuttoned his shirt to reveal his massive, powerful chest covered with black hair. His fingers fumbled with the buttons on her granny gown.

Looking up into his eyes, Aly found them burning with desire for her alone. "Ever since I met you, I've never wanted anyone else, darling. I need you, too." His shirt fell open, and she slid her hands beneath it, pulling it off his magnificent shoulders. Taking in a breath, Aly confided, "You're so beautiful."

Joy surged through Clay as he removed the gown from her shoulders, allowing it to pool around her hips. "And you," he said thickly, cupping her exquisite small breasts, "are even more beautiful...."

She drew in a quick gasp of air as he leaned over, his mouth seeking, finding a soft pink nipple. A little cry escaped her as Clay pulled her into his arms, their flesh meeting hotly for the first time. A thrilling arc of lightning danced through Aly as he sucked upon each nipple in turn, drawing them to budding life with his slow, cajoling movements. She lost sense of time, of direction.

Dazed, Aly watched through lowered lashes as Clay divested himself of his trousers. He was a consummate male animal, the darkness of his hair emphasizing his power, his promise of meeting and matching her hungry femininity. Reaching out, Aly welcomed him back into her arms, arching to graze his taut body with her own.

"Love me," she tremored close to his ear. "I need you, want you so badly, Clay..." She pressed her hip against his hardness resting between them. Each touch of his mouth upon her was explosive. As he teethed one nipple, his hand slid down the damp length of her long torso, slipping gently between her thighs, asking her to give him entrance.

Her breathing became erratic as his hand sought and found her moist womanhood, the center of her longing. Gripping his shoulder, feeling his powerful muscles flex and tighten, she cried out, twisting toward him, begging him with her eyes to enter her.

Clay smiled tenderly, sensing her every desire. She was so wet, so hot. Her lips upon his neck, spreading a sheet of fire across his chest, caused him to groan out in pleasure. He started his silken assault upon her, her thighs taut and trembling as he began to wreak pleasure from her.

"Let me show you how much I love you," he whispered against her cheek, kissing her hungrily. "Give yourself to me, sweet woman of mine...."

The shattering fire exploded to life as he teased her core, and she could do nothing but cry out, pulled tautly against his hard male body.

Clay laughed shakily. "You're so hot, so vibrant with life," he murmured as he eased across her glistening form, finding her, sliding into her liquid depths.

A gasp escaped Aly as she welcomed Clay into her. This was so right, so perfect, she thought as she rose and fell with the rhythm he'd established for them. His eyes shone with love as she looked up into them, nearly drowning in his lambent gaze. Her lips parting as she felt their mutual need quicken, Aly slid her hands around his corded neck, kissing him, taking his groan of pleasure as he released his life deep within her. A heartbeat later, a rainbow explosion tremored through her as she sought and found release within his strong, powerful arms. Her cry was drowned within his mouth as he kissed her long and fiercely.

Clay kissed her cheek, her closed eyes and that aristocratic nose of hers. Sweat glistened off the planes of his face as he lay within her, savoring her in every way. "Open your eyes," he breathed raggedly. Aly opened them, and he could see moonlight in their dazed, sated depths. He shifted some of his weight, smiling down at her.

"I've never seen you so happy."

Languidly, Aly reached up, her fingers trailing through those damp, errant strands of hair across his brow. "It's your fault, darling. All of it."

He kissed her swollen lips gently, soothing them with his tongue in the aftermath. "This is one time I'll take the blame for everything."

A softened laugh escaped her in a breathy rush. Aly sifted her fingers through his hair, memorizing the joyous flame in his gray eyes, that arrogant, self-confident smile on his male mouth. "I love you, Clay Cantrell. Even that inflated ego of yours."

Clay sobered, caressing her copper-colored hair. "And I love you, Aly Trayhern. *All* of you. Past, present and future." His voice grew hoarse. "I want you to know that, honey—that the past doesn't bother me the way it did. You helped me understand you're the way you are because of your family." He gave her a little smile, wiping the perspiration from her brow with his fingers. "You couldn't be this giving, unselfish and unconditionally loving unless you'd been raised in that kind of environment."

Tears gathered in Aly's eyes as she heard and felt Clay's admission. With a cry, she threw her arms around him. "Thank you," she whispered. "I was so afraid the past would get in our way again."

He gently left the sweet confines of her body and turned over on his back. "Come here," Clay called her softly, pulling Aly on top of him. Once she was comfortable, he cupped her face between his hands, looking deeply into her sultry eyes, sparkling with tears. "We are what we are because of our families. You've taught me that each person is an individual within that unit."

"We've worked through and understood our past. Now, we have the present and future to build on, Clay." She sighed, realizing they were both freed. "I like the idea of being Mrs. Alyssa Cantrell," she told him huskily.

His smile was very male and very tender. "Tomorrow morning, let's call your parents and tell them the good news."

Aly sniffed and nodded. "I think they already know we're in love with each other."

He kissed the two tears away, bringing her against him, her head on his shoulder. "Good, then they won't mind us dropping in on them a few days from now. Think they'll balk if we want to get married, say, two weeks from now, down at their home?"

Aly sighed, sliding her hand across his chest. She could hear the solid beat of his heart beneath hers. "No. The more you know of my family, the more you'll realize that we're flexible on a moment's notice.''

Clay closed his eyes, content as never before. ''And strong, and enduring, and so very, very loving,'' he murmured, kissing her brow.

Aly smiled wistfully, nuzzling beneath Clay's chin. ''I can hardly wait until tomorrow, darling....''

''I can't, either, little hellcat.'' Clay brought up the sheet, covering them both, his arms settling around Aly. Embracing her, he murmured again, ''I can't, either....''

* * * * *

RETURN OF A HERO

Chapter One

It was raining. *Or is the sky crying?* Morgan Trayhern wondered as he climbed out of the black limousine. The dawn sky above Washington, D.C., was a funereal gray, mirroring his feelings. Water ran down the planes of his tense face as he walked up a red brick path toward an old Georgian manor tucked away behind a number of sycamore and elm trees.

Fatigue lapped at Morgan as he hunched more deeply into his trench coat. Yesterday he'd received a directive from the commandant of the French Foreign Legion to report to headquarters. Orders had come from American officials, asking him to return at once to Washington for an unspecified reason. The commandant assured him that although the marine corps officials had urgently requested his presence, once the meeting was over, he could return to France and resume his duties as an officer in the Legion.

Further, this unexpected trip was top secret. His commanding officer couldn't even name the man who had issued the orders that had brought him stateside after a seven-year absence. The whole situation made Morgan apprehensive, and a nine-hour flight from France, coupled with time changes, had stripped him, leaving him raw and uneasy.

Morgan saw that the door to the manor was open. A marine corps general in a dark-green uniform filled the entranceway, peering out at him through the pall. Wrestling with his surprise and the sudden pounding of his heart, Morgan clenched one of his fists. So, General Kip Young, his commanding officer back in 1970, wanted to see him. The bastard.

As Morgan approached the door, the bulldog-jawed general with thinning gray hair beckoned him to enter. "Captain Morgan Trayhern?"

Flooded with unexpected anger, Morgan nodded. "You know it is." Maybe his black mustache had changed his appearance more than he'd realized.

Shutting the door, the general stepped back, allowing the maid to take Morgan's trench coat. "General Jack Armstrong is dying. As you know, he was in charge of your battalion."

Glaring at Young, Morgan straightened his dark pin-striped jacket. "Is he dying of guilt, sir?"

"Now you look here," Young snarled, coming within inches of him. "You keep a civil tongue in your head. Jack Armstrong saved your life seven years ago."

A thin, cutting smile slashed across Morgan's mouth. "And I'm supposed to be grateful for his turning me into a convenient scapegoat and purported traitor to my country so that he and all his cronies could escape the blame for Hill 164?'' Morgan defiantly held Young's steely stare.

''Even though you're in the French Foreign Legion, I expect military courtesy from you, Captain.'' Young's square face turned scarlet. ''I'm the one who sent the request to have you fly here. Jack Armstrong is my best friend, and he's dying. There are some things he wants to get off his chest and they involve you.''

Taking a quick look around the impressive home whose walls were filled with war mementos from Armstrong's thirty-year military career, Morgan shrugged. ''I'm following orders from Commandant Gérard. I didn't want to come, General. If I'd realized you were behind this visit—or that Armstrong wanted to talk to me—I'd have refused. As soon as this charade's over, I'm catching a plane back to France.'' His voice grew deep. ''And you can keep your filthy little secret.''

''Excuse me,'' a maid called to the general. ''The doctor says you must hurry.''

Young made a chopping motion toward the walnut-paneled hallway. ''Fourth door on the left. Jack is lucid, but Dr. Bonner says he won't last until sundown today. Whatever your personal feelings over this, Captain, I hope you can respect the fact that he's dying.''

Girding himself, swallowing his anger as he'd been doing for the past year, ever since he'd regained his memory of how he'd been used by Armstrong, Morgan gave a brusque nod to indicate that he understood. He followed the worried-looking maid, quickening his stride. The house was dark and shadowy. Young trailed at a safe distance as they moved down the carpeted hallway.

The maid opened the door to the master bedroom, and Morgan stood uncertainly at the entrance. His heart wouldn't stop pounding; so many old emotions were erupting from within him. His gaze took in the room, from the cheerless brown drapes to the massive carved oak bed, where a frail, emaciated Armstrong lay. Everything was morbidly dark in this house. As Morgan stepped inside, Young edged past him and crossed to the bed. Morgan felt his stomach knot with despair.

Dr. Bonner, a robust man of middle age, slipped back into the shadows, his face grim. Young placed his hand on the shoulder of his dying friend.

"Jack?"

The man in the bed stirred briefly. "Kip?"

"It's me."

"You brought him?"

Young looked over at Morgan and motioned him forward. "Yes, he's here. He's standing at the foot of your bed."

His palms suddenly sweaty, Morgan had the wild urge to wipe them on the pin-striped slacks he wore. Instead he stood stiffly, watching the man in the bed. Jack Armstrong's was the first face Morgan had seen when he'd regained consciousness in a hospital in Japan after the slaughter on Hill 164. The same razor-thin face that he had come to hate was now pinched with illness, the cheeks sunken and the skin stretched like parchment across them. Morgan took a deep breath, wanting to run as Armstrong's lashes fluttered and finally lifted. Those once-piercing green eyes were dull as they settled on him. Morgan felt a scream starting to unwind in his gut, just as it had a year ago when he'd finally realized the truth of who he was and what Armstrong had done to him.

"You...came," Armstrong rasped. One corner of his mouth lifted upward briefly.

"Did I have a choice?" Morgan's voice rolled through the hushed room. He saw Young shoot him a warning look that spoke volumes. To hell with all of them. He wasn't going to be kind or courteous after what they'd done to him.

"C-come closer, Morgan. I-I need to tell you—" The old man took several shallow breaths.

Reluctantly Morgan moved to stand next to the general's bed. "Say it, Armstrong."

"I deserve your anger, Morgan," he whispered. "I wanted you to know the full truth. I didn't want to die with this on my conscience...."

Clenching his teeth, Morgan tasted the hate that had eaten at him for a year. "You lied to me, Armstrong. You and whoever else was in on this scheme."

Weakly lifting a hand, Armstrong silenced him. "The CIA persuaded us to send a company of men into an active NVA area. They said it was safe." He took a breath, then closed his eyes for several moments before going on. "My staff and I backed the CIA appraisal of the situation. It was a chance to make a major coup."

"You thought putting my company on Hill 164 would earn you another star," Morgan hissed. "And it did, didn't it?"

"Y-yes. One that I've worn with guilt ever since." Armstrong opened his eyes and stared fiercely up at Morgan. "I had removed all air support to another part of Vietnam, thinking your company would be safe. I left you defenseless—but not on purpose. It was a horrible tactical error. By the time our helicopter got there, only two of you were left alive. You and Private Lenny Miles."

"And you chose me as your scapegoat, didn't you, Armstrong?" Though anger thrummed through Morgan, this specter on the bed before him brought out only a pathetic numbness.

"We had no choice," Armstrong cried softly, tears welling in his eyes. "My entire staff would have been sent home in disgrace. There would have been court martials. I couldn't see the lives of five good officers destroyed like that." Wheezing, he sank back into the pillows, gathering strength. "A plan was brought to my attention after we found you alive. You had received massive wounds to the head and chest. By the time we got you to Japan for treatment, the doctors told us you'd sustained brain damage, as well. They didn't think you'd survive. So we sent word to the press and our superiors that you had deserted your post, leaving your company of men open to NVA attack. I thought it would be only a matter of hours before you died. That's why I let you be the scapegoat."

"And what about Lenny Miles?" Morgan ground out.

"He was only slightly wounded, but he'd been on drugs, so we had him. We threatened him with court martial if he didn't go along with our plan. Miles didn't want to end up at a military prison, busting rocks for the next thirty years."

"So he agreed."

"He had no choice."

"And when I managed to survive my wounds, that threw a chink into your plans, didn't it, Armstrong?"

The general sighed. "Yes. On the suggestion of someone in the CIA, I flew to your bedside. The doctors told me you had amnesia and couldn't recall anything about your family or past—not even your name. So, as you remember, I sat there telling you how you'd been wounded as a CIA operative behind the lines in Laos. You had no recall of 164 or losing your company of men, so you swallowed the story line."

A harsh smile shadowed Morgan's mouth. "I can still remember you at my bedside, filling me in on every detail, Armstrong. You gave me a new name—Morgan Ramsey. And you told me I had no family, that I was an orphan." His voice trembled. "You gave me an entirely different life. For six years I didn't really know who I was or what had happened to my company. I believed everything you told me, because I couldn't remember a thing. I didn't see a newspaper in Japan for the first three months because I was lapsing in and out of a mild coma state. By the time I could read or watch television, the furor over my 'desertion' and role in the destruction of my company was over."

"After nine months in the hospital, you'd recovered sufficiently to be sent to the French Foreign Legion."

"Where I thought I was being patriotic by becoming a CIA mole within that organization."

"Yes." Armstrong's eyes watered. "And until a year ago, you didn't really know who or what you were."

"I lived in hell for that year," Morgan said, an edge to his voice, "thanks to you."

"I—I just wanted to say I'm sorry it had to be someone like you. Sometimes one good man has to be sacrificed for the good of all...." He closed his eyes.

Morgan stood, a violent storm of emotions flooding him. He watched the doctor move to the bed and pick up Armstrong's wrist to take his pulse. Bonner looked over at him.

"I think you'd better leave, Captain Ramsey. He won't be with us much longer. His pulse is failing."

A powerful urge to scream settled over Morgan. He turned on his heel and jerked open the door, his breath coming in sharp rasps as he moved down the dreary hall toward the foyer. All he wanted to do was escape.

"Captain!" Young caught up with him in the foyer and gripped him by the arm.

Morgan wheeled around, wrenching out of the officer's grasp. "Stay the hell away from me," he breathed savagely. His trench coat hung in the closet, and he yanked it off the hanger.

Young's face broadcast wariness. "What are you going to do now that you know what really happened?"

Shrugging into the trench coat, Morgan glared at Young. "Not a damn thing, General. I know that if I tried to clear my name, you'd make sure I was stopped at every turn."

"You're right. I think it's best if you catch the next flight back to France. At least there you have a good life."

The urge to punch the arrogant general in his flushed face was strong. "Good life!" he spit. "I have parents who grieve for me. I have a brother and sister I haven't seen for years. You've not only hurt me—you've hurt them, as well.'' Punching a finger into Young's chest, Morgan whispered harshly, ''If I didn't have to involve them in clearing my name, I'd do it in an instant, Young. But I know the Pentagon and I know the military machine. You'd use the press to your advantage and put such ungodly pressure on my family that it wouldn't be worth it.'' His breathing was ragged as he straightened and tied the belt around his waist. ''Don't look so worried, Young. I'll keep my cover. I've got reenlistment papers for another five-year stint waiting for me back in Marseilles. They want to make me a major if I sign over.'' His nostrils flared. ''I can live out my life in a dingy third world country, fighting wars I couldn't care less about.''

Young backed off. ''The limo will take you out to the airport,'' he said stiffly. ''Thank you for coming.''

''You're a pack of bastards,'' Morgan snarled, opening the door. Outside, he felt the rain slash at his face as he walked down the brick path. The water cooled the hot frustration inside him. He lifted his face and deeply inhaled the wet springtime air.

Inside the limo, he snapped at the chauffeur, ''Get me the hell out of here and back to the airport.''

Sinking into the gloom of the back seat, Morgan closed his eyes. Tears welled beneath his lids, and he swallowed against his constricted throat. The sky was crying. He was on U.S. soil for the first time in seven years and Clearwater, Florida, where his parents lived, was only an hour-and-a-half flight from D.C.

He dragged in a shaky breath, then opened his eyes and glared out into the gray light. The beauty of Georgetown escaped him as he focused on the pain in his heart. How was Noah? One week before Morgan's company had been wiped out, Noah's Coast Guard career had been in high gear. And Aly... Tears squeezed from beneath his short, spiky lashes. Groaning, he covered his face with his large, scarred hand. Had her dreams of getting an appointment to Annapolis been fulfilled? Had she graduated to go on to Pensacola? All she'd ever wanted was to fly.

It hurt to think of them like this. In France his life revolved around his men, a barracks and soldiering duty on Corsica, where the Legion had one of its forts. The men who were in the Legion came from around the world. Most of them had changed their names, never discussing their pasts with anyone.

Wiping his eyes, Morgan fought to get a hold on himself. The last time he'd cried was when his memory had returned. Over the years, he'd had dreams, seen faces, but had never been able to put them together. Then, on a cliff-climbing exercise in France, his rope had snapped and he'd plummeted thirty feet to the ground. When he'd regained consciousness, the memory of who and what he really was had started to come back.

The limo eased to a halt at a concrete island in front of Pan Am Airlines. The rain was worsening. Morgan muttered his thanks to the driver and got out. All he had was a small leather satchel containing one set of clean clothes. Cars were whizzing by, coming and going like frantic bees to a hive.

The rain was soothing, and Morgan stood on the concrete island, lifting his face to the cleansing power of it. The tormented desire to stay and see his family warred with reality. He couldn't just walk back into their lives unannounced. If the press found out he was back, they'd have a field day. The mustache helped change the look of his face. So did the long scar that ran from his temple down his cheek and followed the square line of his jaw. No, it was unlikely that even his family would recognize the proud young marine captain of 1970 who'd posed with his company of men weeks before the tragedy.

Morgan opened his eyes, tasting the salt of his tears in the corners of his mouth. It was eight in the morning. The sidewalk was jammed with people, and hordes of businessmen were streaming into the busy airport facility. They were all dressed in dark trench coats and carried umbrellas and expensive briefcases. Suddenly the color pink caught his attention.

Directly across the four lanes of traffic, standing on the curb and trying to cross, was a woman in her late twenties. Morgan seized upon her; she was like a bright flower among the grays, browns and blacks of the business suits and coats. Small and slender, she reminded Morgan of a swan. Maybe she was one, he decided, trying to put his suffering behind him. There was a serenity to her oval face. Was it her large blue eyes? Or her delicate mouth that curved naturally upward at the corners? Her blond shoulder-length hair was dampened by the rain as she stood impatiently on first one heel, then the other, trying to time her crossing to where he stood.

Beautiful wasn't the word Morgan would have used to describe her. *Intriguing*, yes. The pink raincoat emphasized her slimness. Her eyes were a deep blue, and they sparkled with life. Morgan yearned to feel what the woman exuded. She was like a springtime flower—alive, young and filled with hope. He glanced up at the gray, turbulent sky, and realized he'd been staring at her. But just looking at her calmed him.

Laura watched the swiftly moving traffic with mounting frustration. Each time she tried to cross, another van or limo raced by, sending up sheets of rain in its wake. Something really ought to be done about this, she fumed. Checking the gold watch on her left wrist, she saw that time was running short. If she wanted to make that interview with General Cunningham over at McLean, Virginia, she was going to have to hurry!

Agitated with the arrogant Washington drivers, who never seemed to respect pedestrians, she looked across to the concrete island where she'd be able to catch a taxi. Her attention focused on one man standing among the others. His face was lifted to the rain, as if he were enjoying the sensation of water trickling down it. He was tall and powerful looking, even in the trench coat. Laura was drawn to his face: square, with harsh lines around his mouth and crinkles at the corner of each eye. He was darkly tanned, telling her that he wasn't from this area. April in D.C. was cloudy and dreary with rain. Sunshine was at a premium. The black mustache emphasized the breadth of the man's features. His gray eyes were sharp and intelligent.

The word *mercenary* sprang to Laura's mind, and she chastised her overactive imagination. But there was nothing peaceful about the man's face or his stance. Even from this distance, she could feel the tension in him. Despite his demeanor, Laura's heart went out to him the instant his eyes met and held hers. There was incredible sadness and turmoil in them. He looked as if he'd just lost his best friend. The rain made his face glisten, but she could almost swear he was crying. Could that be? A scar ran the length of the right side of his face, giving his expression an impenetrable quality.

A gasp broke from Laura. She watched in sudden horror as the man stepped off the curb—and right into the oncoming traffic. Didn't he see that gray limo?

Laura leaped from the safety of the curb, her hand raised in warning. "Look out!" she cried. Desperately she caught his attention, but he seemed dazed, perplexed by her warning. The limo bore down on him. It would be only seconds before he was struck. With a foolhardy lunge, she threw herself at him. Her hands connected solidly with his left shoulder, spinning him around and backward.

She heard the screech of tires on the pavement. Just as the man was thrown off his feet and out of the range of the limo, she felt the impact. One second she was on her feet; the next, she was flying through the air.

Morgan landed heavily against the curb as the limo screamed to a halt beside him. The smell of burned rubber filled the air. Wet and confused, he stumbled to his feet. The woman in the pink raincoat was sprawled ten feet in front of the limo. She had saved his life. The limo driver leaped from the vehicle, his face filled with terror. Cries and shrieks erupted around Morgan, but he ignored them as he ran to the woman's side. Struggling out of his trench coat, he threw it across her to protect her from the downpour. He knelt, his hand going immediately to her small shoulder. She was unconscious, a large, bloody cut on the side of her head, near her left eye. She looked like a bird with a broken wing, so fragile and vulnerable. Dammit!

He looked up at a policeman who had worked his

way through the gathering crowd. "Get an ambulance!" Morgan snarled. "Now!" More people ran over. Morgan's hand on her shoulder tightened. My God, she looked dead, her skin waxen. Was she? Shakily he slid his wet fingers around her wrist. There was a pulse—a weak one. Numbed by the events, he stared down at her wrist. The bones of her hand were tiny in comparison to his. Her flesh was so white and smooth; his sun-darkened, with years of calluses built up on the palms.

The vigilant throng pressed closer. Morgan glared up at them. "Give her room to breathe!" he ordered and they enlarged the circle. He leaned over, gently cupping her cheek with his palm. "Hang on," he begged her. "Just hang on, lady. Help's coming...." He dared not move her. She might have broken bones. She could be paralyzed. And all because of his utter stupidity. God, why hadn't he looked for oncoming traffic before he'd stepped off that curb?

By the time the ambulance arrived, some ten minutes later, Morgan was ready to explode at the cold-blooded curiosity of the people milling around. He hated passersby who gawked. Protecting the woman from the rain, he picked up her purse, tucking it beneath his arm. Anguish filled him as he stared down at her delicate features, now colorless. Why had she done such a foolish thing to save his worthless neck? Yet Morgan knew he'd have done the same thing.

Funny little swan, your courage isn't any match for that tiny body you live within. Her blond lashes lay against her high cheekbones; her lips were parted and slack. The paramedics raced over, bags in hand, carrying an oak body board with them. Morgan moved from his crouched position to stand to one side.

"You know her?" the chief paramedic asked, quickly examining her.

"No, but that doesn't matter. I'm coming with you. She saved me from getting hit by this limo."

The paramedic nodded. "Fine by me. Frank, let's get her on the body board. She might have sustained a back injury."

Numbly Morgan watched them transfer the woman to a thin oak board, then strap her snugly to it. Next came the blankets that would keep her warm. The policeman who'd been directing traffic around the accident came up to him.

"We'll follow you to the hospital, mister. I need to make out a report on this."

"Fine," Morgan agreed tautly, walking toward the rear of the ambulance, where the doors had been thrown open. His mind spun with possibilities. He glanced around. So far no reporters were on the scene. If he was lucky, he'd escape the glare of the cameras. Although his face was altered, he couldn't stand the thought that his family might recognize him, beginning their pain all over again.

Ducking into the ambulance, Morgan sat on the seat opposite the gurney where the woman lay, unconscious. Frank stayed in back with her while his partner drove. He worked quickly, taking a blood pressure reading.

"You got her purse?" he demanded.

Morgan produced it. "Yeah."

"Look for ID. We're gonna need some information for Admissions when we get her to the hospital."

The purse was small and neat, just as she was. Morgan felt shaky inside, adrenaline making him tremble. He opened the wallet and looked at the driver's license. Laura Bennett. Pretty name. Like her.... He searched the rest of the wallet for the name of a person to contact about the accident.

A frown formed on his damp brow. "Her name is Laura Bennett," he muttered, glancing over at her. "Is she going to live?"

"Her pulse and respiration are slow. She's in shock. Looks like a major head injury. Rest of her doesn't show any broken bones. But she could have internal injuries—I just don't know."

Flinching, Morgan gripped the wallet. Head injury. That had been the cause of his amnesia. Desperation filled him, and he kept his eyes on Laura. How could someone so small and exquisite have such a brave heart? He reached out and pressed his hand to her shoulder.

"Fight back, Laura," he told her. "Don't give in. I'll be here to help you."

Thankfully, the ride to the hospital was a short one. The ambulance rolled up to the Emergency entrance. *Hurry!* Morgan thought, staying out of the way when the attendants flung open the doors. Grimly he climbed out, following the paramedics through the sliding glass doors. In his hand was Laura Bennett's purse, her identity. And right on his heels were the police officers.

Chapter Two

Chaos reigned as the gurney bearing Laura Bennett was wheeled into the hospital. Morgan stared helplessly at the swinging emergency room doors. He had been pushed aside by a nurse, doctors and paramedics, who had disappeared with Laura's gurney behind the sign that said No Admittance.

"Can we get your statement, mister?" the redheaded police sergeant asked him.

Distracted, Morgan turned to the waiting officers. He held up the purse. "Yeah…just a minute. Let me give this to the admitting nurse."

His mind swung between concern for Laura's condition and awareness of the watchful officers as he dropped the purse off at the desk. Pushing several strands of damp hair off his brow, he dug into the breast pocket of his business suit and produced his passport for the police.

The sergeant took it and opened it. ''Morgan Ramsey, U.S. citizen. You live in France?''

Putting a tight clamp on his emotions, Morgan kept his voice low and devoid of feeling. ''That's right.''

''French Foreign Legion?'' The cop appraised him for a long time, a look of awe on his meaty face.

''I came on military business. I was about to take a plane back to France when this happened.'' He didn't intend to add anything to pique the cop's curiosity. The Legion had a mystique to it, and Morgan credited the officer's interest to that. Glancing out the doors to the parking lot, Morgan wondered if the press had been notified. He didn't dare allow his photo to be taken.

''Can you tell us what happened?''

''I stepped off the center island at the airport without looking,'' Morgan explained. ''I should have been more careful, but I was thinking about something else at the time. The woman came from the opposite direction and pushed me out of the way of an oncoming limo, and then she got hit.''

''Do you know this woman?''

''No.''

''She's sure got guts,'' the other cop muttered, a note of admiration in his voice as he continued to scribble down notes for his report.

The nurse from Admittance came over. ''Sergeant Amato, we've searched Ms. Bennett's belongings, and there's nothing to indicate whom we should notify about her injury.'' She held up an insurance card. ''We called her insurance agent and he said she's got no family.''

''No family?'' Morgan asked, his eyebrows lifting.

''Probably an orphan. Or adopted,'' Amato volunteered, rummaging through the contents of Laura's wallet.

Morgan felt as if a hand were squeezing his heart, and he rubbed his chest distractedly. "Are you sure?" He turned to the nurse. "Where does she live?"

"In McLean, Virginia. We've already called her residence, but there's only an answering machine to take messages."

Scowling, Morgan said, "Then I'll be her family until someone can be located."

The sergeant smiled. "She saved your neck. That's a nice gesture, Mr. Ramsey. What about that plane back to France you were going to catch?"

"It'll wait until I know she's in capable hands." He was responsible for what happened, and he wasn't going to leave her in the lurch.

"Once Ms. Bennett becomes conscious, she'll be able to tell us more," the nurse said hopefully. "I'm sorry, Mr. Ramsey, but you can't just assume responsibility for her unless she gives us permission."

Rules. They were made to be broken sometimes, Morgan thought darkly, and this was one of those times. But he held his counsel. "I understand. Just let me know as soon as you can what her condition is."

The nurse nodded briskly. "Of course."

The sergeant finished his report by taking down what little information there was regarding Laura Bennett. He glanced at Morgan. "Thanks for your help, Mr. Ramsey. We might need to talk with you again, so please leave an address and phone number where we can reach you at the nurses' station."

Morgan nodded. "I'm not going anywhere until I hear about Ms. Bennett. After that I'll find a local hotel."

"Good enough. Thanks."

Morgan watched the officers leave. The nurse directed him to a waiting room, and, choosing a brown plastic lounge chair, he sat. Resting his elbows on his long thighs, he clasped his hands, staring down at the black-and-white tiles, his mind whirling with questions, his emotions in utter tumult. He'd memorized Laura's face, from her haunting blue eyes to that delicious mouth of hers. Who was she? And why had he been mesmerized by her? Rubbing his face tiredly, he leaned back and rested his head against the wall, utterly drained. For a long time he'd forgotten there was a God, but now he prayed for the life of Laura Bennett.

Intermittent pain stabbed through Laura's head. Groggily she fought to awaken from the darkness that enveloped her. She heard lowered women's voices somewhere in the distance. As she dragged her hand upward, her fingertips came in contact with the bandages around her eyes. What was going on? Struggling to remember, she focused her attention on the dressing.

"Ms. Bennett?" a woman called.

Laura felt the woman's hand come to rest on her shoulder, and she answered, "Y-yes."

"I'm Nurse Karen Mylnar. You're at Washington Memorial Hospital. Four hours ago you were struck by a car at the airport. Do you remember?"

Licking her dry lips, Laura frowned. She sensed people around her. "Hospital?"

"Yes. You're in a private room. Dr. Taggert is here to speak with you. He's the physician on your case."

John Taggert leaned over her and squeezed her

hand. "Laura, I'm Dr. Taggert. Do you have someone we can notify about your injury?"

She took in a deep breath. "No."

"Are you an orphan?"

"I'm adopted, but both my parents are dead."

"I see. Do you remember rushing out in front of a car to save a man from getting hit?"

Laura licked her dry lower lip, the man's grief-stricken face wavering in her memory. How could she ever forget those haunted gray eyes? "Y-yes, I remember…"

"Well, he's safe, but you got hit, instead. You were brought here for treatment. You've got some nasty bruises on your left shoulder and hip, but no internal injuries."

The memory of the man with the black mustache walking out in front of the limo flashed across her mind once again. She remembered his eyes, and how she thought he'd been crying. The rest of the doctor's words were lost as she relived the accident.

"Did you hear me, Ms. Bennett?"

"No…I-I'm sorry," Laura whispered, her head aching fiercely.

"You've sustained a deep cut to your right temple, very close to your eye." Taggert frowned. "Right now, neither of your eyes is responding to light."

"I don't understand." She felt infinitely exhausted.

"It's probably temporary. Tissue swelling could account for the lack of response. We're going to have to wait a couple days for the edema in that area to recede to be sure."

"Sure? Of what?" Suddenly the urge to have that mercenary at her side nearly overwhelmed her. Laura had learned to live alone. She had learned to overcome obstacles without the help of others. His sad gray eyes loomed in her memory.

"You're blind right now, Ms. Bennett. But if I'm correct, it's probably temporary. The blow you took to your head caused it."

Blind? A gasp tore from her, and her hand flew to her bandaged eyes. "No!"

"Easy," Taggert said, capturing her hand and pulling it away from the gauze dressing. "Don't panic yet, Ms. Bennett. In forty-eight hours I'll have a better idea whether your condition is temporary or not."

Panic flooded. "But—I can't be blind!" Her voice cracked.

Patting her hand absently, Taggert said, "Give her a sedative, nurse. Please calm down, Ms. Bennett."

Hot, stinging tears flooded her eyes. Darkness surrounded her. Laura sobbed, fighting to sit up. Her entire body ached. "I don't want a sedative!"

"Take it easy," the doctor murmured. "Listen, the man you saved is outside, waiting to talk to you. His name is Morgan Ramsey, and he won't leave without seeing you."

Morgan Ramsey. Laura leaned back against the pillows, running his name again and again through her mind. "He's here?" Suddenly she needed him. The look in his eyes, despite the harsh cast of his face, told her he was a man of honor, someone she could trust.

"Yes. Maybe talking with him will make you feel better."

"Please, send him in," Laura said, her voice quavering. She wrapped her arms around her gowned body, suddenly very cold and very afraid. Her career depended on her eyes. She couldn't be blind. She just couldn't!

Slipping into the room at Taggert's request, Morgan stood in the ebbing silence after the medical team left. Laura's eyes were bandaged, and he could see that her right cheek was puffy and scratched. She had her arms wrapped against herself, and he sensed her terror.

"Laura, my name is Morgan Ramsey," he said quietly, walking over to her bedside. He allowed his hand to rest on her slumped shoulder. "I'm the guy whose neck you saved."

"Morgan..." His touch was firm, steadying, and his voice was deep, calming her panic. Gradually Laura allowed her arms to relax, and she dropped her hands into her lap. "They said you weren't hurt," she said softly.

Her voice was a sandpapery whisper. Morgan took a pitcher and poured water into a glass, placing it in her hand. "I'm fine. You're the one I'm worried about. Drink this. Maybe you'll feel better."

The water was cooling and bathed her dry throat. Grateful for his sensitivity, Laura handed the glass back to him. "Thank you."

Morgan realized she was trembling as he took the glass from her and set it back on the table. Capturing her hand, he said, "Look, this is awkward as hell, but I owe you my life. I stepped off that curb in another world. If you hadn't pushed me out of the way of that limo, I'd probably be dead by now."

The flesh of his hand was tough, but his grasp was warm and comforting. Laura clung to his hand, needing the stability he automatically provided. "I didn't think. I just reacted," she offered lamely.

He sat down carefully on the edge of the bed, facing her. "Do you always do things out of instinct?" he teased, trying to get her to relax.

Managing a shaky laugh, Laura murmured, "Usually."

"Well, there aren't too many people in this world who would have put their life on the line for the likes of me." He squeezed her cold, damp fingers. "Dr. Taggert told me you can't see. He feels it's temporary, but won't be sure for a couple of days. What can I do for you while you're recovering?"

His voice was incredibly soothing. Laura fought the urge to lean forward and rest against him. "You were at the airport. Surely you have a flight to catch. Not to mention a family and job to go home to. You can't stay here with me."

Morgan felt a slight smile soften his features. "I have no wife or children, Laura. And as for my job, it's overseas and can wait." He had thirty days' leave coming to him and he would wire the commandant of the Legion, requesting it. "They said you have no family," he added. "Maybe I can fill in for a while. Or do you have a friend who can stay with you?"

Laura hung her head, trying to think. Ann Roher, her best friend, was in Europe on assignment for a magazine. Other than that, she had many acquaintances, but no real friends. "My friend Ann is overseas for the next month. I could hire someone—"

"I won't hear of it." Morgan watched her beautifully shaped mouth compress with pain. "Look," he said, reluctantly releasing her hand and standing, "you get some rest. I'll take care of everything."

"But—"

"I know I'm a stranger to you, but you can trust me—" his voice grew hoarse "—with your life."

A shiver shot through Laura as she heard the distinct catch in his tone. "I believe you, Morgan, but I just can't ask you or anyone to—"

"I learned a long time ago that when you're wounded, you should always lean on a buddy for help. It's an old military custom. You're in one hell of a predicament because of me, Laura, and I won't desert you."

Overwhelmed by the incredible twist of events, Laura sank back into the pillows. His voice was fierce with barely veiled emotion, as if she'd struck a raw nerve in him.

Morgan took her silence to mean no. "Look, I'll get a room at a hotel near your house. I don't intend to make a burden of myself. You're going to need someone to get groceries and cook for you. And I can drive you where you need to go. Taggert seems to feel you'll have your eyesight back very soon. A little of my time is small payment for what you did for me today."

"All right, I surrender," Laura said with a sigh.

"There are keys in your purse. Are they to your car?"

"Yes. It's a red Toyota MR2 sports car. I have it parked at the airport. The validation ticket is in my wallet."

"I'll get your car, then. How about at home? Any pets to feed?"

Some of Laura's panic was being assuaged by Morgan Ramsey's sensible practicality. His reference to being wounded triggered her curiosity, but there would be time later to find out more about this mysterious stranger who had crashed into her life. ''Yes, I've got a baby robin at home. She fell out of the apple tree in my backyard a week ago and broke her leg.''

Morgan frowned. ''A robin?'' Anguish surged through him, and with it, old, poignant memories of another baby robin that had touched his life. Was there no end to the pain this day was creating for him? The only positive was Laura. She looked incredibly frail in the stark hospital bed.

''Oh, dear... Will you know how to feed the little bird? She needs worms and fruit—''

''I know all about robins,'' Morgan told her abruptly. ''Any other pets?''

''Just my dog, Sasha. She's a Saint Bernard.''

Unexpected laughter surged through Morgan. ''A big old Saint Bernard with a delicate name like Sasha?''

His laughter feathered across her, and Laura managed a painful smile. ''She's very dainty for a Saint Bernard, Mr. Ramsey.''

Morgan liked Laura's fighting spirit. ''Call me 'Morgan.' We might as well be on a first-name basis. Okay, lady, I'll take care of your menagerie. You just lie back, sleep and get better.''

She heard his footsteps retreating. ''Morgan?''

He halted at the door. ''Yes?''

''Are you sure you want to do this?''

Looking at her soft mouth and listening to her husky voice snapped the tension he'd held in check since this morning. ''Yeah, I'm very sure, Laura. You don't leave a wounded comrade stranded. You're stuck with me.''

She mustered a small smile. ''Okay. Thanks...''

Pulling the door open, Morgan glanced back over his shoulder. "It's one o'clock. I'll be back tonight at visiting hours to report on your household."

"Tonight, then." Laura heard the door shut quietly, and the room suddenly seemed very lonely. Morgan Ramsey's larger-than-life presence was gone, and so was the confidence she'd felt while he was there with her. He'd made the pain go away, too. Touching her bandages gingerly, she prayed with all her heart that the blindness wasn't permanent. Exhaustion eroded her already unraveling emotions, and as she slid into a deep, healing sleep, she wondered what Morgan would think of her small home.

The rain drizzled to a halt as Morgan drove up the narrow asphalt driveway of Laura Bennett's home. The two-story brick home sat back off the road, surrounded by thirty-foot-tall, blossoming pink and white rhododendron bushes. Morgan shut off the red sports car's engine and leaned back to take stock of the house. Three large elm trees towered above it, their branches like arms creating a protective umbrella over the roof. The white shutters at each of the many windows gave the house a quaint appearance, reminding him of the neatly kept homes in the English countryside.

Not able to put his finger on what he felt about the place, Morgan slowly unfolded himself from the small car. The MR2 was excellent for someone of normal size, but his six-foot-five frame and two hundred thirty pounds of tightly packed muscle didn't fit well in such confines.

A white picket fence enclosed Laura's small front yard, he noted, and tulips, hyacinths and yellow daffodils crowded along the front of the house, creating a rainbow of welcoming color. A slight smile thawed the line of Morgan's mouth. The fairy-tale exterior of the house reflected the story-book innocence that flowed from its owner. An idealistic statement, Morgan decided, putting the key in the front door and opening it.

The cold nose of a Saint Bernard poked through the crack in the door, and Morgan spoke gently to the dog, not wanting to startle her. The animal stood in the entrance, enthusiastically wagging her thick brown-and-white tail. A grin crossed Morgan's mouth as he entered and shut the door behind him. Sasha was small for a Saint. He allowed her to sniff at him all she wanted, using the interlude to inspect Laura's residence.

The fairy-tale effect was even more pronounced inside the house. Filmy ruffled white curtains hung over each window, heightening the femininity of the residence. There were pots of African violets on a number of windowsills and sitting on Queen Anne tables, plus a variety of lush greenery in each corner.

"Antique and otherworld," Morgan said. He felt Sasha's pink tongue adoring his hand. Leaning over, he patted her large, broad skull, noting the dancing lights in her huge brown eyes.

"You're just like your mistress, aren't you?" he demanded. "Trusting and naive." Not a good combination for this world, Morgan thought as he moved through the lavender carpeted rooms. The wallpaper was ivory colored, with tiny violets sprinkled across it. No doubt Laura loved the Victorian era, a very romantic period. He shook his head, unable to get her beautiful blue eyes out of his mind.

The baby robin was in a small cage sitting on the kitchen countertop. Morgan scowled down at the bird, who had a wide yellow beak, sparkling black eyes and a cheep that filled the room.

"Hungry, huh?" He turned to go to the refrigerator, and nearly tripped over Sasha. The dog gazed up at him lovingly and Morgan swallowed his reprimand. The kitchen was sunny, with two walls of windows that overlooked the backyard. Morgan wasn't surprised that the yard resembled an English garden in every sense of the word. He could see the round, rectangular and square areas formed by bricks. There were probably different herbs or flowers in each area, he thought, noting green shoots. Opening the door to the refrigerator, Morgan bent down and spotted a carton with "worms" written on the side of it.

The robin hopped onto his finger the moment he put the carton into the cage, and grudgingly Morgan fed the bird a couple of worms. Sated, she sat contentedly on his finger afterward, emitting contented little cheeps.

"Wish it took so little to satisfy everything else in life," Morgan told the robin, putting her back on the perch in the cage. Sasha whined at the back door, wanting out. Morgan shut the wire door to the cage and walked over, allowing the Saint Bernard out into the enclosed yard.

Drawn to explore the entire house, Morgan tried to ask himself why. His world consisted of minding his own business. The men of the Legion lived only in the present, never the past—or the future. But Laura haunted him, like a beautiful dream after he'd awakened. She was like elusive fog that disappeared when the sun shone directly on it. He snorted softly as he walked down the hall and into another room. Maybe he was dreaming and was really on a jet back to France.

Standing at the entrance to a room, he realized that this was her office. A computer terminal sat on a large, elegantly carved cherry desk. Floor-to-ceiling bookshelves lined two of the walls. Morgan wandered over to the terminal and looked at several papers beside it. Frowning, he picked them up.

"'The Buildup of Soviet Military Power' by L. Bennett," he muttered. He stood reading the carefully typed ten-page manuscript. "I'll be damned." His fairy-tale Laura was a technical writer. Obviously a good one, because she had an insider's knowledge of Soviet hardware.

He dropped the manuscript back on the desk and turned around. Looking at the rows of books, he noticed that two of them had been written by her. Taking the first off the shelf, he saw that the book dealt with tactics and strategy in World War II. The second was a detailed account of all the major battles during the Korean War.

Scratching his head, he put both books back on the shelf. She was some kind of military expert. How? Most women had little interest in that topic, much less any expertise in it. "Laura Bennett, you're one hell of an interesting person," he said, leaving the room.

She was going to need a robe and some other items for her stay in the hospital. He had to find her bedroom.

When he did he was speechless. Laura's bedroom was a Victorian fantasy. He stood at the threshold of the large room, staring at the flowery print covering the canopied bed. The elegantly carved bureau shouted her refined taste. A bowl of dried lavender flowers filled the room with a clean scent. He entered the dark-blue carpeted room, pulling himself out of the dreamy state the room induced. White French doors concealed two walk-in closets. Feeling as though he were trespassing, Morgan opened the closet door and found three cotton gowns hanging there. They were delicately embroidered with flowers, with pastel ribbons at the neckline and puffed sleeves. He folded the gowns carefully, located a small suitcase and placed them and other necessary items in it.

Then, going to the back door, he called Sasha. The Saint Bernard bounded back into the house, panting happily. Grinning, Morgan reached down, patting her thick, broad head. ''I'll be back a little later to make sure you don't get housebound, big girl.''

Morgan lingered in the front room, suitcase in hand. The feeling of serenity in the clean, neatly kept house was overwhelming. He wanted to relax, kick off his shoes and stretch out. Sasha came and sat, ladylike, at his side, her pink tongue lolling out the side of her mouth, her brown eyes sparkling. Morgan laughed harshly at himself as his shoulders, usually tense and drawn up, relaxed of their own accord. What kind of magic did Laura Bennett weave? He gazed around at the transparent draperies gracing each window. Laura's home was the direct opposite of what he was used to: a bunk in a sterile barracks with a highly polished floor and no sign of individual expression. Life in the Legion was hard and demanding. This house mirrored the opposite: softness and gentleness. With a sigh, he told the dog goodbye and reluctantly closed the front door.

The next order of business was to find a nearby

hotel. And then he'd have to wait until eight o'clock. Suddenly Morgan found himself restless, wanting to talk at length with Laura, to explore this intriguing young woman.

Laura sensed Morgan's arrival. The door to her private room had opened and closed a number of times previously, but somehow she knew it was him.

"Morgan?"

He halted at the foot of her bed, thinking she looked a bit better than last time. "How did you know?"

Nervously Laura made a gesture with her hand. "Just a feeling around you."

"So," he murmured, bringing the suitcase near her bed and sitting down in a chair, "you're intuitive on top of everything else."

His voice feathered through her, easing her anxiety over her blindness. Laura released a sigh and sat back against several pillows that had been arranged for her earlier. "What's that supposed to mean?"

Hungrily Morgan absorbed her delicate beauty. "It was a compliment. Your home reflects you."

She grinned slightly. "Ann teases me unmercifully about my house. She calls it Sleeping Beauty's Castle."

"I like your place." Morgan caught the sadness in his tone and tried to cover it up. "There's a romantic Victorian aspect to you."

But Laura had caught the sadness, too. She quelled her urge to ask him about the source of his grief. "I love that era. Did you see my leather-bound volumes by Victorian authors in my office?"

She was like sunlight, Morgan decided, warming

beneath her honeyed voice, which was breathless with enthusiasm. Her blond hair had been washed and now hung in graceful abandon around her small shoulders.

"Yeah, I saw your library." He rubbed his jaw. "I also saw a manuscript on your desk about Soviet hardware."

All Laura's fears began to erode in Morgan's presence. He'd think her foolish if she confided that he made her feel safe, as if everything about this experience were going to turn out positively. "You don't miss much, do you?"

"Not when my life can depend on it."

Laura tilted her head, assimilating his brusque answer. It was on the tip of her tongue to ask him about his frequently military references, but she decided to wait. "I make a living writing books and articles for the military establishment," she explained, then wrinkled her nose. "I know it's probably strange for a woman to be in that line of business, but I find it fascinating."

"Oh?"

She rested her hands on her blanketed lap. "I guess my fascination started because my adoptive father was in the marine corps."

Tension thrummed through Morgan, blips of his past flashing before his mind, as they always did in such moments. Scowling, he said, "Marine corps?"

"Yes. Dad was killed in 1970 in Saigon, during the closing days of the Vietnam conflict."

"I'm sorry," he muttered. "A lot of good men died over there at that time." The pain in his chest widened. His past, which had haunted him daily since he'd regained his memory, loomed like an ugly, festering sore before him.

"He believed in what he was doing, Morgan. Dad always believed in fighting for what he felt was right. I was raised around the military and found it interesting from a psychological viewpoint."

"So you were weaned on a military tradition. What about your adoptive mother?"

Laura gestured briefly with her hand. "She died in 1975 in a car accident."

"So now you're alone."

"It's not so bad." Laura managed a brave smile. "Except for times like this when I can't see."

Morgan wanted to get to another topic besides war. All it did was dredge up the faces of ghosts that stalked him nightly. "How are you feeling?"

"Better." *Much better since you're here,* Laura wanted to add, but squelched the urge. Lightly she touched her bandages. "Everyone's positive that when the swelling goes down, I'll be able to see again."

Morgan wanted to reach out and run his fingers down her long, elegant hand. "I've got a hunch you'll see."

"I hope so...I mean, my livelihood depends on my sight, Morgan."

To hell with it. Morgan leaned over and captured her hand. Her fingers were damp and cool. "No one's going to turn your life inside out," he promised her.

His hand was callused and warm, and Laura released a shaky breath. "I'm scared, Morgan. Scared to death. What if I don't see again? How am I going to write? How will I be able to interview? I mean, I spend half my life at the Pentagon, going through tons of files in the basement complex, looking for unclassified material for my articles and books."

He placed both his hands on hers. "Now listen to me, Laura, that isn't going to happen."

With a little laugh of desperation, Laura said, "God, I hope not. But bad things happen to good people, no matter what our intent was at the time."

Morosely Morgan agreed. "Yeah, bad things do happen to innocent people. You just have to be at the right place at the wrong time." As he had been on Hill 164 with his company of men seven years ago. As Laura had been for him today....

"I know so little about you, and yet I feel I've known you forever," Laura said softly. Removing her hands from his, she lay back against the pillows, her voice lowering with feeling. "When I first saw you across that roadway, I thought you were a mercenary. You looked so hard and tough. And that scar on your face made me think you were a soldier. But now... Well, you're far more caring than I'd first thought." She shook her head. "Just goes to show, you can't judge any book by its cover."

Reluctantly Morgan allowed her to reclaim her hands. "I've got a face that was rearranged by a Mack truck," he jested, trying to tease her out of her fear of being permanently blind.

"No! I didn't mean it that way," Laura said quickly. "You're far from ugly." Heat flowed into her neck and cheeks, and she knew she was blushing. "You have character. Every line has a story behind it. I'd much rather look at a face that's interesting than one that's got nothing on it."

Morgan chuckled. "Then you're going to like old age, lady. Everyone gets wrinkles by that time. I just got some of mine a little early, that's all."

She laughed with him. "Thanks for letting me walk out of the noose I prepared for myself."

"No harm done," Morgan assured her. "I look at this mug every morning when I shave, and so far I haven't broken too many mirrors."

His humor stirred her heart. He was always castigating himself in some small way. "Morgan, you haven't told me anything about yourself. If you're going to be stuck with me for a while, I'd like to know something about you."

With her military background and expertise Laura would most likely know about his company being slaughtered in 1970. Maybe it was just as well that she was temporarily blind—that way she couldn't possibly identify him. With time, though, he was afraid Laura would put two and two together. And he couldn't have that happen. Not ever. No, he'd stay with her long enough to make sure she was going to be fine, and then he'd disappear back into Europe to his other life. There was no alternative.

Laura took his silence as a reply. "I don't mean to be snoopy," she began awkwardly.

"Sorry," Morgan muttered, "I was thinking about something else."

"There's an accent to your speech. Are you from a foreign country?"

Her ability to pick up little things like that shouldn't surprise him, but it unnerved him. "I'm American, but I live in France." It wasn't a lie, but it wasn't the total truth, either. "For the past six years, I've been putting my engineering skills to work for the French."

"An engineer," Laura marveled. "I was right. You looked as if you could build things. Your hands are square and large, and you looked as if you get a lot of physical exercise.''

Damn, she didn't miss much at all. ''Right on all accounts. I build bridges.'' That was true, but he also dug ditches, canals and roads wherever the Legion wanted them.

''You're a man with wanderlust in his heart, always on the move.''

Morgan squirmed because he didn't want to lie to her. ''I do travel around,'' he said. ''I've got enough foreign countries under my belt to last me a lifetime.''

''Do I hear longing in your voice?'' Laura asked. ''Maybe you want to settle down and get some good home cooking and a family atmosphere for a bit.''

He laughed, staring down at his scarred, callused hands. ''Yeah, I dream about that every so often.'' Just as he wondered daily how his father and mother were doing down in Clearwater. The itch to pick up a phone and call them was excruciating. But Morgan didn't want to renew their heartbreak over his disappearance. Seven years had healed their grief. He didn't want to add to it now.

''I'm not such a bad cook,'' Laura hinted wryly. ''If you help me in the kitchen, I can promise you some great home-cooked meals.''

''I haven't had a decent meal in a long time,'' Morgan said fervently. He couldn't get that house out of his mind, or her beautiful bedroom. His vivid imagination was torturing him again, and he savagely slammed a lid on his needs. His dreams had died in 1970. There was no future for him. Ever.

Laura smiled gently. ''You sound like a man starved for a little bit of home life.''

Reluctantly Morgan rose. ''I'm not going to answer

on the grounds that it might incriminate me,'' he teased her, watching her lips move into a smile that touched his cold, aching heart.

''You're leaving?''

She must have heard him get up from the chair. ''For being temporarily blind, you don't miss much, do you?''

Disappointed that he was going, Laura tried to mask her reaction. ''Blame it on my dog ears. My parents always told me I was supersensitive to everything. I guess it's true.''

Morgan reached over and patted her shoulder. ''You wear it well. Look, I brought you a suitcase with some items you'll probably want while you're here in the hospital. I'll get a nurse to take care of unpacking them for you.''

His touch on her shoulder was hesitant, almost shy, and Laura's senses told her that Morgan, despite his size and harshly carved face, was a gentle man underneath. ''Thank you for everything, Morgan.''

He walked to the door, taking one last glance at her. She looked like a waif in that dreary light-blue hospital gown. ''You just get a good night's sleep. I'll go home and check on your pets. Then I'll be at the Grand Hotel. The nurses' station will have my phone number in case you need me.''

Fear started to stalk her once more, and Laura tried to swallow it. ''When will I see you again?''

Her mouth was delicious, but the corners were pulled in, as if she were experiencing either pain or fear. Morgan shrugged. ''Considering I'm the guy who caused you to be in this predicament, I wouldn't think you'd want to see much of me too often.''

''No...please, come back soon. Visiting hours start

at eleven in the morning,'' Laura blurted. She compressed her lips, realizing that she sounded like a frightened little girl incapable of caring for herself. ''I mean—'' she rubbed her brow, the ache beginning again ''—it gets lonely here, and I miss Robby and Sasha so much....''

''I understand,'' Morgan said quietly. He forced himself to open the door, instead of walking back over to her bed and enfolding her in his arms. Right now she needed a little care. That was what he was best at: caring. It came naturally to him. ''I'll be here at eleven, then. That's a promise.''

Chapter Three

"It's final, Dr. Taggert, I'm leaving."

Morgan stood in the open doorway of Laura's hospital room, listening to her raised voice. Taggert was standing at her bedside, an agitated look on his face.

"I'm glad you've arrived, Mr. Ramsey," the doctor muttered.

Laura turned her attention from the physician. "Morgan?"

He allowed the door to shut, painfully aware of the desperation in her tone. "It's me. What's going on?" Halting on the other side of her bed, he was surprised as Laura lifted her hand, trying to make contact with him. He took her hand firmly. Her fingers were icy cold.

"Morgan, I've made a decision," Laura said, speaking rapidly because she didn't want the doctor to interrupt. "I had a terrible night's sleep here. I feel good enough to leave. I need my home in order to heal.'' Her grip on him tightened. ''Please take me home. I told Dr. Taggert I'd sign the release papers.''

Automatically Morgan soothed her by stroking her hand. ''Take it easy, Laura.'' He lifted his gaze to the physician, who was standing with crossed arms, a scowl deepening on his brow. ''Doctor, is it safe for her to leave this soon?''

''She ought to stay here for at least forty-eight hours—for observation after any kind of head injury,'' he muttered defiantly. ''That trauma to her head could cause a hemorrhage. She should remain at least another day so we can make sure that isn't going to happen.''

Laura's nostrils flared. ''Morgan, the X-rays on my hard head came back without any sign of a concussion!''

''It's only twenty-four more hours, Ms. Bennett.''

''Morgan,'' Laura pleaded huskily, ''will you take me home?''

''Yeah, hold on just a minute.'' He directed his attention back to Taggert. ''She's obviously upset at having to stay, Doctor. And some people recuperate better in a familiar setting.'' He ought to know. Six months in a hospital bed in Japan had nearly driven him crazy while he'd recovered from his massive wounds. He understood Laura's need to get out of these sterile confines.

Scratching his head, Taggert walked toward the door. ''If she insists on going home, she shouldn't be left alone.''

''Think you can stand me underfoot for twenty-four hours?'' he asked Laura.

''Yes.'' She fought to keep the wobble out of her

voice. "Just let me go home, Morgan. You know what I need...."

He squeezed her hand, then placed it back in her lap. "I do," he agreed quietly. "Okay, Doctor, set things in motion. Ms. Bennett is going home."

Shrugging, Taggert pulled open the door. "Fine. A nurse will be down shortly with the forms to sign and a wheelchair."

Releasing a sigh, Laura sagged back against the pillows. "Thank you, Morgan. I'm sorry you had to walk in on our argument."

He grinned. "That's all right. I've been in a few crossfires before and managed to survive them."

"I knew you'd understand. I slept terribly last night, and I'm a grouch today. My head's fine. It's just my silly eyes." She made a graceful gesture with her hand. "My home is everything to me. It's safety. It's peace. Here I can't do anything except lie in bed. I feel so damned helpless!"

Morgan reached over and massaged her left shoulder gently. "Calm down, my flighty swan, I'll take you home."

His touch was firm and Laura relaxed the instant his hand rested on her shoulder. "I'm sorry to be such a pain in the rear. You probably think I'm—"

"You're not being unreasonable, Laura. I spent a lot of months in a hospital many years ago, and I almost went crazy. I wanted to go home, too, but I couldn't. I know how you're feeling. There's no apology needed. Okay?"

"Okay," Laura whispered. Rallying, she reached up, finding his hand and holding it between hers. "Thanks. At least when I get home, I can get up and move around or work on my article."

"Whoa, one thing at a time. Let's see how it feels

just to get up and walk around. You took a severe bump to your head. You might get dizzy.''

He was right, Laura conceded. ''I never realized how much I disliked hospital environments until last night,'' she grumped. ''You're right. I'll take it one step at a time.''

Already color was coming back into her pale cheeks. He wanted to lean over and brush that slope of cheek to find out if Laura was as soft as she appeared to be. Morgan put a clamp on the simmering desires that automatically surfaced whenever he was around her.

''Morgan?''

''Yes?''

''Did you sleep well last night?''

He grinned. ''No, I had a lousy night's sleep.'' He always did, but he didn't want to say that.

''Look, I know it's terribly awkward for you, having to stay at my house one night just to play babysitter. We barely know each other, but I trust you.''

''I think I'll manage to sleep under your roof,'' he said dryly.

''You don't mind?''

''No.'' In all honesty he was looking forward to sleeping in a real home.

The nurse came in with a clipboard holding several papers. Another nurse followed her. For the next fifteen minutes, Morgan was busy taking instructions on how to dress Laura's eyes twice daily and bandage them. She signed the forms with his help, and then a wheelchair was ushered into the room.

Morgan gripped her hand. ''You ready to fly this place?'' he asked.

Eagerly Laura threw off the covers, exposing the long cotton nightgown. ''Just get me my chenille robe and we're gone.'' Right now all she wanted was home.

''Sasha!'' Laura cried, throwing her arms awkwardly around the whining Saint Bernard. Laughter bubbled up in her throat as she hugged her dog affectionately.

Morgan stood back, suitcase in one hand, and quietly closed the front door behind him. Sunlight poured through the east windows, illuminating the living room, alive with life. Laura looked tiny in comparison to the huge, tail-wagging Saint, who panted happily and whined a joyous greeting to her mistress.

Laura stood, her hand moving outward, connecting with Morgan's. He was always there, somehow sensing when she needed his help. ''Oh, Morgan, it's so wonderful to be home!'' Her voice trembled, but she didn't care.

He smiled, holding her hand more firmly. ''I know... Come on, let's get you to your bedroom.''

''No, take me to the bathroom, will you? I want to fill the tub with orange blossom bubble bath and soak off this hospital smell!''

Her enthusiasm was infectious, and he chuckled. ''Okay, little swan, let's fly to your bath so you can smell like oranges instead of antiseptic.''

Morgan led her into the long, rectangular bathroom that had a green carpet and sunny wallpaper covered with white and yellow daisies. He marveled over his and Laura's innate ability to work as a team without any conversation. Laura started filling the bath and poured the bubble liquid into the water, the scent of orange blossoms filling the air. He left and went to her bedroom. In no time he had chosen a pair of tan slacks, a pink blouse and lingerie for her to wear after her bath. Placing them on the vanity, he shut the door and left.

It was past noon and he was hungry. Walking out to the kitchen, he fed the noisy baby robin, then attended to the details of a lunch for himself and Laura. Sasha sat at his feet, thumping her thick tail, as he made peanut butter sandwiches. "No," he told the dog, "this other sandwich is for your mistress."

Sasha tilted her head, whining.

"Oh, all right...." Morgan threw her a slice of bread and watched it disappear inside her cavernous mouth. "Good thing you're friendly. I'd hate to get bitten by the set of choppers you've got," Morgan muttered, and went back to making lunch.

Laura emerged half an hour later. Using her hand, she followed the hallway wall until it intersected with the kitchen. "Are you in here?" she asked.

Morgan looked up from where he was sitting in the sunny breakfast nook. "Yes. Hold on, I'll help you over to the table."

Laura held up her hand. "No, stay there. I've got to get around on my own, Morgan." Smiling, she added, "I feel a hundred and ten percent better! Did I button this blouse right, or is it hanging at an angle?"

He got to his feet, quietly coming to her side, just in case she stumbled on her way across the kitchen. "You look fine." Hell, she looked breathtakingly beautiful. She had taken off the bandage and washed her hair, then replaced the dressing afterward. Her golden hair hung damply around her shoulders. The fragrance of orange blossoms filled his nostrils as he remained close to her. The pale-pink blouse was excruciatingly feminine, the ruffles around her slender neck emphasizing her delicate beauty. The mobility of her lips entranced him, and Morgan felt heat uncurling deep within him. A gnawing hunger made him all too aware of how she affected him.

Making contact with the wooden chair, Laura pulled it out and sat down. "Success!" she declared, laughing.

"You're doing fine," Morgan congratulated her. "Here's lunch." He placed the plate with the sandwich in front of her. "I made some coffee. You want some?"

Famished, Laura picked up the sandwich. "Yes, please." She smelled it. "Peanut butter. One of my favorites. Thanks for making it."

Heat nettled Morgan's face as he poured coffee into the dainty china cup decorated with pansies. Her gratefulness made him feel as if he'd given her the most beautiful gift in the world. "I'm afraid my skills as a cook are lacking, Laura."

"Why do you always belittle what you do, Morgan?"

Settling back at the table, opposite her, he scowled. "What do you mean?"

Laura placed the half-eaten sandwich on the plate in front of her, hearing the carefully veiled pain in his voice. "You're always cutting yourself down in some way," she murmured. "That self-deprecating humor isn't deserved."

Pushing the cup around on the saucer, Morgan scowled. "Yes, it is," he said, and let it go at that. One look at her face, however, and he realized she wasn't going to let him off the hook that easily. "You're too damn good at being a writer," he griped.

"What do you mean?"

"You pick up nuances in people."

"Does it make you uncomfortable?"

"Yes."

She chuckled. "Why? Because you have something to hide?"

He winced. She was close to the truth. "There isn't a human being alive who doesn't have some secret," he parried.

Laura warmed to their conversation. He was so easy to talk to. "And how many secrets are you carrying, Morgan Ramsey?" she teased.

The china cup looked small in comparison to Morgan's darkly tanned hands. "More than I'd like," he admitted hesitantly.

Sobering, Laura leaned forward. "I'm a great secret keeper, Morgan. Lord knows, when I interview the generals and admirals over at the Pentagon, they sometimes slip and tell me things that could never go into print."

He eyed her. "You're just a regular Pandora's Box, huh?"

"You could say that. I've been rubbing shoulders with the Pentagon people for the past seven years, and they've come to trust me. I hold what they say in confidence." Laura straightened and grinned. "And those things go to the grave with me."

Frowning, he muttered, "Well, you came too damn close to the grave the other day by saving my neck."

"I wouldn't have had it any other way, Morgan."

The sudden quaver in Laura's voice sent a wave of yearning through him. He stared hard at her. There was an underlying strength to her, despite her innate femininity. "I believe you," he whispered.

Laura detected an opening in the wall that so thoroughly protected Morgan Ramsey. "When I first came here after graduating from college, I rented this house." She gestured around the room with her hand.

"I fell in love with it. At the time my dad was over in Vietnam, and I sent him pictures of every room." Her voice grew warm with love. "He was so excited for me. We traded letters for six months on how I was going to decorate each room. Of course, Mom got in on it, too. We'd send him swatches of material, wallpaper samples and photos from magazines of the furniture I someday wanted to be able to afford." She picked up the cup, sipping the cooling coffee. "I think my letters and dreams for this house helped my dad. It was a piece of reality from a world other than the one he fought in daily." Laura shook her head. "I still have all his letters...."

A lump formed in Morgan's throat. "Letters from home meant everything to me—" He caught himself. Damn!

"You were in Vietnam?" Of course, he would have been the right age.

A frown furrowed his brow. "Yeah, I was over there." The words came out harsh and clipped.

Biding time because she heard his anger and pain, Laura drank her coffee. She'd met many veterans who didn't want to discuss what had happened to them over there, and she felt Morgan was like that, too. Gently she steered the conversation back to her father. "The living room was Dad's idea—the colors and the fabric. And so was the kitchen." Fondly she laughed. "At the time we were playing this silly game, I really didn't have any money for redecorating. But that didn't matter. At least it offered Dad some sanity while he was over there. And Mom didn't worry as much, because she had something to do, too."

Morgan could no longer sit still. The ghosts were rising in his memory again—the anger and frustration along with them. He paced slowly around the kitchen.

"So how did you manage to get this house bought and decorated?"

Leaning back, Laura sensed he'd moved away from the table. There was a new and different energy around him, and she felt his tension. "Dad was killed in a rocket attack in the seventh month of his tour. What I didn't realize was that he'd taken out nearly half a million dollars in insurance before he left for Vietnam, just in case he did get killed. My mother and I found out about it when the lawyer read his will to us three weeks later." She rose, picking up her cup and saucer and moved carefully to the drainboard. "So I bought this house instead of renting it, and Mom and I took each room, just as we'd planned it in our letters to Dad, and decorated."

Morgan stood in the center of the kitchen, staring at Laura. There was a sad smile on her lips. "It must have been hard," he said, his voice hoarse.

"No, just the opposite really. I cried a lot, because he was a wonderful father and friend to me. So did Mom. But wallpapering and painting each room, then buying the furniture helped us expend our grief and get over his passing." She patted the drainboard. "This home reflects the love we had as a family. That's why I love it so much." She gave him a shy look. "Maybe now you can understand why I wanted to come home from the hospital. I work through trauma better here than anywhere else."

Morgan tried to fight his need to hold her, but he walked up to her. Gently placing his hands on her shoulders, he looked down at her. "You're like this home," he told her, his voice rough with emotion, "warm, caring and beautiful. Your parents gave you a lot of love, and it shows in many ways."

It felt so natural to lean her head against his chest

and rest for just a moment. Laura sighed as Morgan's arms slid around her shoulders, drawing her gently against him. ''Right now, I don't feel very strong, Morgan.''

She fitted against his tall frame, Morgan thought, a willow in comparison to an oak. The fragrance that was hers alone filled his nostrils. He fought to keep his touch light and comforting, not intimate, as he wanted. ''You're stronger than you think,'' he told Laura gruffly, his mouth near her ear. Caressing her back with his hands, he felt the firm softness of her flesh beneath the silk blouse. If he didn't step back, he'd kiss her, and that wouldn't be right. The timing was all wrong—as usual.

Laura felt bereft as Morgan gently disengaged himself. ''I—I'm sorry. I shouldn't have—''

''Shh,'' Morgan remonstrated, keeping one hand on her upper arm as she swayed. ''That's one of many things I like about you, Laura Bennett—your ability to show your feelings. If you're feeling weak, you lean. If you're feeling strong, you get feisty.'' He grinned. ''You're one hell of a woman, did you know that?''

She shook her head, forcing herself to retreat from him. Shaken by the unexpected contact, Laura found herself wanting more. ''No, you're wrong,'' she whispered, her voice strained, ''you're the one who's special.''

Snorting vehemently, Morgan got busy and cleared the rest of the dishes from the table. ''I'm special all right,'' he growled. *Just ask the press or the Pentagon. They'll tell you all about me.* He glanced at her after setting the dishes in the sink. Her lips were pursed, as if she were deep in thought. All this seemed like a fevered dream. This house that throbbed with life, the beauty and generosity of Laura, were all baubles being dangled cruelly in front of him and his harsh existence. If she found out he was Morgan Trayhern, the traitor, she'd scorn him. Sadness flowed through him, effectively squelching the fires of longing for her. Morgan hadn't fully realized just how tough it would be to stay around Laura. Somehow he'd have to contain his unraveling emotions. Maybe by tonight things would settle into a routine, and he'd be able to control the feelings that Laura brought to brilliant, yearning life within him. Maybe…

"The fire feels wonderful," Laura murmured, sitting with her back to the fireplace. "April nights are always chilly in D.C." Sasha lay directly in front of the fire, snoring fitfully.

Morgan sat nearby in an overstuffed chair. He marveled at Laura's hair, golden threads highlighted by the fire. She had dressed for bed and was wearing a long white cotton gown, her lavender chenille robe wrapped about her slender body. "You give April nights a new meaning," he admitted, his voice deeper than usual.

She drew her knees up, resting her cheek on them, a soft smile on her lips. "It sounds as if in your business you spend a lot of time outdoors. I imagine a quiet night like this *is* different for you."

The magazine in Morgan's lap was a poor substitute for staring like a starving wolf at Laura. He was disgusted with himself, taking advantage of her blindness by watching her for minutes at a time. It wasn't as if he couldn't have a woman if he wanted. That wasn't the issue at all. The issue was Laura and her Dresden doll delicacy, her graceful motions with her hands, that heart-grabbing laughter that made him want to drag her into his arms and crush her against him, never letting her go.

Morgan cleared his throat. "I do spend a lot of time outside," he admitted. Did she hear the longing in his voice? God, he hoped not. She trusted him completely, and he wouldn't reward that trust by letting her know of his insatiable need for her.

Lulled by the peace swirling gently between them, Laura confessed, "When I saw you standing there in the rain at the airport, I sensed this terrible tragedy and loneliness in you, Morgan. That scar on your face..."

Uncomfortable, he placed the magazine on the coffee table. "I'd just gotten some bad news that morning," he said gruffly.

"That scar...did you get it in Vietnam?" Somehow Laura sensed that the suffering surrounding Morgan stemmed from that time in his life. The need to get to the real him, the man she sensed beneath all that weight he carried on his powerful shoulders, was forcing her to ask deeply personal questions.

Automatically Morgan's fingers went to the ridge of the scar, and he scowled. "Yeah, I got it there."

"Tell me how?"

His stomach knotted. If Laura had been pushy or curious, it would have been easy to tell her to mind her own business, but the quaver in her voice unstrung him, and he leaned back, closing his eyes. "I got it in hand-to-hand combat. My company and I were led into a trap and we had to defend a hill," he said in a low, hard voice.

"My God," she whispered. Slowly she got up from her spot near the fireplace. Hand outstretched, she took small steps in the direction of where Morgan sat.

Her lips parted as his fingers wrapped strongly around her arm and he guided her to the chair near him. She sat back down on the floor, nestled at his feet, her back against the chair. "I didn't mean to pry," she told him softly. "But you wear sadness around you like a good friend, Morgan." She took a deep breath and dove in. "We barely know each other, and I know your personal life isn't any of my business, but I just can't seem to help myself. If I'm being nosy, tell me to quit asking questions."

He lifted his hand, and noticed it was trembling. Laura's face was tilted in his direction, her lips parted, pleading. Stroking her hair, Morgan managed a tortured smile. "Sweet Laura," he said thickly, "your heart is pure, so you can see straight through a person." Her hair was clean, and the strands flowed like molten gold between his scarred fingers.

Her breath caught in her throat as his fingers trembled across her hair, again and again. "I don't need eyes to hear the pain in your voice, Morgan," Laura whispered. "I—there's something special we share. I can't define it, but it's there." She placed her hand on his knee, lifting her face more in his direction. "Something tragic happened to you yesterday morning. That's why you stepped off that curb without looking. Please, let me help, if I can...." She moistened her lips. "If nothing else, I'm a good listener, Morgan. And I care..."

Pain, like a volcano inside his chest, exploded violently within him. It seared his heart, soaring up into his throat, and he leaned forward, resting his cheek against the top of Laura's head ever so lightly, needing the comfort she offered. Without a word, he gripped her shoulders, simply holding her, his breathing ragged.

A little cry escaped Laura's lips, and she placed her arm around his shoulder. ''Morgan, what is it? You're shaking.''

Shutting his eyes tightly, he fought to find his voice. ''This isn't real,'' he said gruffly. ''None of this is real, especially you....''

His hands were splayed across her back, and Laura relaxed within them. Something was terribly wrong. Blindly she groped with her hand, her fingers coming in contact with his face. She could feel the thick welt of the scar that ran the length of his face. ''You're wrong,'' she said, her voice quavering. ''This is all real, Morgan. Especially me. I can feel your pain.... Talk to me about it. Whatever it is, I can deal with it.''

The desire to spill the horrible facts surrounding his life dealt him an almost lethal blow. Her fingers were warm against his chilled flesh. He fought the overpowering urge to tilt her face upward and crush those pleading lips beneath his mouth. His heart pounded erratically in his chest, and his breathing was harsh. ''N-no,'' he whispered, ''I can't.''

''Can't or won't?'' Laura asked, gently running her fingers across the scar.

If he didn't push her away, he'd take her, and Laura didn't deserve that. He released her slender form, keeping his hands on her shoulders as he drew away. ''Both,'' he said thickly.

He'd been so close to allowing that awful load he carried to slide into her waiting arms. Laura swallowed her disappointment. She managed a small smile and lifted her hands so that they came to rest on his forearms. The tightly muscled power in them fairly vibrated through her fingertips. ''From the moment I saw you, I knew you were special, Morgan.''

A startled laugh broke from him. He gave her a gentle shake. ''Special? You've got your priorities skewed, sweet swan.''

She laughed softly. ''Swan? Is that how you see me? Tall and skinny with my bird-size bones?''

Her laughter melted the wall of pain that threatened to engulf him. It was a miracle in itself, and Morgan stared down at her. ''Yeah, you're a beautiful, graceful swan.'' He released her shoulders and picked up one of her wrists, turning it over carefully in his large hands. ''You're tiny but mighty.''

His touch was evocative, sending warming threads of yearning up Laura's arm, the heat flowing through her like an awakening river of molten lava. ''So, you see my backbone of steel?'' She ached to lean upward, find his mouth and kiss him.

''A beautiful spine and a set of small, but very strong shoulders,'' he murmured. All he had to do was lean forward—mere inches—to kiss her. He shut his eyes, fighting the overwhelming urge.

''Make me a promise, Morgan?''

He felt her hands tighten on his arms. ''What?''

''You know I'm strong enough to hear anything you might tell me. Promise me that if you want to talk, you'll unload your burden on me?''

Smiling gently, he placed a chaste kiss on her wrinkled brow. ''Sweet, guileless swan. Come on, you've had a long day, and it's time for bed.''

Morgan's kiss had been fleeting. His mouth had been strong against her forehead, and Laura felt the heat escalate within her at his unexpected gesture. ''I think you're right,'' she whispered. ''This swan is ready to call it a night.''

Chapter Four

"Be quiet, you little beggar, or you'll wake up Laura," Morgan growled at the robin, who frantically cheeped in her cage. Morning sunlight cascaded through the green curtains at the windows. Rubbing his face tiredly, Morgan went through the motions of feeding the baby bird. Who could believe this almost featherless creature could cause such a ruckus?

Morgan knew he'd overslept. He'd been unable to sleep for a long time after his conversation with Laura by the fireplace. And then his sleep had been broken with nightmarish memories intermixed with Laura's haunting face dancing before him. Dressed in only a pair of pajama bottoms, Morgan enjoyed the feel of the sunlight against his upper body as he stood at the sink, feeding the robin her morning meal.

"I'll tell you what, little lady, you're lucky I put up with you."

"Morgan?"

He turned, hearing Laura's sleep-filled voice. His heart tightened in his chest as he took in her rumpled appearance. Sasha, who'd slept in her mistress's bedroom, wagged her tail in greeting as she ambled toward Morgan. Sometime during the night Laura's bandage had slipped off. Her blue eyes were incredibly large and thickly lashed. Dragging in a deep breath, he felt that same molten desire explode through him just as it had the night before.

"It's okay," he mumbled. "We both overslept and this little beggar was hungry."

Laura smiled and walked slowly toward Morgan's voice, her hand held out in front of her. "I heard Robby cheeping like crazy. I thought something was wrong," she offered huskily, finding the countertop and halting.

Laura's eyes were puffy with sleep, her hair mussed and framing her face. Morgan swallowed hard, putting the robin back in the cage. "She won't squawk for at least an hour. I stuffed her with four worms."

Laura chuckled and tried to smooth her hair away from her face. "Despite all your snarling and growling about feeding Robby, I really think you like her." Wildly aware of Morgan's overpowering masculinity, Laura sensed she was very close to him. Her dreams had been torrid, centering around her in Morgan's arms.

"You look beautiful just the way you are," Morgan said thickly. He placed the cage back against the wall and turned to her. The white cotton gown was wrinkled, the boat neck revealing her finely sculpted collarbones and emphasizing the smooth expanse of her throat. "And you're going to catch your death of cold if you don't get a robe."

"Oh, dear, I forgot to put it on." Laura pressed both hands to her cheeks, feeling heat steal into them. The gown she wore wasn't sexy in her mind, but she heard the longing in Morgan's tone. "I'm sorry," she began lamely. "I'm so used to padding around here alone in my gown when I get up in the morning."

Squeezing her upper arm, Morgan murmured, "Don't be. Hold on, I'll get the robe for you."

Laura turned toward the sunlight, reveling in the warmth enveloping her. In a minute, Morgan returned and helped her on with the chenille robe.

"Can you see anything yet?" Morgan asked, standing next to her, studying her flawless blue eyes. The pupils were huge and black.

Dejectedly Laura shook her head. "No—nothing." She bit down on her lower lip. "Morgan, what if Dr. Taggert is wrong? What if this isn't temporary?"

He heard the carefully concealed terror in her voice. "I learned a long time ago to live one day at a time, Laura. You do the same."

All her fears surfaced as Morgan's hand came to rest on her shoulder. "My livelihood depends on my being able to see. I've got three articles due at different magazines in the next two weeks. They're typed, but they need to be edited and then a final copy run off on the printer."

"One day at a time, little swan," Morgan urged, sliding his arm around her drawn shoulders. There was no reasoning around Laura, he realized with a pang as he drew her against him. She brought out so many withheld emotions in him, and he responded to them without even thinking. Giving her a quick squeeze and then releasing her, he said, "Let me make breakfast. You have your bath and get dressed. After we're done eating, I'll help you with those articles."

Laura turned, gripping his hand. "Oh, Morgan, would you?"

He smiled down into her eyes, which sparkled with renewed hope. "I'm not very good at typing, but we'll get them done. Let's go to your bedroom and figure out what you want to wear today. Then I'll whip up a breakfast of scrambled eggs and bacon."

"Well," Laura asked, sitting at her office desk, "what do you think of the first article?"

Morgan had brought another chair into the office and placed it next to hers. He'd finished reading the ten-page article on spy satellites. "Very good."

She caught the admiration in his voice. "I can almost hear you asking how a woman could know so much about something so complex, right?"

He grinned up at her. Laura had chosen to wear a pink long-tailed shirt that hung over her curved thighs and a pair of jeans. She had begged him to leave the bandages off her eyes, and he'd agreed. Her blond hair framed her face in a natural page boy, barely grazing her shoulders. The bangs fell softly across her brow, following the gentle slope of her eyebrows.

"No...I'm more impressed with *how* you got this kind of information. Isn't it classified?"

She chuckled. "No. I've got friends down at the Pentagon vaults where all the declassified material is kept. I practically live down there some days, reading through hundreds of pages of information, pulling out interesting tidbits and then compressing them into an article format."

"I'm impressed."

"Will you read the article back to me, sentence by sentence? That way I can listen to it and see if something needs to be changed or tightened up."

"Yeah, and I'll input the edits and then print out a final draft for you."

She reached out, her hand coming in contact with his chest instead of his arm. The tensile strength of his muscles sent a thrill through her. She moved her hand to find his arm, giving it a warm squeeze. "We work well as a team, don't we?"

"Since the beginning," Morgan agreed huskily, lost in the beauty of her eyes. Eyes that showed him the world in a frame of hope, not despair. Rousing himself from his discovery, he grabbed a pencil. "Okay, here comes the first sentence. If we're lucky, we'll be finished by noon."

Morgan dawdled over the noontime meal of tuna salad sandwiches, sweet pickles and potato chips with Laura. The first article was completed. He couldn't recall the last time he'd had so much fun or laughed as hard as he had in that three-hour period. Between editing and the five phone calls that Laura had answered, the article had been revised and printed out to perfection.

Laura licked her fingers after finishing off a third sweet pickle. A new kind of excitement was growing inside her—a sweet euphoria she'd never felt before. It was all due to Morgan, she realized. The need to know more about him never left her. Picking up the paper napkin, she blotted her lips. Sasha sat by her chair, begging for another sweet pickle, a favorite food of hers.

"Every time you feed the robin, you act as if you don't like to do it," Laura noted. "Why?"

Disgruntled once again by her acute hearing and observation, Morgan said, "When I came home from the naval academy on leave for the first time, my sister, Aly, and I went out hunting together. Actually," he went on, frowning, "I was the one who wanted to hunt. Aly was happy just to tag along." He shook his head, a smile edging his mouth. "She was only twelve at the time and had missed her big brother, so she was like my shadow on that first leave."

Laura leaned forward, hearing the nostalgia in Morgan's voice. "It sounds as if Aly idolizes you."

He laughed softly. "Yeah. She was a great kid sister, always hanging around with Noah and me." Glancing up at Laura, he halted, realizing just how much he'd divulged about his past by naming his brother and sister. Would Laura piece things together? Judging from the tenderness in her eyes, Morgan guessed not, and slowly continued.

"I had this .22 caliber rifle I'd grown up with as a kid. My dad and I had gone deer hunting every fall for as long as I could remember. Aly didn't usually like to come with us because she hated to see anything killed. I'd taken the rifle along for the hell of it as we walked through this wooded grove. I wanted to keep up my proficiency shooting, so I was aiming at tree branches in the distance, not birds or animals." Morgan crumpled the napkin in his hands, staring down at the light-green tablecloth.

"I picked out a branch on one tree and fired. There was a robin's nest on it, hidden by leaves, and I hadn't realized it was there. The nest fell out of the tree. Aly ran over to it. When I got there, she was crying."

"Oh, Morgan," Laura whispered, sliding her hand outward, making contact with his. "I'm sorry."

He shrugged, the memory returning powerfully to him. "Two of the three baby robins were dead. The third one had a broken wing, and Aly gently picked it up. She thought we could save it, so I wrapped the bird up in my handkerchief to keep it warm for the walk back to the house.

"When we got home, Aly and I got a shoe box, made a little nest for the bird and kept it warm. She went outside with me to dig worms. I felt terrible, because I'd had no intention of killing anything," Morgan admitted.

Laura tightened her fingers around his. "Did the baby live?"

He sighed. "It died two days later. It must have had internal injuries. The bird should have survived with only a broken wing."

"You both must have been devastated."

Morgan took her hand between his, lightly tracing each of her long, artistic fingers. "Aly cried for hours after the baby died. All I could do was hold her and tell her I was sorry, that I hadn't meant to hurt the robin."

"She wasn't upset with you, was she?"

"No, not Aly. She's just as softhearted as you are."

Sniffing, Laura swallowed back her tears for Morgan's sake. He might misconstrue her compassion for pity. "Robby brings all those memories back to you, doesn't she?"

Looking over at the robin, who slept contentedly in the makeshift nest of grass in the cage, Morgan nodded. "Yeah, the little beggar brings it all back to me. Except maybe this time I won't kill it. Maybe she'll live despite me."

The urge to whisper his name and pull him into

her arms was real. Instead Laura held his hand tightly. "Why do I get this feeling that you think everything you touch is somehow worse off?"

"Not much in my life has had a good ending, Laura," Morgan warned her darkly, getting up. "I don't have to stay in one place long before things turn to hell in a hand basket. Look at you. All you had to do was see me at an airport and you got injured saving my miserable neck."

"I don't believe it," Laura told him fervently. "You're a kind and good person."

"Tell that to the world," he growled, picking up the plates and taking them to the dishwasher. "Come on, let's get back to work on those last two articles."

Phone calls from well-wishers who had found out about her injury via the newspaper, and editors whom Laura had worked with, came in all afternoon. Some flowers arrived, and Morgan brought them into her office. Her enthusiasm over receiving the fragrant bouquet did nothing but remind him that he should have had the sensitivity to bring her some, too. By six o'clock, Morgan was in ill humor.

He got up and went to the kitchen to make them supper. His anger at the situation bred more frustration. What if she was blinded for life? He couldn't just leave her stranded. In his mind, no one who was loyal ever deserted. As he peeled the potatoes, he began to consider the possibility of staying stateside. He now knew he wasn't a CIA mole. So it didn't matter whether he signed up for another five-year stint with the French Foreign Legion or not.

Throwing the potatoes into a pot to boil, Morgan began collecting the vegetables from the refrigerator for a salad.

"Here, little beggar," he muttered, throwing the robin a piece of lettuce. The bird promptly climbed out of her nest in the bottom of the cage and gobbled up the greenery. Morgan grinned tightly, throwing her another piece. "Greedy little thing, aren't you?"

So was he, if he were honest with himself. He liked Laura a hell of a lot—and not for reasons of pity or owing her for saving his life. Looking around at the quiet kitchen, he was astonished, as he always was, by the peace that reigned within this home. Tearing up bib lettuce leaves and putting them in a large bowl, Morgan realized his newfound contentment was due to Laura.

And if Laura's sight came back in two weeks, what would he do? He released a long sigh, grabbing a carrot and methodically beginning to slice it into the bowl. With her background in military information, she'd recognize him sooner or later. Disgruntled, he found himself wanting to stay, but realized it was a stupid dream. This was still nothing more than a beautiful dream that would end very abruptly.

"Mmm, smells good, whatever you're cooking," Laura said, coming into the kitchen. She found a chair in the nook and sat down. "Can I help?"

"I've got chicken in the oven, and I'm working on a salad. Just sit there and look beautiful."

Smiling, Laura murmured, "I wish I could see your face, Morgan Ramsey, when you say that."

"Oh? Why?"

"To see if you're teasing me or if you mean it."

He grinned as he chopped up a scallion. "And if I did mean it, Ms. Bennett, what would you do, I wonder?"

"You're such a rogue," she said with a laugh, clapping her hands delightedly. "And too much of an officer and a gentleman to take unfair advantage of me.''

Scowling, he scooped the scallion into the bowl. The tomato was next. ''Not anymore.''

Undaunted by his growling rejoinder, she sat, enjoying his presence. ''So, you graduated from Annapolis as an officer?''

''Yes.''

''Navy?''

''No…marine corps.''

Her eyebrows moved upward. ''That makes sense.''

''What does?''

''When I saw you, you reminded me of a tough-as-nails soldier. The marine corps image suits you.''

''That's over with now,'' he said in a clipped tone. Moving the bowl of salad to the table, he opened the silver drawer and pulled out the necessary utensils.

''What's the saying? You can take the boy out of the country, but you can't take the country out of the boy? I think that applies to you in a marine corps sense. You're still a marine at heart, Morgan.''

''Probably.'' She'd never know that he used those skills to this very day.

''Were you a lieutenant in Vietnam?''

He placed the silverware on the table, his scowl deepening. ''No, a captain.''

''My dad was a major in the army. He had a company of men to command while he was in Vietnam. Did you?''

Morgan straightened, feeling the tension thrum through him. ''Yeah, I had one hundred sixty men under my command.''

She tilted her head, hearing raw anguish in his voice. ''It's a terrible responsibility,'' Laura whispered. "And knowing you the way I do, I'll bet you cared deeply for each and every one of them."

"Let's get on another subject, Laura. I don't feel like discussing this one very much."

Laura winced at the anger in his voice. She placed her hands in her lap and bowed her head. "Sometimes I can put my foot in my mouth, Morgan...."

He'd seen her face go pale at his snarling order to drop the topic. Cursing himself, he went over and knelt in front of her, scooping up her hands in his. "I'm the one who should apologize," he muttered. "I didn't mean to rip your head off."

"No, it's okay. It's just that some of your mannerisms make me think of Dad. In some ways you're alike."

"A soldier is a soldier," he uttered tiredly. "The uniform may be different, but underneath it, we're all the same. Scared men just trying to do our jobs and uphold our responsibilities."

Murmuring Morgan's name, Laura pulled her hands out of his and slid them across his shoulders. "I feel you're like Dad. You may have been overresponsible, Morgan. Maybe you cared a little too deeply, a little too much.... That can leave an open wound in your heart and memory. Even to this day."

He longed to lean forward and rest his head against Laura. The anguish of the past stared him in the face. "One thing our family prides itself on is responsibility," he told her in a strained tone. "We have a long military tradition of caring for those under our command. My men were more than numbers to me, Laura. More than just sets of dog tags."

She threaded her fingers through his short black hair. "I know," she whispered, "I know...."

A cry lodged in Morgan's throat as she drew him

forward. The softness of her fingertips across his neck and shoulders melted his resolve. He shut his eyes, burying his face against her small, warm body. As she wrapped her arms around his shoulders, he felt a shudder work its way up and out of him. She smelled so good, so fresh and clean, when his world consisted of little more than dirt, sweat and desert. He slid his arms around her small waist, aware of her diminutive size against his bulk and brawn. Yet she was strong in ways that he wasn't right now, and that knowledge shook Morgan to the core.

Closing her eyes, Laura pressed him against her, his head resting on her bosom. When she felt him shudder, she tightened her arms around him. "Oh, Morgan, you're so strong for so many, and I know you're tired," she murmured against his hair. "I understand that. My dad carried the same terrible weight on his shoulders for almost fifteen years. I saw what his care and concern did to him. Every man was like the son he never had. He knew their names, the names of their wives and children. And whenever one of them died, he wrote a long letter to the wife and family." She smiled weakly and caressed his hair. "The war isn't that far away from you, either, is it? It's a living hell for you today, just as it was years ago."

Morgan held her tightly, hearing the fluttering beat of her generous heart beneath his ear. Each stroke of her hand on his head eased a little more of the anguish he'd carried so long by himself. When he felt her lips press against his temple, he groaned. God, he had to get a hold on himself for her sake. He wanted to take Laura, right now. He wanted to love her with wild, hungry abandon and hear her cry out with pleasure. But he wouldn't drag her into his morbid, complicated life. There was no happy ending for them. No, he wasn't going to ruin one more life.

"Listen to me," Morgan commanded harshly, easing out of her arms. He saw huge tears in her lustrous blue eyes, and he winced. "Don't open yourself up to me and my problems, Laura. Dammit, you've got enough worries without taking on mine."

Taking a deep, unsteady breath, she nodded. "It's my nature to get involved, Morgan. I was adopted, and my parents always said I was a fighter for the underdogs of the world."

With his thumbs he wiped away the two tears that trailed down her cheeks. "Then fight for someone who's worth fighting for. I'm not. The die was cast for me many years ago, little swan."

Laura struggled to control her escaping feelings for him—feelings of desire, not pity. Just the roughened touch of Morgan's thumbs against her flesh made her ache to love him. There was some deep inner knowing within her that if she could get him to trust her, she could help him in so many ways.

Forcing a slight smile, she murmured, "I guess I'm letting this trauma get to me."

He caressed her hair. "Yeah, a close call with death can make you do things you're sorry for later."

She nodded, biting down on her lower lip. She wanted to say, *Making love with you, Morgan, would be the most right thing in the world for both of us.* But she didn't. Let him think what he wanted. He brought out all her instincts for nurturing, caring and loving. And every piece of information she'd dragged out of him thus far told her his life was a picture of terrible tragedy. Something had happened to his company in Vietnam. What?

Rising to his feet, Morgan left her side. Despite his

pleading, he saw the stubborn set of her chin and the spark of defiance in her eyes. Still, those warming seconds in her arms did nothing but make him starved to explore Laura. All of her....

"Tomorrow morning," Laura began, her voice low with emotion, "Captain Jim Woodward from the marine corps is coming over. I'll interview him at ten."

Morgan leaned against the counter, scowling. A marine officer. The chances of getting recognized increased a hundredfold. He couldn't risk it.

"No problem. I'll go back to my hotel and—"

"No, that's not what I meant." Why did Morgan always think he was unwanted? "If you could tape the session and run the recorder, it would be of immense help to me."

Shifting uneasily, Morgan grimaced. "Look, I don't want to butt into your personal life."

Laughing, Laura said, "Captain Woodward isn't part of my personal life. He's a long-time associate whom I frequently contact for marine corps articles, that's all." Then she shrugged. "To tell you the truth, I don't have a personal relationship right now. I've spent the past year working on the second of three military history books." She almost added that her engagement to Major Roarke Anderson, an air force pilot, hadn't worked out. He couldn't handle her independence or the fact that she was a celebrated author. But that was a year ago, and her heart had healed, leaving room for someone else. For Morgan, perhaps....

Stymied by her honesty, Morgan paced the room. "I just thought this guy meant something to you."

"Then you'll stay and help me? Please?"

Rubbing his chin, Morgan wondered if Woodward would recognize him. It was a chance he'd have to take. Besides, he was relieved to hear Laura was free of any personal entanglements. "Sure, no problem."

Morgan answered the door. It was exactly ten, and he was sweating, hoping like hell Woodward wouldn't recognize him. He opened the door to a tall, well-built officer in a tan marine corps uniform.

"The name's Ramsey," Morgan said. "Ms. Bennett is expecting you."

Woodward's green eyes narrowed slightly. He hesitated fractionally, then held out his hand. "Captain Jim Woodward."

Morgan shook the officer's hand. It was similar to his own—callused and strong. This man wasn't any desk sitter at the Pentagon. If he wasn't so worried about being recognized, Morgan thought he would like the officer. Part of it was Woodward's proud carriage, his fearless green eyes and the square set of his face. Another part was the confidence and power he radiated. At one time, Morgan remembered, he had, too. "Come in. Ms. Bennett is in her office. Because of her injury, I'll be assisting her today."

"Fine. I know where her office is," Woodward said, taking off his cap and placing it beneath his left arm.

Laura heard both men coming and sat expectantly in her office chair. Today she wore a teal-blue silk blouse and an ivory skirt and jacket—all business. She never appeared for an interview without wearing a suit. Nervously she kept her hands in her lap. Would Jim's discomfort over her blindness interfere with the forthcoming interview?

"Hey, tiger," Jim called from the door. "It's all over the Pentagon that you bumped your head and hurt yourself. How are you feeling?"

Relief swept through her that the two men got along, and she smiled. "Jim Woodward, you're a terrible tease at the best and worst of times. I'm doing well. Come in." She held out her hand. When Jim took it, Laura felt how different his grip was than Morgan's powerful, yet gentle one.

Jim put his hat on the edge of Laura's desk and took the chair next to hers. He searched her features. "Is it true? That you were temporarily blinded? All I see is a nasty cut on the temple and a few scratches on your cheek."

Laura squeezed Jim's hand, then released it. "Put the emphasis on *temporarily*, Jim. The doctor says two weeks at the most in this situation, and I'll be good as new."

Morgan sat down on a chair next to Laura's. She was putting on a sunny smile and brave act for the officer. At least she didn't put on an act for Morgan. But he didn't like the intimacy Woodward had established with her. Was there something between them, despite her earlier protests? Jealousy, an emotion he'd rarely felt before, became screamingly alive within him.

"Actually," Laura went on, "Morgan has been a godsend for me. I saved him from getting struck by that limo at the airport, but he's saved me from a lot of days without help around here."

"Morgan?" Jim Woodward lifted his eyes, looking at him for a long time.

Laura frowned, hearing a question in Jim's voice. "Yes, Morgan Ramsey. I thought you'd introduce yourselves at the door."

Uncomfortable beneath Woodward's sudden scrutiny, Morgan tinkered with the tape in the cassette recorder. "We did, Laura," he managed without reaction. "Are you ready to get this interview underway?"

"Sure. Jim, you set?"

The marine corps officer frowned, reluctantly returning his attention to Laura. "Of course."

Lighting-quick tension shot through the office and it confused Laura. Why was Jim suddenly stiff and formal? And Morgan was acting oddly, too. If only she could see! Had they taken an immediate dislike to each other, after all? Unable to sort out the reasons, Laura had to settle for starting the interview.

With the interview completed, Morgan left the office. For nearly an hour, Woodward had stared hard at him, as if fixing a memory in the back of his mind. Dammit! He went to the kitchen and poured himself a cup of coffee. His face was somewhat altered since 1970, but a mustache wasn't much of a disguise. He broke out in a cold sweat. What if Woodward mentioned his suspicions to Laura? What if he went to the press?

"Laura, do you know anything about this Morgan Ramsey?" Jim asked confidentially.

She smiled. "He's an American who works overseas in France. Why, Jim?"

The officer shook his head. "I don't know. The man looks familiar, but I can't place his face. I could swear I know him."

Laughing lightly, Laura murmured, "With your photographic memory, Jim, I'm sure you'll come up with the answer."

"He was uncomfortable with me being here. You couldn't notice it, but I did."

"I don't think Morgan is used to sitting still in an office for an hour, taping an interview," she returned blithely. "He's strictly the outdoors type."

"Maybe," Jim conceded, getting to his feet. "How'd he get that scar?"

"In Vietnam."

"Oh."

"Yes, he was a captain in the marine corps during the conflict. Why?"

Shaking his head, Jim muttered, "There's something I don't trust about him, Laura. Are you sure you're safe with him here? You live alone—"

"Jim, no one's more trustworthy than Morgan Ramsey. Remember, I've been on the receiving end of his care since the accident." Laura got to her feet.

Undaunted, Jim placed his hand beneath her elbow to lead her from the room. "Maybe," he said. As he guided her to the front door, he lowered his voice. "Look, if you need help, call me. You have my office and home numbers."

Warmed by his protectiveness, Laura placed a hand on his arm. "Thanks, Jim, but everything's fine."

"Who does he work for over in France? Will you find out for me? I want to run a check on that guy. He looks suspicious."

Stopping at the door, Laura grimaced. "Jim, you're overreacting."

"Do you know who he works for?"

Hesitating, Laura bit down on her lower lip. "Well...no, I don't. I assumed it was for an American company."

"Check it out for me, will you, tiger?"

"Jim—"

"Please, Laura? Do me this favor?"

Favors were the name of the game at the Pentagon,

Laura knew from many years of working with the brass there. They were called blue chips. If a chip was tossed in her direction, she had to reciprocate when the chip was called in by the person who had originally granted the favor. Well, Jim had granted this interview, and now she owed him. If she wanted more cooperation from him in the future, she'd have to acquiesce to his request. "All right, Jim, I'll find out."

"And you'll call me right away?"

Upset he was pressing so hard, she muttered. "Yes, I'll call you right away."

Chapter Five

"What's wrong? You look worried." Morgan roused himself from where he was leaning against the drainboard, a cup of coffee in hand.

Laura stood at the entrance to the kitchen. "I do?"

He smiled slightly and walked over, leading her to the chair to sit down. "You never could hide anything with that face of yours."

"Oh."

"That's not a sin. Coffee?"

"No, I'd rather have a glass of orange juice."

Morgan set his cup down on the table and crossed to the refrigerator. "I noticed you and the captain were on pretty friendly terms with each other." He poured the juice into a glass.

She laughed softly. "Morgan Ramsey, are you jealous?"

Disgruntled, he placed the glass in front of her, then sat down at her elbow. "I guess I am."

Reaching over, she found his arm, allowing her fingers to rest on it. "There's nothing to be jealous of. Jim Woodward is a resource for me when I want to write on a topic involving the marine corps. He's their public relations officer at the Pentagon."

Morgan felt his stomach start to knot. Great. That guy would be in a position to have access to more information than most. Had he recognized him? Sweat popped out on his brow. Tearing himself from his fear of being recognized, he gazed over at Laura's serene features. She appeared untouched in a world that had the capability of slashing someone's life apart in seconds.

"So why did you appear upset earlier? Did he say something to you?"

She took a swallow of the juice. "He thinks he knows you, Morgan, but he can't place from where. He asked a favor of me." The unhappiness came out in her voice and she didn't try to disguise it. "Sometimes he gets overly protective of me—just like a big brother."

Morgan held the cup very still between his hands. "What did he want from you?"

"He asked me to find out what company you work for over in France. I told him I thought it was an American one, but wasn't sure." She gripped his arm more tightly. "I'm sorry, Morgan."

He captured her cool, damp fingers by placing his hand on top of hers. "Don't be. That's all he wanted to know?"

"Yes, just the name of your employer. I guess he's going to run a check on you."

Fear cascaded through him. "Isn't he jumping to conclusions? Or is he always this dramatic about another man being in your life?"

Her lips quirked. "I know it's none of his business. He shouldn't be nosing around like this. I'm disappointed in him. I don't know why he's doing it."

"Maybe the guy likes you a lot more than you realized, and he's threatened by the fact that I'm here twenty-four hours a day."

Laura was going to deny Morgan's statement at first, but his reasoning was logical. Jim did ask her out on a date every once in a while, although she always declined. "Oh, dear. Why am I so naive sometimes?"

"Because you see only the best qualities in all of us, Laura," he said quietly. "You're not capable of seeing our worst side—our devious or selfish or greedy side."

His voice was like a balm over her heart, and Laura managed a strangled laugh. "Guilty as charged. Oh, why didn't I realize that Jim's probably jealous?"

"It's a small thing," Morgan said, wrestling with his own fears.

"Tell me where you work so I can rectify this situation in a hurry."

Morgan tightened his hand over hers. "I'm a captain in the French Foreign Legion, Laura. I've been there for the past six years. In a few months I can reenlist, if I want."

"Oh, dear." The French Foreign Legion! Laura knew a great deal about that particular branch of military service. She'd done a long, thorough article on it for a major national magazine a year ago.

Morgan saw the surprise, then confusion in her widening blue eyes. "When Woodward runs a check on me, he's going to find a dead end," he promised. "The Legion never divulges much of anything about the men who serve her."

Laura's mind spun with questions and no answers. "You're right, the Legion keeps every man's identity and record classified." And men from all over the world joined the Legion to escape old ways of life, to make new ones for themselves. "Morgan, why did you join?"

"Is this between you and me, or does this include Woodward?"

"No, just me."

Believing her, Morgan said, "After I recovered from my wounds, I didn't want to come stateside. I'm a good soldier, Laura, and I felt I'd be of use in the Legion." That wasn't a total lie, but it was far from the entire truth. He watched the expression on her face closely. There was compassion in Laura's eyes, and the way the corners of her mouth pulled in, he knew she felt deeply for him. "It wasn't so bad, little swan."

"But, the Legion is so hard on its men! I mean, they're considered the best of the mercenaries."

"Hard, yes. But not cruel."

"And you build bridges for them?"

"Yes, I have a degree in engineering. I build bridges, dig ditches and help clear land for airport runways in some of the most godforsaken spots on this earth. Sometimes we provide protection or perform other military duties."

"But what about your family? It must be terribly hard on them for you to be overseas like that."

He hung his head, real anguish serrating him. "Yeah, it's rough on them," he admitted thickly.

It was on the tip of her tongue to delve further into his past, but Laura sensed the time was not right. Something terrible had happened to his company in Vietnam. That much she was sure of. And whatever it was, Morgan still carried guilt or grief because of it. Had he gone to the Legion to escape his past? So many men did just that. Perhaps over the next week he would share his reasons with her.

Trying to buoy the sudden despair she heard in his voice, Laura found his hand and gripped it. ''I don't know about you, but I'm starved. If you want, we could go to a restaurant and treat ourselves. We've both been housebound, and I can sense that you're restless.''

Morgan smiled, wanting to lean forward the press her ripe lips against his mouth. She was still awkward with her blindness, and to go out in public would be exhausting for her. She'd forsaken her own welfare in order to help him. ''No, let's stay here. I'll make us lunch, and then I'll get to work typing up that interview with Woodward. Maybe by tonight you and I can get it into some kind of article form.''

Laura murmured his name and slid her arms around him. Resting her head against his jaw, she whispered, ''You're so special, Morgan.''

He embraced her for a long moment, relishing her warmth and softness against him. The fragrance of orange blossoms encircled him, and he inhaled the scent deeply. ''Come on, Ms. Bennett, let's get this dog-and-pony show on the road. We've got work to do this afternoon.''

Just being in his arms made her feel safe and loved. She nestled her head against Morgan's shoulder, content as never before. ''I'll be so glad when I get my sight back, Morgan. So glad....''

''You'd think that after seven days I'd at least be able to see some light, Morgan.'' Laura touched the healing cut on her temple as she sat down on the rug in front of the fireplace.

"Dr. Taggert just checked you yesterday, Laura. He said the swelling's going down, but it hasn't disappeared yet. Give it another week, my impatient swan. Here's your popcorn." Morgan brought over a bowl of freshly popped corn and placed it in her lap. She looked fetching in her white cotton gown and lavender robe as she sat in front of the fire. He liked their nightly custom of sitting on the floor, talking, eating popcorn and feeling the warmth of the fire after working all day.

"Thanks." Laura picked disinterestedly at the popcorn. She felt Morgan lie down nearby, always within an arm's distance from her. "I'm just getting panicky, Morgan. What if I don't see?"

He reached over, catching her hand in midair. "You will. I've got a gut feeling on this, Laura. Just hang in there. You're worrying too much, and you aren't sleeping at night the way you should."

She laughed abruptly. "Like last night? I sat up screaming during a nightmare, and you almost killed yourself getting to my room.'

"I thought someone had broken into the house and was attacking you," Morgan said gently. The right toe of his foot still ached from where he'd stubbed it as he ran down the hall to her room.

"Still," Laura murmured, "you hurt yourself." She had fallen into his arms, wildly aware of his rock-hard chest beneath her cheek as he'd embraced her. For the next ten minutes, Morgan had held and rocked her as she cried. They were tears of fear—fear of never being able to see again. His strength was now her strength.

Placing the bowl on the carpeted floor, Laura

stretched out on her stomach, her hands beneath her cheek as she faced him. The silence settled soothingly around them. "Morgan?"

He watched her eyes beneath the thick gold lashes that framed them. If Laura only knew how beautiful she was, or how desirable.... "Yes?" The word stuck in his throat, his heart beginning a slow, sledgehammer pound.

"Tell me about your family. What's Aly like?"

Laura was like an elegant swan, lying prone on the carpet, her face shadowed and thoughtful. Morgan rolled onto his side, only inches away from her. "Spunky," he said, a faraway tone in his voice. "Red haired, tenacious and bold."

"And Noah? Is he older or younger than you?"

Morgan reached out, taming several strands of her blond hair away from her flushed cheek, placing them behind her small ear. "Three years younger. He's the better-looking of the two of us."

Laura smiled, closing her eyes. "That's *your* opinion, Morgan. How would you describe Noah?"

He laid his head down on his arms and stared across at her. There had been tenderness in her voice. "Reliable. And not as hard or driven as I am."

"What drives you, Morgan?"

He sighed. "My dad, I guess. He had thirty years in the air force and came out a general. All his life he expected the three of us to go into the service of our choice. With his illustrious career as an example, I wanted to be exactly like him. You'd have to meet him to understand what I'm saying. He didn't brainwash any of us into going into the military. It was just his presence, his belief in defending this country and the fact that each one of us could make a difference that inspired me, I guess."

Laura heard the wistfulness in Morgan's voice. "How did your parents meet?"

"Mom was a nurse over in Korea during the war. Her MASH unit got overrun by the Communists, and the entire staff was taken prisoner. She escaped from the prison about fifty miles north of the demilitarized zone and was in the process of trying to make her way back to South Korea. Dad was flying his plane over the north when he was jumped by six MIGS and was shot down. He bailed out and my mother followed the parachute to where he landed. They teamed up and spent the next week dodging the Communists trying to recapture them."

Laura rested her head against her hand. "What an exciting way to meet."

"It was pure hell," Morgan said. "Dad was wounded, and Mom ended up being the one who got them back to safe territory."

"And they fell in love during their escape?"

Morgan smiled, watching the sudden animation in Laura's eyes. "Yes, they did. I guess they fought like cats and dogs. Dad can be a bulldog sometimes—a family trait he passed on to all of us, I'm afraid." Morgan chuckled. "He was delirious and swore that south was a certain direction. Mom knew it wasn't. She said they got into a lot of shouting matches on that trip out of enemy territory."

"Sounds like the three of you children inherited the best from both of them," Laura whispered. "You have your father's tenacity and your mother's sensitivity."

Rolling over on his back, Morgan tucked his hands behind his head and stared up at the ceiling. An ache to see his family once again overwhelmed him. "If you met my family," he said thickly, "you'd love them. They're all individuals, but each one is caring and responsible.''

Laura reached out, her hand coming in contact with his chest. She felt his heart beating hard beneath her palm. ''Have you told them you're here in the States yet?''

Her hand eased the ache in his heart. Morgan turned, looking up into her features. ''No—'' Her eyes were shadowed with pain—his pain. ''It wouldn't be wise'' was all he could say.

''Oh, Morgan, are you sure?'' Laura moved into a sitting position, resting her hands in her lap.

''Very,'' he growled, rising to his feet. ''I'm getting tired, Laura. How about you?''

Swallowing against the lump in her throat, Laura got up with his help. Morgan's shields were back in place. She'd pushed too far into his past. ''It's supposed to be sunny and sixty-five degrees tomorrow. I'd like to plant my begonias. Would you help me?''

Her face was guileless, Morgan thought as he stood next to her, his hand gripping hers. ''Yeah, planting something sounds positive,'' he agreed.

The phone on her bedroom nightstand awoke Laura the next morning. Unable to check the time, she groped for and found the receiver.

''Hello?'' she said, her voice husky with sleep.

''Laura? It's Jim Woodward. I'm sorry, did I wake you?''

Sitting up, she rubbed her eyes. ''Uh, that's all right, Jim. What time is it?''

''Nearly nine. Look, I'm sorry to disturb you, but I think you should know something about this guy Morgan Ramsey.''

Pushing the hair away from her eyes, Laura asked, "What?"

"I traced his name through our computers, and there was no Morgan Ramsey in the marine corps during the Vietnam conflict. I know that face, Laura. Right now I'm searching through our photographic files in my spare time. This bothers me. Men don't go into the Foreign Legion unless they want to escape the past. I'm positive Ramsey isn't his real name."

Upset, Laura said, "Look, Jim, I believe him. I *know* Morgan was in Vietnam."

Woodward laughed tightly. "Then it was under another name. I'm sending this info to the CIA. Maybe they can get a handle on him."

"Jim, this isn't necessary!" Her voice had risen, and Laura suddenly realized that Morgan might be able to hear her. She didn't know if the door to her bedroom was open or closed.

"But it is."

"He's not a convict, Jim!"

"Look, I didn't mean to upset you, Laura. It's just that this guy is hiding something. I don't like the fact that he's there with you all the time."

She gripped the phone. "That's really the reason, isn't it, Jim?"

"What?"

"Don't play games with me. I think you're being protective. I don't understand why you're doing this, Jim."

"I've liked you for a long time, Laura—you know that."

Keeping the anger from her voice, she pleaded with him, "Jim, leave Morgan's past alone. Please. He's not a threat to me in any way. The man is simply trying to repay me for saving his life. That's all."

Jim's voice grew dark. "Not from what I could see. You're blind right now, Laura. You don't see how he looks at you. It's as if he's staked his claim, and I don't like it."

"Jim, you're way out of line. My private life is my own, not yours. And he's certainly hasn't 'staked a claim' on me. How can you be so distrusting when the man hasn't done anything to deserve it?"

"Laura, you're angry, and I didn't mean to make you feel that way."

"You're darned right I am. What if someone started snooping into your past?"

"I don't have anything to hide," Jim said tightly. "When I get anything more on him, I'll call you."

Her voice shook with anger. "No, Jim, don't call. You're invading my privacy. You see, I trust Morgan. I don't *care* what his past is. I judge people on how they treat me, not by their names, their pasts or whatever else. Goodbye!" She groped until she found the phone cradle, then dropped the receiver into it. The day wasn't starting off on the right foot at all. Jim Woodward was jealous and protective of her in a way she'd never fathom.

"Men and their games!" she grumped, throwing off the covers. As she placed her feet on the floor, she gasped. The world was no longer black in front of her eyes. It was a dark gray, instead. She placed her hand in front of her face; she could barely make out the outline of it.

She sat for several minutes, assimilating her discovery. Her vision was returning! She was able to discern shadow from light. If she held something close to her eyes, placing it in the sunlight cascading through the ruffled pink curtains, she could make out its general shape, but not the color. Tears streamed from her eyes and ran down her cheeks. She was going to see again! *Oh, God, thank you!*

But her happiness eroded as Jim's phone call came back to haunt her. She sat on the edge of the bed, scuffing her toe into the carpet. She couldn't believe Morgan was lying to her about his family or Vietnam because of the emotion in his voice when he spoke about them.

After getting her morning bath and washing her hair, she put on the clothes Morgan had laid out for her to wear the night before. Troubled, she made her way to the kitchen. She stopped at the entrance, narrowing her eyes, straining to discover if she could see anything. Something moved near the counter—a dark shape against the sunlight pouring in through the windows.

"Morgan?"

Morgan turned, still immersed in thought. "Good morning." Laura looked pretty in the lavender dolman-sleeved blouse and threadbare jeans. Today she wanted to plant begonias and had asked for her worst clothes to wear. Somehow, Morgan thought, feeling his heart squeeze with fresh feelings of happiness, she looked pretty despite her disheveled clothes. Her smile was uncertain, and he noticed she was pale.

"That phone call woke you, didn't it?" he asked, walking over and leading her to the chair at the table.

"Yes."

"Woodward?" he guessed, putting slices of bread into the toaster.

She heard the edge to his tone. "How did you know?"

"A gut feeling." Bad news always traveled fast. "What did he have to say?"

If only she could see the expression on Morgan's

face! It would tell her so much. Laura chewed on her lower lip. "Not much. Just that he swore he recognized you and was now going through photo files at the Pentagon to see if he could find something on you."

Morgan's hands froze over the toast he was buttering. According to what he could find out last year when his full memory had returned, there had been plenty of press and photos on the loss of his men on Hill 164. Sooner or later Jim Woodward would stumble onto the truth. He set the toast aside and divided the scrambled eggs between the two plates. Bringing them over to the table, he set them down.

"Let it pass, Laura. Woodward is chasing up blind alleys for no reason. Come on, let's eat a hearty breakfast and get to planting those begonia bulbs."

Laura hesitated. Should she tell Morgan that her sight was returning? And that she knew Ramsey wasn't his last name? She sensed his nervousness. Something told her that he'd disappear if she admitted either thing. Picking up the fork, she forced herself to eat. The last thing she wanted was for him to walk out of her life.

"Laura?" Morgan reached over, sliding his hand along her shoulder. "What's wrong?"

Just the concerned tenor of his voice unstrung her. Tears welled up in her eyes and she quickly shut them. Morgan must not know how much he'd come to mean to her in such a short time. "N-nothing."

"It's Woodward's phone call that's bothering you, isn't it?"

She put her fork down on her plate. "Yes."

Morgan sat very still. If he told her the truth, she'd want him out of her life. And that shook him like nothing else had in the past year. He absorbed her concerned features. How could someone so small and delicate have captured his heart so thoroughly in one week's time? Suddenly the thought of losing Laura was almost too much to bear.

Miserably Morgan moved the plates aside. He moved his chair next to Laura's and took her hands. "We have to talk," he whispered hoarsely.

Laura gripped his hands. They were cold, almost icy. Morgan's face was heavily lined, and his gray eyes were desolate-looking as he held her gaze. She stilled her joy over her steadily improving eyesight. Morgan's plight was far more important to her heart. "Tell me," she urged softly.

"You won't want me to stay after I tell you, Laura," he warned.

She shook her head, tightening her hands on his. "Let me be the judge of that, Morgan. What happened in your past that still haunts you?"

Taking a deep breath, he let the pain-filled words flow from his conscience and heart. "In January of 1970 I was commanding a company of marines in the I Corps area of Vietnam. My assistant company commander, Lieutenant Stephen Cantrell, was my best friend. Both of us questioned the orders to put our company on Hill 164, which was deep within enemy territory. When I called Colonel Jack Armstrong, he told me the tactical plan had been approved by his superiors, right up the line. He promised we'd have air and artillery support just in case the NVA got aggressive and started testing our defenses."

Morgan shut his eyes, reliving the nightmare. "We were up on that lousy hill for two days, getting the hell rocketed out of us. I was losing men fast. A lot of the time we couldn't even get medevac in to take out the wounded, because the NVA had us pinned down. Every time I requested permission to withdraw, Armstrong insisted we stay.'' His voice grew husky. ''And then they hit us with at least a battalion of NVA. We fought all night. I called for air and artillery, but they weren't available. By dawn there were fifteen of us left. Then came the final attack. It was hand-to-hand combat. The last thing I remember was Stephen getting shot and falling beside me. I saw an NVA officer charge me with his bayonet.'' He pointed to the scar on his face. ''I remember getting cut. And then I blanked out.''

''My God,'' Laura said, her voice quavering, ''I remember now...you're Captain Morgan Trayhern.''

He studied her in silence, watching the myriad emotions play across her face. Morgan expected her to withdraw her hands from his. ''Yeah, that's me.''

Tears stung Laura's eyes, and she sniffed. ''But the press and Pentagon accused you of being a traitor, of leaving your post before your men died.'' She lifted her hand, sliding it across his shoulder, seeing his eyes bleak with pain. ''I can't believe you ran, not after the way you've taken care of me. Morgan, you aren't capable of that.''

A corner of his mouth lifted and he glanced over at her. ''I didn't run, Laura. It was all a fabrication.''

''How?''

He bowed his head, and his words were harsh. ''Twenty-four hours later, according to Colonel Armstrong, they managed to get a relief column to Hill 164. They found two of us alive—me and Private Lenny Miles. The doctors sent me to Japan, to a hospital controlled by the CIA. The surgeons told Armstrong I was going to die. I had a fractured skull and two bayonet wounds in my chest.

Laura cringed. ''Oh, Morgan...''

"That isn't the worst of it," he growled. "After all the surgery and a week in a coma, I survived. Armstrong flew over to Japan and paid me a visit. When I became conscious, I found I'd lost my memory. I didn't know who I was, where I was or anything else. Because of the damage to my brain, the doctors felt I'd never regain my memory or my sense of smell. Armstrong knew it and fabricated a new identity and personal history for me. My name was Morgan Ramsey and I was a CIA operative. I had been wounded in Laos on assignment and was in Japan to recuperate. He said that my next assignment would be to join the French Foreign Legion and act as a mole in that outfit, giving the CIA information as they needed it. Before Armstrong left, he gave me a file covering my life history. I didn't know any differently, so I swallowed my 'past,' never dreaming I'd been lied to."

Horror engulfed Laura, and she placed a hand across her mouth. Morgan's face mirrored his anguish. "What they've done is illegal," she whispered angrily. "They've framed you! Your name and face were splashed across every major television network and newspaper for at least a month. Your poor family..."

"Yeah, they've suffered more than anyone," Morgan ground out. "A year ago I was climbing a cliff face with my company when the rope broke. I fell thirty feet to the ground and struck my head. Luckily I had a helmet on, or I'm sure it would have split open my skull," he said ruefully. "But what the accident did was slowly start to bring my memory back. I'd been seeing the faces of certain people in my dreams for the six previous years, and never knew who they were. Now I knew. They were my parents, my brother, Noah, and my sister, Aly."

"And did you contact General Armstrong once you knew the truth?"

"I did. The CIA operative I'd been working with in Marseilles from time to time suddenly disappeared. I called the Pentagon to talk with General Kip Young, who had been my battalion commander back in 1970, but no one would talk to me." Morgan got up and paced the kitchen. "For the rest of the year, I wondered what the hell to do. I knew from what little I'd investigated about myself that I'd been branded the consummate traitor to this country. And then two weeks ago I got a phone call from the commandant of the Legion. He ordered me to fly to D.C., and wouldn't say why. Of course I had to follow orders. When I got stateside, I found out that Armstrong was dying. He wanted to see me to tell me that sometimes one good man had to be sacrificed for a dedicated group of military officers."

Her heart squeezed with anguish at the hardness and tension in Morgan's face. "Was Armstrong going to clear you?"

"Hell, no!" Morgan exploded, halting in the center of the kitchen. "The bastard just wanted to get things off his chest and make everything right with his Maker. Young warned me that if I tried to stay in D.C. or expose the snafu I wouldn't get anywhere." He ran his fingers through his hair. "I wanted to see my family, but I knew that under the circumstances it was impossible. They've gone through enough pain and hardship for my sake. When you saw me at the airport that morning, I was tied in knots. That's why I stepped in front of that limo without looking. I wasn't thinking straight. I was all wrapped up in my emotions."

Laura sat there, the shock and silence settling over

her. Her mind spun with questions and possible answers. She saw him staring at her, doubt in his eyes. "I believe you, Morgan," she hurried to assure him.

The words fell softly against his throttled anger and fear. The three words offered him hope for once, instead of despair. Laura looked diminutive sitting there, her hands tense in her lap as she gazed up in his direction. "Besides my family, you're the only other person who ever would," Morgan responded bitterly.

Laura got to her feet and walked slowly in his direction, pretending she was still blind by holding out her hand. She lifted her arms once she made contact with Morgan, placing them around his sagging shoulders. There was incredible tension in him as she pressed herself against him. "You're the bravest man I've ever met," she whispered against his ear. "And you're so tired...."

Just Laura's sweet contact broke Morgan. With a groan he swept his arms around her, nearly crushing her. He buried his face in her hair, a sob trying to wrench from deep within him. But he held it back as he always did. He felt her belief in him shatter all his bitterness.

"Just let me hold you," Laura crooned, beginning to stroke his short, black hair with her trembling fingers.

Morgan's world spun around Laura, the strength of her slight form against him giving him sustenance, when he'd had so little the past seven years. He felt her slender arms holding him more firmly, offering solace. The pain in his heart was transformed, and a ragged sigh broke from the tortured line of his mouth.

"You're so damn giving," Morgan rasped, pressing a kiss to her hair. "I couldn't believe you'd stepped out in front of that limo for me. It just exploded my world.'' He nuzzled into the thick strands of her hair. ''You're so small and yet so strong. Strong in ways I'm not, Laura....''

His mouth hungrily trailed a path of fire from her temple to her cheek. ''Morgan,'' she breathed, lifting her lips to his assault, and felt his mouth claim hers with fiery urgency, drinking her into his soul. Surrendering to him, she relaxed within his powerful grip, spiraling into a cauldron of simmering desire. Eagerly she returned his kiss, matching his hunger with her own. He was at once demanding, claiming her, stealing her breath—her heart—as his sweet assault continued. Her senses reeled until her limbs felt weak beneath his onslaught.

Tearing his mouth from hers, Morgan staggered back a step, surprised at his own ferocity and need. Laura swayed uncertainly in his arms, and he gripped her, staring down at her sultry blue eyes, flecked with fire. Her lips were pouty from the strength of his kiss, glistening and wanton in the aftermath. And when her lashes slowly lifted and her eyes met his, it was her soft smile that reached his heavily walled heart.

Laura held his unsure gaze, his gray eyes narrowed and stormy. She cradled his face between her hands. ''Don't say you're sorry, because I'm not,'' she murmured unsteadily. ''This has been coming ever since we met....''

Morgan stared at her. ''And you're not sorry it happened,'' he said wryly.

''No. No regrets, Morgan.'' Making a supreme effort, she locked her knees so that she could stand upright. His kiss had shaken her deeply. Allowing her hands to leave his face, she gripped his upper arms.

''But right now, more important things have to be addressed.''

With her hair mussed she looked wanton. Morgan got a grip on himself. The kiss had been explosive, melding them to each other. ''There's not much else left to be addressed,'' he told her thickly.

Her eyes blazed with indignation. ''Oh, yes, there is, Morgan.'' She pulled out of his arms, noting the surprise on his face at her throaty response. ''Come on, let's sit down and talk.''

Chapter Six

"You know that Armstrong and his cronies framed you. So what are you going to do about it?" Laura asked. She sat down at the table, watching Morgan's face closely. Her heart squeezed with fresh pain as she saw tears in his eyes for just a moment before he forced them away.

Sasha whined and came over, resting her massive head in Laura's lap, as if to give her comfort. Absently she patted the dog.

"Morgan?"

He sat down heavily. "I wasn't going to do anything."

"You mean you were just going to disappear back to France after I got my sight back?" The idea of Morgan leaving her was unbearable. They were so close in so many ways—even if their bond was only a week old. Laura reached out and gripped his hand.

"I wasn't going anywhere until I was sure you had your sight back," he muttered, his voice low with feeling.

"Out of duty to me?" Laura guessed.

"At first it was. But getting to know you, I've stayed because I care about you, Laura. I'll never regret that decision," he said, giving her a sad smile.

"And if my sight returns, you'll leave?" She held her breath, wanting him to say no. Wanting him to recognize that there was something good and positive between them as a man and woman that transcended duty.

Morgan looked up at the ceiling, trying to hold together his unraveling emotions. "I—" With a shake of his head he confessed, "I'm not sure what I was going to do, Laura."

She leaned forward, sliding her hand into his. "Why?"

Her voice reminded him of a whisper of breeze through a meadow in summertime. "I know it hasn't been long, but there's something between us, something that's been missing in my life for as long as I can remember." He studied her long, slender fingers, wondering what it would be like to love her. "Maybe I'm tired of running and hiding. I don't know. Being here with you has made me want to stay and explore what we have." He scowled. "Or haven't had...." A self-deprecating smile cut across his mouth. "My dreamer side wants to stay. My logic tells me that as soon as you can see, I should get the hell out of here and go back to France."

Touched, Laura fought her own reactions. If Morgan saw the tears that wanted to spill from her eyes, he might misinterpret them. Gripping his hand, she murmured, "With or without my sight back, Morgan, I want you to stay."

His eyebrows moving up, Morgan studied her parted lips—lips that had yielded so willingly to him earlier. "Why?"

"My first reaction is unselfish. You were framed by Armstrong and Young. If I were in your shoes, I'd fight back. No one has the right to keep you from your family and cheat you of so much that's rightfully yours." She lowered her voice. "My second reason is selfish. I—I want you to stay. We do have something special between us, and I think we deserve the chance to find out what it is."

The sunlight spilled across the table, highlighting her mussed blond hair. Morgan saw the fire blazing in her wide azure eyes, the stubborn set of her chin and the thinning of those full lips. He gently traced her fingers. "You're a scrappy little thing for being as small as you are," he teased roughly. "And you've got a hell of a lot more backbone than I do, Laura."

"Backbone? Oh, God, Morgan, you've endured seven years of hell! That's real strength."

"There's no way to prove my innocence with the American people, Laura. Young will block me at every turn. It's my word against the Pentagon's if I go public." He shook his head. "Think what it would do to my family if I suddenly reappeared. I can do nothing but continue to make them suffer because I can't prove my innocence."

Anger worked its way through Laura, and she released his hand and stood. "Morgan Trayhern, you're talking like a loser now! How can you forsake your family and your country and slink back to France because of Young?"

She looked like a vengeful Valkyrie without armor.

''Calm down, Laura. The reality of the situation is that I don't have any other recourse.''

''Yes, you do, Morgan!'' She stamped her foot. ''I don't believe this! As close as you seem to be to your family, you're willing to forsake them without a fight!''

''The odds aren't good,'' Morgan parried. ''If I walk back into my family's life, the reporters will get wind of it.''

''So what? It's just another battle, Morgan. And God knows, you've already been through some battles where you should have died. You didn't.''

Morgan got up and walked over to her, bringing her against him. At first Laura resisted, and then, as he kissed her hair, she yielded to him. ''My little warrioress,'' he teased, inhaling her fragrance, absorbing her strength.

''Morgan, I'm not Don Quixote tilting at windmills,'' she warned tightly. Pushing away far enough to look up at him, Laura held his warm gaze, which was filled with longing. The urge to reach up on tiptoe and kiss away the anguish in his compressed mouth nearly unstrung her. ''You forget one thing. I'm an archives expert. I've spent years in the Pentagon file system. Maybe I can discover some unclassified documents, or at least get hold of someone who can help us.''

Leaning down, Morgan kissed the tip of her nose. ''No one in the military is going to help us, Laura. It would cost him his next rank, or politically sandbag him so he'd have to retire.'' He shook his head. ''No, you won't get any help.''

''Damn you!'' Laura grated, gripping his upper arms. ''Fight back! Fight for what's rightfully yours!''

Stunned by her cry, Morgan stood in the ebbing silence, staring at her. Her eyes were filled with tears. He saw them streak down her flushed cheeks.

"If you're really a Trayhern, you'll fight back," she whispered harshly. "Look at what your mother and father did to escape from North Korea. Did they sit down and cry because they were behind the lines? Did they give up because they were fifty miles from safety? No. And you have the gall to stand here and tell me there's no hope for you, Morgan!" Laura wrenched out of his arms and took several steps away from him.

Smarting beneath her attack, Morgan stalked to the counter and leaned heavily against it. He glared out the window at the carefully kept garden in the backyard. "Dammit, Laura, you're refusing to see how *much* is stacked against me!"

Her breath was rapid and shallow. "Only a coward would run from this," Laura shot back.

Morgan spun around, his hands clenched. Eyes blazing, he advanced on her. "Coward?" he snarled into her face.

She held her ground, glaring back at him. "Yes, a *coward*!" she shouted.

"I ought to—"

"What? Strangle me?" Laura laughed sharply and jabbed him in the chest with her finger. "You're running, Morgan. You're admitting defeat before the battle is ever mounted and fought. You've made all the decisions for your mother and father," she stormed. "And for Noah and Aly." With an angry swipe of her hand, she dried the tears from her face. "And you're making a decision for me, too! What if I want you to stay because I happen to like you? How dare you presume to make those decisions for us!"

Morgan blinked once, watching her turn and stalk off to the living room. The air crackled with her anger and hurt. Rubbing his jaw, burning beneath her salvos, he glared down at the carpet. What a little fighter she was. But a beautiful one. Cursing, he, too, stalked out of the kitchen.

Laura stood by the drapes, looking out the window. Her eyesight had returned completely during the heat of their argument. She teetered between the joy of seeing color and shape clearly once again and the anguish she felt for Morgan. The day was sunny and bright—everything she wasn't right now. Torn between sharing her happy news with Morgan and remaining focused on their immediate problem, Laura dragged in a deep breath of air. Hearing him enter, she jerked her head in his direction. All her joy and desire to confide her happiness in him was smashed. She saw the agony in the slash of his mouth. Her anger evaporated as he walked over to where she stood. There was confusion in his features, and she yearned to reach out and comfort him, but she stood woodenly.

"Has anyone ever accused you of being a first-class hellion?" he demanded.

Lowering her gaze, Laura managed a strained laugh. "Yes. My parents."

Morgan closed his eyes, trying to sort through his feelings. "I don't know, Laura," he whispered. "You crashed into my life, and everything's been topsy-turvy ever since. I didn't mean to seem to be making decisions for you and everyone else."

Laura stopped herself from moving into his arms. "Why don't you let your family decide if they want to enter the fray, Morgan?" She lifted her eyes to his.

"And why don't you ask me if I'm willing to help you in your fight to get back your good name?"

Morgan held her tear-filled eyes—blue eyes that were lustrous and gentle with understanding. "I-it's been a long time since someone was on my side, Laura."

"I know." She reached out, finding his hand, holding it. "All you've known since 1970 has been loneliness and the burden of carrying all those memories by yourself. You don't have to now. I'm sure your family would rather see you and help support you in this fight than see you leave for France."

He glanced at her. "You're my biggest fan."

"I've been on the receiving end of your care, remember?" Her voice was hoarse with suppressed sobs. "Morgan, you've proved yourself to me by your actions. It's easy for me to stand here and tell you that I'll help you with every particle of my being. I believe in you."

Lifting Laura's hand, Morgan pressed a kiss to the back of it. Her flesh was firm and warm beneath his mouth. "Okay, little swan, you've convinced me I should try."

Laura moved in front of him. "You've got to stay for yourself, Morgan, not because I want it."

"I understand."

She took a deep breath. "I'm going to test you on that right now."

"What do you mean?" He saw her eyes fraught with fear, not understanding her challenge.

"This morning when I got up, I could see again, Morgan. I've got my sight back."

Stunned, he stared at her for a long moment. Then he grinned. "Wonderful!" he murmured, crushing her against him.

Wanting to share his elation but still uncertain of the consequences of her admission, she allowed him to release her. Relief was etched in his eyes as he cupped her face, staring deeply into hers.

"You can see," he said, his voice quavering.

"Y-yes."

"God, that's good news," Morgan said fervently. If he hadn't been mired in his own self-pity earlier, he thought, he would have noted the dancing highlights in her eyes this morning which hadn't been there before. He sobered suddenly, noticing that Laura wasn't smiling.

"Are you happy?"

She nodded. "Yes, in one way."

"What are you talking about?"

Stepping away from his powerful presence, Laura held his gaze. "I'm no longer blind, Morgan. That frees you of any further obligation to me." She licked her lips. "I don't want you staying here because of what you might owe me. That wouldn't be right. I wanted you to know I can see before you make a final decision on whether you leave for France or stay."

"You've got a lot of courage," he told her.

"I won't lie to you, Morgan. God knows, you've been lied to enough."

He walked over to the couch and sat down. Laura stood at the window, the sunlight caressing her small, proud form. He frowned. "Come here."

Laura came and sat down. Morgan put his arm around her shoulders and drew her to him. Resting her hand against his chest, she could feel the anvil beat of his heart. Weary from the exhilaration and fear of the past half hour, she closed her eyes, resting her head against his shoulder.

"First things first," he told her. "I need to take

you to Dr. Taggert and get a clean bill of health on your eyesight."

"I forgot all about that," Laura admitted.

Chuckling softly, Morgan said, "I figured. You're really like the Trayherns in one way—you've got that bulldog tenacity. Once you bite into something, you won't let go of it."

"You're worth fighting for," Laura murmured, wanting nothing more than to be held.

"Yeah, you've proved that to me." Morgan stared at the fireplace, deep in thought. "If Dr. Taggert says you're fine, I think we should fly down to Florida to visit my parents."

Joy raced through Laura. She lifted her head, drowning in his gray eyes. "Then you're going to stay and fight it out?"

He grinned. "Do I have a choice, little swan?"

She smiled. "Not with me around, you don't."

"You've got my mother's courage—I think my family is going to like you, Laura."

"I already like their elder son. How could I not like them?"

He ran his fingers in an idle pattern on her shoulder and arm. "I don't know which to do—call them or just show up on their doorstep."

"Call them," Laura begged. "Don't shock them by appearing unannounced, Morgan."

She was right. Giving her a hug, he got up. "Come into the kitchen with me. I'll make the call from there."

"Do you still remember their phone number?"

He grinned and grabbed her hand, leading her into the other room. "That phone number haunted me for years before I found out what it meant. After I regained my memory, I knew it was my folks'."

Morgan felt shaky as he picked up the phone and dialed. What would his parents say? What kind of reception would he get? Did they believe he was a traitor? The phone rang three times before it was answered.

"Trayhern residence, Rachel speaking."

Morgan's throat constricted. "Mom? It's Morgan," he rasped unsteadily. "I—I'm calling from Washington, D.C.." The silence seemed to explode with her shock. He heard his mother gasp and utter a small cry.

"Morgan? Morgan, is that really you?"

Tears stung his eyes, and his voice mirrored his emotions. "Yeah, Mom, it's me. Look, I've got a lot of explaining to do, and I don't want to do it over the phone. Can I fly down and see you and Dad?"

"Of course," she sobbed. "Are you all right?"

"Sure, Mom. I'm fine." Morgan glanced over at Laura. She was crying, too. He swallowed hard. "Dad? Is he okay?"

"Fine. Just fine," Rachel assured him. "We didn't know if you were dead or alive. Where have you been? And why haven't you or the Pentagon contacted us?"

"Mom, I'm not a traitor," Morgan whispered, his voice hardening. "Look, I'll answer all your questions once I get there. I'd like to bring a friend of mine along—Laura Bennett. She's important to me...and to what's happened of late."

"Of course, bring her with you."

Exhilaration soared through him. "God, it's good to hear your voice, Mom."

"Oh, honey, you'll never know how much your dad and I prayed for you. I'd let you talk to him, but he's at the golf course right now."

"That's okay. And Noah? Aly? How are they?"

Laughing with joy, Rachel said, "Noah's stationed down in Miami. He's married now and has a beautiful daughter and another baby on the way."

Pain jagged through Morgan. "A daughter?" How much had he missed in seven years?

"Yes. He's married the loveliest woman, Morgan. Her name is Kit, and she's so much like Alyssa."

"How is my little sister?" he asked, choking up again at memories of Aly's red hair in pigtails.

"She's been a navy pilot for a year now. Graduated with honors from Annapolis and the Pensacola flight school."

"I'll bet she's having a hell of a good time." Morgan laughed, feeling the weight of years sliding off his shoulders.

"Aly recently married, too, but she's continuing her career for now."

"Good for her. Look, Mom, let me give the number where I'm staying. When Dad gets in, have him call me?"

"Of course, honey."

Morgan repeated Laura's number. He found himself wanting to continue talking, but knew it was wiser to wait until the family had gathered. "Can Noah and his family make it up to see us?"

Laura smiled, warming when he said "us." She walked over and gripped Morgan's hand, giving him a look of pride. Just the satisfaction in his eyes told her everything. It had been the right decision. For all of them.

"I'm going to call him and Aly right now, Morgan."

"Look, Mom, don't tell anyone except the immediate family that I'm alive and stateside. Promise?"

"Well...sure."

He knew his mother well enough to know that without his warning against it she'd call every one of their relatives with the news. "Listen, I've got a lot of explaining to do. Right now it wouldn't be wise to let the press or anyone we can't trust get a hold of the fact that I'm back. Okay? Legally I'm still considered a traitor. If the authorities found out I was here, they might toss me in jail and throw away the key."

"I understand, honey," his mother agreed. "As soon as your dad gets in, he'll call you. I know he's going to be so happy. So happy...."

Morgan wanted to cry right along with his mother. He managed a lopsided smile filled with emotion. "We'll make plane reservations right now, Mom. Chances are, by the time Dad calls, we'll be booked on tomorrow's flight."

"I'm so happy you're back, Morgan," Rachel said, weeping. "Hurry home to us. We love you so much."

"I love all of you," Morgan replied brokenly. "Goodbye, Mom."

"Hurry home to us, Morgan. Hurry...."

A deluge of stored emotions and memories swelled through Morgan as he gently replaced the phone back in the cradle. He felt Laura slide her arm around his waist, drawing him into her arms. Holding her for a long time, he finally whispered, "That was my Mom. She was glad to hear from me."

Laughing shakily, Laura hugged him tightly. "Of course she was!"

The heavy walls he'd erected around his heart fell beneath Laura's embrace. With a groan Morgan held her close "You're something else, Laura Bennett..."

He pressed his mouth to the smooth slope of her cheek, inhaling her flowery fragrance.

Kissing him quickly and stepping away out of fear at the strength of her own emotions, Laura said breathlessly, "Let me call Dr. Taggert and get this examination out of the way. You should stay here and wait for the call from your dad."

Laura's cheeks were flushed and her eyes sparkled with incredible happiness. Morgan quelled his desire to grab her and bring her back into his arms. "No, I'll go with you. Dad will call back if necessary."

She nodded, unable to stop smiling. "I'm so proud of you, Morgan."

Reaching out, Morgan gripped her fingers. "I've never met anyone like you, Laura. So much bravery in such a little package." He grinned. "What do you say we get this show on the road?"

He was achingly boyish in that split second. Laura saw the years of pain and tension fall away from his lined features. For a moment, the breath was stolen from her as she watched his mobile mouth broaden with a genuine smile. His eyes had lightened in color, the shadows in them no longer present. Yearning to reach out, draw him to her and love him, she said huskily, "Yes, let's get this show on the road, Captain Trayhern. We've got dragons to slay."

Laughing, Morgan spanned her small waist, lifting her off her feet. "Sweetheart, I'm no knight in shining armor. More like Don Quixote with you as Sancho Panza at my side." Gently he set her down, sliding his hands across her shoulders, up her neck to her cheeks. "Be my faithful squire?" he asked, studying her darkening blue eyes dancing with gold highlights.

Sobering, Laura nodded, drowning in the silver fire of Morgan's eyes. "Yes, I'll be your partner in this battle. We can't lose, Morgan. We have truth on our side."

He caressed her lips with his, feeling them part beneath his exploration. "You're so sweet and innocent," he breathed against her.

Closing her eyes, Laura molded her lips to his mouth, feeling the texture and strength that was only him. "My belief in you is all I need."

Groaning, Morgan devoured her offering, kissing her hotly. Laura sagged against him, and Morgan felt his world narrowing to only her unshakable belief in him. As he tasted the depths of her mouth, lost in the sweetness, he knew that, together, their strength would see them through hell, if necessary. Drawing back gently, lightly kissing each corner of her smiling mouth, he admitted that every day presented potential devastation. But looking into Laura's radiant blue eyes, he found the determination he needed.

As he stroked her flaming cheek, threading his fingers through the silky strands of her hair, Morgan could hardly wait to introduce Laura to his family. They would love her on sight, he knew.

The phone rang just as Laura opened the door and entered the foyer of her home. She tossed her coat and purse on the couch, having to reach over a welcoming Sasha to pick up the extension. Elated because Dr. Taggert had said that her eyes were in perfect condition, she answered the phone breathlessly.

"Hello?"

"Laura, this is Jim Woodward."

Her joy dissolved. Morgan was giving her an odd look as he came in and closed the door. "Oh, Jim..."

"Don't sound so happy to hear from me."

Rallying, Laura said, "I'm sorry. What is it you want?"

"Just to make sure you're all right. I'm still doing research on Ramsey. I'm hoping the CIA might shed some light on this for me."

She sat down, rubbing her brow. "Jim, why don't you just drop this?" Frustration built in her. Laura knew Jim's penchant for thoroughness. Often he'd accompanied her down to the photographic vaults in the basement of the Pentagon. Terror leaked through her. If Jim found photos of Morgan, he'd turn the information over to law enforcement officials. And then they would arrest Morgan.

"The guy bothers me," Woodward responded tightly. "His face…I know it! It's bugging me and I want to put all the puzzle pieces together."

Laura sighed, watching how Morgan's features had closed when he found out it was the marine captain on the phone. "Fine. You do what you want, but leave me out of it. I don't want to hear about this again, Jim. Do you understand?"

"I'm sorry I've upset you, Laura. But I've got to pursue this matter. Goodbye."

Laura put the receiver down, giving Morgan a desperate look. "That was Jim Woodward. He's still trying to identify you through photographic files and a CIA search."

Morgan nodded, his eyes hooded. "There's nothing we can do to stop him, Laura. Let's get packed. Our flight is at eight tomorrow morning. I'll take Sasha over to the kennel for you right now."

She rose, all of her happiness returning. Morgan had already agreed to bring the baby robin along in a small cardboard box. He'd assured her that his mother would love the baby bird and probably dote over it. "Okay...."

Taking Laura in his arms, Morgan gave her a game smile. He saw the worry in her eyes. "Hey, this is going to get a hell of a lot worse before it's over, Laura. If you're going to nosedive like this over one snoopy captain, what are you going to do when the heat's really applied?"

Leaning upward, Laura kissed his mouth, relishing the returning strength of his response. The thick hair from his mustache grazed her skin, sending a delightful prickle through her. "You're right," she whispered.

"I've been in tight spots before," Morgan told her, cupping her chin, gazing into her eyes. "Even if Woodward does get something on me, I'll be gone. He won't know we're in Florida because I've given the airlines an assumed name. The tracks leading to me end right here."

"I just hope he doesn't stumble onto your real name," she muttered. "Knowing Jim, he's probably going back year by year through those photo files."

"He's got seven years to plow through before he finds me," Morgan reassured her. "Come on, we've got things to do. And frankly, I can hardly wait to get home."

Chapter Seven

Morgan wiped the nervous sweat from his brow as they drove up to the Trayherns' two-story stucco home on the outskirts of Clearwater, Florida. His heart was pumping hard in his chest, and his mouth was dry as he parked the rented vehicle. He felt Laura's hand on his.

"It's going to be fine," she told him, giving him a warm smile.

"Home," he croaked. "It's just as I remember it...." Palm trees dotted the sloping landscape, and vivid red poinsettias bloomed in colorful profusion along the concrete walk and across the front of the house.

Morgan got out of the car, staring at the front door. He noticed his mother first, then his father. The shock of seeing them rooted him to the spot. All his fear dissolved at the sight of joy and welcome in their faces, not disappointment, as they hurried down the steps to the walk.

"Go ahead," Laura urged, squeezing his hand. "Go meet your parents." She gave him a little shove in their direction, following behind him.

"Oh, Morgan!" Rachel cried, throwing her arms around him.

"Mom—" He folded her tall, thin form against him, a sob tearing from deep within him. His mother was young-looking despite her fifty-six years, with the same sparkling green eyes, winsome smile and short black hair, now textured with silvery gray tones.

Laura stood back, tears in her eyes. She saw Chase Trayhern's piercing blue eyes fall first on her as he approached. Although in his early sixties, he looked much younger. His face was square, with a pronounced aquiline nose and a generous mouth that could either thin in disapproval or... He smiled a welcome to her, and Laura felt as if the sun had embraced her. Holding her hands against her heart, she felt how privileged she was to see Morgan reunited with his parents.

Chase stepped forward, throwing his arms around Morgan's broad shoulders. "It's good to have you back, son," he said, his voice quavering.

Morgan held both his parents, their heads bowed against him, all of them momentarily unable to speak. His mother's quiet weeping, her strong, slender arms around him, broke down the last of the walls holding old grief and pain. He cried with them, time ebbing to a halt around them.

They stood locked in one another's arms for a long time. Finally Morgan raised his head, his eyes awash with tears. His voice was little more than a croak.

"Laura?" He unwrapped his arm from his dad and held his hand out to her. "Come here."

She smiled unsteadily, moving forward to take Morgan's hand. Hastily wiping her tears away, she allowed him to pull her into the circle.

"Mom, Dad, you've got to meet Laura Bennett. If it wasn't for her, I wouldn't be here."

Shyly Laura held out her hand to Rachel Trayhern. Instead Morgan's mother threw her arms around Laura, hugging her tightly.

"We owe you so much," Rachel said, sniffing. "Thank you, Laura."

"Well—I didn't do much—"

Rachel pulled another handkerchief from the pocket of her green apron. "Nonsense. Here you're crying as much as I am," she said, smiling through her tears as she pressed the cloth into Laura's hand.

Blotting her eyes, Laura smiled up into Chase Trayhern's stern features. How much Morgan looked like him, she thought, as she extended her hand to him. Chase gripped it firmly, and rasped, "You've got to be quite a lady to have found our son and brought him back to us. Thank you."

Blushing, Laura was about to correct him, but Morgan interrupted.

"Let's go inside," he urged all of them. "I've got a lot of explaining to do." He gave Laura an unsteady smile as he placed his arm around her shoulders, drawing her to him.

She leaned against Morgan's strong body, deeply moved by the Trayhern family's ability to show their emotions. Somehow Laura had expected "Wolf" Trayhern to be like the other generals she'd met over the years—hard and incapable of displaying feelings. But he had Morgan's sensitivity and warmth beneath that tough skin of his. Walking at Morgan's side, Laura felt her heart lift with euphoria, because, for a while, she would be a part of this incredibly loving family.

"So that's it," Morgan said, concluding the story of what had happened to him in the past seven years. Grimly he studied his parents, who sat opposite him. Shock, disbelief, hurt and outrage showed on their faces. And that was what he felt. He glanced at Laura, who sat next to him. Straightening, he reached out, taking her hand. "And Laura thinks I can clear myself."

Chase leaned forward, a pronounced scowl on his lined face. "I can't believe Armstrong or Young would agree to smear someone like this."

"Dad, there are some officers who put their careers above and beyond honorable conduct," Morgan growled.

Rachel shook her head. "Chase, this is terrible. What are we going to do?" She got up, unable to sit still any longer.

"Take it easy, honey," Chase said soothingly. "Let's look at all facets of this problem. After the rest of the family gets here, we'll put our heads together and plan some strategy." He glanced at his watch. "Noah, Kit and their daughter, Melody, will be here in about an hour."

Morgan grinned. "Was Noah excited about seeing his big brother again?"

Chuckling, Chase rose. "'Excited' isn't the word, son. Your mother and I will get some coffee made. You and Laura just sit back and relax."

"You," Laura murmured, "have wonderful parents."

Morgan drew her into his arms. "After I remembered who I really was, I used to lie on my bunk at night, wondering how my parents would react if I walked back into their lives."

Sliding her hand against his chest, Laura laid her head against his shoulder, contentment flowing through her. "And did your dreams include this kind of welcome?"

Sifting strands of her hair through his fingers, Morgan studied her peaceful face. "I wasn't sure, Laura. I thought they might believe what the press and Pentagon had put out on me."

Each grazing touch of his fingers against her scalp increased the yearning deep within her. Laura raised her lashes, drowning in the warming gray fire in Morgan's eyes as he held her gaze. "You're like your father in many ways. The same bravery and spirit is there. And you look so much alike physically it's uncanny."

Chuckling, Morgan slid his hand down her shoulder to her arm. "Dad always said I was the spitting image of him. I got his square jaw and stubbornness."

"And your mother's warmth and sensitivity."

"You bring that out in me."

Laura sat up. "You've always had that part to you. It just got closed down because of what happened."

The urge to bring her forward and kiss her ripe lips was excruciating. But now was not the time or place. Instead Morgan brushed her cheek with his thumb. "I think you're right. Noah inherited my Mom's temperament. He's more open, more generous in showing his feelings than I ever was."

"I can hardly wait to meet him and his family," Laura said.

* * *

The momentary nervousness that spasmed through Morgan quickly abated as Noah threw his arms around him, holding him tightly for a long time before releasing him. Any doubt he'd had about his brother wondering if he was a traitor disappeared. There were tears in Noah's green eyes. Self-consciously, Morgan wiped the tears from his. He grinned, gripping Noah by his shoulders.

"It's been a hell of a long time," he rasped. He watched the tears trickle down Noah's cheeks.

"Yeah," Noah answered hoarsely. "Too long. God, it's good to see you, Morgan—" And he embraced him hard.

A sob caught in Morgan's throat as he held his younger brother for a long, poignant moment. Noah looked splendid in his uniform of light-blue shirt and dark-blue pants. Morgan felt that Noah embodied all that was good and pure and true about the Trayherns.

Gradually Noah released Morgan and stood back, wiping the tears from his face. He placed an arm around Morgan's shoulders. "Come on, I want you to meet my family."

Morgan made a point of bringing Laura to his side and introducing her to his brother. Noah's delight showed on his face immediately. And then Noah proudly brought his wife and daughter forward. Morgan warmed to Kit, who was decidedly pregnant. It was obvious that Noah and Kit were terribly in love by the tender look they shared. Their sixteen-month-old-daughter, Melody Sue, toddled confidently between the four adults during introductions.

Melody went straight to Morgan, her tiny hands barely reaching his knees, and smiled up at him. Kneeling, Morgan opened his arms to the black-haired, green-eyed little girl. Melody fell into his arms with a giggle, snuggling against him, covering his face with sloppy kisses. Tears drove into Morgan's eyes as he gently gathered Melody into his arms. She smelled so fresh and clean, her laughter light and lifting. Kissing her tiny cheek, Morgan found himself smothered with more returning kisses. Chuckling, he stood up with Melody happily ensconced in his arms.

"She's a little lover," he told Noah and Kit.

Kit's smile broadened, and she patted her swollen belly gently. "In here is Matthew Charles Trayhern. And even at six months he's showing all those famous stubborn traits you have as a family. He won't go to sleep when he's supposed to, and he keeps me up all night."

Laura leaned forward, softly stroking Melody's black hair. "She's so beautiful," she whispered. Melody stretched her arms out to her. Morgan grinned and handed her over to Laura.

"Why don't you two get acquainted?" Kit laughed. "More than anything, Melody loves to be held."

Morgan watched the play of emotions across Laura's radiant face as she took the little girl in her arms. A flush spread across her cheeks, and he saw the luminous joy in her blue eyes as she cradled the child. Looking around, Morgan savored the family that stood around him. Never, in the past seven years, had he dared dream of a moment like this. His throat constricted, he traded a grateful look with his family. They had always believed in him—never giving up on him coming back into their lives.

Noah threw his hands on his hips. "Mom, when are Aly and her husband coming in?"

Rachel brought coffee in on a tray, setting it down on the table in front of the couch. "They'll be here tomorrow afternoon.'' Worried, she looked over at Morgan. ''I guess now is as good a time as any to tell you about Aly's husband.''

Morgan heard the anxiety in his mother's voice. ''What's wrong?''

Chase came over and placed an arm around his wife. ''Son, when Aly was transferred out to the naval air station near San Francisco, she got teamed up with a pilot by the name of Clay Cantrell.''

Shock bolted through Morgan. ''Clay? Stephen's brother?'' He saw his parents nod gravely. ''But—how?''

Grimly Chase said in a low voice, ''We don't know. I suspect foul play at Bupers, in the Pentagon, but I can't prove it. Aly paid hell for being around Clay the first nine months of her duty. He hated her because he thought that you were responsible for his brother's death in Vietnam. And two days after the telegram arrived telling Clay's mother that Stephen had died, she had a major stroke that took her life.''

Reeling from the news, Morgan shut his eyes. He felt Laura's steadying hand on his shoulder. ''My God,'' he croaked, leveling his gaze on his father. ''How did Aly survive?''

''She reached down deep into that Trayhern gene pool and hung in there,'' Chase growled. ''They didn't have a very pretty relationship. Clay was after her to make enough mistakes to get her blackballed at first. Then they were in an air accident that they survived. They spent a week on the tip of the Baja Peninsula before they were able to get help. I guess that during that time Clay and Aly worked out their differences.''

''And they're married?'' Laura murmured, amazed that despite the hatred Clay Cantrell must have had for the Trayherns, love had been able to transcend the situation.

Rachel smiled. "Clay liked her from the beginning, from what he told us. He fought his attraction nearly a year. Unfortunately he let his grief and anger over what happened to Stephen and his mother interfere in his relationship with Aly. After the crash, they resolved those issues and came back here to get married."

Laura glanced up at Morgan, seeing the harshness in his eyes once again. It was a bleak look mired with pain. She tightened her hand on his arm, trying to give him solace. There would be some tense moments when Clay and Morgan met. How would Clay react? Perhaps later, when things quieted down for the evening, she could get Morgan alone, talk with him.

Laura was sitting on the wooden swing in the backyard, watching the sun set behind the wall of palm trees that defined the end of the Trayhern property, when Morgan joined her. Searching his face as he came and sat down with her, she sensed his trepidation.

"It's been one hell of a day." Placing his arm around her shoulders, he drew her against him. "How are you doing?"

She relaxed, savoring the quiet time with him. "I'm doing fine."

"Happy?"

"Very."

Morgan pushed the swing so that it moved gently back and forth. "Noah's got a beautiful wife and little girl, doesn't he?"

"Yes. They're very happy."

"I'm glad for him. After he told us about how he

and Kit met, I realized just how much he'd gone through.''

''Life's never easy on anyone,'' Laura said wryly, glancing up at him. His eyes were shadowed. ''You're worried about meeting Clay, aren't you?''

Nodding, Morgan managed a cutting smile. ''I'll tell you something. The stain Armstrong and Young placed on me has sullied my family even more than me. None of us has escaped the pain they've caused.''

Laura heard the resolve in his voice and exulted at his determination to clear his name. ''Going back to D.C. to start unraveling this mess will take priority,'' she stated.

''You bet it will.'' With a sigh Morgan leaned over and pressed a kiss to her hair. ''Someone's going to pay for all the torture my family has undergone. And soon.''

A little shiver of fear wound through Laura as she watched the sky turn from a brilliant orange to a blood red. The tension in Morgan's voice made his words a ground-out promise. Now she would be witness to the famous Trayhern fighting style.

''Do you know that 'Trayhern' is Welsh for superiron or superstrength?''

''No.''

''Yeah, it means someone with superior strength and endurance. And I'm going to need all the genes I've inherited to uncover this frame-up.''

''I think your father is planning a family conference on what to do, after Aly and Clay arrive.''

Giving her a slight hug, Morgan muttered, ''First things first, though. Somehow I have to convince Clay Cantrell that I didn't desert his brother and leave him to die on that godforsaken hill.''

* * *

Although Clay Cantrell was dressed in civilian dark-brown slacks and a white shirt, Morgan could see the military bearing of his brother-in-law. Aly burst through the door, throwing her arms around Morgan, crying. He mussed her short red hair, kissing her damp cheek, but his eyes never left his brother-in-law, who stood stiffly at the entrance to the house.

Aly wiped the tears from her eyes, holding out her hand to her husband. ''Clay, I want you to meet my brother, Morgan.'' Her voice was husky with feeling. ''And I want you two to shake hands and *not* fight!''

Morgan made the first move, thrusting out his hand to the naval officer. He was aware of the set of Cantrell's mouth and the unsureness in his eyes. ''Stephen talked a lot about you, Clay,'' he offered, holding his hand out to him. ''We were the best of friends.''

Hesitantly Clay took his hand. ''You and I need to talk,'' he said. ''Somewhere private.''

Laura heard the edge to Cantrell's voice and saw the fear in Aly's face. There was so much naked emotion on the surface of each man's face that she ached for both of them. Rachel Trayhern came forward and gave Clay a hug.

''Why don't you and Morgan go take a walk in the backyard? There's a swing out there. Go sit down and resolve your differences. I'll have lunch ready in about an hour.''

Relief sizzled through Laura as Rachel defused the explosiveness that surrounded the two men. Morgan glanced over at her, then turned, heading toward the back door, with Cantrell not far behind.

Laura stood there alone, watching them disappear out the door. She clasped her hands, realizing they were icy cold with nerves. Aly Trayhern came over, giving her a weak smile.

"Mom says you know everything that happened. Maybe we could sit down somewhere and you could fill me in."

Gripping Aly's hand, Laura pointed toward the living room. "Sure. Let's go in there."

It was noon when Laura finished her explanation. The woman pilot sat there, her face devoid of color. She knotted her fists and sat up. "I can't believe this!" she cried softly. "How could they frame Morgan like that?"

"Worse," Laura murmured, "is how Armstrong and Young's decision has affected every one of you."

Rubbing her face tiredly, Aly muttered, "Our family won't let them get away with this. I promise you, we won't." Aly glanced over at her. "It's obvious Morgan couldn't have contacted us without your support."

"Well—uh—"

Her eyes narrowing, Aly studied Laura. "You won't give yourself the credit you deserve. Why?"

"It isn't necessary. What's important is Morgan, and helping him during this time."

A grin spread across Aly's features. "So there is something serious between the two of you. I thought I sensed it."

Heat flamed into Laura's cheeks. "We've known each other less than two weeks."

Chuckling delightedly, Aly got up and stretched. "I met Clay and fell head over heels in love with him the first time I saw him! It took us nine months to admit it, but the love was there from the beginning." She leaned down and patted Laura's shoulder. "Don't worry. I'll keep what I know to myself."

"Morgan has more important things to—"

Rolling her eyes, Aly laughed. "Hey! I know this big brother of mine. I saw the look in his eyes every time he glanced at you, Laura. It's obvious to me Morgan loves you. Maybe he doesn't realize it yet, and maybe you don't, either, but it's there."

Refusing to be pulled into Aly's good-natured baiting, Laura stood. "Anyone ever accuse you of shooting straight from the hip?"

Throwing her arm around Laura, Aly grinned. "That's another one of our endearing family traits, didn't you know? Trayherns never mince words when the truth will do. Come on, I'm starved! And if my eyes don't deceive me, Morgan and Clay are coming in. Let's go meet them."

Laura felt her heart speed up as she walked with Aly to the back door. Clay Cantrell's face was no longer tense. It was softer, perhaps relieved, if she read his expression accurately. Her gaze swung to Morgan, who gave her a game smile.

"I think they've made their peace," Aly murmured, opening the door so the men could step into the house.

"I think you're right," Laura agreed, thankful.

Morgan walked through the door first. He grinned. "What is this? Two snoopy women?"

Aly punched her brother playfully in the arm. "I'll 'snoopy' you, Morgan. Laura just got done filling me in on what happened." She went over to her husband, sliding her arm around his waist, giving him a look filled with love. "Have you two settled things?"

Clay nodded, kissing his wife's cheek. "We have."

"Everything's fine," Morgan said. He slipped his arm around Laura's waist.

Laura was constantly surprised by the fact that Morgan included her, no matter what the importance of the event. She basked in his warming look, content to be embraced by him. When she saw Aly's eyes sparkling in her direction, she avoided the other woman's knowing look.

"Soup's on!" Rachel called from the kitchen.

"Come on," Morgan told all of them, "let's eat."

The dining room was filled with laughter, joking and the pleasant clink of silverware against china plates. Laura sat next to Morgan, absorbing the wonderful atmosphere of gaiety. The Trayhern family was a loving one, and they included her as if she were a member. After lunch Chase Trayhern directed them all into the living room to discuss what could be done to help Morgan clear his name.

"Morgan," Kit said, holding Melody in her arms, "let me try to track down Lenny Miles. My ex-boss over in narcotics at the Miami Police Department might be able to get something on him through department computers."

"Miles was a drug addict," Morgan said. "I had him under arrest at the time we were on Hill 164 because I caught him high on drugs." He glanced over at Laura, who sat close to him. "That's probably why he survived. He was in the bunker at the time of the last attack."

"Miles could have been buried under a lot of those sandbags that make up the walls of the bunker," Clay suggested. "Maybe he hid among them so the NVA couldn't find him and run him through with a bayonet the way they did everyone else."

"Probably," Morgan agreed sourly. He directed his attention back to Kit, who used to be an undercover narcotics police officer for the city of Miami.

"But we still don't know if Miles is even alive. And if he is, which city he's in."

"Doesn't matter, Morgan," Kit interrupted. "Chuck can run a check for us in all major cities. If Miles is still a druggie, he's probably been arrested at one time or another. He'll have a record. We can trace him to a city, then you can go investigate. I'm sure Chuck will see to it that you get help from local law enforcement authorities. I'll tell him you're a friend, without mentioning the fact that your name is Trayhern."

"Good," Morgan muttered. He rubbed his mustache. "Better to keep this thing, I suppose, for now."

Noah sat up, allowing Melody to climb from her mother's arms into his. "Don't shave it off until you're cleared," he warned. Looking around the room, he added, "None of us will say anything about your reappearance. For now, it's a family secret. From my end, I'm going to use the Coast Guard computers to see if Miles has been involved in any drug busts at sea. Between Kit and me, if Miles is around, we'll find him."

"That sounds hopeful," Morgan congratulated them. "Laura is going to begin sifting through mountains of unclassified documents at the Pentagon from the time of the massacre on Hill 164."

"Maybe I can use my top-secret clearance to nose around a little more," Clay suggested. He glanced at Aly. "They'd never let her into certain files knowing she's your sister, Morgan. But if I took some leave, spent some time at the Pentagon, I might be able to find something—anything—that would give us information on the people involved in this coverup."

A powerful thread of hope wound through Morgan.

"From my end," Chase said, "I'm going to put

pressure on people at the Pentagon level who owe me. I doubt they'll help, but it's worth a try."

"The plan sounds solid," Morgan said. "Laura and I both agree that I'll stay at her house. You can contact me there if you stumble onto anything."

"Speaking of Laura," Chase said, directing the family's attention to her, "we owe her more than we can ever repay."

"You're a Trayhern at heart," Rachel put in quietly.

Uncomfortable in the limelight, Laura bowed her head. "Morgan proved himself by staying and helping me while I was temporarily blinded by that accident. He deserves any help I might be able to give him."

Morgan understood her innate shyness at being the center of attention. Gently he squeezed her hand. "Whether you like it or not, you're part of our family now."

Self-conscious, Laura looked at each one of them, a catch in her voice as she said, "I couldn't have wished for a better family than you. You've all been so kind to me."

Aly laughed. "Osmosis, Laura. And frankly, we're proud you're a part of our team. I think Morgan has impeccable taste."

With a groan, Noah stood. "Aly, stop meddling in Morgan's personal affairs. He's capable of handling them himself."

Laura laughed nervously along with everyone else. When she looked up at Morgan, he wasn't laughing. There was pride in his eyes and—something else. Something so tender she wanted simply to throw her arms around him and love him with all her heart.

"Laura and I are going to the beach," Morgan said,

getting to his feet and pulling her upright. ''Anyone want to come along?''

''I see the Pacific Ocean every day from the air station,'' Aly piped up. ''Clay and I are beat from the jet lag. I think we'll hang around the house this afternoon.''

''Noah?'' Morgan asked.

''I see the Atlantic and Caribbean every day from the deck of a cutter. You two are landlocked. Go down and enjoy the beach for us.''

Laura smiled in anticipation of a few hours alone with Morgan. And when she saw that very male look in his eyes, a delicious tremor of anticipation swept through her.

Chapter Eight

The water was warm, easing all the tension out of Laura's shoulders and back. She swam slowly back toward shore, with Morgan at her side. The sunlight was delicious and she allowed the powerful waves to push her forward. Her feet touching bottom, she felt Morgan's arms slide beneath her back and legs, lifting her up against him.

"Morgan!" she gasped, throwing her arms around his neck. His returning laughter flowed through her, and she pressed herself against him.

"I've got you."

Closing her eyes, Laura reached up, seeking, finding his mouth. His lips were warm and cherishing, and she tasted the saltiness of the ocean on them.

"Mmm," Morgan growled, standing in knee-deep water, "you're pure heaven, little swan." And she was, in his book. Those wide, trusting blue eyes of hers would melt even the coldest of hearts, Morgan thought as he walked to the shore and deposited Laura on the blanket.

Pushing the strands of blond hair out of her eyes, Laura lay back, Morgan beside her. "This is what we needed," she whispered, closing her eyes and absorbing the sunlight.

Placing an arm behind his head, Morgan stared up at the building cumulus clouds in the dark-blue sky. "Things are moving pretty fast, aren't they?"

"Yes," Laura said, finding his hand and holding it.

"Scared?"

"A little. You?"

"A lot."

She turned her head and looked at him. "Why?"

"If Jim Woodward exposes me before we can uncover proof for my defense, it could put you and your research in jeopardy." Morgan rolled over, resting his head on one hand. He saw shadows in her blue eyes. "You're more important to me than anything else. I don't want the law to entangle you in this, Laura."

"I'll be fine."

He smiled down at her, thinking how beautifully her neck flowed into her delicate collarbones. Tracing the exquisite length of her throat, he smoothed the droplets of water from her flesh. His hand came to rest on her shoulder.

"I noticed you enjoyed holding Melody."

A soft smile pulled at Laura's lips as she gazed up at him. "I love children."

A frown worked its way across his brow as he studied her. "Are there any plans in your life to have any?"

"I'm twenty-seven now. I figured that by thirty I'd

be married and on my way to having at least two or three children."

With a soft snort Morgan said, "I never even thought of having a family." Until recently. Until he'd met Laura. The gentleness and care she possessed were rare in the world, and he marveled at her abilities. Yes, Laura would be a wonderful mother.

Moving her fingers up his arm, Laura murmured, "There was no room in your life for much of anything except survival, Morgan. How could you think of getting married, much less having a family?"

Her jaw was firm as he cupped it with his hand. "Lately a lot of things in my life have changed."

Laura was unsure how to take his cryptic comment. She met his intense gray gaze that burned with unspoken desire for her alone. "And I'm sure once we get back to Washington, they'll keep on changing. Only this time, Morgan, for the better."

"I hope you're right." He gave her a broken smile laced with longing. "Just seeing Noah and Kit with Melody made me want to have what they've already earned. That little tyke is a charmer. She's got Noah's green eyes, but she's got Kit's personality."

"A nice combination," Laura agreed. There was a hunger in Morgan. She sensed it, felt it in the curve of his fingers as they stroked her cheek and saw it in his eyes. The years of loneliness had caught up with him. And just one day with his supportive, loving family had replaced a bleak and desolate future with a richness of new dreams. She sat up, placing her arms around his neck, kissing him gently.

"First things first," she told him. "We need to get back to Washington so I can begin digging for proof of your innocence."

* * *

"Miss Laura!"

Laura smiled as she walked into one of the many archive vaults far below the main portion of the Pentagon. "Hi, Pop, how are you?"

The elderly man with the balding head smiled from where he sat at his cluttered desk. "Just fine, missy. Where you been? I understand from Captain Woodward that you had a nasty accident a few weeks ago." His thick eyebrows knitted, and he studied her. "You don't look hurt. Matter of fact, you look better than I can ever recall."

Laura stopped at Pop's desk, which was stacked with pancakes of documents waiting to be put back into various files. Picking up a pen, she signed her name to allow her access to the huge, rectangular room that housed row upon row of metal files. "I've recovered now, Pop." And she did feel happier than she could ever recall. But that was due to Morgan's undeniable presence in her life—a presence that must remain a secret for now.

"What you looking for this time?"

Laura hated to lie, but it was necessary. Straightening, she rested her briefcase on the edge of his desk. "Pop, I'm beginning research for my third book about the conflict the U.S. was involved in starting in 1960."

Cackling, Pop pushed up his wire-rimmed spectacles. His brown eyes sparkled as he slowly got up and came around the desk. "So, Vietnam's next?"

"That's right."

"What year you want to start with? 1962?"

"No...I want to start with 1970 and work back."

A little puzzled, he scratched his balding head, which shone beneath the fluorescent lights. "That was close to the end of it, missy."

Laura followed him down one long wall of files. The vault was silent except for the movement of air from a number of strategically placed fans. "I know. But I want to get a perspective on our withdrawal from Vietnam first."

He rounded one corner, then stopped at another row of files, patting one of the cabinets affectionately. "Start here, then. As you know, these are all unclassified documents having to do with any communications regarding the war."

Licking her lips, Laura peered at the small, neatly written tags on each cabinet. "I'm starting with marine corps involvement."

Pop leaned over, placing a hand against his lower back. "Down here," he said, pointing a bony finger at the last cabinet, "then up here in the next section. There are at least three hundred files."

Her heart pounded briefly. "Okay. Thanks, Pop."

Chuckling, he unlevered himself from his stooped position. "The copy machine is working if you want to make duplicates of anything you find."

"Great." Usually the copy machine was broken. Setting down her briefcase, Laura smiled at Pop. Today she had worn a pair of comfortable jeans and a long-sleeved pale-pink sweater. The vaults could get cool on occasion. "Just let me know when lunch rolls around, all right? You know how I get involved in this stuff and don't realize how much time's gone by."

Shuffling down the concrete aisle, Pop nodded. "Don't worry, missy, I'll let you know."

"Pop?"

He stopped and cranked his head in her direction. "Yes?"

"Are you expecting a lot of traffic down here this

coming week?'' Usually people made appointments to utilize the declassified files.

''Nah, it's going to be a quiet week, missy.''

''And Captain Woodward?''

''Oh, he drops in every once in a while. Lately he's been over at the photo vaults most of the time.''

Probably still trying to find out something about Morgan. Hiding her worry, Laura smiled. ''Thanks, Pop. I'll see you later.''

''Sure thing.''

Laura waited until Pop had disappeared back to his guard-dog station at the entrance to this particular vault section. Then she opened the file cabinet, and was faced with hundreds of pieces of paper tightly squeezed into the drawer. Sitting down, she pulled the first handful of papers out into her lap. She was used to this routine, having done it for years when culling for information for a military article or for one of her popular books.

Her mind kept wandering back to Morgan, who had gone over to the main library in Washington, D.C., to dredge up any and all information on Hill 164. Tonight, when they arrived back at her house, they would compare notes.

Morgan lifted his head from the copied papers he was reading. It was 5:30 p.m., and Laura was half an hour late getting home. She appeared at the doorway, her eyes red with tiredness. Sasha bounced out of the kitchen and met her in the living room, whining her welcome, thrashing her thick tail from side to side. Laura leaned over to pat her affectionately.

Getting up, Morgan asked, ''How'd your day go?''

She put her coat over a chair and brought the briefcase to the table. ''So-so. Yours?''

"So-so." She looked lovely, and Morgan was pleasantly surprised as she stepped up to him and placed her arms around his neck. Laura rested her head against his chest, and he folded his arms around her, relishing her firm body next to his.

"You look beat," he murmured, brushing her hair with a kiss.

"Disappointed," Laura admitted, rubbing her cheek against the cotton shirt he wore. "I should know better, Morgan. Things like this take time. I must have read hundreds and hundreds of documents today. Most of them were company commander reports from all over Vietnam. They're not categorized by corps areas, so it's like slogging through peanut butter."

Laughter rumbled in his chest, and he smiled down at her. "Peanut butter, huh?"

The warm invitation in his eyes made Laura vividly aware she was a woman. "Yes, peanut butter. Are you hungry?"

"I am."

Laura heard the huskiness in his voice, and realized her question had dimensions to it beyond food. She saw the amusement in Morgan's eyes and managed a wry smile. "Maybe I should rephrase the question."

"Maybe you should." Morgan felt himself growing turgid with his need of Laura. She was like a light, flexible willow within his arms. The lamp on the ceiling highlighted her blond hair, creating a halo effect about her head. There was an angelic quality to her, Morgan decided, holding her lustrous gaze. His need to make love with her dissolved in the reality of the situation. Right now, he was considered a traitor to the U.S. government. If he couldn't clear his name, there would be no future for him and Laura. And he wanted one with her. Looking deep into her wide, trusting eyes, Morgan realized she was equally serious about him.

All the reasons he should keep his distance melted as he drowned in the warmth of her blue gaze. Without meaning to, Morgan tightened his arms, pressing Laura against him, feeling her softness against his mounting hardness. A groan tore from deep within him as he saw the invitation in her eyes, in the parting of her mouth.

Breath caught in Laura's throat as she read Morgan's intent. She hadn't expected it, was completely unprepared for it as he leaned down, his mouth claiming her—the heat building and then exploding as he moved his lips hungrily against hers. His mouth devoured her, his teeth grazing her lower lip, teasing her into returning his fervent plea. A little cry of surrender arched up through her, and she sagged against him, returning his fire with equal passion. Seconds spun into timelessness as reality melted under the volcanic effects of his mouth devouring her.

Abruptly Morgan broke contact, breathing hard. His eyes narrowed on Laura's flushed features. The pulse at the base of her throat was erratic, telling him just how much his unexpected kiss had affected her. *Fool!* he berated himself, suddenly releasing her and stepping away. It should never have happened! Angrily he swung around, busying himself at the counter.

Stunned, Laura stared at Morgan's powerful shoulders and back. Her lips throbbed from the force of his kiss. Feelings of disappointment swirled amid the clamoring desire he'd suddenly released within her. Morgan was male in every sense of the word, and Laura wanted to worship his strong mouth. But feelings of shame mingled with her excruciating need. Realizing he hadn't meant for the kiss to happen at all, she moved back to the table and pulled out the photocopies she'd made. Her hands shook as she retrieved the papers.

"You might want to look at these while I get dinner." Laura heard the unsteadiness in her voice and winced. Would Morgan notice it, too? She risked everything, looking toward the counter, where he stood cutting up a green pepper.

Morgan barely allowed himself to turn his head. Sweet God in heaven, but Laura was so beautiful and unsure of herself in those moments after his embrace. Guilt tore at him. Her mouth was pouty from the strength of their kiss. Had he hurt her? He hadn't meant to, not realizing until this moment how much he'd been wanting to kiss her, love her. Clearing his throat, he growled, "Yeah, as soon as I get this salad prepared."

Swallowing at the hardness she saw in his eyes, Laura again felt the euphoria he'd given her shatter. He was sorry he'd kissed her. It had been a mistake. Her heart disagreed—she'd been wanting to kiss him, love him.... Forcing more strength into her voice, she asked, "Want some help cooking?"

"I'll finish things," he said gruffly. "Go take it easy for a while. Dinner will be ready in half an hour."

Shaken by his sudden coldness, Laura nodded. He was erecting those walls he hid behind so effectively. "Let me go change," she heard herself say in a monotone. "I'll be out in about fifteen minutes." She needed the time to splash her face with cold water and stop her senses from spinning.

"Fine," Morgan agreed, scowling. He watched

Laura leave the kitchen, with Sasha trotting at her heels. Even the slight sway of Laura's hips enticed him. She was irresistible, he decided, forcing himself to pay attention to what he was doing. A graceful, feminine woman with the ability to help him rise above his own shadowy, uncertain world.

Fifteen minutes later Laura joined Morgan in the kitchen. She'd changed into dark-green slacks and a long-sleeved white blouse with a ruffled collar. Taking an apron from a drawer, she wrapped it around her waist. Whether Morgan wanted help or not, she needed to get rid of the nervousness she still felt after his breath-stealing kiss. Sasha came over and sat on the floor at the end of the counter, watching her mistress with adoring brown eyes.

"I found out Jim Woodward is still snooping around."

Morgan lifted his head, frowning. "Oh?"

Taking out a skillet, Laura set it on the stove. "Yes. But I guess he hasn't found anything yet, because Pop, the guy who takes care of the vault material, said he's down there when time permits."

"If he discovers who I am before we find anything—"

"We'll find it first," Laura insisted, taking two steaks from the refrigerator.

"Getting stubborn about this, aren't you?" Morgan grinned.

"Jim may be a public relations officer, but he isn't an archivist like I am." Laura placed some butter in the skillet and waited for it to melt. "Give me another couple of days with those Vietnam files, and I'll have a good idea of how they're arranged. Once I get a feel for the system, I'll be able to locate Hill 164 documents more quickly."

"Good. I'm going back to the library after dinner. They don't close until ten, and I want to keep reading and taking notes." Morgan grimaced. "They sure as hell drummed me up as a traitor for the whole mess, didn't they?"

Laura felt his pain. "Yes...yes, they did."

"Next week Clay is going to come and start snooping in the classified documents," he said. "Maybe, among us, we'll come up with something."

Let it be sooner, rather than later, Laura thought, placing the steaks in the skillet. Jim Woodward might be slower than her at finding items in the millions of documents kept in the vaults, but he was thorough. How many weeks would it take before she could turn up some scrap of evidence—a finger pointing in the right direction? And if she didn't, then it would be even more important for Clay to come up with something.

"I think," Clay said, looking at both Laura and Morgan, "that this might mean something." Dressed in his khaki uniform, he took off his cap and tossed it on the table. From his leather briefcase he unfolded a piece of paper and handed it to them.

Morgan rubbed his watering eyes. For the past week, he'd been spending long days and nights poring over information that Laura had collected. She leaned over his shoulder as he spread the paper out on the table so they could both read it.

"I found this in a special unclassified part of Section B," Clay explained. "If it had been classified, I couldn't have made a copy and brought it out."

"It's a memo from then General Kip Young to Richard Hadden, CIA Assistant Chief of Operations," Morgan said, his brow wrinkling.

Excitedly Laura pointed to the date. "Look, this memo was written one day after Hill 164." She knew from long experience that certain declassified files were kept in Section B. Only military officials were allowed entry to that area.

Clay leaked a small grin. "Yeah, but look what it says."

Laura reached over, one hand on Morgan's arm. She sensed the strength of his muscles beneath her fingertips, and felt once again how much she was drawn to him. "'Must initiate detailed public relations offense concerning Operation Eagle,'" she read aloud.

Morgan studied it over and over again, his fingers tightening on the paper. "Young was the general over us at the time. Armstrong was a colonel below him."

Snapping her fingers, Laura quickly got up and went over to the kitchen counter, where, over the course of the week, she had begun placing certain documents in specially numbered piles. Rummaging through one stack, she pulled out a piece of paper. Her eyes shone in triumph as she brought it over to the men.

"Look at this." She traced the words "Operation Eagle" in the document. "This is a general communiqué from Armstrong to Young three days after Hill 164."

Morgan read the long, detailed document. "Most of it has to do with taking care of the bodies of my men and getting them stateside," he said. "Operation Eagle is mentioned, it seems, only in passing."

Leaning over his shoulder, Laura read the last line of the communiqué. "'Operation Eagle has been initiated.'" She looked at Morgan. "That could mean you had already been flown to Japan."

Clay rubbed his jaw. ''How can you be sure that Morgan *is* Operation Eagle?''

Straightening, Laura said, ''We can't be. Not yet. But the only coherent thread I've found so far is this Operation Eagle.''

''And if 'Eagle' is in reference to me,'' Morgan added, ''then this implicates Hadden at the CIA.''

''Which,'' Laura pointed out, ''ties in with what Armstrong admitted to you on his deathbed—that the CIA was involved.''

''At least you know *who*,'' Clay said, grinning slightly. He looked at his watch. ''I don't know about you, but it's time for me to hit the sack. I've got an early flight back to San Francisco tomorrow morning.''

Morgan rose, thrusting out his hand to Clay. ''In two days you've done a lot. Thanks.''

Clay's face became solemn. He gripped Morgan's hand. ''Believe me, no one wants to see the scum who really caused this fiasco caught more than I do.'' A twinkle came to his eyes. ''Why don't you two do a little celebrating for me? Good night.''

Laura smiled as Clay rose. She went over and threw her arms around his shoulders, giving him a long embrace. ''Thank you, Clay. I know how hard this must have been for you.''

He hugged her back, then released her, glancing significantly over at Morgan. ''Better keep this woman, Trayhern. She's real special.''

Flushing, Laura whispered good night to Clay and watched him retreat to the door, leaving for his hotel. She turned, and caught the naked look in Morgan's eyes. Shaken by the intensity of his hungry stare, she gathered up the papers.

Morgan stood watching Laura. She had such long,

graceful hands. She made writing a sensuous experience, he decided. His need to love her warred with his caution. The past week had consisted of late nights, early mornings and twelve-hour days of sifting through material at the library or archives. There had been no time for them.

He followed her with his eyes as she walked over to the counter to straighten the pile she had riffled through earlier. Frustration ate at him. He'd like to be able to take her out to a restaurant for dinner, but he couldn't risk being identified. And they were sitting on a time bomb, with Jim Woodward continuing his investigation.

Laura felt Morgan's gaze on her. Nervously she shuffled the papers. The past week Morgan had been moody and withdrawn. That unexpected kiss had been the reason. Still, she ached to be held and kissed by him again.

Frustration claimed Laura. Why was a kiss so wrong between them? He was acting as if it were a federal offense or something. She missed his arms, his mouth strong and hot against hers. Morgan was all the man she'd ever dreamed of—but obviously she wasn't the woman of *his* dreams. She had been a disappointment.... The pain of his rejection cut her deeply, and Laura had no defense against the relentless wall of silence Morgan used as a shield between them. Taking a deep breath, she completed her duties with the documents and turned. Morgan stood in the center of the room, his hands in the pockets of his jeans, staring at her.

Need sizzled through her, and Laura managed a weak smile. "Clay's right. It's time to hit the sack. I've got an eight o'clock start tomorrow morning."

The desire to bring Laura into his arms nearly

drove Morgan to reach out. He forced his hands to stay in the pockets. ''I'll drive Clay to the airport tomorrow morning, then get back over to the library.''

Wistfully Laura nodded. She hesitated at the entrance to the kitchen. ''Good night, Morgan.''

''Good night,'' he said gruffly. He knew sleep would come hard to him tonight—as it had this entire past week. The knowledge that Laura slept down the hall from him, when she could be in his arms, kept him tossing and turning. Sliding his fingers through his hair in agitation, he turned on his heel. If only Noah or Kit had come up with something on Lenny Miles. If only…

The phone was ringing. Muttering an oath, Morgan turned over, blindly groping for the phone that sat next to his bed. What time was it? The clock on the bureau read 4:00 a.m. He checked himself from answering it. No one knew he was still at Laura's. Throwing his legs over the edge of the bed, he reached for the terry-cloth robe and shrugged it on. No phone calls came at this time in the morning unless it was important.

Stumbling out of the room, he saw Laura's door open. Her hair was in disarray around her sleepy features, but she looked hauntingly beautiful in the shadowy darkness. She was struggling to slip the robe across her shoulders, the pristine length of the gown's soft fabric making her agonizingly desirable.

''Laura?'' Morgan halted a foot from where she stood.

''That was Kit. They've got a lead on Lenny Miles,'' she said breathlessly, coming forward and throwing her arms around him. ''He's alive, Morgan!'' She laughed, pressing her head against his shoulder. ''Alive!''

She was warm and tormentingly feminine in his arms. The shock of her body against him made Morgan dizzy for a moment. He placed his arms around her, burying his face in her silky hair. ''Did they say where he is?''

Relishing the kiss he placed on her brow, Laura eased away from him, looking up into the dark planes of his face. ''New York City. Skid row. Kit said they just got the information back from the N.Y.P.D. She's been using the computer at the Miami Police Department every night, searching for him. It was the only time her ex-boss would let her use it. That's why she called at this ungodly hour. Lenny has been in and out of jail on charges of drug trafficking up there since 1970.''

Morgan smoothed the chenille robe against her shoulder. ''Ever since Hill 164.''

Excited, Laura nodded. ''Kit's sending the information up by courier. We should get it no later than tonight. Oh, Morgan, I'm so excited about what this could mean!''

A slight grin curved his compressed mouth. Framing Laura's sleep-ridden face, he looked deeply into her dancing blue eyes. ''It's a good idea,'' he admitted thickly. At one time clearing his name was the only thing that was important to him. Now, looking into Laura's hope-filled features, Morgan was reminded by the soft smile on her lips that she was equally essential to him. His fingers tightened on her flesh. ''You're just as important to me, Laura.''

Shaken by the huskiness in his voice, she nodded. ''I know, Morgan.''

''I don't know about you, but I'll be damned glad

to have this behind us.'' Her lips were tempting, and Morgan steeled himself not to kiss her.

Laura read the torture in his eyes. He was so close, so brazenly male, that she wanted to acquiesce to the burning desire she saw in his gaze. Frustration, like a knife, cut through her. Every fiber in her body screamed for more than just casual contact with him. She couldn't forget the branding, heated kiss that had brought her own deep need to the boiling point. Just seeing the outline of his pursed mouth, remembering the strength and taste of him, made her pulse bound. There was so much they could share. Why wouldn't he? What was he afraid of? ''Let's get back to bed,'' she said, her voice barely above a whisper. ''There's no sense in losing more sleep. Now that we've found out where Lenny Miles is, everything is going to speed up.''

Gently releasing her from his grip, Morgan knew she was right. ''Get some sleep, then, little swan.''

She continued to stare up at the craggy features of his hard face. There was such tenderness in his eyes now. ''Y-yes....''

Turning, she padded back to bed, first closing the door quietly behind her. Laura leaned against it a moment, her knees feeling terribly shaky. ''That man could melt steel with his look,'' she muttered, shedding her robe. Much less melt her heart—her soul. Pulling the covers across her, she dropped her head to the pillow, wildly aware of her heart beating in her breast. ''Steel,'' she fumed. ''He melts *me* every time we get around each other!'' With that she turned on her stomach and buried her head in the pillow, hoping to escape her clamoring needs for Morgan.

Chapter Nine

"It's here," Laura said excitedly, watching as the courier van pulled into her driveway. Glancing at her watch, she saw it was five o'clock. She felt Morgan's presence behind her. The day had dragged for both of them at their respective places of research.

"The package is in your name," Morgan told her. "I'll stay out of sight."

Opening the door and exchanging brief courtesies with the driver, she signed for the hefty packet. Closing the door and turning, she handed it to Morgan. There was a new light burning in his dark-gray eyes.

"Let's go to the kitchen and see what Kit's sent us," he said, putting his arm around her shoulders, then chastising himself for the automatic response to Laura.

Cherishing the unexpected contact with Morgan, Laura leaned against him for a brief moment before pulling away. She led him to the kitchen table. Sitting down, she couldn't contain her excitement as he opened the package.

Morgan's eyes narrowed as he picked up a sheaf of copies. On top was a black-and-white photo of Lenny Miles. He snorted softly. "I wonder if I've changed as much as he has," Morgan said, turning the photo around so Laura could see it.

She studied it. "He looks like a mouse of sorts." Miles's face was triangular, his chin narrowing to a point. His eyes were small and dark, set closely together. The mouse image was emphasized by buck teeth that had never been corrected with braces. Laura almost felt sorry for him. Almost.

"He looks like someone strung out on drugs, doesn't he?" she murmured.

"Yeah. Same face I remember, but with a lot more lines." Morgan began to read the rap sheet on Miles. "He's in New York City. No known address. Kit says on a note attached that he's probably down on skid row, making one of the back alleys or a basement his home."

"That means we'll have to put in a lot of footwork."

Morgan shot her a look. "There's no 'we' to this, Laura. You aren't going into that scummy rat hole looking for Miles. That's my job."

"Hold on. You're not leaving me behind on this. We're partners. Everything we've done so far, we've done together, Morgan."

"It's too dangerous."

"Baloney."

Morgan sat up. He was getting another taste of Laura's stubborn nature. Only this time it was aimed directly at him. ''You're not a cop. And you're not trained to deal with that kind of environment. I am.''

Laura set her lips, her eyes blazing. ''Morgan, I'm not staying behind! You may need me. I can be a second set of eyes and ears as we walk those alleys.''

She was beautiful when she was angry. Morgan almost said it, but caught himself in time. Trying to keep his voice soothing, he said, ''I've got eyes in the back of my head from six years in the Legion. Look, I'm going into an area where drug addicts and pimps make a living, Laura. They don't care who they put a gun to or slip a knife between the ribs of, if they're hunting for money. You'd be at risk, and I won't have it.''

Clenching her hand, Laura asked, ''What if you get into trouble?''

''I can handle it.''

It was her turn to snort. ''Give me a break! You're a marine officer. You know the value of teamwork. No one does anything alone. Even recon marines, the elite of the corps, go in teams. Quit ignoring one of the basic rules of combat, Morgan! Just because I'm a woman doesn't mean I'm a liability.''

There were silver flecks of ire in her eyes. He hadn't counted on Laura using her military knowledge as a lever against his orders. ''I said no.''

''Damn you!'' Laura got up and began pacing the kitchen. She glared at Morgan. ''All those years in the Legion must have made you stupid,'' she ranted.

''Why you—'' Morgan got up and stepped in front of her.

Laura threw her hands on her hips, her chin jutting out at a defiant angle. ''You've been alone so long, you've forgotten how to be a team member, Morgan Trayhern!'' Jabbing a finger into his chest, she went on, "You forget, I was raised as a military brat. I'm extremely self-reliant and able to take care of myself. You can't make me stay behind. I'm going whether you like it or not!"

He almost wanted to strangle her by her long, beautiful neck. But another part of him wanted to love her, to tap into that beckoning fire that radiated from within her. His anger and pride melded with his desire for her. Gripping her by the shoulders, he gave her a little shake. "Dammit, you're not going," he rasped. He leaned down, his face inches from hers. "Did it ever occur to you that I like the hell out of you and don't want to see you get hurt?"

Tears flooded Laura's eyes and she forced back the reaction. Morgan's hands were branding on her shoulders. "I like you enough to go along whether you want me to or not!"

Something snapped within Morgan. With a growl he brought Laura hard against him. Crushing his mouth to hers, he meant to subdue her. Instead her lips parted, allowing him entrance, and he tasted the sweetness of her depths. All his anger melted as her hungry response shattered his resolve. Her arms slid upward, moving against his neck. The feminine scent unique to her entered his flared nostrils, and he inhaled deeply, lost in his need of her. The world ceased to exist for him as she pressed against him. Laura was pure sunlight flooding his dark existence. Needing her, wanting to satisfy the sharpened ache in his lower body, he slid his hands roughly down and across her small shoulders, finding and fitting her breasts into his hands.

A moan escaped him as her flesh became firm beneath his cupping motion. Fire, more violent and seething than he'd ever experienced, erupted deep within him. He could feel the tautness of her nipples beneath the fabric of her blouse. Laura was so warm, so willing....

Just as suddenly Morgan realized what he was doing. He fought the drugging beauty of her mouth, now wet and inviting. It hurt to break contact with her sweet lips. Bare inches separated them, and Laura's eyes were lustrous and dazed. Even more reason to keep her safe from harm, his mind screamed at him.

"You're such a little hellion when you want to be," Morgan grated. Just holding her shoulders to reinforce what he said had a pleasurable effect upon him.

Dizzied by the unexpected ferocity and primal need of Morgan's kiss, Laura stammered breathlessly, "I'm going."

Her lips were pouty, beckoning. He could kiss them again. Laura was so close, and the ache intensified within him. All his anger backwashed. "Didn't you hear me? I care for you, Laura...."

"And trying to make me feel guilty isn't going to work, either, Morgan!" His male scent did nothing but increase her womanly awareness of him. There was an animal gleam in his narrowed eyes. He was the hunter and she was his quarry. Excitement thrummed through Laura as her attention wavered between their words and the heated looks they were trading. Laura didn't want to argue. She wanted to make hungry, passionate love with Morgan. Her voice cracked. "I care for you, too! How can I stay here worrying for days or weeks about you? I couldn't stand the nightmares I'd have of you stabbed in some dark alley." Laura tore from his grasp, pleading with him. "There won't be any police backup. You'll be alone. I'm not about to let you walk into this mess without me at your side."

Hanging his head, Morgan felt Laura's anguish. Even more, his senses cried out as she pulled from his grasp. He wanted to explore that bounding pulse at the spot where her graceful neck intersected with her small but proud shoulders. Giving himself a mental shake, Morgan tried to still his savage want of her. He knew what it was like to be alone. So damned alone. One look into her blue eyes, and he couldn't tell her no. "It won't be easy, Laura. I plan on being out on the street all day and part of the night."

A weakness stole through Laura. She gripped the back of the chair to steady herself. The naked look in Morgan's eyes had stripped her, was making silent love with her. It was so hard to concentrate! Finally, struggling to sound coherent, Laura whispered, "I'll wear sensible shoes, then."

An unwilling grin tugged at the corners of his mouth. "Who could ever believe there was such a spirited hawk beneath that guise of swan you wear?"

Rubbing her arms because she was suddenly cold, Laura shrugged. "I care enough to be with you, Morgan."

"This isn't going to be fun. And there will be danger."

She lifted her chin, holding his suddenly bleak look. All the fire had died in his eyes, leaving only embers of an unfulfilled promise between them. She felt his emptiness just as sharply as she felt her hunger for him. "Together we're strong, Morgan."

With a sigh, he turned back to the table and sat down, making an attempt to concentrate. But how could he? Laura's voice was like a caress. Her eyes promised him a velvet world of love anytime he wanted to take her into his arms. Rummaging through the rest of the background information on Lenny Miles, trying to get a grip on his turmoil of emotions, he rasped, "We're going to have to be."

Even the grate in Morgan's voice was like his hand brushing her sensitized skin. Everything in her responded to his dark tone. Laura closed her eyes, fighting off the wave of dizziness. "I'll call the airlines and make reservations for a flight to New York tomorrow morning," she answered, her voice wispy with barely contained emotion.

Worried for her already, Morgan nodded, saying nothing. His mind and heart swung to Laura's safety. Anything could and did happen in those alleys. There was roving street gangs, kids who wielded knives and guns as easily as he had in the Legion. Only they weren't adults, just children. Rubbing his face tiredly, Morgan closed his eyes. His life took on new importance because of Laura. And there was no way in hell he was going to lose her. No way....

The wind tugged at Laura's overcoat, and she pulled the collar up, protecting her exposed neck. New York at nine o'clock on Monday morning was windy and cold. Eyes focused straight ahead, Morgan appeared impervious to the vicious wind that tore at his dark brown leather jacket, jeans and work boots. He looked like a construction worker. Or perhaps a grim soldier with a mission to accomplish.

She was getting a taste of his other side now. The side that had survived Hill 164 and the Legion. There was no forgiveness in Morgan's set features as his narrowed gray gaze roved down the street. Shivering, she hurried to keep up, feeling sympathy for the drunks who lay on the sidewalk. At each one Morgan would stop. If the person was conscious, he'd pull out a photocopied picture of Lenny Miles and ask if they knew him.

An alley came into view. Morgan halted, searching the trash-scattered depths of the area. Spotting someone lying by a dumpster, he walked in that direction. All the time his senses were screamingly alive. The wind tugged at him, and he bowed his head slightly. Rain was coming, and soon, judging from the darkening clouds above the city.

Leaning down, Morgan tapped the man in the soiled wool coat. "Hey, buddy, are you awake?"

The man growled a curse, slowly unwrapping from a fetal position. He looked up, his eyes red and watery. "What you want?"

Morgan pulled out the picture of Miles from his pocket. "I'm looking for someone." He placed the picture in front of the bloodshot eyes of the drunk. "You ever seen this guy? His name is Lenny Miles."

The drunk rolled back over and curled up. "Get outa here. I ain't seen 'im."

Straightening, Morgan perused the rest of the alley. It was empty. He glanced at Laura. The compassion on her face gripped his heart. Taking her by the arm, he turned her around and headed back out the alley.

"You're not going to make it," he told her tightly.

"I will, too!"

"You're ready to cry."

"So what?" Laura jerked out of his grip, glaring up at him. "Since when can't I feel for these street people? It's cold and windy out here. That old man didn't have enough clothes on to keep him warm. He was shivering!"

Morgan couldn't stand the fact that he'd brought tears to her eyes. He and Laura had been pounding the pavement for almost two hours since their arrival. He'd gotten them two rooms at a hotel not far from skid row, and they had left shortly thereafter to begin the hunt.

"Laura, you aren't cut out for this," he said patiently, walking back toward the street.

"Who is?" Laura shot back, giving him an accusing stare. "You can't tell me you enjoy this. Or that you don't feel sorry for these people."

"We all have our personal hells to deal with," he muttered.

Laura choked in a breath. He was right: the sight of those destitute and helpless people was tearing her up. Somehow she was going to have to steel herself against their misery long enough to help Morgan. She saw the frustration and anger in his eyes.

Morgan glanced up at the sky. "It's going to start raining like hell in a minute." He took in her pale face, her eyes that burned with stubbornness. "Sure you don't want to go back to the hotel?"

"No. As long as you're out on the street, I'm staying with you."

"Okay, wingman, let's get going."

She managed a one-cornered smile at his use of the term *wingman*. No fighter pilot flew without another fighter beside him. It was a protective measure. As they headed deeper into skid row, Laura began to see street gang members; two or three young men wearing the symbol of their gang on the backs of their jackets. There was a tension in Morgan, and suddenly Laura was grateful for his military training and abilities. This was no place for a woman alone.

The rain began violently with huge drops exploding like minibombs all around them. Laura shielded her eyes with her hand. Morgan simply hunched more deeply into the jacket, pulling up the collar to protect the back of his neck. The streets began to clear.

Halting at a basement tavern, Morgan pulled her close beside the ramshackle establishment to protect her from the storm. The paint was peeling off the front and the window was caked with grease and dirt. Frustration thrummed through him. Laura had no business being here! She was like a beautiful lily in the midst of a garbage pile. He tightened his fingers on her arm.

"We're going into this joint. Stick close."

Nodding, she followed on his heels as he opened the creaking door. Clouds of cigarette smoke and the odor of stale alcohol hit her sensitive nostrils. It took precious seconds for her eyes to adjust to the smoky gloom within the tavern. Laura pressed herself against Morgan's back, feeling eyes upon her. There were men and women sitting at round wooden tables, talking in lowered voices. The pungent scent of unwashed bodies assailed her as she moved forward with Morgan toward the bartender behind the counter.

Morgan pulled out the photo, thrusting it under the heavyset bartender's bulbous red nose. "I'm looking for this guy. His name is Lenny Miles. You seen him?"

Scratching his balding head, the bartender took the photocopied picture and held it up to better light.

Morgan felt Laura's hand around his upper arm. She was frightened. Who wouldn't be in a dive like this? The only people in there were drunks or drug addicts, judging from the blankness in their slack, sallow faces. He wanted to soothe her fears, but there was no way to do it. Gazing down the bar, he saw a thin-faced young man in his middle twenties watching them with interest. The man was dressed in a gray silk suit, out of place among the rags worn by the other patrons. He must be a pimp.

"I dunno," the bartender said, placing the photo on the counter. "Sure looks familiar...wha'dja say his name was?"

Morgan divided his attention between the pimp looking Laura over and the bartender. "Lenny Miles. He's a drunk and a drug addict."

Rubbing his nose, the bartender peered down at the picture. "Give me a minute, Mac. I mighta seen him, but I gotta remember."

"Take your time," Morgan said. He stiffened inwardly as the pimp came strolling around the bar directly toward them.

Laura's eyes widened as the man in the suit walked up to her, grinning. She shrank back against Morgan, disgusted by the leer in the man's dark brown eyes.

"Nice filly ya got there, fella. But I gotta tell ya, this is my turf. Nobody does business in here without Rico's permission." He reached out to touch the blond hair lying against Laura's shoulders.

Morgan shot out his hand, capturing Rico's arm in a viselike grip. "Back off, punk, or you'll regret it," he snarled.

Laura uttered a little cry and stumbled backward, hitting a table. She straightened, her hand across her mouth. Rico's thin face went livid as he glared up at Morgan.

"Get your hand off me," Rico sputtered.

"Leave the lady alone."

Rico snorted. "Hey! She's just another piece of meat to sell, buddy. You ain't movin' in on my turf!"

The urge to put his fist right through Rico's snarling face was tempting. With a grin Morgan shoved

Rico away from him. The pimp crashed into another table, then fell to the unswept wooden floor.

Laura gave a small cry of warning as she saw Rico scramble to his feet, drawing a knife from beneath his gray silk suit coat.

"She's mine," Rico whispered, holding the knife outward.

Morgan's eyes glittered. Grabbing a beer bottle, he smashed it against the counter, keeping the jagged remains as a weapon in his hand. He kicked a chair out of the way, then stood in a wide stance for better balance. "No way, punk. The lady's no hooker, and she isn't for sale." The pimp leaped forward, knife hand extended. In one swift motion Morgan lifted his foot, his boot coming into hard contact with Rico's wrist. The pimp cried out as his weapon sailed out of his hand.

Breathing harshly, Morgan caught Rico as he fell off balance from the kick he'd delivered. Grabbing the pimp by the collar of his suit, he slammed him headfirst into the counter. With a groan Rico slumped to the floor, holding his bloodied nose.

"Now get the hell out of here," Morgan snarled, leaning down and jerking Rico back to his feet.

Laura watched as Morgan threw Rico out the front door, then slammed it shut after him. Dizziness assaulted her, but she caught herself, gripping the table for support. She heard snickers from the patrons.

"You all right?" Morgan asked, coming over to her.

"Y-yes, fine."

He cocked his head, studying her darkened eyes and pale skin. "You don't look very good. Here, sit down." Pulling out a chair, he guided Laura over to it.

"Hey, Mac," the bartender called, waving Morgan back over to the counter. "I think I remember now. They call him 'Lenny the Rat.'"

Hesitantly Morgan left Laura's side. She looked as if she were going to faint. "Tell me what you know about him," he ordered, wiping his hands on the thighs of his jeans. Everything about this place was seedy and dirty.

"Not much to tell ya. Lenny's like most of 'em. He sleeps during the day and gets active at night."

"There's a bunch of flophouses about five blocks from here, but it's a real rough area. Even the cops don't go in there unless it's with a couple of cruisers—and then only after a murder's been committed." The bartender rubbed his almost nonexistent chin. He studied Morgan for a moment, then grinned. "But I got a feelin' you can take care of yourself. Anybody who can take on Rico, can take on Hombre."

"The local gang leader?" Morgan guessed.

"Oh, yeah. But Hombre's nasty as they come."

"And you think Lenny the Rat might be over on his turf?"

"I'm pretty sure. He's one of Hombre's dealers, if I remember right."

"Thanks," Morgan said with feeling. He picked up the photo and put it back in the pocket of his plaid shirt. Turning, he focused his attention on Laura. She was completely out of her environment, while he had spent hours at dives like this, thinking and alone.

"Hey, Mac," the bartender called. "You'd better get her outa here. She ain't gonna make it here. Ya know what I mean?"

Grimly Morgan nodded. "Yeah, I understand. Thanks."

Laura stood as Morgan approached. His tense face softened, and she longed simply to fall into his arms. Fighting all her needs, she stood on her own.

"I heard what the bartender said." She heard how strained her voice sounded and she strengthened it. "Wouldn't it be safer to go over and check out those flophouses in daylight?"

Looking around, Morgan saw that every patron was watching them with unparalleled interest. He gripped her arm and led her to the door. They'd do their arguing outside. "Come on," he told her.

Outside the tavern, the wind tore away the smell hovering around her, and Laura appreciated the cleansing rain. She stood huddled next to the tavern wall, her hands shaking so badly she couldn't hide it from Morgan.

Morgan moved behind her to shield her from the driving wind and rain. Water ran in rivulets down his drawn features. "I'm taking you back to the hotel," he growled. "There's no way in hell you're following me into Hombre's territory."

"I'm going, Morgan." There was an edge to her voice, and Laura watched him react to it.

Words were useless and he knew it. Capturing her hand, he pulled her around, heading back toward the hotel. The rain slashed at him, and he lowered his head. Laura tried to jerk out of his grasp. Dammit, he didn't want to hurt her!

"Stop fighting!" he growled, throwing his arm around her shoulders and bringing her against him.

Tears of anger mingled with the cold rain. Her hair wilted around her face, becoming wet ropes. Morgan's strength was too much for her, and she acquiesced, burying her head against his shoulder.

Their middle-class hotel sat on the edge of the skid

row district. Laura was soaked to the skin by the time they arrived at their rooms. Morgan took her key, opened her door and led her inside.

"You're shaking like a leaf," he muttered, throwing his jacket onto a chair. "Come here."

Her teeth were chattering, and Laura allowed him to unbutton her trench coat and peel it off her. She was cold, yes. But fear was making her reaction worse. Grateful for Morgan's hand on her elbow, she let him guide her to the bed, and she sat down.

"I-I'm so cold," she whispered as he knelt to pull the soaked shoes from her feet.

Morgan shot her a knowing look. "You're more scared than cold."

Gripping her hands in her lap, Laura hung her head. "Weren't you frightened when Rico pulled that knife on you?" Off came her socks. Then Morgan got to his feet and pulled her upward.

"No."

Laura started to protest when he began to briskly unbutton her yellow blouse. The material clung to her goose-bumped flesh. "Wh-why?" Each time his fingers grazed her, her skin tingled beneath his touch.

Morgan drew the soaked blouse off her shoulders. His scowl deepened as he threw it on the bed. "Because the punk didn't even know how to hold a knife properly. Sit down."

Numbly Laura obeyed, hotly aware of Morgan's burning gaze on her breasts. Even the silky bra she wore was wet. He unbuttoned and unzipped her jeans, pulling them off her, one leg at a time. Unable to speak because her teeth were chattering, Laura watched as he dragged her chenille robe from her suitcase.

"Get this on. I'm going to start a hot shower for you. You're freezing."

"N-not a shower. I-I don't think I can stand up."

Morgan nodded. "All right, a hot bath." He saw her fumble awkwardly with her robe, her hands shaking.

"Come here," he said huskily, getting her to stand. He helped her on with the robe, wildly aware of the feminine lingerie she wore. It was the first time he had seen her without clothes, and she was beyond his most heated, passionate dreams. Fighting his desire to drag her into a hot shower with him, he closed the robe with the sash, then forced her to sit back down on the bed.

Laura closed her eyes and hunched over, trembling, on the bed. Why couldn't she be more brave? The adrenaline that had shot into her bloodstream when Rico pulled the knife had unhinged her. She had been so frightened for Morgan. Just the mere thought of him getting hurt made her blanch. She hadn't been frightened for herself but for him. Would he understand that?

Minutes later, Morgan came out of the bathroom. And with the same brisk efficiency, he led Laura from the bed to a tub that was rapidly filling with steaming hot water. He stood inches from her, his hands resting on her slumped shoulders. Gently he moved aside her tangled wet hair, grazing her pale cheek.

"Listen, you get a long, hot bath and relax. I'm going to go downstairs and order us some lunch. When you're done soaking, we'll eat here, in your room. How does that sound?" Morgan felt the heat within him threaten to overwhelm him as she lifted those long, thick lashes, her eyes dark and shadowed with fear. Her lower lip trembled. With a groan he felt his heart dissolve beneath Laura's look, pleading with him to kiss her.

Morgan's breath was warm and moist across her cheek as he leaned down to claim her. Laura trembled as his mouth took hers with hungry abandon. She fell against him, hungrily returning the branding kiss that seemed to devour her with fire. As he ran his hands up and down her back and hips, she felt herself drowning in the glory of his ardor, sweeping through her like liquid heat.

Tearing his mouth from her lips, Morgan gripped her. Both of them were breathing raggedly. Laura's lips were wet, inviting. He saw the swell of her breasts outlined by the lavender robe, the nipples pronounced, begging him to touch and tame them. How long could he continue to fight the natural beauty that came straight from her heart? Closing his eyes, Morgan gripped her shoulders hard.

"Get your bath, Laura."

She swayed in his grip, her lips throbbing in the wake of his kiss. "A-all right...."

Tearing himself away from her, Morgan headed blindly out of the bathroom, shutting the door behind him. He stood for nearly a minute, fighting his desire, fighting his primal need for her. Then, rubbing his face savagely, he forced himself to leave her room, lock the door and go downstairs to order their lunch.

Laura stared into her own eyes in the mirror. They were a soft powder blue. Her hands no longer shook as she combed through her just-washed hair. There was color back in her cheeks, but she knew it wasn't so much from the bath as from Morgan's fiery kiss that had claimed her very soul. Setting the comb aside, she applied lipstick, then dressed in a pale-pink blouse, blue jeans and dark fuchsia sweater.

There was a knock at the door. Laura answered it to find Morgan with two sacks of food in his hands.

"Come in," she said breathlessly. Even now, she could see the pewter flame burning in his eyes. She shut the door, watching him place the sacks on the small desk.

Morgan stole a look at Laura as she came over to sit down. She looked vulnerable and beautiful in the jeans and sweater. "You look better," he muttered. Did she hear the desire in his tone? He hoped not.

Laura opened the first sack and pulled out the contents. "I feel much better." It was obvious he didn't want to discuss their torrid kiss. But it was so hard to ignore his powerful masculinity and the desire in his gaze that her heart pounded with a swift staccato beat. She wasn't hungry, but she knew she'd better have something. Morgan had ordered them turkey sandwiches, French fries and coffee.

"Here, you eat first," she said, opening the second sack.

Morgan took a drink of the coffee, scalding his tongue. Damn! Staying around Laura was throwing his feelings into a tailspin. Frowning, he ate in silence. Just the way she held the sandwich in her slender fingers made him ache for her. There was nothing Laura did that wasn't sensual in his eyes.

After lunch, Morgan gathered up the sacks and wrappers. "I'm going back down there." He shot her a dark glance. "And I want you to stay here and rest."

Laura looked out the window of the hotel room. It was pouring. Just the thought of going back into that slashing, freezing rain made her shiver. She watched

Morgan put the sacks into the wastebasket near the bed. His shoulders were incredibly broad, his back strong and powerful. The look on his face told her not to argue with him. "When will you be back, Morgan?"

He picked up his damp leather jacket, shrugging it over his shoulders. "I don't know."

"Please," she whispered, "don't get caught out there after dark, Morgan. Don't...."

Managing a tight smile, he came over to where she sat. "Did I tell you how pretty you look in that sweater?" He caressed her cheek longingly. "Gives color to your face."

Laura cradled his face between her hands. "Morgan, be very careful, do you hear me?" The words *I love you* were nearly torn from her. She brushed her fingers through his damp hair.

"Sweet little swan," he murmured, "I've got everything to live for now." Her lips were soft and pliant beneath his brief, searching kiss. Morgan stood. Laura's eyes were filled with anxiety and fear. "Stay here and keep the door locked. Don't open it for anyone but me. Understand?"

Laura nodded convulsively. Gripping her hands, she watched Morgan leave the room. A coldness swept through her as she sat alone at the desk. Morgan was like warming sunlight to her existence. Uttering a little cry, she pressed her hand to her brow. "I love you, Morgan." The words met a silent room in the wake of his exit. Would he be safe? What if Hombre found him? Suddenly Laura could not sit still. She got up and began pacing the rectangular expanse. Her heart ached with a new pain—one of fear for Morgan's life. He'd nearly given his life for his country once, and had been accused of being a traitor. Now he had to face a different kind of war zone to reclaim his innocence. If only he could find Lenny Miles. If only…

Chapter Ten

"I'm looking for Lenny the Rat," Morgan told a young teenager standing just inside the door of a battered old hotel. The red-haired youth shrugged, blowing cigarette smoke out his pinched nostrils.

"Ain't here."

"Where, then?" Morgan moved inside the hallway, on guard. The boy, who couldn't be more than sixteen, carried a knife in a scabbard just inside the leather jacket he wore.

The youth sized up Morgan with a disgusted look. "You a cop or somethin'?"

"No. I knew Lenny a long time ago, and I'm trying to find him."

"Try the next flophouse down. The Rat usually sleeps in the basement with the rest of the sleaze."

Morgan nodded. "Thanks." He went back into the rain, thrusting his hands deep into the pockets of his jacket. Miserable weather for a miserable day. But he could remember far worse monsoon rains in Vietnam. This was nothing in comparison. Walking quickly down the concrete sidewalk spiderwebbed with cracks, Morgan kept his gaze on the five-story brick structure with broken windows where Lenny might be staying.

There was a group of teenage boys huddled in the doorway of the dilapidated hotel. The windows were patched with cardboard and tape, lending to the beaten image. Pulling his hands out of his pockets, Morgan slowly walked up the steps.

"Hold it right there," a blond-haired boy warned.

Morgan halted within six feet of the group. They all wore the same style of black leather jacket with a tiger emblazoned on the back. "I'm looking for Lenny the Rat."

"What for?" the blond youth challenged, standing with his feet spread, hands on his thin hips.

"I'm a friend of Lenny's. I need to talk with him."

"Frankie, he looks like a cop," a black-haired boy growled.

The blonde grinned, confident with his cohorts surrounding him. "No cop is stupid enough to walk into Hombre's territory alone, Mickey. You lookin' to buy, mister?"

Morgan shook his head. "Drugs aren't my style."

"Then he's a cop!" Mickey cried, pointing a finger at him. "Let's cut 'im up and send 'im back to the precinct."

His eyes hardening, Morgan stared at Mickey, then at Frankie. "You start anything and I'll finish it. I'm not a cop. I'm here to find Lenny."

Frankie lifted his chin, weighing Morgan's growling rejoinder. "It'll cost ya, mister."

"How much?"

Frankie pursed his thin lips. "Say...a hundred bucks."

"Lenny's not worth more than ten bucks."

Laughing sharply, Frankie moved lithely down the stairs, his skinny hand extended. "Deal."

Taking a ten-dollar bill from his pocket, Morgan thrust it into the kid's hand. "Take me to Lenny."

"Hey, Mickey, take this dude to the Rat," Frankie ordered, stepping aside.

The rest of the gang moved to allow Morgan entrance into the flophouse. The hallways were littered with garbage and bottles. An unpleasant odor stung his nostrils. Keying one ear to the gang members who remained at the door, Morgan followed Mickey deeper into the hotel. He didn't trust any of them. He could be jumped at any time.

Mickey stopped and jerked open a door that was hanging by one hinge. "He's down there with the rest of 'em."

Nodding, Morgan moved to the rickety wooden stairs and stood for a minute, allowing his eyes to adjust to the gray light seeping through the pitifully few windows in the basement. Mickey left. Occasionally a snore, or maybe it was a groan, escaped from one of the fifteen or so sleeping figures huddled below him. He was glad Laura hadn't come along. She couldn't have handled this kind of scene.

Quietly Morgan descended into the basement. Most of the men and boys were sleeping, curled up on cardboard, or whatever they could find that was dry, to keep warm. He stopped at each person. Some remained asleep and he could tell they weren't Lenny. Others awakened as he drew near, their eyes malevolent with warning to stay away. Morgan respected their distance as he moved carefully among them.

His disappointment grew stronger with each man he checked. Finally there was only one person left, in the far corner, wrapped in a tattered and filthy olive-green wool blanket. Morgan stepped through the clutter on the floor, making his way toward the sleeping figure.

Leaning over, Morgan gripped the thin shoulder through the damp blanket. Muttering, the man turned his face, his hooded eyes puffy slits.

"Miles." The name came grinding out of Morgan. He tightened his grip on the man's shoulder, forcing him against the wall.

Lenny looked up, his eyes widening. They were glazed over, indicating he was high on drugs. "No!" he croaked, trying to scramble backward but stopped by the wall.

"Hold still!" Morgan hissed, kneeling to grab the ex-soldier by his filthy collar.

Lenny was breathing hard, his voice high and off-key. "Captain Trayhern! No! It can't be...they...they said you were—"

"Shut up, Miles. Shut up and listen." Morgan leaned forward, baring his teeth. "You and I have some talking to do, Miles. I need you to testify for me. You're going to clear my name. Now come on, get up!" He hauled the small man to his feet.

"But," Lenny squealed, "I can't! They'll kill me! They said they'd kill me if I—"

"And I'll kill you if you don't testify about what really happened, Miles," Morgan muttered savagely. He placed one hand on the addict's collar and jerked one arm behind him. "Come on, we're getting out of here."

"You can't do this!" Lenny screamed, fighting weakly against Morgan's superior strength and bulk.

"Like hell I can't. Now move it, Miles." He pushed him toward the stairs.

Lenny Miles was in a weakened state that alarmed Morgan. The guy was nothing but skin hung over bone. He'd gone downhill since Morgan had last seen him. Guiding Miles toward the entrance, Morgan saw that the Hombre gang had disappeared. Good. It would make his job easier getting Miles safely back to the hotel.

As he dragged Miles out of the house and onto the street, Morgan wondered how Laura would react to this disheveled man who had knowingly put the name "traitor" on him.

The heavy, persistent knock at her door sent Laura into a spasm. She leaped off the chair, running to answer it.

"Who is it?"

"Morgan. Meet me over in my room, Laura."

"Okay." She took the key from her purse and quickly opened the door, then walked out into the carpeted hall. Morgan's door was open. As she entered his room, a stench assailed her, and she winced. When she saw Lenny Miles sitting unhappily on a wooden chair, she came to a halt.

Morgan kept a hand on Miles, not trusting him. "This is Lenny Miles," he told her darkly.

Compassion swept through Laura as she stared at the unkempt, thin man. Lenny really did look like a frightened mouse.

"Let me go, Captain," he wailed. "I don't know nothin'!"

"Shut the door, Laura," Morgan ordered grimly.

Lenny cringed when Morgan lifted him to his feet. ''You're sickening, Miles.'' He shoved up the sleeve on the threadbare jacket Lenny wore. There were at least ten needle tracks, attesting to his shooting hard drugs. Turning, Morgan told Laura, ''Get a bath ready. I'm going to scrub him until he squeaks. While I'm doing that, you go downstairs to the men's store and buy him some decent clothes.''

Nodding, Laura did as he asked. In no time the bath was prepared. She laid out several towels, a fresh bar of soap and a razor. Lenny was stinking and dirty. That scraggly brown beard did nothing but make him appear more gaunt.

''The bath's ready, Morgan,'' she called.

Morgan had already stripped Miles of everything but his trousers. ''Thanks. Now go get those clothes. You can take his filthy garments with you.''

Laura had never seen Morgan in this kind of a mood. His face was hard, and so were his eyes. This was his soldier side, the fighter side. ''I'll throw them in a paper sack,'' she said quietly.

''After you get the clothes, put them in my room and then go to yours until I call you,'' he ordered, dragging Lenny toward the bathroom.

Relieved that Morgan was safe and unharmed, Laura nodded and left. From the look on his face, he was ready to drown Lenny instead of wash him. Her hands shaking, she clutched the filthy remains of Miles's clothes and made her way back to her room. She was sure that as soon as Morgan got him decent, he'd begin interrogating him. A cold shiver rippled up her spine. With the mood Morgan was in, he could hurt Lenny Miles badly.

An hour later Morgan called her. He wanted the tape recorder brought over. Grabbing it, Laura left her room and walked those few feet down the hall. The door to Morgan's room was open, and she stepped inside. Morgan looked agitated, his sleeves rolled up on his forearms, the front of his shirt damp from Miles's much-needed bath.

"Laura, you ready with that tape recorder?"

She nodded, placing the microphone on the desk next to where a miserable Lenny Miles sat. "Ready."

Morgan took the other chair, turned it around and threw a leg over it. He sat down only a few feet from Lenny. Dressed in a white shirt and brown trousers, his face scraped clean of a beard, Miles looked almost presentable. Already his hands were beginning to shake because he was coming off the high.

Following standard police procedure, Morgan made Lenny give his full name, present address, then his military rank and where he'd been stationed back in 1970. After Lenny had stammered through the obligatory answers, Morgan pounced on him. "All right, Miles, I want to know what Armstrong and Young put you up to after the massacre on Hill 164."

Standing to one side, Laura made sure the tape was recording properly. She saw the naked fear in Lenny's small, dark eyes. He wrung his hands.

"Look, Captain, I can't say anything! If I do, they'll kill me."

"And I'll kill you if you don't. My life's at stake, Miles. You've helped mess up seven years of it. Now I want the truth."

Lenny hung his head. "Please," he squeaked, "they'll kill me!" Then he added imploringly, "Look, I gotta have a fix or I'm gonna lose it!"

Morgan was about to reach forward and jerk Miles up by his collar, when Laura placed her hand on his shoulder. He glanced at her. There was pain in her blue eyes.

"Let me try," she pleaded.

His nostrils flaring, he nodded.

"Lenny, my name is Laura Bennett. I'm a military archives expert from Washington, D.C."

Gradually Lenny came out of his crouch and raised his head. "The Pentagon?"

"That's right. Certain information was given to Morgan about why he was blamed for Hill 164. General Armstrong himself told Morgan the truth."

Lenny's eyes grew round. "He did?"

"That's right," Laura said, keeping her voice quiet and calming. "Don't you think that if General Armstrong told Morgan the truth, you can tell us what you remember about the plan?"

Chewing on almost nonexistent fingernails, Lenny gazed at the floor for a long time.

Morgan sat tensely. If only Laura could drag the truth out of Lenny. He wanted to wrap his hands around the bastard's neck and wring his life out of him for what he'd done.

Gently Laura squeezed Lenny's shoulder. The man jumped like a frightened mouse. She gave him a pleading smile. "We know about Operation Eagle, Lenny."

He gasped. "Eagle? They told you about Eagle?"

"We know that a CIA chief by the name of Richard Hadden approved the operation."

"Well—I don't understand," he wailed. "If you know all this, you know everything!"

"You see," Laura whispered, trying to get him calmed down again, "we have most of the information. All that's missing is your reason for getting into this mess, Lenny."

He glanced up at her. "Well—I, uh, didn't plan on it."

"I know. You were under arrest and in a bunker when the NVA attacked the hill for the last time," Laura began, hoping he'd continue the story.

"Yeah...well, I was." He glanced apprehensively at Morgan. "The captain saved my life by having me down in that bunker. I was high on drugs and couldn't have hit the broadside of a barn with my M-16." He grimaced. "A rocket hit the bunker and the next thing I knew, I was buried among hundreds of sandbags. That's what saved me, ya know?"

"I'm glad it did. What happened next, Lenny?" Laura coaxed.

"I don't know how long it was before marine reinforcements reached Hill 164. When I heard American voices, I started screaming for help. They dug me out. Colonel Armstrong was there, and he wasn't happy. They took me aside and told me I was the only survivor. The colonel said he wanted me in solitary back at battalion headquarters so he could interrogate me."

"You're doing fine," Laura praised him.

Lenny peeked at Morgan's grim features, then returned his attention to Laura. "I was in solitary for an entire day. The next morning, Armstrong came in with General Young. I repeated what I knew. He told me you were the cause of the massacre. At the time I didn't know any different. I was in the bunker and didn't see anything. And if I went along with their story, they said they'd give me the drugs I wanted." Licking his lips, Lenny blurted, "I needed a fix real bad. They didn't have to twist my arm very hard to get me to sign papers saying the captain was at fault. I figured the captain was dead. What could it hurt?

Then Major Brown and Lieutenant Hardy, interrogation officers who normally questioned the enemy, grilled me for twelve hours solid. They said the press wanted to interview me. I had to answer their questions the way they wanted or else.'' He opened his shaking hands toward Morgan. ''Honest, Captain, I didn't know you were still alive.''

Morgan clenched his fists, feeling a fresh wall of anger rise within him. He felt Laura's hand on his shoulder, as if she'd sensed his grief and anger. Looking up, he saw tears in her eyes. She was sensitive in ways that he was not. If it wasn't for her gentle nature, he'd probably have beaten the answers out of Miles. But she had Miles eating out of her hand. Managing a tight smile, Morgan nodded his praise to her.

''So you went along with the charade because you wanted a fix?'' Laura asked.

Giving a nod, Lenny wiped the tears from his eyes. ''Yeah, I did. I'm sorry, Captain. But it was either roll over on this, or detox. When I got stateside, the press was houndin' me. After three months I was discharged. Then somebody tried to kill me. I took off, realizing I was a liability to those officers.'' He shrugged. ''I didn't wanna die, so I disappeared....''

Morgan glared at Miles. He was a coward of the worst kind. Getting up, he walked around the room. Laura's face mirrored his anguish.

''The only way you'll be safe is if the real truth gets out, Miles. Until then you're living on borrowed time. Those goons who tried to kill you years ago are still around. You know too much. What I need is your testimony in order to clear my name completely. That's the only way you'll truly be safe.'' He halted in front of Miles, gripping the back of the chair with both hands. ''I've lived underground for seven years,

Miles. I haven't been able to see my family or have any kind of decent life for myself. If you feel as badly as you say, you'll help me. Will you?"

Laura saw Lenny begin to squirm. "We already have the evidence," she told him softly. "Please come back to Washington with us, Lenny. You can stay at a drug rehab house and get decent food and care. Morgan won't let anyone harm you."

"Well—" Lenny whispered.

"Please, Lenny," Laura begged. She held his wavering dark eyes. The man was scared to death. The question was, who was he more afraid of? Morgan, or Armstrong and Young's old threat? Holding her breath, Laura waited those agonizing seconds while he made up his mind.

"I ain't had a decent meal since...a long time ago," Lenny admitted. He glanced warily at Morgan, then at Laura. "I guess I'll come. I'm gettin' tired of living in cold basements with cardboard for a bed."

Laura didn't know whether to cry or leap for joy. She held both reactions deep within herself. Morgan moved over to the phone.

"We'll book tickets on the first flight out of here for Washington," he told her grimly.

Lenny's thin eyebrows rose and he craned his neck in Morgan's direction. "You mean, I get to fly?"

Laughing softly, Laura placed her hand on Lenny's pitifully thin shoulder. "Only first class for you, Lenny." Her mind raced with other items that would have to be attended to. On the plane she'd discuss them in detail with Morgan.

"The only attorney you want to represent you is William Wendell," Laura told Morgan in a low tone.

Sweating and nervous, Lenny sat across the aisle on the commuter flight heading for Washington, D.C.

Morgan kept one eye on Miles and keyed his focus to Laura's comment. "I'm going to need a lawyer with the personality of a barracuda to fight the military justice system."

Laughing, Laura slid her hand into his. "Believe me, Bill is the best. He's argued and won cases at the Supreme Court level. Bill is about six-foot-five, with sandy-blond hair and blue eyes. He wears a mustache, too."

Morgan managed a grin, feeling the first real hope in seven years that his life might get turned around. "Then the guy can't be all bad."

"He's the best," she repeated fervently. "I'll call him as soon as we get home."

Gently Morgan raised her hand and kissed the back of it. He held her luminous blue gaze that sparkled with happiness. "No," he said huskily, "you're the best. And I like the way you refer to your house as our home."

A sweet fire blazed through Laura, and she ached to lean those few inches and kiss his so-serious mouth. "It feels right," Laura admitted.

Smoothing several strands of blond hair from her cheek, Morgan said, "When this thing gets past the planning stage and we have all our proof gathered, you and I are going to sit down and have a long talk."

Nodding, she rested her brow against his powerful shoulder. "About the future?"

"About us."

Warmth stole through Laura and she was content to wait. Morgan was being overly cautious about their relationship, but she understood why. He didn't want his dreams to be pulled out from under him as they had once before. His life, his focus, was centered on one day at a time, not future dreams. Squeezing his arm, Laura closed her eyes, suddenly very tired. So much awaited them. Bill Wendell would have to be brought to the house, and a deposition taken from Lenny and Morgan. That would start the wheels of justice turning. Hopefully, in Morgan's favor this time.

"What do you think, Bill?" Laura asked, looking across the kitchen table at the impeccably dressed attorney.

Wendell's sandy-colored eyebrows rose. He glanced at Lenny, who sat at his left arm, then Morgan, who sat at his right. In front of him was all the evidence amassed via the documents. "There's no doubt in my mind that there was a cover-up," he began.

"You'll take my case?" Morgan asked.

Wendell grinned. "I wouldn't miss this one for the world." Thrusting his hand out to Morgan, he said, "Will you retain me as your attorney?"

Gripping Wendell's hand, Morgan nodded. "You bet I will." He liked the tall attorney whose favorite hobby was playing basketball. There was a hunterlike look in his eyes that told Morgan the mild-mannered lawyer possessed the necessary skills to pursue his case to a successful end.

Clapping her hands in delight, Laura got up. She poured everyone another round of coffee. "What now, Bill?"

Leaning back in the chair, Wendell scowled thoughtfully. "There are a number of ways we could proceed. One is through the civil courts right off the bat."

"There are other ways, though," Morgan growled, watching pleasure dance in the attorney's eyes. "Aren't there?"

"You bet there are, Morgan."

"What do you advise?" Laura asked, coming over and standing behind Morgan, her hands resting on his shoulders.

"I think I'm going to make an appointment with Senator Robert Tyler. He's committee chairman for the defense budget committee. Bob and I go back a long way."

"He's pro-defense. What makes you think he'll believe this new proof about Hill 164?" Morgan demanded, worried that a pro-defense senator might want to push anything that could embarrass the military under the carpet to keep the money coming into the services.

"You've been gone for seven years," Bill said. "Bob Tyler is a watchdog of sorts over the military. He can swing for or against them."

"Tyler's a man with a lot of integrity and clout," Laura added, her eyes shining with hope.

"Precisely," Bill agreed. "I want your permission to take depositions from you and Lenny, plus the rest of the proof, to Bob."

Morgan saw the joy on Laura's face. He wanted to see that same joy when he made love to her for the first time. Gently putting aside that aching need, Morgan nodded to the attorney. "Take it all to him, Bill."

"Great." Wendell got up. "I'll send a limousine over to pick up you and Mr. Miles in about an hour. We'll take your depositions and get the ball rolling."

Laura withheld the urge to throw her arms about Morgan after Wendell had left. Lenny Miles sat at the table, still wolfing down the cookies she had set there for all of them earlier. If possible, he was even shakier than he'd been—little more than frayed nerves. Laura was afraid Miles might not be fit to give a deposition as he entered the detox phase of becoming drug-free. As soon as his deposition was completed, Miles would be taken to the nearest rehab center for help and counseling. She followed Morgan into the living room so they could have a bit of privacy. Sasha trailed at their heels, panting happily because they were home.

"Things are falling into place," Morgan murmured, pulling her into his arms.

"I'm so happy."

"I know." He leaned over, claiming her smiling lips, cherishing their softness and eagerness.

The doorbell rang. Morgan raised his head, frowning. "What is this? Grand Central Station?"

Reluctantly Laura pulled from his arms to answer it. "From here on it, I think it will be." She opened the door and her heart slammed against her rib cage. "Jim..."

The marine captain stood grimly before her, his eyes hard. "May I come in, Laura?"

Cold fear washed over her. Jim Woodward had found what he was looking for; there was no doubt. She stepped aside. "Come in."

Jim hesitated. "Is he here?"

"Yes."

Compressing his mouth, the captain entered the house, briefcase clenched in his left hand. His gaze shot to the left.

Laura shut the door, feeling the electric tension between Jim and Morgan. Without thinking, she placed herself between the two men, who bristled like angry dogs. "We know what you've found, Jim," she began quietly, hoping to defuse the explosiveness.

Slowly Jim took off his cap, his eyes never leaving Morgan. "You've been harboring a fugitive, Laura. His real name is Morgan Trayhern. He's a traitor to this country."

"I'm no more a traitor than you are, Woodward," Morgan ground out. What would the captain do with the information? Had he already handed it over to someone else? Called the police? Morgan tried to read the officer's angry features.

"Really?" Jim bit out. His eyes blazed with anger and he turned it on Laura. "You of all people, harboring a bastard like this. I never expected this of you, Laura."

She opened her mouth to defend Morgan, but it was too late. Morgan moved like an attacking tiger, grabbing Jim by the lapels of his khaki uniform and slamming him up against the wall.

"Keep her out of this," Morgan snarled in Jim's face. "Just tell me what you've done with the information you've got on me."

Gasping, Jim dropped the briefcase as Morgan's powerful hands around the neck of his uniform shut off his air. "N-nothing...yet..."

With a curse Morgan released him, breathing hard. "You'd better sit down, Captain. There's some information you *don't* know that's just come to light. In less than an hour, I'm giving a deposition, and so is Lenny Miles, to clear my name and my family's honor."

Blankly the captain looked at Laura, who stood at Morgan's side. "Deposition? Lenny Miles? What are you talking about?"

Gripping the officer's arms, Morgan pulled him

away from the wall. "Get in the kitchen and sit down, Woodward. You're going to hear the real facts concerning Hill 164. Now get moving. I don't have long to convince you that I'm not a traitor."

Laura sat quietly as Miles repeated the story to Jim. Morgan shoved the documents under his nose, and the marine officer inspected them closely. Within half an hour, Jim's demeanor had gone from hostility to disbelief. A dull red color crept into his cheeks as Morgan finished the explanation.

"Looks like I owe you both an apology," Jim said.

Laura sighed. "Don't apologize, Jim. Just keep all this under your hat until Morgan's attorney can contact the right people."

Jim looked at Morgan. "You know what this means, don't you?"

"Clearing my family's name."

"More than that. It means a full congressional investigation. They hung you seven years ago, and if they reopen this case, the press is going to have a field day."

The doorbell rang. It had to be the limo driver to take them to Wendell's office. Morgan got up. "Only this time, Young, Hadden and his cronies are going to be on the hot seat, not me. Miles, let's go."

Lenny nodded, grabbing one more cookie and stuffing it into the pocket of his slacks.

Laura continued to sit opposite Jim. She saw Morgan give her a wink, and she raised her hand in farewell. "Hurry home," she told him, a catch in her voice.

Morgan felt his heart smother with yearning. Laura looked drained. It had been one hell of a day, and it wasn't over yet. "I'll be home as soon as I can," he promised.

Jim gave her an odd look once Morgan and Lenny had left. He pushed the photos of Morgan toward her. "Here, you'd better keep these for now. I retrieved them from the photo files."

Grateful for his loyalty, Laura took them. "Thank you, Jim."

"That guy means something special to you?"

She smiled. "Yes, he does."

"You haven't known him long."

"That's true, but I love him, anyway. I guess I did from the first."

Jim gathered up the rest of the files and placed them in a neat stack in the center of the table. "Lucky bastard." He grinned over at her. "I hope he appreciates you."

"I think he does," Laura admitted softly.

Rising, Jim asked, "Is there anything else I can do for you?"

"Yes. Get that classified document Clay Cantrell located in Section B of the central files on Operation Eagle, Hadden and Armstrong. We'll need it for Morgan's defense."

"No sooner said than done," Jim promised. He picked up his hat and settled it on his head. "You know I'm doing this for you."

Jim had always had a crush on her, Laura realized. "Do it for Morgan. He's a fellow marine and deserves your help."

Nodding, Jim snapped his briefcase shut and took it in his left hand. "You're right. The man's been framed and his entire life destroyed."

Laura stood in the quiet living room after Jim had left. The house felt empty and cool without Morgan's presence. What would tomorrow bring?

Chapter Eleven

Laura went to bed at ten, after receiving a phone call from Morgan. The depositions were taking longer than expected because Bill Wendell wanted every memory, every item that might be important, put down for the record. And Lenny Miles was in worse shape with every passing hour. Exhausted, Laura had taken a bath and slipped into a delicate white cotton gown that brushed her feet.

Her head still spun with worries and anxieties. Would Lenny continue to cooperate? What if he froze and refused to go before a Senate investigative hearing? How would that affect Morgan's case? Sighing, Laura turned on her side, closing her eyes. She missed Morgan more every hour. He'd promised to be home by midnight.

''Be quiet,'' Morgan told Sasha as he entered the foyer of the house. It was a few minutes past midnight.

Sasha whined, thrusting her cold nose into his outstretched hand. Absently Morgan patted the Saint Bernard and tiptoed into the living room. All but one light was out. Laura was in bed, he was sure.

The house was dark and quiet as he walked back toward the bedrooms. His bedroom was all the way down the hall from hers. He glanced at her door and saw that it was ajar. Normally she kept it shut.

"Go to bed, Sasha," he said, and the Saint disappeared into the kitchen to lie down on her blanket.

Morgan moved down the hallway toward Laura's room. He nudged the door open, the light filtering in behind him. Laura lay beneath the pink comforter, asleep. Standing uncertainly, he soaked in her peaceful features hungrily. Her thin cotton gown had a boat neck, emphasizing the clean lines of her beautiful throat and delicate collarbones. His head was pounding with pain from the arduous hours of giving a deposition, but something pushed him farther into her room.

Laura stirred, her groggy senses alerting her to someone's presence. Barely opening her eyes, she saw Morgan's shadowy form backlighted.

"Morgan?" Her voice was raspy with sleep.

He came over and sat down on the edge of her bed, placing his hand over her blanketed hip. "I'm sorry, I didn't mean to wake you." God, but she was beautiful when she was waking up. The comforter lay at her waist, revealing the contour of her small breasts beneath the gown.

Smiling sleepily, Laura turned onto her back, searching his shadowed features. "You look so tired.

It must have been rough to talk about all those things again. Did everything go all right?''

Laura's sensitivity never ceased to amaze Morgan. He reached out to caress her cheek. It was soft, yet firm. ''It went fine. Miles managed to complete his deposition before he went into detox. The rehab people have him now. He'll probably have a rough night of it,'' he answered gruffly, watching the light and dark outline the swell of her breasts.

''It was just as hard on you, though in a different way.''

''I'll have to go through it again in front of a Senate hearing if Wendell gets his way. Every time it gets a little easier.''

Her breasts tightened in anticipation as his gaze lingered on them. Laura felt an almost tangible hunger radiating from him, stirring all her feminine desires to bright life. His hand had come to rest on the side of her neck, stroking her flesh gently. Each touch sent feathery tremors of yearning through her. Sliding her hand up his arm, she managed a soft smile. ''I'll be at your side, just as your family will be. You won't have to go through this alone.''

Morgan traced the graceful curve of her neck with his scarred fingers, watching her lashes flutter closed and her lips part provocatively. He felt her hand tighten on his arm. The screaming need to love her sheared through him. But it wasn't time yet. He hadn't been cleared, and there was no guarantee that he would be. With his thumb, Morgan caressed her collarbone, absorbing her reaction to his touch.

Fighting his desires, fighting what he knew both of them wanted, needed, he said in a low voice, ''Tell me of your dreams, Laura.''

A little sigh escaped her lips. Slowly she opened

her eyes, melting beneath his burning gray gaze. Morgan's hand rested warmly against her shoulder. "Dreams?" she whispered.

A slight smile pulled at his mouth. Laura was shaken. All he would have to do was lie down beside her and take her into his arms. Every nerve in his body begged him to do just that, and quell the fire raging within him. "Yeah, dreams. Your dreams. What do you want out of life?"

It was nearly impossible to think coherently with Morgan continuing to stroke her neck and shoulder. There was such incredible gentleness in his eyes now, and in his voice. "When I was being shuttled from one foster home to another, I dreamed of having a family adopt me," she began in a wispy voice. "And after Mom and Dad did adopt me, I dreamed of making them proud of me."

"And so you graduated with honors from Georgetown University," Morgan said, his voice thick, unsteady.

She ran her fingers up the length of his corded forearm, feeling the muscles tense beneath her caress. "Yes. And then, one by one, they died. Since then, my dreams have changed."

"How?" Morgan lifted his hand, smoothing away the wrinkles on her brow, then began to thread his fingers through her blond hair, which glinted with highlights as he moved the strands.

Her scalp tingled with pleasure as he sifted the hair through his fingers. Laura swallowed convulsively and inhaled sharply, unable to speak.

Laura's answer was far more important than his own selfish desires, and Morgan stopped coaxing his fingers through her hair. Her blue eyes were huge and luminous, telling him of her need of him. "What kind of dreams do you weave in your sleep now?'' Morgan coaxed her huskily.

Breathless beneath his tender onslaught, Laura struggled to contain her yearning. It would be so easy to sit up and slide her arms around his shoulders, drawing him down into bed with her. But their coming together had to be a mutual decision, and she gently acquiesced to that realization.

''Children mean so much to me,'' she began softly. ''My dreams aren't very exciting, Morgan. I hoped to one day find a man I could love. Who would want children as much as I do.''

''You'd make a hell of a mother,'' Morgan told her, still caressing her hair. Forcing himself to stop touching her, he placed his hand at his side. Disappointment was mirrored in her eyes, and he felt like a first-class heel.

Laura lay in the ebbing silence, absorbing Morgan's introspection. ''What are your dreams?''

''I won't have any until this hearing is over.'' Morgan saw the despair come to her eyes. He wanted to tell Laura that he saw her as his wife and the mother of his children. But it was far too soon to say any of those things. They'd barely known each other a month. Everything was moving too swiftly. And yet, as he studied her in the dim light, the soft curves of her face highlighted, Morgan knew that a month was time enough. ''When it's over,'' he whispered, ''I want to share my dreams with you.''

''That time won't come soon enough,'' Laura murmured.

Rising slowly to his feet, Morgan gripped her hand. ''I know... Get some sleep, little swan. I'll see you in the morning.''

Morning. Laura watched Morgan slowly retreat

from her bedroom. As the door was quietly shut, darkness once again descended around her. The love she felt for Morgan was close to exploding. It was so hard not to tell him how she felt. But he'd had so much taken from him already, she knew that he didn't want to risk anything in the future, for fear the present would once again undermine him. Tears stung Laura's eyes, and she blinked them away. The future…their future, hung in precarious balance. Burying her face in the goose down pillow, she wondered how Senator Tyler would react to the evidence Bill Wendell would present to him.

"Senator Tyler wants to see all of us," Wendell told Morgan over the phone late the next afternoon. "I sent the depositions over to his staff this morning, and I just got a call from him."

Grimly Morgan asked, "What's his mood? Does he believe me?"

"The senator, at this point, is incredulous. He wants you, Miles and Laura at his office in an hour. Can you make it?"

Checking his watch, Morgan muttered, "Yes, we'll be there."

"Excellent. I'll have one of the rehab staffers bring Miles over. I guess he's in pretty rough shape this morning. I'll meet you there, Morgan. Goodbye."

Placing the receiver back on its cradle, Morgan glanced up at Laura. She looked like a young girl in her pale-pink cotton dress with lace at the collar. Its pearl buttons gave the dress a decidedly old-fashioned air. She was his Laura, the idealistic dreamer, and she was beautiful in his eyes.

"The senator wants to see us," he said.

Her eyes widened. "He does?"

"All three of us. He's read the depositions, and I think he wants to see if we're real or a figment of Wendell's imagination."

Laura's heart started beating hard. Grabbing her lavender raincoat to face the typically showery April day, she tried to smile. "I'm ready."

Laura waited impatiently in the foyer for Morgan to get his dark-brown corduroy sport coat. He reappeared and shrugged it over his shoulders, offering her a tense smile. *Please,* she prayed, *let the senator believe Morgan.*

Bill Wendell met them outside the senator's office, briefcase in hand. He smiled at them. "Come on, don't look so glum," he chided. "This isn't an inquisition."

Morgan kept his hand cupped over Laura's elbow. "I wish I shared your optimism, Bill."

Wendell slapped him on the back. "Relax. All the senator wants to do is ask you some questions. Miles is already here—a little worse for wear, but he's coherent." He opened the door and stepped in after Laura and Morgan.

Morgan took in the walnut-paneled outer office. Mementos from Senator Tyler's long and illustrious career filled the walls. His secretary, Alice, was dressed in a gray business suit and gave them a welcoming smile. Miles sat quietly on a chair.

"Hello, Bill," Alice said. "Go right on in. The senator's waiting." She stared at Morgan.

Laura felt him tense beneath the secretary's piercing gaze. Was it curiosity or a look damning Morgan as a traitor? She wasn't sure. Following the men, she entered the sumptuous inner office last.

Morgan saw a white-haired man in a pin-striped

suit stand up from behind the huge cherry-wood desk. Tyler was short, reminding Morgan of a bull. His eyes were a piercing dark brown, his jaw set, with sharp creases on either side of his thin mouth. If he didn't know better, Morgan would have mistaken him for a military commander.

Tyler came around the desk and walked energetically over to them. He halted in front of the group, his eyes snapping to Morgan. ''You're Captain Trayhern.''

Morgan nodded, slowly taking the man's parchmentlike hand. Tyler had to be close to seventy. ''Ex-captain, sir.''

''Quite right. Thanks for coming.'' Brusquely Tyler motioned to leather wing chairs that had been placed in front of his desk. ''All of you, sit down.''

The room crackled with energy. Morgan sat on the edge of his chair, his hands clasped between his legs; he was expecting the worst. Tyler's shrewd gaze never left him, and he had the feeling that the senator was sizing him up.

''I've got to tell you, Bill, you sure as hell threw a bomb into my office with this information.'' Tyler jabbed a short, square finger at the depositions.

Wendell smiled slightly. ''Bomb or not, Senator, I think Morgan Trayhern deserves a hearing based upon the evidence.''

Tyler's straight white eyebrows drew together. He addressed Morgan. ''Who else was in that room with you when General Armstrong was dying?''

''Armstrong's doctor and the maid.''

''So there were witnesses.''

''Yes, sir.''

''Young isn't going to willingly testify that Armstrong or he told you anything. You know that?''

"If I were in Young's shoes, I'd roll over and play dead, too," Morgan began slowly. "He's got everything to lose."

Tyler exploded with a bark of laughter. "Son, you've got a string of generals and CIA people who will fall like dominoes if we go into hearings on this. You can bet your last bottom dollar they're going to protect one another's backsides right up the line."

"Just like they did after Hill 164," Morgan ground out.

"I'm afraid so." Tyler leaned back in his chair, surveying him for long, tension-filled moments. "I know your father, Chase, very well. And I'm well aware of your family's prestigious history in defending our country. Every son and daughter of your family has served with distinction. I'll tell you, if Bill had said it was anyone but a Trayhern, I wouldn't have touched this case with a ten-foot pole."

Morgan's heart thumped hard. He swallowed, his eyes widening on the senator. "Then you'll help us?"

Tyler got up and moved around his office. "Earlier today, Captain Jim Woodward came here. He brought me irrefutable proof there has been a cover-up. I'm not at liberty to share those documents with you because they're top secret. Only Committee members for the hearing can read them."

Morgan turned in the chair, watching the senator closely. "Can you give us an idea of what they say?"

Returning to his chair and sitting down, Tyler grinned. "Basically, they tie together all the threads of your documents. Hadden, who is now a CIA assistant chief, was at the bottom of all this. It was his idea to pin the rap for Hill 164 on you. My guess is that Armstrong wanted his general's star more than he wanted to take the heat for the tactical error he and the CIA had made. You know Armstrong was up for promotion at the time of Hill 164?''

"No, sir, I didn't,'' Morgan rasped.

"And Young, who was already a general, had his tail in a sling because he'd approved your company's move to Hill 164. The documentation ties the three of them together, that's all I can say.''

Laura leaned back. Jim Woodward had turned out to be Morgan's friend, not foe. She could hardly wait to throw her arms around the marine captain and thank him for his thorough work on Morgan's behalf.

"So,'' Tyler went on, "I'm calling a secret investigative committee hearing tomorrow morning.''

"Wait a minute,'' Morgan said, rising. "Why secret? If I'm going to be exonerated of these charges, I want it public, Senator.''

"Morgan—'' Wendell protested.

"No!'' Eyes blazing, Morgan looked at both men. "You don't understand. My family has gone through hell. My father was forced to retire. My brother Noah's career with the Coast Guard has been jeopardized. People treat him like a leper, and he's had to bust his butt to get assignments that should have come a hell of a lot easier.'' His breathing became hard with feeling. "And my sister, Alyssa, has been castigated at the Naval Academy *and* Pensacola. She was given the silent treatment all those years.'' Morgan braced his hands on the senator's desk and stared at him. "Do you have any idea what that's like? Frankly, I don't see how Aly stood it. How would you like to be ignored for four years, Senator? No friends. No one to talk to. No one to study with.'' He straightened, anguish in his tone. "This hearing goes public or not at all, Senator. If you won't agree to that, then I'll have Mr. Wendell pursue my case through civil court proceedings. It might take longer, but I intend to vindicate myself and my family publicly. Anything less than that isn't acceptable.''

Tyler slumped back in his leather chair and eyed Morgan. ''You've got your father's fighting spirit, you know that?''

''I don't have a choice in this matter,'' Morgan grated. ''My family's honor is at stake. My *life* is at stake. And to be honest, Senator, I'm fed up with running and hiding.''

Laura bowed her head, fighting back the tears that flooded her eyes at Morgan's pain.

''There are senators and congressmen who will shred you if you go public, Trayhern.''

With a sharp laugh, Morgan straightened. ''What the hell can they possibly do to me that hasn't already been done?''

''Your family will be put through more public scrutiny,'' he warned. ''Do you want Noah and Alyssa to take more pressure from their peers?''

Morgan snarled, ''If they've made it this far, they'll hang tough the rest of the way. Our family was bred to win, Senator, not lose. We don't give up.''

Rubbing his pronounced chin, Tyler muttered, ''That's obvious.'' He stared down at his desk for well over a minute, then said finally, ''You realize that if the inquiry were in secret, General Young and Hadden would be more apt to come clean. In a public hearing, they're going to hire the best criminal defense lawyers they can to appear before the television cameras.''

''America believes I'm a traitor,'' Morgan said fervently, ''and they believe my family is little better than that. If I can't clear my name in front of the public, no one in my family, including me, will ever have a decent life. It's bad enough my life has been screwed up. But to see my brother and sister, not to mention *their* children continue to carry this burden, is asking too much.''

Tyler shot Wendell a grizzled look. ''He's right, you know.''

Wendell nodded. ''Will you contact someone over at the Justice Department? Warrants will have to be served on Young and Hadden.''

''I'll make that call as soon as you leave.'' Tyler looked over at Lenny. ''Mr. Miles, you will be given protective custody by my committee. They'll make sure you have a place to stay during this hearing. Does that meet your requirements?''

Lenny nodded, unable to meet the senator's piercing gaze. His brow was beaded with sweat, and he squirmed uncomfortably in the wing chair. ''Uh... yes, sir.''

Laura stood. ''Wait a minute,'' she pleaded. Everyone quieted and looked at her. ''I'm sorry for barging in, but I have a question, Bill.''

''Well...sure. What is it?''

Nervously Laura said, ''If Morgan were to have a wire placed on him and he went back to Young and Hadden to force them to admit their part in the cover-up, could that possibly cut short a long hearing? I mean—'' she licked her lower lip, glancing at the senator ''—if Morgan got their admission, how could they refute it in a public hearing?''

''Young lady, you're right,'' Tyler agreed with a grin. ''That's something neither of us thought of, Bill.''

Wendell nodded.

Hope shone in Laura's eyes as Morgan went to her

side. He gave her a tender smile. ''You're something else,'' he told her.

''I'll call the Justice Department and talk to them about that possibility. Morgan, would you be prepared to try it?''

He turned, slipping his arm around Laura's waist. ''Yes, sir.''

''It might be dangerous,'' Tyler warned. ''If Young and Hadden can throw your life away to protect theirs, to say nothing of the threats made to Mr. Miles, they might resort to more physical means of getting rid of you this time.''

Gravely Morgan nodded. ''It's a risk I'm willing to take.''

''Fine. I'll have someone from the Justice Department contact you shortly. Planning will have to be done on how we can lure Young and Hadden into meeting you.'' He waved his hand at them, already picking up the phone. ''Nothing we've talked about leaves this room, understood?''

Everyone nodded.

Outside, after Lenny had left with Bill, Morgan drew Laura to a halt.

''That was a good idea,'' he congratulated her.

''I'm not so sure now,'' Laura said, frowning. ''What if Young or Hadden think that killing you is the best way to solve the problem?''

''That,'' he whispered, leaning over to kiss her wrinkled brow, ''isn't going to happen. Come on, let's go home. I don't know about you, but I'm hungry.''

Laura poked at the food on her plate, unable to eat. Things were moving too quickly to suit her. She had barely gotten the meal on the table when Ken Phillips from the Justice Department had called. He would be coming over shortly to discuss Morgan's meeting with Young and Hadden.

"You okay?" Morgan asked, looking across the table at Laura.

"Yes and no."

"I never realized what a worrywart you are, Laura Bennett," he teased gently.

Rallying beneath his cajoling, Laura forced a slight smile. She put her fork aside, her stomach tied in knots. "I guess I'm not cut out for all this cloak-and-dagger stuff."

He reached out, catching her hand and giving it a squeeze. "But here's the lady who gave us the idea."

She met his deep gray gaze, needing to be held by him but knowing that was impossible right now. "If this will force Young and Hadden's hand, then it's worth it, Morgan."

The doorbell rang. "That must be Phillips," Morgan said. Releasing Laura's cool, damp fingers, he rose and went to answer the door.

Laura cleared the dishes away so that Ken Phillips and Morgan could sit and plan. She liked Phillips immediately. He was in his mid-thirties, with military-short black hair and intelligent hazel eyes. And it was apparent that Morgan liked him, too. Both men were basically military types who appreciated cutting through red tape and getting to the heart of a matter.

"We've placed a tap on Young's and Hadden's residential and office phones," Phillips told him. "Tomorrow morning you're going to call Young and demand a meeting. Tell him you're getting tired of your Legion job and want another assignment. When you meet Hadden and him in person, try to get them both to admit to their parts in the affair."

Morgan nodded, studying the wire he'd wear tomorrow morning. "And you'll have your men in a truck, taping the conversation?"

"Yes. We'll also be providing you protection. If things start going bad, use the code word 'Brazil'. We'll come on the run."

Laura shivered as she placed the plates in the sink. Why wasn't either man particularly upset over the possibility that Young or Hadden could pull a gun?

Phillips grinned. "I don't think they'll wait long to have a meeting with you once that call is placed."

Morgan shook Phillips's thin but strong hand. "Thanks."

"I'll be here at eight in the morning. You'll make the call to Young's office at nine. By then I'll have the wire on you, so you can go directly to the meeting, if necessary."

"Sounds good," Morgan said. He rose and walked Phillips to the door. Ambling back into the kitchen, he saw how upset Laura had become.

"How you doing, little swan?" he asked, bringing her into his arms.

Closing her eyes, Laura slipped her arms around his waist, resting her head against his shoulder. "Okay."

"It will be over soon, sweetheart. I promise."

She stirred at the endearment. "I don't want to lose you, Morgan. Not after all this," she whispered, fighting back tears.

"Shh, you aren't going to lose me." He chuckled and held her tightly, rocking her gently back and forth. "I'm too mean to die. And look at me. I've got everything to live for."

Battling to gather her strewn emotions, Laura choked out, "Just be careful, Morgan."

He released her enough to place a finger beneath her chin. Her blue eyes, once sparkling with hope, were dark with despair. The urge to kiss that trembling lower lip tore him apart. "I'll be very careful," he promised her huskily. If he didn't let Laura go, he was going to carry her into her bedroom and love her. How many times, just before a battle, had he wished to be in a woman's arms, safe and loved?

"Come on, it's almost midnight. Let's turn in. We've got a big day ahead of us tomorrow."

It hurt to move away from Morgan. Swallowing her pain, Laura mutely agreed and left the kitchen to go take her bath. Tonight she wanted to be with Morgan, no matter what he thought or wanted. She shut the door to the bathroom and leaned tiredly against it. Her world as she knew it had suddenly grown bleak. The possibility of losing Morgan to a bullet tore a sob from her. Covering her mouth with her hand, she sat down at the vanity, trying to cry quietly so that Morgan would never hear her.

Chapter Twelve

Morgan had just turned out the light in his bedroom and was getting ready to remove his terry-cloth robe, when there was a knock on the door. He opened it. Laura stood uncertainly before him, dressed in her floor-length cotton gown.

Laura's throat constricted as she raised her gaze to meet his turbulent gray one. Placing a hand against her breast where her heart beat wildly, she whispered, "Don't send me away, Morgan...."

The hesitation, the longing, were all Morgan heard in her low, unsteady voice. Her fragility broke his iron-clad grip on himself, and he offered his hand to her. "Come here," he said thickly.

Stepping forward, Laura reached out, sliding her hand across his cheek where the scar lay in silent testimony to the pain he'd borne alone for so many years. She heard the swift intake of his breath. "Tonight,'' she murmured, ''is for both of us. I don't know what will happen tomorrow. I'm afraid, Morgan....''

With a groan, he swept Laura into his arms, violently aware of the softness of her breasts, of her willowy length sinking against him. ''I am, too,'' he admitted, cradling her face, looking deeply into her lustrous blue eyes.

''Love me?''

He ran his mouth lightly across Laura's parted lips. ''Yes,'' he rasped. ''You're so sweet and kind, my little swan.'' He gathered Laura into his arms, carrying her to his bed. The moon provided just enough light to see her features as he set her gently on the bed. Sitting next to her, he watched as she raised her hands.

Her fingers trembling, Laura unknotted the belt at his waist, then pushed the robe away from his shoulders. His chest was broad and deep, tapering to a flat, hard stomach. Her breath caught, and her eyes filled with anguish. ''Oh, Morgan...'' and she stared at the terrible scars that ran vertically down each side of his heavily muscled chest. ''I didn't realize,'' she cried, touching them, feeling the puckered flesh beneath her fingertips.

He tunneled his fingers through her damp hair, inhaling her sweet scent. ''It's all right,'' he said thickly, trailing a line of kisses from her temple, across her cheek, to seek and then find her lips. Lifting her chin, Morgan imprisoned Laura's face within his hands. ''Don't cry.'' He kissed away the silvery tears that had beaded on her lashes.

''How much you've suffered.'' Laura wept, kissing him hungrily, wanting to absorb his pain and loss—to replace them with joy. Their joy.

Laura was lush as he plundered her mouth, and he heard her moan with pleasure. Just the gentle touch of her hands against his chest took away all his memories. Laura was his present, his future. Her breath came rapidly, sweeping across his face as he devoured yielding lips that drove him beyond every wall he'd ever hidden behind.

Breathing hard, too, Morgan ran his hands across her slim shoulders, pushing aside the straps to her gown, pulling the fabric downward. Her flesh was so soft, yet firm, as she was. He watched her flushed face fill with delight as he cupped her small breasts in his hands. Each was a proud crescent, curved and firming under his. As he grazed each expectant nipple, a little cry broke from her and she swayed in his arms.

''Beautiful,'' he groaned, pressing her back against the bed. She was so small and yet so exquisite as he undressed her. In the moonlight, her skin was translucent ivory, her eyes dark with invitation as he skimmed his hand from her hip back up to her awaiting breasts.

The instant Morgan's mouth captured the first nipple, Laura cried out, pressing herself against his naked body. His flesh was taut, the muscles powerful against her yielding form. His callused fingers incited blazing fires wherever he touched her. Her world dissolved beneath his knowing, exploring hands. The tight knot of need deep within her grew, the moist heat building between her thighs, telling him of her need for him.

''Easy, my little swan,'' Morgan coaxed thickly, bringing her beneath him. She was fire and water, hot and liquid, as he parted her curved thighs. The pleading look in her eyes grew as he slid his hand beneath her hip. He was shaking with need. She was so small, but so incredibly fiery, burning through all his control.

The sheen to her flesh emphasized her beauty as he brought her to him.

Morgan's name was on Laura's lips as he thrust deeply into her. A little cry of pleasure, of triumph, slid from her exposed throat. She moved her hips upward, bringing him deep within her, wanting nothing more. Morgan's body moved slickly against hers and she gripped his shoulders, calling out his name as the heat built, then erupted within her. Sunlight burst within her as she closed her eyes, feeling his lean, powerful thrust. A softened smile pulled at her lips as she felt Morgan stiffen, then grip her hard against him. In that rainbow moment, Laura cried out with him, glorying in their untrammeled union, their love indelibly stamped on each other.

A rivulet of sweat traveled down Morgan's left temple. Laura leaned upward, kissing it away. She fell back into his arms, smiling weakly. ''I love you,'' she whispered.

The words, softened heartbeats to his ears, made him want to hold Laura forever. He smiled down into her shining blue eyes, which were filled with love for him alone. ''How long have you known?'' Morgan asked huskily, running several damp strands of her hair through his fingers.

Laughing weakly, Laura murmured, ''Forever, I think....''

He moved his hips slightly, seeing the desire rekindle in her eyes. She was so small and tight, yet able to accommodate him. Hadn't she been able to deal with him in all ways and all levels from the beginning? ''I used to dream about the woman who would one day be my wife,'' he told her, kissing her temple, then her cheek, his mouth finally coming to rest against her smiling lips. ''She would have the courage to hold me when I was weak. And she would have the fire to stand on her own without me.'' He nibbled at her lower lip, running his tongue across the yielding texture of it. ''And most of all, she would love me and love the children I'd want to share with her.''

Tears gathered in Laura's eyes as she held his tender gaze. Despite the terrible atrocities committed against him, Morgan was able to unveil and share his gentle inner core with her. Sliding her hands up across his cheeks, she whispered, ''You're my dream come true, darling. I don't think I fit all the requirements of your dream, though....''

He chuckled, kissing each of her fingers in turn. ''Nonsense. Inside that little frame of yours is a backbone of pure steel.'' Morgan drew her index finger into his mouth, biting it gently, watching the flame of need grow brighter still in her lustrous blue eyes. ''And fire—'' He groaned, releasing her fingers, ''Little swan, you've got all the fire a man could ask for.'' Sweeping his hand down across her damp form, he angled her hips upward. ''I see the fire right now....''

A moan tore from Laura as she felt his returning power filling her once again with throbbing life. She closed her eyes, bringing him into pulsing rhythm with herself. Each thrust, each groan from him, drove her to new, dizzying heights. His mouth ravished her lips, setting her free, coaxing her to become wanton within his arms. It was so easy giving her heart, her soul, to Morgan. The sunlight burst once more within her, and she fused with him, accepting his love, his need of her as they climbed and reached that pinnacle of beauty simultaneously.

Morgan fell against Laura, his head next to hers. They were both breathing hard, their flesh slick and heated against each other. He rolled off her, then brought her on top of him. Her lips were swollen from the demands of his kisses, but they were beautifully pouted as she smiled down at him. He moved his fingers through her golden hair, glorying in the wonderful smile in her eyes. "You're the woman I want to carry my children, Laura."

The words, filled with raw emotion, made Laura's heart contract with happiness. She closed her eyes, reveling in his fingers as they gently massaged her scalp. "I will," she promised huskily. As she moved her hands across his chest, she once again felt the ridges of those scars. Leaning down, she kissed the length of each one, wanting to take away the memories of years filled only with agony and loneliness.

Morgan lay back beneath her ministrations, feeling the feathery touch of her lips against his chest. He closed his eyes, his hands moving slowly up and down her back, tracing the indentation of her slight but strong spine. Just Laura's worship of his body had begun to erase so many ugly memories that had haunted him. Her fingers were trembling as she lightly stroked the scars on his chest. He forced his eyes open to slits, watching her innocent features bathed in moonlight and shadow. "How can you take pain away?" he asked hoarsely.

Laura smiled wistfully and reached up, sliding her fingers down the scar on his face. "Love takes pain away, darling. It always has."

Her voice was tremulous, a breeze wafting across a summery, flower-filled meadow. Laura was part goddess, part sweet innocent, part fiery woman. Gathering her in his arms, Morgan guided her to his side. Raising up one elbow, he studied her rapturous features in the moonlight. "I love you," he whispered, cradling her cheek, holding her simmering gaze. "And when this is all over, I want the time we deserve together." He brushed a droplet of perspiration from her unmarred brow. "We haven't had any since we met, Laura. Neither of us. We've been on a collision course with life."

"Tell me about it," she said with a laugh, sliding her hands around his neck. His face was completely devoid of tension now, and she realized how boyish he looked in that poignant moment. Sobering, she held his molten gaze. "After this is over, we've got all the time the world has to offer us, Morgan."

Lazily he smiled. "Don't get that worried look in your eyes, sweetheart. Everything's going to be fine tomorrow."

Would it? Laura bit back the words. "One day at a time," she murmured, pushing him down on his back and leaning across him. "Tonight, all I want to do is love you," she said breathlessly.

Her silky hair spilled across his face and he inhaled her special feminine scent as he reached up and kissed her cheek. "Come here, my flighty little swan," he growled, holding her against him, pulling up the sheet. As he closed his eyes and Laura fitted against him, he knew he held his new life, his new world, in his arms.

Morgan awoke slowly. He felt the exploring touch of Laura's hand against his chest, trailing down his torso. With a groan he forced open his eyes. It was dawn, and she looked beautiful sitting there, the sheet gathered around her waist. He saw the concern in her eyes. As her hand moved back up across his chest, he brought her into his arms, kissing her slowly, tasting the depths of her mouth.

"I'm dreaming," he said, his voice rough with sleep.

Laughing softly, Laura shook her head, then rested her brow against his. "No, you're not. I'm sorry I woke you, but I couldn't resist touching you. You've got such a beautiful male body, Morgan Trayhern."

He grinned, running his hands down her spine, cupping her hips. "Adore me all you want, sweetheart."

She smiled and kissed his strong mouth. "Conceited, brazen animal."

The scent of her entered his nostrils, and Morgan nuzzled his face into the strands of her blond hair. "You turn me into an animal, little swan," he growled. "It's all your fault."

Laura struggled out of his arms and knelt beside him, her hand resting against his chest. She could feel the sledgehammer beat of his heart beneath her palm. "Morgan, I want you to know that no matter what the outcome of all this, I'll be with you."

Her sudden seriousness jolted him. Stroking her arm with his fingers, he said, "You've stuck with me through all this."

"No," she said, "you don't understand." She chewed on her lower lip, searching for the right words. "No matter what happens, Morgan—whether you prove your innocence or not—I'm going with you. If that means leaving America, then I'll do it."

The tears in her eyes wrenched at his heart. Sitting up, Morgan put his arms around her. "You'd go back to France with me?"

Laura nodded.

Sighing, Morgan held her for a long time. "When did you decide this?"

"Weeks ago," Laura admitted, her voice choked with tears. "You mean more to me than any country,

Morgan. After we made such beautiful love last night, I don't think I could ever bear to be away from you again.''

''My sweet woman,'' Morgan murmured, kissing her gently. Wiping the tears from her cheeks, he gave her a game smile. ''You've run the gauntlet with me, haven't you? And you'd run it again, if you had to.'' He saw the vulnerability in her stormy blue eyes, but her inherent strength was also there. ''In a few hours, if we're lucky, this whole thing will be over, and we can plan our life here, in America.''

Laura stood in the gloomy light of the police van, listening to the last-minute instructions being given to Morgan by Kevin Phillips. The phone call Morgan had placed to General Young's residence had netted instant results. It was nearly noon, and that was when Morgan was to meet Young and Hadden at the general's country home.

How could they look so calm, when she felt as if her stomach were tearing apart? Phillips wasn't happy about the fact that their van was stationed three miles from the manor. But if they got any closer, Young might spot it and become suspicious. The operation could be compromised, and Morgan's life placed in jeopardy as a result. Morgan would drive to the manor in a rented car. Laura gnawed on her lip, her eyes never leaving him. He wore a white shirt, a tan corduroy blazer and dark-brown slacks. His face was set and hard. There was a gleam in his gray eyes that sent a shiver of dread through her.

Laura leaned against one of the steel counters, near a policeman, who sat at the console with a set of earphones on his head. Tape machinery, radio gear and video equipment were crowded into every nook and cranny of the van. There was hardly any room to maneuver, except up and down a narrow aisle. Morgan would drive up the long quarter-of-a-mile asphalt road to the manor. He'd have no weapon on him except for a deadly looking military knife, strapped to the inner calf of his right leg and hidden by the trouser.

Phillips glanced at the watch on his wrist. "It's time for you to leave. We'll follow at a safe distance."

Morgan nodded his thanks to the agent and moved to where Laura stood. He saw the absolute terror in her eyes. Giving her a smile meant to defuse her worry, he took her into his arms. She came, warming the coldness he carried deep within him. Kissing her hair as she buried her face against his shoulder, Morgan whispered, "Everything's going to be all right, Laura."

Tears gathered unexpectedly in Laura's eyes. She blinked them away. Morgan didn't need her weeping right now; he needed her strength. Standing on tiptoe, she kissed him longingly. His mouth was hot as it claimed hers with an urgency that ripped the breath from her.

Tearing his mouth away, Morgan looked deeply into her gray eyes. "I love you," he rasped. "Never forget that...."

And he was gone. Laura sat down, her knees wobbly in the aftermath of Morgan's claiming kiss. Phillips came over and sat down next to her as the van started up, ready to follow Morgan's car at a safe distance.

"He's going to be fine, Laura."

"I hope so."

Phillips smiled. "Morgan's a soldier first, and he's

as tough and smart as they come. I don't think many men can outfox him when the chips are down.''

The praise for Morgan's abilities left her cold. ''If he's going up against men carrying weapons, he doesn't have a chance.''

''You're forgetting one thing.''

Laura chewed on her lower lip. ''What?''

''He's a Trayhern. That says it all.''

After parking the car next to a Mercedes-Benz and a BMW, Morgan got out. The manor where Young lived was an impressive three-story brick home with white columns in front, testament to its Southern heritage. Thirty-foot-high rhododendrons blossomed in pink and white profusion around the residence, creating a protective green wall.

The cries of birds filled the wooded area surrounding the manor, as Morgan sauntered up the brick walk. His senses were screamingly alert, and his nostrils flared to catch any unusual or foreign scents. In the large picture window he saw a tall, spare man with black horn-rimmed glasses watching him intently. That was Richard Hadden. Earlier Phillips had shown him pictures of the CIA agent. There was a dangerousness to Hadden. He had the face of a weasel with those dark, deeply set eyes, gleaming with a fanatical light.

Before Morgan could knock, General Paul Young pulled open the door. His jowly face was set, his hazel eyes narrowed and assessing.

''Come in, Trayhern,'' he growled.

Morgan entered the spacious, highly polished foyer. Everything about the house bespoke understated wealth. Young was dressed in a gray cardigan, a white shirt and black slacks. His mouth was compressed.

"In there," the general ordered gruffly, pointing toward the living room.

The hair on Morgan's neck stood on end as he walked into the room filled with antiques and green plants. Hadden waited tensely, his hands knotted. Hatred flowed through Morgan as he studied the thin agent. He swung his attention to Young, who stood by the picture window after closing the drapes.

"Now what's this all about?" Young demanded.

"Not so fast," Hadden growled, advancing toward Morgan. "Let's search him. I don't trust—"

Morgan gripped Hadden's hand as he extended it toward him. "And I don't trust you, Hadden," he snarled softly, holding the man's glare. If the agent discovered the wire, the operation was doomed. Morgan tightened his fingers around Hadden's wrist and pushed him away.

Rubbing his arm, Hadden backed off. "How do we know you aren't armed?"

"How do I know you aren't?" Morgan shot back. There could be a pistol in a holster beneath the agent's green wool sport coat.

"Richard, relax," Young snapped. He turned his attention to Morgan. "Now what do you want?"

"I've got my full memory back, General."

Young's brows furrowed. "So?"

"So I know that you and Armstrong lied to me about being a CIA mole in the Legion. I'm not really a mole, am I?"

The general reached into a humidor, then jammed tobacco into a pipe. "Nonsense. The CIA has a file on you. Legally you're working for them."

Morgan maneuvered around so that his back was

to a wall and he could see both entrances to the living room while keeping an eye on the two men. ''I want a new assignment. Living in the Legion isn't exactly rewarding.''

''Money?'' Hadden muttered. ''Is that what this is about? You want us to pay you to keep your mouth shut?''

''What do I have to spill, Hadden?''

''Plenty!'' the agent shot back, going over to a wing chair and sitting down. ''Unfortunately, before Armstrong died he admitted he set you up.''

''You set me up, Hadden.''

''So what if I did? It was in the best interests of this country.''

Anger serrated Morgan. He put a clamp on it. ''I have to hand it to you,'' he told the agent. ''That was a pretty creative answer for the way Armstrong and Young screwed up on sending my company to Hill 164.''

Rolling his eyes, Hadden muttered, ''Look, Trayhern, a lot of good officers' careers were at stake.''

''It was more than that,'' Young growled. ''Don't forget, Richard, it was *your* decision and plan we reluctantly agreed to in sending Trayhern's company in there in the first place.''

The agent waved his hand airily. ''I wasn't the only one who made mistakes on gathered intelligence data, Paul.''

''No, but your faulty decision making cost my men's lives,'' Morgan whispered, wanting to advance across the room and beat the living hell out of the smug agent.

''Look, Trayhern, it wasn't my fault you lived. Word came back that you'd survived with brain damage.'' A catlike smile crossed his mouth. ''The two tough military geniuses were panicking. Armstrong and Young were ready to throw in the towel, until I came up with the idea of altering your past. And it was pure brilliance on my part to place you on assignment in the French Foreign Legion. You were out of sight, out of mind, and the American public accepted you as the scapegoat.''

Morgan held on to his disintegrating self-control. ''What about Lenny Miles?'' he ground out.

Hadden shrugged. ''He was a junkie. I couldn't pin the rap on him. He was too unstable. So I had the interrogation officers scare the hell out of him and make him sign a confession that you were at fault.'' He scowled. ''The hophead disappeared stateside three months after we discharged him. He's probably dead in some back alley by now.''

''Quick, clean and simple,'' Morgan said, hatred vibrating in his voice.

The general lit his pipe and puffed hard on it. ''Look, we're sorry it had to be you. But that's the past, Trayhern. What is it you want now? A new billet? More money? Tell us, and we'll get this settled. I can't afford to have you loitering around in the U.S. Someone might recognize you.''

Hadden got to his feet, his hand moving inside his sport coat in one smooth action. ''Don't move, Trayhern,'' he snarled as he held out a Walther P-38 pistol with a silencer on it.

''Richard! What the hell are you doing?'' Young exploded.

The agent grinned. ''Hands up, Trayhern. I'm sure Miles is long dead. Now it's time to get rid of the last survivor of Hill 164. You and I are going for a long walk behind the general's house.''

Slowly Morgan raised his hands. His heart thudded

hard in his chest. He watched Hadden advance on him, a lethal look in his squinted eyes. ''You kill me, and you've got murder on your hands,'' he whispered.

Young cursed. ''Don't do this, Richard! Dammit, I don't want any more blood spilled!''

''Shut up, Paul. You've always been the squeamish one about Operation Eagle.'' He waved the pistol to the right. ''Down that hall, Trayhern. Keep those hands above your head. Any dumb moves, and I'll shoot. Move!''

''Tell me something,'' Morgan snarled, ''you ever been to Brazil?'' He knew the code word for help would bring Phillips and his people on the run. But would it be soon enough?

Startled by the question, Hadden laughed. ''Pal, I'm not interested in discussing travel plans with you. Get moving!''

How long before Phillips and his people could arrive? Morgan slowly turned, in no hurry to leave the house. Even if they did get here in time, that was no guarantee they could save his neck. As he walked down the shadowy hall toward the rear door, his mind swung sharply to Laura. My God, she had heard this conversation—she was in the van with Phillips and his team. All her fears had come true.

''Open the door,'' Hadden growled. ''And hurry up!''

Sunlight poured through the trees bordering the well-kept backyard. The beauty of the daffodils, tulips and hyacinths contrasted starkly with the terror Morgan felt. The lawn sloped toward a dirt path that went through a heavily wooded area. Hadden jabbed the barrel of the Walther into his back as they headed toward it.

"Get moving or I'll blow your head off right here!"

Increasing his pace, Morgan entered the woods. By the time Phillips arrived, it would be too late.

"Why are you doing this?" Morgan asked.

"I don't want any loose ends. I've got my pension coming in two years. I'm not jeopardizing my neck for yours. No one will know the real story behind Hill 164. You'll die the traitor the public thinks you are, Trayhern."

Hatred twined with anger, and the word *traitor* grated across Morgan. In one swift motion he turned, lifting his right leg and aiming the toe of his shoe at the pistol Hadden held. He saw the agent's eyes widen, but it was too late. The tip of his shoe met Hadden's arm. The Walther discharged, the shot muted by the silencer.

"Sonofabitch!" Hadden screamed as the pistol flew high into the air. He lurched after it.

Morgan tripped Hadden, throwing himself on top of him. They landed hard on the path. Hadden struck upward, the punch connecting solidly with Morgan's jaw. He tasted the salt of blood in his mouth. Parrying a second blow, he doubled his fist and smashed it into Hadden's sneering face. Pain soared up his wrist and into his arm. There was a sharp crack. Hadden screamed, blood flowing heavily from his broken nose.

Breathing hard, Morgan threw the agent onto his belly and pinned one arm behind his back. The Walther lay only a few feet away from them, to the left of the path. Hitching up Hadden's arm until he screamed in pain, Morgan eased off the agent, using his foot to bring the pistol within reach. Gripping it, he loosened his hold on Hadden's arm.

"Get up," Morgan rasped, straightening and backing away. "Hands behind your head, Hadden."

The agent crawled slowly to his knees. Glaring at Morgan, he staggered to his feet, doing as he was instructed.

Morgan wiped the blood from his lip and chin, and jerked his thumb in the direction of the manor. "Let's go back. The Justice Department is waiting for you." He grinned, even though it hurt like hell.

"Wh-what are you talking about?" Hadden stumbled up the path, weaving unsteadily.

"Our entire conversation was taped, Hadden. I'm wearing a wire." Elation soared through Morgan at the agent's gasp of disbelief. They made their way out of the woods and climbed up the expanse of lawn.

Just as Morgan stepped onto the patio, he saw Phillips and two of his men, dressed in flak jackets and armed with M-16 rifles, come bursting through the rear door. Relief showed on Phillips's face as he gestured to the men to halt.

"You okay?" he asked Morgan, surveying Hadden grimly.

"Yeah, just a split lip and some loose teeth." Morgan pushed the agent toward the men with the rifles. "Take him into custody." Glancing at Phillips, he said, "I think we got enough on tape to throw the book at them."

Grinning, Phillips gave orders to have Hadden handcuffed and read his Miranda rights. "You did a damn fine job, Morgan. With this evidence I believe the senator will be able to make a public press statement about your innocence."

"No hearings?"

"Doubtful. Even if Young and Hadden refused to admit to their part in Hill 164, this conversation will incriminate them. Come on, I've got one anxious lady waiting for you in the van. We wouldn't let Laura come in with us under the circumstances. She's about ready to throw a shoe.''

Morgan nodded, taking a handkerchief from his back pocket and holding it to his lips. ''I'll bet she is.'' Hesitating at the door, he turned to Phillips. ''Do me a favor?''

''Sure.''

''Give me a little time to calm the lady.''

Smiling, Phillips slapped him on the shoulder. ''You got it.''

Laura stood by the van, her hands gripped in a tight knot of fear. She'd heard over the taping system that Morgan was alive. When she saw him appear out the front door, she flew down the brick walk.

Morgan halted, opening his arms to her. With a muffled cry, Laura threw her arms around his neck. Laughing softly, he embraced her tightly.

''I'm okay, little swan,'' he murmured, inhaling her delicious scent.

Laura's breath came in huge gulps. ''I was so frightened—''

''Shh, so was I, sweetheart. Everything's fine. Believe me.'' And Morgan gently pushed her away just enough so that she could see he was all right. Tears shimmered in her blue eyes, and he leaned down to kiss them away.

''You're hurt.''

''Just scratches.''

Shakily she touched his injured lip. Blood had splattered across his sport coat and shirt. ''I was so afraid, Morgan.''

"I know," he said, caressing her mussed hair. He gave her a slight smile. "It's over now."

Swallowing her fear, Laura nodded. "Does Phillips think there's enough information to clear your name without a hearing?"

Morgan nodded. "Plenty. The senator will probably call a press conference as soon as he can, and I'll be vindicated." Laura looked clean and untouched after the violence that had surrounded him minutes earlier. Cupping her chin, Morgan smiled down into her eyes, now lustrous with love for him alone. "What do you say we go home, call my folks and then plan the rest of our lives together?"

Laura smiled through the tears and slid her hands upward, brushing the cheek with the scar. "I'd like that."

"I love the hell out of you, Laura." Morgan put his arm around her shoulders, and they walked back to the van. The singing of the birds took on added meaning for him, and so did the bright April sunlight. It was spring, the time of year for new seedlings to sprout, for flowers to poke their heads above the wintry, barren ground and blossom. New beginnings, he mused. He gazed tenderly at Laura, who returned his look with love.

There was so much he was grateful for because of her presence, her loyalty and her undying belief in him. Leaning down, Morgan kissed her temple. "You know what? I'm going to enjoy spending the rest of my life telling and showing you just how much I love you."

Sinking against him, Laura closed her eyes, the terror receding, to be replaced by hope. She felt his strength, his protection, where she was concerned. Meeting his warming gaze, she whispered, "Let's go home. We've run the last of this gauntlet together. The first day of our life is about to begin.''

Morgan nodded, leading her past a bright patch of red tulips toward the rented car in the distance. ''Home,'' he murmured, a catch in his voice, ''sounds good.''

* * * * *

The LOVE AND GLORY series continues with the spine-tingling, heart-touching story of how the Trayhern parents, Rachel and Chase, first met and loved—coming soon from Special Edition!

Arianna Worthington was far more beautiful than the photo he'd seen of her, Rafe realized when he first caught a glimpse of her at the airport. Why did she have to be so beautiful? The only reason he'd grudgingly agreed to meet this rich woman, who wanted a jungle adventure, was the check for a hundred-thousand dollars that Morgan Trayhern would write for him. The money was something Rafe desperately needed if he was to complete his mission to save the people of the Juma. So Rafe had capitulated; coping with a socialite brat for three to six months was nothing if he could help the Indian people he had been charged to protect. Reluctantly, he watched as she approached and tried not to be as interested as he was.

Her hair was gold like the sun itself, the thick strands lying in a gentle frame around her oval features and curling softly about her small shoulders. But it was her eyes that intrigued him; they were large, slightly tilted and the color of the blue sky over the Amazon. She looked younger than twenty-five. Somewhere between a girl and a woman, he grimly decided.

That was all he needed—an immature girl on his hands. Rafe was mature beyond his years. His lifestyle, the inherent danger surrounding it, guaranteed that. She seemed as if she was a frightened rabbit in unknown surroundings. Great. The word *baby-sitter* rang clearly in his head and he felt angry. In his world he was a loner. He had accepted that long ago.

Ari sucked in a huge gasp of air when she caught sight of the man who was to guide her through the Amazon. Gulping, she froze where she was. Rafe Antonio was a tall, gorgeous guy moving among lesser beings. She watched as he lifted his hand and removed his sunglasses, placing them in the pocket of his khaki shirt. When he looked up, she paused. His eyes were a cinnamon color, wide with intelligence and something else…aggravation? Still, she sensed a kindness about this man that simply bowled her over. She wasn't used to feeling anything about a man and it shook her deeply.

Dizzied and feeling terribly inept in his towering presence, Ari felt her oversize purse sliding off her shoulder. Oh no! As it clunked to the floor, she tripped over it. With a cry, she went down on her hands and knees. "Ohhh…" Ari moaned as she looked up to see Rafe leaning down over her. She felt so embarrassed. Her hands shook badly as she tried to pick up her scattered luggage and her purse at the same time.

"Allow me, Señorita Worthington."

His voice was deep, dark honey melting right through to her wildly pounding heart. Ari felt his hands slip around her upper arms to steady her and then he lifted her as if she weighed nothing at all. When she looked up into the warm brown eyes of the man who had rescued her, Ari felt her knees going weak.

"I'm so sorry..." she murmured apologetically. "I'm such a klutz! What a mess I've made."

Rafe gave her a tight smile. "*Señorita,* don't be apologizing. As you can see no one takes offense to what has happened." He picked up her luggage and handed her the purse. Then he took her hand, leaned down, and placed a kiss on the back of it. "Rafe Antonio at your service, Señorita Worthington."

Ari was thrilled at his old world manners. As his strong mouth grazed her flesh, a wild series of shocks leaped up her arm. No one had ever kissed her hand before. She had to remember she was in a foreign country and customs were different here. And she did just that the minute Rafe raised his head and she saw that his brown eyes were hard and merciless looking. Was he unhappy with her? Most likely, Ari thought, her heart filling with pain. Just like her father. She could do nothing to please him either. The thought made her stomach knot.

"Oh...well...thank you, Señor Antonio." She quickly pulled her hand away.

"Call me Rafe," he told her confidently. He didn't want to like her. She was artless. Or was it a disguise like the one his ex-finacée had used on him? Justine had displayed a similar helplessness and innocence and Rafe was wary of women since his experience with her. He gave Arianna a hard look. He couldn't bear to think of spending three to six months with a woman—especially a woman like this.

But then, he had no choice. Morgan Trayhern was counting on him. And Rafe wasn't the kind of man who would shirk his duty.

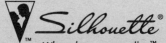

Soldiers of Fortune...prisoners of love.

Back by popular demand, international bestselling author* Diana Palmer*'s daring and dynamic* Soldiers of Fortune *return!

Don't miss these unforgettable romantic classics in our wonderful 3-in-1 keepsake collection. Available in April 2000.*

And look for a **brand-new** *Soldiers of Fortune* tale in May.
Silhouette Romance presents the next book in
this riveting series:

MERCENARY'S WOMAN

(SR #1444)

She was in danger and he fought to protect her. But sweet-natured Sally Johnson dreamed of spending forever in Ebenezer Scott's powerful embrace. Would she walk down the aisle as this tender mercenary's bride?

Then in January 2001, look for THE WINTER SOLDIER in Silhouette Desire!

Available at your favorite retail outlet.
**Also available on audio from Brilliance.*

Silhouette®
Where love comes alive™

Visit us at www.romance.net

PSSOF

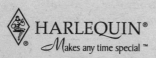

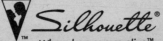